PRAISE FOR *THE KINGDOM OF COPPER*

"With gorgeous world building, compelling characters, and clashing schemes, the second in Chakraborty's Daevabad trilogy will thrill her many fans."
—*BOOKLIST* (starred review)

"With a richly immersive setting and featuring complex familial, religious, and racial ties and divides, Chakraborty's second book in the trilogy wraps readers in a lush and magical story that takes over all the senses." —*LIBRARY JOURNAL* (starred review)

"No series since George R.R. Martin's A Song of Ice and Fire has quite captured both palace intrigue and the way that tribal infighting and war hurt the vulnerable the most."
—*PASTE MAGAZINE*

"Chakraborty manages what many epic fantasy writers have never achieved: a world where everyone can see themselves not only mirrored, but powerful."
—*NEW YORK JOURNAL OF BOOKS*

PRAISE FOR *THE CITY OF BRASS*

"[*The City of Brass*] reads like an invitation for readers from Baghdad to Fairbanks to meet across impossibly divergent worlds through the shared language and images of the fantastical."
—*THE NEW YORK TIMES BOOK REVIEW*

"Chakraborty writes a winning heroine in Nahri — flawed but smart and engaging. And her portrayal of the cultural conflicts in the magical city of Daevabad and of Ali's inner turmoil is compelling and complex, serving as a strong counterpoint to the thrilling action."
—*WASHINGTON POST*

"Against [a] syncretic yet nonderivative and totally credible backdrop, Chakraborty has constructed a compelling yarn . . . culminating in a cataclysmic showdown that few readers will anticipate. . . . Best of all, the narrative feels rounded and complete yet poised to deliver still more. Highly impressive and exceptionally promising."
—*KIRKUS REVIEWS* (starred review)

"*The City of Brass* is more than a promising debut—it beguiles all the way. . . . Chakraborty's research and imagination are equally strong, and she deftly sets up a rich world—and ample suspense—for the rest of this trilogy."
—*VULTURE* (The Ten Best Fantasy Books of 2017)

"I raced to the end of *The City of Brass* and can't wait to see what happens next. I'm eager for more adventures in Daevabad."
—*PETER V. BRETT, New York Times* bestselling auth

"*The City of Brass* is the best adult fantasy I've read stunning and complex and consuming and far
—SABAA TAHIR, #1 *New York Times* bestselling

T0054641

Praise for

The Kingdom of Copper and

Critically Acclaimed Author S. A. Chakraborty

"The second installment of Chakraborty's stunningly rendered Middle Eastern fantasy trilogy. . . . As good or better than its predecessor: promise impressively fulfilled."

—*Kirkus Reviews* (starred review)

"Chakraborty plunges right back into the action set up in *The City of Brass*. . . . This intriguing fantasy series appears to be well on its way to an exciting conclusion."

—*Publishers Weekly* (starred review)

"With gorgeous world building, compelling characters, and clashing schemes, the second in Chakraborty's Daevabad trilogy will thrill her many fans."

—*Booklist* (starred review)

"With a richly immersive setting and featuring complex familial, religious, and racial ties and divides, Chakraborty's second book in the trilogy wraps readers in a lush and magical story that takes over all the senses."

—*Library Journal* (starred review)

"No series since George R.R. Martin's A Song of Ice and Fire has quite captured both palace intrigue and the way that tribal infighting and war hurt the vulnerable the most."

—*Paste* magazine

"Chakraborty manages what many epic fantasy writers have never achieved: a world where everyone can see themselves not only mirrored, but powerful."

—New York Journal of Books

"It was a treat to return to Chakraborty's richly drawn world. . . . . Engaging, satisfying, and left me looking forward to what comes next."

—The Speculative Shelf

Praise for *The City of Brass*

"Highly impressive and exceptionally promising."

—*Kirkus Reviews* (starred review)

"Majestic and magical."

—Shelf Awareness (starred review)

"*The City of Brass* reads like an invitation for readers from Baghdad to Fairbanks to meet across impossibly divergent worlds through the shared language and images of the fantastical."

—*The New York Times Book Review*

"*The City of Brass* is a gorgeous epic as rich in its language as it is in characterization, and I can't recommend it highly enough. Simply one of the best debuts I've read."

—Kevin Hearne, *New York Times* bestselling author of the Iron Druid Chronicles

"An extravagant feast of a book—dizzyingly magical, and still, somehow, utterly believable."

—Laini Taylor, *New York Times* bestselling author of *Strange the Dreamer*

"Compelling and complex. . . . Chakraborty writes a winning heroine in Nahri."

"Beguiles all the way."

"It's hard to describe just how gorgeous and intricate this fantasy novel is."

"An opulent masterpiece. . . . *The City of Brass* is a must-read."

"Readers will lose themselves in the wonder and complexity."

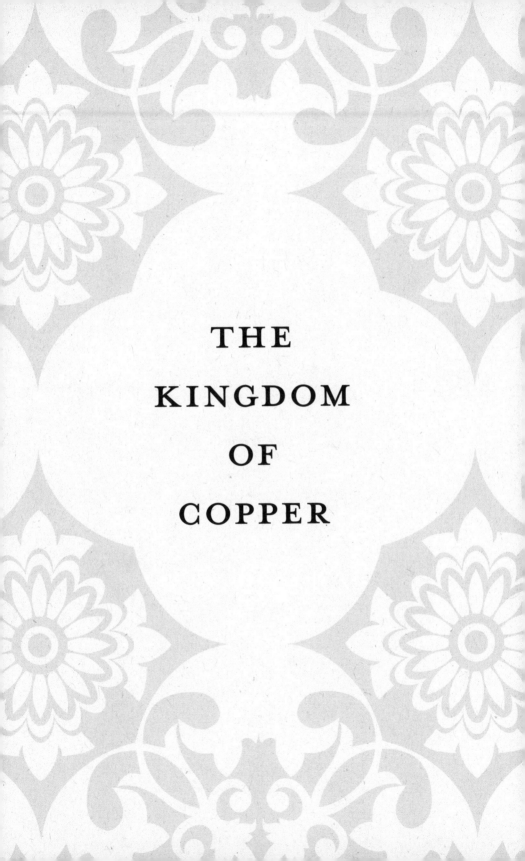

THE
KINGDOM
OF
COPPER

ALSO BY S. A. CHAKRABORTY

The City of Brass

THE
KINGDOM
OF
COPPER

THE DAEVABAD TRILOGY, BOOK TWO

S. A. CHAKRABORTY

HARPER Voyager
An Imprint of HarperCollins Publishers

P.S.™ is a trademark of HarperCollins Publishers.

THE KINGDOM OF COPPER. Copyright © 2019 by Shannon Chakraborty. Excerpt from THE EMPIRE OF GOLD © 2020 by Shannon Chakraborty. All rights reserved. Printed in the United States of America. No part of this book may be used or reproduced in any manner whatsoever without written permission except in the case of brief quotations embodied in critical articles and reviews. For information, address HarperCollins Publishers, 195 Broadway, New York, NY 10007.

HarperCollins books may be purchased for educational, business, or sales promotional use. For information, please email the Special Markets Department at SPsales@harpercollins.com.

Harper Voyager and design are trademarks of HarperCollins Publishers LLC.

A hardcover edition of this book was published in 2019 by Harper Voyager, an imprint of HarperCollins Publishers.

FIRST HARPER VOYAGER PAPERBACK EDITION PUBLISHED 2019.

Designed by Paula Russell Szafranski
Maps by Virginia Norey
Frontispiece art by Aza1976/Shutterstock, Inc.
Half title and chapter opener art by AZDesign/Shutterstock, Inc.

The Library of Congress has catalogued a previous edition as follows:

Names: Chakraborty, S. A., author.
Title: The kingdom of copper / S.A. Chakraborty.
Description: New York, NY : Harper Voyager, 2019. | Series: The Daevabad Trilogy ; Book 2
Identifiers: LCCN 2018036755| ISBN 9780062678133 (hardback) | ISBN 0062678132 (hardcover) | ISBN 9780062870162 (international paperback)
Subjects: | BISAC: FICTION / Fantasy / Epic. | FICTION / Action & Adventure. | FICTION / Fantasy / Historical. | GSAFD: Adventure fiction. | Fantasy fiction.
Classification: LCC PS3603.H33555 K56 2019 | DDC 813/.6—dc23
LC record available at https://lccn.loc.gov/2018036755

ISBN 978-0-06-267814-0 (pbk.)

23 24 25 26 27 LBC 17 16 15 14 13

FOR SHAMIK

CAST OF CHARACTERS

THE ROYAL FAMILY

Daevabad is currently ruled by the Qahtani family, descendants of Zaydi al Qahtani, the Geziri warrior who led a rebellion to overthrow the Nahid Council and establish equality for the shafit centuries ago.

GHASSAN AL QAHTANI, king of the magical realm, defender of the faith

MUNTADHIR, Ghassan's eldest son from his Geziri first wife, the king's designated successor

HATSET, Ghassan's Ayaanle second wife and queen, hailing from a powerful family in Ta Ntry

ZAYNAB, Ghassan and Hatset's daughter, princess of Daevabad

ALIZAYD, the king's youngest son, banished to Am Gezira for treason

Their Court and Royal Guard

WAJED, Qaid and leader of the djinn army

ABU NUWAS, a Geziri officer

KAVEH E-PRAMUKH, the Daeva grand wazir

JAMSHID, his son and close confidant of Emir Muntadhir

ABUL DAWANIK, a trade envoy from Ta Ntry

ABU SAYF, an old soldier and scout in the Royal Guard

AQISA and LUBAYD, warriors and trackers from Bir Nabat, a village in Am Gezira

THE MOST HIGH AND BLESSED NAHIDS

The original rulers of Daevabad and descendants of Anahid, the Nahids were a family of extraordinary magical healers hailing from the Daeva tribe.

ANAHID, Suleiman's chosen and the original founder of Daevabad

RUSTAM, one of the last Nahid healers and a skilled botanist, murdered by the ifrit

MANIZHEH, Rustam's sister and one of the most powerful Nahid healers in centuries, murdered by the ifrit

NAHRI, her daughter of uncertain parentage, left abandoned as a young child in the human land of Egypt

Their Supporters

DARAYAVAHOUSH, the last descendent of the Afshins, a Daeva military caste family that served at the right hand of the Nahid Council, and known as the Scourge of Qui-zi for his violent acts during the war and later revolt against Zaydi al Qahtani

KARTIR, a Daeva high priest

NISREEN, Manizheh and Rustam's former assistant and Nahri's current mentor

IRTEMIZ, MARDONIYE, and BAHRAM, soldiers

THE SHAFIT

People of mixed human and djinn heritage forced to live in Daevabad, their rights sharply curtailed.

SHEIKH ANAS, former leader of the Tanzeem and Ali's mentor, executed by the king for treason

SISTER FATUMAI, Tanzeem leader who oversaw the group's orphanage and charitable services

SUBHASHINI and PARIMAL SEN, shafit physicians

THE IFRIT

Daevas who refused to submit to Suleiman thousands of years ago and were subsequently cursed; the mortal enemies of the Nahids.

AESHMA, their leader

VIZARESH, the ifrit who first came for Nahri in Cairo

QANDISHA, the ifrit who enslaved and murdered Dara

THE FREED SLAVES OF THE IFRIT

Reviled and persecuted after Dara's rampage and death at Prince Alizayd's hand, only three formerly enslaved djinn remain in Daevabad, freed and resurrected by Nahid healers years ago.

RAZU, a gambler from Tukharistan

ELASHIA, an artist from Qart Sahar

ISSA, a scholar and historian from Ta Ntry

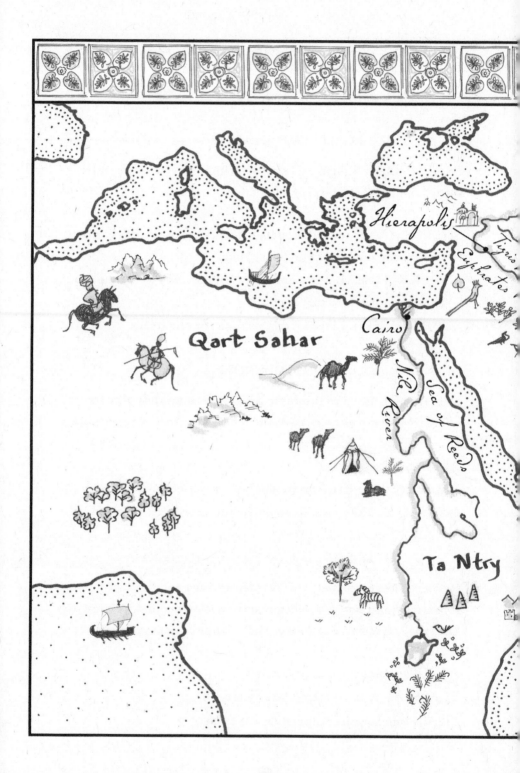

Hierapolis

Tigris

Euphrates

Cairo

Qart Sahar

Nile River

Sea of Reeds

Ta Ntry

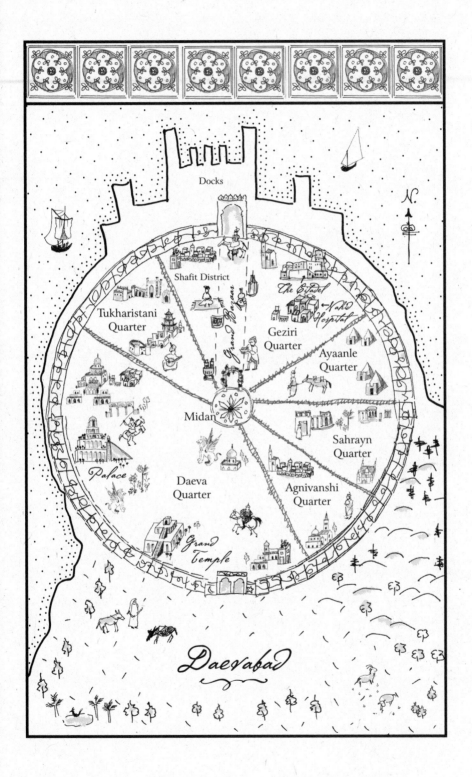

Docks

Shafit District

Tukharistani
Quarter

The Citadel

Nahid
Hospital

Grand Bazaar

Geziri
Quarter

Ayaanle
Quarter

Midan

Sahrayn
Quarter

Palace

Daeva
Quarter

Agnivanshi
Quarter

Grand
Temple

N.

Daevabad

THE
KINGDOM
OF
COPPER

PROLOGUE

ALI

Alizayd al Qahtani didn't make it a month with his caravan.

"Run, my prince, run!" the sole Ayaanle member of his traveling party cried as he staggered into Ali's tent one night when they were camped along a southern bend of the Euphrates. Before the man could say more, a blood-dark blade burst from his chest.

Ali flew to his feet. His weapons already at hand, he slashed the back of the tent open with a strike of his zulfiqar and fled into the darkness.

They pursued him on horseback, but the Euphrates glistened close ahead, black as the star-drenched night reflected in the river's coursing surface. Praying his weapons were secure, Ali plunged into the water as the first arrows flew, one whistling past his ear.

The cold water was a shock, but Ali swam fast, the motion as instinctual as walking, faster than he ever had, with a grace that would have taken him aback had he not been preoccupied with saving his life. Arrows struck the water around him, following his path, and so he dived deep, the water growing murky. The Euphrates was wide, and it took him time to cross, to push through waterweeds and fight the fierce current trying to drag him downstream.

It was only when he was staggering up the opposite bank that the sick realization swept over him: he had not needed to emerge for air the entire time.

Ali gulped, shivering as a cold breeze stole through his wet dishdasha. Nausea rose in his chest, but there was little time to contemplate what had happened in the river—not when mounted archers were pacing on the other side. His tent was aflame, but the rest of the camp looked untouched and eerily still, as though a quiet command had been passed among the other travelers in his party to ignore the screams they might hear tonight.

Ali had been betrayed. And he was not waiting around to find out if either the assassins or his traitorous companions could cross the river. He stumbled to his feet and ran for his life, racing headlong toward the opposite horizon.

Dawn had broken by the time his legs finally gave out. He collapsed, landing hard on the golden sand. The river was long gone. In every direction was desert, the sky a bright, hot bowl turned upside down.

Ali's gaze darted across the still landscape as he fought for breath, but he was alone. Relief and fear warred through him. He was *alone*—with a vast desert before him and enemies at his back, his only possessions his zulfiqar and khanjar. He had no food, no water, no shelter. He hadn't even had time to grab the turban and sandals that might have protected him from the heat.

He was doomed.

You were already doomed, you fool. Your father made that clear. Ali's exile from Daevabad was a death sentence, one obvious to anyone with knowledge of the politics of his tribe. Did he really think he could fight it? That his death would be easy? If his father had wanted to be merciful, he would have had his youngest son strangled in his sleep within the city's walls.

For the first time, a twinge of hate clawed up in Ali's heart. He didn't deserve this. He had tried to help his city and his family, and Ghassan wasn't even generous enough to give him a clean death.

Angry tears pricked his eyes. Ali wiped them away roughly, feeling disgusted. No, this wouldn't be how things ended for him, weeping tears of self-pity and cursing his family as he wasted away in some unknown patch of sand. He was Geziri. When the time came, Ali would die dry-eyed, with the declaration of faith on his lips and a blade in his hand.

He fixed his eyes southwest, in the direction of his homeland, the direction he'd prayed his entire life, and dug his hands in the golden sand. Ali went through the motions to cleanse himself for prayer, the motions he'd made multiple times a day since his mother had first shown him how.

When he finished, he raised his palms, closing his eyes and catching the sharp scent of the sand and salt clinging to his skin. *Guide me*, he begged. *Protect those I was forced to leave behind and when my time comes*—his throat thickened—*when my time comes, please have more mercy on me than my father did.*

Ali touched his fingers to his brow. And then he rose to his feet.

Having nothing but the sun to guide him through the un-broken expanse of sand, Ali followed its relentless path across the sky, ignoring and then growing accustomed to its merci-less heat upon his shoulders. The hot sand scorched his bare feet—and then it didn't. He was a djinn, and though he couldn't drift and dance as smoke among the dunes the way his ancestors had done before Suleiman's blessing, the desert would not kill him. He walked each day until exhaustion overtook him, only stopping to pray and sleep. He let his mind—his despair at how completely he'd ruined his life—drift away under the white, bright sun.

Hunger gnawed at him. Water was no problem—Ali had not thirsted since the marid took him. He tried hard not to think about the implication of that, to ignore the newly restless part of his mind that delighted in the dampness—he refused to call it sweat—beading on his skin and dripping down his limbs.

He could not say how long he'd been walking when the land-scape finally changed, rocky cliffs emerging from the sandy dunes like massive, grasping fingers. Ali scoured the craggy bluffs for any sign of food. He'd heard rural Geziris were able to conjure entire feasts from human scraps, but Ali had never been taught such magic. He was a prince raised to be a Qaid, surrounded by servants his entire privileged life. He had no idea how to survive on his own.

Desperate and starving, he ate any bit of greenery he could find down to the roots. It was a mistake. The following morning, he awoke violently ill. Ash crumbled from his skin, and he vomited until all that came up was a fiery black substance that burned the ground.

Hoping to find a bit of shade in which to recover, Ali tried to climb down from the cliffs, but he was so dizzy that his vision blurred and the path danced before him. He lost his footing on the loose gravel almost immediately and slipped, tumbling down a sharp incline.

He landed hard in a stony crevasse, smashing his left shoulder into a protruding rock. There was a wet pop, and a searing heat burst down his arm.

Ali gasped. He tried to shift and then yelped, a sharp pain shooting through his shoulder. He sucked for air through his teeth, biting back a curse as the muscles in his arm spasmed.

Get up. You will die here if you do not get up. But Ali's weakened limbs refused to obey. Blood trickled from his nose, filling his mouth as he stared helplessly at the stark cliffs outlined against the bright sky. A glance at the crevasse revealed nothing but sand and stones. It was—rather fittingly—a dead place.

He choked back a sob. There were worse ways to die, he knew. He could have been caught and tortured by his family's enemies or hacked apart by assassins eager to claim bloody "proof" of their victory. But God forgive him, Ali was not ready to die.

You are Geziri. A believer in the Most Merciful. Do not dishonor yourself now. Shaking, Ali squeezed his eyes against the pain, trying to find some peace in the holy passages he'd memorized so long ago. But it was difficult. The faces of those he'd left behind in Daevabad— the brother whose trust he'd finally lost, the friend whose love he'd killed, the father who'd sentenced him to death for a crime he hadn't committed—kept breaking through the encroaching darkness, their voices taunting him as he slowly slipped away.

He woke to an impossibly foul substance being forced down his throat.

Ali's eyes shot open and he gagged, his mouth full of something crunchy and metallic and *wrong*. His vision swam, slowly focusing on the silhouette of a broad-shouldered man squatting beside him. The man's face came to him in patches: a nose that had been broken more than once, a matted black beard, hooded gray eyes.

Geziri eyes.

The man laid a heavy hand on Ali's brow and spooned another thick helping of the disgusting gruel into his mouth. "Eat up, little prince."

Ali choked. "W-what is that?" His voice was barely a whisper in his parched throat.

The other djinn beamed. "Oryx blood and ground locusts."

Ali's stomach immediately rebelled. He turned his head to

throw up, but the man clamped his hand over Ali's mouth and massaged his throat, forcing the revolting mixture back down.

"Aye, do not be doing that. What kind of man turns down food that his host has so thoughtfully prepared?"

"Daevabadis." A second voice spoke up, and Ali glanced down at his feet, catching sight of a woman with thick black braids and a face that might have been carved from stone. "No manners." She held up Ali's zulfiqar and khanjar. "Lovely blades."

The man held up a gnarled black root. "Did you eat something like this?" When Ali nodded, he snorted. "Fool. You're lucky not to be a pile of ash right now." He shoved another spoonful of the bloody gristle at Ali. "Eat. You'll need your strength for the journey home."

Ali pushed it weakly away, still dazed and now thoroughly confused. A breeze swept through the crevasse, drying the dampness that clung to his skin, and he shivered. "Home?" he repeated.

"Bir Nabat," the man said as if it was the most obvious thing in the world. "Home. It is but a week's travel west."

Ali tried to shake his head, but his neck and shoulders had gone stiff. "I can't," he rasped out. "I . . . I'm going south." South was the only direction he could think to go; the Qahtani family originally hailed from the forbidding mountain chain along Am Gezira's humid southern coast, and it was the only place he could think to find allies.

"*South?*" The man laughed. "You are mostly dead and you think to cross Am Gezira?" He thrust another spoonful into Ali's mouth. "There are assassins looking for you in every shadow of this land. Word is the fire worshippers will make rich the man who kills Alizayd al Qahtani."

"Which is what *we* should be doing, Lubayd," the other raider cut in. She nodded rudely at the gruel. "Not wasting our provisions on a southern brat."

Ali swallowed back the vile concoction with difficulty, narrowing his eyes at her. "You'd kill a fellow Geziri for foreign coins?"

"I'd kill a Qahtani for free."

Ali started at the hostility in her voice. The man—Lubayd—sighed and shot her an annoyed look before turning back to Ali. "You'll forgive Aqisa here, prince, but it's not a good time to be visiting our land." He put down the clay cup. "We haven't seen a drop of rain in years. Our spring is drying up, we're running out of food, our babies and old folk are dying . . . So we send messages to Daevabad pleading for help. And do you know what our king says, our fellow Geziri king?"

"*Nothing.*" Aqisa spat at the ground. "Your father doesn't even respond. So do not speak of tribal ties to me, al Qahtani."

Ali was too tired to be frightened by the hatred in her face. He eyed the zulfiqar in her hands again. He kept his blade sharp; at least this ordeal would finally end quickly should they choose to execute him with it.

He choked back another wave of bile, the oryx blood thick in his throat. "Well . . . ," he started weakly. "In that case I agree. You needn't waste that on me." He nodded at Lubayd's gruel.

There was a long moment of silence. Then Lubayd burst into laughter, the sound ringing out across the crevasse.

He was still laughing when he grabbed Ali's injured arm without warning and pulled it firmly straight.

Ali cried out, black spots blossoming across his vision. But as his shoulder slid back into place, the searing pain immediately lessened. His fingers tingled, sensation returning to his numb hand in excruciating waves.

Lubayd grinned. He removed his ghutra, the cloth headdress worn by northern Geziri djinn, and quickly fashioned it into a sling. Then he hauled Ali to his feet by his good arm. "Keep your sense of humor, boy. You're going to need it."

A massive white oryx waited patiently at the mouth of the crevasse; a line of dried blood crossed one flank. Ignoring Ali's protests, Lubayd shoved him up onto the animal's back. Ali clutched its long horns, watching as Lubayd wrestled his zulfiqar away from Aqisa.

He dropped it in Ali's lap. "Let that shoulder heal and perhaps you'll swing this again."

Ali gave the blade an incredulous look. "But I thought . . ."

"We'd be killing you?" Lubayd shook his head. "No. Not yet, anyway. Not while you are doing *that*." He motioned back to the crevasse.

Ali followed his gaze. His mouth fell open.

It wasn't sweat that had soaked his robe. A miniature oasis had sprung up around him while he lay dying. A spring gurgled through the rocks where his head had been, trickling down a path shrouded with new moss. A second spring bubbled up through the sand, filling the depression his body had left. Bright green shoots covered a bloody patch of gravel, their unfurling leaves wet with dew.

Ali took a sharp breath, scenting the fresh moisture on the desert air. The potential.

"I have no idea how you did that, Alizayd al Qahtani," Lubayd said. "But if you can draw water into a barren patch of sand in Am Gezira, well . . ." He winked. "I'd say you're worth far more than a few foreign coins."

NAHRI

It was very quiet inside Emir Muntadhir al Qahtani's apartment.

Banu Nahri e-Nahid paced the room, her bare toes sinking into the sumptuous carpet. Upon a mirrored table, a bottle of wine rested beside a jade cup carved in the shape of a shedu. The wine had been brought in by the calm-eyed servants who'd helped

Nahri out of her heavy wedding clothes; perhaps they'd noticed the Banu Nahida's trembling and thought it would help.

She stared at the bottle now. It looked delicate. It would be easy to break it, easier still to conceal a glass shard under the pillows of the large bed she was trying not to look at and end this evening in a far more permanent way.

And then you will die. Ghassan would put a thousand of her tribesmen to the sword, make Nahri watch each one, and then throw her to his karkadann.

She tore her gaze from the bottle. A breeze came from the open windows, and she shivered. She'd been dressed in a delicate blue silk shift and soft hooded robe, neither of which did much to ward off the chill. All that was left of the overly elaborate outfit in which she'd been wed was her marriage mask. Made of finely carved ebony and secured by copper clasps and chains, the mask was engraved with her and Muntadhir's names. It was to be burned upon consummation, the ash marking their bodies the next morning proof of the marriage's validity. It was—according to the excited Geziri noblewomen teasing her earlier at the wedding dinner—a beloved tradition of their tribe.

Nahri didn't share their excitement. She'd been sweating since she entered the room, and the mask kept sticking to her damp skin. She pulled it slightly loose, trying to let the breeze cool her flushed cheeks. She caught the reflection of her movement in the massive bronze-edged mirror across the room and averted her eyes. However fine the clothes and mask, they were Geziri, and Nahri had no desire to see herself in the garb of her enemy.

They're not your enemy, she reminded herself. "Enemy" was Dara's word, and she was not going to think about Dara. Not tonight. She couldn't. It would break her—and the last Banu Nahida of Daevabad was not going to break. She'd signed her wedding contract with a steady hand and toasted Ghassan without trembling, smiling warmly at the king who'd threatened her with the murder of Daeva children and forced her to disown her Afshin with the crudest of charges. If she could handle all of that, she could handle whatever happened in this room.

Nahri turned to cross the bedroom again. Muntadhir's vast apartment was located on one of the upper levels of the enormous ziggurat at the heart of Daevabad's palace complex. It was filled with art: paintings on silk screens, delicate tapestries, and finely wrought vases, all of which had been carefully displayed and all of which seemed to carry an aura of magic. She could easily envision Muntadhir in this wondrous room, lounging with a cup of expensive wine and some cosmopolitan courtesan, quoting poetry and bantering about the useless pleasures of life that Nahri had neither the time nor inclination to pursue. There was not a book in sight. Not in this room, nor in the rest of the apartment she'd been guided through.

She stopped to stare at the closest painting, a miniature of two dancers conjuring flamelike flowers that sparked and flashed like hearts of ruby as they twirled.

I have nothing in common with this man. Nahri couldn't imagine the splendor in which Muntadhir had been raised, couldn't imagine being surrounded by the accumulated knowledge of millennia and not bothering to learn how to read. The only thing she shared with her new husband was one awful night upon a burning ship.

The bedroom door opened.

Nahri instinctively stepped back from the painting, pulling her hood low. There was a soft crash from outside, followed by a curse, and then Muntadhir entered.

He wasn't alone; indeed, she suspected he might not have made it alone, for he was leaning heavily on a steward, and she could practically smell the wine on his breath from across the room. A pair of female servants followed, and Nahri swallowed as they helped him out of his robe, unwinding his turban with a number of what sounded like teasing jests in Geziriyya, before leading him to the bed.

He sat heavily on the edge, looking drunk and somewhat stunned to find himself there. Heaped with cloudlike linens, the bed was big enough to fit a family of ten—and given the rumors she'd heard whispered about her husband, she suspected he'd filled it on many an occasion. Frankincense smoldered in a corner burner beside a chalice of sweetened milk mixed with apple leaves—a traditional Daeva drink brewed for new brides hoping to conceive. That, at least, would *not* be happening—Nisreen had assured her. One did not assist Nahid healers for two centuries without learning a number of nearly foolproof methods to prevent pregnancy.

Even so, Nahri's heart beat faster as the servants left, closing the door softly behind them. Tension filled the air, thick and heavy and at awkward odds with the sounds of celebration in the garden below.

Muntadhir finally glanced up, meeting her eyes. Candlelight played on his face. He might not have had Dara's literally magical beauty, but he was a strikingly handsome man, a charismatic man, she'd heard, one who laughed easily and smiled often . . . at least with people who weren't her. His thick black hair was cut short, his beard stylishly trimmed. He'd worn his royal regalia for the wedding, the gold-trimmed ebony robe and patterned blue, purple, and gold silk turban that were the hallmarks of the ruling al Qahtani family, but he was dressed now in a crisp white dishdasha edged with tiny pearls. The only thing detracting from his careful appearance was a thin scar dividing his left eyebrow—a remnant from Dara's scourge.

They stared at each other for a long moment, neither one moving. She saw that beneath the edge of drunken exhaustion, he too looked nervous.

Finally he spoke. "You're not going to give me plague sores, are you?"

Nahri narrowed her eyes. "Excuse me?"

"Plague sores." Muntadhir swallowed, kneading the embroidered covering on the bed. "That's what your mother used to do to men who looked at her too long."

Nahri hated that the words stung. She wasn't a romantic—on the contrary, she prided herself on her pragmatism and her ability to set aside her emotions—that's what had led her to this room, after all. But it was still her *wedding night*, and she might have hoped for a word of kindness from her new husband; for a man eager to touch her, rather than one worried she would curse him with some sort of magical disease.

She let her robe drop to the floor without ceremony. "Let's get this over with." She approached the bed, fumbling with the delicate copper fixtures holding her marriage mask in place.

"Be careful!" Muntadhir's hand shot out, but he jerked it back when he brushed her fingers. "Forgive me," he said quickly. "It's just—the mask clips were my mother's."

Nahri's hands stilled. No one in the palace ever spoke of Muntadhir's mother, Ghassan's long-dead first wife. "They were?"

He nodded, taking the marriage mask from her hands and deftly unhooking the clips. In comparison to the opulent room and the glittering jewelry they were both wearing, the clips were rather plain, but Muntadhir held them as if he'd just been handed Suleiman's seal ring.

"They've been in her family for centuries," he explained, running his thumb over the fine filigree work. "She always made me promise to have my own wife and daughter wear them." His lips quirked into a sad smile. "She said they brought good fortune and the best of sons."

Nahri hesitated and then decided to press forward; long-lost mothers might be the only topic they had in common. "How old were you—"

"Young," Muntadhir cut in, his voice a little raw, as if the question caused him pain. "She'd been bitten by a nasnas out in Am Gezira when she was a child, and the poison stayed with her. She'd have the occasional reaction, but Manizheh could always treat it." His expression darkened. "Until one summer Manizheh decided dawdling in Zariaspa was more important than saving her queen."

Nahri tensed at the bitterness lingering in his words. So much for a connection between them. "I see," she said stiffly.

Muntadhir seemed to notice. A flush came to his cheeks. "I'm sorry. I shouldn't have said that to you."

"It's fine," Nahri replied, though in truth she was regretting this marriage more with each passing moment. "You've never hid how you feel about my family. What was it you called me to your father? The '*lying Nahid whore*'? The one who seduced your brother and ordered my Afshin to attack your men."

Muntadhir's gray eyes flashed with regret before he dropped his gaze. "That was a mistake," he said, defending himself weakly. "My best friend and my little brother were at death's door." He rose to his feet, moving toward the wine. "I wasn't thinking straight."

Nahri dropped to sit on the bed, crossing her legs under the silk shift. It was a pretty thing, the fabric so thin it was nearly sheer, chased through with impossibly fine gold embroidery and adorned with delicate ivory beads. At another time—with another person—she might have delighted in the teasing way it brushed her bare skin.

She was decidedly not feeling that way now. She glared at Muntadhir, incredulous that he believed such an excuse sufficient justification for his actions.

He choked on his wine. "That's not helping me forget about plague sores," he said between coughs.

Nahri rolled her eyes. "For God's sake, I'm not going to hurt you. I can't. Your father would murder a hundred Daevas if I so much as put a scratch on you." She rubbed her head and then held out a hand for the wine. Maybe a drink *would* make this more bearable. "Pass that over."

He poured her a cup, and Nahri drank it down, her lips puckering at the sour taste. "That's awful."

Muntadhir looked wounded. "That's an antique ice wine from Zariaspa. It's priceless, one of the rarest vintages in the world."

"It tastes like grape juice that's been passed through a rotting fish."

"A rotting fish . . . ," he repeated faintly. He rubbed his forehead. "Well . . . what do you like to drink then, if not wine?"

Nahri paused but then answered honestly, seeing little harm in it. "Karkade. It's a tea made from hibiscus flowers." The lump grew in her throat. "It reminds me of home."

"Calicut?"

She frowned. "What?"

"Isn't that where you're from?"

"No," she replied. "I'm from Cairo."

"Oh." He looked a bit nonplussed. "Are they close?"

Not at all. Nahri tried not to cringe. He was supposed to be her husband, and he didn't even know where she was from, the land whose essence still flowed in her blood and beat in her heart. Cairo, the city she missed so fiercely it took her breath away at times.

I don't want this. The realization, swift and urgent, swept through her. Nahri had learned the hard way not to trust a soul in Daevabad. How could she share a bed with this self-centered man who knew nothing of her?

Muntadhir was watching her. His gray eyes softened. "You look like you're about to be sick."

She did flinch now. Maybe he wasn't completely blind. "I'm fine," she lied.

"You don't look fine," he countered, reaching for her shoulder. "You're trembling." His fingers brushed her skin, and Nahri tensed, fighting the urge to jerk away.

Muntadhir dropped his hand as though he'd been burned. "Are *you* afraid of *me*?" he asked, sounding shocked.

"No." Nahri's cheeks burned with embarrassment, even as she bristled. "It's just . . . I haven't done this before."

"What, slept with someone you hate?" His wry smile vanished when she bit her lip. "Oh. *Oh*," he added. "I had assumed that you and Darayavahoush—"

"No," Nahri said quickly. She couldn't hear that sentence completed. "Things weren't like that between us. And I don't want to talk about him. Not with you."

Muntadhir's mouth tightened. "Fine."

Silence grew between them again, punctuated by the shouts of laughter that drifted in from the open window.

"Glad to know everyone's so happy we're uniting our tribes," Nahri muttered darkly.

Muntadhir glanced at her. "Is that why you agreed to this?"

"I *agreed*"—her voice turned sarcastic on the word—"because I knew I would otherwise be forced to marry you. I figured I might as well go willingly and take your father for every coin of dowry I could. And maybe one day convince you to overthrow him." It probably wasn't the wisest response, but Nahri was finding it harder and harder to care what her new husband thought.

The color abruptly left Muntadhir's face. He swallowed and then tossed back the rest of his wine before turning to cross the room. He opened the door, speaking in Geziriyya to whoever was on the other side. Nahri inwardly cursed the slip of her tongue. Her feelings toward Muntadhir aside, Ghassan had been hell-bent on marrying them, and if Nahri ruined this, the king would no doubt find some ghastly way to punish her.

"What are you doing?" she asked when he returned, anxiety rising in her voice.

"Getting you a glass of your strange flower tea."

Nahri blinked in surprise. "You don't have to do that."

"I want to." He met her gaze. "Because, quite frankly, you terrify me, wife, and I wouldn't mind staying on your good side." He retrieved the marriage mask from the bed. "But you can stop shaking. I'm not going to hurt you, Nahri. I'm not that kind of man. I'm not going to lay another finger on you tonight."

She eyed the mask. It was starting to smolder. She cleared her throat. "But people will be expecting . . ."

The mask burst into cinders in his hands, and she jumped. "Hold out your hand," he said, dumping a fistful of ash into her palm when she did so. He then ran his ash-covered fingers through his hair and around the collar of his tunic, wiping them on his white dishdasha.

"There," he deadpanned. "The marriage has been consummated." He jerked his head at the bed. "I've been told I toss and turn terribly in my sleep. It will look like we've been doing our part for peace between our tribes all night long."

Heat filled her face at that, and Muntadhir grinned. "Believe it or not, it's nice to know *something* makes you anxious. Manizheh never showed any emotion, and it was terrifying." His voice grew gentler. "We'll need to do this eventually. There will be people watching us, waiting for an heir. But we'll take it slow. It doesn't have to be a horrible ordeal." His eyes twinkled in amusement. "For all the handwringing that surrounds it, the bedroom *can* be a rather enjoyable place."

A knock interrupted them, which was a blessing, for despite growing up on the streets of Cairo, Nahri didn't have a retort for that.

Muntadhir crossed back to the door and returned with a silver platter upon which a rose quartz pitcher rested. He placed it on the table next to the bed. "Your karkade." He pulled back the sheets, collapsing into the small mountain of pillows. "Now if I'm not needed, I'm going to sleep. I'd forgotten how much dancing Daeva men did at weddings."

The worry inside her unknotted slightly. Nahri poured herself a glass of karkade, and, ignoring her instinct to retreat to one of the low couches arranged near the fireplace, carefully slipped into the bed as well. She took a sip of her tea, savoring the cool tang.

The familiar tang. But the first memory that came to Nahri wasn't of a café in Egypt, it was of Daevabad's Royal Library, sitting across from a smiling prince who'd known the difference between Calicut and Cairo quite well. The prince whose knowledge of the human world had drawn Nahri to him in a way she hadn't realized was dangerous until it was too late.

"Muntadhir, can I ask you something?" The words burst from her before she could think better of them.

His voice came back to her, already husky from sleep. "Yes?"

"Why wasn't Ali at the wedding?

Muntadhir's body instantly tensed. "He's busy with his garrison in Am Gezira."

His garrison. Yes, that's what every Geziri said, almost down to the word, when asked about Alizayd al Qahtani.

But secrets were difficult to keep in Daevabad's royal harem. Which is why Nahri had heard rumors that Zaynab, Ali and Muntadhir's sister, had cried herself to sleep every night for weeks after her little brother was sent away. Zaynab, who had looked haunted ever since, even at the wedding festivities this evening.

The real question slipped from her. "Is he dead?" she whispered.

Muntadhir didn't respond right away, and in the silence Nahri felt a tangle of conflicting emotions settle into her chest. But then her husband cleared his throat. "No." The word sounded careful. Deliberate. "Though if you don't mind, I would rather not discuss him. And, Nahri, about what you said before . . ." He looked at her, his eyes heavy with an emotion she couldn't quite decipher. "You should know that when it comes down to it, I'm a Qahtani. My father is my king. I will always be loyal to that first."

The warning was clear in his words, uttered in a voice that had lost all hint of intimacy. This was the emir of Daevabad speaking now, and he turned his back to her without waiting for a response.

Nahri set her glass down with a thud, feeling the slight warmth that had risen between them turn to ice. Annoyance sparked in her chest.

One of the tapestries across the room shuddered in response. The shadows falling across Muntadhir's form, outlining the palace window, suddenly lengthened. Sharpened.

Neither surprised Nahri. Such things had been happening lately, the ancient palace seeming to awaken to the fact that a Nahid dwelled within its walls again.

DARA

In the crimson light of a sun that never set, Darayavahoush e-Afshin slumbered.

It was not true sleep, of course, but something deeper. Quieter. There were no dreams of missed opportunities and unrequited love, nor nightmares of blood-drenched cities and merciless human masters. He lay on the felt blanket his mother had woven for him as a boy, in the shade of a cedar glen. Through the trees, he caught glimpses of a dazzling garden, one that occasionally tugged at his attention.

But not now. Dara did not entirely know where he was, nor did it seem to matter. The air smelled of his home, of meals with his family and the sacred smoke of fire altars. His eyes fluttered open briefly now and then before the sounds of birdsong and a distant lute lulled him back toward sleep. It was all Dara wanted to do. To rest until the weariness finally slipped from his bones. Until the scent of blood left his memory.

A small hand nudged his shoulder.

Dara smiled. "Coming to check on me again, sister?"

He opened his eyes. Tamima knelt at his side, grinning a gap-toothed smile. A shroud draped his little sister's small form, her black hair neatly plaited. Tamima looked far different than she had when Dara had first set eyes on her. When he had arrived in the glen, her shroud had been drenched in blood, her skin carved and scored with names written in Tukharistani script. It was a sight that had made him wild; he'd torn the glen apart with his bare hands again and again until he finally collapsed in her small arms.

But her marks had been fading ever since, along with the black tattoo on his own body, the one that looked like rungs on a twisting ladder.

Tamima dug her bare toes into the grass. "They are waiting to talk to you in the garden."

Apprehension stole through him. Dara suspected he knew all too well the judgment that awaited him in that place. "I am not ready," he replied.

"It is not a fate to fear, brother."

Dara squeezed his eyes shut. "You do not know the things I have done."

"Then confess them and free yourself of their weight."

"I cannot," he whispered. "If I start, Tamima . . . they will drown me. They—"

A burst of heat suddenly seared his left hand, and Dara gasped, the pain taking him by surprise. It was a sensation he'd started to forget, but the burn vanished as quickly as it had come. He raised his hand.

A battered iron and emerald ring was on his finger.

Dara stared at it, baffled. He pushed to a sitting position, the heavy mantle of drowsiness falling from his body like a cloak.

The glen's stillness ebbed away, a cold breeze sweeping aside the smells of home and sending the cedar leaves dancing. Dara shivered. The wind seemed like a thing alive, pulling at his limbs and tousling his hair.

He was on his feet before he realized it.

Tamima grabbed his hand. "No, Daru," she pleaded. "Don't go. Not again. You're finally so close."

Startled, he glanced at his sister. "What?"

As if in response, the shadows in the cedar grove deepened, emerald and black writhing and twisting together. Whatever magic this was . . . it was intoxicating, tugging hard at his soul, the ring pulsing against his finger like a beating heart.

It was suddenly obvious. Of course, Dara would go. It was his duty, and he was a good Afshin.

He obeyed.

He pulled free of his sister's hand. "I will come back," he said. "I promise."

Tamima was weeping. "You always say that."

But his sister's sobs grew distant as Dara walked deeper into the grove. The sound of birdsong vanished, replaced by a low humming buzz that set his nerves on edge. The air seemed to close in around him, uncomfortably hot. The tug came again from his hand, the ring smoldering.

And then he was seized. *Stolen,* an unseen force snatching him like a rukh and dragging him into its maw.

The cedar glen vanished, replaced by utter blackness. Nothingness. A blazing, tearing pain ripped through him, worse than any sensation he could imagine, a thousand knives seeming to shred every fiber of his body as he was pulled, *dragged* through a substance thicker than mud. Disassembled and reformed from pieces as sharp as broken glass.

A presence thundered to life in his breast, pounding like a drum. Rushing liquid swirled through new veins, lubricating the growing muscles, and a smothering heaviness settled upon his chest. He choked, his mouth reforming to draw air into his lungs. His hearing returned, bringing with it screams.

His screams.

Memories slammed into him. A woman shouting his name, whispering his name. Black eyes and a sly smile, her mouth on his as their bodies pressed together in a darkened cave. Those same eyes filled with shock, with betrayal, in a ruined infirmary. A drowned man covered in scales and tentacles looming over him, a rusting blade in his dripping hand.

Dara's eyes shot open, but he saw only blackness. The pain was fading but everything felt wrong, his body both too light and yet too real, pulsing in a way he hadn't experienced in decades. Centuries. He choked again, gasping as he tried to remember how to breathe.

A hand clamped down on his shoulder, and a wave of warmth and calm surged into his body. The pain vanished, his heart slowing to a steady beat.

Relief flooded through him. Dara would know the healing touch of a Nahid anywhere. "Nahri," he breathed. Tears burned his eyes. "Oh, Nahri, I am sorry. I am so sorry. I never meant—"

The words died in his mouth. He'd caught sight of his hand.

It was fire-bright, tipped in deadly sharp claws.

Before he could scream, a woman's face swam into view. Nahri. No, not Nahri, though Dara could see the ghost of her in the woman's expression. This Daeva was older, her face slightly lined. Silver stole through the black hair roughly shorn at her shoulders.

She looked almost as shocked as Dara felt. Delighted—but shocked. She reached up to stroke his cheek. "It worked," she whispered. "It finally worked."

Dara stared down in horror at his burning hands. The hated emerald slave ring glittered back. "Why do I look like this?" His voice broke in panic. "Have the ifrit—"

"No," the woman assured him quickly. "You're free of the ifrit, Darayavahoush. You're free of *everything*."

That answered nothing. Dara gaped at the incomprehensible sight of his fiery skin, dread rising in his heart. In no world he knew did djinn and daevas look as he did now, even when brought back from slavery.

In a distant corner of his mind, Dara could still hear his sister begging him to return to the garden of his ancestors. *Tamima.* Grief rushed through him, and tears streamed down his cheeks, sizzling against his hot skin.

He shuddered. The magic coursing through his blood felt raw: new and ragged and uncontrollable. He drew a sharp breath, and the walls of the tent they were in undulated wildly.

The woman grabbed his hand. "Calm yourself, Afshin," she said. "You are safe. You are free."

"*What am I?*" He glanced again at his claws, sick at the sight. "What have you done to me?"

She blinked, looking taken aback by the despair in his voice. "I've made you a marvel. A miracle. The first daeva to be freed of Suleiman's curse in three thousand years."

Suleiman's curse. He stared at her in disbelief, the words echoing in his head. That wasn't possible. That . . . that was *abominable*. His people honored Suleiman. They obeyed his code.

Dara had killed for that code.

He shot to his feet. The ground shook beneath him, the tent walls flapping madly in a gust of hot wind. He staggered outside.

"Afshin!"

He gasped. He had been expecting the darkly lush mountains of his island city, but instead, Dara faced a desert, vast and empty. And then with horror, he recognized it. Recognized the line of salt cliffs and the single rocky tower that stood sentinel in the distance.

The Dasht-e Loot. The desert in southern Daevastana so hot and inhospitable that birds dropped dead from the sky while flying over it. At the height of the Daeva rebellion, Dara had lured Zaydi al Qahtani to the Dasht-e Loot. He'd caught and killed Zaydi's son in a battle that should have finally turned the war in the Daevas' favor.

But that was not how things had ended for Dara in the Dasht-e Loot.

A cackling laugh brought him sharply to the present.

"Well, there is a wager I have lost . . ." The voice behind him was smoothly clever, pulled from the worst of Dara's memories. "The Nahid actually did it."

Dara whirled around, blinking in the sudden brightness. Three ifrit were before him, waiting in the crumbling ruins of what might have once been a human palace, now lost to time and the elements. The same ifrit who'd hunted him and Nahri across the Gozan River, a desperate encounter they'd barely survived.

Their leader—Aeshma, Dara remembered—dropped from a broken wall, sauntering forward with a grin. "He even looks like us," he teased. "I suspect that's a shock."

"It's a pity." The ifrit who spoke next was a woman. "I liked the look of him before." She gave him a sly smile, holding up a battered metal helmet. "What do you think, Darayavahoush? Want to see if it still fits?"

Dara's eyes locked on the helmet. It had gone bluish-green with rust, but he instantly recognized the ragged edge of the brass shedu wings that sprouted from its sides. Shedu feathers, passed down from father to son, had once lined the helmet's crest. Dara could still remember shivering the first time he had touched them.

With rising horror, he looked again at the crumbling bricks. At the dark hole they enclosed, a black void upon the moonlit sand. It was the well down which he'd been callously thrown centuries ago to be drowned and remade, his soul enslaved by the ifrit now casually spinning his helmet on one finger.

Dara jerked back, clutching his head. None of this made any sense, but it all suggested something unfathomable. Unconscionable.

Desperate, he reached for the first person on his mind. "N-nahri," he stammered. He'd left her screaming his name upon the burning boat, surrounded by their enemies.

Aeshma rolled his eyes. "I did tell you he would ask for her first. The Afshins are like dogs for their Nahids, loyal no matter how many times they're whipped." He turned his attention back to Dara. "Your little healer is in Daevabad."

Daevabad. His city. His Banu Nahida. The betrayal in her dark eyes, her hands on his face as she begged him to run away.

A choked cry came from his throat, and heat consumed him. He whirled around, not certain where he was going. Only knowing that he needed to get back to Daevabad.

And then in a crack of thunder and flash of scalding fire, the desert was gone.

Dara blinked. Then he reeled. He stood upon a rocky shore, a swiftly coursing river gleaming darkly beside it. On the opposite bank, limestone cliffs rose against the night sky, glowing faintly.

The Gozan River. How he had gotten here from the Dasht-e Loot in the blink of an eye was not a thing Dara could begin to comprehend—but it didn't matter. Not now. The only thing that mattered was returning to Daevabad and saving Nahri from the destruction he'd wrought.

Dara rushed forward. The invisible threshold that hid Dae-vabad away from the rest of the world was mere moments from the riverbank. He had crossed it countless times in his mortal life, returning from hunting trips with his father and his assign-ments as a young soldier. It was a curtain that fell instantly for anyone with even a drop of daeva blood, revealing the misty green mountains that surrounded the city's cursed lake.

But as he stood there now, nothing happened.

Panic swept him. This couldn't be. Dara tried again, criss-crossing the plain and running the length of the river, struggling to find the veil.

On what must have been the hundredth attempt, Dara crashed to his knees. He wailed, flames bursting from his hands.

There was a crack of thunder and then the sound of running feet and Aeshma's annoyed sigh.

A woman knelt quietly at his side. The Daeva woman whose face he'd awoken to, the one who resembled Nahri. A long moment of silence stretched between them, broken only by Dara's ragged breaths.

He finally spoke. "Am I in hell?" he whispered, giving voice to the fear that gnawed at his heart, the uncertainty that had kept him from taking his sister's hand to enter the garden. "Is this punishment for the things I've done?"

"No, Darayavahoush, you are not in hell."

The soft assurance in her calm voice encouraged him to con-tinue, and so he did. "I cannot cross the threshold," he choked out. "I cannot even find it. I have been damned. I have been turned away from my home and—"

The woman gripped his shoulder, the powerful magic in her touch stealing his words. "You have not been damned," she said firmly. "You cannot cross the threshold because you don't carry Suleiman's curse. Because you are free."

Dara shook his head. "I do not understand."

"You will." She took his chin in her hands, and Dara found himself turning to look at her, feeling strangely compelled by the urgency in her dark eyes. "You've been granted more power than any daeva in millennia. We will find a way to return you to Daevabad, I promise." Her grip tightened on his chin. "And when we do, Darayavahoush . . . we are going to *take* it. We're going to save our people. We're going to save Nahri."

Dara stared at her, desperate for the chance her words offered. "Who are you?" he whispered.

Her mouth curved in a smile familiar enough to break his heart. "My name is Banu Manizheh."

NAHRI

Nahri closed her eyes, lifting her face to the sun and enjoying its heat on her skin. She inhaled, savoring the earthy smell of the distant mountains and the fresh breeze off the lake.

"They're late," Muntadhir complained. "They're always late. I think they like the sight of us waiting in the sun."

Zaynab snorted. "Dhiru, you haven't been on time for a single event in your life. Is this truly a fight you wish to pick?"

Nahri ignored their bickering, taking another deep breath of the crisp air and reveling in the stillness. It was rare she was allowed such freedom, and she intended to savor what she could of it. She'd learned the hard way that she had no other choice.

The first time Nahri had attempted sneaking out of the palace had been shortly after the night on the boat. She had been desperate for a distraction, aching to wander parts of the city she'd yet to visit, places where thoughts of Dara wouldn't haunt her.

In response, Ghassan had her maid Dunoor brought out before her. He hexed the girl's tongue for not reporting the Banu Nahida's absence, stealing her ability to ever speak again.

The second time, Nahri had been moved by a surge of defiance. She and Muntadhir were soon to be wed. She was the Banu Nahida. Who was Ghassan to lock her away in her ancestor's city? She had taken better care, making sure her companions had alibis and using the palace itself to cloak her in shadows and guide her through the most unused of corridors.

Still, Ghassan had found out. He dragged in the sleeping gate guard she'd tiptoed past and had the man scourged before her until there was not a strip of unbloodied skin on his back.

The third time, Nahri hadn't even been sneaking around. Newly married to Muntadhir, she had merely decided to walk back to the palace from the Grand Temple on a sunny day, instead of taking her guarded litter. She'd never imagined Ghassan—now her father-in-law—would care. On the way, she'd stopped inside a small café in the Daeva Quarter, passing a lovely few moments chatting with its surprised and delighted proprietors.

The following day Ghassan had the couple brought to the palace. This time, he didn't have to harm anyone. Nahri had no sooner seen their frightened faces than she dropped to her knees and swore never to go anywhere without permission again.

Which meant she now never turned away a chance to escape the palace walls. Aside from the royal siblings' squabbling and the cry of a hawk, the lake was entirely silent, the air wrapping her in a blessed, heavy peace.

Her relief didn't go unnoticed.

"Your wife looks like someone just released her from a century in prison," Zaynab muttered from a few paces away. She kept her voice low, but Nahri had a talent for listening to whispers. "Even I'm starting to feel bad for her, and one of the vines in her garden ripped my cup from my hand the last time we had tea."

Muntadhir shushed his sister. "I'm certain she didn't mean it. Sometimes that just . . . happens when she's around."

"I heard one of the shedu statues bit a soldier who slapped her assistant."

"Maybe he shouldn't have slapped her assistant." Muntadhir's whisper turned sharper. "But enough of such gossip. I don't want Abba hearing things like that."

Nahri smiled beneath her veil, pleasantly surprised by his defense. Despite being married now for nearly five years, Muntadhir rarely defended her against his family.

She opened her eyes, admiring the view before her. It was a beautiful day, one of the few in which not a single cloud marred the bright, fathomless blue of Daevabad's sky. The three of them were waiting at the front of the city's once grand port. Though the docks were still serviceable, the rest of the port was in ruins and apparently had been for centuries. Weeds grew through the cracked paving stones and the decorative granite columns lay smashed. The only hint of the port's ancient grandeur was behind her, in the gleaming brass facades of her ancestors on the city's mighty walls.

Ahead was the lake, the misty-green mountains of the opposite shore melting into a thin, pebbly beach. The lake itself was still, its murky water cursed long ago by the marid during some forgotten feud with the Nahid Council. It was a curse Nahri tried very hard not to think about. Nor did she let her gaze drift southward to where the high cliffs beneath the palace met the dark water. What had happened on that stretch of the lake five years ago was a thing she didn't dwell on.

The air shimmered and sparked, pulling Nahri's attention to the center of the lake.

The Ayaanle had arrived.

The ship that emerged from the veil looked like something out of a fairy tale, slipping through the mists with a grace that belied its size. Nahri had grown up along the Nile and was used to boats, to the thicket of sleek feluccas, fishing canoes, and loaded trade transports that glided over the wide river in a ceaseless flow. But this ship was nothing like any of those. It looked large enough to fit hundreds, its dark teak dazzling in the sunlight as it floated lightly upon the lake. Teal banners adorned with the icons of studded golden pyramids and starry silver salt tablets flew from the masts. Its many amber-colored sails—and Nahri counted at least a dozen—dwarfed the glimmering decks. Segmented and ribbed, the sails looked more like wings than anything that belonged on a boat, and they shivered and undulated in the wind like living things.

Awed, Nahri drew closer to the Qahtani siblings. "How did they get a *ship* here?" The only land beyond the magical threshold that embraced Daevabad's vast lake and misty mountains was composed of immense stretches of rocky desert.

"Because it's not just any ship." Zaynab grinned. "It's a sandship. The Sahrayn invented them. They're careful to keep the magic behind them a secret, but a skilled captain can fly across the world with one of those." She sighed, her gaze admiring and rueful. "The Sahrayn charge the Ayaanle a *fortune* to use them, but they do make a statement."

Muntadhir didn't look as impressed by the lovely ship. "Interesting that the Ayaanle can afford such a thing when Ta Ntry's taxes have been chronically short."

Nahri's gaze flickered to her husband's face. Though Muntadhir had never directly spoken to her of Daevabad's economic problems, they were obvious to everyone—especially the Banu Nahida who healed the training injuries of soldiers as they griped about reduced rations and undid the hexes the increasingly frazzled Treasury secretaries had begun hurling at one another. Fortunately, the downturn had yet to largely affect her Daevas—mostly because they'd cut themselves off from trading with the other tribes after Ghassan had tacitly allowed the Daeva stalls to be destroyed and their merchants harassed in the Grand Bazaar after Dara's death. Why take the risk of trading with djinn if none would stand up to protect them?

The Ayaanle ship drifted nearer, its sails fanning out as deckhands in brightly striped linen and thick gold ornaments dashed about the boat. On the top deck, a chimeralike creature with a feline body covered in ruby scales strained at a golden harness, flashing horns that shone like diamonds and whipping a serpentine tail.

The ship had no sooner docked than a knot of passengers made their way toward the royal party. Among them was a man dressed in voluminous teal robes and a silver turban that wrapped his head and neck.

"Emir Muntadhir." He smiled and bowed low. "Peace be upon you."

"And upon you peace," Muntadhir returned politely. "Rise."

The Ayaanle man did so, aiming what seemed to be a far sincerer grin at Zaynab. "Little princess, how you've grown!" He laughed. "You do this old coin-changer a great honor, coming to greet me yourself."

"The honor is mine," Zaynab assured him with a grace Nahri would never have the patience to emulate. "I pray your journey went well?"

"God be praised." The man turned to Nahri, his gold eyes lighting in surprise. "Is this the Nahid girl?" He blinked, and Nahri didn't miss the way he stepped back ever so slightly.

"This is my wife," Muntadhir corrected, his voice considerably cooler.

Nahri met the man's eyes, drawing up as she pulled her chador close. "I am the Banu Nahida," she said through her veil. "I hear you are called Abul Dawanik."

He bowed. "You hear correctly." His gaze didn't leave her, the examination making her skin crawl. He shook his head. "Astonishing. I never imagined I'd meet a real Nahid."

Nahri gritted her teeth. "Occasionally we're allowed out to terrify the populace."

Muntadhir cleared his throat. "I have made room for your men and your cargo at the royal caravanserai. I would be happy to escort you there myself."

Abul Dawanik sighed. "Alas, there's little cargo. My people needed more time to prepare the tax caravan."

Muntadhir's civil mask didn't waver, but Nahri sensed his heartbeat pick up. "That was not the arrangement we agreed on." The warning in his voice was so reminiscent of Ghassan, her skin prickled. "You are aware of how close Navasatem is, yes? It is a bit difficult to plan a once-in-a-century celebration when tax payments are consistently late."

Abul Dawanik threw him a wounded look. "Straight to all this talk of money, Emir? The Geziri hospitality I'm used to typically involves chattering about polite nonsense for at least another ten minutes."

Muntadhir's response was direct. "Perhaps you would prefer my father's company to mine."

Abul Dawanik didn't look cowed; if anything, Nahri saw a hint of slyness in his expression before he responded. "No need for threats, Your Highness. The caravan is but a few weeks behind me." His eyes twinkled. "No doubt you will enjoy what it brings you."

From behind the city walls, the adhan sounded, calling the faithful to noon prayer. It rose and fell in distant waves as new muezzins picked it up, and Nahri fought a familiar twinge of homesickness. The adhan always made her think of Cairo.

"Dhiru, surely this can wait," Zaynab said, clearly trying to alleviate the tension between the two men. "Abul Dawanik is our guest. He has had a long journey. Why don't the two of you go pray together and then visit the caravanserai? I can take Nahri back to the palace."

Muntadhir didn't look pleased, but he didn't protest. "Do you mind?" he asked Nahri courteously.

Do I have a choice? Zaynab's bearers were already bringing their litter over, the pretty cage that would return Nahri to her gilded prison. "Of course not," she muttered, turning away from the lake to follow her sister-in-law.

They didn't talk much on the way back. Zaynab appeared absorbed in her thoughts, and Nahri was happy to rest her eyes before returning to the bustling infirmary.

But the litter shuddered to a stop too soon. Nahri jolted from her half doze and rubbed her eyes, frowning as she caught sight of Zaynab hastily pulling off some of her jewelry. Nahri watched as she piled it on the cushion beside her, and then from beneath the brocade-covered seat, retrieved two plain cotton abayas, pulling one over her silk gown.

"Are we being robbed?" Nahri asked, half-hoping it might be true. Being robbed would mean a delay in returning to the palace and Ghassan's constant, watchful presence.

Zaynab neatly wrapped a dark shawl around her hair. "Of course not. I'm going for a walk."

"A *walk*?"

"You're not the only one who wants to escape sometimes, and I take my opportunities when they arise." Zaynab tossed the second abaya at Nahri. "Quick, put this on. And keep your face veiled."

Nahri stared at her in surprise. "You want me to come?"

Zaynab eyed her. "I've known you for five years. I am not leaving you alone with my jewelry."

Nahri hesitated, tempted. But the terrified faces of the people Ghassan had punished in her place immediately flooded her mind, and her heart seized in fear. "I can't. Your father—"

Zaynab's expression softened. "He hasn't caught me yet. And I'll take the responsibility if he does today, I swear." She beckoned Nahri forward. "Come. You look like you need this even more than I do."

Nahri quickly considered her options. Ghassan did have a soft spot for his only daughter, so after another moment of indecision, temptation won out. She pulled free her most visibly royal jewels, slipped into the garment Zaynab had offered her, and followed her out of the litter.

With a quiet word and a knowing wink between the princess and one of her guards—Nahri sensed this was a well-honed routine—the two women were pulled into the crush of pedestrians. Nahri had been to the Geziri Quarter plenty of times with Muntadhir to visit his relatives, but she hadn't seen anything beyond the curtains of the litters in which they traveled and the sumptuous interiors of mansions. Palace women were not expected to mix with commoners, let alone wander the city streets.

At first glance, the Quarter looked small—despite a Geziri family ruling the city, most of their tribesmen were said to prefer the rugged terrain of their homeland. But it was a pleasant glance, nonetheless. Windtowers loomed far above, sending lake-fresh breezes past neat rows of tall brick buildings, their pale facades adorned with copper shutters and white stucco filigree. Ahead was the market, protected from the hot sun by woven reed mats and a glistening water channel cut into the main street, filled with enchanted ice. Across from the market was the quarter's main mosque, and next to the mosque was a large floating pavilion, shaded by date and citrus trees, where families feasted on dark halwa, coffee, and other treats from the market.

And over it all loomed the stark tower of the Citadel. The home of the Royal Guard, the Citadel threw shadows over the Geziri Quarter and the neighboring Grand Bazaar, jutting up against the brass walls that separated Daevabad from its deadly lake. Nisreen had once told her—in one of her many dark warnings about the Geziris—that the Citadel had been the first structure Zaydi al Qahtani built upon seizing Daevabad from the Nahid Council. He'd ruled from there for years, leaving the palace a deserted ruin stained with the blood of her ancestors.

Zaynab chose that moment to take her arm, pulling her toward the market, and Nahri happily let herself be towed. Almost unconsciously, she palmed a ripe orange from a fruit stand as they passed. Stealing it was probably reckless, but there was something so freeing about strolling crowded city streets. It might not be Cairo, but the rustle of impatient passersby, the aroma of street food, and knots of men emerging from the mosque were familiar enough to briefly ease her homesickness. She was anonymous again for the first time in years, and it was delightful.

They slowed to a stroll once they entered the shadowed depths of the market. Nahri looked around, dazzled. A glassworker was turning hot sand into a speckled bottle with her fiery hands while across the lane a wooden loom worked by itself, bright woolen threads wrapping and twisting to pattern a half-completed prayer mat. From a stall packed with flowers came a rich aroma, a perfumer sprinkling rosewater and musk over a glittering tray of molten ambergris. Next door, a pair of hunting cheetahs in jeweled collars lounged on elevated cushions, sharing a storefront with squawking firebirds.

Zaynab stopped to stroke the large cats while Nahri wandered ahead. Down an adjacent lane was a row of booksellers, and she immediately headed for them, captivated by the volumes laid out in rows on rugs and tables. While a few books had an aura of magic, their covers bound in scales and pages shimmering gently, the majority looked human-made. Nahri wasn't surprised; of all the djinn tribes, the Geziris were said to be closest to the humans with whom they silently shared their land.

She browsed the nearest stall. Most of the books were in Arabic, and the sight sent an odd pang through her. It was the first language she'd learned to read, and a skill she could never entirely divorce in her mind from the young prince who'd taught her. Not wanting to think of Ali, she glanced idly at the next table. A book with a sketch of a trio of pyramids rested in its center.

Nahri was there the next moment, reaching for the book like she might have grabbed a long-lost friend in an embrace. They were Giza's famed Pyramids, all right, and as she flipped through the pages, she recognized more of Cairo's distinctive landmarks: the twin minarets of the Bab Zuweila gate and the vast interior of the Ibn Tulun mosque. There were women in the black dresses Nahri had once worn gathering water from the Nile, and men sorting piles of sugarcane.

"You have a good eye, miss." An older Geziri man ambled forth. "That's one of my newest human acquisitions, and I've never seen anything like it. A Sahrayn trader picked it up crossing the Nile."

Nahri ran her hands over the first page. The book was written in a script she'd never seen. "What language is this?"

The man shrugged. "I'm not certain. The lettering appears similar to some of the old Latin texts I have. The trader who picked it up didn't stay in Egypt long; he said it looked as though the humans were engaged in some sort of war."

Some sort of war. Her fingers pressed harder on the book. Egypt had been freshly subjugated by the French when Nahri left, ruled by the Ottomans before that—it was seemingly Nahri's destiny to belong to an occupied people wherever she went. "How much do you want for this?"

"Three dinars."

Nahri narrowed her eyes at him. "Three *dinars*? Do I look as though I'm made of gold?"

The man seemed shocked. "That . . . that is the price, miss."

"Maybe for someone else," she said scornfully, masking her glee while feigning insult. "I won't give you a coin over ten dirhams."

He gaped. "But that's not how we—"

Zaynab was suddenly there, seizing Nahri's arm in a tight grip. "What are you *doing*?"

Nahri rolled her eyes. "It's called bargaining, sister dear. I'm sure you've never had to do such a thing but—"

"Geziris do not *bargain* in our community markets." Zaynab's words dripped with revulsion. "It breeds discord."

Nahri was scandalized. "So you just pay whatever they ask?" She couldn't believe she'd married into such a naive people. "What if they're cheating you?"

Zaynab was already handing three gold coins to the bookseller. "Perhaps it would be better to stop thinking that everyone is cheating you, no?" She pulled Nahri away and pushed the book into her hands. "And stop making a scene. The point is to *not* get caught."

Nahri clutched the book to her chest, a little abashed. "I'll pay you back."

"Don't insult me." Zaynab's voice turned gentler. "You're not the first outspoken fool for whom I've bought overpriced human books on this street."

Nahri darted a look at the princess. She wanted to press her as much as she wanted to change the subject. And that, in essence, was how she felt about Alizayd al Qahtani.

Let it go. There were plenty of other ways to pester her sister-in-law. "I'm hearing rumors you're being courted by a noble from Malacca," she said brightly as they resumed walking.

Zaynab drew to a stop. "Where did you hear that?"

"I like to converse with my patients."

The princess shook her head. "Your patients should learn to hold their tongues. *You* should learn to hold your tongue. Surely,

I deserve that much for buying your book about odd human buildings."

"Do you not want to marry him?" Nahri asked, peeling the orange she'd stolen.

"Of course, I don't want to marry him," Zaynab replied. "Malacca is across the sea. I'd never see my family." Disdain entered her voice. "Besides which, he has three other wives, a dozen children, and is approaching his second century."

"So refuse the match."

"That's my father's decision." Zaynab's expression tightened. "And my suitor is a very wealthy man."

Ah. Muntadhir's concerns about the state of the city's treasury suddenly made more sense. "Can't your mother object?" she asked. Queen Hatset thoroughly intimidated Nahri, and she couldn't imagine the woman allowing her only daughter to be packed off to Malacca for any amount of gold.

Zaynab seemed to hesitate. "My mother has a more important battle to fight right now."

They'd wandered down a quieter street that ran past the Citadel. Its heavy stone walls loomed high overhead, blocking the blue sky in a way that made Nahri feel nervous and small. Through a pair of open doors came the sound of laughter and the distinctive sizzling clash of zulfiqar blades.

Not certain how to respond, she handed Zaynab half of her orange. "I'm sorry."

Zaynab stared at the fruit, uncertainty blooming in her gray-gold eyes. "You and my brother were enemies when you married," she said haltingly. "Sometimes it seems like you *still* are. How . . . how did you . . . ?"

"You find a way." The words unfurled from a hard place within Nahri, one that she'd retreated to countless times since she'd been plucked from the Nile and dropped in Cairo, alone and afraid. "You'd be amazed by the things a person can do to survive."

Zaynab looked taken aback. "You make me feel as though I should tell Muntadhir to keep a blade under his pillow."

"I'd advise against your brother keeping anything sharp in his bed," Nahri said as they continued walking. "Considering the number of visitors—" She choked, the orange falling from her fingers as a wave of coldness stole through her.

Zaynab instantly stopped. "Are you all right?"

Nahri barely heard the question. It felt as though an unseen hand had grasped her chin, turning her head to stare down the gloomy street they'd just passed. Tucked between the Citadel and the mottled brass of the city's outer walls, it looked as though the block had been razed centuries ago. Weeds and dirt covered the broken paving stones and scorch marks scarred the bare stone walls. At the very end was a crumbling brick complex. Broken windows faced the street, the black spaces looking like missing teeth in a gaping mouth. Beyond the front portico were the lush tops of wildly overgrown trees. Ivy covered the buildings, strangling columns and dangling over smashed windows like so many nooses.

Nahri took a few steps in and then inhaled sharply, a buzz racing down her skin. She'd swear the heavy shadows had lifted slightly when she moved.

She turned to see Zaynab had followed her. "What is this place?" she asked, her voice echoing against the stone.

Zaynab gave the complex a skeptical glance. "A ruin? I'm not exactly an expert when it comes to moldering buildings in a three-thousand-year-old city."

The street warmed beneath Nahri's feet, hot enough to feel through her sandals. "I need to go in there."

"You need to do *what*?"

But Nahri was already walking, thoughts of the princess, even fears of Ghassan's gruesome punishments all falling away. She felt almost compelled, her gaze locked on the mysterious complex.

She stopped outside a pair of large brass doors. Pictograms were carved into their surface—a leaping oryx and a ship's prow, a Daeva fire altar and a pair of scales—and magic all but simmered off the brass. Though Nahri couldn't imagine anyone living in such a place, she raised a hand to knock.

Her knuckles hadn't even grazed the surface when the door swung open with a groan, revealing a yawning black hole.

There was no one on the other side.

Zaynab had caught up. "Oh, absolutely not," she said. "You're with the wrong Qahtani if you think I'm about to go wandering into this haunted wreck."

Nahri swallowed. Had she been back in Egypt, this might have been the start of a tale told to frighten children, one of mysterious ruins and terrifying djinn.

Except she was technically the terrifying djinn, and the icy grip the building had on her heart had only tightened. It was reckless; it was an impulse that made no sense—but she was going inside.

"Then stay out here." Nahri dodged Zaynab's hand and ducked inside.

The darkness instantly swallowed her. "Naar," she whispered. Flames blossomed in her palm, throwing light on what must have once been a grand entrance chamber. Remnants of paint clung to the walls, outlining the forms of winged bulls and prancing phoenixes. Pockmarks were everywhere, places gems had likely been pried from the walls.

She stepped forward, raising her flames. Her eyes widened.

In fragments and shadows, the Nahids' creation story spread on the wall before her. Suleiman's ancient temple rising over the heads of its laboring daeva workers. A woman with pointed ears kneeling in a blue-and-gold chador at the feet of a human king. As Nahri stared in wonder at the mural, she'd swear the figures started to move and merge: a scattering of glazed paint becoming a flock of soaring shedus, the bare line drawing of veiled Nahid healers mixing potions filling with color. The faint sound of marching boots and cheering spectators whispered in her ear as a parade of archers trooped by, wearing ceremonial helmets crested with swaying feathers.

Nahri gasped, and as she did, the flame twirled away from her palm, pinpricks of light dancing away to illuminate the rest of the chamber. It was a burst of unconscious magic, the kind she associated with the palace, the royal heart of the Nahids whose power still coursed in her blood.

The murals abruptly stopped moving. Zaynab had entered and was gingerly picking her way over the debris littering the floor.

"I think this place belonged to my family," Nahri whispered, awed.

Zaynab gave the room a wary look. "To be fair . . . I believe that could be said of much of Daevabad." Her expression turned exasperated when Nahri glared. "Excuse me if it's difficult to be diplomatic when I'm afraid the building is going to come down at any moment. Now can we *please* leave? My father will have me packed off to Malacca tomorrow if his Nahid gets crushed under a pile of falling bricks."

"I'm not his Nahid, and I'm not leaving until I figure out what this place was." The tingle of magic on Nahri's skin had only increased, the humid heat of the city oppressive in the close chamber. She pulled free her veil, thinking it unlikely they would come upon anyone, and then, ignoring Zaynab's warning, Nahri climbed over one of the crumbling walls.

She landed lightly on her feet in a long, covered corridor, a succession of sandstone arches separating a row of doors from an overgrown courtyard garden. The walkway was in far better shape than the foyer: the floor appeared freshly swept, the wall plastered and covered in swirls of colorful paint.

With a curse, Zaynab followed. "If I've not said it lately, I think I hate you."

"You know, for a magical being, you have a terrible sense of adventure," Nahri replied, touching one of the eddies of paint, a blue swell that looked like a wave. An ebony boat was outlined against it. At her touch, the wave rose as if alive, sending the boat careening down the wall.

Nahri grinned. Thoroughly intrigued, she kept walking, peeking inside the rooms she passed. Save for the occasional broken shelf and rotting bits of carpet, they were all empty.

Until they weren't. Nahri abruptly stopped outside the last room. Cedar shelves bursting with scrolls and books covered the walls, stretching to the distant ceiling. More texts were stacked in precarious, towering piles on the floor.

She was inside before she noticed the floor desk wedged between two of the piles. A figure was hunched over its paper-strewn surface: an elderly looking Ayaanle man in a striped robe that nearly swallowed his wizened body.

"No, no, no . . . ," he muttered in Ntaran, scratching out whatever he'd just written with a charcoal pencil. "That makes *no* sense."

Nahri hesitated. She couldn't imagine what an Ayaanle scholar was doing in a book-stuffed room in a ruined building, but he looked harmless enough. "Peace be upon you," she greeted him.

The man's head snapped up.

His eyes were the color of emeralds.

He blinked rapidly and then yelped, pushing back from his cushion. "Razu!" he cried. "*Razu!*" He snatched up a scroll, raising it like a sword.

Nahri instantly backed away, brandishing her book. "Stay back!" she shouted as Zaynab ran to join her. The princess held a dagger in one hand.

"Oh, Issa, *whatever* is the problem now?"

Nahri and Zaynab both jumped and whirled around. Two women had emerged from the courtyard so swiftly they might have been conjured. One looked Sahrayn, with reddish black locks that fell to the waist of her paint-streaked galabiyya. The taller woman—the one who'd spoken—was Tukharistani, dressed in a dazzling cape of visibly magic design that fell like a mantle of molten copper across her shoulders. Her gaze locked on Nahri. Green eyes again. The same bright hue Dara's had been.

The Ayaanle scholar—Issa—peeked past his door, still wielding his scroll. "It looks human, Razu! I swore they would never take me again!"

"That is no human, Issa." The Tukharistani woman stepped forward. Her brilliant gaze hadn't left Nahri's. "It is you," she whispered. Reverence swept over her face and she dropped to her knees, bringing her fingers together in respect. "Banu Nahida."

"*Banu Nahida?*" Issa repeated. Nahri could see him still trembling. "Are you certain?"

"I am." The Tukharistani woman gestured to an emerald-studded iron cuff on her wrist. "I can feel the tug in my vessel." She touched her chest. "And in my heart," she added softly. "Like I did with Baga Rustam."

"Oh." Issa dropped the scroll. "Oh, dear . . ." He attempted to bow. "Apologies, my lady. One can never be too careful these days."

Zaynab was breathing heavily beside her, her dagger still raised. Nahri reached out and pushed her arm down. Thoroughly mystified, she stared at the strange trio, her gaze darting to each of them in turn. "I'm sorry . . . ," she started, lost for words. "But who are you all?"

The Tukharistani woman rose to her feet. Her silver-and-gold-streaked black hair was held back in an intricate lace net, and her face well-lined; had she been human, Nahri would have guessed she was in her sixties. "I am Razu Qaraqashi," she said. "You have already stumbled into Issa, and this is Elashia," she added, affectionately touching the shoulder of the Sahrayn woman next to her. "We are the last ifrit slaves in Daevabad."

Elashia instantly scowled, and Razu bowed her head. "Forgive me, my love." She glanced back at Nahri. "Elashia does not like to be called a slave."

Nahri fought to keep the shock from her face. Quietly, she let her abilities expand. Small wonder she thought she'd been alone: hers and Zaynab's were the only hearts pounding in the entire complex. The bodies of the djinn before her were entirely silent. Just as Dara's had been.

Because they're not true bodies, Nahri realized, recalling what she knew of the slave curse. The ifrit murdered the djinn they took, and in order to free them, the Nahids conjured new forms, new bodies to house their reclaimed souls. Nahri knew little else about the process; slavery was so feared among the djinn, it was rarely spoken of, as if simply mentioning the word "ifrit" would get one dragged off to a fate considered worse than death.

A fate the three people before her had survived. Nahri opened her mouth, struggling for a response. "What are you doing here?" she finally asked.

"Hiding," Issa responded mournfully. "No one else in Daevabad will have us after what happened to the Afshin. People fear we're liable to go mad and start murdering innocents with ifrit magic. We thought the hospital the safest place."

Nahri blinked. "This was a *hospital*?"

Issa's bright eyes narrowed. "Is it not obvious?" he asked, gesturing inexplicably to the crumbling ruins around them. "Where do you think your ancestors practiced?"

Razu quickly stepped forward. "Why don't you two come with me for some refreshments?" she suggested kindly. "It is not often

I have guests as esteemed as Daevabadi royals." She smiled when Zaynab shrank back. "Do not fear, my princess, it is otherwise a lovely disguise."

With the word "hospital" ringing in her ears, Nahri followed at once. The courtyard was in the same sorry state as the rest of the complex, with roots snaking over its shattered blue and lemon-yellow tiles, yet there was something lovely about its ruin. Dark roses grew lush and wild, their thorny vines twining around a long-fallen shedu statue and the air rich with their fragrance. A pair of bulbuls splashed and sang in a cracked fountain set in front of the cascading boughs of a stand of shade trees.

"Do not mind Issa," Razu said lightly. "His social graces could use some work, but he's a brilliant scholar who's lived an extraordinary life. Before the ifrit took him, he spent centuries traveling the lands of the Nile, visiting their libraries and sending copies of their work back to Daevabad."

"The Nile?" Nahri asked eagerly.

"Indeed." Razu glanced back. "That is right . . . you grew up there. In Alexandria, yes?"

"Cairo," Nahri corrected, her heart giving its familiar lurch.

"Forgive the error. I'm not sure there was a Cairo in my day," Razu mused. "Though I'd heard of Alexandria. All of them." She shook her head. "What a vain, upstart youth Alexander was, naming all those cities after himself. His armies terrified the poor humans in Tukharistan."

Zaynab gasped. "Do you mean to say you lived in the same era as *Alexander the Great*?"

Razu's smile was more enigmatic this time. "Indeed. I'll be twenty-three hundred at this year's generation celebration. Anahid's grandchildren were ruling Daevabad when the ifrit took me."

"But . . . that's not possible," Nahri breathed. "Not for ifrit slaves."

"Ah, I suspect you've been told that we're all driven mad by the experience within a few centuries?" Razu quirked an eyebrow. "Like most things in life, the truth is a bit more complicated. And my particular circumstances were unusual."

"How so?"

"I offered myself to an ifrit." She laughed. "I was a terribly wicked thing with a fondness for tales of lost fortune. We convinced ourselves that we'd find all sorts of legendary treasures if we could recover the powers we'd had before Suleiman."

"You *gave* yourself to the ifrit?" Zaynab sounded scandalized, but Nahri was starting to feel a bit of a kinship for this mysterious hustler.

Razu nodded. "A distant cousin of mine. He was a stubborn fool who refused to submit to Suleiman, but I liked him." She shrugged. "Things were a little . . . gray between our peoples back then." She raised her palm. Three black lines marred the skin. "But it was foolish. I set my masters chasing after fantastical prizes my cousin and I planned to retrieve after I was freed. I was digging through some old tombs with my third human when the entire thing collapsed, killing him and burying my ring under the desert."

She snapped her fingers and a bolt of silk spun out from a basket sitting beneath a neem tree, arching and expanding in the air to form a swing. She motioned for Nahri and Zaynab to sit.

"It took two thousand years for another djinn to stumble upon me. He brought me back to Daevabad, and here I am today." Razu's bright eyes dimmed. "I never did see my ifrit cousin again. I suppose a Nahid or Afshin caught up with him, in the end."

Nahri cleared her throat. "I'm sorry."

Razu nudged her shoulder. "You needn't apologize. I was certainly more fortunate than Issa and Elashia; the few human masters I had never abused me. But when I returned, my world was gone, any descendants lost to history, and the Tukharistan

I knew a legend in the eyes of my own people. It was easier to begin anew in Daevabad. At least until recently." She shook her head. "But here I am rambling about the past . . . what brings *you* two here?"

"Carelessness," Zaynab muttered under her breath.

"I . . . I don't quite know," Nahri confessed. "We were passing by and I felt . . ." She trailed off. "I felt the magic emanating from this place, and it reminded me of the palace." She glanced around wonderingly. "Was this truly a hospital?"

Razu nodded. "It was." With another snap of her fingers, a smoking glass ewer appeared alongside three chalices. She poured Nahri and Zaynab each a glass of a cloud-colored liquid. "I spent some time here as a patient after failing to dodge one of my creditors."

Zaynab took a cautious sip and then promptly spit it most inelegantly back into the cup. "Oh, that's definitely forbidden."

Curious, Nahri tested her own glass, coughing at the intense burn of alcohol as it ran down her throat. "What is this?"

"Soma. The preferred drink of your ancestors." Razu winked. "Regardless of Suleiman's curse, the daevas of my day had yet to entirely lose our wildness."

Whatever soma was, it admittedly left Nahri feeling more relaxed. Zaynab looked ready to bolt, but Nahri was enjoying her time more and more with each allusion to Razu's felonious past. "What was it like back then—when you were a patient, I mean?"

Razu gazed pensively at the hospital. "It was an astonishing place, even in a city as magical as Daevabad. The Nahids must have treated thousands, and it all hummed along like a well-oiled wheel. I'd been hexed with a rather contagious streak of despair, so I was treated in quarantine over there." She tilted her head toward a crumbling wing, then took a sip of her drink. "They took excellent care of us. A bed, a roof, and warm meals? It was almost worth being sick."

Nahri leaned back on her palms, contemplating all that. She knew hospitals fairly well; she'd often snuck into Cairo's most famous—the majestic, old bimaristan in the Qalawun complex—to steal supplies and wander its depths, fantasizing about joining the ranks of the students and physicians crowding its lofty corridors.

She tried to imagine how that bustle would look here, the hospital whole and filled with Nahids. Dozens of healers consulting notes and examining patients. It must have been an extraordinary community.

A Nahid hospital. "I wish I had something like that," she said softly.

Razu grinned, raising her chalice in Nahri's direction. "Consider me your first recruit should you attempt to rebuild."

Zaynab had been tapping her foot, but now she stood. "Nahri, we should go," she warned, motioning to the sky. The sun had disappeared behind the hospital walls.

Nahri touched Razu's hand. "I'm going to try and come back," she promised. "The three of you . . . are you safe here? Is there anything you need?" Though Razu and her companions were probably more capable than Nahri at taking care of themselves, she felt suddenly protective of the three souls her family had freed.

Razu squeezed her hand. "We are fine," she assured her. "Though I do hope you come back. I think the place likes you."

2

ALI

Ali gazed at the edge of the rocky cliff, squinting in the desert's bright sunlight. His heart was beating so fast he could hear it in his ears, his breath coming in ragged bursts. Nervous sweat beaded on his brow, soaking into the cotton ghutra he'd wrapped around his head. He raised his arms, shifting back and forth on his bare feet.

"He's not going to do it," he heard one of the other djinn goad. There were six of them there atop the cliffs bordering the village of Bir Nabat, and they were all fairly young, for what they were doing required the sort of recklessness youth provided. "Little prince isn't risking his royal neck."

"He'll do it," another man shot back—Lubayd, Ali's closest friend in Am Gezira. "He *better* do it." His voice rose. "Ali, brother, I've got coin riding on you. Don't let me down!"

"You shouldn't be gambling," Ali shot back anxiously. He took another shaky breath, trying to work up his courage. This was so dangerous. So unnecessary and foolish, it was almost selfish.

From beyond the cliff, there was the sound of reptilian snuffling, followed by the sharp, unpleasant tang of burnt feathers. Ali whispered a prayer under his breath.

And then he took off, sprinting toward the cliff edge. He ran as fast as he could and when the cliff gave way to air, he kept going, hurling himself into empty space. For one petrifying moment, he was falling, the distant, rock-strewn ground he was about to be dashed upon rushing up . . .

He landed hard on the back of the zahhak that had been roosting along the cliff face. Ali gasped, a thrill racing through his blood as he let out a cry that was equal parts terrified and triumphant.

The zahhak clearly didn't share his enthusiasm. With an offended screech, the flying serpent took to the sky.

Ali lunged for the copper collar that a far more enterprising djinn had slipped over the zahhak's neck years ago, tightening his legs around the creature's sleek, silver-scaled body as he'd been instructed. Four massive wings—misty white and billowing like clouds—beat the air around him, snatching the breath from his lungs. Resembling an overgrown lizard—albeit one with the ability to shoot flames from its fanged mouth when harassed by djinn—this particular zahhak was said to be over four hundred years old and had been nesting in the cliffs outside Bir Nabat for generations, perhaps favoring the familiarity of its nesting spot enough to deal with the antics of the Geziri youth.

One of those youths squeezed his eyes shut now; the rush of the wind and the sight of the ground whizzing beneath him sending another rush of fear into Ali's heart. He clutched the collar, huddling against the zahhak's neck.

Look, you fool. Considering there was a chance this ended with him in pieces on the sand below, Ali might as well appreciate the view.

He opened his eyes. The desert spread before him, great sweeps of red-gold sand stretching to meet the bright blue horizon, broken by proudly jutting stands of rocks, antique formations sculpted by the wind over countless millennia. Jagged paths marked the line of long-vanished wadis, a distant stand of darkly lush palms forming a tiny oasis to the north.

"God be praised," he whispered, awed by the beauty and magnificence of the world below him. He understood now why Lubayd and Aqisa had been goading him into taking part in this most deadly of Bir Nabat's traditions. Ali might have grown up in Daevabad, but he'd never experienced anything as extraordinary as flying like this.

He squinted at the oasis, growing curious as he noticed black tents and movement between the distant trees. A group of nomads perhaps—the oasis belonged to humans according to custom long set, the djinn of Bir Nabat not daring to take even a cup of water from its wells.

He leaned forward against the creature's neck for a better look, and the zahhak let out a smoky grumble of protest. Ali coughed, his stomach turning at the stench of the creature's breath. The gristle of roasted prey crusted its stained fangs, and though Ali had been warned about the smell, it still left him light-headed.

The zahhak obviously didn't think much of him either. Without warning, it banked, sending Ali scrambling to keep his grip, and then the creature hurtled back the way they'd come, cutting through the air like a scythe.

Ahead, Ali could see the entrance to Bir Nabat: a forbiddingly dark, empty doorway built directly into the cliffs. Stark sandstone carvings surrounded it: crumbling eagles perched upon decorative columns and a sharp pattern of steps that rose to meet the sky. The carvings had been done eons ago by Bir Nabat's original human settlers, an ancient group lost to time whose ruined settlement the djinn now called home.

His companions were just below, waving their arms and beating a metal drum to draw the ire of the zahhak. It dived for them, letting out a screech. Steeling himself, Ali waited until the zahhak drew close to his friends, opening its jaws to breathe an angry plume of scarlet fire that they narrowly ducked. Then he jumped.

He tumbled hard to the ground, Aqisa yanking him back just before the zahhak scorched the place he'd landed. With another offended shriek, it soared off, clearly having had enough of djinn for one day.

Lubayd hauled Ali to his feet, clapping his back and letting out a whoop. "I told you he would do it!" He grinned at Ali. "Worth the risk?"

Every part of his body ached, but Ali was too exhilarated to care. "It was amazing," he gushed, trying to catch his breath. He pulled away the ghutra the wind had plastered to his mouth. "And guess what? There's a new group of humans at the—"

Groans interrupted him before he'd even finished the sentence.

"No," Aqisa cut in. "I am not going to spy on humans with you again. You are obsessed."

Ali persisted. "But we could learn something new! You remember the village we explored in the south, the sundial they used to regulate their canals? That was very helpful."

Lubayd handed Ali his weapons back. "I remember the humans chasing us away when they realized they had 'demonic' visitors. They were firing quite a lot of those explosive stick . . . things. And I don't intend to learn if there's iron in those projectiles."

"Those 'explosive stick things' are called rifles," Ali corrected. "And you are all sadly lacking a spirit of enterprise."

They made their way down the rocky ledge that led to the village. Etchings covered the sandstone: letters in an alphabet Ali couldn't read, and carefully hewn drawings of long-vanished animals. In one high corner, an enormous bald man loomed over simple line drawings of figures, stylized flames twisting around his fingers. An original daeva, the village djinn believed, from before Suleiman blessed them. Judging from the figure's wild eyes and sharp teeth, they must have terrorized the human settlers.

Ali and his friends crossed beneath the entrance facade. A pair of djinn were drinking coffee in its shade, ostensibly guarding it. On the rare occasion a curious human got too close, they had charms capable of conjuring rushing winds and blinding sandstorms to frighten them off.

They looked up as Ali and his companions passed. "Did he do it?" one of the guards asked with a smile.

Lubayd wrapped an arm around Ali's shoulders proudly. "You'd think he'd been riding zahhak since he was weaned."

"It was extraordinary," Ali admitted.

The other man laughed. "We'll make a proper northerner out of you yet, Daevabadi."

Ali grinned back. "God willing."

They crossed through the dark chamber, passing the empty tombs of the long-dead human kings and queens who once ruled here—no one would ever give Ali a straight answer as to exactly *where* their bodies had gone and he wasn't sure he wanted to know. Ahead was a plain stone wall. To a casual observer—a human observer—little would mark it as special save the slight glow emanating from its oddly warm surface.

But it was a surface that all but sang to Ali, magic simmering from the rock in comforting waves. He placed his palm upon the wall. "Pataru sawassam," he commanded in Geziriyya.

The wall misted away, revealing the bustling greenery of Bir Nabat. Ali paused, taking a moment to appreciate the newly fertile beauty of the place he'd called home for five years. It was a mesmerizing sight, far different from the famine-stricken shell it had been when he first arrived. Though Bir Nabat had likely been a lush paradise at the time of its founding—the remnants of water catchments and aqueducts, as well as the size and artistry of its human-crafted temples, indicated a time of more frequent rains and a flourishing population—the djinn who'd moved in after had never matched their numbers. They'd gotten by for centuries with a pair of remaining springs and their own scavenging.

But by the time Ali arrived, the springs had dwindled down to almost nothing. Bir Nabat had become a desperate place, a place willing to defy their king and take in the strange young prince they'd found dying in a nearby crevasse. A place willing to overlook the fact that his eyes occasionally gleamed like wet bitumen when he got upset and his limbs were covered in scars no blade could draw. That didn't matter to the Geziris in Bir Nabat. The fact that Ali had uncovered four new springs and two untapped cisterns, enough water to irrigate Bir Nabat for centuries, did. Now small but thriving plots of barley and melons hemmed new homes, more and more people opting to replace tents of smoke and oryx hide with compounds of quarried stone and sandblasted glass. The date trees were healthy, thick and towering to provide cool shade. The village's eastern corner had been given over to orchards: a dozen fig saplings growing strong between citrus trees, all carefully fenced off for protection from Bir Nabat's booming population of goats.

They passed by the village's small market, held in the shadow of the enormous old temple that had been carved into the cliff face, its carefully sculpted columns and pavilions laden with magical goods. Ali smiled, returning the nods and salaams of various djinn merchants, a sense of calm stealing over him.

One of the vendors quickly stepped to block his path. "Ah, sheikh, I've been looking for you."

Ali blinked, pulled from his euphoric daze. It was Reem, a woman from one of the artisan-caste families.

She waved a scroll in front of him "I need you to check this contract for me. I'm telling you . . . that shifty southern slave of Bilqis is cheating me. My enchantments have no equal, and I know I should be seeing higher returns on the baskets I sold him."

"You do realize *I'm* one of those shifty southerners, correct?" Ali pointed out. The Qahtanis originally hailed from Am Gezira's mountainous southern coast—and were rather proud descendants of the djinn servants Suleiman had once gifted Bilqis, the human queen of ancient Saba.

Reem shook her head. "You're Daevabadi. It doesn't count." She paused. "It's actually worse."

Ali sighed and took the contract; between spending the morning digging a new canal and getting tossed around by a zahhak in the afternoon, he was beginning to yearn for his bed. "I'll have a look."

"Bless you, sheikh." Reem turned away.

Ali and his friends kept walking but didn't get far before Bir Nabat's muezzin came huffing over to them.

"Brother Alizayd, peace and blessings upon you!" The muezzin's gray eyes flitted over Ali. "Aye, you look half-dead on your feet."

"Yes. I was about to—"

"Of course, you were. Listen . . ." The muezzin lowered his voice. "Is there any way you could give the khutbah tomorrow? Sheikh Jiyad hasn't been feeling well."

"Doesn't Brother Thabit usually give the sermon in his father's place?"

"Yes, but . . ." The muezzin lowered his voice even further. "I can't deal with another of his rants, brother. I just can't. The last time he gave the khutbah, all he did was ramble about how the music of lutes was leading young people away from prayer."

Ali sighed again. He and Thabit didn't get along, primarily because Thabit fervently believed all the gossip coming out of Daevabad and would rail to anyone who would listen that Ali was an adulterous liar who'd been sent to corrupt them all with "city ways." "He won't be happy when he learns you asked me."

Aqisa snorted. "Yes, he will. It will give him something new to complain about."

"And people enjoy your sermons," the muezzin added quickly. "You choose very lovely topics." His voice turned shrewd. "It is good for their faith."

The man knew how to make an appeal, Ali would grant him that. "All right," he grumbled. "I'll do it."

The muezzin pressed his shoulder. "Thank you."

"You're dealing with Thabit when he hears about this," Ali said to Aqisa, half-stumbling down the path. They had almost reached his home. "You know how much he hates—" Ali broke off.

Two women were waiting for him outside his tent.

"Sisters!" he greeted them, forcing a smile to his face even as he inwardly swore. "Peace be upon you."

"And upon you peace." It was Umm Qays who spoke first, one of the village's stone mages. She gave Ali a wide, oddly sly grin. "How does this day find you?"

Exhausted. "Well, thanks be to God," Ali replied. "And yourselves?"

"Fine. We're fine," Bushra, Umm Qays's daughter spoke up quickly. She was avoiding Ali's eyes, embarrassment visible in her flushed cheeks. "Just passing through!"

"Nonsense." Umm Qays yanked her daughter close, and the young woman gave a small, startled yelp. "My Bushra has just made the loveliest kabsa . . . she is an extraordinarily gifted cook, you know, can conjure up a feast from the barest of bones and a whisper of spice . . . Anyway, her first thought was to set aside a portion for our prince." She beamed at Ali. "A good girl, she is."

Ali blinked, a little taken aback by Umm Qays's enthusiasm. "Ah . . . thank you," he said, catching sight of Lubayd covering his mouth, his eyes bright with amusement. "It is much appreciated."

Umm Qays was peeking in his tent. She tutted in disapproval. "A lonely place this looks, Alizayd al Qahtani. You are a great man. You should have a proper home in the cliffs and someone to return to."

God have mercy, not this again. He stammered out a reply. "I-I thank you for your concern, but really I'm quite content. Being lonely."

"Ah, but you're a young man." Umm Qays clapped his shoulder, giving his upper arm a squeeze. A surprised expression came over her face. "Well, my goodness . . . God be praised for such a thing," she said admiringly. "Certainly, you have *needs*, dear one. It's only natural."

Heat flooded Ali's face—more so when he realized Bushra had slightly lifted her gaze. There was a flicker of appraisal in her eyes that sent nerves fluttering in his stomach—and not entirely unpleasant ones. "I . . ."

Mercifully, Lubayd stepped in. "That's very considerate of you, sisters," he said, taking the dish. "We'll make sure he appreciates it."

Aqisa nodded, her eyes dancing. "It smells delicious."

Umm Qays seemed to recognize temporary defeat. She wagged a finger in Ali's face. "One day." She gestured inside as she left. "By the way, a messenger came by with a package from your sister."

The women were barely around the bend when Lubayd and Aqisa burst into peals of laughter.

"Stop it," Ali hissed. "It's not funny."

"Yes, it is," Aqisa countered, her shoulders shaking. "I could watch that a dozen more times."

Lubayd hooted. "You should have seen his face last week when Sadaf brought him a blanket because she felt his bed 'needed warming.'"

"That's enough." Ali reached for the dish. "Give me that."

Lubayd ducked away. "Oh no, this is my reward for saving you." He held it up, closing his eyes as he inhaled. "Maybe you should marry her. I can intrude upon all your dinners."

"I'm not marrying anyone," Ali returned sharply. "It's too dangerous."

Aqisa rolled her eyes. "You exaggerate. It has been a year since I last saved you from an assassin."

"One who got close enough to do this," Ali argued, arching his neck to reveal the faint pearly scar running across his throat just under the scruff of his beard.

Lubayd waved him off. "He did that and then his own clan caught him, gutted him, and left his body for the zahhak." He gave Ali a pointed look. "There are very few assassins foolish enough to come after the man responsible for half of northern Am Gezira's water supply. You *should* start building a life here. I suspect marriage would vastly improve your temperament."

"Oh, immeasurably so," Aqisa agreed. She glanced up, exchanging a conspiratorial grin with Lubayd. "A pity there is no one in Bir Nabat to his taste . . ."

"You mean someone with black eyes and a penchant for healing?" Lubayd teased, cackling when Ali glared at him.

"You know there's no truth to those idiotic rumors," Ali said. "The Banu Nahida and I were merely friends, and she is married to my brother."

Lubayd shrugged. "I find the idiotic rumors enjoyable. Can you blame people for spinning exciting tales out of what happened to all of you?" His voice took on a dramatic edge. "A mysterious Nahid beauty locked away in the palace, an evil Afshin set to ruin her, an irritable prince exiled to the land of his forefathers . . ."

Ali's temper finally snapped as he reached for the tent flap. "I am not *irritable*. And you're the one spinning most of those tales!"

Lubayd only laughed again. "Go on inside and see what your sister sent you." He glanced at Aqisa, holding up the dish. "Hungry?"

"Very."

Shaking his head, Ali kicked off his sandals and ducked inside his tent. It was small yet cozy, with ample space for the bed cushion one of Lubayd's cousins had mercifully lengthened to Ali's "ludicrous" height. In fact, everything in the room was a gift. He'd arrived in Bir Nabat with only his weapons and the bloodstained dishdasha on his back, and his belongings were a record of his years here: the extra robe and sandals that were the first things he'd scavenged from an abandoned human caravan, the Qur'an that Sheikh Jiyad had given him when Ali started teaching, the pages and pages of notes and drawings he'd taken while observing various irrigation works.

And something new: a sealed copper tube the length of his forearm and wide as a fist, resting upon his neatly folded cushion. One end had been dipped in jet black wax, a familiar signature carved around its perimeter.

With a smile, Ali picked up the tube, peeling off the wax to reveal the blade-sharp pattern it had been protecting. A blood seal, one that ensured none but a blood relation of Zaynab's would be able to open it. It was the most they could do to protect their privacy . . . not that it mattered. The man most likely to have their communication intercepted was their own father and he could easily use his own blood to read their messages. Likely he did.

Ali pressed his arm against the edge. The scroll top smoked away the moment the blades drew blood, and Ali tilted it, emptying the contents onto his cushion.

A bar of gold, a copper armband, and a letter, several pages in length. Attached to the armband was a small note in Zaynab's elegant hand.

For the headaches you keep complaining about. Take good care of this, little brother. The Nahid horribly overcharged me for it.

Ali fingered the armband, eying the gold bar and the letter. *God preserve you, Zaynab.* Bir Nabat might be recovering, but it was still a hard place and that gold would go a long way here. He only hoped sending it hadn't gotten his sister in any trouble. He'd written her multiple times trying to warn her off providing him with supplies, and she'd ignored him, flouting his advice as thoroughly as she defied their father's unofficial decree that no Geziri was to aid him. Zaynab was probably the only one who could get away with such a thing; Ghassan had always been soft-hearted when it came to his daughter.

He fell on his bed cushion, rolling onto his stomach to read the letter, Zaynab's familiar script and barbed observations like a warm hug. He missed his sister terribly; theirs was a relationship he'd been too young and self-righteous to appreciate until now, when it was reduced to the occasional letter. Ali would never see Zaynab again. He wouldn't sit by the canal on a sunny day to share coffee and family gossip, nor be proudly at her side when she married. He'd never meet her future children, the nieces and nephews he would have spoiled and taught to spar in another life.

He also knew it could be worse. Ali thanked God every day he'd landed with the djinn of Bir Nabat rather than in the hands of any of the dozens who'd tried to kill him since. But the ache when he thought of his family never quite went entirely away.

Then maybe you should start building one here. Ali rolled onto his back, basking in the warmth of the sun glowing against the tent. In the distance, he could hear children laughing and birds chirping. Bushra's quiet interest played across his mind, and alone in his tent, Ali would not deny it sent a slight thrill through his body.

Daevabad seemed a world away, his father apparently content to forget him. Would it truly be so terrible to allow himself to settle more permanently here, to quietly seize the kind of domestic life he would have never been allowed as Muntadhir's Qaid?

Dread crept over him. *Yes,* it seemed to answer, swallowing the simple fantasies running through his mind's eye. For in Ali's experience, dreaming of a better future had only ever led to destruction.

3

NAHRI

Well, one thing was clear: her Daeva elders did not share Nahri's enthusiasm about the Nahid hospital.

Nisreen stared at her. "You slipped away from your guards? *Again?* Do you have any idea what Ghassan will do if he finds out?"

"Zaynab made me do it!" Nahri defended herself. Then—realizing it was perhaps a little ungrateful to blame her sister-in-law for an outing she rather enjoyed—she quickly added, "She said she takes such walks often and hasn't been caught yet. And she promised to take the blame if we were."

Kartir looked openly alarmed. The grand priest was normally more indulgent of Nahri's . . . unorthodox ways, but this latest misadventure seemed to have shaken his calm. "And you trust her?" he asked, his wiry brows knitting in worry.

"On this, yes." Nahri's relationship with her sister-in-law was a prickly one, but she recognized a woman eager for a little bit of freedom when she saw one. "Now will the two of you stop fretting over everything? This is exciting! Can you imagine it? A Nahid hospital?"

Kartir and Nisreen shared a look. It was quick, but there was no denying the way the priest's cheeks flushed in guilt.

Nahri was instantly suspicious. "You already know of this place? Why wouldn't you tell me?"

Kartir sighed. "Because what happened to that hospital is neither pleasant nor wise to discuss. I doubt anyone besides the king and a few devoted Daevabadi historians even know anything about it."

Nahri frowned at the vague words. "Then how do you two?"

"Because Banu Manizheh learned of its existence—and of its fate," Nisreen said quietly. "She was always poring over her family's old books. She told us."

"What do you mean, 'its fate'?" When neither replied, Nahri's impatience got the better of her. "Suleiman's eye, must everything be a seecret here? I learned more from Razu in five minutes than I have from the two of you in five years!"

"Razu? Baga Rustam's Razu?" Relief lit Kartir's face. "Thank the Creator. I feared the worst when her tavern was burned."

Nahri felt a pang of sorrow for the kind gambler who'd welcomed her so warmly. "I'm the Banu Nahida. I should have known ifrit slaves were being hunted down."

Nisreen and Kartir exchanged another glance. "We thought it best," Nisreen said finally. "You were still so deep in grief over Dara, and I didn't want to burden you with the fate of his fellows."

Nahri flinched at Dara's name; she could not deny she had fallen apart in the weeks after his death. "It still wasn't a decision you should have made on my behalf." She eyed them. "I cannot be Banu Nahida in the Temple and infirmary and then be treated like a child when it comes to political matters you believe upsetting."

"Political matters we think could get you killed," Nisreen corrected bluntly. "There is more room for error in the Temple and infirmary."

"And the hospital?" Nahri pressed. "What political reason could there be to have kept me in the dark about its existence?"

Kartir stared at his hands. "It's not because of its existence, Banu Nahida. It's because of what happened to it during the war."

When he fell silent again, an idea struck Nahri. "If you can't give me a better explanation than that, you'll force me to find a way back. One of the freed djinn was a historian, and I'm sure he knows."

"Absolutely not," Nisreen cut in quickly, but then she sighed, sounding resigned. "The hospital was the first place to fall when Zaydi al Qahtani took Daevabad. The Nahids inside didn't even have a chance to flee back to the palace. The shafit revolted the moment Zaydi's army breached the city walls. They stormed the hospital and murdered every Nahid inside. *Every single one,* Banu Nahri. From elderly pharmacists to apprentices barely out of childhood."

Kartir spoke up, his voice grave as the blood left Nahri's face. "It was said to have been quite brutal. The Geziris had their zulfiqars, of course, but the shafit fought with Rumi fire."

"Rumi fire?" Nahri asked. The term sounded slightly familiar.

"It's a human invention," Nisreen explained. "A substance that sticks like tar and burns even Daeva skin. 'Fire for the fire worshippers,' the shafit were said to have shouted." She dropped her gaze, looking sick. "Some still use it. It's how the djinn thieves who murdered my parents set our family's temple ablaze."

Guilt swept through Nahri, hard and fast. "Oh, Nisreen, I'm sorry. I had no idea."

"It's not your fault," Nisreen replied. "In truth, I suspect what happened at the Nahid hospital was far worse. I didn't read the accounts Banu Manizheh did, but she barely spoke for weeks after finding them."

"There were some indications that it was an act of revenge," Kartir added carefully. "The violence . . . it seemed purposeful."

Nisreen scoffed. "The djinn do not need a reason to be violent. It is their nature."

The priest shook his head. "Let's not pretend our tribe doesn't have blood on its hands, Lady Nisreen. That is not the lesson I would impart to a young Nahid." A shadow passed across his face. "Banu Manizheh used to speak like that. It was not good for her soul."

Nisreen's eyes narrowed. "She had reason to speak as she did, and you know it."

There was a knock on the door. Nisreen instantly fell silent. They might be in the Temple, but one still needed to be wary of speaking ill of the Qahtanis in Daevabad.

But the man who poked his head in was anything but a spy. "Banu Nahida?" Jamshid tented his fingers together in respect. "I'm sorry to interrupt, but the palace sent a litter for you."

Nahri scowled. "Because Creator forbid I spend one unauthorized moment in my own temple." She stood up, glancing at Nisreen. "Are you coming?"

Nisreen shook her head. "I have some matters to finish here." She gave Nahri a stern look. "Please resist the urge to take another side trip, I beg you."

Nahri rolled her eyes. "I bet my own mother would have been less controlling than you."

Nisreen touched her wrist as she passed, an act technically forbidden in the Temple. Her eyes were soft. "But she's *not* here, child, so it's up to us to protect you."

The genuine worry in her face cut through some of Nahri's annoyance. For their many arguments, Nisreen was the closest thing Nahri had to family in Daevabad, and she knew her mentor cared dearly for her. "Fine," she grumbled, bringing her hands together in blessing. "May the fires burn brightly for you both."

"And for you, Banu Nahida," they replied.

"SIDE TRIP?" JAMSHID ASKED ONCE THE DOOR WAS closed. "You have the look of someone freshly scolded."

"A new, rather grisly lesson in Daevabad's history." Nahri made a face. "Just once, I'd like to learn of an event that was nothing but our ancestors conjuring rainbows and dancing in the street together."

"It's a bit more difficult to hold a grudge over the good days."

Nahri wrinkled her nose. "I suppose that's true." She set aside thoughts of the hospital, turning to face him. In the dim light of the corridor, the shadows under Jamshid's eyes were well-pronounced and the planes of his cheekbones and nose stood out sharply. Five years after Dara's attack had nearly killed him, Jamshid was still recovering—at a gruelingly slow pace no one could understand. He was a shadow of the healthy archer Nahri had first seen deftly shooting arrows from upon the back of a charging elephant. "How are you feeling?"

"As though you ask me that question every day, and the answer is always the same?"

"I'm your Banu Nahida," she said as they emerged into the Temple's main prayer hall. It was a vast space, designed to fit thousands of worshippers with rows of decorated columns holding up the distant ceiling and shrines dedicated to the most lionized figures in their tribe's long history lining the walls. "It's my duty."

"I'm fine," he assured her, pausing to look at the bustling temple. "It's crowded here today."

Nahri followed his gaze. The temple was indeed packed, and it seemed like many were travelers: ascetics in worn robes and wide-eyed pilgrim families jostling for space with the usual Daevabadi sophisticates.

"Your father wasn't joking when he said people would start arriving months before Navasatem."

Jamshid nodded. "It's our most important holiday. Another century of freedom from Suleiman's imprisonment . . . a month of celebrating life and honoring our ancestors."

"It's an excuse to shop and drink."

"It's an excuse to shop and drink," Jamshid agreed. "But it's supposed to be an extraordinary spectacle. Competitions and parties of every kind, merchants bringing all the newest and most exciting wares from across the world. Parades, fireworks . . ."

Nahri groaned. "The infirmary is going to be so busy." The djinn took merrymaking seriously and the risks of overindulgence far less. "Do you think your father will be back by then?" Kaveh had left recently to visit the Pramukhs' ancestral estate in Zariaspa, ranting about a union dispute among his herb growers and a particularly pernicious plague of ravenous frogs that had besieged their silver-mint plants.

"Most certainly," Jamshid replied. "He'll be back to help the king with the final preparations."

They kept walking, passing the enormous fire altar. It was beautiful, and Nahri always paused for a moment to admire it, even when she wasn't conducting ceremonies. Central to the Daeva faith, the striking altars had persisted through the centuries and consisted of a basin of purified water with a brazierlike structure rising in its middle. Inside burned a fire of cedarwood, extinguished only upon a devotee's death. The brazier was carefully swept of ash at dawn each day, marking the sun's return, and the glass oil lamps that bobbed in the basin were relit to keep the water at a constant simmer.

A long line of worshippers waited to receive blessings from the priest; Nahri caught the eye of a little girl in a yellow felt dress fidgeting next to her father. She winked and the girl beamed, tugging her father's hand and pointing excitedly.

At her side, Jamshid misstepped. He stumbled, letting out a hiss of pain, but waved Nahri off when she moved to take his arm.

"I can do it," he insisted. He tapped the cane. "I'm hoping to be done with *this* come Navasatem."

"An admirable goal," Nahri said gently, worry rising in her as she studied the stubborn set of his features. "But take care not to exhaust yourself. Your body needs time to heal."

Jamshid made a face. "I suppose being cursed has its drawbacks."

She immediately stopped, turning to look at him. "You're not cursed."

"Do you have a better explanation for why my body reacts so badly to Nahid healing?"

No. Nahri bit her lip. Her skills had come a long way, but her inability to heal Jamshid gnawed at her confidence. "Jamshid . . . I'm still new at this, and Nisreen isn't a Nahid. It's far more likely there's some magical or medical reason that your recovery is taking so long. Blame *me*," she added. "Not yourself."

"I would not dare." They were nearing the shrines that lined the Temple wall. "Though on that note . . . I would like to have another session soon if possible."

"Are you certain? The last time we tried . . ." Nahri trailed off, trying to find a diplomatic way to point out that the last time she'd healed him, he'd barely lasted five minutes before he was screaming in agony and clawing at his skin.

"I know." He kept his gaze averted, as if he was struggling to keep both the hope and despair from his face; unlike many in Daevabad, Jamshid had never struck Nahri as a good liar. "But I'd like to try." His voice dropped. "The emir . . . his father forced him to appoint another captain to his personal guard."

"Oh, Jamshid, it's just a position," Nahri replied. "Surely you know you're Muntadhir's closest companion regardless. He never stops singing your praises."

Jamshid shook his head, stubborn. "I should be protecting him."

"You almost died protecting him."

They came into view of Dara's shrine at that rather inopportune time, and Nahri felt Jamshid tense. Dara's shrine was among the most popular; roses garlanded his brass statue, that of a Daeva warrior on horseback, standing proudly upright in his stirrups to aim an arrow at his pursuers, and offerings littered the floor around the statue's base. No blades were allowed in the temple, so small ceramic tokens depicting a variety of ceremonial weapons— mostly arrows—had been brought instead.

An enormous silver bow hung on the wall behind the statue, and as Nahri gazed at it, a lump rose in her throat. She'd spent a lot of time staring at that bow, though never in the company of a man—a friend—she knew had every right to hate the Afshin who'd wielded it.

But Jamshid wasn't looking at the bow. He was instead squinting at the statue's foot. "Is that a *crocodile*?" he asked, pointing to a small charred skeleton.

Nahri pressed her lips together. "Looks like it. Alizayd the Afshin-slayer." She said the title softly, hating everything about it.

Jamshid looked disgusted. "That's obscene. I am no fan of Alizayd's, but the same sentiment that calls the Ayaanle crocodiles calls us fire worshippers."

"Not everyone shares your tolerance," she replied. "I've seen the skeletons here before. I suppose some people think Dara would enjoy having his murderer burned before him."

"He probably would," Jamshid said darkly. He glanced at her, his expression shifting. "Do you do that often? Come here, I mean?"

Nahri hesitated, uncertain how to respond. Dara was a raw nerve within her, even five years after his death—an emotional bramble that only grew more tangled when she tried to cut through it. Her memories of the grumbling, handsome warrior she'd grown to care for on their journey to Daevabad warred with the knowledge that he was also a war criminal, his hands drenched with the blood of Qui-zi's innocents. Dara had stolen his way into her heart and then he'd shattered it, so desperate to save her despite her own wishes that he'd been willing to risk plunging their world into war.

"No," she finally replied, checking the tremor in her voice. Unlike Jamshid, Nahri was accomplished at hiding her emotions. "I try not to. This isn't a shrine to the Dara I knew."

Jamshid's gaze flickered from the shrine to her. "What do you mean?"

Nahri considered the statue, the warrior caught in action. "He wasn't a legendary Afshin to me. Not originally. Qui-zi, the war, his rebellion . . . he didn't tell me about any of that." She paused. It had been here in the Temple that she and Dara had come closest to speaking aloud of what had grown between them, a fight that had dragged them apart and offered Nahri the first true glimpse of how much the war had stolen from Dara—and how much the loss had warped him. "I don't think he wanted me to know. In the end . . ." Her voice softened. "I don't think that was the man he wanted to be." She flushed. "I'm sorry. I shouldn't be burdening you of all people with this."

"You can burden me," Jamshid said quietly. "It's hard to watch the way this city ruins the ones we love." He sighed and then turned away, leaning on his cane. "We should head back."

Lost in thought, Nahri said nothing as they left the Temple and crossed its manicured grounds to the waiting palanquin. The sun blinked past the distant mountains, vanishing into the green horizon, and from deep inside the temple, a drum began to beat. Across the city, the djinn call to prayer answered it in waves. In marking the departure of the sun, the djinn and Daeva faithful were briefly united.

Once inside the palanquin, she relaxed into the cushions, the rocking motion lulling her toward sleep as they made their way through the Daeva Quarter.

"Tired?" Jamshid asked as she yawned.

"Always. And I had a patient who went late last night. An Agnivanshi weaver who inhaled the vapors she uses to make her carpets fly." Nahri rubbed her temples. "Never a dull day."

Jamshid shook his head, looking amused. "I can help when we get back."

"That would be appreciated. I'll have the kitchens send us up some dinner."

He groaned. "Not your strange human food."

"I like my strange human food," Nahri defended. One of the palace cooks was an old man from Egypt, a shafit with a knack for knowing when to prepare the comforting dishes of her former home. "And anyway—"

From beyond the palanquin, a woman's cry pierced the air. "Let him go! *Please!* I beg you. We did nothing wrong!"

Nahri shot upright. The palanquin lurched to a stop, and she yanked back its brocade curtain. They were still in the Daeva Quarter, on a quiet street that ran past some of the city's oldest and finest homes. In front of the largest, a dozen members of the Royal Guard were rooting through a pile of furnishings. Two Daeva men and a boy who couldn't be out of his teens had been bound and gagged, pushed into kneeling positions on the street.

An older Daeva woman was pleading with the soldiers. "Please, my son is only a boy. He wasn't involved!"

Another soldier exited the smashed and dangling doors of the home. He shouted excitedly in Geziriyya and then tossed a carved wooden chest to the cobblestone street with enough force to break it. Coins and uncut jewels spilled out, glittering on the wet ground.

Nahri leapt from the litter without a second thought. "What in God's name is going on here?" she demanded.

"Banu Nahida!" Relief lit in the woman's wet eyes. "They're accusing my husband and his brother of treason and trying to take my son!" She choked back a sob, switching to Divasti. "It's a lie! All they did was hold a meeting to discuss the new land tax on Daeva properties. The king heard of it and now's he's punishing them for telling the truth!"

Anger surged through Nahri, hot and dangerous. "Where are your orders?" she demanded, turning to the soldiers. "I can't imagine they gave you permission to loot this home."

The officers looked unimpressed by her attempt at authority. "New rules," one replied brusquely. "The Guard now gets a fifth of whatever is confiscated from unbelievers—and that would be you Daevas." His expression darkened. "Strange how everyone in this city is suffering save the fire worshippers."

The Daeva woman dropped to her knees in front of Nahri. "Banu Nahida, please! I told them they could have whatever money and jewelry they want, but don't let them take my family! I'll never see them again once they're in that dungeon."

Jamshid came to their side. "Your family isn't going any-where," he assured her. He turned to the soldiers, his voice steely. "Send one of your men to the emir. I don't want another hand laid on these people until he's here."

The djinn officer snorted. "I take my orders from the king. Not from the emir and certainly not from some useless Afshin pretender." Cruelty edged his voice as he nodded at Jamshid's cane. "Your new bow isn't quite as intimidating as your old one, Pramukh."

Jamshid jerked back like he'd been slapped, and Nahri stepped forward, enraged on his behalf. "How dare you speak so disrespectfully? He is the grand wazir's son!"

In the blink of an eye, the soldier had his zulfiqar drawn. "His father is not here and neither is your bloody Scourge." He gave Nahri a cold look. "Do not try me, Nahid. The king made his orders clear, and believe me when I say I have little patience for the fire worshipper who loosed her Afshin on my fellows." He raised his zulfiqar, bringing it dangerously close to Jamshid's throat. "So, unless you'd like me to start *executing* Daeva men, I suggest you return to your palanquin."

Nahri froze at the threat—and the implication that accompanied its open hostility. Ghassan had an iron grip on Daevabad: if his soldiers felt comfortable intimidating two of the most powerful Daevas in the city, it was because they weren't worried about being punished.

Jamshid stepped back first, reaching for Nahri's hand. His was cold. "Let's go," he said softly in Divasti. "The sooner we're gone, the sooner I can get word of this to Muntadhir."

Heartsick, Nahri could barely look at the woman. In that moment, though she hated the memory of the warrior Dara, she couldn't help but wish he was here, bringing shedu statues to life and drawing his bow against those who would hurt their people. "I'm sorry," she whispered, cursing her inability to do anything more. "We'll talk to the emir, I promise."

The woman was weeping. "Why bother?" she asked, bitter despair lacing into her voice. The words she spoke next cut Nahri to the core. "If you can't protect yourself, how can you possibly protect the rest of us?"

4

DARA

In the deep quiet of a snowy night, Dara made his way through a black forest.

He did so in complete silence, moving stealthily alongside the five young Daeva men mirroring his every action. They had bound their boots in cloth to muffle their steps and smeared their woolen coats with ash and dirt to mimic the pattern of the skeletal trees and rocky ground. There were magical ways—better ways—to conceal oneself, but what they were doing tonight was as much test as it was mission, and Dara wanted to challenge his young recruits.

He stopped at the next tree, raising a hand to signal his men to do the same. He narrowed his eyes and studied their targets, his breath steaming against the cloth that covered the lower part of his face.

Two Geziri scouts from the Royal Guard, exactly as rumored. Gossip in this desolate part of northern Daevastana had been buzzing with news of them. They had apparently been sent to survey the northern border; his sources had told him it was normal, a routine visit completed every half-century or so to harass the locals about their taxes and remind them of King Ghassan's reach. But Dara had been suspicious of the timing and thus quietly relieved when Banu Manizheh ordered him to bring them to her.

"Would it not be easier to kill them?" had been his only protest. Contrary to the rumors he knew surrounded him, Dara did not relish killing. But neither did he like the prospect of two Geziris learning of his and Manizheh's existence. "This is a dangerous land. I can make it look as though they were attacked by beasts."

Manizheh had shaken her head. "I need them alive." Her expression had grown stern, his Banu Nahida perhaps coming to know him a bit too well in the few years he'd served her. "Alive, Darayavahoush. That's nonnegotiable."

Which is why they were here now. It had taken them two weeks to find the scouts, and two days to quietly drive them off course, his men shifting the boundary stones in waves to send the Geziris off the established path to the village of Sugdam and deep into the thick forest that belted the nearby mountains.

The scouts looked miserable, wrapped in furs and felt blankets and huddled together under a hastily erected tarp. Their fire was a weak one, slowly losing the battle against the steady snowfall. The older scout was smoking a pipe, the sweet smell of smoldering qat scenting the air.

But it wasn't pipes Dara was concerned with, nor the khanjar daggers tucked in their belts. After a moment of scanning the camp, he spotted the zulfiqars he'd been looking for on a bed of raised stones just behind the scouts. Their leather scabbards had been wrapped in a layer of felt to protect the blades from the snow, but Dara could see a hilt poking free.

He silently cursed. Skilled zulfiqaris were treasured, and he'd been holding out hope that the king hadn't bothered sending such valuable warriors on what should have been a rather dull mission. Invented during the war against the Nahid Council—or stolen from the angels who guarded Paradise, as the more fanciful stories went—the zulfiqar at first appeared to be a normal scimitar, its copper construction and two-pronged end a bit unusual but otherwise unremarkable.

But well-trained Geziris—and only Geziris—could learn to conjure poisoned flames from the zulfiqar's deadly edge. A single nick of the skin meant death; there was no healing from the wounds, not even by the hand of a Nahid. It was the weapon that had turned the war and ended the rule of his blessed and beloved Nahid Council, killing an untold number of Daevas in the process.

Dara glanced at the warrior nearest him. Mardoniye, one of his youngest. He'd been a member of the Daeva Brigade, the small contingent of Daeva soldiers once allowed to serve in the Royal Guard. They'd been run out of the Citadel after Dara's death on the boat, ordered from their barracks by djinn officers they considered comrades and sent into the Grand Bazaar with only the clothes on their backs. There, they'd been met by a shafit mob. Unarmed and outnumbered, they'd been brutally assaulted, several men killed. Mardoniye still bore Rumi fire burns on his face and arms, remnants of the attack.

Dara swallowed against the worry rising in his chest. He'd made it clear to his men that he would not aid them in capturing the Geziris. He considered it a rare opportunity for them to test their training. But fighting zulfiqaris wasn't the same as fighting regular soldiers.

And yet . . . they needed to learn. They would face zulfiqaris one day, Creator willing. They'd fight Daevabad's fiercest, in a battle that would need to be decisively won.

The thought sent more smoldering heat into Dara's hands. He fought it back with a tremble, this new, raw power he'd yet to entirely master. It simmered beneath his skin, the fire aching to escape. He struggled with it more when he was emotional . . . and the prospect of the young Daevas he'd mentored for years being cut down by the blade of a sand fly certainly made him so.

You've spent a lifetime training warriors. You know they need this. Dara pushed aside his misgivings.

He let out a low hoot, the approximation of an owl. One of the djinn glanced up but only briefly. His men fanned out, their dark eyes darting back to him as they moved. Dara watched as his archers nocked their arrows.

He clicked his tongue, his final signal.

The archers' pitch-soaked arrows burst into conjured flames. The djinn had less than a second to spot them before they shot past, striking the tarp. In the blink of an eye, the entire thing was blazing. The larger Geziri—an older man with a thick salt-and-pepper beard—whirled around to grab the zulfiqars.

Mardoniye was already there. He kicked away the blades and then threw himself on the Geziri. They rolled into the snow, scrabbling at each other.

"Abu Sayf!" The younger scout lunged for his companion—an unwise move that left his back exposed when the rest of Dara's men emerged. They threw a weighted net over his head, dragging him back and ensnaring his arms. In seconds, his khanjar had been ripped away and iron cuffs—meant to dampen his magic—clasped around his wrists.

Mardoniye was still struggling. The Geziri man—Abu Sayf—struck him hard across the face and then lunged to grab a zulfiqar. It burst into flames. He whirled back on Mardoniye.

Dara's bow was off his shoulder, an arrow nocked before he even realized what he was doing. *Let him fight!* the Afshin in him demanded. He could all but hear his father's voice, his uncles' voices, his own. There was no room for mercy in the heat of the battle.

But by the Creator, he did not have it in him to watch another Daeva die. Dara drew back his bow, his index finger on the twitching feather fletch, the string a whispered brush against his cheek.

Mardoniye threw himself at the Geziri's knees with a howl, knocking him into the snow. Another of Dara's archers ran forward, swinging his bow like a club at the Geziri man's hand. Abu Sayf dropped the zulfiqar, and the flames were gone before it hit the ground. The archer struck the djinn hard across the face, and he collapsed.

It was over.

The scouts were secured by the time Dara stomped out their campfire. He quickly checked the unconscious one for a pulse. "He's alive," he confirmed, silently relieved. He nodded at the small camp. "Check their supplies. Burn any documents you find."

The conscious djinn was indignant, straining against his binds. "I don't know what you fire worshippers think you're doing, but we're Royal Guard. This is treason! When my garrison commander learns you interfered with our mission, he'll have you executed!"

Mardoniye kicked at a large sack, and it let out a jingle. "All the coins they've been stealing from our people, I suspect."

"Taxes," the Geziri cut in savagely. "I know you're all half feral out here, but surely you have some basic concept of governance."

Mardoniye scoffed. "Our people were ruling empires while yours were scavenging through human trash, sand fly."

"That's enough." Dara glanced at Mardoniye. "Leave the coins. Leave everything but their weapons and retreat. Take them at least twenty paces away."

The Geziri soldier struggled, trying to twist free as they hauled him to his feet. Dara began unwrapping his headcloth, not wanting it to burn when he shifted. It briefly caught on the slave ring he was still too nervous to remove.

"You're going to hang for this!" the djinn repeated. "You filthy, sister-fucking, fire-worshipping—"

Dara's hand shot out as Mardoniye's eyes flashed again. He knew all too well how quickly tensions built between their peoples. He grabbed the djinn by the throat. "It is a long walk back to our camp," he said flatly. "If you can't be *polite*, I am going to remove your ability to speak."

The djinn's eyes traveled over Dara's now uncovered face, landing on his left cheekbone. That was all it took for the color to leach from his skin.

"No," he whispered. "You're dead. You're dead!"

"I was," Dara agreed coldly. "Now I'm not." He could not keep the edge of bitterness out of his voice. Annoyed, he shoved the Geziri back at his men. "Your camp is about to be attacked by a rukh. Best step away."

The djinn let out a gasp, looking up at the sky. "We're about to be *what*?"

Dara had already turned his back. He waited until the sounds of his men faded away. The distance wasn't only for their protection.

Dara didn't like anyone to see him when he shifted.

He pulled off his coat, setting it aside. Heat rose in hazy waves from his tattooed arms, the snow melting in the air around him before the flakes came close to brushing his skin. He closed his eyes, taking a deep breath as he steeled himself. He hated this part.

Fire burst from his skin, flushed light sweeping down his limbs, washing away the normal brown. His entire body shook violently, and he fell to his knees, his limbs seizing. It had taken him two years to learn how to shift between his original form—that of a typical man of his tribe, albeit an emerald-eyed one—and that of a true daeva, as Manizheh insisted on calling him, the form their people had taken before Suleiman changed them. The form the ifrit still held.

Dara's vision sharpened, the taste of blood filling his mouth as his teeth lengthened into fangs. He always forgot to prepare for that part.

His clawed hands clenched at the icy ground as his raw jittery power settled completely. It only ever happened in this form, a peace he obtained by becoming something he hated. He exhaled, burning embers leaving his mouth, and then he straightened back up.

He raised his hands, smoke swirling up from around them. With a quick snap of his claws across his wrist, a shimmer of golden blood dripped down to merge with the smoke, growing and twisting in the air as he shaped it. Wings and talons, a beak and glittering eyes. He fought for breath, the magic draining him.

"Ajanadivak," he whispered, the command still foreign on his tongue. The original language of the daevas, a language only a handful of ifrit still remembered. They were Manizheh's "allies," pressed into teaching a reluctant Afshin the ancient daeva magic that Suleiman had stripped away.

Fire burst from the rukh, and it let out a screech. It rose in the air, still under Dara's command, destroying the camp in a matter of minutes. He took care to let it crash through the canopy and rake its talons over the tree trunks. To anyone with the misfortune of coming across this place—any members of the Royal Guard looking for their two lost fellows, though Dara doubted they'd ever make it out here—it would appear as though the scouts had been eaten, the fortune in taxes left untouched.

He released the rukh, and it disintegrated, cinders raining over the ground as its hazy form dissipated. With a final burst of magic, Dara shifted back, stifling a gasp of pain. It always hurt, like shoving his body into a tight, barbed cage.

Mardoniye was at his side in moments, reliably loyal. "Your coat, Afshin," he said, offering it out.

Dara took it gratefully. "Thank you," he said, his teeth chattering.

The younger man hesitated. "Are you all right? If you need a hand—"

"I am fine," Dara insisted. It was a lie; he could already feel the black pitch churning in his stomach, a side effect of returning to his mortal body while his new magic still swirled in his veins. But he refused to show such weakness before his men; he would not risk it getting back to Manizheh. If the Banu Nahida had her way, Dara would stay forever in the form he hated. "Go. I'll be along shortly."

He watched, waiting until they were out of view. Then he dropped to his knees again, his stomach heaving, his limbs shaking, as the snow fell silently around him.

THE SIGHT OF THEIR CAMP NEVER FAILED TO EASE Dara's mind, the familiar plumes of smoke promising a hot meal, the gray felt tents that blended into the horizon a warm bed. These were appreciated luxuries for any warrior who'd just spent three days trying hard not to rip the tongue out of a particularly irritating djinn's mouth. Daevas bustled about, hard at work cooking, training, cleaning, and forging weapons. There were about eighty of them, lost souls Manizheh had come upon in her years of wandering: the sole survivors of zahhak attacks and unwanted children, exiles she'd rescued from death and the remnants of the Daeva Brigade. They swore allegiance to her, offering loyalty in an oath that would rot their tongues and hands should they attempt to break it.

He'd shaped about forty of them into warriors, including a

handful of young women. Dara had at first balked at that, finding it unorthodox and improper. Then Banu Manizheh had bluntly pointed out that if he could fight *for* a woman, he could fight beside one, and he had to admit she'd been right. One of the women, Irtemiz, was by far his most talented archer.

But his good mood vanished the second he caught sight of their corral. A new horse was there: a golden mare whose finely tooled saddle hung over the fence.

Dara's heart dropped. He recognized that mare.

Kaveh e-Pramukh had arrived early.

A gasp from behind stole his attention. "This is your camp?" It was Abu Sayf, the zulfiqari who'd nearly killed Mardoniye and yet had oddly proven far less maddening on their return trek than his younger tribesman. He asked the question in fluent Divasti; he'd told Dara that he'd been married to a Daeva woman for decades. His gray eyes scanned the neat row of tents and wagons. "You move," he noted. "Yes, I suppose you would. Easier to stay hidden that way."

Dara met his gaze. "You would do well to keep such observations to yourself."

Abu Sayf's expression dimmed. "What do you plan to do with us?"

I do not know. It was also not a thing Dara could think about—not when the sight of Kaveh's horse was making him so anxious he felt sick.

He glanced at Mardoniye. "See that the djinn are secured, but get them water for washing and something hot to eat." He paused, glancing at his tired band of soldiers. "And do the same for yourselves. Your rest is well earned."

Dara turned toward the main tent. Emotions swirled inside him. What did one say to the father of a man they had nearly killed? Not that Dara had meant to do so; he remembered nothing about his assault on the warship. The time between Nahri's strange wish and Alizayd tumbling into the lake that ill-fated night was shrouded in fog. But he remembered what he'd seen afterward far too well: the body of the kind young man he'd taken under his wing slumped on the boat deck, his back riddled with Dara's arrows.

His stomach fluttering with nerves, Dara coughed outside the tent flap, alerting those inside to his presence before he called out. "Banu Nahida?"

"Come in, Dara."

He ducked inside and immediately starting coughing more as he inhaled the cloud of acrid purple smoke that greeted him—one of Manizheh's many experiments. They lined the enormous slate table she insisted on lugging around with them, her equipment taking up an entire wagon.

She was at the table now, seated on a cushion behind a floating glass flask and holding a long pair of forceps. A lilac-hued liquid boiled inside the flask, giving off the purple smoke.

"Afshin," she greeted him warmly, dropping a small, wriggling silver object into the boiling liquid. There was a metallic squeal, and then she stepped back, pulling aside her facecloth. "Your mission was a success?"

"The Geziri scouts are being secured as we speak," he said, relieved that Kaveh was nowhere to be seen.

Manizheh's brow arched. "Alive?"

Dara scowled. "As requested."

A small smile lit her face. "It is much appreciated. Please tell your men to bring me one of their relics as soon as possible."

"Their relics?" Djinn and Daeva alike all wore relics—a bit of blood, sometimes a baby tooth or lock of hair, often paired with a holy verse or two, all bound in metal and worn on the person. They were safeguards, to be used to bring a soul back into a conjured body should one be enslaved by an ifrit. "What do you want with their . . ."

The question died on his lips. Kaveh e-Pramukh had emerged from the inner room to join them.

Dara just managed to keep his mouth from falling open. He wasn't sure what surprised him more: that Kaveh had stepped out of the small, private chamber in which Manizheh slept, or that the grand wazir looked terrible. He might have aged fifteen years, not five, his face scored by lines and his hair and mustache mostly silver. He was thin, the shadowed swells under his eyes indicating a man who had seen too much and not slept enough.

But by the Creator, did those eyes find him. And when they did, they filled with all the anger and betrayal that had undoubtedly been seething inside him since that night on the boat.

Manizheh caught the wazir's wrist. "Kaveh," she said softly.

The practiced words of regret vanished from Dara's mind. He crossed the room, falling to his knees.

"I am so sorry, Kaveh." The apology tumbled inelegantly from his lips. "I never meant to hurt him. I would have taken a blade to myself had I—"

"Sixty-four," Kaveh cut in coldly.

Dara blinked. "What?"

"Sixty-four. It is the number of Daevas who were killed in the weeks following your death. Some died after being interrogated, innocents who had nothing to do with your flight. Others because they protested what they saw as your unjust murder at the hands of Prince Alizayd. The rest because Ghassan let the shafit attack us, in an effort to muscle our tribe back into compliance." Kaveh's mouth thinned. "If you are going to offer useless words of remorse, you should at least be reminded of the extent of what you're responsible for. My son lives. Others do not."

Dara's face burned. Did Kaveh not think he regretted, down to his marrow, what his actions had led to? That he wasn't reminded of his mistake every day as he watched over the traumatized remnant of the Daeva Brigade?

He gritted his teeth. "So in your eyes I should have stood silently by as Banu Nahri was forced to marry that lecherous sand fly?"

"Yes," Kaveh said bluntly. "That is *exactly* what you should have done. You should have bowed your damn head and taken the governorship in Zariaspa. You could have quietly trained a militia for years in Daevastana while Banu Nahri lulled the Qahtanis into a false sense of peace. Ghassan is not a young man. Alizayd and Muntadhir could have easily been manipulated into warring against each other once Muntadhir took the throne. We could have let the Geziris destroy themselves and then swept in to take over with minimal bloodshed." His eyes flashed. "I told you we had allies and support outside Daevabad because I *trusted* you. Because I didn't want you to do something rash before we were prepared." His voice turned scornful. "I never imagined the supposedly clever Darayavahoush e-Afshin, the rebel who almost beat Zaydi al Qahtani, would risk us all because he wanted to run away."

The fire under Manizheh's flask flared, and with it, Dara's anger. "*I was not running—*"

"That's *enough*," Manizheh cut in, glaring at them both. "Afshin, calm yourself. Kaveh . . ." She shook her head. "Whatever the consequences, Dara acted to protect my daughter from a fate I fought for decades. I cannot fault him for that. And if you think Ghassan wasn't looking for a reason to crack down on the Daevas the instant a Nahid and Afshin strolled through the gates of Daevabad, you clearly do not know him at all." She gave them another sharp look. "Tearing each other apart is not why we are here." She gestured to a heap of floor cushions arranged around her fire altar. "*Sit.*"

Chastened, Dara obeyed, rising to his feet and moving toward the cushions. After a few moments, Kaveh did the same, still glowering.

Manizheh placed herself between them. "Would you conjure some wine?" she asked Dara. "I suspect you could both use it."

Dara was fairly certain that the only thing Kaveh wanted to do with wine was throw it in his face, but he obeyed. With a snap of his fingers, three brass goblets appeared, filled with the dark amber hue of date wine.

He took a sip, trying to calm himself. Causing fires to explode was not going to alleviate Kaveh's concerns about his temper. "How is he?" he asked carefully. "Jamshid. If I may inquire."

Kaveh stared at the altar. "He didn't wake for a full year. It took another for him to be able to sit up and use his hands. He's walking with a cane now, but . . ." His voice broke, his hand trembling so hard he nearly spilled his wine. "He hasn't handled being injured well. He loved being a warrior . . . he wanted to be like *you*."

The words were like a blow. Ashamed, he dropped his gaze, though not before he caught sight of Manizheh. Her hand was clenched around her goblet so tightly that her knuckles were turning white.

She spoke. "He will be all right, Kaveh. I promise you. Jamshid will be healthy and whole and have *everything* that has been denied him."

The intensity in her voice took Dara aback. In the years he'd known her, Manizheh's calm was constant. Rather reassuring, in fact. The type of absolute unflappability he preferred in a leader.

They are friends, he reminded himself. Small surprise she was so protective of Kaveh's son.

Deciding Jamshid was perhaps not the safest subject, Dara moved on, all while quietly working to calm the magic pulsing through his veins. "And how is Banu Nahri?" he asked, forcing a bland distance into his voice.

"Surviving," Kaveh replied. "Ghassan keeps her on a tight leash. All of us. She was wed to Muntadhir less than a year after your death."

"He no doubt forced her," Manizheh said darkly. "As I said, he tried to do the same to me for decades. He was obsessed with uniting our families."

"Well, he certainly underestimated her. She took Ghassan for everything she could during the marriage negotiations." Kaveh sipped his wine. "It was actually a bit frightening to watch. But Creator bless her. She ended up signing the bulk of her dowry over to the Temple. They've been using it for charitable work: a new school for girls, an orphanage, and assistance for the Daevas ruined in the assault on the Grand Bazaar."

"That must make her popular with our people. A clever move," Manizheh assessed softly before her expression turned grim. "And regarding the other part of their marriage . . . Nisreen is keeping an eye on that situation, yes?"

Kaveh cleared his throat. "There will be no child between them."

Dara's insides had been churning as they spoke, but Kaveh's carefully worded response made his skin prickle. It did not sound like Nahri had much of a say in that either.

The words were leaving his mouth before he could stop them. "I think we should tell her the truth about what we are planning. Your daughter," he burst out. "She is smart. Strong-willed. She could be an asset." Dara cleared his throat. "And she did not quite seem to . . . appreciate being left in the dark the last time."

Manizheh was already shaking her head. "She is safe in the dark. Do you have any idea what Ghassan would do to her if our conspiracy were uncovered? Let her innocence protect her a bit longer."

Kaveh spoke up, more hesitant. "I must say Nisreen has been suggesting the same, Banu Nahida. She's grown very close to your daughter and hates lying to her."

"And if Nahri knew, she might be able to better protect herself," Dara persisted.

"Or she might reveal us all," Manizheh countered. "She is young, she is under Ghassan's thumb, and she has already shown a predilection for cutting deals with djinn. We cannot trust her."

Dara stiffened. The rather curt assessment of Nahri offended him, and he struggled not to show it. "Banu Nahida—"

Manizheh raised a hand. "This is not a debate. Neither of you know Ghassan like I do. You do not know the things he is capable of. The ways he finds to punish the ones you love." A flicker of old grief filled her eyes. "Ensuring that he cannot do such things to another generation of Nahids is far more important than my daughter's feelings about being left in the dark. She can yell at me about that when Ghassan is ash."

Dara lowered his gaze, managing a bare nod.

"Perhaps we can discuss our preparations then," Kaveh said. "Navasatem is approaching, and it would be an excellent time to attack. The city will be caught up in the chaos of celebration and the palace's attention focused on the holiday."

"*Navasatem?*" Dara's head jerked up. "Navasatem is less than eight months away. I have forty men."

"So?" Kaveh challenged. "You're free of Suleiman's curse, aren't you? Can you not tear down the Citadel with your hands and let your blood beasts loose on the city? That is what Banu Manizheh has told me you can do. That is the reason you were brought back."

Dara gripped his cup tightly. He knew he was viewed as a weapon—but this unvarnished assessment of his worth still stung. "It is more complicated than that. I am still learning to control my new abilities. And my men need more training."

Manizheh touched his hand. "You are too humble, Darayavahoush. I believe you and your warriors are more than ready."

Dara shook his head, not as ready to concede on military matters as he was on personal ones. "We cannot take Daevabad with forty men." He looked between them urgently, willing them to listen. "I spent years before the ifrit killed me contemplating how to best capture the city. Daevabad is a fortress. There is no scaling the walls, and there is no tunneling under them. The Citadel has thousands of soldiers—"

"Conscripts," Kaveh cut in. "Poorly paid and growing more mutinous by the day. At least a dozen Geziri officers defected after Alizayd was sent to Am Gezira."

Thoughts of besieging Daevabad vanished from Dara's mind. "Alizayd al Qahtani is in Am Gezira?"

Kaveh nodded. "Ghassan sent him away within days of your death. I thought it might have been temporary, until things calmed, but he hasn't returned. Not even for Muntadhir's wedding." He took another sip of his wine. "Something is going on, but it's been difficult to discern; the Geziris hold their secrets close." A little relish filled the other man's face. "Admittedly, I was happy to see him fall from favor. He's a fanatic."

"He is more than that," Dara said quietly. A buzz filled his ears, smoke curling around his fingers. Alizayd al Qahtani, the self-righteous brat who'd cut him down. The young warrior whose dangerous combination of deadly skill and unquestioning faith had reminded Dara a little too much of his younger self.

He knew quite well how that had turned out. "He should be dealt with," he said. "Swiftly. Before we attack Daevabad."

Manizheh gave him a skeptical look. "You do not think Ghassan would find it suspicious should his son turn up dead in Am Gezira? Presumably in whatever brutal fashion you're currently imagining?"

"It is worth the risk," Dara argued. "I too was a young warrior in exile when Daevabad fell and my family was slaughtered." He let the implication linger. "I would strongly suggest you not let such an enemy have a chance to grow. And I wouldn't be brutal," he added quickly. "We have time aplenty for me to track him down and get rid of him in a way that would leave nothing for Ghassan to question."

Manizheh shook her head. "We don't have time. If we are to attack during Navasatem, I can't have you spending weeks wandering the Am Gezira wastelands."

"We are not going to be able to attack during Navasatem," Dara said, growing exasperated at their stubbornness. "I cannot yet even cross the threshold to *enter* Daevabad, let alone conquer it."

"The threshold is not the only way to enter Daevabad," Manizheh replied evenly.

"What?" Dara and Kaveh said the word together.

Manizheh took a sip of her wine, seeming to savor their shock. "The ifrit think there might be another way to enter Daevabad . . . one for which you may have Alizayd al Qahtani to thank. Or the creatures pulling his strings anyway."

"The creatures pulling his strings," Dara repeated, his voice growing hollow. He'd told Manizheh everything about that night on the boat. About the magic that had overpowered him and stolen his mind. About the prince who'd climbed out of Daevabad's deadly lake covered in tentacles and scales, whispering a language Dara had never heard, raising a dripping blade. She'd come to the same impossible conclusion. "You don't mean . . ."

"I mean it is time we go speak to the marid." A little heat entered Manizheh's expression. "It is time we get some vengeance for what they have done."

5

ALI

"Sheen," Ali said, marking the letter in the damp sand before him. He glanced up, his gaze turning severe at the sight of two boys tussling in the last row. They immediately stopped, and Ali continued, motioning for his students to copy the letter. They obediently did so, also on the sand. Slates and chalk required resources Bir Nabat didn't have to spare, so he taught his lessons in the cool grove where the canals met and the ground was reliably wet. "Who knows a word that starts with 'sheen'?"

"Sha'b!" a little girl in the center piped up while the boy sitting beside her shot his hand into the air.

"I start with sheen!" he declared. "Shaddad!"

Ali smiled. "That's right. And do you know who you share your name with?"

His sister answered. "Shaddad the Blessed. My grandmother told me."

"And who was Shaddad the Blessed?" he asked, snapping his fingers at the boys who'd been fighting. "Do either of you know?"

The smaller one shrank back while the other's eyes went wide. "Um . . . a king?"

Ali nodded. "The second king after Zaydi the Great."

"Is he the one who fought the marid queen?"

The grove went dead silent at the question. Ali's fingers stilled on the damp sand. "What?"

"The marid queen." It was a little boy named Faisal who'd spoken up, his face earnest. "My abba says one of your ancestors defeated a marid queen, and that's why you can find our water."

The simple words, said so innocently, went through Ali like a poisoned blade, leaving sick dread creeping through his limbs. He'd long suspected quiet rumors circulated in Bir Nabat about his affinities with water, but this was the first time he'd heard himself mentioned in relation to the marid. It was probably nothing; a half-remembered folktale given new life when he started discovering springs.

But it was not a connection he could let linger. "My ancestors never had anything to do with the marid," he said firmly, ignoring the churning in his stomach. "The marid are gone. No one has seen them in centuries."

But he could already see eager curiosity catching ahold of his students. "Is it true they'll steal your soul if you look too long at your reflection in the water?" a little girl asked.

"No," an older one answered before Ali could open his mouth. "But I heard humans used to sacrifice *babies* to them." Her voice rose in fear-tinged excitement. "And if they didn't give them up, the marid would drown their villages."

"*Stop*," one of the youngest boys begged. He looked near tears. "If you talk about them, they'll come for you in the night!"

"That's enough," Ali said, and a few children shrank back,

his words coming out sharper than he'd intended. "Until you've mastered your letters, I don't want to hear anything more about—"

Lubayd ran into the grove.

"Forgive me, brother." His friend bent over, clutching his knees as he caught his breath. "But there is something you need to see."

THE CARAVAN WAS LARGE ENOUGH TO BE VISIBLE FROM a fair distance away. Ali watched it approach from the top of Bir Nabat's cliffs, counting at least twenty camels moving in a steady, snaking line toward the village. As they left the shadow of a massive sand dune, the sun glinted off the pearly white tablets the animals were carrying. Salt.

His stomach plummeted.

"Ayaanle." Lubayd took the word from Ali's mouth, shading his eyes with one hand. "And with a fortune . . . that looks like enough salt to pay a year's taxes." He dropped his hand. "What are they doing *here*?"

At his side, Aqisa crossed her arms. "They cannot be lost; we are weeks' travel from the main trade route." She glanced at Ali. "Do you think they could be your mother's kin?"

They better not be. Though his companions didn't know it, his Ayaanle mother's kin were the ones who'd truly gotten Ali banished from Daevabad. They'd been behind the Tanzeem's decision to recruit him, apparently hoping the shafit militants would eventually convince Ali to seize the throne.

It had been a ludicrous plot, but in the chaos following the Afshin's death, Ghassan wasn't taking the chance of anyone preying on Ali's conflicted sympathies—let alone the powerful lords of Ta Ntry. Except, of course, the Ayaanle were difficult to punish in their wealthy, cosmopolitan homeland across the sea. So it had been Ali who suffered, Ali who was ripped from *his* home and tossed to assassins.

Stop. Ali checked the vitriol swirling within him, ashamed of how easily it had come. It was not the fault of the entire Ayaanle tribe, only a handful of his mother's scheming relatives. For all he knew, the travelers below were perfectly innocent.

Lubayd looked apprehensive. "I hope they brought their own provisions. We won't be able to feed all those camels."

Ali turned away, resting his hand on his zulfiqar. "Let's go ask them."

THE CARAVAN HAD ARRIVED BY THE TIME THEY climbed down from the cliffs, and as Ali waded through the crowd of bleating camels, he realized Lubayd had been right about the fortune they were carrying. It looked like enough salt to provision Daevabad for a year and was most certainly some type of tax payment. Even the glossy, bright-eyed camels appeared costly, the decorated saddles and bindings covering their golden-white hides far finer than was practical.

But Ali didn't see the large delegation he would have expected making small talk with Sheikh Jiyad and his son Thabit. Only a single Ayaanle man stood with them, dressed in the traditional bright teal robes that Ayaanle djinn on state business typically donned, their hue an homage to the colors of the Nile headwater.

The traveler turned around, the gold glittering from his ears and around his neck dazzling in the sunlight. He broke into a wide smile. "Cousin!" He laughed as he took in the sight of Ali. "By the Most High, is it possible a prince is under all those rags?"

The man crossed to him before Ali could offer a response, flabbergasted as he was. He held out his arms as if to pull Ali into an embrace.

Ali's hand dropped to his khanjar. He swiftly stepped back. "I do not hug."

The Ayaanle man grinned. "As friendly as people said you would be." His warm gold eyes shone with amusement. "Peace be upon you either way, Hatset's son." His gaze traveled down Ali's body. "You look awful," he added, switching to Ntaran, the language of his mother's tribe. "What have these people been feeding you? Rocks?"

Offended, Ali drew up, studying the man, but no recognition came to him. "Who are you?" he stammered in Djinnistani. The common tongue felt strange after so long in Am Gezira.

"Who am I?" the man asked. "Musa, of course!" When Ali narrowed his eyes, the other man feigned hurt. "Shams's nephew? Cousin to Ta Khazak Ras on your mother's maternal uncle's side?"

Ali shook his head, the tangled lines of his mother's family confusing him. "Where are the rest of your men?"

"Gone. May God have mercy upon them." Musa touched his heart, his eyes filling with sorrow. "My caravan has been utterly cursed with every type of misfortune and injury, and my last two comrades were forced to return to Ta Ntry due to dire family circumstances last week."

"He lies, brother," Aqisa warned in Geziriyya. "No single man could have brought a caravan of such size here. His fellows are probably hiding in the desert."

Ali eyed Musa again, growing more suspicious. "What is it you want from us?"

Musa chuckled. "Not one to bother with small talk, are you?" He pulled free a small white tablet from his robe and tossed it to Ali.

Ali caught it. He rubbed his thumb over the grainy surface. "What am I supposed to do with a lump of salt?"

"Cursed salt. We bewitch our cargo before crossing Am Gezira, and none but our own can handle it. I suppose the fact that you just did means you're Ayaanle, after all." He grinned as if he had said something enormously witty.

Looking doubtful, Lubayd reached to take the salt from Ali's hands and then let out a yelp. His friend yanked his hand away, both the salt and his skin sizzling from the contact.

Musa wrapped a long arm around Ali's shoulder. "Come, cousin. We should talk."

"ABSOLUTELY NOT," ALI DECLARED. "WHETHER OR NOT Ta Ntry's taxes make it to Daevabad is not my concern."

"Cousin . . . show some compassion for family." Musa sipped his coffee and then made a face, setting it aside. They were in Bir Nabat's central meeting place: a large sandstone chamber in the cliffs, its corners dotted with tall columns wrapped in ribbons of carved snakes.

Musa lounged against a worn cushion, his tale of woe finally complete. Ali kept catching sight of curious children peeking past the entrance. Bir Nabat was extremely isolated; someone like Musa, who flaunted the Ayaanle's legendary wealth so openly in his sumptuous robe and heavy gold ornaments, was probably the most exciting thing to happen since Ali's own arrival.

Musa spread his hands; his rings winked in the firelight. "Are you not headed home for Navasatem anyway? Certainly the king's own son would not miss the generation celebrations."

Navasatem. The word rang in Ali's mind. Originally a Daeva holiday, Navasatem was now when all six tribes celebrated the birth of a new generation. Intended to commemorate the anniversary of their emancipation and reflect upon the lessons taught by Suleiman, it had turned into a frenetic celebration of life itself . . . Indeed, it was an old joke that there was typically a *swell* in life ten months after because so many children were conceived during the wild festivities. Like most devout djinn, Ali had mixed feelings about a full month of feasts, fairs, and wild revelry. Daevabad's clerics—djinn imams and Daeva priests alike—typically spent the time clucking their tongues and admonishing their hungover flock.

And yet, in his previous life, Ali had looked forward to the celebrations for years. Navasatem's martial competitions were legendary and, young age notwithstanding, he'd been determined to enter them, to sweep them, earning his father's admiration and the position his name had already bought: Muntadhir's future Qaid.

Ali took a deep breath. "I am not attending Navasatem."

"But I need you," Musa implored, sounding helpless. "There is no way I can continue on to Daevabad alone."

Ali gave him an incredulous look. "Then you shouldn't have left the main route! You could have found assistance at a proper caravanserai."

"We should kill him and take his cargo," Aqisa suggested in Geziriyya. "The Ayaanle will think he perished in the desert, and the lying fool deserves it."

Lubayd touched her fingers, easing them away from the hilt of her zulfiqar. "People won't think much of our hospitality if we start killing all the guests who lie."

Musa glanced between them. "Am I missing something?"

"Just discussing where we might host you for the evening," Ali said lightly in Djinnistani. He pressed his fingers together. "Just so I'm clear. You left the main route to come to Bir Nabat—an outpost you knew could not afford to host you and your animals—in order to foist your responsibilities upon me?"

Musa shrugged. "I do apologize."

"I see." Ali sat back and gave the circle of djinn a polite smile. "Brothers and sisters," he started. "Forgive the burden, but would you mind giving me a few moments alone with my . . . what did you call yourself again?"

"Your cousin."

"My cousin."

The other djinn rose. Thabit gave him a pointed look. He clearly knew Ali well enough to hear the danger in his voice even if Musa did not. "Do not get blood on the rugs," he warned in Geziriyya. "They are new."

The others were barely gone before Musa let out an overwrought sigh. "By the Most High, how have you survived for so long in this *backwater*?" He shuddered, picking at the goat that had been prepared for him, a goat one of the villagers had been readying for his daughter's wedding and happily offered when he learned they had a guest. "I didn't think djinn still lived like—ah!" he cried out as Ali grabbed him by his silver-embroidered collar and threw him to the ground.

"Does our hospitality not please you?" Ali asked coldly, drawing his zulfiqar.

"Not current—wait, don't!" Musa's gold eyes went bright with terror as flames licked down the copper blade. "Please!"

"Why are you really here?" Ali demanded. "And don't give me any more nonsense about your travel woes."

"I'm here to help you, you wild fool! To provide you with a way to return to Daevabad!"

"*Help me?* Your scheming was the reason I was sent away in the first place!"

Musa held up his hands in surrender. "To be fair . . . that was another branch of the family—stop!" he shrieked, scrambling back as Ali pressed the blade closer. "Are you crazy? I'm your blood! And I'm under guest-right!"

"You are not my guest," Ali countered. "I am not from Bir Nabat. And Am Gezira is a dangerous—what did you call it?—*backwater*?" He spat in offense. "Traders disappear all the time. Especially ones foolish enough to go traipsing about alone with such wealth."

Musa's eyes locked on his. There was determination under the fear. "I made it very clear where I was headed. If my cargo doesn't make it to Daevabad in time to pay for Navasatem, the king will come looking for it." He lifted his chin. "Would you invite such trouble upon your new brothers and sisters?"

Ali stepped back, the flames vanishing from his blade. "I'm not getting drawn into another scheme. And I will kill you myself before you threaten these people."

Musa rolled his eyes. "I was warned you had a temper." He straightened up, brushing the sand off his robe. "And a rather alarmingly close relationship with your zulfiqar." He crossed his arms. "But I'm not leaving without you. A not-inconsiderable amount of risk and cost went into this. Another man might be grateful."

"Find him, then," Ali shot back.

"And that would be it? You'd really go back to picking through human trash and selling dates when I'm offering to help you return to Daevabad before it falls apart?"

"Daevabad is not *falling apart*."

"No?" Musa stepped closer. "Does news from the capital not make it to this forsaken place? Crime is soaring, and the economy is so bad that the Royal Guard can barely afford to feed its soldiers, let alone provision them with proper weapons."

Ali gave him an even look. "And what part did the Ayaanle play in those economic woes?"

Musa spread his hands. "Why should we be fair to a king who exiles our prince? A king who turns his back on his own family's legacy and does nothing as shafit are sold at auction blocks?"

"You're lying." Ali eyed the man with scorn. "Not that your people would care about the shafit or the city. Daevabad is a game to the Ayaanle. You sit in Ta Ntry, counting your gold and playing with other people's lives."

"We care far more than you think." Musa's eyes flashed. "Zaydi al Qahtani wouldn't have taken Daevabad without the Ayaanle. *Your* family would not be royalty without the Ayaanle." His mouth lifted in a slight smile. "And let's be honest . . . rising crime and political corruption do have a tendency to disrupt business."

"And there it is."

"That's not all it is." Musa shook his head. "I don't understand. I thought you'd be thrilled! I'd be heartbroken if I was banished from my home. I know I'd do anything to return to my family. And your family . . ." His voice softened. "They're not doing well."

Apprehension raced down Ali's spine. "What are you talking about?"

"How do *you* think your mother responded to your being exiled? You should be relieved she's restricted herself to a trade war rather than an actual one. I hear your sister is heartbroken, that your brother falls further into drink every day, and your father . . ." Musa paused, and Ali did not miss his calculated tone when he spoke again. "Ghassan's a vengeful man, and his wrath has fallen directly on the shafit he believes stirred you to treason."

Ali flinched, the last line finding its mark. "I can't do anything about any of that," he insisted. "Every time I tried, it hurt the people I cared about. And I have even less power now than I did then."

"*Less* power? Alizayd the Afshin-slayer? The clever prince who has learned to make the desert bloom and travels with a pack of Am Gezira's fiercest warriors?" Musa eyed him. "You underestimate your appeal."

"Probably because I know intimately how much of that is nonsense. I'm not going to Daevabad." Ali crossed to the entrance to beckon his companions back. "My decision is final."

"Alizayd, would you just—" But Musa was wise enough to fall silent as the others joined them.

"My cousin apologizes for abusing the hospitality of Bir Nabat," Ali announced. "He intends to depart at dawn and says we may take a fifth of his inventory to compensate our loss."

Musa whirled on him. "What?" he said hotly in Ntaran. "I certainly did not!"

"I will gut you like a fish," Ali warned in the same tongue before slipping back into Djinnistani: ". . . *to compensate our loss*," he repeated firmly, "and refill the bellies of the children gone hungry while his camels gorge. Additionally, have someone take his provisions and replace them with locusts and dates." He watched as Musa went from incredulous to outraged. "You said you were feeling weak. I suggest a change in diet. Such food has made us very hardy." He clicked his teeth. "You get used to the crunch."

Indignation simmered in Musa's eyes, but he didn't speak. Ali stood, pressing a hand to his heart in the traditional Geziri salute. "If you'll excuse me, I have work to do. I'll wake you at dawn for prayer."

"But of course," Musa said, his voice newly cool. "One must never forget their obligations."

Ali didn't like the look in his eyes, but having made his point, he turned for the exit. "Peace be upon you, cousin."

"And upon you peace, prince."

ALI SLEPT HARD; HE ALWAYS DID HERE. HE DREAMT HE was back in Daevabad on the lovely pavilion overlooking the harem gardens, lost in his books. A cool breeze, a wet breeze, gently swung his hammock. The water soaked through the fabric, through his dishdasha, clammy and cold fingers upon his skin . . .

"Ali!"

Ali's eyes snapped open. His hand flew to his khanjar, the dagger a silver gleam in the dark tent. He caught sight of Lubayd, the other man staying wisely out of reach, and dropped the blade.

It landed with a splash in the pool of water nearly level with his bed cushion. Ali shot up in alarm at the sight of his flooded tent, then flew to his feet, quickly snatching up his books and his notes.

"Come," Lubayd said, already holding open the tent flap. "It looks to be the worst rupture we've had."

The scene outside was mayhem. The water in the courtyard was waist high, and judging from its turbulence, still gushing out of the cistern below. The cairns Ali used to block off the canals were nowhere to be seen, probably washed away.

He swore. "Wake the rest. Anyone with a working pair of hands needs to get down to the fields and orchards. Don't let the soil get oversaturated."

Lubayd nodded, his usual humor vanished. "Don't drown."

Ali pulled off his robe and waded through the courtyard. He made sure Lubayd was gone before he submerged to check on conditions underground. Drowning didn't worry him.

It was the fact that he couldn't that did.

THE SUN WAS WELL RISEN OVER A SOGGY BIR NABAT BY the time the rupture was fixed. Ali was so tired he had to be helped from the cistern. His fingers were swollen from groping the rock, his senses numb from the cold water.

Lubayd pushed a cup of hot coffee into his hands. "We've salvaged what we could. I don't think there was much harm to any crops, but several of the aqueducts will need to be repaired. And there was rather extensive damage to the trellis in the fig orchard."

Ali nodded mutely. Water streamed down his limbs, echoing the cold rage welling inside him. "Where is he?"

Lubayd's reluctant silence confirmed Ali's suspicions. He'd known as soon as he dived into the cistern and found that the rocks limiting the spring had been moved. No Geziri would have swum so deep, and none would have ever dared sabotage a well. But an Ayaanle man who'd been taught to swim as a child? One who'd never gone thirsty? He might have.

"Gone, departed in the chaos," Lubayd finally answered. He cleared his throat. "He left his cargo."

Aqisa dropped down next to them. "We should let it rot in the desert," she said bitterly. "Salvage what we can, sell what we can't, and let the rest sink below the sands. To hell with the Ayaanle. Let them explain to the king."

"They will find a way to blame us," Ali said softly. He stared at his hands. They were shaking. "Stealing from the Treasury is a capital offense."

Lubayd knelt before him. "Then we'll take the damned salt," he said firmly. "Aqisa and I. You'll stay in Am Gezira."

Ali tried to clear the lump growing in his throat. "You can't even touch it." Besides, this was his family's mess; it wasn't right to foist responsibility for dealing with it on the people who'd saved him.

He stood up, feeling unsteady. "I . . . I'll need to organize repairs first." The words made him sick. The life he'd been carefully putting together in Bir Nabat had been turned upside down in a night, carelessly cast aside by outsiders in the name of their own political calculations. "We'll leave for Daevabad tomorrow." The words sounded odd in his mouth, unreal somehow.

Lubayd hesitated. "And your cousin?"

Ali doubted they would find Musa, but it was worth a try. "No man who would sabotage a well is kin of mine. Send a pair of fighters after him."

"And should they find him?"

"Drag him back. I'll deal with him when I return." Ali's hands tightened on his cup. "And I *will* return."

6

NAHRI

"*Ow!* By the Creator, are you doing that on purpose? It didn't hurt nearly as bad last time!"

Nahri ignored her patient's complaint, her attention focused instead on his neatly splayed lower midsection. Metal clamps held open the skin, white-hot to keep the wound clean. The shape-shifter's intestines shimmered a pale silver—or at least they would have shimmered had they not been studded with stubborn bits of rocky growths.

She took a deep breath, centering herself. The infirmary was stifling, and she'd been working on this patient for at least two grueling hours. She had one hand pressed against his flushed skin to dull the pain of the procedure and keep it from killing him. With the other, she manipulated a pair of steel tweezers around the next growth. It was a complicated, time-consuming operation, and sweat beaded her brow.

"Damn it!"

She dropped the stone into a pan. "Stop *turning into a statue*, and you won't have to deal with this." She briefly paused to glare at him. "This is the third time I've had to treat you . . . people are not meant to shift into rocks!"

He looked a little ashamed. "It's very peaceful."

Nahri threw him an exasperated look. "Find another way to relax. I beg you. Stitches!" she called aloud. When there was no response, she glanced over her shoulder. "Nisreen?"

"One moment!"

From across the crowded infirmary, she caught sight of Nisreen dashing between a table piled high with pharmaceutical preparations and another with instruments due for a magical scalding. Nisreen picked up a silver tray, holding it over her head as she navigated the tightly packed cots and huddles of visitors. The infirmary was standing room only, with more people pushed into the garden.

Nahri sighed as Nisreen squeezed between a bouncing Ayaanle artist hexed with exuberance and a Sahrayn metalworker whose skin was covered in smoking pustules. "Imagine if we had a hospital, Nisreen. An enormous hospital with room to breathe and staff to do your busywork."

"A dream," Nisreen replied, setting down her tray. "Your stitches." She paused to admire Nahri's work. "Excellent. I never get tired of seeing how far your skills have progressed."

"I'm barely allowed to leave the infirmary, and I work all day. I'd hope my skills had progressed." But she couldn't entirely hide her smile. Despite the long hours and grueling work, Nahri took great satisfaction in her role as a healer, able to help patients even when she couldn't fix the myriad other problems in her life.

She closed the shapeshifter up quickly with the enchanted thread and then bound the wound, pressing a cup of opium-laced tea into his hands. "Drink and rest."

"Banu Nahida?"

Nahri glanced up. A steward dressed in royal colors peeked in from the doors leading to the garden, his eyes going wide at the sight of her. In the moist heat of the infirmary, Nahri's hair had grown wild, black curls escaping her headscarf. Her apron was splashed with blood and spilled potions. All she needed was a fiery scalpel in one hand to look like one of the mad, murderous Nahids of djinn lore.

"What?" she asked, trying to keep her irritation in check.

The steward bowed. "The emir would like to speak with you."

Nahri gestured to the chaos around her. "*Now?*"

"He is waiting in the garden."

Of course he is. Muntadhir was practiced enough in protocol to know she couldn't entirely snub him if he showed up in person. "Fine," she grumbled. She washed her hands and removed her apron, then followed the steward outside.

Nahri blinked in the bright sunshine. The wild harem garden—more jungle than garden, really—had been pruned back and tamed on the land facing the infirmary by a team of dedicated Daeva horticulturists. They'd been giddy at the assignment, eager to recreate the glorious palace landscapes the Nahids had been famous for, even if only in miniature. The infirmary's grounds were now starred with silver-blue reflecting pools, the walkways lined with perfectly pruned pistachio and apricot trees and lush rosebushes laden with delicate blooms that ranged from a pale, sunny yellow to the deepest of indigos. Though most of the herbs and plants used in her work were grown in Zariaspa on the Pramukh family estates, anything that needed to be fresh when used was planted here, in neatly manicured corner plots bursting with shuddering mandrake bushes and dappled yellow henbane. A marble pavilion overlooked it all, set with carved benches and invitingly plump cushions.

Muntadhir stood there now, his back to her. He must have come from court because he was still dressed in the smoky gold-edged black robe he wore for ceremonial functions, his brightly colored silk turban dazzling in the sun. His hands rested lightly upon the balustrade, the lines of his body commanding as he gazed upon her garden.

"Yes?" she asked brusquely as she stepped into the pavilion.

He glanced back, his gaze traveling down her body. "You look a sight."

"I'm working." She wiped away some of the sweat from her forehead. "What do you need, Muntadhir?"

He turned to face her fully, leaning against the railing. "You didn't come last night."

That was what this visit was about? "I was busy with my patients. And I doubt your bed was cold for long." She couldn't resist adding the last part.

His lips twitched. "This is the third time in a row you've done this, Nahri," he persisted. "You could at least send word instead of leaving me waiting."

Nahri took a deep breath, her patience with Muntadhir—already a thing in short supply—diminishing with each second. "I apologize. Next time I'll send word so you can head straightaway to whatever wine-soaked salon you're frequenting these days. *Now* are we done?"

Muntadhir crossed his arms. "You're in a good mood today. But no, we're not done. Can we talk somewhere more private?" He gestured to the bright citrus trees in the distance. "Your orange grove, perhaps?"

A protective instinct surged in Nahri's heart. The orange grove had been planted long ago by her uncle Rustam, and it was precious to her. While not as talented a healer as her mother, Manizheh, Rustam had been a famed botanist and pharmacist. Even decades after his death, the carefully selected plants within the grove grew strong and healthy, their healing powers more potent and their fragrance headier. Nahri had requested the grove be restored to its original glory, enchanted by the privacy and shade afforded by the glen's thick screen of leaves and brambles, and the feeling of standing on soil once worked by her family's hands.

"I don't let anyone in there," she reminded him. "You know that."

Muntadhir shook his head, used to her stubbornness. "Then let's just walk." He moved toward the steps without waiting for her.

Nahri followed. "What's happened with the Daeva family I told you about?" she asked as they made their way along the snaking path. If Muntadhir was going to pull her away from work, she might as well take advantage of it. "The ones who were abused by the Royal Guard?"

"I'm looking into it."

She stopped. "*Still?* You told me you'd speak to your father last week."

"And I did," Muntadhir replied, sounding annoyed. "I can't exactly go around setting criminals free against the king's command because you and Jamshid are upset. It's more complicated than that." He eyed her. "And the more you interfere, the harder you make it. You know how my father feels about you getting involved in political matters."

The words struck hard, and Nahri drew up. "Fine," she said bitterly. "You can go tell him his warning has been passed on."

Muntadhir grabbed her hand before she could turn away. "I'm not here at his command, Nahri," he protested. "I'm here because I'm your husband. And regardless of how either of us feels about that, I don't want to see you hurt."

He led her toward a shaded bench that faced the canal. It was tucked behind a timeworn neem tree whose boughs curved down in a thick cascade of emerald leaves, effectively curtaining them from view.

He sat, pulling her down beside him. "I hear you had quite the adventure with my sister the other week."

Nahri instantly tensed. "Did your father—"

"No," Muntadhir assured. "Zaynab told me. Yes," he clarified, perhaps noticing the surprise on Nahri's face. "I know about her little jaunts in the Geziri Quarter. I found out about them years ago. She's clever enough to keep herself safe, and her guard knows he can come to me if she's ever in trouble."

"Oh." That took Nahri aback. And oddly enough, it made her a little jealous. The Qahtanis might be her ancestral enemies and a bunch of backstabbing opportunists, but the quiet loyalty between the siblings—borne out of the type of familial love Nahri had never known—filled her with a sad sort of envy.

She pushed it away. "I take it she told you about the hospital?"

"She said she'd never seen you so excited."

Nahri kept her face carefully blank. "It was interesting."

"It was *interesting*?" Muntadhir repeated in disbelief. "You, who barely stops talking about your work in the infirmary, discovered your ancestors' old hospital and a group of freed ifrit slaves, and your only comment is 'It was interesting'?"

Nahri chewed her lip, debating how to respond. The hospital had been far more than interesting, of course. But the fantasies she'd been spinning since her visit seemed a fragile thing, safest kept to herself.

Muntadhir clearly wasn't so easily fooled. He took her hand again. "I wish you would talk to me," he said softly. "I know neither of us wanted this, Nahri, but we could try to make it work. I feel like I have no idea what goes on in your head." His tone was imploring but there was no hiding a hint of exasperation. "You have more walls up than a maze."

Nahri said nothing. Of course, she had walls up. Nearly everyone she knew had betrayed her at least once.

He rubbed his thumb against her palm. Her fingers twitched, and she made a face. "Lots of stitching today, and I think my internal healing abilities have stopped recognizing aching muscles as an abnormality."

"Let me." Muntadhir took her hand in both of his and began to massage it, pressing the joints as though he'd been doing it for years.

Nahri exhaled, some of the tension immediately leaving her sore fingers. "Who taught you how to do this?"

He pulled at her fingers, stretching them out in a way that felt heavenly. "A friend."

"Were you and said friend wearing clothes at the time of this lesson?"

"You know, considering the friend . . . it is rather likely we weren't." He gave her a wicked smile. "Would you like to know what else she taught me?"

Nahri rolled her eyes. "I won't unburden myself to you, so now you're trying to seduce me using knowledge you gained from another woman?"

His grin widened. "Political life has taught me to be creative in my approaches." He brushed his fingers lightly up her wrist, and Nahri couldn't help a slight shiver at his touch. "You're clearly too busy to come to my bed. How else to sustain the peace our marriage alliance was supposed to build?"

"You have no shame; do you know that?" But the edge was gone from her voice. Muntadhir was damnably good at this.

His fingers were tracing delicate patterns on the skin of her wrist, his eyes dancing with mirth. "You don't complain about that when you *do* find your way into my bed."

Heat flooded her cheeks—not all of it from embarrassment. "You've slept with half of Daevabad. I'd hope that would teach you some skill."

"That sounds like a challenge."

The mischief in his expression was not helping with the utterly traitorous unspooling of heat in her belly. "I have work," she protested as he pulled her onto his lap. "At least a dozen patients waiting. And we're in the garden. Someone could . . ."

She trailed off as he pressed his mouth to her neck, lightly kissing her throat.

"No one can see anything," Muntadhir said calmly, his voice sending a brush of warmth against her skin. "And you clearly need to relax. Consider it a professional duty." His hands slipped underneath her tunic. "Surely your patients will be better served by having a Banu Nahida who's not in such a snappish mood."

Nahri sighed, pressing closer to him despite herself. His mouth had moved lower, his beard tickling her collar. "I am *not* snappish . . ."

There was a polite cough from behind the tree, followed by a squeaked "Emir?"

Muntadhir removed neither his hands nor his lips. "*Yes?*"

"Your father wishes to speak with you. He says it's urgent."

Nahri stilled, the mention of Ghassan making her go cold.

Muntadhir sighed. "Of course it is." He pulled away to meet her gaze. "Have dinner with me tonight?" he asked. "I will order your strange flower tea and you can insult my shamelessness to your heart's content."

Nahri had little desire to dine with him but admittedly wouldn't mind continuing what they'd just started. She *had* been under a great deal of stress lately, and she often got more sleep the nights she spent in Muntadhir's room; people usually had to be actively dying for a servant to muster up the courage to interrupt the emir and his wife there.

Besides which, the flicker of hope in his eyes was pulling on the one shred of tenderness left in her heart; for all his flaws—and there were a great number—her husband did not lack in charm. "I'll try," she said, biting back a smile.

He grinned back, looking genuinely pleased. "Excellent." He untangled his limbs from hers.

Nahri hastily straightened her tunic; she was not going back to the infirmary looking like . . . well, like she had just been doing what she had been doing. "Good luck with whatever your father wants."

Muntadhir rolled his eyes. "I am sure it is nothing." He touched his heart. "In peace."

She watched him go, taking a minute to enjoy the fresh air and the trill of birdsong. It was a beautiful day, and her gaze drifted lazily over to the herb garden.

It landed on a shafit man scurrying through the bushes.

Nahri frowned, watching as the fellow hurried past a patch of sage to stop in front of a willow tree. He wiped his brow, looking nervously over his shoulders.

Odd. While there were some shafit among the gardeners, none were allowed to touch the Nahid plants, nor was this particular man familiar. He took a pair of shears from his belt and opened them, as though he meant to cut away one of the branches.

Nahri was on her feet in an instant, her silk slippers and a lifetime of cat burglary disguising the sound of her steps. The man didn't even look up until she was nearly on top of him.

"What do you think you're doing to my tree?" she demanded.

The shafit man jumped up, whirling around so fast that his cap tumbled off. His human-hued hazel eyes went wide with horror.

"Banu Nahida!" he gasped. "I . . . forgive me," he begged, bringing his hands together. "I was just—"

"Hacking at my willow? Yes, I see that." She touched the maimed branch, and a sprinkling of new bark spread beneath her fingers. Nahri had a bit of a talent for botany herself, though she hadn't yet attempted to develop it further, much to Nisreen's chagrin. "Do you know what would happen if someone else had caught . . ." She trailed off, the sight of the man's bare scalp stealing her attention. It was disfigured, his hair long around his temples, but prickly and patched at the top as if recovering from a rushed shave. The flesh there was mottled purple and slightly swollen, surrounding an oddly flat patch in the size and shape of a coin. A half-moon of scar tissue edged the patch—it had been stitched, and skillfully so.

Overwhelmed by curiosity, Nahri reached out and lightly touched the swollen flesh. It was soft—too soft. She let her Nahid senses expand, confirming what seemed impossible.

A small section of the man's skull had been removed beneath the skin.

She gasped. It was healing; she could sense the spark of new bone growth, but even so . . . She dropped her hand. "Did someone *do* this to you?"

The man looked petrified. "I had an accident."

"An accident that neatly bored a hole through your skull and then stitched it shut?" Nahri knelt beside him. "I'm not going to hurt you," she assured him. "I just want to know what happened— and make certain someone isn't going around Daevabad cutting coins out of people's skulls."

"It was nothing like that." He bit his lip, glancing around. "I fell off a roof and cracked my head," he whispered. "The doctors told my wife that blood was swelling under the bone and that re- moving part of the skull might relieve the pressure and save my life."

Nahri blinked. "The *doctors*?" She looked at the tree he'd been taking the cuttings from. Willow. Of course. Both the leaves and bark were valuable, easily distilled into medicine for aches and pains . . . for *human* aches and pains. "Did they ask you for this as well?"

He shook his head, still trembling. "I offered. I saw a picture in one of their books and thought I remembered seeing a tree like it when I worked on the roof here last year." He gave her an imploring look. "They're good people, and they saved my life. I wanted to help."

Nahri was having trouble containing her excitement. Shafit

doctors who could do surgery and had medical books? "Who?" she asked eagerly. "Who are these doctors?"

He dropped his gaze. "We're not supposed to talk about them."

"I don't mean them any harm." She touched her heart. "I swear on my ancestors' ashes. I'll bring them some willow myself, and more. I have plenty of medicines that are safe for shafit in my apothecary."

The man looked torn. Nahri studied him again, noting his bare feet and ragged galabiyya. His heavily calloused hands.

Hating herself a little, Nahri pulled a gold ring from her pocket. She'd forgotten to remove it before starting work in the infirmary and had settled for slipping it in there. Small rubies, set in a floral pattern, were embedded in its surface.

She placed it in his hand. "A name and a location." His eyes went wide, locking on the ring. "I'm not going to hurt them, I promise. I want to help."

Longing filled his face; Nahri imagined the money a ring like that could fetch would go a long way for a shafit laborer.

"Subhashini Sen," he whispered. "The house with the red door on Sukariyya Street."

Nahri smiled. "Thank you."

A SMALL ARMY OF SERVANTS WAS WAITING FOR NAHRI when she finished her work, and she'd no sooner set foot in the steamy hammam than they descended, taking her blood- and potion-splattered clothes away to be washed and then giving her a thorough scrub, rinsing her skin with rosewater, massaging her limbs with precious oils, and attempting to coax her wild curls into an elegant crown of braids.

Never one content to give up control, Nahri had, however, insisted on picking out her own clothes. Tonight she'd selected a gown cut from the finest linen she'd ever touched. It was sleeveless, falling to her ankles in a pale buttery sheath and held together by an ornate collar of hundreds of beads: lapis lazuli, gold, carnelian, and topaz. It reminded Nahri of home, the pattern looking like one that might have been copied from an ancient temple back in Egypt.

A servant had just finished clasping the delicate collar when another approached, bearing a discreet ivory cosmetics pot. "Would you like me to powder your skin, my lady?" she asked.

Nahri stared at the vessel. An innocent question, but one that always caused her stomach to tighten. Instinctively, she glanced up, catching sight of her reflection in the polished silver mirror perched on her dressing table.

Though the line between the shafit and the purebloods in Daevabad was a hard one, carved by centuries of violence and enshrined in law, the differences in their appearances were not as great as their divide in power suggested. The purebloods had their pointed ears and metal-toned eyes, of course, the color varying by tribe. And their skin had a gleam to it, a shimmer and a haze that reflected the hot, jet-colored blood that simmered in their veins. Depending on ancestry and luck, shafit had a mix of human and djinn features: human hazel eyes paired with perfectly pointed ears, or perhaps the tin-toned gaze of the Agnivanshi without the glimmer to their skin.

And then there was Nahri.

At first glance, there was *nothing* magical about Nahri's appearance. Her ears were as rounded as a human's and her skin an earthy matte brown. Her black eyes were dark, to be certain, but she'd always felt like they lacked the same shining ebony depths that marked one as Daeva. Hers was a face that had once convinced Dara she was a shafit with the barest drop of magical blood in her veins. And it was a face that was apparently a lie, the product of a marid curse—or so the ifrit who'd hunted her had claimed, a claim Ghassan had seized upon in order to publicly declare her a pureblood.

Privately, of course, he'd said something very different. Not that it mattered. Nahri suspected she would never fully discern the truth of her origins. But the laissez-faire approach to her appearance had changed when she married Muntadhir. The future queen of Daevabad was expected to look the part, and so hairdressers arranged her braids to cover the tips of her ears. Ash was mixed into her kohl to make her eyes look darker. And then the cursed ivory pot appeared. It contained an incredibly expensive powder made from the Creator only knew what that when brushed upon her skin gave Nahri the shimmer of a pure-blood for hours.

It was an illusion, a waste of time and an utter facade—and all for a future queen who couldn't even protect her tribesmen from being beaten and robbed in front of her. And the fact that it was her shafit servants who were forced to create an image of the blood purity that circumscribed their lives . . . it made Nahri feel ill. "No," she finally replied, trying not to let her revulsion show. "I don't need that."

There was a knock on the door and then Nisreen entered.

Nahri groaned. "No. I need a night off. Tell whoever it is to heal themselves."

Her mentor gave her a wounded smile. "It is not *always* work that I seek you for." She glanced at Nahri's maids. "Would you mind leaving us?"

They obeyed at once, and Nisreen joined her at the dressing table. "You look very pretty," she said. "That dress is beautiful. Is it new?"

Nahri nodded. "A gift from a Sahrayn seamstress happy to no longer have silver-pox."

"Your husband will be hard-pressed to take his eyes off you in that."

"I suppose," Nahri said, fighting embarrassment. She wasn't sure why she was even bothering. Muntadhir had married her for her name, not her face, and her husband was so constantly surrounded by djinn who were breathtakingly gorgeous—men and women who had voices like angels and smiles that could lure humans to madness—that it seemed a waste of time to even attempt to attract his eye.

Nisreen's gaze darted to the door before she set down the small silver chalice that had been casually concealed in the folds of her shawl. "I've prepared your tea."

Nahri stared at the chalice, the sharp scent of herbs wafting from pale green liquid. They both knew what kind of "tea" it was: the kind Nahri drank only when she visited Muntadhir. "I still worry we're going to get caught."

Nisreen shrugged. "Ghassan probably has his suspicions, but you're a Nahid healer. On this, he's going to have a hard time out-maneuvering you, and it's worth the risk to buy you a bit of time."

"A *bit* of time is all it's buying." Ghassan hadn't overly pressed on the topic of grandchildren yet. Djinn didn't conceive easily, and it was entirely reasonable the emir and his wife had yet to be blessed with an heir. But she doubted he'd hold his tongue for long.

Nisreen must have heard the uncertainty in her voice. "That is enough for now." She pushed the cup into Nahri's hands. "Take things here day by day."

Nahri gulped the tea and then stood, pulling a hooded robe over her dress. "I should go." She was early, but if she left now, she could sneak through the back passages and have a few minutes to herself rather than being escorted by one of Muntadhir's stewardesses.

"I won't delay you." Nisreen stood as well, and when she met Nahri's eyes, there was conviction in her gaze. "Have faith, my lady. Your future here is brighter than you realize."

"You always say that." Nahri sighed. "I wish I had your confidence."

"You will one day," Nisreen promised. She shooed her off. "Go on then. Don't let me keep you."

Nahri did, taking one of the private corridors that led from the harem garden to the royal apartments on the upper level of the palatial ziggurat, a level with an excellent view of Daevabad's lake. All the Qahtanis had quarters up there save Zaynab, who preferred the garden below.

Just as Ali had. The thought came to her unbidden—and unwelcome. She hated thinking about Ali, hated that five years after that night, a sting of humiliation still pierced her when she recalled how her supposed friend had quietly led her and Dara into a deadly trap. The naive young prince should have been the last one capable of duping her, and yet he had.

And she hated that despite everything, part of her still worried about him. For it was damnably clear—no matter what the Qahtanis pretended—that Ali was not merely "leading a garrison" in the peace of his ancestral land. He'd been cast out, and under terms Nahri suspected were rather dire.

She emerged onto the expansive balcony that ran the length of Muntadhir's apartment. Like everything he owned, it was achingly sophisticated, its trellised wooden railings and screens carved in the semblance of a garden, with embroidered panels of silk draped to mimic a tent. Frankincense smoldered inside a fiery brazier across from a pile of brocaded cushions that sat angled toward the best view of the lake.

Cushions that were very much *not* empty. Nahri abruptly stilled, catching sight of Jamshid and Muntadhir sitting across from each other. Jamshid's presence there didn't surprise her—but the fact that they were clearly arguing did.

"Tell your father to send him *back!*" Jamshid was insisting. "Is there any reason he can't drop his damned cargo on the beach and turn right around?"

"I tried." Muntadhir sounded nearly hysterical. "I begged my father, and do you know what he told me?" He let out a choked, humorless laugh. "To go *put an heir in my Nahid wife* if I was so worried about my position. That's all we are to him. Pawns in his damned political game. And now his favorite, sharpest piece is returning."

Nahri frowned in confusion. Pushing aside the guilt she felt for eavesdropping—more on account of Jamshid, her friend, than for the sake of her politician of a husband, who almost certainly had a loyal spy or two installed in her infirmary—she crept closer, tucking herself into a niche between a potted fern and an ornamental carved screen.

She took a deep breath. The palace's magic was as unpredictable as it was powerful, and though Nahri had been quietly working to learn how to better call upon it, doing so was always a risk—she had no doubt that if Ghassan got an inkling of what she was up to, she'd be promptly punished.

But sometimes a little risk was worth it. Nahri focused on the shadows at her feet. *Grow*, she urged, beckoning them closer and allowing her fear of getting caught to expand. *Protect me.*

They did so, the shadows sweeping up to envelop her in a cloak of darkness. Breathing a bit easier, Nahri moved closer to the screen to peer through the cutouts in the wood. The two men were alone, Jamshid seated on the edge of a cushion as he watched Muntadhir with open concern.

Muntadhir shot to his feet, visibly trembling. "His mother's going to kill me." He paced, pulling anxiously at his beard. "The Ayaanle have wanted this for years. He'll no sooner be back in Daevabad than I'll be waking up with a cord around my neck."

"That's not going to happen," Jamshid said sharply. "Muntadhir, you need to calm down and think this—*no*." His hand shot out to grab Muntadhir's as her husband lunged for the bottle of wine on the table. "Stop. That's not going to help you."

Muntadhir offered a broken smile. "I disagree," he said weakly. He looked close to tears. "Wine is reportedly an excellent companion during one's downfall."

"There's not going to be any downfall." Jamshid pulled Muntadhir onto the cushion beside him. "*There's not*," he repeated when Muntadhir looked away. "Muntadhir . . ." Jamshid hesitated, and when he spoke again, there was a wary edge to his voice. "It's a long journey back to Daevabad. A dangerous one. Surely you have people who—"

Muntadhir violently shook his head. "I can't. I don't have that in me." He bit his lip, staring in bitter resignation at the floor. "Not yet anyway." He wiped his eyes and then took a deep breath, as if to compose himself before speaking again. "I'm sorry. I shouldn't burden you with this. God knows you've suffered enough for my family's politics."

"Don't be ridiculous." Jamshid touched Muntadhir's cheek. "I want you to come to me with things like this." He smiled. "To be honest . . . the rest of your companions are fairly useless sycophants."

That drew a laugh from her husband. "Whereas I can always rely on you to honestly insult me."

"And keep you safe." Jamshid's hand had moved to cradle Muntadhir's jaw. "Nothing's going to happen to you, I swear. I won't let it, and I'm obnoxiously honorable about these things."

Muntadhir laughed again. "That I know." He took another breath and then suddenly closed his eyes as if in pain. When he spoke again, his voice was heavy with sorrow. "I miss you."

Jamshid's face twisted, the humor vanishing from his expression. He seemed to realize what he was doing with his hand, his gaze falling to her husband's mouth. "I'm sorry," he whispered. "I didn't mean to—"

The rest of his explanation didn't leave his lips. Because Muntadhir was suddenly kissing him, doing so with a desperation

that was clearly returned. Jamshid tangled his hand in Muntadhir's dark hair, pulling him close . . .

And then he pushed him away. "I can't," Jamshid choked out,
his entire body shaking. "I'm sorry, but I can't. Not anymore. I
told you when you got married. She's my Banu Nahida."

Nahri stepped back from the screen, stunned. Not by the allusion to past intimacy between them—there were times it seemed
Muntadhir had literally slept with half the people he knew. But
those affairs all seemed so casual—flirtations with various foreign
ministers, dalliances with poets and dancing girls.

The anguish radiating off her husband now was *not* casual.
Gone was the emir who'd confidently pulled her into his lap in
the garden. Muntadhir had rocked back like he'd been punched
when Jamshid had pushed him away, and it looked like he was
struggling not to cry. Sympathy stole through her. For all the
trappings of power and glamour of the court, she could not help
but be struck by how utterly lonely this place had made them all.

Muntadhir stared at the ground. "Of course." It sounded
like he was fighting to regain his composure. "Then maybe you
should go," he added, his voice stiff. "I'm expecting her and I
would hate to put you in an uncomfortable position."

Jamshid sighed, pulling himself slowly to his feet. He leaned
on his cane, looking resignedly down upon Muntadhir. "Have
you had any luck freeing the Daeva men Nahri and I told you
about?"

"No," Muntadhir replied, his response far flatter than it had
been with her on the topic. "It's difficult to free people when
they're guilty of the crime they're charged with."

"It's a crime now to discuss the implications of your father's
financial policies in a public setting?"

Muntadhir's head jerked up. "Daevabad is restless enough
without such gossip being spread. It hurts morale and causes
people to lose faith in their king."

"So does arbitrarily arresting people who happen to have wealth and land that can be confiscated for the Treasury." Jamshid's eyes narrowed. "Of course, by 'people' I mean 'Daevas.' We all know the rest of the tribes aren't suffering the same treatment."

Muntadhir was shaking his head. "He's trying to keep the peace, Jamshid. And let's not pretend your people make that easy."

Jamshid's mouth pressed into a disappointed line. "This isn't you, Muntadhir. And since we've established I'm the only one who's honest with you . . . let me warn you that you're going down the same path you say ruined your father." He turned away. "Give my greetings to Nahri."

"Jamshid—"

But he was already leaving, making his way toward the place where Nahri was hiding. Quickly, she retreated to edge of the steps as though she'd just arrived.

"Jamshid!" she said, greeting him with false cheer. "What a lovely surprise!"

He managed a smile, though it didn't meet his eyes. "Banu Nahida," he replied, his voice a little hoarse. "Apologies. I didn't mean to intrude upon your evening."

"It's all right," she said gently, hating the heartbreak still writ clearly across his face. Muntadhir wasn't looking at them; he'd walked to the edge of the balcony, his attention focused on the twinkling fires of the city below. She touched Jamshid's shoulder. "Come see me tomorrow. I have a new poultice I want to try on your back."

He nodded. "Tomorrow." He moved past her, disappearing down into the palace.

Nahri took a few steps forward, feeling uncertain. "Peace be upon you," she called out to her husband. "If it's a bad time . . ."

"Of course not." Muntadhir turned around. Nahri had to give him credit: though he was pale, his face was swept of the emotion that had been there only moments ago. She supposed a few decades in Daevabad's royal court taught one that ability. "Sorry." He cleared his throat. "I was not expecting you so soon."

Obviously. She shrugged. "I finished early."

Muntadhir nodded. "Let me call a servant," he suggested, crossing the balcony. "I'll have them bring some food."

Nahri caught his wrist. "Why don't you sit?" she suggested softly. "I'm not hungry and I thought we could talk first."

They'd no sooner sunk into the cushions than Muntadhir was reaching for the wine bottle. "Would you like some?" he asked, filling his cup to the top.

Nahri watched. She wasn't Jamshid, and she didn't feel comfortable stopping him. "No . . . thank you." He drank back most of his cup and then refilled it. "Is everything well?" she ventured. "The meeting with your father . . ."

Muntadhir winced. "Can we talk about something else? For a little while at least?"

She paused. Nahri was madly curious to discover what he'd been discussing with Ghassan that had led to his fight with Jamshid, but perhaps a change in subject would pull him from his dark mood.

And she certainly had a subject ready to discuss. "Of course. Actually, I came across someone interesting in the garden after you left. A shafit man with a hole in his skull."

Muntadhir choked, coughing a spray of wine into his hand. "You found a *dead shafit in your garden*?"

"Not dead," Nahri corrected lightly. "He looked quite well otherwise. He said a surgeon had done the procedure to save his life. A *shafit surgeon*, Muntadhir." Admiration crept into her voice. "Someone skilled enough to bore a hole in a man's skull, sew it back up, and keep him alive. And it looked *perfect*. I mean, it felt a bit spongy where the bone was gone, but—"

Muntadhir raised a hand, looking slightly ill. "I don't need to hear the details." He glanced at his crimson wine, a little revulsion passing across his face, and then set it down. "So what of it?"

"*What of it?*" Nahri exclaimed. "That speaks to extraordinary talent! That physician might have even trained in the human world. I convinced the man in the garden to give me a name and the street where he works."

"But why would you want such information?" Muntadhir asked, looking perplexed.

"Because I want to find him! For one . . . I *am* the Banu Nahida. I should ensure he's a real doctor and not some . . . con artist taking advantage of desperate shafit." Nahri cleared her throat. "But I'd also just love to meet him. He could be a valuable asset; after all, I still find much of what Yaqub taught me relevant."

Muntadhir seemed even more confused. "Yaqub?"

Her stomach tightened. Nahri wasn't used to talking about her passions, the ones closest to her heart, and Muntadhir's bewilderment wasn't making it easier. "The pharmacist I worked with back in Cairo, Muntadhir. The old man. My friend. I know I've mentioned him to you before."

Muntadhir frowned. "So, you want to find some shafit doctor because you once had a pharmacist friend in the human world?"

Nahri took a deep breath, seeing her opening. Maybe it wasn't the best time, but Muntadhir *had* said he wanted her to talk to him more freely, and right now, her heart was bursting. "Because I want to see if there's a way we can work together . . . Muntadhir, it's so hard being the only healer here," she confessed. "It's *lonely*. The responsibility is crushing. There are times I barely sleep, I barely eat . . ." She checked the emotion growing in her voice. "I thought . . . the old Nahid hospital . . ." She stumbled over her words, trying to explain the dreams that had been spinning in her head since her visit to those ruins. "I wonder if maybe we could rebuild it. Bring in a shafit physician to share the patient load and . . ."

Muntadhir's eyes went wide. "You want to *rebuild* that place?"

Nahri tried not to shrink back at the horrified disbelief in his expression. "You . . . you told me that I could come to you, talk to you—"

"Yes—but about *plausible* things. If you want to bring another Daeva to court or take part in the preparations for Navasatem. What you're suggesting . . ." He sounded shocked. "Zaynab said the building was in a shambles. Do you have any idea of the effort and expense it would take to restore?"

"I know, but I thought—"

Muntadhir stood, pacing in agitation. "And to work alongside *shafit*?" He said the word with thinly veiled disdain. "Absolutely not. My father would never allow it. You shouldn't even be looking for this doctor. You must realize that what he's doing is illegal."

"*Illegal?* How is helping people illegal?"

"The shafit . . ." Muntadhir rubbed the back of his neck, shame creeping across his face. "I mean . . . they're not—*we're* not—supposed to act in a manner that . . . encourages their population to increase."

Nahri was silent for a moment, shock freezing her tongue. "Tell me you don't really believe that," she said, praying he'd misspoken, that she'd imagined the distaste in his voice. "You're a Qahtani. Your ancestors overthrew mine—*slaughtered mine*—to protect the shafit."

"That was a long time ago." Muntadhir looked beseechingly at her. "And the shafit are not the innocents you might imagine. They hate the Daevas, they hate *you*."

She bristled. "Why should they hate me? I was raised in the human world!"

"And then you came back here at the side of a man famous for using a scourge to determine the color of someone's blood," Muntadhir pointed out. "You have a reputation with them, Nahri, like it or not."

Nahri flinched, but let the charges slide past her. This conversation had taken enough of a horrifying turn without bringing her broken Afshin and his bloody crimes into it. "I had nothing to do with Qui-zi," she said, defending herself. "None of us alive today did."

"It doesn't matter." Muntadhir's eyes filled with warning. "Nahri, there's too much history between the Daevas and the shafit. Between *most* of the purebloods and the shafit. You don't understand the hatred they feel for us."

"And *you* do? You've probably never spoken to a shafit in your life!"

"No, but I've seen the human weapons they've smuggled here in hopes of sparking unrest. I've listened to their preachers spout poisonous lies and aim threats toward *your* people just before being executed." A look she couldn't decipher crossed his face. "And believe me when I say I know all too well how clever they are in recruiting others to their cause."

Nahri said nothing. She felt sick—and not because of the reminder that she and the Daevas were in danger.

It was because she suddenly realized her husband—the Qahtani she'd assumed cared little about blood purity—might share the worst prejudices of her tribe. Nahri still didn't know what about her appearance made Ghassan so certain she was both Nahid *and* shafit, but he'd made it clear it was the possession of Suleiman's seal that brought him such insight.

And one day Muntadhir would have it. Would take it and see truly the woman he'd married.

Her heart stuttered. "None of what you're suggesting sounds politically stable, Muntadhir," she said, choosing her words carefully. "If things have gotten so bad, wouldn't it be better to try and work with the shafit? You and I were married to foster peace between the Geziris and the Daevas. Why can't we attempt the same with the mixed-bloods?"

Muntadhir shook his head. "Not like this. I feel bad for the shafit, I do. But theirs is a problem generations in the making, and what you're suggesting is too risky."

Nahri dropped her gaze. She caught sight of the beaded collar of her pretty new dress, and she pulled her robe more tightly over it, suddenly feeling very foolish.

He is never going to be the ally I need. The blunt truth resounded through her: Muntadhir's refusal to address the shafits' persecution and Jamshid's accusations churned in her mind. Oddly enough, Nahri couldn't hate him for it. She too had been beaten down by Ghassan, and she wasn't even his son. There was no denying Muntadhir's anguish over Jamshid and the genuine regret when he'd mentioned—and then promptly dismissed—the shafits' plight.

But Ghassan hadn't worn her down, not yet, not entirely. And she didn't want to bend any further than she already had, even if it meant standing alone.

Muntadhir must have registered the change in her expression. "It's not a no forever," he said quickly. "But it's not the right time to propose something so drastic."

Nahri gritted her teeth. "Because of Navasatem?" If one more thing got blamed on that damned holiday, she was going to burn something.

He shook his head. "No, not because of Navasatem. Because of the reason my father wanted to see me today." His jaw clenched, and his gaze fixed on the distant lake, the black water reflecting the scattered stars overhead. "Because my brother is coming back to Daevabad."

7

DARA

Dara studied the smoky map of Daevabad he'd conjured, using his fingers to spin it this way and that as he thought. "On the chance we *do* find a way to pass the threshold and cross Daevabad's lake, getting into the city itself poses the next problem." He glanced up at his band of warriors. He'd chosen the group carefully: his ten cleverest, the ones he was grooming for leadership. "What would you suggest?"

Irtemiz paced the map, almost stalking it. "Is there a way we could scale the walls?"

Dara shook his head. "The walls cannot be scaled, nor can they be tunneled under or flown over—Anahid herself raised them, may she be blessed."

Mardoniye spoke up, nodding at the city gates. "The gates are poorly defended. The Royal Guard keeps an eye out for boats crossing the lake—not for warriors arriving directly upon the beach from the water itself. We could force our way through."

"And enter directly in the middle of the Grand Bazaar," Dara pointed out.

Mardoniye's eyes flashed with hatred. "Is that a bad thing?" He ran a hand over his scarred face, the skin mottled where it had come into contact with Rumi fire. "I would not mind getting some vengeance for what the shafit did to us."

"Vengeance is not our mission," Dara chided. "And right now we are merely discussing strategy—I want you to *think*. The Grand Bazaar is only blocks from the Citadel." He nodded at the Citadel's tower, looming over the Grand Bazaar from its perch beside the brass wall. "We would have hundreds—thousands—of Royal Guard down on us in minutes. We'd be annihilated before we even reached the palace."

Bahram, another survivor from the Daeva Brigade, spoke next. "We could split up," he suggested. "Half of us stay behind to delay the Guard while you take the lady and the rest to the palace."

A chill went down Dara's spine at how easily he suggested it. "It would be certain death for the warriors left behind."

Bahram met his gaze, his eyes glittering. "We are all prepared to make that sacrifice."

Dara glanced at his group. He didn't doubt Bahram was right. The faces of his young soldiers were fierce with conviction. It should have filled Dara with pleasure. He'd poured himself into their training; he should be proud to stand at their side.

But by the Creator, he had fought at the side of so many young Daevas whose faces had sparked with equal conviction. He'd collected their bodies afterward, consigning them to the flames as martyrs in what was beginning to feel like a war with no end.

He sighed. This one *would* have an end, Dara would make sure of it—but he'd also take greater care with his men. "It would only be a delay. They'd slaughter you and be on the rest of us before we got far."

"What about ghouls?" another man suggested. "The ifrit are our allies now, are they not? One of them was boasting about how he could summon an entire army of ghouls. The skinny one."

Dara's face twisted in disgust at the mention of the ifrit, whom he hated in particular, escalating ways. The remark about them being allies and the memory of their ghouls only fueled his revulsion. Not to mention that Vizaresh—the ifrit they were speaking of now—had once threatened Nahri. Threatened "to grind her soul into dust" for blood-poisoning his brother . . . a threat Dara wouldn't be forgetting anytime soon. "I do not wish to see those foul things in our city," he said shortly.

Irtemiz grinned. "The ghouls or the ifrit?"

Dara snorted. His soldiers were all like family to him, but he had a particular fondness for Irtemiz, whose innate talent with a bow had come a long way under Dara's careful hand and who'd managed to keep her good humor even during the hardest of training sessions.

"Both," he replied. Then he gestured back at the map. "I want you to think about this and discuss solutions with each other while I'm away." Dara didn't quite share Manizheh's confidence that some mysterious meeting with Aeshma and the marid would result in his being able to cross the magical threshold protecting Daevabad, but on the off chance it did, he wanted to be prepared.

"Should we keep practicing with Abu Sayf?"

Dara considered that. He'd managed to convince Abu Sayf to spar with his soldiers . . . well, no, perhaps convince wasn't the right term. He'd threatened to scourge the younger, more irritating Geziri scout to death if the older man didn't comply. They were going to face zulfiqars in their fight to retake Daevabad, and they'd been handed a rare opportunity to learn to fight against them with the two Geziri scouts as their prisoners. Dara had not liked making such a ghastly threat, but there was little he was unwilling to do if it would help prepare his young warriors.

But only under his eye; he didn't trust the Geziris not to try something in his absence. "No. I do not want either of them unchained for even a moment." He dismissed the group. "Now go. I will join you for dinner before I leave."

He raised a hand to sweep the map away as they left, watching the buildings tumble together in a smoky wave. The miniature palace collapsed, the Citadel's tower dissolving over the wall.

Dara stilled. He snapped his fingers, conjuring and then crushing the tower again, letting it topple. It was tall enough that the upper half could crash through the wall, ripping a hole into the heart of the Citadel itself—and creating an entrance into the city.

That is magic beyond me. Manizheh might think him invincible, but Dara was learning that the fantastic tales told about the powers of their mighty ancestors in the time before Suleiman were best taken with a little salt. He was willing to break himself to reclaim Daevabad, but he couldn't afford to exhaust his magic at the very beginning of the invasion.

He tucked the idea away, crossing to the large carpet rolled in one corner. Dara hadn't flown one in years, not since journeying to Daevabad with Nahri. He ran a hand down its woolen length.

I will find a way to get back to you. I promise.

But first Dara had a meeting with the devil himself.

HE AND MANIZHEH FLEW EAST, TRAVELING ACROSS A stunning landscape that spread before them like crumpled silk, emerald hills and dusty plains blending into each other, marked by deep blue lines of twisting rivers and streams. The sight brought Dara a rare peace. Khayzur, the peri who'd once nursed him back to health, had tried to teach Dara to appreciate such moments, to let the solace and beauty of the natural world sweep him away. It had been a difficult lesson to internalize. The first time he'd been brought back, Dara had awakened to the news that his world had died fourteen centuries earlier and that he was nothing but a blood-soaked memory to his people.

Not to everyone. It was impossible to sit on this rug as it cut through the sky and not think of the first days he'd spent with Nahri—days that had driven him to drink. He'd found her very existence a scandal, physical proof one of his blessed Nahids had broken their most sacred code and lain with a human. That she'd been a cunning thief who lied as easily as she breathed seemed proof of every negative stereotype Dara had heard about the shafit.

But then . . . she became so much more. He had felt shockingly free with her—free to be a normal man and not the celebrated Afshin or the despised Scourge, free to exchange flirtatious barbs with a quick-witted, beautiful woman, and delight in the unexpected stirring her magnetic, mocking grin caused in his shuttered heart. All because Nahri *hadn't* known their history. She was the first person Dara had spoken to in centuries who knew nothing about his past—and so he'd been able to leave it behind.

He'd known theirs was foolish affection, had known it couldn't last, and yet Dara had been desperate to keep the worst from her—a decision he still regretted. Had he been honest with Nahri and confessed it all . . . given her a chance to make her own choice . . . he could not help but wonder if she would have chosen to escape Daevabad at his side without him putting a blade to Alizayd al Qahtani's throat.

Not that it mattered now. Nahri had seen exactly what Dara was on the boat that night.

"Are you all right?" Startled, Dara glanced up to find Manizheh watching him, a knowing expression on her face. "You look to be contemplating something weighty."

Dara forced a smile. "You remind me of your ancestors," he said, evading the question. "When I was a child, I used to think they could read minds."

Manizheh laughed, a rare sound. "Nothing so fantastical. But when you spend two centuries attuned to every heartbeat, skin flush, and inhalation that surrounds you, you learn to read people." She gave him a pointed look. "The question remains."

Dara flinched. At first glance, there wasn't much resemblance between Manizheh and her daughter. Manizheh was shorter and more compact, reminding him in no small way of his own mother, a woman who could cook up a meal for fifty, then break a spoon over her knee to stab a man. Manizheh's eyes, though, the sharp black eyes that tugged down slightly at the outer edge—those were Nahri's. And when they lit with challenge, they cut through Dara rather effectively.

"I am fine." He swept his hand toward the distant ground. "Appreciating the scenery."

"It is beautiful," she agreed. "It reminds me of Zariaspa. Rustam and I used to spend summers with the Pramukhs when we were young." Her voice turned wistful. "They were the happiest days of my life. We were always dashing about, climbing mountains, racing simurgh, experimenting with whatever forbidden plants and herbs we could." A sad smile crossed her face. "The closest thing to freedom we experienced."

Dara cocked his head. "Perhaps you are fortunate you did not have an Afshin. That all sounds terribly risky. We never would have permitted it."

Manizheh laughed again. "No, there weren't any legendary guardians around to ruin our fun, and the Pramukhs were fairly indulgent as long as we brought Kaveh along. They seemed not to realize he was equally irresponsible." She saw Dara's skeptical expression and shook her head. "Do not let his stern grand wazir face fool you. He was a mud-splattered country boy when I met him, more accomplished at sneaking out to hunt for fire salamanders than reining in two restless Nahids." She stared into the distance, her eyes dimming. "We weren't permitted to go to Zariaspa as frequently when we were older, and I always missed him."

"I suspect he felt the same," Dara said carefully. He had seen the way Kaveh looked at Manizheh, and no one at camp had missed the fact that their visitor had yet to sleep in the tent they'd prepared for him. *That* had thrown Dara; clearly the prim grand wazir did have a hidden side. "I am surprised you didn't bring him with us."

"Absolutely not," she said at once. "I don't want the ifrit to know anything more than necessary about him."

Dara frowned at the fierceness in her voice. "Why not?"

"Would you die for my daughter, Darayavahoush?"

The question surprised him, and yet the answer was already leaving Dara's lips. "Yes. Of course."

Manizheh gave him a knowing look. "And yet, would you let her die for you? Suffer for you?"

She has already suffered for me. "Not if I could help it," Dara said quietly.

"Precisely. Affection is a weakness for people like us, a thing to be concealed from those who would harm us. A threat to a loved one is a more effective method of control than weeks of torture."

She said the words with such cold certainty that a chill raced down his spine. "You sound as though you speak from experience," he ventured.

"I loved my brother very much," she said, staring into the distance. "The Qahtanis never let me forget it." She dropped her gaze, studying her hands. "I will confess that my desire to attack during Navasatem has a personal edge."

"How so?"

"Because Rustam spent the last one in the dungeons. I lost my temper, said something unwise to Ghassan's father. Khader." The name fell like a curse from her tongue. "An even harder man than his son. I don't remember what it was, petty nonsense from an angry young woman. But Khader took it as a threat. He had my brother dragged from the infirmary and thrown into a light-less cell at the bottom of the palace. They say . . ." She cleared her throat. "They say that the bodies of those who die in the dungeon aren't removed. You lie with corpses." She paused. "Rustam spent the entire month of Navasatem there. He didn't speak for weeks. Even years later . . . he could only sleep if lamps were blazing all night long."

Dara felt sick. He thought unwillingly of his sister's fate. "I am sorry," he said softly.

"As am I. I've learned since that anonymity is far safer for those I love." Her mouth twisted bitterly. "Though not without its own cruel drawbacks."

He hesitated; Manizheh's words indicated something that he couldn't let pass. "Do you not trust the ifrit?" he asked. He'd made his poor opinion of the ifrit clear more than once, but Manizheh never wanted to hear it. "I thought they were your allies."

"They are a means to an end, and I do not trust easily." She leaned back on her palms. "Kaveh is dear to me. I will not have the ifrit learn that."

"Your daughter . . ." Dara's throat constricted. "When I said I would die for her, I hope you know I would do so for any Nahid. It was not because . . ." He grew flustered. "I would not overstep my station."

A glint of amusement lit her face. "How old were you when you died, Afshin? The first time?"

Dara tried to recall. "Thirty?" He shrugged. "It was so long ago, and the last years were difficult. I do not remember exactly."

"That's what I thought."

"I do not understand."

She gave him a wry smile. "At times you speak like a young man who's yet to see a half-century. And as we discussed . . . I am a Nahid with a skill you compared to mind-reading."

Heat filled his cheeks before he could check it, his heart skipping a beat . . . the very signs, of course, that he knew she'd been looking for.

Manizheh shaded her eyes. "Ah, I do believe that is the lake where we are to meet Aeshma. You can take us down."

He flushed again. "Banu Manizheh, I pray you know . . ."

She met his eyes. "Your affections are yours, Afshin." Her gaze turned a little harder. "But do not let them be a weakness. In any way."

Embarrassed, he merely nodded. He raised a hand, and the rug dipped, speeding toward a distant gleam of azure. The lake was enormous—more sea than lake—the water a brilliant aquamarine, the tropical hue at stark odds with the snowcapped mountains ringing its shore.

"Lake Ossounes," Manizheh said. "Aeshma says it's been sacred to the marid for millennia."

Dara gave the lake an apprehensive look. "I am not flying over that much water on a rug."

"We needn't." Manizheh pointed to a thin trail of smoke drifting from the easternmost shore. "I suspect that is him."

They flew closer, zooming over rocky red bluffs and a narrow, marshy beach. It really was a stunning place. Lines of evergreens stood as sentinels against jutting hills and grassy valleys. A few clouds streaked the pale sky, and a hawk circled overhead. The air smelled fresh, promising cold mornings around pine-scented fires.

Longing stole into his heart. Though Dara had been born in Daevabad, this was the type of country he loved. Open skies and staggering vistas. One could take a horse and a bow and disappear into a land like this to sleep under the stars and explore the ruins of kingdoms lost to time.

Ahead, a fire blazed on the beach, the flames licking the air with a bit too much malicious delight.

Dara inhaled, catching the scent of ancient blood and iron. "Aeshma. He is near." Smoke curled from under his collar. "I can smell that foul mace he carries, thick with the blood of our people."

"Perhaps you should shift back into your natural form."

Dara scowled. "This is my natural form."

Manizheh sighed. "It isn't, and you know it. Not anymore. The ifrit have warned you that your magic is too much for this body." She tapped his tattooed arm, the skin pale brown and very much not aflame. "You leave yourself weak."

Their carpet fluttered to the ground. Dara didn't respond, but he didn't shift either. He would do so if and when the marid appeared.

"Ah, there are my erstwhile allies."

At the sound of Aeshma's voice, Dara's hand dropped to the long knife at his side. The bonfire split, and the ifrit strolled through the break with a black-fanged grin.

It was a grin that made Dara sick. That was what he looked like now when he shifted, his fire-bright skin, gold eyes, and clawed hands a mirror of the demons who'd enslaved him. That his ancestors had looked the same before Suleiman's curse was of little comfort. It hadn't been his ancestor's grin he'd seen just before the fetid water of the well closed over his face.

Aeshma sauntered closer, his smile widening as if he could sense Dara's displeasure. He probably could; it was not a thing Dara tried to conceal. Balanced on one shoulder was his mace, a crude metal hammer studded with barbs. Aeshma seemed to enjoy the effect it had on Dara's temper, and took special delight in mentioning the times it had been bathed with Nahid and Afshin blood.

Our allies. Dara's hand curled around the hilt of his knife.

"A knife?" Aeshma clucked his tongue in disappointment. "You could summon a sandstorm that would throw me across the lake if you would leave that useless body behind you." His eyes brightened with viciousness. "And surely if you're going to use a weapon, we might as well get a look at your famous scourge."

Manizheh's hand shot out as the air sparked with heat. "*Afshin*," she warned him before fixing her attention on Aeshma. "I received your signal, Aeshma. What have you heard?"

"The same whispers and premonitions that started up when you brought your Scourge back to life," the ifrit replied. "My companions have gone burning through all the marid haunts they know without response. But now there's something else . . ." He paused, seeming to savor the moment. "The peris have left the clouds to sing their warnings on the wind. They say the marid have overstepped. That they broke the rules and are to be called to account—punished by the lesser being to whom they owe blood."

Dara stared at him. "Are you drunk?"

Aeshma grinned, his fangs gleaming. "Forgive me, I forget at times one must speak simply to you." His voice slowed to a mocking crawl. "The marid killed you, Afshin. And now they owe you a blood debt."

Dara shook his head. "They might have been involved, but it was a djinn who wielded the blade."

"And?" Manizheh cut in. "Think back on what you've told me of that night. Do you truly believe some al Qahtani brat was capable of cutting you down on his own?"

Dara hesitated. He'd put arrows in the prince's throat and lungs and knocked him into the lake's cursed depths. Alizayd should have been dead twice over and instead he'd climbed back onto the boat looking like some sort of watery wraith. "What do you mean by a blood debt?" he asked.

Aeshma shrugged. "The marid owe you a favor. Which is convenient, because you want to break into their lake."

"It's not their lake. It's ours."

Manizheh laid a hand on Dara's wrist as Aeshma rolled his eyes. "It was once theirs," she said. "The marid helped Anahid build the city. Surely you were taught some of this? It's said that the jeweled stones that pave the Temple grounds were brought by the marid as tribute."

Afshin children were not exactly schooled in the finer points of their people's history, but Dara had heard the story of the Temple's stones. "So how does that get me across the threshold?"

"Forget your threshold," Aeshma said. "Do you imagine water beings crossing deserts and mountains? They use the waters of the world to travel . . . and they once taught your Nahid masters to do the same." Resentment flashed in his eyes. "It made hunting *my* people that much easier. We dared not even go near a pond lest some blood-poisoning Nahid spring from its depths."

"This is madness," Dara declared. "You want me to threaten the marid—the *marid*, beings capable of turning a river into a serpent the size of a mountain—based on the supposed whispers of peris and tales of a legendary magic neither Banu Manizheh nor I were alive to witness." He narrowed his eyes. "You wish to kill us, is that it?"

"If I wanted to kill you, Afshin, believe me I'd have come up with a far simpler method and spared myself your paranoid company," Aeshma replied. "You should be excited! You get to avenge yourself on the marid who killed you! You get to be their Suleiman."

The comparison instantly extinguished Dara's anger, replacing it with dread. "I am no Suleiman." The denial surged from his mouth, his skin prickling at the thought of such blasphemy. "Suleiman was a prophet. He was the man who set our laws and granted us Daevabad and blessed our Nahids—"

Aeshma burst into laughter. "My, you really do rattle that off. I remain forever impressed by the training your Nahid Council beat into you."

"Leave him alone," Manizheh said sharply. She turned back to Dara. "No one is asking you to be Suleiman," she assured him, her voice gentler. "You are our Afshin. That is all we need you to be." The confidence in her eyes helped calm him. "But this blood debt is a good thing. A *blessed* thing. It might get us back to Daevabad. To my daughter."

Nahri. Her face played in his memory. The betrayal in her dark eyes as Dara forced her hand in the infirmary, her screams as he was cut down.

Sixty-four, Kaveh had said coldly. Sixty-four Daevas who died in the chaos Dara had caused.

He swallowed the lump growing in his throat. "How do we summon the marid?"

Violent delight danced across the ifrit's face. "We anger them." He turned away. "Come! I've found something they're going to be *very* upset to lose."

We anger them? Dara stayed rooted to the sand. "My lady . . . this could be quite dangerous."

"I know." Manizheh's gaze was locked on the retreating ifrit. "You should shift."

This time, Dara obeyed, letting the magic take him. Fire raced down his limbs, claws and fangs bursting forth. He sheathed the knife, conjuring a new weapon from the smoke that swirled around his hips. He raised it, the familiar handle of the scourge warming in his hand.

It would not hurt to remind Aeshma of what he was capable of.

"Don't believe everything they tell you," Manizheh said, suddenly sounding on edge. "The marid. They are liars." She turned abruptly on her heel, following Aeshma through the flames.

Dara stared at her another moment. *What would they possibly have to tell me?* Bewildered, he followed her, his unease growing.

Behind the veil of smoke, a figure writhed on the sandy beach. His hands and legs were bound, his mouth gagged. He was sobbing against the ball of fabric stuffed in his mouth, his wrists bloody where he'd tried to tear away his binds.

Crimson blood.

Manizheh spoke first. "A human? You plan to use a human to summon the marid?"

"Not just any human," Aeshma explained. "A devotee of the marid—one who was hard to find. Humans have been giving up the old ways, but I spied him conducting rituals at high tide." He inhaled, looking disgusted. "He's theirs. I can smell it."

Dara frowned. He could too, as a matter of fact. "Salt," he said softly. He studied the human. "And something else . . . like a heaviness upon him. Something dark. Deep."

Aeshma nodded, swinging his mace in one hand. "He's been claimed."

Manizheh was staring at the human, her expression unreadable. "And that claim is important to them?"

"Very," Aeshma replied. "There's power in worship, and the marid don't have many followers left. They're going to be very upset to lose one."

The ifrit's plan became horribly clear in Dara's head. "Lose one . . . you cannot mean you intend—"

"*I* do not." Aeshma gave them both a careful look. "If I'm wrong about the blood debt, the marid will be within their rights to slaughter whoever kills their acolyte." He held the mace out to Manizheh. "This risk is yours, Banu Nahida."

Dara instantly stepped between them. "No. Banu Manizheh . . . there—there are rules," he stammered. "Our tribe has always obeyed Suleiman's code; it's what separates us from the djinn. We do not touch humans. We certainly do not kill them!"

She shook her head, grim resignation in her eyes as she reached for the mace. "We have to find a way to get into Daevabad, Afshin. We're running out of time."

Dread clawed up in his chest, but he lowered her hand. "Then

I will do it." This was not a sin he could let his Nahid commit herself.

Manizheh hesitated. Her lips were pressed tight, her spine rigid. And then she nodded, stepping back.

Dara took the mace. He headed for the human, closing himself off from the man's sobs, from the voice screaming inside his own head.

He smashed his skull in with a single strike.

A moment of horrified silence seemed to hang in the air. Then Aeshma spoke, his voice strained. "Burn him. In the water."

Sick to his soul, Dara grabbed the human he'd murdered by his bloody collar and dragged him farther into the shallows. The smell of viscera swept over him. Around the dead man's wrist was a blue string knotted with jade beads. Had someone given that to him? Someone who'd be waiting for him to return?

Demon. The whispered accusations that followed Dara in Daevabad rose in his mind. *Murderer.*

Scourge.

Crimson blood stained the clear water, ballooning out from the body like a storm cloud overtaking the sky. The water simmered against his ankles. Dara hated it. He hated everything about this. Fire poured down his hands, rushing to consume the man's body. For a moment, Dara could not help but wish it would consume him as well.

A high, thin screech tore the air—and then the lake attacked.

The water drew up so fast Dara didn't even have time to move. A wave twice his height lunged for him, towering over him like a ravenous bear . . .

And then the wave fell apart, collapsing around his body with an angry hiss of steam. The water tried again, flattening and then twisting around his legs as if to drag him down and drown him. And again it lurched back, as though it were an animal that had been burned.

"Afshin!" he heard Manizheh cry. "Watch out!"

Dara looked up. His eyes went wide. In the churning depths, a ship was re-forming. Barnacle-covered wooden ribs and broken deck planks rushed together, a skeleton of sunken wrecks. An enormous anchor, the metal orange with rust, flew into place on the bow like some sort of battering ram.

Dara stepped back as the boat rushed forward, his first instinct to protect Manizheh.

"Stand your ground!" Aeshma shouted. "Command it!"

Command it? Too shocked to argue and at an utter loss for how *else* to confront the nightmarish wreck hurtling toward him, Dara found himself raising his hands. "Za marava!" he cried, using the words the ifrit had taught him.

The ship burst into ash. The flakes drifted in the acrid air, falling like snow, and Dara stumbled, shaking badly.

But the lake wasn't done. Water dashed over the dead human, frothing as it doused the flames covering his body.

And then the man stood up.

Water streamed from his limbs, seaweed wrapping his arms and crabs skittering up his legs. Triangular fins spiked from his shoulders, tracing down to meet reptilian clawed hands. Mollusks covered his crushed skull, and scales crept across his bloodied cheeks, a snarled mess of shells and decayed fishing nets replacing his soiled clothing. He straightened his broken neck with an abrupt crack and blinked at them, the whites of his eyes vanished under an oily dark film.

Dara recoiled in horror. "That is what Alizayd looked like," he gasped as Manizheh and Aeshma rejoined him. "By the Creator . . . it really was them."

The dead man eyed them, and the temperature plummeted, the air growing clammy with moisture.

"*Daevas*," it hissed, speaking Divasti in a reedy, whispering voice that set Dara's teeth on edge.

Aeshma stepped forward on the smoking sand. "Marid!" he greeted it, sounding almost cheerful. "So you salt-blooded old fiends *are* still around. I was beginning to fear your sea-beast of a mother had devoured you all."

The marid hissed again, and Dara's skin crawled. The thing before them, a dead, twisted nightmare from the depths of the dark water, seemed wrong in every sense of the word.

It bared a set of reptilian teeth. "You killed my human," it accused him.

"You killed *me*," Dara snapped. He had no doubt now, and fresh fury was coursing through him. "One of you did anyway. And for what? I did nothing to your people!"

"Ours was not the hand that slayed you," the marid corrected, an odd defensiveness creeping into its breathy voice. A muddy snail glided along the scaled fin of its shoulder. "You were killed by a man of your own race."

"So kill him again," Aeshma said casually. "He has murdered your acolyte and set aflame your holy waters. Smash him to bits with another ship. Drown him." The ifrit stepped closer, ignoring the glare Dara threw at him. "But you can't, can you? It's being whispered all around. Your people broke the rules . . ." His tongue darted across his lips, hungry anticipation on his fiery face. "He could burn the world's waters and you could do nothing."

The marid hesitated. "An error was made in taking the boy," it finally said.

"An *error*?" Fire burst from Dara's hands. "You slaughtered me in cold blood and *taking Alizayd* was the error?"

The marid made an angry clicking sound, and a thick fog rose from the water. "Blame your Nahid," it hissed, glaring at Manizheh with hate in the glittering depths of its eyes. "She who was warned, she who seeks to upend what was wrought in blood!" The unnatural fog slid over his skin like a snake and Dara shiv-

ered. "If you could see the destruction you portend, Darayavahoush e-Afshin, you would throw yourself in the sea."

Shock froze Dara's tongue, but Aeshma waved a dismissive
hand. "Ignore it. The marid like to pretend at prophecy, but they
are demented fools whose wits are as scattered as their waters."
His bright golden eyes filled with scorn. "A millennium or two
ago, I remember these shores being lined with shining temples,
a ceaseless horde of humans willing to throw themselves in your
waters and declare you their gods. Your kind laughed as Suleiman punished my people." His face was dark with anger. "I am
glad I have lived to see the same done to you."

The marid hissed again. "This creature is no Suleiman." Its
oily eyes narrowed on Dara. "He is nothing but a blood-soaked
pawn."

"And yet you owe him a debt." Manizheh's cool voice cut
through the charged air like a knife. "A debt you would presumably like to be free of. So perhaps we could have a conversation
instead of arguing over old wars."

The marid tilted its head, considering them. The water at
its feet contracted and surged out, as if the creature was taking a
breath. "Speak," it finally replied.

"We wish to return to Daevabad." Manizheh pointed at Dara.
"My Afshin can no longer cross the mountain threshold, but
there are legends that my ancestors had another way. That they
could slip into the lake as though it were a doorway and reemerge
in whichever waters were on their minds, in any place in the
world their hearts most desired."

"That was magic never meant for daevas. The lake was *ours*.
It was sacred." Hurt crept into the creature's voice. "It was the
birthplace of Tiamat. She enchanted it so that we could pay homage to her from any water."

"Tiamat?" Dara repeated, confused. "As in Bet il Tiamat?
The southern ocean?"

"Not precisely," Aeshma replied. "Tiamat was one of their gods, their mother. A giant sea monster born in the chaos of creation with a penchant for destroying whatever dirt-blood civilizations provoked her ire." He grinned. "She *hated* daevas."

"She had cause to hate daevas," the marid hissed. "Anahid stole her lake. We removed the enchantment when Anahid's descendants grew too weak to control us. They deserved to be torn apart for daring to enter our waters." It turned on Manizheh, snapping its teeth. "And it is not just Daevabad you seek, daughter of Anahid. Do not think us so easily fooled. You are after Suleiman's seal."

Manizheh shrugged, unruffled as ever. "I am after what belongs to me. Daevabad was granted to the Nahids by the Creator, as was Suleiman's seal. Their return is equally ordained." She gestured to Dara. "Why would our greatest warrior be given back to us with such extraordinary abilities if it was not the will of the Creator?"

The marid gestured to its murdered human husk. "This is not the will of the Creator. It is the ill-fated scheme of a power-hungry woman." Its gaze flickered to Dara. "And you are worse. Twice undead and with the blood of thousands on your hands . . . and still you serve those who made you into this abomination."

The sudden charge took Dara aback and then it cut him deep, striking the darkest part of his heart, a shadowed part he dared not touch.

There is a city called Qui-zi.

The calm with which those words had been spoken, by an authority Dara was raised never to doubt. The screams of the people who lived there, the shafit that the Nahid Council had assured him were soulless deceptions. The belief he'd desperately clung to until he'd met a shafit woman—Nahri—whose company made him fear that everything he'd been told about the mixed-bloods was a lie.

Except Nahri wasn't shafit. *That* had been the lie, a deception put in place by the very creature before him. A marid curse, a marid lie.

"*Can* you do it?" he demanded of the marid, abruptly done with these games. "Is it possible for us to travel through the waters back to Daevabad?"

"We will not help a Nahid retake Suleiman's seal."

"That is not what I asked," he said through his teeth. "I asked if you *could*."

The marid drew up. "We do not take commands from fire-born devils."

That was answer enough for Dara.

It took very little to call up the raw power burning bright and angry inside him. Dara had spilled so much blood. It couldn't be for nothing, and if the marid needed to learn that lesson the hard way, so be it.

He scorched the ground in a burst of heat that baked the clay beneath his feet, shaking the entire lake bed. The water churned as it came to a vicious boil, steaming away in gigantic clouds of vapor. More fire poured down his hands, dashing to consume everything that had been safely nestled in the lake's embrace. The waterweeds that had been dancing and the fossilized teeth of creatures lost to time; a pair of writhing eels and the remains of countless fishing boats. A flock of cranes beat a hasty retreat, the frightened cry of birds filling the air.

The marid howled as its sanctuary burned, falling to its knees and screeching in pain as if it had taken the blow itself. Its clawed hands scrabbled at the dust.

Dara approached, kneeling at its side. He took the marid by its chin, its skin like pebbles beneath his fingertips. He forced its oily gaze to meet his. "You take commands from this fire-born devil," he said coldly. "You will obey those commands or I will burn every water you consider sacred, every place your kind has *ever* called home. I will reduce it all to ash and dust and murder every human follower you have left on the wreckage of your shores."

The marid jerked free. It stared at its burning sanctuary. In the puddles that remained, writhing fish were ablaze, looking like a sick parody of a Daeva fire altar.

The marid's gaze lingered on the charred remains of a water snake. "When Suleiman punished your people, he shed no blood. He offered a choice . . . a choice to spend your penance *building a temple to the Creator*, not a command to take part in a war."

The words came far easier to Dara now. "I am no Suleiman."

"No," the marid agreed. "You are not." It seemed to have grown smaller, its teeth and scales dull.

A moment passed, the only sound the crackling of flames. The fire was spreading to the trees, to the evergreen forest he'd briefly longed to escape into.

The marid spoke again, its voice lower. "You will consider the blood debt paid if we let you pass through Daevabad's lake?"

A loud crack from ahead caught his attention. The flames had taken a large tree on the opposite shore. It had stood alone, a towering sentinel, but as Dara watched, it broke, shattering from its base. It fell, landing across the smoking lake like the husk of a bridge.

He went very still. "No. That is not my only price," he said softly. "Before you killed me on the lake, you attacked me at the Gozan. You transformed the river itself into a serpent, a beast as large as a mountain. Could you do that to the lake?"

"Perhaps." The marid tensed. "Briefly. The lake is Tiamat's birthplace. Its waters are not easily controlled." It frowned. "Why would you want to do such a thing?"

Dara's eyes returned to the burning tree. "I want to bring down a tower."

8

ALI

Daevabad's lake stretched before him, a pane of murky green glass.

No ripples played upon the dark water, nor did any leaping fish break its surface. The only movement came from the clumps of dead leaves that floated past. The thick, cold air smelled of earthen decay and lightning, an eerie silence hanging over the boat. The lake looked dead, a place cursed and left abandoned long ago.

Ali knew better.

As if in a trance, he stepped closer to the deck's edge, his skin prickling as he watched the ferry course through the water. Its stern looked like a blunt knife dragged through oil, leaving not a single wave in its wake. They had yet to pass the veil, and with the morning's thick fog, nothing was visible behind them. It felt as though they were suspended in time, the lake endless.

Tell me your name. Ali shivered at the memory, the marid's soft whisper like a finger of ice stroking his spine. The soft buzzing of insects rose in his ears. The water really was so close. It would be nothing to climb over the ship's railing. To trail his hands in its cool depths. To submerge.

Aqisa's hand came down on his wrist. "A little close to the edge, don't you think?"

Ali started, pulled from his daze. He was holding the railing, one foot slightly raised though he had no memory of doing so. And the buzzing sound was gone.

"I . . . did you hear that?" he asked.

"All I hear is Lubayd emptying the contents of his stomach," Aqisa replied, jerking a thumb at their friend as he did just that, violently retching over the boat's railing.

Ali shivered again, rubbing his arms. It felt as though something damp and heavy had been clinging to his skin. "Odd," he muttered.

Lubayd made his staggering way over to them, his face pale. "I hate this blasted thing," he declared. "What kind of djinn sail *boats?* We're fire creatures, for the love of God."

Ali gave him a sympathetic look. "We're almost there, my friend. The veil should be falling before us at any moment."

"And have you a plan yet for when we arrive?" Aqisa asked.

"No?" Ali had sent missives to the palace several times during the journey to Daevabad, suggesting that Ayaanle traders be sent out from the capital to intercept them. He'd even offered to simply leave the cargo on the beach outside the city. Each letter received the same reply, written in the hand of a different scribe. *Your return pleases us.* "I suppose the only thing we can do is wait and see how we're received."

Another hush descended, and this time all three of them went still. The scent of smoke washed over him, along with the familiar tingling as they crossed the veil.

And then Daevabad was towering before them.

The city dwarfed their ship, a lion to a gnat. The thick fog was a mere skirt around its massive, glinting brass walls, and its looming bulk blotted out the sky. Peeking over the wall were the tops of sandblasted glass minarets and delicate floating stupas, ancient mud-brick ziggurats and brightly tiled temples. And guarding all of them was the stark crenellated tower of the Citadel, standing tall and proud as a symbol of Am Gezira.

Lubayd exhaled. "*That's* Daevabad? *That's* where you're from?"

"That's where I'm from," Ali echoed softly. The sight of his old home made him feel as though someone had reached into his chest and turned over his heart. He looked up at the facades of the long-dead Nahids carved into the city's brass walls as the boat drew near. Their distant metal gazes seemed ethereal, bored, the arrival of some exiled sand-fly prince a mere footnote in the long history they'd witnessed. Though the Nahid Council had been overthrown centuries earlier, no one had torn down their statues. The common refrain was that the Qahtanis didn't care: they were so confident and secure in their reign that they weren't bothered by ruined remembrances of the defeated Nahids.

But as with many things in Daevabad, the truth was more complicated. The facades *couldn't* be torn down. Not by anyone. Zaydi's workers had no sooner taken a chisel to their surface than boils broke out across their skin, brass erupting through the fetid wounds until all that was left was ashy bone and puddles of cooling metal.

No one had tried since.

The docks were silent and deserted, save for a pair of cargo dhows and a Sahrayn sandship, the port in even worse repair than it had been when Ali left. Even so, the decay only added to the majesty. It was like stepping into some long-abandoned paradise, a massive world built by beings they could scarcely understand.

"Praise God . . . ," Lubayd whispered as they slid past a statue of a warrior holding a bow twice Ali's height and familiar enough to make his stomach turn. "I did not expect to ever see such a sight in my life."

"I did," Aqisa muttered darkly. "I just assumed we'd have an army behind us when it happened."

A dull ache pounded in Ali's head. "You can't talk like that here," he warned. "Not even in jest. If the wrong person in Daevabad hears you . . ."

Aqisa snorted, caressing the hilt of her khanjar. "I'm not worried." She gave Ali a pointed stare. "I saw how well their future Qaid survived in the desert."

Ali threw her a wounded look.

Lubayd groaned. "Can we delay bloodshed for at least a few days? I didn't cross a cursed lake in a giant wooden bowl so I could be beheaded for treason before I had a chance to sample some royal cuisine."

"That's not the punishment for treason," Ali murmured.

"What's the punishment for treason then?"

"Being trampled to death by a karkadann."

Lubayd paled and this time, Ali knew it wasn't due to seasickness. "Oh," he choked out. "Don't you come from an inventive family?"

Ali returned his gaze to the brass walls. "My father doesn't deal lightly with disloyalty." He ran his thumb over the scar on his neck. "Believe me."

THEY LEFT THE CAMELS AND THE BULK OF THEIR cargo at the caravanserai beside the city gate, Lubayd affectionately cooing into the ears of the animals of which he'd grown fond while Aqisa and Ali waited impatiently. Half-expecting to be arrested the moment they docked, Ali was surprised to find no one waiting for them. Uncertain of what else to do, he ordered two camels loaded with the most precious pieces of the Ayaanle's cargo: trunks of raw gold, cases of finely worked jewelry, and a crate of rare books for the royal library that he'd broken into more than once during the long journey.

The gifts secure, they'd headed for the palace. Ali wrapped one end of his ghutra across his face before they set out; his mixed Ayaanle and Geziri features were not entirely uncommon in cosmopolitan Daevabad, but throw a zulfiqar in the mix, and he might as well shout his name from the rooftops.

The Grand Bazaar was a riot of color and chaos, the crowd thick with arguing shoppers, wide-eyed tourists, and beasts of various magical persuasions. The sound of haggling in a dozen different tongues filled Ali's ears, the competing scents of shafit sweat, djinn smoke, fried sweetmeats, enchanted perfumes, and bins of spices making him heady with nostalgia. He dodged a baby simurgh as it belched a plume of green fire, accidentally stepping on the foot of a Sahrayn woman in a snakeskin cape who cursed him in such vulgar terms they bordered on artistry.

Ali only grinned, his giddiness hidden beneath his ghutra. However he'd been brought back to Daevabad, there was no denying that the spectacle of his old home made his heart beat faster. The mysterious whispers on the lake seemed distant, the prickling in his mind gone for now.

But as they moved deeper into the crowd, the conditions of the bazaar swept away his nostalgia. Never clean to begin with—in fact, Ali had threatened to cut out the tongue of the openly corrupt sanitation minister during his brief tenure as Qaid—Daevabad's streets looked positively filthy now. Rotting garbage collected in piles, and the narrow canals cut into the road to drain away rain and sewage were overflowing with debris. More unsettling was the fact that he saw few members of the Royal Guard patrolling the streets—and those he did see were dressed in threadbare uniforms, the younger ones armed with regular swords instead of the costlier zulfiqars. He pressed on, growing more troubled by the minute. Musa had claimed that Daevabad had fallen upon hard times, but Ali had dismissed it as a means of goading him into returning home.

They were halfway to the midan, crossing a crowded intersection deep in the heart of Daevabad's shafit district, when a child's scream split the air.

Ali stopped, pulling the camel he was leading to a halt. The sound had come from a crude platform standing among the ruins of a stone building. Upon the platform was a Geziri man clad in brightly patterned yellow silk. He was forcing another man, a shafit in a dirty waist-wrap, to the front of the platform.

"*Baba!*" The scream came again, and then a little girl burst from a wooden stockade set behind the platform. She ran to the shafit man, throwing herself in his arms.

Ali stared, struggling to comprehend what was happening. A crowd of djinn stood below the platform, all dressed in rather expensive-looking garb. There were more shafit as well—men, women, and children—trapped behind the stockade, hemmed in by several well-armed djinn.

The shafit man was refusing to let go of his daughter. He was shaking, rubbing her back and whispering into her ear as she sobbed. He stepped back as the guards made a halfhearted attempt to pull his daughter away, glaring at them.

The Geziri djinn crossed his arms over his fine silks and then sighed, striding to the front of the platform.

A too-wide grin came over his face. "How's this pair for you who've not yet had the good fortune to spot some weak-blooded kin? They're both Daevabadi-born and fluent in Djinnistani. And our friend here is a talented cook. We found him running a snack stall in the bazaar. He'd be an asset in the kitchen of *any* long-lost relation."

What? Ali stared in incomprehension at the sight before him.

Aqisa was clearly not as confused. "They're selling them," she whispered in rising horror. "They're *selling* shafit."

"That can't be." Lubayd looked sick all over again. "That . . . that is forbidden. No Geziri would ever . . ."

Ali wordlessly pressed the reins of his camel into Lubayd's hands.

Lubayd grabbed his arm. Ali tried to wrench away, and Lubayd nodded at the line of men guarding the stockade. "*Look, you rash fool.*"

Ali stared—but it wasn't because of the guards. Familiar landmarks drew his eye: a pottery shop with a blue-striped door, the distinctive way two of the narrow alleys ran close but never touched, the slightly slumped minaret in the distance. Ali knew this neighborhood. He knew what had once stood here, what the building in ruins before him once was.

It was the mosque at which Sheikh Anas, the martyred former leader of the Tanzeem, had preached.

Ali inhaled, suddenly breathless. His father might as well have twisted a knife in his heart. But he knew the punishment hadn't been directed at the son in faraway Am Gezira; it had been aimed at the shafit whose plight had pushed him into disloyalty . . . the ones being auctioned off before his eyes.

The girl began to cry harder.

"To hell with this," Aqisa snapped, striding forward.

Ali followed her, leaving Lubayd cursing in their wake and struggling with the camels. The Geziri trader must have noticed them because he broke off from his vile pitches, his steel eyes lighting with anticipation.

"By the Most High, you two look like you just blew in from a sandstorm." The trader laughed. "Certainly not my usual customers, but I suppose one can find blood kin anywhere." He lifted a dark brow. "As long as that kin can pay."

Aqisa's hand dropped to her sword. Ali swiftly stepped in front of her. "When did Daevabad start selling its shafit citizens?" he demanded.

"*Selling?*" The man clucked his tongue. "We're not selling anyone." He sounded aghast. "That would be illegal. We are merely facilitating the search for this man's pureblood family . . . and then taking a fee to support our work." He touched his heart. "Easier to find relatives when he's standing in front of them, no?"

It was a pathetically flimsy cover, and at his side, Aqisa snarled. Ali could only imagine how awful his home must look to his friends. Like many Geziris, the djinn of Bir Nabat kept their mixed-blood relatives with them, ignoring the law that demanded they be brought to Daevabad to live out their lives. The few shafit in Bir Nabat were treated as equals, roles found for them no matter their abilities with magic.

Ali gritted his teeth. "It doesn't look like he desires to find any pureblooded kin," he said. "You said he had a livelihood? Why not let him return to it?"

The trader shrugged. "The shafit are like children. Should we let children choose their fate as well?"

At that, Aqisa elbowed Ali hard in the stomach and then took advantage of his distraction to push him out of her way. She pulled free her khanjar, her eyes flashing. "I should cut out your tongue," she snapped in Geziriyya. "You're a traitor to our tribe, to everything our people stand for!"

The trader raised his hands as several of his guards flanked him. "Nothing we're doing here is illegal," he said, the oily tone leaving his voice. "And I don't need some northern garbage-picker getting everyone riled up . . ."

"What is your price?" The question was poison in Ali's mouth. "The price for the man and his daughter both?"

The trader shrugged in the direction of a djinn in shocking spotted robes. "The gentleman from Agnivansha offered twelve hundred dinars for the girl alone."

Twelve hundred dinars. A disgustingly low amount at which to value a life and yet far more than what he and his companions could muster up. Ali was as poor as the rest of Bir Nabat, his wealth stripped away when his father banished him. The camels they towed were loaded with gifts, but all of it was carefully inventoried, a gift from the Ayaanle to the palace.

Reaching down, Ali pulled his zulfiqar from his robes.

Now the trader did more than flinch. He blanched and stepped back in open fear. "Now, wait a minute. I don't know who you stole that from, but—"

"Would this be enough?" Ali's fingers tightened on the hilt of his beloved blade. Then he swallowed hard and offered it to the trader.

A shrewd look entered the man's eyes. "No," he said bluntly. "Not with all the soldiers trying to pawn them before they desert back to Am Gezira. I'll give you the father, but not the girl."

The shafit man had been watching them haggle in what looked like numb shock. But at the trader's offer, his daughter let out a cry, and the man clutched her close.

"*No.*" The word burst from his mouth. "I won't let you put her back in that cage. I won't let you take her away from me!"

The despair in his voice shoved Ali past his tipping point. "A *Qahtani* zulfiqar." He threw it at the man's feet and then pulled away the ghutra covering his face. "Surely *that* will pay your price?"

The trader's mouth fell open, the golden tone of his skin turning a green Ali hadn't realized was possible. He dropped to his knees. "Prince Alizayd," he gasped. "My God . . . f-forgive me," he stammered. "I would never have spoken with such disrespect had I known it was you."

The crowd parted in a way that reminded Ali of how djinn in Am Gezira jumped from horned vipers. His name carried on the wind, whispers in various tongues rustling through the throng.

Ali tried to ignore them, instead letting a little of his old arrogance leach into his voice. "Come now," he challenged. He jutted his chin at the zulfiqar, heartsick at the thought of giving over the weapon that had kept him alive during his exile. "My personal blade. It's been in my family for generations—certainly this will cover them both?"

A mix of greed and fear flitted across the trader's face. "Is this what you used to kill the Scourge?"

Ali was repulsed by the question. But suspecting it would help sway the man, the lie came easily. "The very blade."

The man grinned. "Then I would say it is very good doing business with you, my prince." He bowed and motioned for Ali to join him. "Please . . . the contracts will only take a moment . . ."

The shafit man was looking at him in stunned disbelief. "But you . . . people say—" His eyes darted toward the crowd of pure-bloods, and he abruptly changed the subject. "Please don't separate us, Your Highness." He hugged his daughter closer. "I beg you. We'll serve however you like, but please don't separate us."

"No," Ali said quickly. "That's not what this is." The trader returned with the contracts, and he read through them before adding his signature. Then he handed them to the shafit father.

The other man looked bewildered. "I don't understand."

"You're free," Ali said. "As you should be." He shot the trader his coldest glare, and the man flinched away. "Those who peddle in lives will be among the first to burn in hell."

"And we shall leave it at that!" Lubayd had finally made his way to them, pulling both bleating camels through the crowd. He shoved the reins into Aqisa's hands and seized the hem of Ali's robe, dragging him off the platform.

Ali glanced around, but the shafit father was gone, vanished into the crowd with his daughter. Ali didn't blame him. He could feel the eyes of the bystanders boring into them as Lubayd started trying to rewrap Ali's ghutra around his face.

"Wh-what are you doing?" Ali demanded as his friend poked him in the eye. "Ow! Will you stop . . ." The words died in his mouth as he spotted the reason he suspected Lubayd was trying to hustle him away.

A dozen members of the Royal Guard had joined them.

Ali stood awkwardly, his ghutra askew, uncertain how to greet his former companions. There was a moment or two of hesitant staring, until one of the officers stepped forward. He brought his hand to his heart and brow in the Geziri salute. "Peace be upon you, Prince Alizayd," he greeted him solemnly. "Your father has asked that I retrieve you."

"IT IS A VERY LOVELY PLACE TO BE EXECUTED, I WILL grant you that," Lubayd said conversationally as they were escorted down a deserted palace corridor. Sweet-smelling purple flowers climbed the columns, dappled sunlight playing through the wooden screens.

"We're not going to be executed," Ali said, trying to keep the feeling that they were walking to their doom from his face.

"They took our weapons," Lubayd pointed out. "Well, they took Aqisa's and my weapons . . . you gave yours away. Brilliant move, by the way."

Ali threw him a dark look.

"In here, my prince." The officer stopped, pulling open a blue-painted door with a pattern of leaping gazelles carved around it. It led to a small courtyard garden, enclosed by high walls of pale cream stone. In the center was a sunken pavilion shadowed by lush palms. Water bubbled merrily in a stone fountain shaped like a star and tiled with sunbursts, and across from it was a carpet laden with silver platters of rainbow-hued pastries and jewel-bright fruit.

"Your father will join you shortly. It is an honor to meet you, my prince." The officer hesitated, then added, "My family is from Hegra. The work you did on our well last year . . . it saved them."

His eyes met Ali's. "I hope you know how fond many of us in the Royal Guard remain of you."

Ali considered the carefully worded statement. "A fondness well returned," he replied. "What is your name, brother?"

The man bowed his head. "Daoud."

"A pleasure to meet you." Ali touched his heart. "Send your people my greetings when next you meet."

"God willing, my prince." He bowed again and then left, pulling the door shut behind him.

Aqisa gave him a look. "Making friends?"

Allies. Though Ali didn't like how swiftly his mind settled on that word. "Something like that."

Ahead, Lubayd had fallen upon the food. He took a bite of a honeyed confection studded with sugared flowers, and his eyes closed in bliss. "This is the best thing I've ever tasted."

"It is likely poisoned," Aqisa said.

"It is worth death."

Ali joined him, his stomach rumbling. It had been years since he'd seen such delicacies. As usual, they'd been piled to impress—an amount not even Ali and his hungry companions would be able to finish. It was a practice he hadn't thought much about when he was younger, but recalling the visible poverty in Daevabad's streets, he suddenly saw it as sinfully wasteful.

The door creaked open. "Little Zaydi!"

Ali glanced up to see a barrel-chested man in an officer's uniform and crimson turban stride into the garden. "Wajed uncle!" he cried happily.

The beaming Qaid pulled Ali into a crushing hug. "By God, boy, is it good to see you again!"

Ali felt some of the tension leave him, or perhaps Wajed's embrace was merely turning him numb. "You too, uncle."

Wajed pushed him back, holding him at arm's length to look him over; there were tears in the older man's eyes, but he laughed, clearly delighted at the sight of Ali. "Where is the gangly boy I taught to swing a zulfiqar? My soldiers were whispering that you resembled Zaydi the Great, striding up to the palace in your rags with your companions in tow."

That was not a comparison Ali suspected would sit well with his father. "I don't think anyone would mistake me for Zaydi the Great," he demurred quickly. "But meet my friends." He took Wajed's arm. "Aqisa, Lubayd . . . this is Wajed al Sabi, the Qaid of the Royal Guard. He all but raised me when I was sent to the Citadel."

Wajed touched his heart. "An honor," he said sincerely. A little emotion crept into the Qaid's gruff voice. "Thank you for protecting him."

Ali heard the creak of the door again. His heart skipping a beat, he glanced back, expecting his father.

But it was Muntadhir who stepped into the sunlight.

Ali froze as his brother met and then held his gaze. Muntadhir looked paler than Ali remembered, shadows dark under his eyes. Two thin scars marked his left brow—a remnant of the Afshin's scourge. But they did little to detract from his appearance. Muntadhir had always been the dashing one, the handsome, rakish prince who won over adoring nobles as swiftly as Ali put them off. He looked striking in the Qahtani royal regalia: the gold-trimmed black robe that swirled like smoke around his feet and the brilliant turban of twisted blue, purple, and gold silk that crowned his head. A length of luminous black Geziri pearls circled his neck and a ruby winked like a drop of human blood from the gold ring on his thumb.

Wajed bowed his head. "Emir Muntadhir," he greeted him respectfully. "Peace be upon you."

"And upon you all peace," Muntadhir returned politely. The familiar sound of his brother's voice sent a wave of emotion crashing through Ali. "Qaid, my father requests that you escort Prince

Alizayd's companions to the Citadel's guest quarters. Please ensure that they want for nothing." He touched his heart and then aimed a dazzling smile at Aqisa and Lubayd. "We are forever grateful for the welcome you provided my brother in your village."

Ali narrowed his eyes at the pleasantly worded lie, but neither Aqisa nor Lubayd responded with their usual sarcasm. Instead, they looked rather awestruck by the sight of Daevabad's emir.

Yes, I suppose he makes for a more gripping image than a soaked, starving prince dying in a crevasse.

Lubayd recovered first. "Is that all right with you, brother?" he asked Ali.

"Of course it is," Muntadhir cut in smoothly. "You'll understand that we're eager to spend some time alone with Prince Alizayd."

Ali didn't miss his brother's aggressive use of "we," a manner of speaking he associated with their father. There was a terseness lurking under Muntadhir's charming words that Ali didn't like. And though it probably didn't bode well for him, he suddenly didn't mind his friends being far away. "You'll look after them?" he asked Wajed.

Wajed nodded. "You have my word, my prince."

It would have to do. Ali trusted Wajed as much as he could trust anyone here. He glanced at Lubayd and Aqisa and attempted a smile. "I'll see you soon, God willing."

"You better," Lubayd replied, snatching another pastry before rising to his feet.

Aqisa pulled him into a quick embrace. Ali went stiff with shock at the utter inappropriateness of it, but then something hard was sliding into the fold of his belt. "Do not die," she hissed in his ear. "Lubayd would be inconsolable."

Fairly certain she'd just passed him God only knew what weapon she'd manage to smuggle into the palace, Ali nodded, silently grateful. "Take care."

Wajed squeezed his shoulder. "Get over to the Citadel when you have a chance. Show my Daevabadi-born brats how we fight back home."

As soon as they left, the temperature seemed to dip, and the politely vacant smile vanished from Muntadhir's face. "Alizayd," he said coolly.

Ali flinched; his brother rarely called him by his formal name. "Dhiru." His voice caught. "It's really good to see you."

Muntadhir's only reaction was a slight grimace, as though he'd bitten into something sour. He turned, ignoring Ali to descend into the pavilion.

Ali tried again. "I know we didn't part under the best circumstances. I'm sorry." His brother said nothing, pouring a cup of wine and sipping it as though Ali wasn't there. Ali persisted. "I hope you've been well. I was sorry to miss your wedding," he added. Despite his efforts, he could hear the stiffness in his words.

At that, Muntadhir looked up. "All the blandly diplomatic things you could blather about, and you go straight to her."

Ali flushed. "I only meant—"

"How's your cousin?"

Ali started. "My what?"

"Your cousin," Muntadhir repeated. "The Ayaanle one who conveniently fell ill and needed you to continue on in his place."

The sarcastic implication that Ali had played a part in Musa's plot set his teeth on edge. "I had nothing to do with that."

"Of course not. One Ayaanle plot gets you sent away, another one brings you back. And there remains Alizayd, innocent and oblivious to it all."

"Come on, Dhiru, surely—"

"Don't call me that," Muntadhir interrupted. "I meant what I told you that night—you must remember, it was just before you brought the ceiling of the infirmary down on my head—I'm done protecting you." He took another sip from his cup. His hands were shaking, and though his voice didn't waver, Muntadhir's gaze flickered away as though the sight of his little brother caused him pain. "I don't *trust* you. I don't trust myself with you. And that's not a weakness I intend to let drag me down."

Stung, Ali struggled for a response, emotions swirling in his chest.

Hurt responded first. "I saved your life. The Afshin . . . the boat . . ."

"I'm well aware." Muntadhir's voice was curt, but this time Ali didn't miss the flicker of emotion in his brother's eyes. "So let me return the favor. Leave."

Ali stared at him. "What?"

"*Leave*," Muntadhir repeated. "Get out of Daevabad before you blunder into something else you don't understand and get a score of innocent people killed." A fierce protectiveness crept into his voice. "And stay away from Zaynab. I know she's been helping you. That ends. I will kill you myself before I let you drag my little sister into one of your messes."

Ali recoiled, struck speechless by the open hate in his brother's face. He hadn't expected Muntadhir to greet him with open arms, but this . . .

It was of course at that moment that the door opened again, and their father entered the courtyard.

Training and a lifetime of being scolded to respect his elders had Ali bowing before he even realized what he was doing, his hand moving from his heart to his brow.

But he caught himself before he let a certain word slip. "My king," he greeted Ghassan solemnly. "Peace be upon you."

"And upon you peace, my child," Ghassan replied.

Ali straightened up, taking in the sight of his father as he approached. Ghassan had aged far more than Ali expected. Stress lines bored deep around the king's eyes, echoing the gaunt shadows under his cheeks. A heaviness seemed to have settled on his shoulders, making him appear, if not frail, at least older. He suddenly seemed like a man who'd lived two centuries, a king who'd seen and done far too much.

Ghassan stared back, gazing at Ali with open relief. He stepped closer, and Ali dropped to one knee, reaching out to take his father's hand and press it to his brow. It wasn't a thing the Qahtanis did in private, but Ali suddenly found himself retreating into formality, wanting the distance that ceremony and ritual provided. "May God preserve your reign," he murmured.

He stood and stepped back, but Ghassan grabbed his wrist. "Stay, boy. Let me look at you a moment longer."

Aware of Muntadhir watching them, Ali tried not to cringe. But when his father touched his face, he could not help but stiffen.

Ghassan must have noticed; there was a brief moment of hurt in his lined eyes, gone in the next instant. "You can sit, Alizayd," he said softly. "I know you've had a long journey."

Ali sat, crossing his legs underneath him. His heart was racing. "I pray you can forgive my sudden return, my king," he rushed on. "Bir Nabat could not sustain the Ayaanle caravan, and when that wretched trader abandoned it, I had little choice. I was the only man who could handle the untreated salt."

"You could have butchered the animals for food and stolen the cargo," Muntadhir suggested casually. "The djinn of Bir Nabat are raiders like the rest of the north, no?"

"No," Ali said, matching his brother's even tone. "We are farmers, and it was a small fortune due to the Treasury. I didn't want the village to land in any trouble."

Ghassan raised a hand. "No explanation is necessary, Alizayd. I suspected your mother's people would cook up some trick eventually to get you back here."

Muntadhir looked at his father in disbelief. "And you really think he played no part in this, Abba?"

"He looks ready to leap from his cushion and jump on the first carpet that will whisk him back to the desert. So no, I do not think he played any part." He poured a cup of wine. "He also sent me a letter from every caravanserai between here and Am Gezira suggesting different ways he could avoid this very encounter."

Ali flushed. "I wanted to be thorough."

"Then let us be thorough." Ghassan motioned to the long-healed scar high upon Ali's cheekbone—the spot where the marid had carved Suleiman's seal into his skin. "That looks worse."

"I took my khanjar to it before I reached Am Gezira," Ali explained. "I didn't want anyone recognizing it."

Muntadhir blanched, and even his father looked slightly taken aback. "That wasn't necessary, Alizayd."

"Being exiled made me no less loyal to maintaining our family's secrets," Ali replied. "I wished to be discreet."

"Discreet?" His brother scoffed. "Alizayd the Afshin-slayer? The hero out battling muwaswas and turning Am Gezira green while his relatives laze about Daevabad's palace? That's what you consider discreet?"

"It was just one muwaswas," Ali defended, recalling the incident with the rampaging magical sandfish quite well. "And I'm hardly turning Am Gezira green. It's simple irrigation work, searching for springs and digging canals and wells."

"And I wonder, how did you find those springs, Alizayd?" his father mused idly. "Those springs locals had never managed to discover themselves?"

Ali hesitated, but there was no lie his father would believe. "I have myself under control. What happened in the infirmary . . . I haven't been like that in years."

Ghassan looked grim. "Then it is a side effect of the marid possession."

Ali pressed his palms against his knees. "It's nothing," he insisted. "And no one there cares. They're too busy trying to survive."

His father didn't seem convinced. "It is still risky."

Ali didn't argue. Of course it was risky, but he hadn't cared. The sight of dying Bir Nabat, the thin bodies of its people, and the children whose hair was streaked with the rust of famine had driven those concerns from his heart.

He met his father's gaze. "Northern Am Gezira had been suffering for years. I wanted to do some good for the people who sheltered me before I was murdered by assassins."

He let the charge lie, and though Ghassan's calm expression slipped slightly, his voice was even when he replied. "And yet you still live."

Resisting the urge to offer a sarcastic apology, Ali responded simply. "All praise is due to God." Muntadhir rolled his eyes, but Ali continued. "I have no desire to play politics in Daevabad. My companions need only a short time to rest, and I intend to make the Ayaanle provision us in exchange for the transport of their goods. We can be gone in a week."

Ghassan smiled. "No. As a matter of fact, Alizayd, you cannot."

Dread snared Ali's heart, but Muntadhir reacted first, straightening up like a shot. "Why not? Do you hear him? He wishes to leave."

"It will look suspicious if he goes back too soon." Ghassan took another sip of his wine. "He hasn't been home in five years and leaves in days? People will talk. And I won't have rumors of our rift spreading. Not with the Ayaanle already meddling."

His brother's face shuttered. "I see." He was gripping his knees as though resisting the urge to throttle someone. Ali, most likely. "Then when *is* he leaving?"

Ghassan tented his hands. "When he has my permission to do so . . . permission I'm granting to you now, Muntadhir. Ask the servant at the gate to retrieve the case from my office on your way. He will know what you mean."

Muntadhir didn't argue. He didn't say another word, in fact. He got to his feet smoothly and departed without looking at Ali again. But Ali watched his brother until he vanished, a lump rising in his throat that he couldn't quite swallow.

Ghassan waited until they were alone before he spoke again. "Forgive him. He's been fighting with his wife more than usual lately, and it puts him in a foul mood."

His wife. Ali wanted to ask after her, but he dared not make the situation worse.

But his father had clearly noticed his reticence. "You used to speak far more freely. And loudly."

Ali stared at his hands. "I was young."

"You are young still. You've not even reached your first quarter century."

Silence fell between them, awkward and charged. He could feel his father studying him, and it sent a prickle down his spine. It wasn't the fear of his youth, Ali realized, but something deeper, more complicated.

It was anger. Ali was angry. He was angry about the cruel sentence his father had handed him and angry that the king was more worried about gossip in Am Gezira than its people going hungry. He was beyond angry at what was happening to Daevabad's shafit in the ghastly ruins of Anas's mosque.

And he was angry that feeling this way about his own father still filled him with shame.

Fortunately, a servant came in at that moment, bearing a plain leather box about the size of a turban case. He bowed and set it at Ghassan's side. As he turned to leave, the king motioned him close and whispered an order in his ear Ali couldn't make out. The man nodded and left.

"I will not keep you, Ali," Ghassan said. "It's a long journey and I can only imagine how eager you are for a hot bath and a soft bed. But I have something that should have been given over to you long ago, in keeping with our traditions." He motioned to the box.

Apprehensive, Ali took it. Aware of his father's keen gaze, he opened it carefully. Nestled inside was a beautifully crafted straight blade—a Daeva blade.

A familiar blade. Ali frowned. "This is Nahri's dagger, isn't it?" She had often worn it at her waist.

"It actually belonged to Darayavahoush," his father replied. "He must have given it to her when he first left Daevabad." Ghassan leaned back in his cushion. "Her room was searched after his death, and I wasn't eager to allow such a weapon to remain in her possession. You killed him. You earned it."

Ali's stomach gave a violent turn. They'd stolen this from Nahri to give to him? As though it was some sort of prize?

"I don't want this." Ali closed the box with a snap and shoved it away. "The marid killed him. They just used me to do it."

"That is a truth not to be repeated," Ghassan warned, his words quiet but sharp. When Ali made no move to touch the box, he sighed. "Do with it as you please, Alizayd. It is yours. Give it to the Daevas if you don't want it. They've a shrine to him in the Grand Temple they think I don't know about." He rose to his feet.

Ali quickly followed. "What Muntadhir asked . . . when *can* I go back to Am Gezira?"

"After Navasatem."

Ali swayed on his feet. His father had to be joking. "Navasatem is not for seven months."

Ghassan shrugged. "There is not a soul in Daevabad who would believe my youngest son—one of the best zulfiqari in our world—would leave before the grandest martial competitions in a century if things were amicable between us. You will stay and celebrate Navasatem with your family. Then we will discuss your leaving."

Ali fought panic. There was no way he could stay in Daeva-bad that long. "Abba," he begged, desperation pulling the word from him. He had not intended to use it with the man who'd sent him to die in the desert. "Please. I have responsibilities in Am Gezira."

"I'm sure you can find responsibilities here," Ghassan said breezily. "There will be plenty to go around with the holiday approaching. And Wajed could always use you in the Citadel." He gave his son a pointed look. "Though he was instructed to thrash you should you get too close to the city gates."

Ali didn't know what to say. He felt like the walls were closing in on him.

Ghassan seemed to take his silence as acquiescence. He touched Ali's shoulder—and then pressed the box containing the Afshin's dagger into his hands. "I intend to hold a feast at the end of the week to welcome you properly. For now, rest. Abu Sara will take you to your quarters."

My quarters? Ali remained speechless. *I still have quarters?* Numbly, he headed for the door.

"Alizayd?"

He glanced back.

"I've arranged to have some other property returned to you as well." There was a note of warning in Ghassan's voice. "Take care not to lose it again."

9

ALI

Ali glanced around his old quarters, dazed. The room looked untouched, books laying haphazardly on the desk where he'd left them five years ago, the clothes he'd rifled through while packing for Am Gezira still strewn across the floor. A crumpled sheet of paper—a letter he'd intended to write Nahri and then abandoned for lack of words—was balled up next to his favorite quill and the nub of candle wax he remembered meaning to replace. Though everything was dusted and freshly swept, it was otherwise clear nothing had changed.

Nothing except Ali. And if Ghassan thought to slip his youngest son back into his old life so easily, he was wrong.

Ali took a deep breath, and as he did, smelled a hint of frankincense and the sour tamarind wine his father preferred. A well-worn cushion sat on the floor where Ali once performed his prayers, and Ali recognized one of his caps laid neatly on its surface. He picked it up, and his father's particular scent came more strongly. The cap was well worried, with creases marring the linen from where it had been repeatedly folded.

He shivered as he continued into the inner room, his sleeping area still as sparse now as it had been five years ago. It was beginning to feel like he was visiting his own grave. He glanced at the bed. He blinked.

Resting on the neatly folded quilt was his zulfiqar.

Ali was across the room in the next moment, dropping the Afshin's knife box to the bed. The zulfiqar was indeed Ali's, the heft and hilt as familiar as his own hand. And if he'd had any doubts, the contracts he'd signed had been resting beneath it.

Marked by a royal scribe nullifying them.

Ali collapsed on the bed as though his knees had been cut out from under him. He scanned the pages, hoping he was wrong, but the evidence was spelled out in clear legal terms before him. The shafit father and daughter had been returned to the Geziri trader.

He shot to his feet. *No.* Those people had been innocent. They weren't Tanzeem fighters, they were no threat to anyone. But as he reached for his zulfiqar, his father's warning came back to him. Ghassan had done this to teach him a lesson. He'd destroyed the lives of two shafit because Ali had dared to interfere.

What would he do if Ali fought?

Ali closed his eyes, nausea rising in his chest as the little girl's tear-streaked face sprang to his mind. *God forgive me.* But it wasn't just her. Sheikh Anas and Rashid, Fatumai and her orphans. The auction block erected from the ruined mosque.

Every person I try to help, he breaks. He breaks us all.

He jerked his hand away from the zulfiqar. His skin was crawling. Ali couldn't stay here. Not in this carefully preserved room. Not in this deadly city where every wrong move of his got someone else hurt.

Abruptly, he thought of Zaynab. Ali dared not get further entangled with his mother, but surely his sister could help him. She could get him out of this.

Muntadhir's warning echoed in his ears, and the flicker of hope that had sparked in his chest at the thought of his sister sputtered out. No, Ali could not risk her. He squeezed his eyes shut, fighting despair. Water was pooling in his hands, a thing that hadn't happened in years.

Breathe. Pull yourself together. He opened his eyes.

His gaze fell on the box.

Ali was across the room in the next breath. He threw open the box, grabbed the dagger, and slipped it into his belt.

To hell with his father's commands.

HE WAS HALFWAY TO THE INFIRMARY BEFORE HE started to wonder if he wasn't being a bit rash.

Ali slowed on the path, one of the many that meandered through the heart of the harem garden. It wasn't as though he was actually planning to *visit* Nahri, he reasoned. Ali would wait for a servant outside the infirmary and then ask to speak to her assistant, Nisreen. He could give Nisreen the dagger and a message, and if Nahri didn't want to see him, that was fine. Completely fine. Hell, maybe Muntadhir would find out and murder him for trying to speak to his wife, and then Ali would no longer have to worry about staying in Daevabad through Navasatem.

He took a deep breath of the humid air, rich with the smell of rain-soaked earth and dew-damp flowers, and his chest unknotted slightly. The mingled sounds of the rushing canal and the water dripping off leaves were as soothing as a lullaby. He sighed, taking a short moment to watch a pair of small, sapphire-colored birds dart through the dark trees. If only the rest of Daevabad could be so peaceful.

A surge of cool moisture wove through his fingers. Startled, Ali glanced down to find a ribbon of fog swirling around his waist. As he watched, it curved over his shoulder like the embrace of a long-missed friend. His eyes went wide. *This* had certainly never happened in Am Gezira. And yet he grinned, enchanted by the sight of the water dancing upon his skin.

His smile vanished as quickly as it had come. He glanced quickly at the greenery around him, but thankfully the path was deserted. The whispers on the boat came back to him, the strange tug of the lake and the speed with which water had beaded from his skin in his room. Ali had not given thought to how much harder it might be to hide his new abilities in misty, water-rich Daevabad.

Then you'd better figure it out. He couldn't get caught. Not here. The villagers of Bir Nabat might be willing to overlook his occasional strangeness—Ali had saved them, after all—but he couldn't take the risk with Daevabad's far more mecurial population. The marid were feared in his world. They were the monsters djinn parents evoked in frightening bedtime stories, the unknowable terror djinn travelers wore amulets to ward against. Growing up, he'd heard a dark tale of a distant Ayaanle relative who'd been thrown in the lake after being unjustly accused of sacrificing a Daeva child to his supposed marid lord.

Suppressing a shudder, Ali continued toward the infirmary. But when he reached the grounds, he stopped short again, amazed at the transformation. The formal gardens for which the Daevas were famous made a beautiful sight, with raised beds of bright herbs bordering trellises heavy with flowers, and fruit trees shading glass birdhouses and gently burbling fountains. At its very center, between two rectangular pools, was a striking orange grove. The trees had been planted close together, the branches carefully manicured and coaxed to intertwine as if to form a ceiling. A little enclosure, he realized, the foliage so thick with plump fruit and snowy white flowers one couldn't see through it.

Charmed, he kept walking, drawn to the place. Whoever had planted it really had done an extraordinary job. It even had an archway pruned from the leaves to create . . .

Ali halted so fast, he almost fell backward. Nahri was very much not in the infirmary. She was here, surrounded by books, as though she'd stepped straight out of his fondest memories.

And more—she looked like she *belonged* here, the royal Banu Nahida in the palace of her ancestors. It had nothing to do with jewels or rich brocade; on the contrary, she was dressed simply in a white tunic that fell to her calves and loose purple trousers. A raw silk chador in shimmering umber was pinned just above her ears with diamond clips, thrown back over her shoulders to reveal the four black braids that fell to her waist.

Are you surprised? What had Ali expected of Nahri? That she'd be a faded version of the sharp woman he'd known, grieving for her lost Afshin, pale from being trapped for long hours in the infirmary? That had not been the Banu Nahida he'd once called a friend.

Ali shut his mouth, suddenly aware that it had fallen open, that he was staring like an addled fool, and that he was *very* much somewhere he shouldn't be. A glance revealed neither guards nor servants nearby. Nahri was alone, perched in a wide swing, an enormous volume open in her lap, notes scattered haphazardly on an embroidered rug below her, along with a tray holding an untouched cup of tea. As Ali watched, she frowned at the text as if it had personally offended her.

And suddenly all he wanted to do was step forward and drop down by her side. To ask her what she was reading and resume their bizarrely companionable friendship of hunting through the catacombs of the Royal Library and arguing about Arabic grammar. Nahri had been a light for him during a very dark time, and Ali hadn't realized until he was standing here quite how much he'd missed her.

Then stop stalking her like a ghoul. Nerves fluttering in his stomach, Ali forced himself to approach. "Sabah el-noor," he greeted softly in the Egyptian dialect she'd been teaching him.

Nahri jumped. The book fell from her lap as her startled black eyes swept his face.

They locked on the zulfiqar at his waist, and the earth buckled beneath his feet.

Ali cried out, stumbling as a root burst from the grass to snake around his ankle. It jerked forward, and Ali fell hard, the back of his head hitting the ground.

Black spots blossomed across his vision. When they cleared, he saw the Banu Nahida standing over him. She did not look pleased. "Well . . . ," Ali started weakly. "Your powers have come a remarkably long way."

The root tightened painfully around his ankle. "What the hell are you doing in my garden?" Nahri demanded.

"I . . ." Ali tried to sit up, but the root held firm. It twisted up his ankle, disappearing under his robe to snake around his calf. The feeling was far too similar to the weeds that had grabbed him under the lake, and he found himself fighting panic. "Forgive me," he blurted out in Arabic. "I only—"

"*Stop.*" The flat word in Djinnistani was like a slap across the face. "Don't you dare speak Arabic to me. I won't hear my language on your lying tongue."

Ali stared at her in shock. "I . . . I'm sorry," he repeated in Djinnistani, the words coming more slowly to him. The root was at his knee now, hairy tendrils sprouting and spreading. His skin crawled, a painful prickle shooting down the scars the marid had left on him.

He squeezed his eyes shut, and water beaded on his brow. *It's just a root. It's just a root.* "Please, can you get that thing off me?" It was taking every bit of strength he had not to reach for his zulfiqar and hack it off. Nahri would probably let the earth swallow him whole if he drew his blade.

"You didn't answer my question. *What are you doing here?*"

Ali opened his eyes. There was no mercy in Nahri's expression. Instead, she was slowly spinning one finger, a mirror of the movement the root was making around his leg.

"I wanted to see you." The words rushed from him as though she'd dosed him with one of her ancestor's truth serums. And it was the truth, he realized. Ali had wanted to see her, Darayavahoush's dagger be damned.

Nahri dropped her hand, and the root released. Ali took a shaky breath, embarrassed by how deeply it had frightened him. By the Most High, he could face assassins armed with arrows and blades and yet a root reduced him to near tears?

"I'm sorry," he said for the third time. "I shouldn't have come here."

"You certainly shouldn't have," she snapped back. "I have one place in Daevabad that's mine, one place not even my husband will set foot in, and here you are." Her face twisted in anger. "But I suppose Alizayd the Afshin-slayer does whatever he likes."

Ali's cheeks burned. "I'm not," he whispered. "You were there. You know what killed him."

Nahri clucked her tongue. "Oh no, I was corrected. Firmly. Your father said he'd murder every Daeva child in the city if I dared utter the word 'marid.'" Tears were brimming in her eyes. "Do you know what he made me say instead? What he made me say Dara tried to do? What you supposedly *interrupted*?"

Her words cut him to the bone. "Nahri . . ."

"*Do you know what he made me say?*"

Ali dropped his gaze. "Yes." The rumors had followed him to Am Gezira—there was a reason, after all, that people had no trouble believing the otherwise mild-mannered prince had killed another man.

"I saved you." She let out a high, humorless laugh. "I healed you with my own hands. More than once, even. And in return, you said *nothing* as we got on that boat, though you knew your father's men would be waiting. My God, I even offered to let you come with us! To escape your father's wrath, to escape this *cage* and see the rest of the world." She hugged her arms around herself, pulling her chador close as if to put a wall between them. "You should be proud, Ali. Not many people can outwit me, but you? You had me believing you were my friend until the very end."

Guilt crashed over him. Ali had no idea she'd felt that way. Though he'd considered her a friend, Nahri had seemed to keep him at a careful distance, and the realization that their relationship had meant more to her—and that he'd destroyed it—made him sick.

He fought for words. "I didn't know what else to do that night, Nahri. Darayavahoush was acting like a madman. He would have started a war!"

She trembled. "He wouldn't have started a war. I wouldn't have let him." Her voice was curt, but it looked like she was struggling to maintain her composure. "Is this enough for you, then? You've seen me. You've intruded upon my privacy to dredge up the worst night of my life. Is there anything else?"

"No, I mean, yes, but . . ." Ali inwardly cursed. It scarcely seemed the right moment to pull out Dara's dagger and admit his father had stolen it and kept it as some sort of war trophy. He tried another tack. "I . . . I tried to write you . . ."

"Yes, your sister gave me your letters." She tapped the ash on her forehead. "They made good fodder for my fire altar."

Ali glanced at the mark. In the shadowy grove, he hadn't noticed it at first, and it surprised him. In the time he'd known her, Nahri had never seemed all that keen on the religious rituals of her people.

She saw him take it in and her eyes lit with challenge. He couldn't blame her. He'd been rather . . . loud when voicing his opinions about the fire cult. A bead of cold sweat dripped down his neck, soaking into the collar of his dishdasha.

Her gaze seemed to trace the movement of the water trickling down his throat. "They're all over you," she whispered. "If you were anyone else, I would have heard your heartbeat, sensed your presence . . ." She raised a hand and he flinched, but thankfully, no plants attacked. Instead, she simply studied him. "They changed you, didn't they? The marid?"

Ali went cold. "No," he insisted, to himself as much as to her. "They did nothing."

"Liar," she taunted softly, and he couldn't keep the anger from his face at that. "Oh, do you not like being called a liar? Is that worse than being a man who strikes a bargain with a water demon?"

"A bargain?" he repeated in disbelief. "You think I *asked* for what happened that night?"

"For aid in killing your people's greatest enemy? For the fame of finally finishing off the man your ancestor couldn't?" Scorn filled her eyes. "Yes, Afshin-slayer, I do."

"Then you're wrong." Ali knew Nahri was upset, but she wasn't the only one whose life had been turned upside down that night. "The marid wouldn't have been able to use me to kill your Afshin if he hadn't knocked me into the lake in the first place. And how they took me, Nahri?" His voice broke. "They *ripped through my mind and made me hallucinate the deaths of everyone I loved.*" He yanked up his sleeve. His scars were stark in the faded sunlight: the ragged marks of triangular teeth and a strip of ruined flesh that twisted around his wrist. "And that's while they were doing this." He was shaking, the memory of the awful visions stealing over him. "Some bargain."

He would swear he saw a flicker of shock on her face, but it lasted only a second. Because between being thrown to the ground and pulling up his sleeve, Ali realized too late what had become visible at his waist.

Nahri's gaze locked on the distinctive hilt of Darayavahoush's dagger. The leaves in the grove shuddered. "What are you doing with that?"

Oh no. "I-I meant to give it to you," Ali said quickly, fumbling to pull the dagger from his waist.

Nahri lunged forward and ripped it from his hands. She ran her fingers over the hilt, gently pressing the carnelian and lapis stones as wetness brimmed in her eyes.

He swallowed, aching to say something. Anything. But no words would erase what was between them. "Nahri . . ."

"*Get out.*" She said it in Arabic, the language that had once been the foundation of their friendship, the one with which he'd taught her to conjure flames. "You want to avoid a war? Then get out of my garden before I bury this in your heart."

10

NAHRI

Nahri sank to her knees as Ali vanished beyond the trees. Dara's dagger was heavy in her hands. *No, like this,* she remembered him correcting her when he taught her how to throw it. Dara's hot fingers grazing her skin, his breath tickling her ear. His laugh on the wind when she swore in frustration.

Tears blurred her eyes. Her fingers curled around the hilt, and she pressed her other fist hard against her mouth, fighting the sob rising in her chest. Ali was probably still close and she'd be damned if he was going to hear her cry.

I should have buried this in his heart anyway. Leave it to Alizayd al Qahtani to intrude upon her one sanctuary in Daevabad and upend all her emotions. She was as angry at his nerve as at her own reaction; Nahri rarely lost her composure so badly. She argued plenty with Muntadhir, she looked forward to the day Ghassan burned on his funeral pyre with open relish, but she didn't weep before them like some sad little girl.

But they hadn't tricked her. Ali had. Despite Nahri's best intentions, she'd fallen for his friendship. She'd liked spending time with someone who shared her intellect and her curiosity, with someone who didn't make her feel self-conscious about her ignorance of the magical world or her human skin. She'd liked *him*, his endearing exuberance when he rattled on about obscure economic theory, and the quiet kindness with which he'd treated the palace's shafit servants.

It was a lie. Everything about him was a lie. Including what he'd just been spouting about the marid. It had to be.

She took a deep breath, unclenching her fist. The stones on the dagger's hilt had left an impression in her palm. Nahri had never expected to see Dara's blade again. In the wake of his death, she'd once asked Ghassan about the dagger, and he said he'd had it melted.

He'd lied. He'd given it as a prize to his son. His Afshin-slaying son.

She wiped her eyes with trembling hands. She hadn't known that Ali was already back. In fact, she'd been making a conscious effort to avoid hearing news of him. Muntadhir's stress—and the increasingly shaky grip he had on his wine consumption—had been all the information she'd needed about his brother's progress toward the city.

Footsteps approached on the other side of the grove. "Banu Nahida?" a female voice squeaked. "Lady Nisreen asked me to retrieve you. She said Jamshid e-Pramukh is waiting."

Nahri sighed, glancing at the book she'd been studying before Alizayd had interrupted her. It was a Nahid text on curses that were said to prevent healing. One of the novitiates at the Grand Temple had found it while sorting their old archives, and Nahri had it brought immediately to her. But the Divasti was so confusing and archaic, she feared she was going to have to send it right back for translation.

Not that Jamshid would wait. He'd been pleading with her for weeks to try healing him again, his desperation mirroring Muntadhir's spiral. Nahri didn't have to ask why. She knew not being able to personally protect Muntadhir as the captain of his guard was killing Jamshid.

She took a deep breath. "I'll be right there." She set the book aside—on top of an Arabic volume about hospitals. Or at least Nahri thought it was about hospitals; she hadn't actually had time to read it. Muntadhir might have shot down her nascent dreams of restoring her ancestors' hospital, but Nahri wasn't ready to give up.

She rose to her feet, slipping the dagger's sheath in her waistband, beneath her gown. She forced herself to put Ali out of mind. To put *Dara* out of mind. Her first responsibility was to her patients, and right now it might be a relief to let work swallow her.

THE INFIRMARY WAS ITS USUAL LIVELY SELF, CROWDED and smelling of sulfur. She passed through the patient area and behind the curtain that sectioned off her private work space. The curtain was slippery in her hands, its silk enchanted to dampen noise on both sides. She could step back here and talk frankly with Nisreen about a poor diagnosis without someone overhearing them.

The curtain could also hide the sounds of a man screaming in pain.

Jamshid and Nisreen were waiting for her, Jamshid lying on a pallet, looking pale but determined.

"May the fires burn brightly for you, Banu Nahida," he greeted her.

"And for you," Nahri returned, bringing her fingertips together. She tied her scarf back to hold her braids and washed her hands in the basin, splashing some cold water on her face.

Nisreen frowned. "Are you all right?" she asked. "Your eyes . . ."

"I'm fine," Nahri lied. "Frustrated." She crossed her arms, deciding to throw the emotions Ali had upset in a different direction. "That book is written in some blasted ancient script I can't decipher. I'll have to send it back to the Grand Temple for a translation."

Jamshid glanced up, his panic clear. "But surely that doesn't mean we can't have a session today?"

Nahri paused. "Nisreen, would you leave us for a moment?"

Nisreen bowed. "Of course, Banu Nahida."

Nahri waited until she was gone to kneel at Jamshid's side. "You're rushing this," she said, as gently as she could. "You shouldn't be. Your body is recovering. It just needs time."

"I don't have time," Jamshid replied. "Not anymore."

"You do," Nahri argued. "You're young, Jamshid. You have decades, centuries before you." She took his hand. "I know you want to be at his side again. Capable of jumping on a horse and firing a dozen arrows. And you will be." She met his gaze. "But you need to accept that it might take years. These sessions . . . I know how badly they hurt you, the toll they take on your body . . ."

"I want to do this," he said stubbornly. "The last time you said you'd gotten close to fixing the damaged nerves you believe are causing most of the weakness in my leg."

God, how Nahri suddenly wished she had another decade in the infirmary behind her, or a senior healer at her side to guide her through this conversation. The look in her patients' eyes when they begged her for certainty was difficult enough when they weren't friends.

She tried another tactic. "Where is Muntadhir? He usually comes with you."

"I told him I changed my mind. He has enough to worry about without seeing me in pain."

By the Creator, he really wasn't making this any easier. "Jamshid—"

"Please." The word cut through her. "I can handle the pain, Nahri. I can handle being bedridden for a few days. If you think it's going to do worse than that, we can stop."

She sighed. "Let me examine you first." She helped him out of the shawl wrapping his shoulders. "Lie back." They had done this so many times, the steps came automatically to them both. She took a blunt brass rod from the tray Nisreen had laid out, running it down his left leg. "Same numb burning?"

Jamshid nodded. "But it's not weak like the right leg. That's what's causing me the most trouble."

Nahri eased him onto his belly. She flinched at the sight of his bare back; she always did. Six scars, the ridged lines marking the spots where Dara's arrows had plunged into him. One had lodged in his spine, another had punctured his right lung.

You should be dead. It was the uneasy conclusion Nahri came to every time she looked at the evidence of his wounds. At a cruel order from Ghassan meant to goad Kaveh into finding Dara's so-called accomplices, Jamshid had been left untreated for a week, the arrows still in his body. He should have died. That he hadn't was a mystery on a par with the fact that he reacted so poorly to her magic.

Her gaze drifted past the small black tattoo on the inside of his shoulder. She had seen it many times, three swirling glyphs. It was a faded ghost of the striking, elaborate tattoos that had decorated Dara's skin—family sigils and clan marks, records of heroic deeds and protective charms. Jamshid had rolled his eyes when she asked about it. Apparently, the custom of the tattoos had mostly died out in the generations of Daevas born after the war, particularly in Daevabad. It was an old-fashioned superstition, he'd jokingly complained, one that gave away his rural roots.

Nahri touched his back, and Jamshid tensed. "Would you like some wine?" she asked. "It might dull the pain."

"I downed three cups just to work up the courage to come here."

Lovely. She took up a length of cloth. "I'd like to bind your hands this time." She gestured for him to grip the posts of the pallet. "Hold on to this. It will give you something to squeeze."

He was trembling now. "You have something I can bite?"

She silently handed him a skinny block of opium-infused cedarwood and then laid her hands on his bare back, glancing over to make sure the curtain was fully closed. "Ready?"

He nodded jerkily.

Nahri closed her eyes.

In seconds, she was there, his body open to her. The beat of his racing heart, pumping simmering ebony blood through a delicate map of veins. The gurgling of stomach acid and other humors. His lungs steadily expanding and contracting like bellows.

Her fingers pressed his skin. She could almost see the nerves of his spine in the blackness of her mind, brilliantly colored, dancing filaments protected by the bony ridges of vertebrae. She moved her fingers lower, tracing the bumpy scar tissue. And not just on the skin, but deeper as well: ruined muscles and frayed nerves.

She took a steadying breath. This much she could do without hurting him. It was only when she acted upon him that his body fought back. Were he anyone else, Nahri could urge those nerves to knit back together, could dissipate the scar tissue that had grown over the muscle, leaving him stiff and in pain. It was powerful magic that exhausted her—she might have needed a few sessions to heal him entirely—but he'd have been back on a horse, bow in hand, years ago.

Nahri concentrated on a small section of the flailing nerves. She steeled herself and then commanded them to reconnect.

Magic slammed into her, raw, protective, and powerful, like a blow to her very mind. Prepared, Nahri fought back, pinning a torn nerve back into place. Jamshid seized beneath her, a grunt escaping his clenched teeth. She ignored it, focusing on the next nerve.

She'd fixed three when he started groaning.

He bucked beneath her, pulling at his bindings. His skin burned under her fingertips, scorching to the touch, every pain receptor firing. Nahri held on, sweat pouring down her face. There were only five nerves left in this particular spot. She reached for another one, her hands shaking. It took strength to fight his body's reaction and perform the magic, strength she was rapidly losing.

One more nerve melded back into place, glowing faintly in her mind's eye. She seized the next.

The block fell from Jamshid's mouth, his shriek cutting the air. Ash was powdering on his skin, and then with a burst of magic, the binds holding his hands erupted into flames.

"Jamshid?" A *very* unwelcome voice spoke from behind her. *"Jamshid!"*

Muntadhir rushed inside. The shock of the interruption threw her, and then whatever power was within Jamshid's body took the opportunity to *actually* throw her, a surge of energy so fierce that Nahri stumbled back, her connection severed.

Jamshid fell still. Despite the pounding in her head, Nahri flew to her feet to check his pulse. It was fast, but it was there. He'd only passed out. She quickly smothered the flames around his wrists.

Enraged, she whirled on Muntadhir. "What the hell were you thinking?" she snapped. "I was making progress!"

Muntadhir looked aghast. "Progress? He was on fire!"

"He's a *djinn*! He can handle a little fire!"

"He's not even supposed to be here!" Muntadhir argued back. "Did you convince him to try this again?"

"Did *I* convince him?" Nahri seethed, fighting to control the emotions rising in her. "No, you fool. He's doing this for you. If you weren't so selfish, you'd see that!"

Muntadhir's eyes flashed. His usual grace had deserted him, his movements jerky as he pulled the shawl over Jamshid. "Then you shouldn't have let him. You're being reckless, so eager to prove yourself that—"

"I was not being *reckless*." It was one thing to fight with Muntadhir about politics and family; she would not have him throwing her doubts about her healing abilities in her face. "I knew what I was doing, and he was prepared. *You're* the one who interrupted."

"You were hurting him!"

"I was healing him!" Her temper broke. "Maybe if you'd shown this concern when your father was willing to let him die, he'd be in better shape!"

The words ripped from her, an accusation that for all their many fights, Nahri had never intended to let slip. She knew too well the fear Ghassan used to keep his people in line, the terror that clawed up in her own throat when she thought of his wrath.

And she knew damn well how Muntadhir felt about Jamshid.

Her husband jerked back like she'd slapped him. Shocked hurt—and a good deal of guilt—flashed across his face, spots of angry color rising in his cheeks.

Nahri instantly regretted her words. "Muntadhir, I only meant—"

He raised a hand, cutting her off as he pointed a shaking finger at Jamshid. "The only reason he's hurt is because of Darayavahoush. Because of *you*. Because a lost little girl from Cairo thought she was living in some sort of fairy tale. And because for all her supposed cleverness, she couldn't see that the dashing hero who saved her was actually its monster. Or maybe she just didn't care." His voice grew colder. "Maybe all he had to do was tell one of his sad stories and bat his pretty green eyes, and you were all too happy to do whatever he wanted."

Nahri stared at him, speechless, the words reverberating in her head. She'd seen Muntadhir drunk before, but Nahri had not known he could be so cruel.

She had not known he could cut her so deep.

She inhaled, shaking with hurt betrayal. *This* was why she had walls up, why she tried to hide away her heart. Because it was clear she couldn't trust a damn soul in this city. Her blood boiled. And who was Muntadhir to say such things to her? *Her?* The Banu Nahida in her own infirmary?

The palace seemed to agree, her ancestors' magic swirling in her blood. The flames in her firepit soared, licking out like they might seize him, this newest incarnation of the sand flies who'd stolen their home.

Then Nahri's rage felt different. Purposeful. She could sense Muntadhir as though she were laying hands upon him. The rapid beat of his heart and the flush in his skin. The very delicate vessels in his throat. The bones and joints that could be commanded to break.

"I think you should leave, Emir." It was Nisreen, standing at the edge of the curtain. When she'd gotten there, Nahri didn't know, but the older Daeva woman had obviously heard enough to be gazing at Muntadhir with barely concealed contempt. "The Banu Nahida is in the middle of treating your companion, and it is better for him that they not be disturbed."

Muntadhir's mouth clamped into a stubborn line. He looked like he had more to say . . . and he was clearly unaware of how close Nahri had come to doing something she might not have been able to take back. But after another moment, he touched Jamshid's hand, briefly sliding his fingers through the other man's. Then, without looking at Nahri or Nisreen, he pushed to his feet, turned, and left.

Nahri exhaled, her entire body shivering as the dark urge left her. "I think . . . I think I could have just killed him."

"He would have deserved it." Nisreen crossed to check on Jamshid, and after another moment, Nahri joined her. His pulse was a little rapid and his skin still hot, but his breathing was slowly returning to normal. "Do not ever let that foul drunk touch you again."

Nahri felt like she was about to be sick. "He's my husband, Nisreen. We're supposed to be working to bring peace between the tribes." Her voice was weak, the words almost laughable.

Nisreen pulled over the ice-filled bucket that had been left next to the pallet, dampening a cloth in the cool water and placing it on Jamshid's back. "I would not overly worry about the future of your marriage," she muttered darkly.

Nahri stared at Jamshid. A wave of despair swept her as she remembered his pleading. She felt so utterly useless. It was all too much: the crush of her responsibilities and her constantly deflected dreams. The deadly dance she was forced to do with Ghassan and the pleading eyes of the Daevas who prayed to her to save them. Nahri had tried, she had. She'd married Muntadhir. But she had nothing left to give.

"I want to go home," she whispered, her eyes growing wet. It was a completely nonsensical desire to have, a pathetically childish urge, and yet her heart ached with a longing for Cairo so strong it stole her breath.

"Nahri . . ." Embarrassed, Nahri tried to turn away, but Nisreen reached for her face, cupping her cheeks. "Child, look at me. *This is your home.*" She pulled her into a hug, stroking the back of her head, and Nahri couldn't help but sink into her embrace, the tears finally spilling from her eyes. It was a type of physical affection no one here gave her, and she took it gratefully.

So gratefully in fact that she didn't question the fervor in Nisreen's voice when she continued speaking. "I promise you, my lady. It is going to be all right. You will see."

11

ALI

Ali smashed his zulfiqar into Wajed's, spinning off the momentum to duck Aqisa's blade as it passed over his head.

How did you expect Nahri to react? You gave her no warning and you arrived carrying Darayavahoush's dagger. Did you think she'd invite you to talk about books over tea?

He brought his weapon up to block Wajed's next strike.

I still can't believe she thinks I wanted any of this. After all, Ali didn't exactly *ask* to get kidnapped and shot by her precious Afshin. And he didn't believe for a second that Nahri had gone these five years without learning about Qui-zi and Darayavahoush's other innumerable crimes. How could she still defend him?

He pushed off the Qaid's blade, whirling around to face Aqisa again, narrowly parrying her next blow.

Love—for it was apparent even to Ali, who was typically oblivious to such things, that there had been a bit more than the usual Afshin-to-Nahid devotion between Nahri and that brutish demon of a man. *What a useless, distracting emotion.* How ridiculous to be flashed a pretty smile and lose all sense of—

Aqisa smashed him across the face with the flat part of her sword.

"Ow!" Ali hissed in pain and then lowered his zulfiqar. He touched his cheek, his fingers coming away bloody.

Aqisa snorted. "It isn't wise to spar while distracted."

"I wasn't distracted," he said heatedly.

Wajed lowered his weapon as well. "Yes, you were. I've been training you since you were waist high. I know what you look like when you're not focusing. You, on the other hand . . ." He turned to Aqisa, his expression admiring. "You're excellent with that zulfiqar. You should join the Royal Guard. You'd get your own."

Aqisa snorted again. "I don't take orders well."

Wajed shrugged. "The offer remains." He gestured to the opposite corner of the Citadel courtyard where Lubayd appeared to be holding court before an enthralled group of young recruits, no doubt telling some highly sensationalized tale of the trio's adventures in Am Gezira. "Why don't we take a break and join your loud friend for some coffee?"

Aqisa grinned and headed off, but Wajed held Ali back another moment.

"Are you all right?" he asked, lowering his voice. "I know you, Ali. You're not just distracted, you're holding back. I've seen you get the same look in your eyes when you're training others."

Ali pressed his mouth in a thin line. Wajed had struck closer to the truth than he liked. Ali *was* holding back, though not quite in the way the Qaid meant. And it wasn't only memories of Nahri that were distracting him.

It was the lake. It had been pulling on him since he arrived at the Citadel, drawing Ali to the walls more times than he could count to press his hands against the cool stone, sensing the water on the other side. When he closed his eyes, the whispers he'd heard on the ferry rushed back: an incomprehensible buzz that made his heart pound with an urgency he didn't understand. His marid abilities felt closer—wilder—than they had in years, as though with a single snap of his fingers, he could fill the Citadel's courtyard with a blanket of fog.

None of which he could tell Wajed. Or frankly, anyone at all. "It's nothing," Ali insisted. "I'm just tired."

Wajed eyed him. "Is this about your family?" When Ali grimaced, sympathy flooded the Qaid's face. "You didn't even give the palace a day, Ali. You should go home and try to talk to them."

"I am home," Ali replied. "My father wanted me raised in the Citadel, didn't he?" As he spoke, his gaze caught a pair of guards heading out on duty. Both wore uniforms that had been heavily patched, and only one of them had a zulfiqar.

He shook his head, thinking of Muntadhir's jewelry and the sumptuous platter of pastries. It was clear he wasn't alone in noticing the discrepancy: he'd overheard plenty of grumbling comments since arriving at the Citadel. But while Ali suspected some of Daevabad's economic woes could be traced to the Ayaanles' quiet interfering—Musa had implied as much—he doubted his fellow soldiers knew to look so far. They'd only seen Daevabad's feasting nobles and complacent palace denizens. They certainly didn't seem to blame *him*; Ali had been warmly welcomed back with only a few teasing remarks about the reduced meals of lentils and bread he now shared with them.

Commotion at the main gate caught his attention, and Ali glanced over to see several soldiers scurrying toward the entrance . . . and then promptly backing away in a clumsy mob, a few men tripping over their feet as they dropped their gazes to the ground.

A single woman strode in. Tall, and with a willowy grace Ali recognized immediately, she wore an abaya the color of midnight, embroidered with clusters of diamonds that shone like stars. A long silver shayla had been drawn across her face, concealing all but her gray-gold eyes.

Angry gray-gold eyes. They locked on Ali's face, and then she lifted her hand, gold bangles and pearl rings shimmering in the sunlight, to make a single rude beckoning motion before she abruptly turned around, marching straight back out.

Wajed looked at him. "Was that your sister?" Concern filled his voice. "I hope everything is well. She almost never leaves the palace."

Ali cleared his throat. "I . . . I may have come to the Citadel without stopping to see her and my mother."

Ali hadn't known Daevabad's Qaid—a massively built man who wore two centuries of war scars with pride—could go so pale. "You haven't gone to see your mother?" He drew back as if to physically distance himself from what was about to happen to Ali. "You better not tell her I let you stay here."

"Traitor." Ali scowled but couldn't deny the trickle of fear he felt as he moved to follow his sister.

Zaynab was already seated in the litter by the time he climbed inside. He pulled the curtain closed. "Ukhti, you really didn't—"

His sister slapped him across the face.

"You ungrateful ass," she seethed, yanking her shayla away from her face. "Five years I spend trying to save your life and you can't be bothered to come see me? Then when I finally track you down, you think to greet me with a lecture on *propriety*?" She raised her hand again—a fist this time. "You self-righteous—"

Ali ducked her fist and then reached out and gripped her shoulders. "That's not what this is, Zaynab! I swear!" He let her go.

"Then what is it, brat?" Her eyes narrowed in hurt. "Because I've half a mind to order my bearers to toss you in a trash pit!"

"I didn't want to get you in trouble," Ali rushed on. He reached for her hands. "I owe you my life, Zaynab. And Muntadhir said—"

"Muntadhir said what?" Zaynab interrupted. Her expression had softened, but anger still simmered in her voice. "Did you care to ask my opinion? Think for a moment that maybe I was perfectly capable of making a decision *without* my older brother's permission?"

"No," Ali confessed. All he'd been thinking about was getting away from the palace before he hurt someone else. And of course, in doing so, he had hurt someone else. "I'm sorry. I panicked. I wasn't thinking and . . ." Zaynab yelped, and Ali abruptly released her hands, realizing he'd been squeezing them. "Sorry," he whispered again.

Zaynab was staring at him, worried alarm replacing the anger in her face as her eyes swept his bloody face and filthy robe. She picked up his hand, running her thumb over his ragged fingernails.

Ali flushed, embarrassed at their state. "I'm trying to stop biting them. It's a nervous tic."

"A nervous tic," she repeated. Her voice was trembling now. "You look terrible, akhi." One of her hands lifted to his cheek, touching the ruined flesh where Suleiman's scar had been carved.

Ali attempted and failed to force a weak smile. "Am Gezira wasn't as welcoming as I'd hoped."

Zaynab flinched. "I thought I'd never see you again. Every time I had a messenger, I feared they were coming to say that you . . . that you . . ." She seemed unable to finish the words, tears brimming in her eyes.

Ali pulled her into a hug. Zaynab clutched him, letting out a choked sob.

"I was so worried about you," she wept. "I'm sorry, Ali. I begged him. I begged Abba every day. If I'd been able to convince him . . ."

"Oh, Zaynab, none of this is your fault." Ali held his sister close. "How could you think that? You are a blessing; your letters and supplies . . . you have no idea how much I needed them. And I'm okay." He pulled back to look at her. "Things were getting better there. And I'm here now, alive and already irritating you." He managed a small smile this time.

She shook her head. "Things aren't okay, Ali. Amma . . . she's so angry."

Ali rolled his eyes "I haven't been back *that* long. How mad could she be?"

"She's not angry at *you*," Zaynab retorted. "Well . . . she is, but that's not what I'm talking about. She's angry at *Abba*. She came back to Daevabad in a rage when she learned what happened to you. She told Abba that she was going to drive him into debt."

Ali could only imagine how that conversation had gone. "We'll talk to her," he assured her. "I'll find a way to fix things. And forget all that for now. Tell me how *you* are." He didn't imagine any of this was easy for Zaynab, being the only one of them still on speaking terms with all of her squabbling relatives.

Zaynab's composure cracked for a moment, but then a serene smile lit her face. "Everything's fine," she said smoothly. "God be praised."

Ali didn't believe that for a moment. "Zaynab . . ."

"Truly," she insisted, though a little of the spark had left her eyes. "You know me . . . the spoiled princess without a care."

Ali shook his head. "You're not that." He grinned. "Well, perhaps a little bit of the first part." He ducked when she tried to swat him.

"I hope you guard your tongue better when you're in front of Amma," Zaynab warned. "She didn't think highly of your dashing back to the Citadel and had some rather choice words to say about the fate that befalls ungrateful sons."

Ali cleared his throat. "Anything . . . specific?" he asked, repressing a shiver.

Zaynab smiled sweetly. "I hope you've been saying your prayers, little brother."

QUEEN HATSET'S SPRAWLING APARTMENTS WERE LO-cated on one of the highest levels of the palatial ziggurat, and Ali could not help but admire the view as they climbed the stairs. The city looked like a toy below, a sprawl of miniature buildings and scurrying ant-size inhabitants.

They ducked through the intricately carved teak door that led to his mother's pavilion, and Ali held his breath. Designed to mimic the enchantments of her beloved homeland, the pavilion first appeared to be the ruins of a once magnificent coral castle, like the many human ones dotting the coast of Ta Ntry. But then with a teasing swirl of smoke and magic, it shimmered back to its glory before his eyes: a lush salon of gem-studded coral archways, lined with planters of rich marsh grasses, emerald palms, and Nile lilies. The pavilion had been a marriage gift from Ghassan, meant to ease the homesickness of his new Ayaanle bride—a gesture that spoke to a kinder version of his father than Ali had known. The air smelled of myrrh, and the sounds of a lute and laughter drifted from behind gently billowing purple and gold linen curtains.

Familiar laughter. Ali steeled himself as they passed the curtain. But whatever he was expecting . . . the scene before him was certainly not it.

Queen Hatset sat on a low couch, half bent over a beautifully carved lapis lazuli game board, chuckling with a shafit man and woman. A little girl sat in her lap, toying with the gold ornaments in his mother's braids.

Ali stared in astonishment. It was the shafit girl and her father from the auction, the ones he'd feared he'd doomed. Here they were, with smiles on their faces, dressed in clothing befitting Ayaanle nobles.

Hatset glanced up. Delight, relief, and not a little bit of mischief lit her gold eyes. "Alu! How lovely to *finally* see you." She patted the little girl's cheek and then handed her to the other woman—her mother, judging from the resemblance. "I've been teaching your friends how to play senet." She rose to her feet gracefully, crossing the pavilion. "It seems I had quite a bit of time on my hands, waiting for you."

Ali was still at a loss for words when his mother reached him. "I . . ."

She pulled him into a fierce hug. "Oh, baba," she whispered, holding him tight. Her cheeks were wet. "God be praised for letting me look upon you again."

Ali was caught off guard by the wave of emotion that swept him upon being in his mother's arms again for the first time in years. Hatset. The woman who'd birthed him, whose family had betrayed him and then schemed to drag him away from the life he was building in Bir Nabat. He should have been furious—and yet as she pulled back to touch his cheek, he felt some of the anger he'd been carrying evaporate. God, but how many times had he looked at her face as a child and held the edge of her shayla, followed her absentmindedly through the harem, and cried for her in Ntaran during his first lonely, frightening nights at the Citadel?

"Peace be upon you, Amma," he managed. The curious gazes of the shafit family brought him back to the present, and Ali stepped away, trying to clamp down on his emotions. "How did you—"

"I heard about their misfortune and decided to help." Hatset glanced back at the shafit family with a smile. "I suggested they join my service here at the palace rather than return to their home. It is safer."

The shafit woman touched her heart. "We are much indebted to you, my queen."

Hatset shook her head and then pulled Ali forward firmly. "Nonsense, sister. It is a crime that you were ever even briefly separated."

The woman blushed, bowing her head. "We'll give you some time with your son."

"Thank you." His mother pushed him into the couch with what seemed like unnecessary force and then glanced at the remaining attendants. "My ladies, would you mind seeing if the kitchens can prepare some proper Ntaran food for my son?" She smiled pleasantly at him. "He looks like an underfed hawk."

"Yes, my queen." They vanished, leaving Ali alone with his mother and sister.

In a second, the two women whirled on him, looming over the couch into which he'd been shoved. Neither looked happy.

Ali immediately raised his hands in a gesture of surrender. "I was going to come see you, I swear."

"Oh? When?" Hatset crossed her arms, her smile gone. "After you'd seen everyone else in Daevabad?"

"It's only been two days," he protested. "It was a long journey. I needed time to recover—"

"And yet you had time to visit your brother's wife."

Ali's mouth dropped. How had his mother known *that*? "Do you have spies among the birds now?"

"I do not share a palace with vengeful Nahids and their apothecary of poisons without knowing what they're up to at all times." Her expression darkened. "And that was not a visit you should have made alone. People talk."

He bit his lip but stayed silent. He couldn't exactly argue with her on that point.

His mother's gaze trailed him, lingering on the scar on his temple. "What is that?"

"Just a scar," Ali said quickly. "I injured myself quarrying rock for Bir Nabat's canals."

Hatset continued studying him. "You look like you just robbed a caravan," she assessed bluntly and then wrinkled her nose. "Smell like it too. Why have you not been to the hammam and changed into something that doesn't have the blood of God only knows who all over it?"

Ali scowled. He had a very good reason for avoiding the hammam: he didn't want anyone catching a glimpse of the scars covering his body. "I like this robe," he said defensively.

Zaynab looked like she was struggling not to laugh. She fell into the seat beside him. "I'm sorry," she rushed to say when Hatset threw her an exasperated glare. "I mean . . . did you think his personality would improve out there?"

"Yes," Hatset replied sharply. "I'd hope after being sent to Am Gezira to die, he'd be sharper. Your appearance shapes your public image, Alizayd, and wandering around Daevabad in bloody rags looking like a lost sheep is not particularly impressive."

A little offended, Ali retorted, "Is that what you're doing with that poor family, then? Dressing them up, parading them around in order to shape your image?"

Hatset narrowed her eyes. "What are their names?"

"What?"

"Their names. What are the names of the people *you* put a target on?" She pressed on when Ali flustered. "You don't know, do you? Then I'll tell you. The woman is Mariam, a shafit from Sumatra. Her husband is Ashok and their daughter is Manat. Despite the city's problems, they've been managing fine. So well, in fact, that Ashok's success in running a food stall attracted the jealousy of one of their neighbors, who gave them up to that foul trader's roaming goons. But Ashok likes cooking, so I've gotten him a position in the palace kitchens and rooms where he may live with his wife while she attends me in the harem and her daughter takes lessons with the other children."

Ali was chastened, but not enough to be unsuspicious. "And why would you do such a thing?"

"Someone needed to fix my son's mistake." When Ali flushed, she continued, "I'm also a believer, and it is a great sin to abuse the shafit. Trust me when I say I find what's happening in Daevabad to be as abhorrent as you do."

"My 'cousin' Musa said a very similar thing before sabotaging my village's well in an effort to force his cargo upon me," Ali replied. "I take it you were behind that as well?"

There was a moment of silence, the two women exchanging a look before Zaynab spoke up, her voice uncharacteristically abashed. "That . . . that might have been my idea." When Ali spun on her, she gave him a helpless look. "I was worried you would never come back! My messengers said it seemed like you were settling in!"

"I was! It was *nice*." Ali couldn't believe what he was hearing. He pressed his hands against his knees, fighting his temper. The plot might have been Zaynab's, but this was a game his mother had started. "But maybe if we're going to speak so *plainly* we can talk about the reason I was sent to Am Gezira in the first place."

His mother actually smiled. It was a little unnerving, seeing that sharp delighted grin he'd been told more than once that he shared. The years had not aged Hatset like they had his father. She was every inch the queen, and she straightened up as if he'd issued her a challenge, adjusting her shayla like it was battle armor.

"Zaynab, my love . . . ," she started slowly, not taking her eyes from Ali. A prickle of fear danced over the nape of his neck. "Would you mind leaving us?"

His sister glanced between them, looking alarmed. "Maybe I should stay."

"You should go." His mother's careful smile didn't waver as she took a seat on the opposite couch, but her voice had an authoritative edge. "Your brother clearly has some things he'd like to say to me."

Zaynab sighed and stood. "Good luck, akhi." She squeezed his shoulder again and was gone.

"Alu," Hatset said, in a tone that made Ali fairly certain he was about to be slapped again, "I know you're not insinuating that the woman who carried and birthed you, enormous potato head and all, was involved in that idiotic conspiracy with the Tanzeem."

Ali swallowed. "Abba said they had Ayaanle backers," he said, defending himself. "That one of them was your cousin—"

"Indeed, one of them was. *Was*," his mother repeated, the deadly intent clear in her voice. "I don't deal lightly with those who risk the lives of the ones I love. And on some half-baked scheme at that." She rolled her eyes. "A revolution. How unnecessarily bloody."

"You sound more annoyed by the *method* than by the idea of treason."

"And?" Hatset picked up a fragrant cup of tea from a nearby table, taking a sip. "You're looking at the wrong person if you expect me to defend your father's rule. He's been going astray for years. You clearly agreed with that assessment if you were willing to join the Tanzeem."

He winced, her words finding their mark. He had disagreed—violently—with his father's handling of the shafit. He still very much did. "I was just trying to help the shafit," he insisted. "There was nothing political in it."

His mother gave him an almost pitying look. "There is nothing nonpolitical about someone named 'Zaydi al Qahtani' trying to help the shafit."

At that, Ali dropped his gaze. His name didn't feel like an inspiration these days—it felt like a burden. "He was certainly better at it than I."

Hatset sighed and then moved to sit beside him. "You are still so much the boy I remember," she said, her voice softer. "From the time you could walk, you'd follow me through the harem, babbling about everything you could see. The smallest things would fill you with delight, with wonder . . . The other women declared you the most curious child they'd ever encountered. The sweetest." Her eyes flashed with old betrayal. "Then Ghassan took you from me. They locked you away in the Citadel, put a zulfiqar in your hand, and taught you to be your brother's weapon." Her voice hitched on the last word. "But still I see that innocence in you. That goodness."

Ali didn't know what to say to that. He ran his fingers over the striped blue silk of the couch. It felt soft as a rosebud, far finer than anything he'd sat on in Am Gezira, and yet that was where he ached to be, assassins be damned. A place where helping others was a simple matter of digging a well. "That goodness has gotten me nowhere in Daevabad. Everyone I try to help ends up worse off."

"You don't stop fighting a war just because you're losing battles, Alizayd. You change tactics. Surely, that's a lesson you learned in the Citadel."

Ali shook his head. They were veering too close to a conversation he didn't want to have. "There's no war to be won here. Not by me. Abba wanted to teach me a lesson, and I've learned it. I'll stay in the Citadel with a zulfiqar in my hand and my mouth firmly shut until Navasatem."

"While down the street, shafit are auctioned off like cattle?" Hatset challenged. "While your brothers in the Royal Guard are reduced to training with blunt knives and eating spoiled food so nobles can feast and dance during the holiday?"

"*I can't help them.* And you're hardly innocent in this," Ali accused. "Do you think I don't know the games the Ayaanle are playing with Daevabad's economy?"

Hatset returned his glare. "You are far too clever to believe the Ayaanle are the only reason for Daevabad's financial problems. We are a scapegoat; a slight diminishment in taxes does not do the damage I know you've seen. Keeping a third of the population in slavery and squalor does. Oppressing another third to the point where they self-segregate does." Her tone grew intent. "People do not thrive under tyrants, Alizayd; they do not come up with innovations when they're busy trying to stay alive, or offer creative ideas when error is punished by the hooves of a karkadann."

Ali rose to his feet, wishing he could refute her words. "Go tell these things to Muntadhir. He is the emir."

"Muntadhir doesn't have it in him to act." Hatset's voice was surprisingly kind. "I like your brother. He is the most charming man I know, and he too has a good heart. But your father has carved his beliefs into Muntadhir deeper than you realize. He will reign as Ghassan does: so afraid of his people that he crushes them."

Ali paced, fighting the water that wanted to burst from his hands. "And what would you have me do, Amma?"

"*Help* him," Hatset insisted. "You don't need to be a weapon to be an asset."

He was already shaking his head. "Muntadhir hates me," he said bitterly, the blunt statement salting the wound his brother had inflicted when Ali first returned. "He's not going to listen to anything I say."

"He doesn't hate you. He's hurt, he's lost, and he's lashing out. But those are dangerous impulses when a man has as much power as your brother, and he's going down a path from which he might not be able to return." Her voice darkened. "And that path, Alu? It might present you with choices far worse than talking to him."

Ali was suddenly conscious of the water in the pitcher on the table next to him, in the fountains lining the pavilion, and in the pipes under the floor. It pulled on him, feeding off his mounting agitation.

"I can't talk about this right now, Amma." He ran his hands over his face, pulling at his beard.

Hatset stilled. "What is that on your wrist?"

Ali glanced down, his heart skipping as he realized the sleeve of his damn robe had fallen back once more. He kicked himself. After his encounter with Nahri, he'd sworn he'd find something new to wear. But uniforms at the Citadel had been scarce, and he hated to inconvenience the already struggling men.

Hatset was on her feet and at his side before Ali could respond; he hadn't actually realized his mother could move so quickly. She grabbed his arm. Ali tried to pull back, but not wanting to hurt her—and underestimating her strength—he was not fast enough to block her before she'd shoved the sleeve back to his shoulder.

She gasped, pressing the bumpy edge of the scar that wrapped his wrist. "Where did you get this?" she asked, alarm rising in her voice.

Ali panicked. "Am-Am Gezira," he stammered. "It's nothing. An old injury."

Her gaze trailed his body again. "You haven't been to the hammam . . . ," she said, echoing her earlier words. "Nor taken off this filthy robe." Her eyes darted to his. "Alu . . . are there more of these scars on your body?"

Ali's stomach dropped. She'd asked the question far too knowingly.

"Take it off." His mother was pulling the robe from his shoulders before he could move. Underneath, he wore a sleeveless tunic and a waist-wrap that came to his calves.

Hatset inhaled. She grabbed his arms, examining the scars that crossed his skin. Her fingers lingered at the ragged line crocodile teeth had torn just below his collarbone, and then she picked up his hand, touching the seared impression of a large fishing hook. Horror filled her eyes. "Alizayd, *how did you get these?*"

Ali trembled, torn between the promise he'd made to his father not to speak of that night and his desperate desire to know what had happened to him beneath the lake's dark water. Ghassan had implied that the Ayaanle had an ancient tie to the marid—that they'd used them to aid in the conquest of Daevabad—and during his darkest days, Ali had been terribly tempted to find someone from his mother's homeland and beg for information.

He said no one could know. Abba said no one could ever know.

Hatset must have seen the indecision warring in his expression. "Alu, look at me." She took his face between her hands, forcing him to meet her gaze. "I know you don't trust me. I know we have our differences. But this? This goes beyond all that. I need you to tell me the truth. *Where did you get these scars?*"

He stared into her warm gold eyes—the eyes that had comforted Ali since he was a child skinning his elbows while climbing trees in the harem—and the truth tumbled out. "The lake," he said, his voice the barest of whispers. "I fell in the lake."

"The lake?" she repeated. "*Daevabad's lake?*" Her eyes went wide. "Your fight with the Afshin. I heard he knocked you overboard, but that you caught yourself before you reached the water."

Ali shook his head. "Not quite," he replied, his throat catching.

She took a deep breath. "Oh, baba . . . here I am discussing politics . . ." She held on to his hands. "Tell me what happened."

Ali shook his head. "I don't remember much. Darayavahoush shot me. I lost my balance and fell in the water. There was something in it, some sort of presence tearing at me, tearing through my mind, and when it saw the Afshin . . ." He shuddered. "Whatever it was, it was so *angry*, Amma. It said it needed my name."

"Your name?" Hatset's voice rose. "Did you give it?"

He nodded, ashamed. "It forced these visions upon me. Daevabad destroyed, all of you murdered . . ." His voice broke. "It made me see them again and again, all while it attached itself to me, biting and ripping at my skin. Zaynab and Muntadhir were screaming for me to save them, to give my name and I . . . I broke." He could barely say the last words.

Hatset pulled him into a hug. "You didn't break, child," she insisted, stroking his back. "You couldn't have fought them."

Nerves fluttered in his stomach. "You know what it was, then?"

His mother nodded, pulling back to touch the hooked scar in his palm. "I'm Ayaanle. I know what leaves these marks."

The word lay unsaid between them another moment, and then Ali couldn't bear it. "It was a marid, wasn't it? A marid did this."

He didn't miss the way her gold eyes flickered around the pavilion before she replied—that she did so for this and not while discussing treason was telling. And not reassuring. "Yes." She let go of his hands. "What happened after you gave your name?"

Ali swallowed. "It took over me. Muntadhir said it looked like I was possessed, that I was speaking a strange language." He bit his lip. "It used me to kill Darayavahoush, but I don't remember anything between giving my name and waking up in the infirmary."

"The infirmary?" His mother's voice was sharp. "Does that Nahid girl know—"

"No." The danger in the question and a tug of old loyalty pushed the lie from his lips. "She wasn't there. Only Abba and Muntadhir know what happened."

Hatset's eyes narrowed. "Your father knew the marid did all this to you and *still* he sent you to Am Gezira?"

Ali grimaced but could not deny the relief coursing through him. It felt so good to finally talk about all this with someone who knew more, someone who could help him. "I'm not sure I would have survived Am Gezira if the marid hadn't possessed me."

She frowned. "What do you mean?"

He looked at her in surprise. "My abilities, Amma. You must realize that's what's behind my irrigation work."

Too late, he recognized the horror crossing her face. "Your *abilities*?" she repeated.

His heart raced at the shock in her voice. "My . . . my abilities with water. Abba said the Ayaanle had a relationship with the marid. You recognized their marks . . ." Desperate hope clawed up in Ali's chest. "That means this happens to djinn back in Ta Ntry, doesn't it?"

"No, baba . . ." Hatset took his hands in hers again. "Not like this. We find . . ." She cleared her throat. "We find bodies, love. Bodies with marks like yours. Djinn fishermen who stay out past sundown, human children lured to the riverbank. They're murdered, drowned, and drained."

Ali reeled. *Bodies?* "But I thought . . ." He choked on the words. "Didn't our ancestors revere the marid?"

Hatset shook her head. "I don't know what was between our ancestors, but the marid have been a terror as long as I've been alive. We keep it to ourselves; we'd rather handle our own business than invite foreign soldiers into Ta Ntry. And the attacks are rare. We've learned to avoid the places they like."

Ali was struggling to comprehend what he was hearing. "Then how did I survive?"

His mother—his always savvy mother—looked equally at a loss. "I don't know."

A door hinge creaked, and Ali yanked his robe back on so fast he heard some of the stitches tear. By the time a pair of servants joined them, Hatset's face was calm; but he didn't miss the grief with which she'd watched him move.

She offered a small smile to the servants as they set down a tray of covered silver platters. "Thank you."

They removed the tops, and Ali's heart and stomach gave a leap at the familiar smells of the Ntaran dishes he'd loved as a child. Fried plaintains and anise-spiced rice, fish steamed in banana leaf with ginger and grated coconut, and syrupy dumplings.

"I remember your favorites," Hatset said softly when they were alone again. "A mother doesn't forget something like that."

Ali didn't respond. He didn't know what to say. The answers he'd wanted for years about the marid had left worse questions and more mysteries in their wake. What happened to him wasn't something that happened to other Ayaanle. The marid were a terror in Ta Ntry, monsters to be feared.

Monsters who had saved him. Ali shifted, completely on edge. The possession in the lake had been vicious, but his abilities after had felt . . . calming. The solace when he ran his hands through a canal, the near playfulness with which new springs bubbled beneath his feet. What was that all supposed to mean?

His mother touched his wrist. "Alu, it's okay," she said, breaking the silence. "You're alive. That's all that matters now. Whatever the marid did to you . . . it's over."

"That's just it, Amma . . . it's not over," Ali said softly. "It's getting worse. Ever since I came back to Daevabad . . . I feel like these things are *inside* me, slipping over my skin, whispering in my head . . . and if I lose control . . ." He shivered. "People used to kill djinn they suspected of cavorting with the marid."

"That's not going to happen," she declared firmly. "Not to you. I'll take care of this."

Ali bit his lip, wanting to believe her but seeing little way out of a mess it was clear neither of them understood. "How?"

"First, we fix . . . this," she said, waving a hand over his body. "You'll use my hammam from now on. Send the servants away with one of your rants about modesty, and they'll have no problem letting you bathe alone. I also have an Agnivanshi tailor I trust completely. I'll tell him your scars are from the Afshin and you want them hidden. I'm sure he can design you some new clothes to do so."

"Alizayd the Afshin-slayer," he repeated grimly. "How fortunate that I'm known for killing a man who liked to scourge his opponents."

"It's a stroke of fortune I'll take," Hatset replied. "In the meantime, I'm going to reach out to a scholar I'm acquainted with. He can be a bit . . . *difficult*. But he probably knows more about the marid than anyone else alive."

Hope rose in Ali's voice. "And you think he can help us?"

"It's worth a try. For now, put this business with the marid out of your mind. And *eat*." Hatset pushed the platters at him. "I'd like to have you looking like less of a wraith by week's end."

Ali picked up a pitcher of rosewater to rinse his hands. "Why by week's end?"

"Because that's when your father is holding a feast to celebrate your return."

Ali scowled, plucking a bit of rice and stew from the plate with his fingers. "I wish he'd hold a feast to send me somewhere that isn't a marid-haunted island surrounded by a cursed lake."

"He's not going to be sending you anywhere if I have any say in it." She poured a cup of tamarind juice and pushed it in his direction. "I just got you back, baba." Her voice was fierce. "And if I have to fight some marid to keep you, so be it."

12

NAHRI

Because a lost little girl from Cairo thought she was living in some sort of fairy tale. And because for all her supposed cleverness, she couldn't see that the dashing hero who saved her was its monster.

Nahri closed her eyes, quietly obeying the whispered commands of the servants painting her face. Muntadhir's cruel taunt played ceaselessly in her mind; she'd been thinking about his words for days now, the accusation all the more haunting because for the life of her, Nahri could not help but fear it contained a kernel of truth.

One of her maids approached with a selection of ornate hair combs shaped like various birds. "Which would you like, my lady?"

Nahri stared at the jeweled combs, too glum to even silently assess their value. Her braids were already undone, her black curls spilling wildly to her waist. She touched her hair, twisting one lock around a finger. "It's fine like this."

Two of her maids exchanged nervous looks, and from the corner of the room where she'd been watching Nahri dress with open concern, Nisreen coughed.

"My lady, with all respect . . . between your hair and the dress, you do not quite appear to be going to a ceremonial event," her mentor said delicately.

No, I probably look like I'm about to visit my husband's bed, which is ironic because I'm damn well never doing that again. Nahri had again chosen to wear the sleeveless linen gown with the elaborate beaded collar that reminded her of Egypt. The prospect of interacting with the Qahtanis left her anxious and she wanted to cling to something familiar.

And she didn't really care what anyone else thought about it. "I'm going like this. It's a Geziri feast, and there won't be any men in the women's section to see me either way."

Nisreen sighed, perhaps recognizing defeat. "I take it I am still to come up with some sort of emergency so that you can leave early?"

"Please." Nahri couldn't entirely snub the feast, but she could make sure she spent as little time there as possible. "Did you happen to notice if Jamshid left?"

"He did. He insisted on helping me restock the apothecary shelves and then departed. I told him he needed another day to recover, but—"

"But he wants to be at Muntadhir's side." Nahri waited until the maids had left to finish the sentence. "Muntadhir doesn't deserve him."

"I don't disagree." When Nahri moved to stand, Nisreen touched her shoulder. "You'll take care with the queen tonight?"

"I always do." It was the truth; Nahri evaded Hatset like she owed the older woman money. From what Nahri had observed, the queen was Ghassan's equal in cunning and resource, but whereas the king desired Nahri as an ally—in name at least—Hatset wanted nothing to do with her, treating her with the wary disdain someone might show an ill-mannered dog.

Which was fine with Nahri, especially tonight. She would steal a few minutes to eat—possibly *actually* steal one of the gold carving knives used during state functions just to make herself feel better—and then be gone without having to talk to either of the Qahtani princes.

Draping a snow-white chador embroidered with sunbursts of sapphires over her head, she followed a female steward through the open corridor that led to the formal gardens in front of Ghassan's throne room. Globes of enchanted flames in rainbow-bright hues nestled in the fruit trees, and fine carpets embroidered with hunting scenes had been laid upon the trimmed grass. Tiny jade hummingbirds glittered as they sang and swooped between delicate copper feeders, their song mingling with the strumming of lutes. The air was fragrant with jasmine, musk, and roasted meat. The last made her stomach rumble sadly; Nahri hadn't touched meat since committing to her role as Banu Nahida.

Directly ahead was an enormous tent constructed with swaths of silver silk that shimmered under the moonlight. The steward pulled aside one of the pearly curtains, and Nahri stepped inside the perfumed interior.

Its opulence was a mockery of the tents the nomadic Geziris would have once called home. Stunning hand-loomed rugs in a riot of colors lay thick upon the ground, and an illusionist had conjured up a constellation of miniature fireworks to swirl and sparkle overhead. Fire burned in wide, open golden lamps—the djinn had a strong aversion to the small, closed ones often used as slave vessels by the ifrit.

The tent was warm and packed; Nahri slipped out of her chador, handing it off to a waiting attendant and blinking as her eyes adjusted to the crowded, firelit interior. Past the bustle of servants and guests lingering near the entrance, she caught a glimpse of Queen Hatset and Princess Zaynab holding court on a raised marble dais scattered with ebony and gold cushions. Cursing the etiquette that required her to greet them first, Nahri made her way across the floor. She was determined to ignore the raised eyebrows she knew her dress would attract, so she refused to look at the other women . . . which meant she realized too late that many had pulled their various shaylas and veils over their heads.

The reason why sat between his mother and sister.

It took Nahri a moment to recognize the finely dressed young man in the robes of an Ayaanle noble as the traitorous former friend she'd contemplated murdering in her garden a few days ago. Gone were the filthy traveling robe and ragged ghutra. Over a rich, black dishdasha trimmed with pale moonstone beads, Ali wore a grass-green robe patterned in silver ikat, a cheerfully colored garment deeply uncharacteristic of the taciturn prince. A beautiful silver turban crowned his head, wrapped in the Geziri style that revealed the copper relic bolted to his ear.

Ali looked equally taken aback by the sight of Nahri, his shocked gaze traveling from her uncovered head down her bare arms. She heard him take a sharp breath, and she bristled; given Ali's conservative views, he probably thought the dress even more inappropriate than Nisreen had.

"Banu Nahida," Hatset greeted her, beckoning Nahri closer with a hand that sparkled with golden rings. "There you are. Come, join us!"

Nahri approached, bowing her head as she brought her hands together. "Peace be upon you all," she said, in her best attempt at ingratiating politeness.

"And upon you peace, dear daughter." Hatset gave her a warm smile. The royal women looked stunning, as usual. Hatset wore a silk abaya dyed in saffron and crimson, the fabric shimmering like a flame under a midnight-colored shayla trimmed in Geziri pearls. Zaynab—who could drive men to their knees dressed in an ill-fitting sack—was clad in a gown that looked like a waterfall had come to life and decided to worship her, a cascade of teal, emerald, and cobalt blue held together by a collar of real lotus flowers. "I was beginning to fear something might have happened to you when you didn't arrive with your husband."

The words were said with far too much intent, but Nahri wasn't surprised: there seemed to be very little Hatset didn't know about the domestic happenings of the palace. Nahri had no doubt a few of her maids were in the queen's employ—and that news of her argument with Muntadhir had already been relayed.

But Nahri was not discussing her marital woes with this woman. She feigned a smile. "Forgive my tardiness. I had a patient."

Hatset's golden eyes twinkled. "No apology necessary." She gestured to Nahri's dress. "That is quite lovely. A little different, to be sure, but very beautiful." Her voice took on a teasing tone. "Alu, doesn't she look pretty?" she asked her son.

Ali's gaze was darting everywhere but at Nahri. "I, er, yes," he stammered. "I should go. The men will be expecting me."

Hatset grabbed his wrist. "Remember to talk to people . . . and about things *other* than hadith and economics, for the love of God, Alizayd. Tell some exciting stories about Am Gezira."

Ali rose to his feet. Nahri hated to admit such a thing, but he looked striking in his new clothes, the beautifully dyed robe highlighting his haughty features and luminous dark skin. She supposed that's what happened when you let your mother dress you.

He kept his gaze on the floor as he passed her. "In peace," he said softly.

"Go jump in the lake," she returned under her breath in Arabic. She saw him tense but he didn't stop.

Hatset smiled as she watched him walk away, her expression both proud and fiercely protective.

Of course she's proud; she's probably been conspiring to get him back here for years. Nahri had been turning over in her mind the conversation she'd overheard between Muntadhir and Jamshid since her run-in with Ali. She wondered if there was any truth to her husband's concerns about the deadly intentions of the "mother" she now knew was Hatset.

The queen's gaze shifted back to Nahri. "Dear one, why are you still standing? Sit," she commanded, gesturing to the cushion next to Zaynab. "My daughter has already accidentally knocked aside the tent panel in front of us to improve our view. And you always hide yourself away at these things." She nodded at the platters surrounding them. "I've had the kitchens bring out some vegetarian dishes for you."

Nahri went from baffled to suspicious in one fell swoop. Hatset was clearly up to something—so much so that the queen was barely attempting to hide it with her question about Muntadhir and her exuberant friendliness. And the rather obvious comment to Ali about her dress.

Nahri's cheeks suddenly burned. Oh, no . . . she was not letting herself get dragged between the estranged brothers that way. She had enough problems of her own. But neither could she be rude. Hatset was the queen—wealthy, powerful, and with as much of an iron fist when it came to the harem as her husband held over the city. Daevabad's royal harem was enormously influential; here marriages between their world's most powerful families were debated, and here posts and contracts were given out that changed lives . . . all under the watchful eye of the djinn queen.

So when Hatset again gestured to the cushion next to Zaynab, Nahri sat.

"I take it you knock aside tent panels with the same frequency that your empty litter dallies in the Geziri bazaar?" she whispered to her sister-in-law. Zaynab rolled her eyes, and Nahri continued, gesturing at the platters of fruit and pastries spread before her.

"This reminds me of the first time we met. I mean . . . before you purposely got me so intoxicated I passed out."

Zaynab shrugged. "I was trying to be a good host," she said airily. "How was I to know the potency of such forbidden substances?"

Nahri shook her head, stealing a glance through the billowing tent partitions at the men's section. The jeweled stakes pinning the silk had indeed been knocked aside in front of them, giving Nahri a fairly good view. Ahead, the Qahtani men sat with their closest retainers on a beautiful white jade platform that floated upon the lush grass. The platform was stunning, its edges carved with an assortment of leaping oryxes, sly-eyed sphinxes, and soaring simurghs. Precious stones and gems highlighted the length of a horn, the sweep of a tail, and the delicate array of feathers on a wing. The men reclined upon silk cushions, wine cups and spun glass water pipes scattered about them.

At the center of course, was Ghassan al Qahtani. Nahri's skin prickled as she looked at the djinn king. It always did—there was far too much history between them. The man who held her life in his hands, who controlled her as thoroughly as if he'd locked her away, her chains the lives of the Daevas and friends he would destroy if she so much as thought about stepping out of line.

He looked calm and as inscrutable as ever, dressed in royal robes and his striking silk turban—a turban Nahri couldn't look at without recalling the cold way he'd revealed the truth about Dara and Qui-zi to her on that rain-soaked pavilion five years ago. Early in her marriage, Nahri had quietly asked Muntadhir to take his off before they were alone—a request he had granted without comment and one he'd religiously followed.

Her gaze went to him now. She hadn't spoken to her husband since their fight in the infirmary, and seeing him there, dressed in the same official robes and turban as his father, deepened her unease. Jamshid was at his side, of course, their knees brushing, but there were others as well, most of whom Nahri recognized. Wealthy, well-connected men all of them . . . but they were also Muntadhir's friends, true ones. One appeared to be telling Muntadhir a story, while another passed him a water pipe.

It looked as though they were trying to keep his spirits up—or perhaps distract him from the other side of the platform, where Ali had taken a seat. Though he lacked his older brother's dazzling array of jewelry, the starkness of his attire seemed to elevate him. At Ali's left were several officers from the Royal Guard, along with a thickly bearded man with an infectious grin and a severe-eyed woman in male dress. On his right, the Qaid appeared to be telling a story at which Ghassan gave a hearty laugh. Ali remained silent, his gaze flitting between his companions and a large glass pitcher of water on the rug before him.

And though it was a beautiful night in an enchanted garden, filled with guests who looked like they might have stepped from the pages of a book of legends, Nahri had a sense of foreboding. The things Muntadhir had whispered to Jamshid, whatever Hatset was up to . . . Nahri could see it playing out in the scene before her. Daevabad's sophisticated elites—the literati noblemen and wealthy traders—had flocked to Muntadhir. The rougher men who wielded blades, and the ones who could stand before the Friday crowds and fill their hearts with holy purpose . . . they were with Ali.

And if those brothers remained divided, if those groups turned on each other . . . Nahri didn't see it ending well for her people—for any of them.

Her stomach rumbled. Impending civil war or not, there was little Nahri could do to save her tribe on an empty stomach. Not particularly caring about etiquette, she pulled over a tiled glass dish of knafeh and a reed platter of fruit, fully determined to gorge herself on cheese pastry and melon.

The nape of her neck prickled. Nahri glanced back up.

Through the narrow opening, Ali was watching her.

She met his troubled gray eyes. Nahri typically tried to close herself off from her abilities in crowds like this, the competing heartbeats and gurgling humors an irritating distraction. But for a moment she let them expand.

Ali stood out like a spot on the eye, a deep silence in the ocean of sounds.

You're my friend, she remembered him declaring the first time she'd saved his life, with the utter confidence the haze of opium had instilled. *A light,* he'd added when he begged her not to follow Dara.

Annoyed by the unwanted, unsettling feeling the memory caused, she snatched up one of the serving knives. Still holding his gaze, she plunged it deep into a piece of melon, then began carving it with surgical precision. Ali drew up, looking both startled and somehow still snobbish. Nahri glared, and he finally looked away.

Ahead, Ghassan clapped his hands. Nahri watched as he gazed warmly at the crowd.

"My friends, I thank you for honoring my family with your presence here tonight." He beamed at Ali. "And I thank God for allowing me the joy of seeing my youngest again. It is a blessing whose value I didn't quite realize until he came striding into my palace dressed like some northern raider."

That brought a chuckle to the mostly Geziri crowd, and Ghassan continued. "Prince Alizayd, of course, wanted none of this. If he had his way, we'd share a single platter of dates and perhaps a pot of the coffee I hear he now brews himself." Ghassan's voice turned teasing. "Then he would likely give us a lecture on the benefit of estate taxes."

Ali's companions burst into laughter at that. Muntadhir was clenching his wine cup, and Nahri didn't miss the quiet way Jamshid lowered her husband's hand.

"I will, however, save you from such a thing," Ghassan said. "Indeed, I've something else planned. My chefs have been furiously attempting to outdo each other in advance of Navasatem, so I issued them a challenge this evening. Prepare their finest dish, and my son will choose the best cook to design the menu for the generation celebrations."

Nahri grew a bit intrigued at that. Five years in Daevabad had yet to completely inure her to its marvels, and she was sure whatever the royal chefs conjured would be magnificent indeed. She watched as more servants wound their way through the royal platform, some pouring rosewater over the hands of the men while others refilled cups. Turning away a wine bearer, Ali beckoned politely to a young man holding a glass pitcher icy with condensation.

Before the servant could reach the prince, Jamshid stopped him, holding out his arm in a slightly rude—or perhaps inebriated—manner. He took the pitcher and poured his own glass of what Nahri recognized as tamarind juice, before pushing it back at the other man. He took a sip and then set his cup down, reaching out to quickly squeeze Muntadhir's knee.

Ghassan clapped his hands again and then Nahri wasn't looking at Jamshid.

Because a damned boat had joined them.

Carved from teak and large enough to fit the royal family, the boat swept in on a wave of conjured smoke, a miniature version of the great sewn ships said to sail the Indian Ocean. On its silk sail, the emblem of the Sahrayn tribe had been painted, and indeed the man accompanying it was Sahrayn, his striped hood thrown back to reveal red-streaked black hair.

He bowed low. "Majesty, Your Royal Highnesses, peace be upon you all."

"And upon you peace," Ghassan replied, looking bemused. "An impressive presentation. What do you have for us, then?"

"The finest of delicacies from Qart Sahar: cave eels. They are found only in the deepest, most forbidden cisterns of the Sahara. We capture them alive, bringing them back in great vats of saltwater, and then prepare them in a scented broth of the most delicate perfumes and preserved vinegars." He beamed, gesturing to the boat . . . no, to the vat, Nahri realized, catching sight of several sinuous shapes churning in the dark liquid filling the bottom. "They have been swimming in there a whole fortnight."

The look on Ali's face was almost enough to make the whole evening worth it. He choked on his tamarind juice. "Swimming . . . they're still *alive*?"

"But of course." The Sahrayn chef gave him a puzzled look. "The thrashing makes the meat sweeter."

Muntadhir finally smiled. "Sahrayn eels. Now that is an honor, brother." He took a sip of his wine. "I believe the first bite belongs to you."

The chef beamed again, looking ready to burst with pride. "Shall I, my prince?"

Ali looked ill but motioned for him to continue.

The chef plunged a glittering brass trident into the vat, provoking a metallic shriek that drew startled yelps from the audience. The eel was still squirming as he quickly spun it into a nest and then placed it gingerly on a brightly patterned tile. He presented it to Ali with a flourish.

Muntadhir was watching with open delight on his face, and Nahri had to admit that in this, she and her husband were united.

Ali took the tile and choked down a bite of eel, swallowing hard before he spoke. "It's . . . it's very good," he said weakly. "It certainly tastes like it did a lot of thrashing."

There were tears in the chef's eyes. "I will carry your compliments to my grave," he wept.

The next two competitors did not offer quite the same level of presentation, though the diners looked considerably more pleased by the skewers of minced rukh kebab—Nahri could only imagine how someone had caught one of those—grilled with golden Tukharistani apples, studded with whole spices, and served while still aflame.

They were removing the largest platter of kabsa Nahri had ever seen, a shrewd move made by the Geziri chef who probably suspected a prince living in the countryside might long for comfort food after some of the competition's more "creative" dishes, when Ghassan frowned.

"Strange," he said. "I did not see the competitor from Agni—"

A simurgh soared into the garden with a shriek.

The glittering firebird—twice the size of a camel—swept over the crowd, its smoking wings setting an apricot tree aflame. By the time it fluttered to the ground, half the men had reached for their weapons.

"Hah! It worked!" A grinning Agnivanshi man with a singed mustache joined them. "Peace be upon you, my king and princes! How do you like my creation?"

Nahri watched hands slowly move away from dagger hilts. And then she clapped in delight when she realized what the man meant. The simurgh wasn't a simurgh, not really. It was a composite, constructed from what appeared to be a dizzying array of sweets in every color of creation.

The chef looked inordinately proud of himself. "A little different, I know . . . but what is the purpose of Navasatem if not to celebrate the sweetness of relief from Suleiman's servitude?"

Even the king looked dazzled. "I'll grant you points for creativity," Ghassan offered. He glanced at Ali. "What say you?"

Ali had risen to his feet to better examine the simurgh. "A stunning enchantment," he confessed. "I've never seen anything like this."

"You've never tasted anything like this either," the chef said smoothly. He tapped the simurgh's glass eye and it fell neatly into his hands, a waiting platter. He made a swift selection and then bowed as it was passed toward the prince.

Ali smiled, biting into crumbly pastry covered in silver foil. Appreciation lit his face. "That is delicious," he admitted.

The Agnivanshi chef shot a triumphant look at his competitors as Ali took a sip from his goblet and then tried another sweet. But this time, he frowned, reaching for his throat. He hooked his fingers around the collar of his dishdasha, tugging at the stiff fabric.

"You'll excuse me," he said. "I think I just . . ." He reached for his cup and then stumbled, knocking it over.

Ghassan straightened up, a look Nahri had never seen in his eyes. "Alizayd?"

Coughing, Ali didn't answer. His other hand went to his throat, and as the confusion in his expression turned to panic, his eyes met Nahri's again through the tent panel.

There was no anger there, no accusation. Just pained regret that sent a wave of cold dread through her before Ali even fell to his knees.

He gasped, and with the sound, Nahri was back on the boat, back in that horrible night five years ago. Dara had gasped like that, a hushed sound of true fear—an emotion she hadn't thought her Afshin could feel—as he fell to *his* knees. His beautiful eyes had met hers and then he'd gasped, his body crumbling into dust as she screamed.

From the corner of her eye, she saw Hatset fly to her feet. "Alizayd!"

And then it was chaos.

Ali collapsed, choking and clawing at his throat. Hatset burst through the tent, propriety abandoned as she raced to her son's side. Zaynab screamed, but before she could lunge forward, a pair of female guards descended, nearly knocking Nahri aside in their effort to pull the princess to safety. The Royal Guard was doing the same on the men's side, soldiers hustling a stunned Muntadhir back. The Qaid drew his zulfiqar and then actually grabbed Ghassan, locking him in a tight, protective grip.

No one stopped Hatset. Well, one of the guards tried, and she smashed the heavy goblet she was holding into his face, then dropped at Ali's side, shouting his name.

Nahri didn't move. She could see Dara's tear-streaked face before hers. *"Come with me. We'll leave, travel the world."*

His ashes on her hands. His ashes on the wet robe of his killer.

Everything seemed to go very still; the screams of the crowd faded, the thud of running feet fell away. A man was dying before her. It was a scene she knew well from the infirmary, one of desperate family members and scrambling aides. Nahri had learned not to hesitate, learned to shut her emotions off. She was a healer, a Nahid. The doctor she always wanted to be.

And in her dreams—her foolish dreams of being an apprentice to the great physicians in Istanbul, of taking her place in one of Cairo's famed hospitals—in those dreams, she was not the kind of doctor to sit and watch a man die.

She jumped to her feet.

She was halfway to Ali, close enough to see the shimmering silver vapors escaping the gashes he'd clawed in his skin, when Suleiman's seal crashed down upon her.

Nahri swooned, fighting for air herself, weak and bewildered by the sudden clash of incomprehensible languages. She spotted the seal glowing on Ghassan's face and then Hatset whirled on her, brandishing the goblet. Nahri froze.

Ali started screaming.

Blood blossomed from his mouth, from his throat and neck, silver shards emerging from his skin in bloody bursts. The silver vapors, Nahri realized. They'd turned to solid metal the instant Ghassan called upon the seal; their misty form must have been magical.

Ghassan had just killed his son trying to save him.

Nahri ran. "Lift the seal!" she shouted. "You're killing him!" Ali was seizing as he clutched his shredded throat. She dropped beside Hatset, snatching up one of the silver shards and holding it before the terrified queen. "Look for yourself! Did you not just see this change?"

Hatset glanced wildly between the shard and her dying son. She turned on Ghassan. "Lift it!"

The seal was gone in an instant, Nahri's powers surging back through her. "Help me turn him over!" she shouted as Ali's companions rushed to join them. She thrust a finger down his throat until he gagged and then pounded his back, black blood mingling with the silver gushing from his mouth. "Get me a board! I need to get him to the infirmary immediate—"

A blade whipped past her face.

Nahri jerked back, but it hadn't been meant for her. There was a heavy thump and then a muffled scream as the servant who'd served Ali's juice fell dead at the garden's entrance, the khanjar belonging to Ali's female companion buried in his back.

She didn't have long to dwell on it. Ali's eyes snapped open as they laid him on a stretched portion of cloth.

They were as black as oil. As black as they'd been when the marid took him.

Hatset clamped a hand over them, a little too fast. "The infirmary," she agreed in a shaky voice.

13

NAHRI

It took the rest of the night to save him. Though he'd vomited up most of the poison, what remained was pernicious, racing through his blood to whirl into solid form as it burst through his skin seeking air. Nahri would no sooner lance, clean, and heal a silver boil than another would bloom. By the time she was finished, Ali was a bloody wreck, and silver-soaked rags lay everywhere.

Fighting a wave of exhaustion, Nahri pressed a hand upon his damp brow. She closed her eyes, and that strange sensation rushed back: a deep, impenetrably dark curtain through which she could barely detect the thud of his heart. The scent of salt, of a cold and utterly alien presence.

But no hint of the destructive poison. She sat back, wiping her own brow and taking a deep breath. A violent tremor went through her body. It was a sensation that often overtook her after a particularly terrifying bit of Nahid healing, her nerves catching up only after she was done.

"He is all right?" Ali's friend—Lubayd, as he'd introduced himself—spoke up. He was the only one in the room with her, her own bedroom. Ghassan had commandeered it, insisting on privacy for his son, and in response, Nahri had kicked both him and Hatset out, declaring that she couldn't work with Ali's worried parents hovering over her.

"I think so." She hoped so anyway. She had dealt with poisonings—both intentional and not—plenty of times since arriving in Daevabad, but nothing that worked with such speed and deadliness. Though it was obvious the silver vapors would have eventually choked him, the way they'd turned to metal shards when Ghassan had used Suleiman's seal . . . that was a diabolical bit of cruelty, and Nahri had no idea who might have devised something so vicious.

Looking relieved, Lubayd nodded and retreated to a corner of the room while Nahri returned to her work, leaning closer to Ali to examine one of the wounds on his chest. The poison had burst perilously close to his heart there.

She frowned, catching sight of a bumpy ridge of skin above the wound. A scar. A meandering, savage line as if some sort of spiked vine had crawled across his chest before being ripped away.

Her stomach knotted. Before she could think twice, Nahri yanked close a basin Nisreen had filled with water, dampened a cloth, and wiped away the blood that covered his limbs.

The scars were everywhere.

A ragged line of puncture marks on his shoulder where teeth the size of her thumb had pierced him. The imprint of a fishing hook in his left palm and whirls of ruined flesh that called to mind waterweeds and tentacles. Pocked divots over his stomach, like fish had attempted to feast on him.

She covered her mouth, horrified. The memory of him climbing back onto the boat came to her: his body covered in lake detritus, a crocodile snout clamped on his shoulder, fishing hooks snarled in his skin. Nahri had thought him already dead, and she'd been so panicked that she and Dara were about to follow that she'd given little thought to what had happened to him. The stories about "Alizayd the Afshin-slayer" gallivanting across Am Gezira certainly made it sound like he was fine. And Nahri hadn't seen him again after the boat.

But Nisreen had. She'd treated Ali . . . and she'd never said anything about this.

Nahri stepped away from the bed, beckoning for Lubayd to follow as she passed. "We should give the king and queen a moment with him."

Hatset and Ghassan were standing on opposite sides of the pavilion outside her room, neither one looking at the other. Zaynab and Muntadhir were sitting on the bench between them, Muntadhir holding one of his sister's hands.

"Is he all right?" Hatset's voice shook slightly.

"For now," Nahri answered. "I've stopped the bleeding and there's no trace of the poison left. That I can detect," she clarified.

Ghassan looked as though he'd aged a half-century. "Do you know what it was?"

"No," she said flatly. This wasn't an answer she could risk massaging. "I have no idea what that was. I've never seen or read of anything like that." She hesitated, remembering the fleeing cupbearer—and the thrown dagger that had interrupted that flight. "I don't suppose his cupbearer . . ."

The king shook his head, grim. "Dead before he could be questioned. One of Alizayd's companions acted a bit too rashly."

"I daresay those companions and their rashness are probably the only reason our son is still alive." Hatset's voice was sharper that Nahri had ever heard it.

Muntadhir rose to his feet. "So he'll live?"

Nahri forced herself to meet her husband's eyes, not missing the tangle of emotion in them. "He'll survive this."

"All right." Muntadhir's voice was low and troubled enough that Nahri saw Hatset narrow her eyes at him. He didn't seem to notice, instead turning abruptly away and disappearing down the steps that led to the garden.

Zaynab hurried after him. "Dhiru . . ."

Ghassan sighed, watching them for a moment before turning back to Nahri. "May we see him?"

"Yes. I need to prepare a tonic for his throat. But don't wake him. He lost a lot of blood. I don't even think he should be moved. Let him stay here for at least a few days."

The king nodded, heading toward her room. But Hatset caught Nahri's wrist.

"Do you truly know nothing about this poison?" she asked. "Nothing in your mother's old notes?"

"We're healers, not assassins," Nahri shot back. "And I'd be a fool to get involved with anything like this."

"I'm not accusing you," Hatset said, a little of the edge leaving her voice. "I just want to make sure if you think of anything—*suspect* anything—you come to me, Banu Nahida." Her expression grew intent. "I am not my husband," she added softly. "I reward loyalty—I don't terrorize people into it. And I'll not forget what you did for my son tonight."

She let go of Nahri's wrist, following Ghassan without another word. Her mind spinning, Nahri continued on to the infirmary.

Nisreen was already at work on the tonic, transferring a spoonful of bright orange, freshly ground salamander skin from a stone mortar into a honey-colored potion simmering in a glass flask suspended over an open flame. A puff of smoke burst from the flask and then the mixture turned crimson, uncomfortably close to the color of human blood.

"I started without you," Nisreen called over her shoulder. "I figured you could use the help. It just needs another moment or two to simmer."

Nahri's stomach tightened. Reliable Nisreen, always two steps ahead of what Nahri needed. Her mentor and closest confidante.

The only person left in Daevabad that she thought she could trust.

She joined her, pressing her hands against the worktable and fighting the emotion bubbling up inside her. "You lied to me," Nahri said quietly.

Nisreen glanced up, looking taken aback. "What?"

"You lied to me about Ali. After Dara's de—after that night on the boat." Her voice was unsteady. "You said Ali was fine. You said he had *scratches*." She gave Nisreen an incredulous stare. "There's not a patch of skin on him bigger than my palm that isn't scarred."

Nisreen stiffened. "You'll forgive me not thinking much of his wounds when Dara and a dozen other Daevas lay dead, and Ghassan was contemplating executing you."

Nahri shook her head. "You should have told me. You dismissed me when I tried to talk about that night, you had me doubting my very memories . . ."

"Because I didn't want them to consume you!" Nisreen put down the mortar, turning her full attention on Nahri. "My lady, you were singing to shadows and cutting open your wrists to try and bring Dara back. You didn't need to know more."

Nahri flinched at the blunt depiction of her grief, but Nisreen's last words still set her blood boiling. "Whether or not I needed to know more was not your decision to make. Not with this, not with the hospital, not with *anything*." She threw up her hands. "Nisreen, I can't have this. I need at least one person in this cursed city I can trust, one person who will tell me the truth no matter what."

Nisreen's dark eyes flicked away. When she spoke again, her voice was soft with both pity and disgust. "I didn't know what to tell you, Nahri. He was barely recognizable as a djinn when they brought him in. He was hissing and spitting like a snake, shrieking in some language no one could recognize. The things clinging to his skin attacked us as we removed them. We had to tie him down after he tried to strangle his own father!"

Nahri's eyes widened, but Nisreen clearly wasn't done. "What do you think brought down the ceiling of your infirmary?" She jerked her head up. "It was Alizayd, whatever was *in* Alizayd." Nisreen lowered her voice further. "I assisted your mother and uncle for a century and a half, and I witnessed things I could never have imagined, but, Banu Nahri . . . nothing comes close to what I saw happen to Alizayd al Qahtani." She reached for the simmering glass flask with a gloved hand and poured the potion into a jade cup that she then thrust at Nahri. "His friendship was a weakness you should have never permitted yourself and now he's a threat you barely understand."

Nahri made no move to take the cup. "Taste it."

Nisreen stared at her. "What?"

"Taste it." Nahri jerked her head toward the door. "Or get out of my infirmary."

Without dropping her gaze, Nisreen lifted the cup to her mouth and took a sip. She put it back down with a thud. "I would never risk you like that, Banu Nahida. *Never.*"

"Do you know who might have been capable of making that poison?"

Nisreen's black gaze didn't so much as waver. "No."

Nahri took the cup. Her hands were shaking. "Would you tell me if you did? Or would that be another truth I'm not capable of handling?"

Nisreen sighed. "Nahri . . ."

But she was already walking away.

LUBAYD WAS ON THE PAVILION STEPS, SOME DISTANCE from the entrance to her bedroom.

"I wouldn't interrupt them if I were you," he warned.

Nahri brushed past. "They're the ones interrupting me." She continued toward her room but paused at the curtained door, stepping into the shadow of a rose lattice. She could hear the voices of the royal couple inside.

"—should burn in hell for sentencing your child to such a fate. He was *eighteen*, Ghassan. Eighteen and you sent him to die in Am Gezira after some lake demon tortured him!"

"Do you think I wanted to?" Ghassan hissed. "I have three children, Hatset. I have thirty *thousand* times as many subjects. Daevabad comes first. I have always told you that. You should have concerned yourself with his safety before your relatives and their dirt-blooded friends attempted to lure him into treason!"

Nahri stood utterly still, well aware that the two most powerful people in Daevabad were having an argument it seemed to be courting death to overhear. But she couldn't make herself turn away.

And Hatset wasn't done. "*Daevabad comes first,*" she repeated. "Fine words for a king doing his best to destroy everything our ancestors fought for. You're letting the shafit be sold off to the highest bidder while your emir drinks himself into an early grave."

"Muntadhir is not *drinking himself into a grave,*" Ghassan said, defending his son. "He has always been more capable than you grant him. He's making peace with the Daevas, a peace long overdue."

"This isn't peace!" Rage and exasperation warred in Hatset's voice. "When will you realize that? The Daevas don't want your peace; they want us *gone*. Manizheh despised you, your grand wazir would cut your throat in your sleep if he could, and that girl you bullied into marrying Muntadhir is not going to forget what you've done to her. The moment she gets pregnant, *you'll* be the one poisoned. She and the Pramukhs will shuffle Muntadhir off into an opium den, and just like that, we'll be under Nahid rule again." Warning laced into her voice. "And the Daevas will pay us back in blood for everything your family has done to them."

Nahri stepped back, her hand going to her mouth in shock. The queen had just neatly and horribly pulled together the strands of a future Nahri hardly dared consider—and the tapestry it created when presented by the other side was awful. A calculated scheme of revenge, when Nahri only wanted justice for her tribe.

Justice was what Dara wanted too, wasn't it? And look at the price he was willing to pay for it. Nahri swallowed, her legs feeling a bit unsteady.

Ghassan raised his voice. "And this is why Alizayd talks and acts the way he does. Why he recklessly throws himself into aiding every shafit he comes across. Because of you."

"Because he wants to fix things, and all you've ever told him to do is shut his mouth and wield a weapon. I've heard the stories coming out of Am Gezira. He has done more good for people there in five years than you have in fifty."

Scorn filled Ghassan's voice. "It is not his leadership in Am Gezira that you desire, wife. Do not think I am so naive. And I will not have you interfere again. The next time you overstep, I *will* send you back to Ta Ntry. For good. You will never see either of your children again."

There was a moment of silence before the queen responded. "And that, Ghassan?" Her voice was chillingly quiet. "That you would reach for such a threat with the mother of your children? That is why people hate you." Nahri heard the door open. "And it breaks my heart when I remember the man you used to be."

The door shut. Nahri leaned in and peered through the roses, catching sight of Ghassan staring at his unconscious son. He inhaled sharply and then was gone, sweeping out in a swirl of black robes.

Nahri was shaking as she entered her room. *I should have been more aggressive in my dowry demands*, she suddenly thought. Because she had *not* been paid enough to marry into this family.

She returned to Ali's side. His chest was rising and falling in the light of her fireplace, reminding her of the first time she'd healed him. The quiet night she'd accidentally killed her first patient and then saved a prince, the first time she'd had to grudgingly admit to herself that the man she insisted was only a mark was becoming the closest thing she had to a friend.

Nahri squeezed her eyes shut. Ali and Nisreen. Muntadhir. *Dara.* Everyone she let get a glimpse past the walls Muntadhir had accused her of keeping around her heart had lied to her or used her. Nahri had once quietly feared that it was her, that growing up alone on Cairo's streets with abilities that terrified everyone had broken her, shaped her into a person who didn't know how to forge a genuine bond.

But it wasn't her. Or at least not *just* her. It was Daevabad. Daevabad had crushed everyone in it, from its tyrant king to the shafit laborer scurrying through her garden. Fear and hate ruled the city—built up by centuries of spilled blood and the resulting grievances. It was a place where everyone was so busy trying to survive and ensure their loved ones survived that there was no room to build new trust.

She let out a breath, opening her eyes to see Ali stir in his sleep. A pained grimace creased his face, breath rasping in his throat. The sight shook away her dark thoughts and reminded her of the potion still clutched in her hand. Her work was not done.

She pulled a cushioned stool closer. Besides his scars, Ali looked like he'd lived a rougher life in Am Gezira than she would have imagined, his body lean and wiry and his nails bitten low. She frowned as she caught sight of another mark just under his jaw. Rather than the ragged imprints the marid left, this one was a clean slash.

It looks like someone tried to cut his throat. Though Nahri couldn't imagine who would be foolish enough to attempt to assassinate a Qahtani prince in the depths of Am Gezira. She reached out and touched his chin, his skin clammy beneath her fingertips as she turned his head to examine a mottled patch of scar tissue on his temple. She could no longer make out the lines of the eight-pointed star that had been carved there—a version of Suleiman's seal, apparently by way of the marid—but she hadn't forgotten the sight of it flashing on his face that night.

She stared at him. *What did they do to you?* And perhaps a question that burned even more—*why?* Why had the marid been so determined to come after Dara?

Movement near her hand caught her eye. Nahri started. The potion in the cup was moving, the liquid's surface rippling like it was being struck by invisible drops.

Ali's eyes fluttered open, his gaze dazed and feverish. He tried to draw a breath and then coughed, pain twisting his face.

Nahri reacted immediately. "Drink this," she commanded, sliding her hand under his head to raise him up. "*No*, don't try to talk," she added as he moved his lips. "Your throat was shredded. Even you can hold your tongue for a moment."

She helped him finish the contents of the cup. Ali was shivering violently, and she eased him back onto the pillow when he was done. "Does anything feel sharp in your body?" she asked. "Anything like a buzzing beneath your skin?"

"No," he croaked. "What-what happened?"

"Someone tried to poison you. Obviously."

Despair swept his face. "Oh," he whispered, his gaze dropping to his hands. "Even in Daevabad then," he added with a soft bitterness that took her aback. The tonic was clearly doing its job, his voice smoother though filled with misery. "I thought they might stop."

Nahri frowned. "Who might stop?"

Ali shook his head stiffly. "It doesn't matter." He glanced up, worry flashing in his eyes. "Was anyone else hurt? My mother—"

"Your mother is fine." That was a lie, of course. Hatset had watched her son almost die in her arms. "No one else was hurt, but your cupbearer was killed trying to escape."

Ali looked pained. "I wish they had not done that. He was only a boy." He covered his mouth as he began to cough again, his hand coming away flecked with blood.

Nahri refilled the cup with water from her pitcher. "Drink," she said, pressing it into his hands. "I suspect your throat will be raw for the next few days. I've done what I could, but the poison was a powerful one."

He took a sip, but his eyes didn't leave her face. "I thought you had done it," he said quietly.

She drew back, annoyed that the accusation hurt. "Yes, I know. You and everyone else. Your people don't make secret what they think of me."

Guilt blossomed in his eyes. "I didn't mean it like that." He lowered the cup, running his thumb against the edge. "I only meant that I wouldn't have blamed you if you wanted me dead."

"Wanting you dead and actually killing you are very different things," she said sharply. "And I'm no murderer."

"No, you're not," Ali said. "You're a healer." He met her eyes again. "Thank you for saving my life." He bit his lip, a little desperate humor creeping across his face. "I think this is the fourth time."

Nahri struggled to remain expressionless, cursing the part of her heart that wanted to soften at his words. His breathing ragged and his eyes bright with pain, Ali didn't look the "Afshin-slayer" right now; he looked sick and weak—a patient who needed her. An old friend who missed her.

A weakness. Not trusting her emotions, Nahri abruptly stood up. "It's my duty," she said brusquely. "Nothing more." She turned for the door. "A servant will bring you fresh clothing. I have other patients."

"Nahri, wait," he rasped. "Please."

Hating herself, she stopped. "I'm not doing this with you, Ali."

"What if I told you that you were right?"

Nahri glanced back at him. "What?"

Ali stared her, his expression beseeching. "You were right. About that night, about the boat." Shame filled his face. "I did know the Royal Guard would be waiting for us."

She shook her head. "Glad to know you're just as brutal when being honest as you are when lying."

He tried to push up, wincing in pain. "I didn't know what else to do, Nahri. I'd never fought someone who could use magic the way Darayavahoush did. I'd never *heard* of someone who could use magic the way he did. But I knew . . . so much else about him." Sick regret crossed his face. "All those books I didn't want you to read. If he had taken you, if he had killed me—our people would have gone to war." Ali shuddered. "And I knew all too well the kinds of things he did during wars."

Do you know why he's called the Scourge of Qui-zi? The regret that hung on Dara like a cloak, the open fear his name had provoked. "He wouldn't have started another war," she tried to insist, her voice hoarse. "I wouldn't have let him." But even as she said it, she knew she didn't quite believe it. There was a reason Muntadhir's accusation had struck so close to the bone.

Because on that awful night, a desperate Dara had shown how far he would go. He had forced her hand in a way she hadn't considered him capable of, with a reckless violence that had stunned her.

And a small part of her still wondered if she should have seen it coming.

"I couldn't take that risk." Ali's face was drawn, a sheen of dampness on his brow. "You're not the only one with a duty."

Silence fell between them. Nahri struggled to maintain her composure, hating that Ali's haunted confession touched her. She almost wanted to believe him. To believe that the boy who'd taught her to conjure a flame was real, and that the man he'd become was not manipulating her yet again, to believe that not everyone and everything in this miserable city had to be second-guessed.

A weakness. Nahri shuttered the thought, ignoring the loneliness that pierced her chest upon doing so. "And the rest?"

He blinked. "The rest?"

"The marid," she prompted, steadying her voice.

He stared at her in disbelief, turning his palms to reveal his scars. "You can't believe I wanted this."

"What did the *marid* want? Why did they use you to kill Dara?"

Ali shivered. "We weren't exactly having a conversation down there. They were showing me things . . . the destruction of Daevabad, of Am Gezira. They said he was going to do it. Showed him doing it . . . but it didn't look like him."

Nahri narrowed her eyes. "What do you mean?"

Ali frowned as though he were trying to remember. "They showed him turning into something else. His skin and eyes were like fire, his hands black claws . . ."

A chill went down her spine at the description. "They showed Dara becoming an *ifrit*?"

"I don't know," Ali replied. "I try not to think about that night."

You're not the only one. Nahri stared at him, a wary, charged tension filling the space between them. She felt raw, the dredged-up details of that awful night—a night she tried so hard not to dwell on—leaving her more exposed than she liked.

But it was a vulnerability she could see echoed in Ali's face, and though her heart was warning her to get out of this room, she couldn't turn away an opportunity to learn more about the dangerous rift she feared was growing in the family that controlled her life.

"Why are you back in Daevabad, Alizayd?" she asked baldly.

Ali hesitated but answered. "An Ayaanle trader, a cousin of mine, fell ill while crossing Am Gezira." He shrugged—a poor attempt at casualness. "I offered to do him the favor of taking his cargo, thinking I'd enjoy the opportunity to celebrate Navasatem with my family."

"Surely you can lie better than that."

He flushed. "That's the reason I'm here. There's nothing more to it."

Nahri drew closer. "Your mother seems to think there's more to it. *Muntadhir* seems to think there's more to it."

Ali's gaze shot to hers. "I could never hurt my brother."

That lay between them for another long moment, Nahri crossing her arms and holding his gaze until he looked away, still a little shamefaced.

His attention fell on the books stacked haphazardly on the table next to her bed. He cleared his throat. "Er . . . are you reading anything interesting?"

Nahri rolled her eyes at the blatantly obvious attempt to change the subject. "Nothing that concerns you." And nothing that should have concerned her. She was never going to rebuild the hospital, let alone find some mysterious shafit surgeon to work with her.

Clueless as usual, Ali didn't seem to pick up on the malice in her voice. "Who is ibn Butlan?" he asked, leaning close to read from the Arabic scrawled on the top book. "*The Banquet of the Physicians?*"

She reached possessively for the armful of books. "Mind your own business. Were you not just weeping about how many times I've saved your life? Surely you owe me some privacy."

That shut him up, but as Nahri crossed to dump the books on her couch, something clicked into place in her head.

Ali *did* owe her. She turned over Ghassan and Hatset's argument. He was reckless when it came to the shafit, so self-righteous about helping them that he flung himself into things without thinking them through.

She straightened up, turning to him. "You know the shafit neighborhoods."

His eyebrows knit together in confusion. "Yes . . . I mean, I suppose so."

She tried to tamp down the excitement swirling in her chest. No. This was a fool's quest. If Nahri had any sense, she'd be staying away from Ali and holding her tongue about the hospital.

And will you do so forever? Was Nahri going to let Ghassan destroy her ability to hope for a better future, to harden her into the threat Hatset suggested she would one day become? Was that the life she wanted in Daevabad?

Ali drew back. "Why are you looking at me like that? It is alarming."

She scowled. "I'm not looking at you like anything. You don't know me." She snatched the cup. "I'm going to get you some food. Touch my books again and I'll put ice spiders in your coffee. And don't die."

Confusion rippled across his face. "I don't understand."

"You owe me a debt, al Qahtani." Nahri strode off, yanking her door open. "I don't intend to let it go unpaid."

14

DARA

They were holding the Geziri scouts in a crude hut of lashed branches that Dara took care to keep wet and covered in snow. He had originally conjured their prisoners a small tent, a place that would have been warmer, but the pair had returned the favor by setting the felt aflame in the middle of the night and arming themselves with the support beams, breaking the bones of two of his warriors in an attempt to flee. Whatever else they were, the Geziris were a wily people, used to finding ways to survive in inhospitable environments, and Dara would not grant them another chance to escape.

His boots crunching on the snow as he approached the hut, Dara called out a warning. "Abu Sayf, tell your fellow that if he greets me with a rock again, I'm going to shove it down his throat."

There was a flurry of conversation in Geziriyya inside at that, Abu Sayf sounding weary and exasperated and the younger one—who still refused to give his name—irritable before Abu Sayf spoke. "Come in, Afshin."

Dara ducked inside, blinking in the dim light. It was fetid and cold, and smelled of unwashed men and blood. After their last escapade, the djinn were kept in irons and given blankets only during the coldest nights. And while Dara understood the need for security measures, the crude conditions made him increasingly uneasy. He had not taken Abu Sayf and his companion on the field of battle as combatants. They were scouts: a young man on what Dara suspected was his first posting, and an old warrior with one foot in retirement.

"Ah, look, it's the devil himself," the younger djinn said heatedly as Dara entered. He looked feverish but was glaring with as much hate as he could muster.

Dara matched his glare and then knelt, putting down the platter he'd been carrying and shoving it toward the younger man's feet. "Breakfast." He glanced at Abu Sayf. "How are you today?"

"A little stiff," Abu Sayf confessed. "Your warriors are getting better."

"A thing I have to thank you for."

The younger Geziri snorted. "Thank? You told him you'd flay me alive if he didn't spar with your band of traitors."

Abu Sayf shot the other djinn a look, adding something in their incomprehensible language before nodding at the tray. "This is for us?"

"It is for him." Dara crossed to Abu Sayf and struck his irons off. "Come with me. A walk will ease your limbs."

Dara led the other man out and toward his own tent, a fittingly bare place for a man who belonged nowhere. He rekindled his fire with a snap of his fingers and waved for Abu Sayf to sit upon the carpet.

The Geziri did so, rubbing his hands before the fire. "Thank you."

"It is nothing," Dara returned, taking a seat across from him. He snapped his fingers again, conjuring a platter of steaming stew and hot bread. The burst of magic while in his mortal form made his head pound, but he felt the other man deserved it. This was the first time he'd invited Abu Sayf to his tent, but not the first time they'd shared conversation. He might have been an enemy, but Abu Sayf's fluency in Divasti and his two centuries serving in the djinn army made him an easy companion. Dara had great affection for his young recruits and was deeply loyal to Manizheh—but Suleiman's eye, sometimes he just wanted to gaze upon the mountains and exchange a few words about horses with an old man who was equally weary of war.

Dara passed over a cloak. "Take this. It has been cold." He shook his head. "I wish you would let me conjure you a proper tent. Your companion is an idiot."

Abu Sayf pulled over the stew, ripping off a piece of the bread. "I prefer to stay with my tribesman. He is not handling this well." A weary sadness fell over his face. "He misses his family. He learned just before we were posted that his wife was pregnant with their firstborn." He glanced at Dara. "She is in Daevabad. He fears for her."

Dara pushed away a stab of guilt. Warriors left wives behind all the time; it was part of their duty. "If she were back in Am Gezira, where you all belong, she would be plenty safe," he offered, forcing a conviction he didn't entirely feel into his voice.

Abu Sayf didn't take the bait. He never did. Dara suspected he was a soldier through and through and didn't care to defend politics in which he had little voice. "Your Banu Nahida came to take blood again," he said instead. "And she hasn't returned my friend's relic."

At that Dara reached for his goblet, watching it fill with date wine at his silent command. "I am certain it is nothing." In truth, he didn't know what Manizheh was doing with the relics, and her secrecy was starting to grate on him.

"Your men say she intends to experiment on us. To boil us alive and grind our bones for her potions." Fear crept into the other man's voice. "They say she can capture a soul like the ifrit and bind it away so it never sees Paradise."

Dara kept his face blank, but annoyance with his soldiers—and with himself for not checking their behavior sooner—sparked in his chest. Animosity toward the djinn and shafit ran high in their camp: many of Manizheh's followers had suffered at their hands, after all. Admittedly, Dara hadn't thought much of it when he was first brought back. During his own rebellion fourteen centuries ago, he and his fellow survivors had expressed similar hatred—and carried out darker acts of vengeance. But they'd been raw with grief over the sack of Daevabad and desperate to save what was left of their tribe. That was not the situation his people were in today.

He cleared his throat. "I'm sorry to hear they've been harassing you. Believe me when I say I'll speak to them." He sighed, looking to change the subject. "May I ask what has kept you in this part of Daevastana for so long? You said you've lived here a half-century now, yes? This does not seem an ideal posting for a man from the desert."

Abu Sayf smiled slightly. "I have come to find the snow lovely even if the cold remains brutal. And my wife's parents are here."

"You could have taken a posting in Daevabad and brought them with you."

The other man chuckled. "You have never had in-laws if you say something so easily."

The comment threw him. "No," Dara said. "I was never married."

"No one ever caught your eye?"

"Someone did," he said softly. "But I could not offer the future that she deserved."

Abu Sayf shrugged. "Then you will have to take my opinion on the matter of in-laws. And regardless, I did not wish to take a posting in Daevabad. It would have led to orders I do not care for."

Dara met his gaze. "You speak from experience."

The other man nodded. "I fought in King Khader's war when I was young."

"Khader was Ghassan's father, no?"

"Correct. The western half of Qart Sahar tried to secede during his reign, about two hundred years ago."

Dara rolled his eyes. "The Sahrayn have a habit of that. They tried to do the same just before I was born."

Abu Sayf's mouth quirked. "To be fair . . . I do believe secession was somewhat in fashion in your time."

He grunted. Had another djinn said that to him, Dara would have been irked, but considering Abu Sayf was his prisoner, he held his tongue. "Fair point. You fought the Sahrayn, then?"

"I'm not sure 'fought' is the best description," Abu Sayf replied. "We were sent to crush them, to terrorize a set of tiny villages on the coast." He shook his head. "Amazing places. They built directly from the sand of the seabed, blasting it into glass to create homes along the cliffs. If you pulled up the rugs, you could watch fish swim beneath your feet, and the way the glass glittered in the sun when we first arrived . . ." Wistfulness filled his eyes. "We destroyed them all, of course. Burned their ships, threw their bound leaders into the sea, and took back the boys for the Guard. Khader was a hard man."

"You were following orders."

"I suppose," Abu Sayf said quietly. "Never seemed right, though. It took us *months* to get out there, and I never really understood what kind of threat some little villages on the edge of the world could present to Daevabad. Why they had anything to do with Daevabad."

Dara shifted, not liking the fact that he'd essentially been backed into defending a Qahtani. "Surely if you wonder why Daevabad rules a distant Sahrayn village you should wonder why a Geziri family commands a Daeva city?"

"I suppose I never really thought of Daevabad as a Daeva city." Abu Sayf looked almost surprised. "Feels like the center of our world should belong to us all."

Before Dara could respond, there was the sound of running outside his tent. He shot to his feet.

Mardoniye appeared at the entrance the next instant, out of breath. "Come quickly, Afshin. There has been a letter from home."

15

ALI

"Okay, we're here," Ali said, throwing out his arm to prevent Nahri from slipping past. "Now will you tell me why you *had* to visit Sukariyya Street?"

Nahri was the very image of calmness at his side, her dark eyes studying the bustling shafit neighborhood like a hunter might survey its prey. "The house with the red door," she remarked softly under her breath.

Perplexed, Ali followed her gaze to a narrow, three-story wooden house that looked like it had been crammed between the two larger stone buildings on either side of it. A small open porch fronted the house, surrounding a red door painted with orange flowers. It was a cloudy afternoon, and shadows swallowed the building, obscuring it in gloom.

His unease instantly grew. The windows were boarded over, but with enough cracks that one could easily spy on the street from the inside, and a man sat on the steps of the neighboring building, reading a pamphlet with a bit too much studied disinterest. At a café across the street, two others sat ostensibly playing backgammon, their gazes occasionally flitting over to the red door.

Ali wasn't Citadel-trained for nothing. "It's being watched."

"Why do you think I brought you?" Nahri asked. A strangled sound of disbelief left his mouth, and she threw him a scornful look. "By the Most High, could you stop acting so jumpy?"

He stared at her. "*Someone tried to murder me a week ago.*"

Nahri rolled her eyes. "Let's go." She was off without another word.

Aghast, Ali watched as she strode purposefully towards the guarded house. Admittedly, there was little to give her away. Dressed in a rough-spun abaya and shawl, Nahri blended into the crowd of gossiping shafit shoppers and arguing laborers with ease.

Certainly a different look from the gold dress she wore to the feast. Ali's face abruptly filled with heat. No, he was not thinking about that dress. Not again. Instead, he hurried after her, cursing himself for getting dragged into whatever mysterious business Nahri claimed to have in the shafit district. He still wasn't sure what foolishness had made him agree to this; the days since he'd been poisoned were nothing but a pain-wracked blur of his mother's hovering, endless questions from the Royal Guard's investigators, and increasingly foul-tasting potions from the Banu Nahida.

She probably hexed you into agreeing. The Nahids could do that, couldn't they? Because surely not even Ali was reckless enough to sneak his sister-in-law out of the palace—*and* to agree to take the blame if they were found out—without being hexed.

By the time he caught up, Nahri was walking with a hand on her lower belly. There was suddenly a bump there, and her bag was gone from her shoulder. When she'd slipped it under her abaya,

God only knew, but she was sniffling by the time they neared the house. She wiped her eyes, a feigned limp affecting her walk.

The man next door dropped his pamphlet and rose to his feet, stepping in her path. "Can I help you, sister?"

Nahri nodded. "Peace be upon you," she greeted him. "I . . ." She sucked in her breath, clutching her exaggerated belly. "I'm sorry. My cousin said there was someone here . . . someone who helps women."

The man's gaze swept over them. "If indeed your cousin said such a thing, you'd know to bring her so she could vouch for you." He stared at Ali. "Is this your husband?"

"I didn't tell her it was I who needed help." Nahri lowered her voice. "And this isn't my husband."

The blood left Ali's face. "I—"

Nahri's hand darted out and she grasped his arm in a viselike grip. "Please . . ." She gasped, curling in on herself. "I'm in a lot of pain."

The man flushed, glancing helplessly down the street. "Oh, all right . . ." He crossed the porch, swiftly pulling open the red door. "Come quick."

Ali's heart raced, his mind screaming warnings of entrapment—this was, after all, not the first time he'd been tricked into entering a crumbling shafit building—but Nahri was already dragging him up the steps. They creaked underfoot, the wood soft from Daevabad's misty air. The shafit man shut the door behind them, throwing them into a gloomy darkness.

They were standing in a fairly simple entrance hall, with lacquered wooden walls and two doors. There were no windows, but the ceiling had been left open to the cloudy sky, making it feel as though they'd been dropped into a pit. The only other light came from a small oil lamp that sat burning next to a platter piled with sweets, in front of a garlanded rice-paper painting of a well-armed woman sitting astride a roaring tiger.

His patience with Nahri abruptly vanished. Someone had tried to kill him less than a week ago. He was drawing a line at lurking in some mysterious shafit house while pretending he'd impregnated his brother's wife.

Ali turned on her, selecting his words carefully. "My *dear*," he started. "Would you please explain what we're doing here?"

Nahri was gazing about the foyer with open curiosity. "We're here to meet a shafit doctor named Subhashini Sen. This is where he works."

The man who'd brought them in abruptly straightened up. "*He?*" Suspicion blossomed across his face, and he reached for his waist.

Ali was faster. He drew his zulfiqar in a breath, and the shafit man stepped back, his hand frozen on a wooden baton. He opened his mouth.

"Don't scream," Nahri said quickly. "Please. We don't mean anyone here harm. I only want to talk to the doctor."

The man's gaze darted nervously to the door on his left. "I . . . you can't."

Nahri looked baffled. "Excuse me?"

The shafit man swallowed. "You don't understand . . . she's very particular."

Curiosity lit Nahri's eyes. She must have also noticed the door the shafit man glanced at—because she was reaching for the handle in the next moment.

Ali panicked, not thinking. "Nahri, wait, don't—"

The shafit man's mouth fell open. "*Nahri?*"

God preserve me. Ali charged after her as she slipped into the room. Discretion be damned, they were getting out of here.

A clipped female voice with a thick Daevabadi accent cut him off the moment he passed the threshold.

"I have told all of you . . . at least a dozen times . . . if you interrupt me while I'm doing this procedure, I'm going to perform it on you next."

Ali froze. Not so much at the warning, but at the sight of its source. A shafit woman in a plain cotton sari knelt before them at the side of an elderly man lying on a cushion.

She had a needle inserted in his eye.

Aghast at the grisly sight, Ali opened his mouth to protest, but Nahri clapped a hand over it before he could speak.

"Don't," she whispered. She'd drawn back her veil, revealing the open delight dancing across her features.

The shafit guard joined them, wringing his hands. "Forgive me, Doctor Sen. I would never have interrupted you. Only . . ." He glanced nervously between Ali and Nahri, his eyes seeming to trace Ali's height and his zulfiqar anew. "You appear to have some guests from the palace."

The doctor hesitated. But only for a moment, and neither her hands nor attention so much as twitched. "Whether that's true or some symptom of madness, all of you can take a seat *right now*. I still have part of this cataract to remove."

There was no room for disobedience in the woman's stern voice. Ali backed up as quickly as the guard, dropping into one of the low couches lining the wall. He looked around the room. Full of light from an adjoining courtyard and copious lanterns, it was large enough to fit perhaps a dozen people. Three pallets were set low on the ground, the two not being used loosely covered in crisp linen. Cupboards lined one wall, and beside them a desk faced the courtyard, stacked high with books.

Nahri, of course, had ignored the doctor's command, and Ali watched helplessly as she drifted toward the desk and began flipping through a book, a grin on her face. He'd seen that look back when they'd been friends: when she'd read her first sentence correctly and when they'd gazed upon the moon through a human telescope, ruminating on the source of its shadows. Her desire to learn had been one of the things that had drawn him to her, a thing they had in common. He had *not*, however, expected

it to lead them to a shafit doctor in one of the city's more dangerous neighborhoods.

The sound of a crying infant broke the silence. The door
creaked open again, the wailing growing louder.

"Subha, love, are you already done, then?" A new voice, a
man's low rumble. "The baby is hungry, but she won't eat any of
the . . . *oh*." The man trailed off as he stepped into the infirmary.

The newcomer was enormous, easily one of the largest men Ali
had ever see. A mop of messy black curls fell past his shoulders,
and his nose looked like it had been broken multiple times. Ali
instantly raised his zulfiqar, but far from being armed, the man
held only a wooden spoon and a small baby.

Ali lowered his weapon with some embarrassment. Maybe
Nahri had a point about him being jumpy.

"And that's the last of it," the doctor announced, setting down
her needle and sitting back. She reached for a tin of salve and
then quickly bandaged the man's eyes. "You'll be keeping this on
for a full week, understand? Don't pester it."

She rose to her feet. The doctor looked younger than Ali
would have expected, but that might have been thanks to her
djinn blood, which was quite apparent. Though her dark brown
skin didn't have the telltale shine of a pureblood, her ears were as
peaked as his own and there was only a glimmer of brown in her
Agnivanshi-tin eyes. Her dark hair was plaited in a thick braid
that fell to her waist, a line of vermilion neatly set in the part.

She wiped her hands on a cloth tucked into her waistband and
then looked them over, a muscle working in her cheek. It was an
appraising gaze, one that flickered from the crying baby to linger
on Ali and Nahri before returning to the child.

Far from ruffled, she appeared unimpressed and rather irritated. "Manka . . . ," she started, and the doorman's head snapped
up. "I want you to help Hunayn to the recovery room. Parimal,
bring the baby here."

Both men instantly obeyed, one helping the groggy patient out while the other handed the baby over. The doctor took her child, her gaze not once leaving Ali and Nahri's faces as she rearranged her sari over her chest and the baby's sobs turned to happy suckling.

Ali swallowed, fixing his gaze upon the opposite wall. Nahri didn't seem bothered by any of this; she was still standing at the desk with a book in her hand.

The doctor narrowed her eyes, glaring at the Banu Nahida. "If you wouldn't mind . . ."

"But of course." Nahri set down the book and then took a seat next to Ali. "Was that cataract surgery you were doing?"

"Yes." The woman's voice stayed clipped. She took a seat on a wooden stool across from them. "And it's a complicated, delicate procedure . . . one I don't like interrupted."

"We're sorry," Ali rushed to say. "We didn't mean to barge in."

The woman's expression didn't change. He tried not to squirm; it felt like being confronted by Hatset crossed with the most terrifying of his old tutors.

The doctor pursed her lips, nodding at the zulfiqar. "Mind putting that away?"

He flushed. "Of course." He quickly sheathed the sword and then pulled down his face covering. It didn't seem right to intrude upon these people and remain anonymous. He cleared his throat. "Peace be upon you," he offered weakly.

Parimal's eyes went wide. "*Prince Alizayd?*" His gaze darted to Nahri. "Does that mean you're—"

"Daevabad's newest Nahid?" the doctor cut in, her voice filled with scorn. "Seems likely. So are the two of you here to shut us down, then? Planning to haul me off to the bronze boat for trying to help my people?"

The mention of the bronze boat sent ice into his veins; Ali had once been forced to do just that to a number of shafit caught in a riot his father had engineered to provoke the Tanzeem. "No," he said quickly. "Absolutely not."

"He's right," Nahri said. "I only wanted to meet you. I came across one of your patients recently. A man with a hole in his skull, like someone had cut—"

"Drilled." Nahri blinked and the doctor pressed on, her voice cold. "It is called a trepanation. If you believe yourself a healer, you should use the correct terms."

Ali felt Nahri tense slightly at his side, but her voice stayed calm. "Drilled, then. He claimed you were a physician, and I wanted to see if that was true."

"Did you?" The doctor's brows knit together in incredulity. "Is the little girl who makes potions for good luck and tickles away bad humors with a simurgh feather here to assess my training?"

Ali's mouth went dry.

Nahri bristled. "I'd daresay what I do is a bit more advanced than that."

The doctor lifted her chin. "Go on, then, make your examination. You've already intruded, and I don't suppose we can protest." She jerked her head at Ali. "That's why you brought your prince, no?"

"I'm not her prince," Ali corrected swiftly, glaring when Nahri threw him an annoyed look. "I said I'd take you to Sukariyya Street," he said, defending himself. "Not sneak you into some doctor's house by pretending that we . . . that you . . ." Very unhelpfully, the memory of Nahri's gold dress appeared again in his mind, and mortified heat stole over his face. "Never mind," he stammered.

"Traitor," Nahri said, her tone withering as she added something even less kind in Arabic. But it was clear neither Ali's desertion nor the doctor's hostility would stop her. She rose to her feet, crossing to the bookshelf.

"This is an impressive collection . . . ," she remarked, longing in her voice. She pulled two volumes loose. "Ibn Sina, al Razi . . . where did you get all this?"

"My father was a physician in the human world." The doctor gestured to her pointed ears. "Unlike me, he could pass, and so he did. He traveled and studied wherever he liked. Delhi, Istanbul, Cairo, Marrakesh. He was two hundred and fifty when some loathsome Sahrayn bounty hunter found him in Mauritania and dragged him to Daevabad." Her eyes lingered on the books. "He brought everything he could."

Nahri looked even more awed. "Your father spent *two hundred years* studying medicine in the human world?" When the doctor nodded, she pressed on. "Where is he now?"

The doctor swallowed hard before responding. "He died last year. A stroke."

The eagerness faded from Nahri's face. She carefully put the book back. "I'm sorry."

"As am I. It was a loss for my community." There was no self-pity in the doctor's voice. "He trained a few of us. My husband and I are the best."

Parimal shook his head. "I'm a glorified bonesetter. Subha is the best." There was affectionate pride in his voice. "Even her father said so, and that man did not compliment easily."

"Do the other doctors he trained practice here as well?" Nahri asked.

"No. It's not worth the risk. Purebloods would rather we die from coughs than live to procreate." Subha's grip on her baby tightened. "The Royal Guard comes in here and any number of my instruments could land me in prison under the weapons ban." She scowled. "Nor are the shafit entirely innocent. These are desperate times, and there are people who believe we're rich. I had a talented surgeon from Mombasa working here until a band of thieves kidnapped his daughter. He sold everything he owned to ransom her back and then fled. They were going to try and smuggle themselves out of the city." Her face fell. "I've heard nothing since. Many of the boats don't make it."

The boats? Ali stilled. Daevabad wasn't an easy place to escape. The courage—the desperation—it must take to load one's family onto a rickety smuggler's boat and pray it made it across the murderous waters . . .

We have failed them. We have utterly failed them. He took in the little family before him, remembering the shafit his mother had saved. There were thousands more like them in Daevabad, men and women and children whose potential and prospects had been coldly curtailed to suit the political needs of the city in which they had no choice but to live.

Lost in his thoughts, Ali only noticed Nahri reaching for a cabinet door when Parimal lunged forward.

"Wait, Banu Nahida, don't—"

But she'd already opened it. Ali heard her breath catch. "I take it this is for protection from those kidnappers, then?" she asked, pulling out a hefty metallic object.

It took Ali a moment to recognize it, and when he did, his blood ran cold.

It was a pistol.

"Nahri, put that down," he said. "Right now."

She threw him an irritated look. "Oh, give me some credit. I'm not going to shoot myself."

"It is a tool of iron and gunpowder and you are the Banu Nahida of Daevabad." When she frowned, looking confused, his voice broke in alarm. "It explodes, Nahri! We are literally creatures of fire; we don't go near gunpowder!"

"Ah." She swallowed and then set it back down, carefully easing the door shut. "Probably best to be careful, then."

"It's mine alone," Parimal said quickly, an obvious lie. "Subha knew nothing."

"You shouldn't have that here," Ali warned. "It's incredibly dangerous. And if you got caught?" He looked between the two. "Shafit possession of even a small amount of gunpowder is punished with execution." Granted, Ali suspected that was a punishment driven by fear of the shafit as much as it was of gunpowder—no pureblooded djinn wanted a weapon around that the shafit could handle with more finesse. "Add a pistol? This entire block would be leveled."

Subha gave him a wary look. "Is that a warning or a charge?"

"A warning," he replied, meeting her eyes. "One I'd beg you heed."

Nahri returned to his side, her swagger gone. "I'm sorry," she said softly. "Truly. I wasn't sure what to think when I saw that man. I've heard rumors of how desperate the shafit are, and I know how easily people can prey upon that type of fear."

Subha stiffened. "That you would think such a thing of me says far more about you."

Nahri winced. "You're probably right." She dropped her gaze, looking uncharacteristically chastened, and then reached for her bag. "I . . . I brought you something. Healing herbs and willow bark from my garden. I thought you could use them." She offered the bag.

The doctor made no move to take it. "You must know nothing of your family's history if you think I'd ever give 'medicine' prepared by a Nahid to a shafit." Her eyes narrowed. "Is that why you're here? To spread some new disease among us?"

Nahri recoiled. "Of course not!" Genuine shock filled her voice, tugging at Ali's heart. "I . . . I wanted to help."

"Help?" The doctor glared. "You broke into my practice because you wanted to *help*?"

"Because I wanted to see if we could work together," Nahri rushed. "On a project I'd like to propose to the king."

Subha was staring at the Banu Nahida as if she'd sprouted another head. "You want to work with *me*? On a project you intend to propose to the king of Daevabad?"

"Yes."

The doctor's gaze somehow grew even more incredulous. "Which is . . . ?"

Nahri pressed her hands together. "I want to build a hospital."

Ali gaped at her. She might as well have said she wished to throw herself before a karkadann.

"You want to build a hospital?" the doctor repeated blankly.

"Well, not so much *build* one as rebuild one," Nahri explained quickly. "My ancestors ran a hospital before the war, but it's in ruins now. I'd like to restore and reopen it."

The *Nahid hospital*? Certainly she couldn't mean . . . Ali shuddered, searching for a response. "You want to recover the Nahid hospital? The one near the Citadel?"

She looked at him with surprise. "*You* know about that place?"

Ali fought very hard to keep his face composed. There was nothing in Nahri's voice that suggested she'd asked the question in anything other than innocence. He dared a glance at Subha, but she looked lost.

He cleared his throat. "I . . . er . . . might have heard a thing or two about it."

"A thing or two?" Nahri pressed, eyeing him closely.

More. But what Ali knew about that hospital—about what had been done there before the war, and the brutal, bloody way the Nahids had been punished for it—those facts were not widely known and certainly not ones he was about to share. Especially with an already arguing Nahid and shafit.

He shifted uncomfortably. "Why don't you tell us more about your plan?"

Her eyes stayed on his, heavy with scrutiny for another moment, but then she sighed, turning back to Subha. "A single cramped infirmary is no place to treat the entirety of Daevabad's population. I want to start seeing people who *didn't* have to pay a bribe to gain access to me. And when I reopen the hospital, I want it open to all."

Subha narrowed her eyes. "To all?"

"To all," Nahri repeated. "Regardless of blood."

"Then you're delusional. Or you're lying. Such a thing would never be permitted. The king would forbid it, your priests would die of shock and horror . . ."

"It will take some convincing," Nahri cut in lightly. "I know. But I think we can make it work." She pointed at the bookshelf. "There are more books like that in the Royal Library; I've read them. I healed people in the human world for years, and I know the value in those methods. There are still plenty of times I prefer ginger and sage to zahhak blood and incantations." She gave Subha an imploring look. "That's why I came to find you. I thought we could work together."

Ali sat back, stunned. Across from him, Parimal appeared equally astonished.

Subha's expression turned colder. "And should I bring to this hospital a shafit man dying of a stroke . . ." Her voice trembled slightly, but her words were precise. "An ailment I suspect you could heal with a single touch . . . are you going to lay hands on him, Banu Nahida? In the presence of witnesses, of your pureblood fellows, would you use Nahid magic on a mixed-blood?"

Nahri hesitated, a wash of color sweeping over her face. "I think . . . initially . . . it might be better if we treated our own."

The shafit doctor laughed. It was bitter and utterly without humor. "You don't even see it, do you?"

"Subha . . . ," Parimal cut in, his voice thick with warning.

"Let her speak," Nahri interrupted. "I want to hear what she has to say."

"Then you will. You say you mean us no harm?" Subha's eyes flashed. "You are the very essence of harm, Nahid. You're the leader of the tribe—the faith—that calls us soulless, and the last descendant of a family that culled shafit for centuries as though we were rats. You were the companion of the Scourge of Qui-zi, a butcher who could have filled the lake with the shafit blood he spilt. You have the arrogance to burst into my infirmary—my *home*—uninvited, to inspect me as though you are my superior. And now you sit there offering pretty dreams of hospitals while I am wondering how to get my child out of this room alive. Why would I *ever* work with you?"

Thunderous silence followed Subha's fiery words. Ali felt the urge to speak up for Nahri, knowing her intentions had been good. But he also knew the doctor was right. He had seen firsthand the destruction that pureblood blunderings could cause the shafit.

A muscle worked in Nahri's cheek. "I apologize for the manner of my arrival," she said stiffly. "But my intent is sincere. I might be a Nahid and a Daeva, but I want to help the shafit."

"Then go to your Temple, renounce your ancestors' beliefs in front of the rest of your people, and declare us equals," Subha challenged. "If you want to help the shafit, deal with your Daevas first."

Nahri rubbed her head, looking resigned. "I can't do that. Not yet. I'd lose their support and be of use to no one." Subha snorted and Nahri glared at her, appearing angry now. "The shafit are hardly innocent in all of this," she retorted, heat creeping into her voice. "Do you know what happened to the Daevas caught in the Grand Bazaar after Dara's death? The shafit fell upon them like beasts, hurling Rumi fire and—"

"*Beasts?*" Subha snapped. "Ah, yes, because that's what we are to you. Ravaging animals who need to be controlled!"

"It isn't a terrible idea." The words slipped from Ali's mouth before he could think, and when both women whirled on him, he fought to stay composed. He was nearly as surprised as they were that he was speaking . . . but it *wasn't* a terrible idea. It was . . . actually sort of brilliant. "I mean, if my father approved this, and you proceeded carefully, I think the Daevas and the shafit working together would be extraordinary. And to build a hospital, something Daevabad could truly use? It would be an incredible achievement."

He caught Nahri's gaze then. Her eyes swam with an emotion he couldn't decipher . . . but she didn't look entirely pleased by his sudden support.

Nor did Subha. "So, you're also a part of this plan?" she asked him.

"No," Nahri said flatly. "He isn't."

"Then you're not good at convincing people to work with you, Nahid," Subha replied, putting her daughter against her shoulder to burp her. "With him at your side, I might actually believe some of this newfound concern you seem to have for the shafit."

"You'd work with *him*?" Nahri repeated in outraged disbelief. "You do realize it's his father currently persecuting your people?"

"I'm quite aware," Subha retorted. "There's also not a shafit in Daevabad who doesn't know how the prince feels about it." She turned her attention back to Ali. "I heard about the father and daughter you saved from the traffickers. People say they're living like nobles in the palace now."

Ali stared at her, his heart dropping. For the first time he thought he might have seen a flicker of interest in Subha's eyes, but he couldn't bear the thought of lying to her.

"They were very nearly returned to that trafficker because I wasn't careful enough. I think the Banu Nahida's plan is admirable, I do. But when things go wrong in Daevabad . . ." He gestured between Nahri and himself. "People like us rarely pay the same price as the shafit."

Subha paused. "It seems neither of you are good at convincing others to work with you," she said calmly.

Nahri swore under her breath, but Ali held his ground. "A partnership founded in deceit is no partnership at all. I would not wish to lie and bring you into danger unwarned."

Parimal reached out to touch a lock of the baby's curly hair. "It might be a good idea," he said softly to Subha. "Your father used to dream about building a hospital here."

Ali glanced at Nahri. "Well?"

She looked murderous. "What do *you* know about building hospitals?"

"What do you know about building anything?" he asked. "Have you given thought to how to collect and administer the funds needed to restore a ruined, ancient complex? It's going to be incredibly expensive. Time-consuming. Will you be assessing contracts and hiring hundreds of workers in between patients at the infirmary?"

Nahri's glare only intensified. "Those were some very pretty words about founding relationships in deceit."

Ali flinched, their fight in the garden coming back to him. "You said I owe you," he replied carefully. "Let me pay my debt. Please."

Whether or not that resonated, Ali couldn't tell. Nahri drew up, the emotion vanishing from her face as she turned back to Subha. "Fine, he's with me. Is that enough for you?"

"No," the doctor said bluntly. "Get the king's permission. Get money and draw up actual plans." She nodded at the door. "And don't come back until you do. I won't have my family caught up in this mess otherwise."

Ali stood. "Forgive us for our intrusion," he apologized in a rasp; his still-healing throat didn't seem to appreciate all the arguing he'd just done. "We'll be in touch soon, God willing." He snapped his fingers, trying to get Nahri's attention. She'd turned back to the desk and its treasures, not seeming particularly eager to leave. "*Nahri.*"

She dropped her hand from the book she'd been reaching for. "Oh, fine." She touched her heart, offering an exaggerated bow. "I look forward to speaking again, Doctor, and hearing what new invective you have to hurl upon my ancestors and tribe."

"An endless supply, I assure you," Subha responded.

Ali ushered Nahri out before she could reply. His hands were shaking as he secured the tail of his turban across his face and then pulled the outer door closed behind them. Then he leaned hard against it, the full meaning of what he'd just agreed to hitting him.

Nahri didn't seem as bothered. She was gazing upon the busy shafit neighborhood below. And though she'd pulled her niqab back over her face, as a man swept past carrying a board of steaming bread, she inhaled, and the cloth pulled close against her lips in a way Ali cursed himself for noticing.

She glanced back. "This doesn't make us friends again," she said, her voice sharp.

"What?" he stammered, thrown by the bald statement.

"Us working together . . . it doesn't mean we're friends."

He was more stung than he wanted to admit. "Fine," he replied, unable to check the snippiness in his tone. "I have other friends."

"Sure you do." She crossed her arms over her abaya. "What did Subha mean when she mentioned that shafit family and traffickers? Surely things haven't gotten that bad here?"

"It's a long story." Ali rubbed his aching throat. "But don't worry. I suspect Doctor Sen will be more than happy to tell it to you, among other things."

Nahri made a face. "If we can even do this. How do you propose we start?" she asked. "Since you seemed so convinced of your skills inside."

Ali sighed. "We need to talk to my family."

16

DARA

Dara sat in shocked silence in Manizheh's tent, attempting to process what Kaveh had just read aloud from the scroll. "Your son poisoned *Alizayd al Qahtani*?" he repeated. "Your son? Jamshid?"

Kaveh glared at him. "Yes."

Dara blinked. The words in the letter Kaveh held did not match Dara's memory of the merry, kindhearted young archer with a regrettably sincere attachment to his Qahtani oppressors. "But he is so loyal to them."

"He's loyal to *one* of them," Kaveh corrected. "Creator curse that bloody emir. Muntadhir's probably been in a drunken, paranoid spiral since his brother returned. Jamshid *would* do something foolish to help him." He threw an annoyed look at Dara. "You might remember whose life Jamshid took six arrows to save."

"Saving a life and taking one are very different matters." A concern Dara didn't like was shaping up in his mind. "And how would he even know *how* to poison someone?"

Kaveh raked a hand through his hair. "The Temple libraries, I suspect. He's always been quite taken with Nahid lore. He used to get in trouble when he was a novitiate for sneaking into their archives." His eyes darted to Manizheh. "Nisreen said this looked somewhat similar to . . ."

"To one of my experiments?" Manizheh finished. "It is, though I doubt anyone but she would recognize that. Jamshid must have stumbled upon some of my old notes." She crossed her arms, her expression grave. "Does she think anyone else suspects him?"

Kaveh shook his head. "No. They believe it was his cupbearer, and the boy was killed in the melee, though she warned they were still interrogating the kitchen staff. She also said that if . . . that if Jamshid fell under suspicion, she was prepared to take the blame."

Dara was stunned. "*What?* Forgive me, but why should she? It is your son who is at fault, and foolishly so. What if his ingredients are followed back to the infirmary? Nahri might be blamed!"

Manizheh took a deep breath. "You are certain this letter was not traced in any way?"

Kaveh spread his hands. "We took all the precautions you taught us. She was only to contact me in an emergency. And respectfully, Banu Nahida—we are running low on time." He nodded at her worktable. "Your experiments . . . have you had luck figuring out how to limit—"

"It doesn't matter. Not anymore." Manizheh exhaled. "Tell me our plans once again," she commanded.

"We cross into the city and take the Royal Guard with the assistance of the marid and the ifrit," Dara answered automatically. "A contingent of my men stay behind with Vizaresh and his ghouls"—he had to fight to keep the distaste from his voice—"while we continue on to the palace." He glanced between them. "You told me you have a plan for taking care of the king?"

"Yes," Manizheh said briskly.

Dara paused. Manizheh had been cagey about this for months, and while he didn't want to step out of bounds, he felt now would be a good time to understand the full scope of their plans. "My lady, I am your Afshin; it might be helpful if you would tell me more." His voice rose in warning. "We don't know how my magic might react to Suleiman's seal. If the king is able to cripple me—"

"Ghassan al Qahtani will be dead before either of us sets foot in the palace. It's being arranged, and I will be in a position to tell you more in a few days. But speaking of Suleiman's seal . . ." Her gaze flickered from Dara to Kaveh. "Have you learned anything more about the ring?"

The grand wazir's face fell. "No, my lady. I have bribed and cajoled everyone I know, from concubines to scholars. Nothing. There is no one ring he wears consistently, and there are no records of how it's passed to a new owner. A historian was executed last year simply for attempting to research the seal's origins."

Manizheh grimaced. "I fared no better, and I spent decades scouring the Temple archives. There are no texts, no records."

"Nothing?" Dara repeated. "How is that possible?" The success of their plan hinged on Manizheh taking possession of Suleiman's seal ring. Without it . . .

"Zaydi al Qahtani probably had all the records burned when he took the throne," Manizheh said bitterly. "But I remember Ghassan going into seclusion for a few days after his father's funeral. When he reappeared, he looked as though he'd been ill—and the seal mark was on his face." She paused, considering this. "He never left the city again. He used to enjoy hunting in the lands beyond the Gozan when he was young. But after he became king, he never strayed farther than the mountains inside the threshold."

Kaveh nodded. "The seal ring may be tied to Daevabad—it's certainly never been used to stop any wars outside the city." He glanced at Dara. "Unless things were different in your day?"

"No," Dara replied slowly. "The members of the Nahid Council would pass it among each other, taking turns serving with it." He thought hard, trying to recall what he remembered—it always hurt to think about his old life. "But I only knew that because of the mark on their face. I do not recall ever seeing a ring."

After another moment, Manizheh spoke again. "Then we need his son. We'll have to make sure Muntadhir survives the initial siege so he can tell us how to take the seal. He's Ghassan's successor. He must know." She eyed Kaveh. "Can you find a way to do this?"

Kaveh looked apprehensive. "I don't think that's information Muntadhir is going to give up easily . . . particularly in the wake of his father's death."

"And I don't think it's going to be difficult to force Ghassan's wastrel son to talk," Manizheh countered. "I imagine the very prospect of being alone in a room with Dara will have him spilling any number of royal secrets."

Dara dropped his gaze, his stomach tightening. Not that he should be surprised she'd use him as a threat. He was the Scourge of Qui-zi, after all. No one—least of all the man Nahri had been forced to wed—would want to be on the receiving end of his supposed vengeance.

Kaveh's face seemed to momentarily display equal misgivings, but then the other man bowed. "Understood, Banu Nahida."

"Good. Kaveh, I would like you to prepare for your journey back to Daevabad. If there's a conflict brewing between those sand-fly princes, make sure our people—not to mention our respective children—stay out of it. Dara will enchant a carpet for you and teach you how to fly it." Manizheh turned back to her worktable. "I need to finish this."

Dara followed Kaveh out of the tent, grabbing his sleeve as soon as they were clear. "We need to talk."

Kaveh threw him an annoyed look. "Surely you can teach me how to fly one of your Creator-forsaken tapestries later."

"It is not about that." He pulled Kaveh toward his tent. This was not a discussion he wanted anyone to overhear—nor a topic he suspected Kaveh would take well to.

Kaveh half stumbled inside and then glanced around Dara's tent, his expression souring further. "Do you sleep surrounded by weapons? Do you truly not have a single personal possession that doesn't deal death?"

"I have what I require." Dara crossed his arms over his chest. "But we are not here to discuss my belongings."

"Then what do you want, Afshin?"

"I want to know if Jamshid's loyalty to Muntadhir is going to be a problem."

Kaveh's eyes flashed. "My son is a loyal Daeva, and considering what you did to him, you have some nerve questioning anything he does."

"I am Banu Manizheh's Afshin," Dara said flatly. "I am in charge of her military conquest and the future security of our city . . . so yes, Kaveh, I need to know if a well-connected, well-trained former soldier—*who just poisoned Muntadhir's political rival*—is going to be a problem."

An expression of pure hostility swept over Kaveh's face. "I am done with this conversation." He turned on his heel.

Dara took a deep breath, hating himself for what he was about to do. "My slave abilities came back to me that night . . . before the boat," he called out as Kaveh reached the tent flap. "It was brief—quite frankly, I still don't know what happened. But when I was in that dancer's salon, I felt a surge of magic, and then I could see her desires, her wishes all spread before me." Dara paused. "She had at least a dozen. Fame, money, a leisurely retirement with a lovesick Muntadhir. But when I saw into Muntadhir's mind next . . . it was not the dancer who occupied it."

Kaveh halted, his hands in fists at his sides.

"There was no throne either, Kaveh," Dara said. "No riches, no women, no dreams of being king. Muntadhir's only desire was your son at his side."

The other man was trembling, his back still turned.

Dara continued, his voice low. "I mean Jamshid absolutely no harm, I swear to you. I swear on the Nahids," he added. "And what we say here never has to leave this tent. But, Kaveh . . ." His tone grew imploring. "Banu Manizheh is relying on us both. We need to be able to talk about this."

A long moment of silence stretched between them, the cheerful chatter and clash of his sparring men beyond the tent at odds with the tension rising inside it.

And then Kaveh spoke. "He did nothing," he whispered. "Jamshid took six arrows for him and all Muntadhir did was hold his hand while his father let my boy suffer." He turned around, looking haunted—and old, as though the very memory had aged him. "How do you do that to someone you claim to love?"

Dara unwittingly thought of Nahri, and he didn't have an answer for the man. Suddenly, he felt quite old himself. "How long"—he cleared his throat, suspecting it still wouldn't take much for Kaveh to storm out—"have they been involved with each other?"

Kaveh's face crumpled. "At least ten years," he confessed softly. "If not longer. He was careful to hide it from me in the beginning. I suspect he feared I would disapprove."

"Such a fear is understandable," Dara said, quietly sympathetic. "People have often looked askance at such relationships."

Kaveh shook his head. "It wasn't that. I mean . . . it was in part, but our name and our wealth would have shielded him from the worst. *I* would have shielded him," he said, his voice growing fiercer. "His happiness and safety are my concerns, not the gossip of others." He sighed. "*Muntadhir* was the problem. Jamshid thinks because he is charming and speaks Divasti and loves wine and entertains his cosmopolitan court that he is different. He is not. Muntadhir is Geziri to the core and will always be loyal to his father and his family first. Jamshid refuses to see that, no matter how many times that man breaks his heart."

Dara sat on his cushion. He patted the pillow next to him, and Kaveh fell into it, still looking half reluctant. "Does Banu Manizheh know?"

"No," Kaveh said quickly. "I would not trouble her with this." He rubbed his silvering temples. "I can keep Jamshid away during the invasion and for those first few days—I'll lock him up if need be. But when he finds out about Muntadhir—about what happens after Manizheh gets what she needs . . ." He shook his head, his eyes dimming. "He'll never forgive me for that."

"Then blame me," Dara offered, his stomach twisting even as he said it. "Tell him Muntadhir was to be kept alive as a hostage, and I killed him in anger." He looked away. "It is what everyone expects from me anyway." Dara might as well use it to quietly ease the grief between the Pramukhs. He'd already hurt them enough.

Kaveh stared at his hands, twisting the gold ring on his thumb. "I don't know that it matters," he said finally. "I'm about to become one of the most infamous traitors in our history. I don't think Jamshid will ever look at me the same way again, regardless of what happens to Muntadhir. I don't think anyone will."

"I wish I could tell you that it becomes easier." Dara's gaze swept over his tent, the accumulated weapons that were his only possessions. His only identity in this world. "I suppose our reputations are small prices to pay if it means our people will be safe."

"Small consolation if our loved ones never speak to us again." He glanced at Dara. "Do you think she'll forgive you?"

Dara knew who Kaveh meant, and he knew all too well the answer, deep in his heart. "No," he said honestly. "I do not think

Nahri will ever forgive me. But she'll be safe with the rest of our people and reunited with her mother. That is all that matters."

For the first time since he'd seen Kaveh again, there was a hint of sympathy in the other man's voice. "I think they'll get along well," he said softly. "Nahri has always reminded me of her mother. So much so that it hurts at times. As a girl, Manizheh delighted in her cleverness exactly the way Nahri does. She was sharp, she was charming, she had a smile like a weapon." Tears came to his eyes. "When Nahri claimed to be her daughter, it felt like someone stole my breath."

"I can imagine," Dara said. "You thought she was dead after all."

Kaveh shook his head, his expression turning grim. "I knew Manizheh was alive."

"But . . ." Dara thought back to what Kaveh had told him. "You said you were the one who found her body . . . you were so upset . . ."

"Because that part was true," Kaveh replied. "All of it. I *was* the one who found Manizheh and Rustam's traveling party after they vanished. The fire-scorched plain, the torn remains of their companions. Manizheh—or the woman I thought was Manizheh— and Rustam with their heads . . ." He trailed off, his voice shaking. "I brought their bodies back to Daevabad. It was the first time I saw the city, the first time I met Ghassan . . ." Kaveh wiped his eyes. "I remember almost nothing of it. Had it not been for Jamshid, I would have thrown myself on her funeral pyre."

Dara was stunned. "I don't understand."

"She planned for me to find them." Kaveh's expression was vacant. "She knew I was the only one Ghassan would believe and hoped my obvious grief would protect her from his pursuit. Those are the lengths that demon pushed her to."

Dara stared at him, completely lost for words. He could not imagine coming upon the body of the woman he loved in such a way; he probably *would* have thrown himself on the funeral pyre, though knowing his cursed fate, someone would have found a way to drag him back. And the fact that Manizheh had done such a thing to Kaveh—a man she clearly loved—spoke to a dark ruthlessness he hadn't thought she possessed.

Then another thought struck him. "Kaveh, if Manizheh was able to feign her own death in such a manner, you do not think Rustam . . ."

Kaveh shook his head. "It was the first thing I asked her when we met again. All she would tell me was that he attempted a magic he should not have. She does not speak of him otherwise." He paused, old grief crossing his face. "They were very close, Dara. Sometimes it seemed like Rustam was the only one who could keep her feet on the ground."

Dara thought of his own sister. Tamima's bright smile and constant mischief. The brutal way she'd been killed—punished in Dara's stead.

And now he was about to introduce more brutality, more bloodshed into their world. Guilt wrapped his heart, constricting his throat. "You should try to do what you can to pull Jamshid and Nahri away from the Qahtanis, Kaveh. From all of them," he clarified, having little doubt Alizayd was already trying to worm his way back into Nahri's good graces. "It will make what is to come easier."

Silence fell between them again until Kaveh finally asked, "Can you do it, Afshin? Can you truly take the city? Because this . . . we cannot go through all of this again."

"Yes," Dara said quietly. He had no choice. "But if I may ask something of you?"

"What?"

"I am not certain of my fate after the conquest. I am not certain . . ." He paused, struggling for the right words. "I know what I am to people in this generation. What I did to Jamshid, to

Nahri . . . There may come a day that Manizheh will find it easier to rule if the 'Scourge of Qui-zi' is not at her side. But you will be there."

"What are you asking, Afshin?"

That Kaveh did not protest such a future spoke volumes, but Dara pushed aside the sickness rising within him. "Do not let her become like them," he rushed on. "Manizheh trusts you. She'll listen to your guidance. Do not let her become like Ghassan." Silently, in his heart, he added the words he could not yet speak. *Do not let her become like her ancestors, the ones who made me into a Scourge.*

Kaveh stiffened, a little of his usual hostility returning. "She won't be another Ghassan. She never could be." His voice was shaky; this was the man who loved Manizheh and spent his nights at her side, not the cautious grand wazir. "But frankly, I would not blame her if she wanted some vengeance." He rose to his feet, not seeming to realize his words had just sent Dara's heart to the floor. "I should go."

Dara could barely speak. He nodded instead, and Kaveh swept out, the tent flap blowing in the cold wind.

This war is never going to end. Dara stared at his weapons again, and then closed his eyes, taking a deep breath of the snow-scented air.

Why do you make those? The memory of Khayzur came to him. After finding Dara, the peri had taken him to the desolate icy mountains he called home. Dara had been a wreck in those early years after slavery, his soul shattered, his memory a blood-colored mosaic of violence and death. Before he could even recall his own name, he had taken to making weapons out of everything he found. Fallen branches became spears, rocks were chipped into blades. It was an instinct Dara hadn't understood, and he hadn't been able to answer Khayzur's gentle quizzing. None of the peri's questions made sense. *Who are you? What did you like? What makes you happy?*

Confused, Dara had simply stared at him. *I am an Afshin*, he'd reply each time—as though that answered everything. It took years for him to remember the better parts of his life. Afternoons with his family and galloping on horseback across the plains surrounding the Gozan. The dreams he'd harbored before his name became a curse, and the way Daevabad had hummed with magic during feast days.

By then, Khayzur's questions had changed. *Would you like to go back?* The peri had suggested a dozen different ways. They could attempt to remove his Afshin mark and Dara could settle in a distant Daeva village under a new name. He'd never lose the emerald in his eyes, but his people treaded lightly around former ifrit slaves. He might have made a life for himself.

And yet—he had never wanted to. He remembered too much of the war. Too much of what his duty had cost him. Dara had to be dragged back to his people, and that was a truth he hadn't even told Nahri.

And now here he was again, with his weapons and his cause.

It will end, he tried to tell himself, pushing away memories of Khayzur.

Dara would make sure.

17

NAHRI

It should have been a lovely morning. They'd gathered at a pavilion high upon the palace wall, the same place Ali and Nahri had once stargazed. The sun was warm, and there was not a cloud in the sky, the lake stretching like a cool glass mirror below them.

A plush embroidered rug deeper than Nahri's hand and large enough to sit fifty had been laid out under painted silk awnings and spread with a sumptuous feast. Every fruit one might imagine lay spread before them, from slivers of golden mango and bright persimmon to gleaming silver cherries that made a distinctly metallic crunch when chewed and trembling crimson custard apples whose similarity to a beating heart made Nahri shudder. Delicate pastries of creamed honey, sweetened cheese, and roasted nuts shared space between bowls of yoghurt strained and shaped into herb-brushed balls and platters of spiced semolina porridge.

And even better, a dish of fried fava beans with onions, eggs, and country bread, an unexpected delight indicating that the quiet old Egyptian cook who served in the palace kitchens had a hand in the morning's meal. In the earliest and darkest months after Dara's death, Nahri had noticed a number of dishes from her old home making their way into her meals. Nothing fancy, but rather, the comfort fare and street food she most loved. During a bout of homesickness, Nahri had once tried to find the cook, a meeting that hadn't gone well. The man had burst into tears when she smilingly introduced herself, his fellows in the kitchen later telling her that he rarely spoke and was considered slightly touched in the head. Nahri had dared not intrude upon him again, but he'd kept quietly preparing food for her, often slipping small tokens next to her dishes: a garland of jasmine, a reed folded to resemble a felucca, a carved wooden bangle. The gifts charmed her as much as they saddened her: reminders of the way Daevabad walled her off from a former countryman.

"Did Muntadhir tell you we found a troupe of conjurers, Abba?" Zaynab asked, pulling Nahri from her thoughts. The princess had been valiantly trying to make small talk with them all since they sat down, a task Nahri didn't envy. Muntadhir was sitting across from her, so stiff he might have been embalmed, and Hatset was slapping Ali's hand every time he reached for a dish without letting her try it first, because "your father's tasters are clearly useless." "They're excellent," Zaynab continued. "They summoned up a whole menagerie of birds that sang the loveliest of melodies. They'll be perfect for Navasatem."

"I hope they've signed a contract, then," Ghassan said lightly. Oddly enough, the djinn king seemed contentedly amused by this barbed family breakfast. "The last few Eids, I've found the entertainers I've hired suddenly lured away to Ta Ntry by promises of fees that are mysteriously always twice the amount we'd agreed to."

Hatset smiled, passing another loaded plate to Ali. "Alu-baba, enough with all those scrolls," she chided, gesturing at the pile of papers next to Ali. "What work could you possibly already have?"

"I suspect those scrolls have to do with his reason for arranging all this," Ghassan said knowingly, taking a sip of his coffee.

Muntadhir straightened up even further. "You didn't tell me Alizayd arranged this."

"I didn't want you finding a reason not to attend." Ghassan shrugged. "And waking before noon for once will not harm you." He turned back to his youngest. "How are *you* feeling?"

"Fully recovered," Ali said smoothly, touching his heart with a nod in Nahri's direction. "A thing I owe entirely to the Banu Nahida."

Ghassan's attention turned to her. "And has the Banu Nahida made any progress in discovering more about the poison used?"

Nahri forced herself to meet his gaze. Ghassan was her captor, and she never forgot it—but right now, she needed him on her side. "Regretfully, no. Nisreen thinks it might have been something in his tamarind juice designed to react to the sugar in the sweets. The prince is known to favor the drink in place of wine."

Muntadhir snorted. "I suppose that's what you get for being so obnoxious about your beliefs."

Ali's eyes flashed. "And how very interesting, akhi, that it was always you who was loudest about mocking me for them."

Hatset cut in. "Have *you* learned anything more about the poison?" she demanded, staring at Ghassan. "You told me you were having the kitchen staff questioned."

"And I am," Ghassan replied tersely. "Wajed is overseeing the investigation himself."

The queen held her husband's eye another moment, looking unimpressed, but then glanced at her son. "Why don't you tell us why you've brought us here?"

Ali cleared his throat. "It's not actually me alone. While I've been recovering, the Banu Nahida and I have been discussing working together on a very promising project. Her infirmary . . . it's very crowded."

He stopped as if this explained everything, and seeing confusion on their faces, Nahri swept in, silently cursing her partner. "I want to build a hospital," she said plainly.

"*We,*" Ali muttered, tapping on his mountain of scrolls. "What?" he asked defensively when she gave him an annoyed look. "I didn't fiddle with numbers all week just so you can cut me out."

Muntadhir set his cup down so hard that the dark plum liquid inside sloshed out. It did not look like juice. "Of course you went to him. I try to talk sense into you, and your response is to race to your blockhead of a tutor the minute he comes riding back—"

"Should it make a *difference,*" Ghassan interrupted, with a look that silenced them all, "I would like to hear them out." He turned to Nahri. "You want to build a hospital?"

Nahri nodded, trying to ignore the daggers Muntadhir was shooting at her from his eyes. "Well, not so much build a new one as restore an old one. I hear the complex my ancestors once used remains near the Citadel."

Ghassan's gaze was so calmly appraising it made the hairs on the back of her neck rise. "And where, dear daughter, did you hear such a thing?"

Her heart skipped a beat; she had to tread carefully or some poor Daeva would suffer for it, of that she had no doubt. "A book," she lied, trying to keep the strain from her voice. "And some rumors."

Zaynab was blinking at her with barely concealed alarm, Muntadhir studying the rug as though it were the most fascinating one he'd ever seen. Nahri prayed they'd stay silent.

"A book," Ghassan repeated. "And some rumors."

"Indeed," Nahri replied, rushing on as if she hadn't noticed the suspicion in his voice. "The descriptions of the hospital in its heyday are extraordinary." She casually picked up her teacup.

"I've also heard a trio of djinn freed from ifrit slavery are living in the remains."

"That's quite a lot of information to glean from some rumors."

Help came from a very unexpected direction. "Oh, stop menacing the poor girl, Ghassan," Hatset interrupted. "She's not wrong. I know about those former slaves as well."

Nahri stared at her. "You *do*?"

Hatset nodded. "One of them is a kinsman of mine." Nahri didn't miss the quick dart of her eyes to Ali. "A brilliant scholar— but a deeply eccentric man. He refuses to return to Ta Ntry, so I keep an eye on him and make sure he doesn't starve himself. I've met the two women there as well. The eldest, Razu, can spin some rather exciting tales of the hospital's past. Their magic is quite formidable, and I suspect she and her partner would be happy to help restore the place."

Nahri swallowed as the queen looked at her; there was far too much knowing in her eyes. But Nahri also suspected Hatset wouldn't betray her—not with Ali at her side. "That's my hope as well."

Ghassan was studying his family with open suspicion, but he let it go, returning his attention to Nahri. "That sounds like an admirable fantasy, Banu Nahida, but even if you had a building, you're barely able to keep up with your patients now. How could you possibly treat an entire hospital's worth?"

Nahri was prepared for the question. Her mind had been turning since she'd left the Sens. Subha's father had arrived alone in Daevabad with two centuries of medical knowledge and used it to train others. Surely, Nahri could do the same. "I'll have help," she explained. "I want to start teaching students."

Genuine surprise lit the king's face. "Students? I was under the impression most of the healing you do couldn't be accomplished by someone without your blood."

"A lot can't," Nahri admitted. "But many of the basics can. With proper training, I could shift some of my workload to others. We could see more people, and I could let them stay on to properly recover instead of booting them out of the infirmary as quickly as possible."

Ghassan took a sip of his coffee. "And earn some acclaim from your tribe, no doubt, for recovering an institution once so important to the Daevas."

"This isn't about tribal politics or pride," Nahri argued. "And I don't intend to only teach Daevas; I'll take students from any background if they're bright and willing."

"And between your duties in the infirmary now and teaching students, when exactly are you going to have time to oversee the rebuilding of a ruined, ancient hospital? Not to mention the cost . . . ah." His eyes narrowed on Ali. "The 'we.' A preposterously expensive public works project. Little wonder you have involved yourself."

"You did tell me to find something to do," Ali replied, a petty edge in his voice. Nahri clenched her teacup, resisting the urge to hurl it at his head. If she could check her temper, so could he. "But it wouldn't be preposterously expensive if handled correctly," Ali continued, gesturing to the armful of scrolls he'd brought. "I've been running estimates with people at the Treasury, and we've devised numerous proposals." He plucked up one of the fatter scrolls. "I know how important financials are, so I haven't spared any details."

Ghassan held up a hand. "Spare the details. We will be sitting here until Navasatem if I let you start talking about the specifics. I can have my own accountants check your proposals later." He tilted his head. "I am, after all, quite aware of your cleverness when it comes to numbers."

The words hung between them for a moment. Unwilling to

let whatever drama swirled around her in-laws eclipse her hospital, Nahri spoke quickly. "I'm willing to offer a portion of my dowry as well, enough to cover the materials and room and board for an initial class of twenty students. And once we start seeing patients, we can charge those who can pay on a sliding scale."

"I also thought the queen might assist me in meeting with the Ayaanle trade envoy," Ali added. "Should Ta Ntry find a way to make restitutions for its unfortunate tax situation, we could use the revenue to fix a lot of things in Daevabad."

Hatset raised her palms, smiling sweetly. "It can be difficult to predict financial matters."

Ali returned her smile. "Not when they can be audited, Amma," he said pleasantly.

Hatset drew up, looking taken aback, and Nahri saw a far more genuine smile spread across Ghassan's face.

But it was not a pleasure that erased his skepticism. "And the staffing cost?" he asked. "However formidable their magic, a handful of freed djinn are not going to be able to build and maintain a complex of that size."

Before Nahri could respond, Ali spoke up again. "I had been thinking in another direction." He toyed with a length of prayer beads looped around his wrist. "I'd like to tear down the shafit . . . *exchange* . . . in the Grand Bazaar and reuse its materials, as well as free those being held there. I'll offer them—and any shafit qualified and interested—employment in the hospital restoration."

Nahri blinked, surprised but pleased at the suggestion. She wasn't sure what exchange Ali was talking about—though the naked disdain in his voice made clear his opinion of it. But Subha's accusations about Nahri's complicity in the oppression of Daevabad's shafit had struck deep. Nahri *didn't* know much about the lives of a people she quietly belonged to, but this seemed like a good way to help some of them.

But Ghassan's expression had darkened. "I thought you'd learned to be warier about getting involved with the shafit, Alizayd."

"It's not just him," Muntadhir cut in. His gaze locked on hers. "And I suspect that's not all they want. This has to do with that shafit physician you were so eager to track down, doesn't it?" He turned back to his father. "She came to me with this weeks ago, talking about how she wanted to start working with shafit doctors and treating shafit patients."

Shock fell across the pavilion, so thick she could almost feel it. Zaynab dropped her cup, the queen taking a sharp breath.

Nahri silently cursed; it wasn't enough for Muntadhir to dis-agree, apparently. He also needed to undermine her by rudely letting slip a risky plan she'd wanted to be far more precise in proposing.

Ghassan recovered first. "You intend to *heal* shafit?"

Nahri answered honestly, though she loathed the words. "No. Not myself . . . not at first. We'd work and study alongside each other, the djinn using magic and the shafit using human tech-niques. I'm hoping it might prove a fresh start for the Daevas and the shafit, and that maybe, in the future, we'll be able to cross those lines."

Ghassan shook his head. "Your priests would never approve of such a thing. I am not certain *I* approve of such a thing. The first time a shafit doctor hurts a Daeva—or the reverse—people will be rioting in the streets."

"Or they might learn to get along a bit better." It was the queen, still looking slightly taken aback, though her words were encouraging. "It is the Banu Nahida who is proposing this project. The Daevas are obliged to obey her, are they not?" She shrugged lightly, as though the conversation hadn't turned fraught. "It is her responsibility and her risk if she wants to provoke them."

"Your support is appreciated," Nahri replied, checking her sarcasm. "I figured we could start the rebuilding effort first—of that I am certain my people would approve. I will go to the priests afterward and tell them of my plans regarding the shafit. *Tell* them," she clarified. "I'll listen to their concerns, but as the queen pointed out, I am the Banu Nahida. What I wish to share of my abilities at my hospital is my decision."

Ghassan leaned back. "If we're speaking so frankly . . . what do *we* get out of this? You're asking me to lay out money and risk to restore a monument to your ancestors . . . people who, as you may recall, were the enemies of mine." He arched a dark eyebrow. "The health of Daevabadis aside, I am not naive to the fact that this empowers you, not me."

"But what if it was truly a joint project?" Zaynab spoke this time, softly at first, though her voice grew more assured as she continued. "An extension of your outreach to the Daevas, Abba. It would be greatly symbolic, especially in light of the generation celebrations." She smiled at her father. "Maybe we could even try to finish it in time for Navasatem? You could open it yourself, as a crowning achievement for your rule."

Ghassan inclined his head, but at his daughter's warm smile, his expression had softened. "A rather plain appeal to vanity, Zaynab."

"Because I know you well," she teased. "Peace between the tribes is why you wished to see Muntadhir and Nahri marry, isn't it? Perhaps he could even go with her to the Temple to seek the priests' blessing."

Nahri had to work to keep her expression neutral at that. She was glad for Zaynab's support, but she knew how protective her people were of their customs. "Only Daevas are permitted to enter the Temple. It's been that way for centuries."

Hatset gave her a pointed look. "If you're willing to take djinn money for your hospital, Banu Nahida, I think you'd be willing to let one of us darken the doorstep of your Temple." She laid a hand on her son's shoulder. "But it should be Alizayd. He is the one who wishes to partner with you."

"It should be Muntadhir," Zaynab corrected, pleasantly firm. "He is her husband, and his history is a bit less . . . complicated . . . when it comes to the Daevas." She plucked a pink milk-sweet from one of the silver platters, taking a delicate bite. "Would it not be good to see them work together, Abba? I think it would do much to quell all this unnecessary and divisive talk from some of the other tribes."

Nahri did not miss the sugary smile Zaynab aimed at her mother . . . nor the way Hatset carefully nodded once, not so much in agreement, but in quiet approval of her daughter's maneuvering.

Muntadhir was looking at the three women with outrage. "Me? I don't even agree with this! Why do I have to convince the priests of anything?"

"I'll do the convincing," Nahri said sharply. She wasn't letting Muntadhir ruin this. "You might even enjoy it," she added quickly, trying for more tact. "Jamshid gives a wonderful tour."

Her husband glowered in response but stayed silent.

Ghassan seemed to study her again. It was the same look she'd seen when he'd welcomed her to Daevabad. The same look he'd worn the first time they'd negotiated her betrothal, the look of a gambler willing to bet a great deal if the risk was carefully calculated.

The first time she'd seen that expression it had set her at ease; Nahri had always preferred pragmatists. But now it made her skin crawl. Because she'd seen what Ghassan was capable of when his gambles didn't pay off.

"Yes," he finally said, and her heart skipped. "You may proceed. With *extreme* caution. I intend to be consulted on every development and every snag." He wagged his finger in Ali's direction. "You, in particular, are to be careful. I know how passionate you get about all of this. You are to build a hospital, not start climbing up on minbars and giving the masses sermons about equality, understand?"

Ali's eyes flashed and Nahri did not miss the quick way Zaynab "accidentally" struck his knee, reaching rather purposefully for a serving knife. "Yes, Abba," Ali said hoarsely. "I understand."

"Good. Then you may tell your priests you have my blessing, Banu Nahida, and take Muntadhir with you. But you are to make it clear this is your idea, not ours. I won't have any Daeva spreading rumors that we dragged them into this."

She nodded. "Understood."

The king regarded them all. "This pleases me," he declared, rising to his feet. "It will be good for Daevabad to see us working together in peace." He hesitated and then snapped his fingers at Ali. "Come, Alizayd. If you're going to brag about your financial acumen, you might as well help me. I've a meeting with a particularly slippery governor from Agnivansha and could use you."

Ali looked uncertain, but after a nudge from his mother, he stood. Nahri started to do the same.

Muntadhir's hand fell lightly on her wrist. "*Sit,*" he hissed under his breath.

With a quick glance between them, Zaynab rose hastily. Nahri didn't blame her; Muntadhir's handsome face was furious, a vein jumping in his temple. "Enjoy the Temple, akhi," she teased.

"About that . . ." Hatset pulled Zaynab close. "Take a walk with me, daughter."

The door leading to the steps closed, and then they were alone, save for the wind and the gulls.

Muntadhir turned to her, a shaft of sunshine illuminating the tired shadows under his eyes. It looked as though he hadn't slept in days. "Is this because of our fight?" he demanded. "Are you really ready to throw in with Alizayd and his lunatic ideas because of what I said?"

Nahri's temper flared. "I'm not *throwing in* with anyone. I'm doing this for myself and for my people. And as you'll recall, I came to you first. I tried to talk to you about these things—things close to my heart—and you dismissed me." She fought to keep the bitterness from her voice. "I suppose I shouldn't have been surprised. You made plain what you think of the foolish girl from Cairo."

He pressed his lips into a grim line, dropping his gaze. The moment stretched, silent and tense.

"I shouldn't have said that," he finally said. "I'm sorry. I was upset about Jamshid, and about Ali returning . . ."

"I've had enough of men hurting me because they were upset." Her voice was hard, so much so that Muntadhir looked startled. But Nahri didn't care. She rose to her feet, placing her chador over her head. "I won't have it from the man I call my husband. Not anymore."

Muntadhir's eyes darted to hers. "What are you saying?"

Nahri paused. What *was* she saying? As in Cairo, divorce was permissible in Daevabad—and rather widely practiced considering djinn life-spans and temperaments. But Nahri and Muntadhir were royals, their marriage blessed by Ghassan himself. It wasn't as though she could run to a judge down the street with her grievances.

But there were lines her husband wouldn't cross, and he'd made one of them clear on their wedding night.

"I'm doing this, Muntadhir. For my people, for myself—with or without you. I want to build this hospital. I want to see if there's a way to make peace with the shafit. If you'd like to join me, I will gladly welcome you to my people's Temple. If you cannot bring yourself to visit me there . . ." She paused, choosing her words carefully. "I'm not sure you should be visiting me anywhere."

Stunned incredulity crossed his face, and Nahri turned away. He could stew on the implications of that for a time.

Her hand was on the door when he finally responded.

"He is so much more dangerous than you realize." Nahri glanced back, and Muntadhir continued, his voice low. "I understand, believe it or not. I know you. I know Ali. I suspect you really were friends. I bet it was nice. The palace can be a lonely place, after all. And I know damn well he cared about you."

Nahri stilled.

"And that's just it, Nahri. He does care . . . recklessly so. Passionately so. About the shafit. About his village in Am Gezira. He cares so much he's willing to risk himself and everyone around him, unwilling to accept a shade of gray or a lesser evil in service to a greater good." Warning laced into his voice. "My brother would die for his causes. But he's a prince of Daevabad, so he's not the one who pays that price. Other people do. And you have an entire tribe of such people to protect."

Nahri twisted the edge of her chador in her fists, wishing she could say he was wrong. Except Ali had risked incurring his father's wrath to sneak out of the palace with her because he'd felt guilty. He'd all but warned Subha off working with them because he didn't want to lie. They'd come here today to beg a favor from the king, and he'd been rude, brimming with his usual self-righteousness.

It doesn't matter. Nahri had set herself on this path for the right reasons, and she now had the resources to try and bring her dream to fruition. Ali was a means to an end, and she wouldn't let him be a weakness again.

She opened the door. "Nisreen is expecting me in the infirmary," she said, forcing a steadiness she didn't feel into her voice. "I'll send word when we're visiting the Grand Temple."

NAHRI ALMOST GROANED WHEN SHE SAW JAMSHID waiting in the private section of the infirmary. She didn't need him begging for another healing session or talking about

Muntadhir right now. But then she noticed the anxiety that was all but radiating off his body, one leg jiggling while he passed his cane nervously back and forth between his hands. Nisreen paced before him, her expression harried.

Odd. Nisreen typically doted on him. Nahri frowned as she approached. "Everything all right?"

Jamshid glanced up, his eyes too bright above the shadows lingering under them. "Banu Nahida!" His voice sounded oddly strained. "May the fires burn brightly for you." He cleared his throat. "Of course everything is all right." He blinked at Nisreen. "Everything is all right?"

Nisreen glowered at him. "I certainly hope so."

Nahri looked between the two of them. "Is something wrong at home? Has there been news of your father?"

Nisreen shook her head. "Nothing is wrong. But as a matter of fact, I did recently write to his father. Just after the prince's feast," she added, and Jamshid flushed. "Creator willing, he'll be headed back to Daevabad soon."

Let him delay. Nahri didn't think the powerful—and rather orthodox—Daeva grand wazir was going to think much of her plans for the hospital or the shafit.

Which meant she'd need to set them in motion quickly. "That's good, then. But since you're both here, I want to talk." She took a seat across from Jamshid and motioned for Nisreen to do so as well. "I've just gotten back from meeting with the Qahtanis . . ." She took a deep breath. "We're going to rebuild the Nahid hospital."

It took a moment for her words to land, and then Jamshid's face lit up in intrigue as swiftly as Nisreen's darkened.

"There's a Nahid hospital?" he asked brightly.

"There's an ancient ruin soaked in the blood of your ancestors," Nisreen cut in. She stared at Nahri in shock. "You told *Ghassan* about your visit?"

"I left that part out, actually," Nahri said lightly. "But yes, we're going to restore it. The king agreed."

"Who exactly is 'we,' my lady?" Nisreen asked, though it was clear she already knew the answer.

"The Qahtanis, of course," Nahri replied, deciding it was best not to be precise.

"You're going to rebuild the Nahid hospital with the Qahtanis?" Nisreen repeated faintly. "*Now?*"

Nahri nodded. "We're hoping to have it open in time for Navasatem." That seemed wildly optimistic to her, but if that was the price for Ghassan's blessing, she and Ali would have to find a way to get it done. "I want to change things around here. We'll rebuild the hospital, hire the freed djinn currently living there, start training apprentices . . ." She grinned, hopeful in a way she hadn't been for a very long time. A little happy, even.

"Delay it," Nisreen said bluntly. "Don't do this. Not now. Things are too tense."

Nahri felt some of her spirits drain; she'd hoped her mentor would share at least a touch of her excitement. "I can't. Ghassan only agreed so we could present it as a tribal unity gesture for the celebrations. And anyway, I don't want to delay it," she added, a little hurt. "I thought you'd be thrilled."

"That all sounds extraordinary," Jamshid enthused. "I didn't know about the hospital, but I'd love to see it."

"I'd like to have you do more," Nahri replied. "I want to make you my first student."

His cane clattered to the floor. "What?" he whispered.

Nahri bent to pick it up and then smiled. "You're smart. You're excellent with the other patients here, and you've been a great help already." She touched his hand. "Join me, Jamshid. It might not be the way you originally thought to serve our tribe . . . But I think you'd be a wonderful healer."

He took a deep breath; he seemed stunned by the offer. "I . . ." His gaze darted to Nisreen. "If Nisreen does not object . . ."

Nisreen had the look of a woman wondering what she had done to deserve her current misfortune. "I . . . Yes. I think Jamshid might have quite the . . . knack for healing." She cleared her throat. "Though *perhaps* he might exercise a bit more caution when putting away ingredients in the apothecary—and when reading old texts." She returned her gaze to Nahri. "It seems Jamshid came across some of Manizheh's notes archived in the Temple."

"Really?" Nahri asked. "I'd love to see them."

Jamshid paled. "I . . . I'll try to find them again."

Nahri grinned. "Then I think this would be perfect for you! Though it won't be easy," she warned. "I don't have a lot of time, and neither will you. You'll need to all but take up residence in this place, reading and studying every second you're not working. You might hate me by the end."

"Never." He gripped her hand. "When do I start?"

"There's one more thing before you say yes." She glanced at Nisreen. Her assistant looked like she was fighting panic, which Nahri thought a complete overreaction—Nisreen couldn't hate the Qahtanis so much that she wouldn't want a hospital. "Nisreen, would you mind leaving us? I'd like to speak with Jamshid alone for a moment."

Nisreen let out a huffed sound. "Would it matter if I did mind?" She rose to her feet. "A hospital with the Qahtanis before Navasatem . . . The Creator have mercy . . ."

"What is this 'one thing'?" Jamshid asked, pulling her attention back to him. "Not sure I like the sound of it," he teased.

"It's a sizable one thing," she confessed. "And I'll need you to keep it to yourself for now." She lowered her voice. "I intend to open the hospital to all. Regardless of their blood."

Confusion wrinkled Jamshid's brow. "But . . . that's forbidden. You . . . you can't mean to heal mixed-bloods, Banu Nahida. You could lose your magic that way."

The remark—a prejudice she'd heard uttered by many a fearful Daeva—stung no less for having been said in earnest ignorance. "That's not true," she said firmly. "I'm proof that it isn't. I healed humans for years in Egypt before coming to Daevabad, and it never affected my magic."

He must have heard the heat in her response, for he drew back. "Forgive me. I didn't mean to doubt you."

She shook her head. If she couldn't handle Jamshid's doubt, she wouldn't survive the reactions from the priests at the Grand Temple. "No, I want you to question me. I'm hoping you can help me convince the rest of our tribe. You're a Temple-trained noble, the son of the grand wazir . . . what could sway someone like you to support this?"

He drummed his fingers against his leg. "I'm not certain you could. Let alone what Suleiman's law says about sharing magic with them . . . the shafit despise us. You know what they did to the Daevas they caught after Dara's death. They'd probably murder us all in our beds if they could."

"Does that not make peace sound rather desirable?"

He sighed. "I don't see how that's possible. Look to our history. Whenever the shafit rise, we're the ones who pay a price."

"Jamshid, have you ever even had a conversation with a shafit lasting longer than ten minutes?"

He had the grace to blush. "We're not supposed to interact with the human-blooded."

"No, what we're not supposed to do is creep through the human world, seducing virgins and starting wars. It doesn't say anywhere that we can't talk to them." He fell silent but didn't look convinced. "*Speak*, Jamshid," she pressed. "Call me a fool, a tyrant, but say something."

She saw him swallow. "Why should we have to?" he burst out. "This is *our* home. We're not the ones responsible for the shafit. Let the djinn build them hospitals. Why should we be the ones to offer this peace when they've done nothing to deserve it?"

"Because it *is* our home," she said gently. "And there's got to be a better way to protect it, to protect all of us. Do you have any idea the size of the shafit neighborhoods, Jamshid? How crowded they are? There are probably more shafit in Daevabad than the rest of the djinn tribes put together, and we can't rely on the Qahtanis to keep us from each other's throats forever." These were thoughts that had been swirling in her head for five years, solidifying more and more each day. "Doing so leaves us vulnerable."

He seemed to contemplate that. "That'll be your argument," he finally said. "People are afraid. Convince them that this is the best way to ensure our safety."

I can do that. "Excellent. Now, I should be starting my rounds."

His face lit up. "Wonderful! May I . . ."

She laughed. "Oh, no." She pointed to the nearest desk. Well, Nahri knew it was a desk. At the moment, its surface wasn't visible: it was entirely covered in stacks upon stacks of books, messy notes, pens, inkpots, and empty teacups. "You aren't touching any of my patients. Work your way through those books first and then we'll talk."

Jamshid's eyes went wide. "All of them?"

"All of them." She pulled over a blank piece of parchment. "Write your attendants and have them send over some of your things." She nodded to the couch. "That's yours. Feel free to make yourself comfortable here."

He looked dazed, but still eager. "Thank you, Banu Nahida. I hope you know how much this means to me."

She winked. "We'll see if you're still saying that in a month."

She moved toward the curtain, but then stopped and looked back. "Jamshid?"

He glanced up.

"You . . . you should know that Muntadhir doesn't support this. He thinks I'm being reckless, and I'm sure he'll have words about how I'm going to be the downfall of Daevabad the next time you see him." She paused. If Muntadhir had turned to Jamshid when he found out his brother was returning, she had no doubt he'd do the same after their conversation on the terrace. "If that puts you in an awkward position . . ."

"You're my Banu Nahida." He hesitated, and Nahri could see warring loyalties play across his face. Oddly enough, the way it made his dark eyes crease struck her as familiar. "And I'm Daeva first. You have my support." He gave her a hopeful smile. "Maybe I can convince him to do the same."

A mix of relief and guilt flared in her. Nahri didn't want to put Jamshid in the middle of her marriage, but she would take every advantage she could get. And truthfully, it was clear he was already there. "That would be appreciated." She nodded at the books and grinned. "Now get to work."

18

NAHRI

Two weeks after her barbed family breakfast, Nahri found
herself back in the hospital, watching Razu with rapt attention.
"Beautiful," she said admiringly, as the ancient Tukharistani
gambler swapped the jewels again, a sleight of hand that betrayed nothing as Razu set down a brilliant glass gem in front
of her—a pretty bauble, but certainly not the ruby that had
vanished. "And it's not magic?"

"Not at all," Razu replied. "One cannot overly rely on magic.
What if your hands were bound in iron, and you needed to hide
away the key you'd snatched?"

"Is that a situation you've found yourself in?"

The other woman gave her a cryptic smile. "Of course not.
I am a . . . what are we telling your law-abiding friends again?"

"A former trader from Tukharistan who ran a respectable inn."

Razu laughed. "Respectability was the last thing my old tavern
was known for." She sighed. "I am telling you . . . a couple glasses

of my soma and your doctor and prince will be agreeing to your every suggestion."

Nahri shook her head. She was fairly certain a single sip of Razu's soma would knock Ali out cold, and Subha would probably think they were poisoning her. "Let's try a more orthodox approach first. Though I would not be averse to you teaching me how to do that," she said, pointing to the glass gem.

"I am at my Banu Nahida's service," Razu replied, placing the gem in Nahri's palm and adjusting her fingers. "So you twist your hand like this and . . ."

From the other side of the courtyard came a disapproving cluck. Elashia, the freed djinn from Qart Sahar, was painting a turtle she'd carved from cedarwood. Nahri had brought her the paints, an act that had been greeted with wet eyes and a fierce hug.

But right now Elashia was looking at Razu with open disapproval. "What?" Razu asked. "The child wants to learn a skill. Who am I to deny her?" When Elashia turned back around with a sigh, Razu flashed Nahri a conspiratorial smile. "When she is out of sight, I will teach you a spell to give even a rock the appearance of a jewel."

But Nahri's gaze was still on the Sahrayn woman. "Does she ever speak?" she asked softly, switching to Razu's archaic dialect of Tukharistani.

Sadness swept the older djinn's face. "Not often. Sometimes with me, when we are alone, but it took years. She was freed decades ago, but she never speaks of her time in slavery. A companion of mine brought her to my tavern after finding her living on the streets, and she's been with me since. Rustam told me once he believed his grandfather freed her, and that she had been enslaved for nearly five hundred years. She is a gentle soul," she added as Elashia blew on the turtle and then let it go, smiling as it came to life and tottered along the edge of the fountain. "I cannot imagine how she survived."

Nahri watched her, but it wasn't Elashia she saw in her mind's eye. It was Dara, whose captivity had been three times as long as

Elashia's. However, Dara had remembered almost nothing of his imprisonment—and the few recollections they'd shared together had been ghastly enough that he'd confessed to being relieved such memories were gone. Nahri hadn't agreed at the time—it seemed appalling to lose such a huge portion of one's life. But maybe there had been a mercy in it she hadn't realized, one of the few Dara had enjoyed.

A crashing came from the entrance. "I take it your friends are here," Razu said.

Nahri rose to her feet. "I would not call us friends."

Ali and Subha entered the courtyard. They couldn't have looked more different: the djinn prince was smiling, his eyes bright with anticipation as he gazed about the ruins. In contrast, apprehension was written in every line of Subha's body, from her pursed lips to her tightly crossed arms.

"Peace be upon you all," Ali said in greeting, touching his heart as he caught sight of them. He was in plain Geziri dress today: a white dishdasha that fell to his sandaled feet and a charcoal-colored turban, his zulfiqar and khanjar tucked into a pale green belt. On one shoulder, he was carrying a leather bag full of scrolls.

"And upon you peace." Nahri turned to Subha, offering a polite bow. "Doctor Sen, it is lovely to see you again. Razu, this is Doctor Subhashini Sen and Prince Alizayd al Qahtani."

"An honor," Razu said, bringing her left hand to her brow. "I am Razu Qaraqashi, and this is Elashia. You'll excuse our third companion for hiding in his room. Issa does not do well with guests."

Ali made his way forward. "Did you see the seals on the door?" he asked eagerly.

Nahri thought back to the carved pictograms she'd noticed when she first found the hospital. "Yes. Why? What are they?"

"The old tribal sigils," Ali explained. "They were used before we had a shared written language. The great scholar Grumbates once said—"

"Can we not have a history lesson right now? *Another* one?" Subha clarified, in a tone that made Nahri suspect the walk to the hospital in the company of the chatty prince had been a long one. Her gaze darted around the courtyard like she expected some sort of magical beast to leap out and attack. "Well . . . it certainly looks like this place has been abandoned for fourteen centuries."

"Nothing we can't fix." Nahri plastered a grin on her face. She was determined to win over the other healer today. "Would you like some refreshments before we take a tour? Tea?"

"I'm fine," Subha replied, her expression displeased. "Let's just get this over with."

The blunt refusal of her hospitality ruffled something very deep in the Egyptian part of her heart, but Nahri stayed polite. "Certainly."

Ali stepped in. "I tracked down the hospital's old plans and had a Daeva architect at the Royal Library go through them with me to draw up notes for us to follow."

Nahri was taken aback. "That was a good idea."

"Yes. It is almost as if history lessons are useful," he sniffed, plucking out one of his scrolls and spreading it before them. "This was always a courtyard. The architect said there were notes about it containing a garden."

Nahri nodded. "I'd like to keep it that way. I know my patients in the infirmary enjoy the occasional chance to walk around my gardens now. It lifts their spirits." She glanced at Subha. "Does that seem correct to you?"

The doctor narrowed her eyes. "You did see where I worked, yes? Do you imagine us getting some air near the local uncollected trash piles?"

Nahri flushed. She was itching to find a commonality with this fellow female healer, a physician who, in the brief time Nahri had watched her, seemed to have an abundance of the professional confidence Nahri was still pretending at. She doubted Subha shook like a leaf before new procedures, or desperately prayed she didn't kill someone every time she performed surgery.

Ali was peering at his notes. "According to this . . . that domed chamber there was used for humoral disorders of air. It says that tethers were set in the floor to prevent people from injuring themselves while floating . . ."

"And that?" Nahri prompted, pointing to a line of crumbling columns. She suspected Subha was not ready to discuss rooms designed to enclose flying djinn. "It looks like a corridor."

"It is. It leads to a surgical wing."

That sounded more promising. "Let's start there."

The three of them headed down the twisting path. The dirt was soft underfoot, the sun shining in bright swaths through the overgrown trees. The air smelled of old stone and fresh rain. It was humid, and Nahri fanned herself with an edge of her linen chador.

The silence between them was heavy. Awkward. And try as she might, Nahri couldn't forget that the last time Daevas, Geziris, and shafit had been together in this place, they had all been brutally killing one another.

"I've been discussing funding options with the Treasury," Ali said, an oddly pleased smile playing across his mouth. "And after a visit from my companion Aqisa, I find the Ayaanle trade envoy suddenly far more eager to offer financial assistance."

Subha shook her head, glancing about in dismay. "I cannot imagine turning this into a functioning hospital in six months. With several miracles, perhaps you could do it in six years."

A golden-brown monkey chose that particular moment to leap over their heads with a screech, jumping from the trees to land upon a broken pillar. It glared at them as it munched a mushy apricot.

"We'll, ah, have the monkeys cleared out right away," Nahri said, mortified.

The corridor came to an abrupt stop. The surgical wing was enclosed by thick brass walls that towered overhead, and the one in front of them was covered in scorch marks, the brass melted into an impenetrable barrier.

Nahri touched one of the marks. "I don't think we'll be getting in there."

Ali stepped back, shading his eyes. "It looks as though part of the roof has collapsed. I can climb up and see."

"You're not going to be able to—" But Ali was gone before the words left her mouth, his fingers hooking around handholds she couldn't see.

Subha watched him scale the wall. "If he breaks his neck, I am not taking responsibility."

"You were never here." Nahri sighed as Ali pulled himself on the roof and vanished out of sight. "Your daughter is with your husband today?" she asked, determined to continue the conversation.

"I do typically advise that infants steer clear of decaying ruins."

Nahri had to bite her tongue to keep from saying something sarcastic in return. She was reaching the end of her diplomatic rope. "What's her name?"

"Chandra." Subha said, her face softening slightly.

"That's very pretty," Nahri replied. "She looked healthy too. Strong, mashallah. She's doing all right?"

Subha nodded. "She was born earlier than I'd like, but she's thriving." Her eyes dimmed. "I've seen it go the other way too many times."

Nahri had too, both in Cairo and in Daevabad. "I had one last week," she said quietly. "A woman from out in northern Daevastana rushed here after being bitten by a basilisk. She was in her last month of pregnancy, and she and her husband had been trying for decades. I was able to save her, but the child . . . a basilisk bite is terribly poisonous and I had no good way to administer the antidote. He was stillborn." Her throat tightened at the memory. "The parents . . . I don't think they quite understood."

"They never do. Not really. Grief clouds the mind, makes people say terrible things."

Nahri paused. "Does . . ." She cleared her throat, suddenly embarrassed. "Does it get easier?"

Subha finally met her gaze, her tin-toned eyes understanding if not warm. "Yes . . . and no. You learn to distance yourself from it. It's work; your feelings don't matter. If anything, they can interfere." She sighed. "Trust me . . . one day you'll go from witnessing the worst of tragedies to smiling and playing with your child in the space of an hour, and you'll wonder if that's for the best." She gazed upon the ruined hospital. "The work is what matters. You fix what you can and keep yourself whole enough to move on to the next patient."

The words resonated through Nahri, her mind drifting to another patient: the only one she couldn't heal. "Could I ask you something else?"

Subha nodded briefly.

"Is there anything you recommend for spinal injuries? For a man struggling to walk?"

"Is this about your friend, the grand wazir's son?" When Nahri's eyes widened in surprise, Subha tilted her head. "I do my research before agreeing to work with someone."

"It's about him," Nahri admitted. "Actually, you'll probably meet him soon. He's my apprentice now. But he took several arrows to the back five years ago, and I haven't been able to heal him. He's getting better slowly with exercise and rest but . . ." She paused. "It feels like a failure on my part."

Subha looked contemplative, perhaps the medical nature of

the conversation drawing her out. "I can examine him if he's willing. There are some therapies I know that might work."

Before Nahri could respond, Ali leapt down to join them, landing so silently that she jumped and Subha yelped.

His expression didn't inspire much hope. "Well . . . the good news is, it does indeed look like this was a surgical wing. There are even some tools scattered about."

"What sort of tools?" Nahri asked, her curiosity kindled.

"Hard to say. Much of it is underwater. It appears that a base-ment collapsed." Ali paused. "And there are snakes. Lot of them."

Subha sighed. "This is madness. You are never going to be able to restore this place."

Nahri hesitated, resignation beginning to seep through her. "Maybe you're right."

"Nonsense," Ali declared, drawing up when Subha glared at him. "Don't tell me the two of you are ready to give up so soon. Did you think this would be easy?"

"I didn't think it would be *impossible*," Nahri countered. "Look around, Ali. Do you have any idea how many people we would need to even get started?"

"I will by the end of the week," he said confidently. "And lots of work is not a bad thing—it means we need lots of workers. It means new jobs and training for hundreds, people who will then have money for food and school and shelter. This project is an opportunity. One we haven't had in generations."

Subha made a face. "You sound like a politician."

He grinned. "And you sound like a pessimist. But that doesn't mean we can't work together."

"But the money, Ali," Nahri replied. "And the *timing* . . ."

He made a dismissive gesture. "I can get the money." An ea-ger glint entered his eye. "I could have trade guilds built around waqfs and increase the tax on luxury imports . . ." Perhaps seeing that the two healers looked lost, he stopped. "Never mind. The two of you tell me what a hospital needs, and I'll worry about getting it done." He turned around without waiting for a response. "Now come. The plans say that building ahead was once the apothecary."

Subha blinked, looking a little bewildered, but she followed Ali, muttering under her breath about youth. Nahri was equally taken aback—but also grateful. Their personal history aside, maybe partnering with Ali wasn't the worst idea. He certainly seemed confident.

They continued down the weed-covered path, pushing aside wet palm fronds and glistening spider webs. Columns lay smashed on the ground, half swallowed by thick, twisting vines, and a large black snake sunned itself on the remains of a small pavilion.

They crossed under a forbidding arch and into the darkened chamber of the ancient apothecary. Nahri blinked as her eyes adjusted to the loss of light. Whatever floor had been there was long gone, swallowed by dirt, and only scattered sections of broken masonry were left behind. The distant ceiling had likely once been beautiful; blue and gold bits of tile still clung to its delicately carved and stuccoed surface. A swallow's nest had been built into one elaborate cornice.

A burst of light briefly blinded her. Nahri glanced back to see that Subha had conjured a dancing pair of flames in one hand.

A challenge lit her face at Nahri's astonishment. "Surely you know there are shafit capable of magic?"

Better than you would imagine. "Ah, of course," Nahri said weakly. "I'd been told that." She turned to study the room. The opposite wall was covered in hundreds of drawers. Though rusted over now, they were linked in a clever structure of metal and marble, their contents held behind securely fastened brass doors. Dozens were still clamped shut, their scrollwork surfaces tarnished by green and red rust.

"Care to see what mysterious magical ingredients look like after being locked away for fourteen centuries?" Nahri jested.

"I would rather not," Subha replied, knocking Ali's hand away when the prince reached for one of the handles. "*No.* The two of you can sate your curiosity when I'm gone."

Nahri hid a smile. The doctor still looked exasperated, but Nahri would take that over openly hostile. "I think there will be more than enough room for all our supplies here."

"I suspect so, considering my pharmaceuticals fit inside a single chest," Subha replied. "I usually have to send patients to buy their own medicines for me to prepare. It's an expense we can't spare."

"You won't have to pay another coin yourself," Nahri said smoothly. "Well, as long as our royal backer remains so sure of himself." She smiled sweetly at him, relishing his glower.

A metal glint caught her eye from the ground. Remembering Ali's comments about seeing tools in the surgical wing, Nahri knelt. Whatever it was was partially buried, half hidden behind a tree root that had burst through the floor and littered the broken tile with mounds of dark soil.

"What's that?" Subha asked when Nahri reached for it.

"It looks like a scalpel," Nahri replied, brushing the dirt away. "But it's stuck."

Ali leaned over her. "Pull a bit harder."

"I *am* pulling hard." Nahri gave another determined yank, and the blade abruptly came free, bursting out of the dirt with a spray of dark soil—and the skeletal hand still holding it.

Nahri dropped it, falling backward with a startled shriek. Ali grabbed her arm, yanking her back as his other hand went to his zulfiqar.

Subha peered past them. "Is that a *hand*?" Her eyes went wide with horror.

Ali quickly let Nahri go. "This place was destroyed during the war," he said haltingly. Guilt flashed in his eyes. "Maybe . . . maybe not all those killed were put to rest."

"Obviously not," Nahri said acidly. Had Subha not been there, she would have had far sharper words, but Nahri didn't dare start fighting about the war in front of the already apprehensive doctor.

It was Subha, however, who continued. "It seems a terrible thing to attack a place like this," she said grimly. "No matter how just a war's cause."

Ali was staring at the bones. "Maybe that's not all that happened here."

"And what exactly do you think happened here that justified destroying a hospital and slaughtering its healers?" Nahri shot back, infuriated by his response.

"I didn't say it was justified," Ali defended. "Just that there might be more to the story."

"I think I've had enough of this particular story," Subha interrupted, looking ill. "Why don't we move on and leave digging in the floors to people who can properly take care of these remains?"

Remains. The word seemed cold, clinical. *Family*, Nahri silently corrected, knowing there was a good chance the person murdered here still clutching a scalpel had been a Nahid. She removed her chador, draping it carefully over the bones. She'd come back here with Kartir.

By the time she straightened up, Subha was already through the apothecary door, but Ali was not.

Nahri grabbed his wrist before he could leave. "Is there something about this place you're not telling me?"

His gaze darted away. "You're better off not knowing."

Nahri tightened her grip. "Don't you dare condescend to me like that. Wasn't that your reasoning when it came to Dara as well? All those books I wasn't 'prepared' for? How did that turn out for you?"

Ali jerked free. "Everyone knew about Darayavahoush, Nahri. They just couldn't agree if he was a monster or a hero. What led to this?" He tilted his head to take in the dim room. "It was buried. And if you want a new beginning, it should stay buried."

19

DARA

"We'll attack the second night of Navasatem," Dara said as they gazed at the map he'd conjured: a section of Daevabad's narrow beach, the city walls and looming Citadel tower just behind it. "It is a new moon then and will be lightless. The Royal Guard will not see us coming until their tower is crashing through the lake."

"That's the night after the parade, correct?" Mardoniye asked. "Are you sure that's wise?"

Kaveh nodded. "I may not have witnessed a Navasatem in Daevabad, but I've heard plenty about the first day of celebrations. The drinking starts at dawn and doesn't stop until after the competitions in the arena. By midnight, half the city will be passed out in their beds. We'll take the djinn unaware and the majority of the Daevas will be at home."

"And Nahri will be in the infirmary, yes?" Dara asked. "You are certain Nisreen can keep her safe?"

"For the twentieth time, yes, Afshin," Kaveh sighed. "She will bar the infirmary doors at the first sight of your rather . . . creative sign."

Dara wasn't convinced. "Nahri is not the type to be confined against her will."

Kaveh gave him an even stare. "Nisreen has spent years at her side. I'm certain she can handle this."

And I'm certain she has no idea the Nahid under her charge once made a living getting in and out of locked places undetected. Uneasy, Dara glanced at Mardoniye. "Would you go see if Banu Manizheh is ready to join us?" he asked. She had barely left her tent in the past few days, working at a feverish pace on her experiments.

The young soldier nodded, rising to his feet and heading off across the camp. The sky was a pale pink through the dark trees. The snows had finally melted and the dew-damp earth glistened under the sun's first rays. His archers had already left to go practice with their horses in the valley below, and another pair of warriors was leading a yawning Abu Sayf out to their sparring ring. Dara quickly checked to make sure the zulfiqars were still sheathed on the other side of the ring. He had made it clear to his soldiers they were only to practice with Abu Sayf in his presence.

Aeshma snorted, drawing Dara's attention. "I still cannot believe they celebrate what Suleiman did to us," he said to Vizaresh.

Dara's mood instantly darkened. The ifrit had returned to their camp yesterday, and each hour in their presence was more trying. "We celebrate freedom from his bondage," he shot back. "You remember . . . the part where our ancestors obeyed and thus didn't have their magic permanently taken away. And surely you must have once celebrated *some* sort of festivities."

Aeshma looked wistful. "The humans in my land would occasionally sacrifice virgins in my name. They screamed terribly, but the music was enjoyable."

Dara briefly closed his eyes. "Forget the question. But speaking of the attack . . . are the two of *you* prepared? The ghouls will be handled?"

Vizaresh inclined his head. "I'm well-accomplished at such a thing."

"Accomplished enough to keep them from attacking my warriors?"

He nodded. "I will be at the beach with them myself."

That didn't make Dara feel much better. He hated the idea of separating his small militia and leaving a group of his untested warriors on the opposite side of the city. But he had no choice.

Aeshma grinned. "If you're worried, Afshin, I'm sure Qandisha would be happy to join us. She misses you terribly."

The campfire snapped loudly in response.

Kaveh glanced at him. "Who is Qandisha?"

Dara focused on his breath, staring at the flames as he tried to steady the magic surging through his limbs. "The ifrit who enslaved me."

Vizaresh clucked his tongue. "I was very jealous," he confessed. "I never managed to enslave someone so powerful."

Dara cracked his knuckles loudly. "Yes, what a pity."

Kaveh frowned. "This Qandisha is not working with Banu Manizheh?"

"She was, but then *he* wouldn't allow it," Aeshma mocked, tilting his head toward Dara. "He fell to his knees and begged his Nahid to send Qandisha away. Said it was his only condition. Though I can't imagine why." Aeshma licked his teeth. "After all, she's the only one who remembers what you did as a slave. And you must be curious. *Fourteen* centuries' worth of memories . . ." He leaned in. "Think of all the delightful desires you must have fulfilled."

Dara's hand dropped to his knife. "Give me a reason, Aeshma," he seethed.

Aeshma's eyes danced. "Only a joke, dear Afshin."

He didn't get a chance to respond. There was a startled cry from behind him, a thud, and the unmistakable sound of two bodies colliding.

And then the terrible hiss of a zulfiqar flaring to life.

Dara was whirling around, a conjured bow in his hands before he had taken another breath. The scene came to him in pieces. An exhausted Manizheh emerging from her tent. Abu Sayf's two guards on the ground, the fiery zulfiqar in the Geziri man's hands as he lunged toward her . . .

Dara's arrow flew, but Abu Sayf was prepared, raising a plank of wood with a speed and skill that took Dara by surprise. This was *not* the man who'd been sparring with his soldiers. He shot again, a cry rising from his throat as Abu Sayf rushed forward.

Mardoniye flung himself between the Geziri scout and Manizheh, parrying the zulfiqar's strike with his sword, the iron hissing against the conjured flames. He pushed Abu Sayf back, barely meeting the next blow as he inadvertently stepped between Dara and a clean shot.

But it was clear who was the better swordsman . . . and Mardoniye wasn't able to block Abu Sayf's next thrust.

The zulfiqar went straight through his stomach.

Dara was running for them the next moment, his magic surging, ice and snow melting beneath his feet. Abu Sayf pulled the zulfiqar out of Mardoniye and the Daeva man collapsed. He raised it over Manizheh . . .

She snapped her fingers.

Dara heard the bones in Abu Sayf's hand shatter from ten paces away. Abu Sayf cried out in pain, dropping the zulfiqar as Manizheh stared down at him, cold hatred in her dark eyes. By the time Dara reached them, his soldiers had pinned the Geziri. His hand was horrifically broken, the fingers splayed and pointing in different directions.

Dara dropped to Mardoniye's side. A sheen had swept the young man's eyes, his face already pale. His wound was a ghastly, gaping hole, black blood spreading in a pool beneath him. Though a few tendrils of the zulfiqar's telltale greenish-black poison were snaking across his skin, Dara knew that wouldn't be what took him.

Manizheh had gone right to work, ripping open the young warrior's coat. She pressed her hands against his stomach and closed her eyes.

Nothing happened. Nothing would happen, Dara knew. No one—not even a Nahid—healed from a zulfiqar blow.

Manizheh gasped, a choked sound of angry disbelief in her throat as she pressed harder.

Dara touched her hand. "My lady . . ." Her eyes darted to his, wilder than Dara had ever seen them, and he shook his head.

Mardoniye cried out in pain, clutching Dara's hand. "It hurts," he whispered, tears trickling down his cheeks. "Oh, Creator, please."

Dara took him gently into his arms. "Close your eyes," he soothed. "The pain will be gone soon, my friend. You fought well." His throat constricted. The words came automatically to him; he'd done this awful duty so many times.

Blood was trickling from Mardoniye's mouth. "My mother . . ."

"Your mother will be brought to live at my palace, her every need seen to." Manizheh reached out to bless Mardoniye's brow. "I will take her myself to visit your shrine at the temple. You saved my life, child, and for that your eyes will next open in Paradise."

Dara brought his lips to Mardoniye's ear. "It's beautiful," he whispered. "There's a garden, a peaceful grove of cedars where you'll wait with your loved ones . . ." His voice finally cracked, tears brimming in his eyes as Mardoniye jerked and then grew still, hot blood slowly soaking Dara's clothes.

"He's gone," Manizheh said softly.

Dara closed Mardoniye's eyes, gently laying him back on the bloody snow. *Forgive me, my friend.*

He rose to his feet, pulling free the knife he wore at his waist. Flames were licking down his arms and flickering in his eyes before he even approached Abu Sayf. The Geziri man was bloody, his nose broken, held fast by four of Dara's warriors.

Rage tore through him. The knife in his hand transformed, smoking away to reveal a scourge.

"Tell me why I should not flay you piece by piece right now," Dara hissed. "Why I should not do the same to your companion and make you listen as he screams for death?"

Abu Sayf met his eyes, a mix of defeat and grim determination in his expression. "Because you would have done the same thing in my place. Do you think we don't know who you *are*? What your Nahid is doing with our blood and our relics? Do you think we don't know what you have planned for Daevabad?"

"It is not your city," Dara snapped. "I treated you with kindness and this is how you repay me?"

Incredulity crossed Abu Sayf's face. "You cannot be that naive, Afshin. You threatened to torture the young warrior in my care if I didn't train *yours* to murder my kinsmen. Do you think a few shared meals and conversations erase that?"

"I think you are a liar from a tribe of liars." When Dara rushed on, he knew it was not just Abu Sayf he was angry at. "A horde of sand flies who lie and manipulate and feign friendship to gain trust." He raised his scourge. "I think it should be your tongue I take first."

"No." Manizheh's voice cut through the air.

Dara whirled around. "He killed Mardoniye! He would have killed you!" He was nearly as furious with himself as he was with Abu Sayf. Dara should never have allowed this. He knew how dangerous the Geziris were and yet he'd let them remain at camp, let himself be lulled into complacency by Abu Sayf's fluent

Divasti and the comfort of swapping stories with a fellow warrior. And now Mardoniye was dead.

"I am killing him, Banu Nahida," Dara said flatly, the defiance easy for once. "This is a matter of war you do not understand."

Manizheh's eyes flashed. "Do not dare condescend to me, Darayavahoush. Lower your weapon. I will not ask again." She turned to Kaveh without waiting for a response. "Retrieve the serum and the relic from my tent. And I want the other Geziri brought out."

Dara was instantly chastened. "Banu Nahida, I merely meant—"

"I do not care what you meant." Her gaze leveled on him. "You may be dear to me, Darayavahoush, but I am not as ignorant of our history as my daughter. You obey *my* commands. But if it helps . . ." She brushed past him. "I don't plan to leave these men alive."

Kaveh returned. "Here you are, my lady," he said, handing her a small glass bottle stoppered with red wax.

Dara's men returned the next moment, dragging the second Geziri scout as he struggled and swore. He went still the moment he saw Abu Sayf, their gray gazes locking. A look of understanding passed between them.

Of course, you fool. They've probably been plotting this, laughing behind your back at your weaknesses. Again, he cursed himself for underestimating them. His younger self wouldn't have. His younger self would have killed them in the forest.

Manizheh handed the relic to one of his men. "Put it back in his ear. Then tie them . . . here and here," she said, indicating a pair of trees about ten paces apart.

The younger scout was losing his fight against panic. He thrashed out as they shoved the relic back into his ear, his eyes wild.

"Hamza," Abu Sayf spoke softly. "Do not give them that."

A tear ran down the other man's cheek, but he stopped fighting.

Mardoniye, Dara reminded himself. He turned from the frightened Geziri to Manizheh. "What is that?" he asked, looking at the bottle.

"The other part of our plan. A potion I've been working on for decades. A way to kill a man who might be well-guarded. A way too swift to stop."

Dara drew up. "A way to kill Ghassan?"

Manizheh's gaze seemed distant. "Among others." She removed the top from the flask.

A wispy copper vapor rose out, dancing and darting in the air like a thing alive. It seemed to hesitate, to search.

And then, without warning, it dove for Abu Sayf.

The older scout jerked back as the vapor rushed past his face, swarming his copper relic. It dissolved in the blink of an eye, the liquid metal shimmering in a coppery haze that vanished into his ear.

There was a moment of startled, horrified shock on his face, and then he howled, clutching his head.

"Abu Sayf!" the younger djinn cried out.

The other man didn't respond. Blood was streaming from his eyes, ears, and nose, mixed with the coppery vapors.

Kaveh gasped, covering his mouth. "Is that . . . is that what my Jamshid . . ."

"I suspect Jamshid found an earlier version of my notes," Manizheh replied. "This is far more advanced." She fell briefly silent as Abu Sayf grew still, his unseeing eyes fixed on the sky, and then she swallowed loud enough for Dara to hear. "It's attracted to Geziri relics and grows upon consuming them, pressing upon the brain until it kills its bearer."

Dara couldn't take his eyes off Abu Sayf. His bloody body was twisted, his face frozen in a mask of anguish. Manizheh's explanation sent a chill through him, extinguishing the flames swirling over his limbs.

He tried to recover some semblance of his wits. "But it is magic. If you tried this on Ghassan, he would just use the seal."

"It works as well without magic." She pulled free her scalpel. "If you remove the magic as Nahid blood does, as Suleiman's seal does . . ." She cut her thumb, squeezing out a drop of black blood. It landed on a tendril of vapor rising from Abu Sayf's corpse, and a jagged shard of copper fell instantly to the bloody snow. ". . . that's what you get in your skull."

The other scout was still trying to twist free of his binds as he yelled in Geziriyya. And then he started to scream.

The vapor was creeping toward his feet.

"No!" he cried as it wrapped around his body, winding toward his ear. "No—"

His scream cut off, and this time Dara did glance away, fixing his gaze on Mardoniye's body until the second scout fell silent.

"Well," Manizheh said grimly. There was no triumph in her voice. "I suppose it works."

At his side, Kaveh swayed. Dara steadied him, putting a hand on his shoulder. "You want me to give this to Ghassan?" the wazir said hoarsely.

Manizheh nodded. "Vizaresh has designed one of his old rings so that a false jewel may be filled with the vapor. You need merely break it in Ghassan's presence. It will kill every Geziri in the room."

It will kill every Geziri in the room. Kaveh looked like he was about to be sick, and Dara didn't blame him.

Even so, he spoke up. "I can do it. The grand wazir need not risk himself."

"He does," Manizheh countered, though the quiet worry was audible in her voice. "We don't know if Ghassan will be able to use Suleiman's seal on you, Dara. We can't risk finding out. He needs to be dead before you step into the palace, and Kaveh's position ensures him easy and relatively unguarded access."

316 ✧ S. A. CHAKRABORTY

"But—"

"I will do it." Kaveh's voice was no less frightened, but it was determined. "For what he did to Jamshid, I will do it."

Dara's stomach tightened. He stared at the dead scouts, the cool earth steaming as their copper-flecked blood spread. So this was what Manizheh had been working on so diligently the past few months.

Did you think this wouldn't be vicious? Dara knew war. He knew—more than anyone alive—just what the Nahids could be capable of.

But by the Creator, did he hate seeing this violence claim her.

It claimed Mardoniye as well, he reminded himself. *It claimed Nahri and Jamshid.* Ghassan had been terrorizing and killing Daevas for years. If victory for his people meant the king and a few of his guards died painfully, that was not a cost Dara would protest. He would end this war and ensure Manizheh never had to resort to anything like this again.

He cleared his throat. "It sounds as if you should pack, Kaveh. Now, if you will both excuse me . . ." He headed for Mardoniye's body. "I have a warrior to put to rest."

DARA BUILT MARDONIYE'S FUNERAL PYRE WITH HIS own hands and stayed at its side until it was reduced to ash, the smoldering remains throwing a weak light into the dark night. Dara was alone by then; Manizheh had overseen rites and then left to see Kaveh off, while Dara ordered the rest of his soldiers to continue with their duties. He could tell they were shaken—for all their devotion and training, few had witnessed the kind of fighting that led to a man bleeding out on the snow, and he could see the unspoken question in their eyes. Would they too end up this way in Daevabad?

Dara hated that he couldn't tell them no.

A touch upon his shoulder startled him. He glanced back. "Irtemiz?"

The young archer stepped closer. "We thought one of us should check on you," she said softly. Her gaze fell on the smoking pyre. "I still can't believe he's gone." Her voice trembled. "I should have had my bow on hand all the time, like you say . . ."

"It is not your fault," Dara said firmly. "The sand fly was likely waiting for such an opportunity." He pressed her shoulder. "Besides, he blocked my arrows, and surely, you are not suggesting you're better than your teacher?" He feigned offense.

That drew a small, sad smile from her lips. "Give me another decade." Her smile faded. "There . . . there was something else we thought you should see."

Dara frowned at her tone. "Show me."

She led him through the dark trees, their boots crunching on the ground. "Bahram first noticed it when he took the horses out. He said it stretched as far as he could see."

They emerged from the tree line, the valley spreading flat before them. The river was a gleaming ribbon of moonlight that would have normally outshone the surrounding plain.

But the spring grass was not dark. It was glowing with a warm copper hue that exactly matched Manizheh's vapor, a low fog of death clinging to the earth.

"Bahram . . . he rode out far, Afshin. He said it's everywhere." She swallowed. "We haven't told the Banu Nahida yet. We weren't certain it was our place, but surely . . . surely, this does not mean . . ." She trailed off, unable to voice the same awful fear snaring Dara's heart.

"There must be some explanation," he finally replied. "I will talk to her."

He went straight to Manizheh's tent, ignoring the stares of his warriors and the chuckles of the ifrit at their roaring fire. Despite the late hour, she was clearly awake; the light of oil lamps shone through the felt and he could smell the tang of freshly brewed tea.

"Banu Manizheh?" he called. "May I speak to you?"

She appeared a moment later, her familiar chador replaced by a thick woolen shawl. She was clearly readying herself for bed; her silvering black braids had been undone and she looked surprised to see him.

"Afshin," she greeted him, her eyes concerned as they swept his face. "What's wrong?"

Dara flushed, ashamed to have come upon her in such a manner. "Forgive my intrusion. But this is a matter best discussed privately."

"Then come in." She held open the tent flap. "Take some tea with me. And sit. This has been a terrible day."

The affection in her voice set him at ease, stilling some of the dread rising in his heart. He slipped off his boots and hung his cloak before taking a seat on one of the cushions. On the other side of the tent, the curtain partitioning off the small area where she slept was drawn back.

One of Kaveh's caps was still there. Dara looked away from it, feeling like he'd seen something not meant for his eyes. "The grand wazir departed safely?"

"Right after the funeral," she replied, pouring the tea. "He wanted to get some distance covered before the sun set."

Dara took the cup she handed him. "Kaveh is a quicker flier than I would have imagined," he said. "There must be some truth to those stories you tell of racing horses around Zariaspa."

Manizheh took a seat across from him. "He is eager to get back to Daevabad. He's been worried about Jamshid since we received Nisreen's letter." Manizheh took a sip of her drink. "But something tells me Kaveh is not the reason you are here."

"No. Not quite." Dara set down his tea. "My lady, my riders brought something to my attention I think you should know about. The copper vapor that killed the scouts . . . it appears to have spread. It looks fainter to my eye, but it's everywhere, hovering just above the ground as far as the river valley."

Manizheh's expression didn't waver. "And?"

The clipped response set his heart racing. "You said that it is attracted to Geziri relics, that it grows upon consuming them . . ." His voice caught. "Banu Nahida . . . when does it *stop*?"

She met his gaze. "I don't know. That's what I've been working on all these months: I've been trying to find a way to contain its spread and the length of time that it's potent." Her eyes dimmed. "But I haven't had much success, and we are out of time."

"You're going to let Kaveh release that in the palace," Dara whispered. He fought for control as the implication swept through him. "Banu Manizheh . . . there must be hundreds of Geziris in the palace. The scholars in the library, secretaries and attendants. The women and children in the harem. Ghassan's daughter. They all wear relics. If he lets this loose in the middle of the night . . . it could kill every Geziri there."

Manizheh quietly set her cup of tea down, and her silence sent him reeling.

No. Creator, no. "Not just the palace." A gasp left his lips. "You think this could kill every Geziri in Daevabad."

There was no mistaking the soft edge of despair in her voice when she replied, "I think that more likely than not." But then her black eyes hardened. "And what of it? How many Daevas died when Zaydi al Qahtani took Daevabad? How many of your friends and relatives, Afshin?" Scorn filled her voice. "The sand flies are not complete fools. At least a few will figure out what is happening and take out their relics. Which is why the timing must be perfect."

A voice was screaming inside his head, but Dara felt no heat, no magic aching to escape his skin. He was colder than he had ever been. "Do not do this," he said, his entire body shaking. "Do not start your reign with this much blood on your hands."

"I have no choice." When Dara looked away, Manizheh pressed on, her voice growing firmer. "This is how we win. And we *must* win. If Ghassan lives, if our victory is anything less than completely decisive, he will annihilate us. He will not rest until every trace of our people is destroyed. You are mourning Mardoniye? You must realize how many more of your warriors will survive if there are no soldiers left to fight by the time we reach the palace."

"You will make us monsters." The ice around his heart shattered, and Dara began to lose the fight with his emotions. "That is what we are if you let this happen . . . and Banu Nahida, that's not a reputation you'll ever lose." He looked at her, beseeching. "I beg you, my lady. These are innocents. *Children.* Travelers coming to celebrate Navasatem . . ." His memories were stealing over him. This was all too familiar.

Merchants. Traders. Weavers whose finely embroidered silk ran with blood just a touch too crimson. Children who didn't realize the human brown in their eyes sealed their fate. The calm commands and coldly reasoned explanations of another generation of Nahids.

The fabled city of Qui-zi reduced to smoking ruins. The screams and smell of earthy blood that would never leave his memories.

"Then we will be monsters," Manizheh declared. "I will pay that price to end this war."

"It won't end it," Dara argued, desperate. "We will have every Geziri capable of picking up a blade at the banks of the Gozan when they learn we slaughtered their kinsmen without provocation. They will fight us until the Day of Judge—"

"Then I will release this poison into their homeland." Dara jerked back, and Manizheh continued. "Let the djinn tribes know the price for defiance. I do not want this death on my hands, but if it will stifle the rebellions of the Sahrayn and the cunning of the Ayaanle, I will take it. Let the fate of the Geziris weigh on the minds of the Tukharistanis who still curse your name and the Agnivanshis who think their wide rivers protect them."

"You sound like Ghassan," Dara accused her.

Her eyes flashed in anger. "Then maybe he was right to rule so," she said bitterly. "But at least this time, it won't be my family and tribe living in fear."

"Until the next war," he said, unable to check the savage resentment rising in him. "Which I assume I'll be dragged back for, should I happen to die here." He rose to his feet. "You were to be better than this. Better than the Qahtanis. Better than your ancestors!"

He crossed the tent, reaching for his cloak.

"Where are you going?" Manizheh demanded sharply.

Dara shoved on his boots. "To stop Kaveh."

"Absolutely not. You are under *my* command, Darayavahoush."

"I said I'd help you retake Daevabad—not commit another Qui-zi." He reached for the tent flap.

It burst into flames and a searing pain shot down his arm. Dara cried out, more in shock than hurt as he whirled back around.

Manizheh snapped her fingers, and the pain vanished. "We are not done with our conversation," she seethed. "I have risked and lost too much to see my plans fail now because a warrior with more blood on his hands than I can even imagine momentarily grew a conscience." Her expression was cold. "If you have ever called yourself an Afshin, you will sit back down right now."

Dara stared at her in disbelief. "This is not you, Banu Manizheh."

"You do not know me, Darayavahoush. You do not know what you've already cost me."

"What *I've* cost *you*?" The charge was almost laughable. Dara beat a fist against his chest. "*Do you think I want to be here?*" Anger swirled into his heart, and then it was breaking free—the line he'd sworn he'd never cross, the resentment that festered in the darkest part of his soul. "I do not want any of this! Your family destroyed my life—my honor, my reputation! You had me carry out one of the worst crimes in our history, and when it blew up in your faces, you blamed me!"

She glared. "I wasn't the one who put a scourge in your hand."

"No, you are just the one who brought me back. Twice." Tears blurred his eyes. "I was with my sister. I was at *peace*."

Her eyes were blazing now. "You don't get to pine for peace with your family after what you did to mine."

"Your daughter would never agree to *any* of this."

"I'm not talking about my daughter." Manizheh's gaze pinned him. He'd swear he could feel her magic, the ghost of fingers around his throat, a barbed tightness in his chest. "I'm talking about my son."

Confusion coursed through him. "Your son?" But before the word fully left his mouth, Dara's gaze fell upon Kaveh's cap beside her bedroll. He recalled her fierce words about keeping those she loved hidden . . .

He thought, very suddenly, of the kindhearted young man he'd left riddled with arrows.

"No," Dara whispered. "He . . . he has no abilities." Dara couldn't even say his name; it would make the horrified suspicion racing through his mind all too real. "He said his mother was a servant. That she died when he was born . . ."

"He was misinformed," Manizheh said brusquely. "He has no mother because if the Qahtanis ever learned of such a thing, he would have been forced into the same cage I was trapped in. He has no abilities because when he was less than a week old, I had to *brand my infant child* with a tattoo that would inhibit them. In order to give him a life, a peaceful future in the Zariaspa that I loved, I had no choice but to to cut him off from his very birthright." Manizheh's voice was trembling. "Jamshid e-Pramukh is my son."

Dara inhaled, fighting for breath, for words. "That cannot be."

"He's my son," Manizheh repeated. "Your Baga Nahid, should such a thing mean anything to you." She sounded more hurt than angry now. "And because of your heedlessness when it came to my daughter, you nearly killed him. You stole from him the only future he ever wanted and left him wracked with such physical pain Kaveh says there are days he can't leave his bed." Her expression twisted. "What is the punishment for that, Afshin? For sending arrows into a man you should have greeted with your face in the dust?"

Dara was suddenly sitting, though he had little recollection of doing so. His knees felt weak, his head heavy.

Manizheh clearly wasn't done. "I wasn't going to tell you, you know. Not until after we'd won. Until he was safe and I'd burned that damned mark from his back. I thought you'd suffered enough. I feared the guilt might break you."

He could see the truth of that in her eyes, and that did break him—that, and the realization that Manizheh had spent these years Jamshid needed her most at the side of the man who'd injured him. "I am sorry," he whispered.

"I don't want your apology," Manizheh snapped. "I want my children. I want my city. I want the throne, and the seal Zaydi al Qahtani stole from my ancestors. I want my generation of Daevas to stop suffering because of the actions of yours. And quite frankly, Afshin, I do not give a damn if you approve of my methods."

Dara ran his hands through his hair. "There has to be a better way." He could hear the plea in his voice.

"There isn't. Your warriors swore oaths to me. If you go after Kaveh, we will be gone when you return. I will take them to Daevabad, release the poison myself, and hope it kills Ghassan before he realizes what's happening and has Nahri, Jamshid, and every Daeva he can get his hands on slaughtered." She stared at him. "Or you can help me."

Dara's hands curled into fists. He felt more trapped than he had in years, as though a net he'd unknowingly stepped into had snapped up around him. And, Creator forgive him, he could not see a way to escape that wouldn't kill more people he loved.

He dropped his gaze, briefly closing his eyes. *Forgive me, Tamima,* he prayed softly. Manizheh might be right. This brutal act might be enough to force the other tribes into a more permanent submission.

But for standing at her side while she committed it, Dara did not imagine he would ever again see the garden where his sister waited for him.

He opened his eyes. His soul was heavy as iron. "My soldiers are asking questions," he said slowly. "And I do not want this guilt on their consciences." He fixed his gaze on his Nahid and bowed his head once again. "What would you have me tell them?"

20

ALI

"Take the bricks as well," Ali said, shading his eyes against the bright sun to scan the mound of rubble that his workers had unearthed while ripping up the platform erected over Sheikh Anas's ruined mosque. "We'll find a way to reuse them."

One of the men tugged a piece of rotting textile from the pile of debris. "Looks like old carpeting." He tossed it at Ali's feet. "Probably not worth saving, no?"

Ali's eyes locked on the tattered fragment; what remained of the carpet's geometric pattern was instantly familiar. Ali had prayed upon that carpet, had sat in rapturous silence as he listened to Sheikh Anas's thunderous sermons.

"No," he said, his throat thickening at the memory of his murdered sheikh. "Probably not."

A heavy hand dropped on his shoulder, startling him from his thoughts. "The women and children are off with Aqisa," Lubayd announced. "Tents are waiting for them outside the hospital and that grumpy doctor of yours is going to examine them."

"That grumpy doctor has a name," Ali replied wearily. "And I would recommend not getting on her bad side. But thank you."

Lubayd squinted at him. "Everything all right, brother? You don't look well."

Ali sighed, turning away from the carpet. "This isn't an easy place to be." He glanced across the street where a few of the shafit men they'd freed were eating food his sister had sent over from the palace kitchens. Freshly arrived—or rather dragged—to Daevabad from the human world, they had no other homes to return to. "And these aren't easy stories to hear."

Lubayd followed his gaze. "I'd like to toss the purebloods who oversaw this place in the lake. A bunch of thieves and thugs— stealing jewelry, harassing women, beating the men who talked back." He shook his head. "And under the guise of helping shafit newcomers find family. What a rotten scheme."

"Not just newcomers," Ali pointed out. "I've been speaking to plenty of people who were kidnapped and pressed into service, like the father and daughter we first came upon."

"And you said it was a Geziri man at the top, correct? Tariq al whatever?" Lubayd looked disgusted. "Shameful. Such behavior goes against everything we've fought for."

"Money changes people," Ali said. "And I think quite a lot was made here."

They started walking. "Speaking of money, are we threatening any more rich folk today?" Lubayd asked.

Ali shook his head, wiping the dust from his face with the end of his turban. "Not threatening—correcting a fiscal deficit. But no, not today. I've hammered out a repayment plan with Abul Dawanik," he said, naming the Ayaanle trade envoy. "Their first payment should be in the Treasury by month's end, and he agreed to make immediate arrangements to cover the costs of new uniforms for the Royal Guard and zulfiqars for the cadets. Their rations should be improved soon as well. Turns out the official in charge of contracting meals for the Citadel was taking a cut from the money he was granted. His secretary figured it out but was too afraid to approach my father."

"I take it that secretary now has his job?"

Ali smiled. "And my eternal gratitude."

Lubayd clucked his tongue. "Do you ever rest between these tasks? You *do* know most people sleep at night, yes? They don't just hunch over pages of numbers and mutter to themselves."

"I like working hard," Ali retorted. "It keeps my mind off things."

"This seems like the kind of place where you should probably keep your mind *on* things." Lubayd gestured at a trio of djinn pulling partitions from the wreckage. "Soldiers?"

"Friends from when I was a cadet. They had the day off and wanted to help."

"I suspect they're not the only ones." Lubayd lowered his voice. "I've been hearing whispers again, the kind you asked me to keep an ear out for."

Ali stopped. "From the Guard?"

Lubayd nodded. "A lot of soldiers think fondly of you, Ali. *Very* fondly. And when those new uniforms and rations show up at the Citadel, people are going to know you're behind them."

Ali paused. "Good."

Lubayd started. "*Good?*"

"My father spent five years making it clear he didn't care whether I lived or died," Ali said, defending himself. "Should I pretend I'm not pleased people like me . . . particularly when those people are the ones with weapons?"

His friend assessed him shrewdly. "I might not be some Daevabadi courtier, Ali, but even *I* know what it looks like when bitter second sons start making friends with the military." Intent laced into his voice. "That wasn't the plan, remember? The plan was to return to Am Gezira with your head still attached to your neck. With *my* head still attached to *my* neck."

The sound of horses—at least a half dozen, their hooves striking the cobbled stones with speed—interrupted them. Ali glanced up, ready to chide whoever it was for riding at such a pace in the crowded plaza.

The words died on his tongue. It was Muntadhir—and he looked furious. Just behind him rode a coterie of his companions, the wealthy dilettantes who orbited him like particularly useless moons. They stood out in this neighborhood, one of Daevabad's poorest, their jewels glinting in the sun and their vibrant silks gaudy.

Despite the crowd, Muntadhir was across the plaza in moments; he'd always been an excellent horseman. When they reached Ali, his mount came to an effortless stop, as if it could read its rider's thoughts. It was a beautiful animal, silver spots scattered across its ebony hide like a spray of stars in the night sky.

Ali tensed. He wasn't expecting his brother. On the contrary, Muntadhir had been avoiding Ali's increasingly desperate attempts to talk to him with admirable success. His brother ignored him when they were at court and had obviously enlisted his formidable—and loyal—staff in ensuring they were never alone. Ali would no sooner corner him after a meeting than a steward would magically appear to usher Muntadhir off on some "urgent" unspecified errand.

"Emir," Ali greeted, uneasy. Every instinct was warning him to tread carefully. "Peace be upon you."

"Peace is the last thing you've brought me," Muntadhir snapped. He threw a thick scroll at Ali, which Ali instinctively caught. "Is this a joke?"

Baffled, Ali unfurled the scroll. He recognized it at once . . . mostly because he'd thrown it himself, hours earlier, at the men he'd found forcing a new group of stolen shafit into the foul pens Ali's workers had just finished tearing down. It was a royal proclamation declaring the area was now the property of the king, and that any shafit in the vicinity were free to leave.

He frowned. "How did you get this?"

"Strange you should ask: it was given to *my cousin* this morning by one of his servants."

A terrible chill descended over Ali. "Tariq al Ubari is your *cousin*? One of your *relatives* was responsible for this place?"

A Geziri man emerged from Muntadhir's crowd of sparkling friends. He sat in a gilded saddle upon a beautiful red stallion, wearing a fine brocade coat woven with silver thread and jade beads. Ropes of pearls lined his neck, the largest ending in a gold brooch the size of Ali's fist, encrusted with rubies in the shape of a zahhak.

Ali instantly disliked him. "You're Tariq al Ubari, I take it?" he asked.

"Cousin to our emir, God preserve him," Tariq declared coolly, matching Ali's disdain. "Queen Saffiyeh, may her soul rest in peace, and I shared a third great-great-uncle."

Oh. The mention of Muntadhir's mother landed like a heavy stone between them. Ali tried to maintain his calm, and he could see Muntadhir struggling to do the same. His brother rarely spoke about his mother. Ali had never known her—she'd died before he was born, when Muntadhir himself was still a child. But he'd heard she and Muntadhir had been very close, and he'd always known his brother was deeply affected by her loss.

Looking at Tariq of the third great-great-uncle, Ali suspected he knew as well, and was only too happy to take advantage of that grief. Anger stirred in Ali's heart. He didn't need another reason to hate the man behind this abominable place, but the fact that he was so obviously using Muntadhir made his hatred burn a hundred times hotter.

Still, the situation before him was delicate. If Tariq had been a closer relation, Ali would have recognized the name and acted with more discretion. God knew things were already strained enough between him and Muntadhir.

He stepped closer to his brother's horse. "Why didn't you say something sooner?"

Muntadhir flushed. "I wasn't aware. Do you know all your relatives' personal assets?"

"I know none of them made a business of selling shafit like slaves." Ali hissed the words under his breath, but clearly not quietly enough, for Tariq drew up.

"*Slaves?*" Tariq rolled his eyes, the word coming in a condescending drawl. "By the Most High, we're all aware of how sensitive you are when it comes to the shafit, Prince Alizayd, but there were no *slaves* here. God forbid such a thing. There were shafit looking for work, and for their pureblooded kin."

Ali couldn't believe the man's gall. "Looking for work?" he asked incredulously. "The first time I came upon this place, your men were auctioning off a child as she screamed for her father!"

Muntadhir turned toward Tariq in shock. "Is that true?"

Ali had to hand it to Tariq—the man didn't so much as flinch. "Of course not." He touched his heart. "Come, Emir, you know me. And you know how the shafit like to exaggerate their woes . . . particularly before a man known to have an open purse and susceptible heart." He shook his head. "I have no doubt they have been filling your poor brother's ears with all sorts of tales of beatings and abuse."

Lubayd threw out a hand, stopping Ali before he lunged forward. But he couldn't stop Ali's tongue. "You lying snake—"

"Enough," Muntadhir snapped. "Both of you." His brother now looked more annoyed than shaken, the doubt that had flashed in his eyes when Ali mentioned the girl already gone. "We didn't come here to fight, Alizayd. The order came from Abba, and Tariq doesn't plan to contest it. But he wants to be properly compensated."

Ali gritted his teeth. "He was. I outlined terms in the scroll."

"A hundred dinars?" Tariq mocked. "That's nothing. Oh, wait, forgive me . . . *and* passage to Mecca," he added sarcastically. "Clearly more an order than an offer."

It was costing every bit of self-control Ali had not to drag this man from his horse. Had Muntadhir not been there, he probably would have. Feeling water begin to pool in his hands, he quickly clenched his fists; he dared not lose control here. "It is a great honor to be allowed to retire to Mecca," he said in an even voice. "We only allow a handful of new djinn to enter the holy city each year; there are those who would weep for such a prize."

"Well, I'm not one of them," Tariq retorted. "My life and my business are in Daevabad. I'm not leaving, and I insist you properly compensate me."

"I can leave you to the shafit you claim to have been assisting in 'finding jobs and kin,'" Ali suggested coldly. "Would that be proper compensation?"

"*No*," Muntadhir said flatly, his eyes flashing as his cousin paled. "Though if you threaten him again, we're going to be having a very different conversation." He stared at Ali. "This man is my kin," he said, his voice low and laced with purpose. "He's under my protection. Do not dishonor me by treating him so disdainfully. There must be some sort of compromise we can agree to."

Ali met his gaze. He understood quite well the Geziri notions of pride and honor his brother was attempting to appeal to.

But that wasn't the only code their tribe held dear.

"There's no compromise to be made here, Dhiru," Ali replied. "I'm not giving this man another coin. We cannot spare them. You are asking me to take bread out of the mouths of the soldiers who guard your life and bricks from the hospital intended to treat your citizens so an already rich man—a man who twisted our most sacred beliefs—can have his pride soothed?" Ali shook his head. "I will not."

A little too late, Ali realized that much of the crowd had gone quiet and that his words had carried. More people were gathering to watch, shafit and working-class djinn locals from the surrounding neighborhoods, people who were staring at the emir and his overdressed companions with open resentment.

Muntadhir seemed to notice as well. His gray eyes flickered across the growing mob, and Ali saw his hands twitch on the reins.

Tariq pressed on, arrogant. "A very pretty speech to your supporters, Prince Alizayd. I suppose it doesn't matter that it rests on the lies of a bunch of ungrateful dirt-bloods and will ruin one of your kinsmen, a man who escorted the emir's own mother to Daevabad." He stared down his nose at Ali, and when he spoke again, his words were precise. "Perhaps a rather clear lesson to us all in how little family means to you."

Ali was biting his tongue so hard it hurt. He could only thank God it was a dry, sunny day—otherwise he was fairly certain he'd be learning new, murderous things to do with rain. "The shafit aren't lying. I saw with my own eyes—"

"Oh?" Tariq interrupted. "Where are the whips then, Prince Alizayd? The chains and these crying children you claim I have so terribly mistreated?"

"I've sent them away to be cared for." Ali motioned to the debris. "There's no evidence because we've been here since dawn. But you can be damn sure I took down the name of every shafit you abused here, and I'd be happy to present their testimony."

"After you've gilded their tongues, you mean," Tariq snorted. "It is the Ayaanle way, after all."

Ali abruptly lost the battle he'd been waging with his temper. His hand dropped to his khanjar. "Would you like to settle things *our* way?" he hissed in Geziriyya. "You should be *fleeing* to Mecca. If you had any fear of God, you would spend the rest of your days repenting for the evil you've done here before you burn in hell-fire for all—"

"*Enough.*" Muntadhir's voice cracked across the plaza. "Draw that blade, Alizayd, and I'll have you arrested. *No.*" He held up a hand, cutting off Tariq when he opened his mouth. "I've heard enough from both of you. Return to your home, cousin. There's obviously no negotiation to be made here. I'll take care of you and your wife myself." He nodded to the rest of his men. "Let's go."

Ali dropped his hand from his khanjar. "Dhiru, I only meant—"

"I know what you meant. And I told you not to call me that." Muntadhir suddenly looked exhausted, fed up and disgusted with the entire situation. "My God, and to think she almost convinced me to support this madness . . ." He shook his head. "Perhaps I should be grateful for this, in a way."

"Grateful for what?" Ali ventured, even as his stomach twisted in apprehension.

"Grateful for the reminder that you will always choose your beliefs over your family. Which is fine—enjoy having the shafit as your only ally." Muntadhir touched his brow before turning his horse away. "See how far that takes you in Daevabad, little brother."

21

NAHRI

Nahri pounded again on the door to her husband's apartment. "Muntadhir, I don't care who's in there or what you're drinking, open up. We need to go."

There was no response.

Her frustration reached dangerous levels. She knew her husband and early mornings were no companions, but it had taken her weeks to arrange this visit to the Grand Temple, and they were already running late.

She banged on the door again. "If I have to drag you out of bed—"

The door abruptly opened. Nahri nearly tumbled in, narrowly catching herself.

"Banu Nahida . . ." Muntadhir leaned heavily against the door frame. "Wife," he clarified, lifting a jade wine cup to his lips. "Always so impatient."

Nahri stared at him, completely lost for words. Muntadhir was half dressed, wearing what appeared to be a woman's shawl wrapped around his waist and the dramatically peaked court cap of a Tukharistani noble.

A burst of laughter behind him caught her attention, and Nahri glanced past his shoulder to see two dazzling women lounging in similar states of disarray. One was smoking from a water pipe while the second—dressed in nothing but Muntadhir's court turban wrapped in a way it was certainly *not* intended—rearranged game pieces.

Nahri inhaled, fighting the sudden desire to burn the room down. "Muntadhir," she said, her jaw clenching, "do you not remember that we're supposed to be visiting the Grand Temple today?"

"You know . . . I did remember, as a matter of fact." Muntadhir drained his cup.

Nahri threw up her hands. "Then what is *this*? I can't take you to my people's holiest place while you're drunk and wearing your courtesan's scarf!"

"I'm not going."

Nahri blinked. "Excuse me?"

"I'm not going. I already told you: I think this plan to hire and treat shafit is madness."

"But . . . but you agreed to come today. And your father told you to!" Her voice rose in alarm.

"Ah, there you are wrong," Muntadhir declared, wagging a finger in her face. "He did not order such a thing specifically. He said you had our support." He shrugged. "So tell your priests that you do."

"They're not going to believe me! And if you don't show up, they're going to think there's a reason." She shook her head. "I can't risk another excuse for them to oppose me. They'll take this an insult."

Muntadhir snorted. "They'll be relieved. You're the only Daeva who wants to see a Qahtani in your temple."

The other women laughed in the background again, one throwing dice, and Nahri flinched. "Why are you doing this?" she whispered. "Do you really hate me so much?"

His disinterested expression slipped. "I don't hate you, Nahri. But you're going down a path I can't support, with a partner who destroys everything he touches. I will not sit with my future subjects in a place they hold sacred and make promises I don't believe in."

"You could have told me that last week!"

Muntadhir inclined his head. "Last week, Alizayd had yet to threaten my cousin with hellfire in front of a mob of angry mixed-bloods."

Nahri grabbed his wrist. "He did *what*?"

"I did try to warn you. Go ask your sheikh about it. Hell, ask *him* to go to the Temple with you. I'm sure it would be most entertaining." Muntadhir removed his arm from her grasp and then shut the door in her face.

For a full breath, Nahri stood there stunned. Then she slammed her fists against the door. "MUNTADHIR!"

It stayed closed. As her fury grew, a few cracks appeared in the carved wood and the hinges began to smoke.

No. Nahri stepped back. She'd be damned if she was going to humiliate herself begging her drunken wretch of a husband to keep his word. But damn the bloody princes and their idiotic arguments!

She whirled around, charging down the hall. If Alizayd al Qahtani's recklessness ruined her plans today, she *was* going to poison him.

The door to Ali's apartment was closed when she arrived, and a soldier rose to his feet as she approached. Out of patience and with the palace's magic whirling in her blood, Nahri had no sooner snapped her fingers then a corner brazier unfurled, tossing its fiery contents to the floor and snaking around the soldier's ankle. It yanked him to the ground, and the door burst open before her.

She stepped in and then paused, for a moment not certain she'd entered the correct room. Ali's apartment was in chaos. A half-dozen floor desks were being used by harassed-looking secretaries, and scrolls and record books were everywhere, as were people, pushing papers around and arguing in multiple languages.

Ali's irate voice drifted to her from across the room. "—and I told you I've already awarded the contract. I don't care who your boss's uncle is; that's not how I do things. The hospital's plumbing is being installed by a guild *without* a history of hexing their competition."

She made her way toward him, dodging several startled scribes. Ali noticed her approach at once and quickly straightened up . . . so swiftly, in fact, that he upset an ink bottle across his pale blue dishdasha.

"Banu Nahida, p-peace be upon you," he stammered, dabbing at the ink. "Er, aren't you supposed to be at the Grand Temple?"

"I was supposed to be, yes." She pushed away the edge of her chador to poke a finger at his chest. "With my husband. That is what my people and priests are expecting. And yet my *husband* is now in his cups, entertaining company that is definitely not me, and he's saying *you're* responsible. That you were shouting in the streets about how his cousin was going to burn in hell." She jabbed him again. "Do the two of you not have a *single* grain of sense between you?"

Ali's expression instantly grew stormy. "I didn't say he was *going* to burn in hell," he defended. "I suggested he repent before that happened."

Nahri felt the floor shift beneath her feet. She closed her eyes for a minute, willing herself to be calm. "Alizayd. I spent weeks fighting with the priests to allow this visit. If he doesn't come, they'll view it as a slight. And if they view it as a slight—if they don't think I have your family's support—then how do you think they're going to react when I announce I want to overturn *centuries of tradition* to work alongside shafit? I'm staking my reputation on this hospital. If it fails because you can't keep your mouth shut, hellfire is going to be the least of your problems."

She'd swear the air sparked as the threat left her lips, and she didn't miss the speed at which several of the nearest djinn backed away.

Ali swallowed. "I'll fix it. I swear. Go to the Temple and wait for him."

NAHRI WAS NOT FEELING OPTIMISTIC.

At her side, Jamshid shifted. "I wish you'd let me go talk to him."

She shook her head. "This is between me and Muntadhir. And you shouldn't be solving his problems for him all the time, Jamshid."

He sighed, readjusting his cap. Like Nahri, he was in his Temple attire, bloody and ash-stained hospital smocks traded for silk chadors and coats. "Did you tell Nisreen the truth about why we were coming here?"

Nahri shifted on her feet. "No," she confessed. Nisreen had stayed behind to oversee the infirmary, a thing for which Nahri was secretly relieved. She didn't need another voice arguing against her. "We . . . we have not been seeing eye to eye on much lately."

"She doesn't strike me as the type to enjoy being left in the dark," Jamshid observed mildly.

Nahri grimaced. She didn't like the tension that had grown between her and her mentor, but neither did she know how to fix it.

Jamshid glanced at the gate. "Speaking of unhappy elders, I should probably tell you that my father is—"

The clattering of hooves cut him off. Nahri glanced up to see a rider in an ebony robe cantering toward them. Relief flared in her chest.

It lasted only a moment. Because that rider was *not* her husband.

Ali was at their side in seconds, looking, well, rather damn princely on a magnificent gray stallion. He was dressed in royal colors, the first time she'd ever seen him so, the gold-trimmed black robe smoking around his ankles, the brilliant blue, purple, and gold turban wrapped around his head. He'd shaved his scruffy beard into a semblance of order and was even wearing jewelry—a strand of pearls looping his neck, and a heavy silver ring crowned with one of the famed pink diamonds of Ta Ntry on his left thumb.

Nahri gawked at him. "You're not Muntadhir."

"I am not," he agreed, sliding from the horse. He must have prepared in a hurry; he smelled of freshly burned agarwood, and there were drops of water still clinging to his neck. "My brother remains indisposed."

Jamshid was looking at Ali with open hostility. "Are those his clothes?"

"He doesn't seem to need them today." Ali glanced back, peering in the direction from which he'd come. "Where is she?" he asked, seemingly to himself. "She was right behind me . . ."

Jamshid stepped between them. "Nahri, you can't bring him into the Temple," he warned, switching to Divasti. "People *burn him in effigy* in the Temple!"

Nahri didn't get a chance to respond. Another rider had joined them, one even more surprising than Ali.

"Peace be upon you," Zaynab said in a gallant tone as she dismounted. "A lovely day, isn't it?'

Nahri's mouth actually fell open. The Qahtani princess looked even more dazzling than her brother, in billowy gold riding pants beneath a brightly striped indigo tunic. She wore her black shayla lightly, under a headdress of glittering sapphires, her face partially obscured by a silver Geziri mask. Jewels winked from each of her fingers.

Zaynab took her brother's hand, turning a winning smile toward the Daevas who'd gathered to gawk. There was no denying the royal siblings made for an extraordinary sight, something Zaynab seemed to be relishing.

"What-what are you doing here?" Nahri managed to ask.

Zaynab shrugged. "Ali came running and said you needed Qahtanis to help sway your priests. Now you have some. Even better, you have me." Her tone was sugar sweet. "If you're not aware, the two of you"—she motioned between Ali and Nahri—"are rather abrasive." Her gaze slid past Nahri. "Jamshid!" she said warmly. "How are you? How is your father?"

Some of the anger left Jamshid's face at Zaynab's aggressive goodwill. "We are well, Princess. Thank you for asking." He darted a look at Nahri. "Actually, on the matter of my father . . . he is here."

Nahri closed her eyes. This was all beginning to feel like a terrible dream. "Your father is back? Kaveh's *here*?"

Jamshid nodded, swallowing. "He typically goes straight to the Temple after a journey, to thank the Creator for ensuring his safety."

"What a lovely tradition," Zaynab said cheerfully, aiming a sharp look at her brother. At the mention of Kaveh, Ali's face had twisted like he'd sucked on a lemon. "Isn't that right, Alizayd?"

Ali offered something that might have been a nod. "Yes. Lovely."

"Shall we go?" Zaynab said, stepping between the men. "Jamshid, would you give me a tour? Ali and Nahri likely have many extremely boring things to discuss."

"Your *sister*?" Nahri hissed as soon as Jamshid and Zaynab moved out of earshot.

Ali looked at her helplessly. "*Kaveh?*"

"That's a surprise to me as well," she said grimly. "He's very orthodox. He will argue against this."

"And he won't like seeing me here," Ali warned. "We . . . we do not have the most amicable history."

"You and Kaveh?" she asked sarcastically. "I can't imagine why not." She sighed, glancing at the Temple Gates. For all her fears, bringing Alizayd al Qahtani into the Temple was not nearly as bad as saying she intended to work alongside shafit. "Leave your weapons in my litter."

Ali's hand went to the hilt of his zulfiqar like an overprotective mother might clutch a child. "Why?"

"We don't allow weapons in the Temple. *None*," she added, sensing this was a thing to be clear upon with the warrior prince before her.

"Fine," he muttered, removing his zulfiqar and khanjar and placing them delicately inside Nahri's litter. He freed a small knife from a holster around his ankle and then a spike from his sleeve. He turned back, the sunlight glinting off the copper relic in his ear. "Let's go."

Zaynab and Jamshid were already halfway down the main path, Zaynab's lilting voice carrying back to them. The Temple grounds were crowded as usual, with local Daevabadis strolling the manicured grounds and extended families of pilgrims seated on rugs spread under shade trees. People had stopped to look at Zaynab, excitedly peeking and pointing in the princess's direction.

The sight of Ali provoked a very different reaction. Nahri heard a couple of gasps, catching sight of narrowed eyes and open horror.

She ignored it. She straightened her shoulders and tipped her chin up. She would not show weakness today.

Ali gazed upon the Temple complex with visible appreciation, seeming not to notice the hostility around him. "This is beautiful," he said admiringly as they passed a row of towering cedars. "These trees look like they've been here since Anahid's time." He knelt, running his fingers over one of the brightly colored stone disks that made up the Temple's pathways. "And I've never seen anything like these."

"They're from the lake," Nahri explained. "Supposedly the marid brought them up as tribute."

"The marid?" He sounded startled as he straightened up, holding the stone. It was the bright orange of a setting sun, flecked with bits of crimson. "I didn't realize . . ."

The stone in his hand abruptly brightened, shimmering as if under a pale sea.

Nahri knocked it out of his hand.

Ali's eyes were wide. "I-I'm sorry."

"It's fine." Nahri dared a glance around them. People were watching, of course, but it didn't seem anyone had noticed.

She heard Ali swallow. "Do the stones do that often?" he asked hopefully.

"Never, as far as I'm aware." She gave him a sharp look. "Then again, considering the source of these stones . . ."

He cleared his throat, silencing her. "Can we not talk about that here?"

He had a point. "Fine. But don't touch anything else." Nahri paused, recalling just who she was about to bring into the Temple. "And maybe don't say anything. At all."

A disgruntled expression crossed his face, but he remained silent as they caught up with Jamshid and Zaynab at the Temple's entrance.

Zaynab's eyes were shining. "An extraordinary place," she enthused. "Jamshid has been giving me a wonderful tour. Did you know he was once a novitiate here, Ali?"

Ali nodded. "Muntadhir told me you had trained for the priesthood." He looked curious. "What made you leave it for the Guard?"

Jamshid's face was stony. "I wanted to be more proactive in defending my people."

Zaynab swiftly took her brother's arm. "Why don't we go inside?"

As Jamshid led them into the Temple, the healer in Nahri could not help but note that he seemed to be leaning on his cane a bit less. Perhaps the session Muntadhir had interrupted had done some good after all.

"These are our shrines," Jamshid explained, "dedicated to our most honored ancestors." He glanced back at Ali. "I do believe your people killed a number of them."

"A favor they returned more than once, as I recall," Ali replied acidly.

"Maybe we could rehash the war later," Nahri suggested, walking faster. "The longer I am away from the infirmary, the higher the chance of an emergency occurring."

But at her side, Ali suddenly went still. She turned to look at him and saw his gaze was locked on the last shrine. It drew the eye, of course; it was the most popular in the Temple, garlanded with flowers and offerings.

Nahri heard his breath catch. "Is that—"

"Darayavahoush's?" Kaveh's voice rang out from behind them, and then the grand wazir was striding up, still dressed in his traveling cloak. "It is, indeed." He brought his hands up in blessing. "Darayavahoush e-Afshin, the last great defender of the Daeva people and guardian to the Nahids. May he rest in the shade of the Creator."

Nahri saw Jamshid flinch out of the corner of her eye, but he was quiet, obviously loyal to his tribe first in the face of their visitors.

"Grand Wazir," she greeted diplomatically. "May the fires burn brightly for you."

"And for you, Banu Nahida," Kaveh replied. "Princess Zaynab, peace be upon you. An honor and a surprise to see you here." He turned to Ali, the warmth vanishing from his face. "Prince Alizayd," he said flatly. "You returned from Am Gezira."

Ali didn't seem to notice the rudeness. His gaze hadn't left Dara's shrine, and it looked like he was struggling to keep his composure. His eyes flickered to the bow at the back, and then Nahri saw him stiffen. She couldn't blame him—she'd seen Jamshid react the same way to the replica of the weapon that had nearly taken his life.

And then Ali stepped closer, his gaze falling to the base of Dara's statue. Nahri's heart sank. *No. Not today.*

Ali picked up an object from among the pile of tokens. Charred and blackened though it was, its reptilian features were instantly recognizable.

Zaynab softly gasped, the skeleton perhaps too much even for her. "Is that a crocodile?" she asked, her voice laced with anger.

Nahri held her breath. Ali twitched, and she silently cursed whoever had left it. This was it. He was going to explode, he was going to say something so offensive that the priests would want him tossed out, and her plans for the shaft were going to be over before she'd even proposed them.

"I take it this is meant for me?" Ali asked after a moment of silence.

Kaveh spoke first. "I do believe that was the intent." At his side, Jamshid looked ashamed.

"Ali . . . ," Nahri began.

But he was already putting it back. Not on the ground, but at the feet of Dara's stone horse—its hooves stomping the carved sand flies she had no doubt the sharp-eyed prince noticed.

He brought his fingers together. "Then to Darayavahoush e-Afshin," he said, only the faintest hint of sarcasm in his exaggerated politeness. "The best and most terrifying warrior this crocodile has ever fought." He turned back around, flashing an almost frightening smile at Kaveh. "Come, Grand Wazir," he said, throwing his arm around the other man and pulling him close. "It has been too long since we've shared each other's company, and I know our brilliant Banu Nahida is eager to tell you her plans."

ACROSS FROM HER, KARTIR WAS WRINGING HIS HANDS, the elderly priest paler than she'd ever seen. They'd met in a windowless inner chamber with high walls, torches throwing light on the icons of her ancestors that ringed the room. It felt as though even they were staring down disapprovingly at her.

"Shafit? You intend to work with *shafit*?" Kartir finally asked after she finished laying out her plans for the hospital. It sounded as though he were begging her to contradict him.

"I do," Nahri replied. "I have already partnered with one. A physician with far more training and experience than I. She and her husband are incredible practitioners."

"They are *dirt-bloods*," one of the priestesses all but spat in Divasti. "The un-souled spawn of lecherous djinn and humans."

Nahri was suddenly grateful neither Ali nor Zaynab shared their older brother's fluency in the Daeva tongue. "They are as innocent in their creation as you and I." Heat filled her voice. "You forget I was raised in the human world. I will not hear abuse thrown at those who share their blood."

Kartir brought his hands together in a gesture of peace, glaring admonishingly at the priestess. "Nor shall I. Those sentiments do not have a place in the Temple. But, Banu Nahida . . . ," he added, staring at her beseechingly, "please understand that what you suggest is impossible. You cannot use your abilities on a shafit. It is forbidden." Fear filled his dark eyes. "It is said that Nahids lose their abilities upon touching a shafit."

Nahri kept her face composed, but the words hurt. This from the gentle man who'd taught her about their religion, who'd placed Anahid's original altar in her hands and put her doubts and fears to rest on more than one occasion—even he harbored the same prejudices as the rest of her people. As Dara had. As her husband did. As nearly everyone who was dear to her did, in fact.

"An incorrect assumption," she said finally. "But I don't intend to heal shafit myself," she clarified, forcing the despicable words from her tongue. "We'd work and study alongside each other, that's all."

Another priest spoke up. "It is a violation of Suleiman's code to interact with them in any way!"

Nahri was not unaware of Kaveh looking on, the grand wazir's disapproval plain but unvoiced for now; she suspected he was waiting for the right time to strike. "It is not a violation of Suleiman's code," she argued, switching to Djinnistani for Ali and Zaynab's benefit. "It is another interpretation."

"Another interpretation?" Kartir repeated weakly.

"Yes," she replied, her voice firm. "We are in Daevabad, my friends. A protected magical city, hidden from humans. What we do here, how we treat those with their blood, it has no bearing on the human world beyond our gates. Treating those *already in our world* with respect and kindness does not counteract Suleiman's order that we leave humanity alone."

"Does it not?" Kartir asked. "Would it not be condoning such future interactions?"

"No," Nahri said flatly, continuing in Djinnistani. "Whether or not a djinn obeys the law outside our gates is a separate issue from how we treat those inside them." Her voice rose. "Have any of you been to the shafit districts? There are children wading in sewage and mothers dying in childbirth. How can you call your-selves servants of the Creator and think such a thing is permissible?"

That seemed to land, Kartir looking slightly chastened. Ali was staring at her with open pride.

It didn't go unnoticed, and Kaveh finally spoke. "The prince has put these things in your head," he declared in Divasti. "My lady, he is a known radical. You mustn't let his fanaticism about the shafit sway you."

"I need no man to put ideas in my head," Nahri retorted. "You speak out of turn, Kaveh e-Pramukh."

He tented his hands. "I meant no disrespect, Banu Nahida." But there was no apology in his voice; it was the way one would speak to a child, and it grated on her. "What you're suggesting sounds lovely, it indicates a good heart—"

"It indicates a woman who learned her lesson when Ghassan lifted his protection from our tribe after Dara's death," Nahri said in Divasti. "It is kindness as much as pragmatism that moves me. We will never be safe in Daevabad unless we have peace with the shafit. You must see this. They are nearly as numerous in the city as we are. Relying on the djinn to keep us from each other's throats is foolish. It leaves us weak and at their mercy."

"It is out of necessity," Kaveh argued. "My lady, respectfully . . . you are very young. I have seen plenty of overtures of peace to both the djinn and the shafit in my life. They have never ended well."

"That's my choice to make."

"And yet you're asking our blessing," Kartir pointed out gently. "Are you not?"

Nahri hesitated, her gaze drifting to the icons of her ances-tors. The Temple whose construction Anahid had overseen, the people she'd knit back together after Suleiman cursed them.

"I am not," she said, letting the words fall in Djinnistani as she gazed at the elders around her. "I am informing you as a matter of respect. It is my hospital. They are my abilities, and I do not require your permission. I am the Banu Nahida, and believe it or not, *Kaveh*," she said, deliberately leaving out his title, "in my few years in Daevabad, I've learned the meaning and the history behind that title. You would not dare question my ancestors."

Stunned silence met that. The grand wazir stared at her in shock, and a few of the priests drew back.

"Yet the Nahids ruled as a *council*," Kartir pointed out, undeterred. "Your ancestors discussed things among themselves and with their priests and advisors. They did not rule as kings accountable to no one." He looked at neither al Qahtani as he said this, but the implication was there.

"And they were overthrown, Kartir," she replied. "And we have been fighting ever since. It's time to try something new."

"I think it is obvious where the Banu Nahida stands." Kaveh's voice was curt.

"And I." Jamshid hadn't spoken since they entered the room, but he did now, looking his father in the eye. "She has my support, Baba."

Kaveh glanced at the two of them, his gaze inscrutable. "Then I suppose the matter has been decided. If you don't mind . . ." He rose to his feet. "I have had quite a long journey."

His words seemed to disband the meeting, and though Nahri was irked he'd been the one to do so, she was also relieved. She'd made her decision clear, and even if the priests didn't like it, they hardly seemed willing to openly defy her.

Kartir spoke up one more time. "The procession. If you want our support in this, surely you can grant us your presence in that."

Nahri bit back a groan. She should have known it wouldn't be so easy. "Please don't make me do that."

Ali frowned. "Do what?"

"They want to dress me up like Anahid and put me in some parade for Navasatem." She threw Kartir a desperate look. "It's embarrassing."

"It is fun," he clarified with a smile. "The Daeva procession is a favorite part of Navasatem, and it's been centuries since we've had a Nahid to join."

"You had my mother."

He eyed her. "Do the stories I've told you of Banu Manizheh make it seem like she was the type to take part in such a thing?" His face turned beseeching. "Please. Do it for your people."

Nahri sighed, guilt nagging at her. "Fine. If you will support my hospital, I will dress in a costume and smile like a fool." She feigned a glare. "You're slyer than I would have thought."

The elderly priest touched his heart. "The sacrifices one makes for their tribe," he teased.

They left the sanctuary after that, making their way out of the Temple. Sunspots danced across Nahri's vision as they emerged into the bright afternoon light.

Ali paused on the steps. "This place really is lovely," he said, gazing at the lily-dappled reflecting pools. A breeze brought the scent of the cedar trees lining the perimeter. "Thank you for allowing us to visit. The circumstances aside—it was an honor." He cleared his throat. "And I'm sorry about those circumstances. I'm going to try to be more careful, I promise."

"Yes. In turn, thank you for not strangling the grand wazir." But then remembering the chaos of his apartment, Nahri added, a bit reluctantly, "And thank you for the work you've been doing with the hospital. It hasn't gone unnoticed."

Ali turned to look at her, a surprised grin lighting his face. "Was that a compliment?"

"No," she said, forcing a grumpiness she didn't feel into her voice. "It's a simple statement of fact."

They began crossing the garden. "So," Ali continued, a playful edge in his voice, "what is this about dressing up in an Anahid costume?"

She looked up, eyeing him severely. "Don't start, al Qahtani.

Not when you've been admiring your reflection in every shiny surface we've passed since you got off your horse."

Mortification swept the humor off his face. "Was it that obvious?" he whispered.

Nahri paused, savoring his embarrassment. "Only to anyone who looked your way." She smiled sweetly. "So, everyone."

Ali cringed, reaching out to touch his turban. "I never expected to wear this," he said softly. "I couldn't help but wonder how it looked."

"Good luck with that excuse when Muntadhir learns you stole it." Admittedly, Ali did cut a striking figure in the turban, the dazzling gold stripes picking up a warmth in his gray eyes. Still, Nahri didn't like it on him. "It doesn't suit you," she said, as much to herself as to Ali.

"No," he replied tonelessly. "I suppose of the two of us, Muntadhir looks more like what people expect of a Qahtani prince."

She realized too late the double meaning of her words. "Oh, no, Ali. That's not what I meant. Not at all." Every time Nahri pinned her chador over her human-round ears, she had the same feelings about her appearance not matching expectations, and it made her sick to think she might have implied the same to someone else. "It's just I hate that turban. I hate what it represents. The war, Qui-zi . . . it seems so rooted in the worst parts of our past."

Ali stopped, turning to face her fully. "No, I don't suppose a Banu Nahida who just defied a group of men with a collective millennium on her *would* think highly of such a tradition." He smiled, shaking his head. "Your people are blessed to have you as their leader. I hope you know that." He said the words warmly, with what seemed to be all the friendly sincerity in the world.

Nahri's response was immediate. "Maybe one day *your* people will have me as their leader."

She'd meant it as a challenge, and indeed, Ali jerked back, looking slightly startled. But then he broke into a slow grin, his eyes glinting with dark amusement.

"Well, then I guess I better get back to building your hospital." He touched his heart and brow in the Geziri salute, clearly biting back a laugh. "Peace be upon you, Banu Nahida."

Nahri didn't reply—nor did Ali wait for her to do so. Instead he turned away, heading toward Zaynab, who was already waiting at the gate.

Nahri watched him go, suddenly aware of how many other Daevas were doing the same—and the quiet scrutiny with which she suspected many had just observed their interaction.

She let her expression turn severe and she stared at the crowd until people began hastily resuming their own activities. Nahri meant what she'd told the priests; she was going to do this her way, and a good Banu Nahida couldn't show weakness.

So Nahri would make sure she had none.

22

ALI

Ali grinned as he pressed the pump handle with one hand. A rush of cold water splashed to the ground. "Your son's new specialty," he joked to the woman across from him.

Hatset's golden eyes traced the spray of mud across his dish-dasha. "When I envisioned a brighter future for you, baba, you looked distinctly . . . cleaner."

"I like getting my hands dirty." Ali straightened up, wiping his fingers on a rag tucked into his belt. "But what do you think?" he asked, gesturing to the line of bustling workshops in front of the hospital.

"I'm impressed," his mother replied. "Then again, considering the fortune you've shaken out of my tribe since you returned to Daevabad, I'd hope to be impressed."

Ali touched his heart in mock offense. "Ah, what happened to all your words about doing good for my city?" He winked. "Did you think it would be cheap?"

She shook her head, but she was smiling, her gaze lingering on a group of children sitting in the workcamp's school. "It is worth the cost. I'm proud of you. A little exasperated, but still proud."

They continued toward the hospital, and Ali nodded in greeting to a pair of carpenters hammering cabinetry. "It's the shafit doing most of the work," he replied. "I feel more like a glorified task manager than anything; my biggest problem is finding a job for everyone who wants to join us. It's been astonishing to see what people have done with such an opportunity. And in only a few months!"

"A nice thing to watch your beliefs about the shafit made manifest, I take it?"

Ali nodded fervently. "Nothing would make me happier than seeing this place thrive. Let everyone with pretensions of blood purity see what the shafit have accomplished here." He clasped his hands behind his back, toying with his prayer beads. "I wish I could get Abba to see this. We'd have more security investing in the shafit than beating them into obedience."

"Then it sounds as though you should stop pining over this Bir Nabat of yours and work on convincing your father to let you stay in Daevabad." Hatset looked at him intently as they entered the hospital. "The kind of change you want takes time and patience, child. You consider yourself some sort of farmer now, don't you? Do you toss seeds upon the ground only to abandon them in hopes they'll grow untended?"

Ali held his tongue at that. And not just because of the workers bustling around them, but because in truth, with every passing day in Daevabad, he wasn't quite sure what he wanted.

Hatset let out a surprised exclamation as they stepped into the main corridor. "Well, isn't this lovely," she said, admiring the vivid murals Elashia had painted on the walls: dazzling sandships darting through the dunes and the lush oases of Qart Sahar alongside images of its craggy bluffs and azure seas.

"You should see what happens when Nahri passes through," Ali said. "The paintings come alive, the waves crashing over the beach, the trees blooming. The Nahid magic in this place is incredible."

"Yes, it's becoming more and more clear she's cast quite the spell," Hatset said lightly.

Ali leaned over one of the balustrades to check the day's progress. At first glance, the hospital's heart was barely recognizable from the wild, weed-strewn ruin Nahri had first shown him. The feral garden had been transformed into a small slice of paradise, along whose tiled paths visitors and patients might amble, enjoying the sweet-smelling water of the fountains and the coolness of the palms' shade. The interior walls had been rebuilt, and woodworkers were putting together a glasswork roof that would maximize the amount of natural light allowed into the rooms. The main examination chamber was done, awaiting furnishings and cabinetry.

"Prince Alizayd!"

A voice caught his attention, and Ali glanced across the courtyard to see a group of shafit seamstresses seated among a pile of embroidered curtains. A woman who looked to be around his age had risen to her feet, a shy smile on her face.

She continued speaking when their gazes met, a blush rising in her cheeks. "I'm so sorry to bother you, Your Highness. But if you're around later, we were thinking . . ." She gestured to the other women and several giggled. "We hoped you might be able to help us hang these curtains."

"I . . . of course," Ali replied, slightly puzzled by the request. "Let me know when you're ready."

She smiled again, and Ali could not help but note it was to a rather fetching effect. "We'll be sure to hunt you down." She resumed her seat, whispering to her companions.

"It's fascinating," his mother said dryly, "that in this entire magical complex full of building equipment, the only way to hang curtains is to rely on an unmarried, overly tall, handsome young prince."

Ali quickly pulled his gaze from the young women. "I'm sure they meant nothing like that."

Hatset snorted. "Not even you're that naive." She wound her arm through his as they kept walking. "But you know . . . it wouldn't be the worst idea for you to burn a marriage mask with a nice shafit girl. Maybe then you'd actually *visit* your bed instead of working yourself to death."

Embarassed heat swept his face so fast Ali felt he might actually burst into flames. "*Amma* . . ."

"What? Am I not permitted to want some happiness for my only son?"

He was already shaking his head. "You know I'm not allowed to marry."

"No, what you're not allowed is a gaudy ceremony with a noblewoman who could offer you political allies and heirs that might compete with Muntadhir's—which is why I'm not suggesting that." She studied him, her eyes soft. "But I worry about you, baba. You seem lonely. If you would like either Zaynab or me to make inquiries—"

"No," Ali said, trying to keep the ache from his voice. His mother's assessment wasn't wrong—it was simply a part of his life he tried not to dwell on. Growing up as Muntadhir's future Qaid, Ali had attempted to steel himself for what that future would look like—a violent, lonely life in the Citadel for Ali; wealth, a family, and the throne for Muntadhir. Ali had found it easier not to think about the things he'd be denied, the luxuries reserved for his brother.

But those were oaths he'd made as a child, too young to understand their cost. Not that it mattered now. Ali would never be Qaid, and he could not pretend resentment hadn't worked its way into his heart. But there was nothing to be done about it. He'd meant what he said to Lubayd and Aqisa when they teased him about marriage: he would not make vows to an innocent woman if he didn't think he could live up to them, and right now, he was barely capable of protecting himself.

His mother was still looking at him expectantly. "Can we discuss this another time?" he asked. "Perhaps on a day we're *not* trying to force a meeting with a temperamental scholar?"

Hatset rolled her eyes. "There's not going to be any forcing, my dear. I've been dealing with Ustadh Issa for years."

Ali was glad she was so confident. He'd been shocked to learn the Ayaanle scholar his mother hoped could tell them more about the marid and the batty old man barricaded in a room at the hospital were one and the same. Ali had yet to even set eyes on him; upon learning strangers would be entering the hospital, he'd filled the corridor outside his quarters with all manner of magical traps. Finally, after several workers had been bitten by hexed books, Nahri and Razu—the only people Issa would speak to—had been able to negotiate a compromise: no one would be permitted near his room, and in return, he'd stop cursing the corridor.

"We should have asked Nahri to come," Ali said again. "Issa likes her, and she's very skilled at prying information out of people."

His mother gave him a dark look. "You best make sure she's not prying information out of *you*. That woman is the kind of ally you keep at knife's length." They stopped outside the scholar's locked door, and Hatset knocked. "Ustadh Is—"

She hadn't even finished the word when Ali felt a whisper of magic. He yanked his mother back—just before a saber, made from what looked like disassembled astrolabes, sliced across the door frame.

Ali swore in Geziriyya, but Hatset merely shook her head. "Ustadh, now really," she lectured in Ntaran. "We've discussed

being more sociable." A crafty note entered her voice. "Besides . . .
I have a gift for you."

The door abruptly cracked open, but only a handbreadth. Ali
jumped as a pair of emerald-bright eyes appeared in the gloomy
dark.

"Queen Hatset?" Even Issa's voice sounded ancient.

His mother pulled a tiny ash-colored sack from her robe. "I
do believe you were interested in this for your experiments when
last we met?"

Ali inhaled, recognizing the sharp smell. "Gunpowder? You're
going to give him gunpowder? For his *experiments*?"

Hatset shushed him. "A brief chat, Issa," she said smoothly.
"A very brief, *very* confidential chat."

The scholar's luminous eyes darted between them. "There
are no humans with you?"

"We have been over this a hundred times, Ustadh. There are
no humans in Daevabad."

The door swung open, the sack of gunpowder vanishing
from his mother's hand faster than Ali's eyes could track.

"Come, come!" Issa ushered them in, slamming the door
closed when they passed the threshold, whispering what sounded
like an unreasonable number of locking charms under his breath.

Ali was regretting their decision to come here with each passing
moment, but he followed his mother into the cavernous chamber.
Books were stacked to the ceiling and scrolls stuffed into shelves
Issa seemed to have magicked together from salvaged bits of the
infirmary's ruins. A long row of dusty stained-glass windows threw
gloomy light onto a low table crowded with gleaming metal instruments, pieces of parchment, and burning candles. A cot lay tucked
between two towering piles of books and behind a section of the
floor studded with broken glass, as though the scholar feared being
attacked while he slept. Only one small corner of the room was kept
neat, a pair of floor cushions framing a striped ottoman that had

been carefully set with a silver tray that held a teapot, glasses, and, judging from the smell, several of the cardamom-spiced sweets Nahri was fond of.

We really should have brought her, Ali thought again, guilt gnawing at him. God knew he was already keeping enough secrets from Nahri.

The scholar returned to a well-worn pillow on the floor, folding his skinny limbs beneath him like some sort of gangly bird. As a resurrected formerly enslaved djinn, Issa's age was impossible to guess. His face was well lined and his fuzzy brows and beard were entirely snow white. And the disapproving expression on his face was . . . oddly familiar.

"Do I know you?" Ali asked slowly, studying the man.

Issa's green eyes flickered over him. "Yes," he said shortly. "I threw you out of a history lecture once for asking too many questions." He tilted his head. "You were much smaller."

"That was *you*?" The memory came to Ali immediately—not many tutors had dared treat one of Ghassan's sons with such disrespect. Ali had been young, no older than ten, but the man he remembered tossing him out had been a forbidding, furious scholar in fine robes . . . nothing like the frail old man before him. "I don't understand. If you had a position at the Royal Library, what are you doing here?"

Pain filled the scholar's bright eyes. "I was forced to resign."

Hatset took a seat across from Issa, motioning for Ali to do the same. "After the Afshin's rampage, there was a lot of violence directed at the rest of city's formerly enslaved djinn. Most fled the city, but Issa is too stubborn." She shook her head. "I wish you would return home, my friend. You would be more comfortable in Ta Ntry."

Issa scowled. "I am too old for journeying. And I hate boats." He threw an irritated glance in Ali's direction. "The hospital made for a perfectly fine home until this one's workers arrived.

They hammer constantly." He sounded wounded. "*And* they scared away the chimera living in the basement."

Ali was incredulous. "It tried to *eat* someone."

"It was a rare specimen!"

Hatset quickly interjected. "Since you bring up rare specimens . . . we are here to speak to you about another elusive creature. The marid."

Issa's expression changed, alarm sweeping away his cantankerousness. "What could you possibly want to know about the marid?"

"The old tales," Hatset replied calmly. "They've become little more than a legend for my generation of Ayaanle. However, I've heard encounters with the marid were far more common in your time."

"Consider it a blessing they've all but vanished." Issa's expression darkened further. "It is not wise to discuss the marid with our youth, my queen. Particularly overly ambitious ones who ask too many questions." He gave a disgruntled nod in Ali's direction.

His mother persisted. "It's not mere curiosity, Ustadh. We need your help."

Issa shook his head. "I spent my career traveling the length of the Nile and saw more djinn than I care to remember destroyed by their fascination with the marid. I thanked God when I learned it was a madness your generation had forgotten, and it's not one I'll rekindle."

"We're not asking you to rekindle anything," Hatset replied. "And we're not the ones who reached out first—" She grabbed Ali's wrist, swiftly undoing the button that held the sleeve of his dishdasha flush and pushed it back, revealing his scars. "It's the marid who came to us."

Issa's green eyes locked on Ali's scars. He inhaled, straightening up like a shot.

Then he slapped Ali across the face. "Fool!" he shouted. "Apostate! How dare you make a pact with them? What ghastly abomination did you commit to convince them to spare you, Alizayd al Qahtani?"

Ali reeled back, ducking a second blow. "I didn't make a pact with anyone!"

"Liar!" Issa wagged an angry finger in his face. "Do you think I don't know about your previous snooping?"

"My what?" Ali sputtered. "What in God's name are you going on about?"

"I think I'd like to know as well," Hatset said sharply. "Preferably before you start beating my son again."

Issa stormed across the room. With a burst of fiery sparks, a locked chest popped out of the air, landing with a dusty thud. Issa threw it open and plucked out a papyrus scroll, waving it like a sword. "Remember this?"

Ali scowled. "No. Do you have any idea how many scrolls I've seen in my life?"

Issa unfurled it, spreading it on the table. "And how many of those were guides to summoning a marid?" he asked knowingly, as if he'd caught Ali out.

Thoroughly confused, Ali stepped closer. A brilliant blue river had been painted on the scroll. It was a map, he realized. A map of the Nile, from what he could interpret of the roughly drawn borders. That was all he could make out; though there were notations, they were written in a script consisting of bizarre, entirely incomprehensible pictograms.

And then Ali remembered. "This is the map Nahri and I found in the catacombs of the Royal Library."

Issa glared. "So you *do* admit you were trying contact the marid?"

"Of course not!" Ali was rapidly losing patience with this hot-tempered old man. "The Banu Nahida and I were looking into the story that the marid supposedly cursed her appearance and left her in Egypt. We heard this scroll was written by the last djinn to see one in the area. I couldn't read it, so I sent it off for translation." He narrowed his eyes on Issa. "To you, most likely."

Hatset cut in. "Would you please tell me what it is about this map that has you so upset, Ustadh?"

"It's not just a map," Issa replied. "It's an evil thing, meant to serve as a guide to the desperate." He jabbed a gnarled finger at one set of notations. "These mark places on the river believed to be sacred to the marid, and the notes detail what was done—what was *sacrificed*—to call upon them at that particular spot."

Hatset's eyes flashed. "When you say 'sacrifice' . . . surely you don't mean—"

"I mean exactly as I say," Issa cut in. "Blood must be offered to call upon them."

Ali was horrified. "Ustadh Issa, neither Nahri nor I knew anything of this. I've never been to the Nile. And I never desired *any* contact with the marid, let alone sacrificed someone to them!"

"He fell in the lake, Ustadh," Hatset explained. "It was an accident. He said the marid tortured him into giving up his name, and then they used him to kill the Afshin."

Ali whirled on her. "*Amma*—"

She waved him down. "We need to know."

Issa was staring at Ali in shock. "A marid used you to kill another djinn? They *possessed* you? But that makes no sense . . . possession is an acolyte's last act."

Revulsion swept him. "What are you talking about?"

"It's a pact," Issa replied. "A partnership . . . though not a particularly balanced one. If a marid accepts your sacrifice, you're brought under its protection. And they'll give you almost anything you could desire during your mortal life. But in the end? The acolyte owes their lifeblood. And the marid possess them to take it." His eyes swept over Ali. "You don't survive such a thing."

Ali went entirely cold. "I am no marid's *acolyte*." The word left his lips with a savage denial. "I am a believer in God. I would never commit the blasphemy you're suggesting. And I certainly never made any sacrifice," he added, growing heated even as his mother placed a hand on his shoulder. "Those demons tortured me and forced me to hallucinate the deaths of everyone I loved!"

Issa inclined his head, studying Ali as though he were some sort of equation. "But you did give them your name?"

Ali's shoulders slumped. Not for the first time, he cursed the moment he'd broken under the water. "Yes."

"Then that might have been all they needed—they're clever creatures and God knows they've had centuries to learn how to twist the rules." Issa tapped his chin, looking perplexed. "But I don't understand *why*. Plotting the murder of a Daeva—a lesser being—would be risky, even if they used a fellow djinn to do it."

Hatset frowned. "Do they have a quarrel that you know of with the Daevas?"

"It's said the marid cursed the lake after a falling-out with the Nahid Council," Issa replied. "But that must have been over two thousand years ago. As far as I know, they haven't been seen in Daevabad since."

Ali's skin tingled. That, he knew, was not at all true. In the aftermath of his possession, Ali had said the same thing to his father and had been quietly told the marid had indeed been seen—at the side of Zaydi al Qahtani's Ayaanle allies.

But he held his tongue. He'd sworn to his father, sworn on their tribe and his blood, not to reveal that information. Even the slightest whisper that his ancestors had conspired with the marid to overthrow the Nahids would rock the foundations of their rule. Zaydi al Qahtani had taken a throne even he believed God had originally granted to the Anahid and her descendants; his reasons and his methods for doing so had to remain above reproach. And if Hatset and Issa didn't already know, Ali wasn't saying anything.

"How do I get rid of it?" he asked brusquely.

Issa stared at him. "Get rid of what?"

"My connection with the marid. These . . . whispers in my head," Ali rushed on, feeling his control start to fray. "My abilities. I want it all gone."

"Your *abilities*?" the scholar repeated in astonishment. "What abilities?"

Ali abruptly let go of the magic he'd been holding back. Water burst from his hands, a fog swirling around his feet. "*This*," he exhaled.

The scholar scurried back. "Oh," he whispered. "That." He blinked rapidly. "That is new."

"No," Hatset said. "It's not." She gave Ali an apologetic look as he whirled around. "A slight—a *very* slight—affinity with water magic runs in our family. It shows up occasionally in our children and usually vanishes by the time they're in their teens. And it's nothing like what you've told me you can do," she added when Ali's eyes went wide. "A toddler having a tantrum might upset a water pitcher from across the room. Zaynab used to spin little water spouts in drinking cups when she didn't think I was watching her."

Ali gasped. "*Zaynab?* Zaynab has these abilities?"

"Not anymore," Hatset said firmly. "She was very young at the time. She probably doesn't even remember them. I would punish her terribly when I caught her." His mother shook her head, looking grim. "I was so frightened someone would see her." She glanced back at him. "But I never considered it of you. You were so Geziri, even as child. And once you joined the Citadel, you were so loyal to their code . . ."

"You feared I would tell," Ali finished when his mother trailed off. He felt sick. He couldn't even say she was wrong.

There were times when he was a child that he was so determined to prove himself true to his father and brother's tribe, so rigid in his conception of faith, that yes, he would have let slip an Ayaanle secret, and it shamed him. He abruptly sat down, running his wet hands over his face. "But why didn't you say anything when I first told you about the marid possession?"

Her words were gentle. "Alu, you were panicking. You'd been in Daevabad less than a week. It wasn't the time."

Issa was looking between them as though he were suddenly very sorry he'd let them in. "*Stop that*," he warned, waving a hand at the ribbon of fog curling around Ali's waist. "Do you have any idea what would happen if someone saw you doing that? I had a mob chase me from the palace just for these emerald eyes!"

"Then help me," Ali begged, struggling to rein back the water. "Please. It's getting harder to control."

"I don't know how to help you," Issa replied, sounding flabbergasted. He glanced at Hatset, for the first time looking slightly chastened. "Forgive me, my queen. I don't know what you were expecting, but I have never come across anything like this. You should take him back to Ta Ntry. He'd be safer and your family might have answers."

"I cannot take him back to Ta Ntry," his mother said plainly. "Things are too tense in the palace. His father and brother will think I'm preparing him for a coup, and if either of them got wind of this?" She nodded at the still lingering fog. "I do not trust them. Ghassan puts the stability of this city before everything else."

Issa shook his head. "Queen Hatset . . ."

"Please." The word cut through the air. "He is my only son, Ustadh," she pressed. "I will get you everything that's ever been written about the marid. I will get you copies of my family records. All I ask is that you look for a way to help us." Her voice turned a little crafty. "And come now, it must be decades since you've had a good mystery on your hands."

"You might not like the answers," Issa pointed out.

Ill with dread, Ali's gaze had fallen to the floor. Still, he could sense the weight of their stares, the worry radiating from his mother.

Hatset spoke again. "I don't think we have a choice."

THOUGH HIS MOTHER HAD ENDED THEIR MEETING with a firm order for Ali to stay calm and let her and Issa handle things, their conversation at the hospital haunted him. In response, Ali threw himself deeper into his work, trying desperately to ignore the whispers that ran through his mind when he bathed and the fact that the rain—which had not abated in days—came down more heavily each time he lost his temper. He hadn't been sleeping much, and now when he did close his eyes, his dreams were plagued with images of a burning lake and ruined ships, of scaled limbs dragging him beneath muddy waters and cold green eyes narrowing over an arrow's shaft. Ali would wake shivering and drenched in sweat, feeling as though someone had just been whispering a warning in his ear.

The effect it was having on his behavior did not go unnoticed.

"Alizayd." His father snapped his fingers in front of Ali's face as they exited the throne room after court. *"Alizayd?"*

Ali blinked, pulled from his daze. "Yes?"

Ghassan eyed him. "Are you all right?" he asked, a little concern in his voice. "I thought for certain you'd have sharp words for the moneychanger from Garama."

Ali could remember neither a moneychanger nor Garama. "Sorry. I'm just tired."

His father narrowed his eyes. "Problems at the hospital?"

"Not at all," Ali said quickly. "Our work there continues smoothly and we should be on track, God willing, to open by Navasatem."

"Excellent." Ghassan clapped his back as they came around the corner. "Take care not to entirely overwork yourself. Ah . . . but speaking of someone who could stand to overwork himself—Muntadhir," he greeted as his eldest son came into view. "I do hope you have an excuse for missing court."

Muntadhir touched his heart and brow. "Peace be upon you, my king," he said, ignoring Ali. "I do indeed. May we speak inside?"

Ali tried to step away, but Ghassan caught his wrist. "No. You can spare a few minutes. Don't think I've not noticed the two of you avoiding each other. It is deeply childish."

Ali flushed and Muntadhir drew up, giving Ali a short, disdainful glance as though he were some sort of irritating bug before sweeping into the office—which was good because Ali did indeed feel a sudden childish urge to coax the water fountain outside his father's office into ruining the expensive cloak draping his brother's shoulders.

To say things had soured between the princes since Ali visited the Daeva temple in Muntadhir's stead was an understatement. Despite their best efforts, Ali and Zaynab hadn't been able to sneak Muntadhir's regalia back into his wardrobe without getting caught, and Muntadhir—sporting a freshly bruised jaw, no doubt courtesy of their father—had thoroughly upbraided them, shouting at his younger siblings until Zaynab had been on the verge of tears and Ali on the verge of making the bottles of liquid intoxicants scattered about the room explode.

He hadn't tried approaching his brother again. It felt like Muntadhir was constantly watching him, studying him with a ruthless calm that left Ali uneasy and more than a little heartsick. Any hope he had of reconciling with the older brother he'd once adored, the brother he still loved, was beginning to fade away.

Even so, he followed, having little other choice.

"—what do you mean you've solved the problem of the southern Geziri sheikhs?" Ghassan was asking. He'd seated himself at his desk and Muntadhir was standing across from him. "Because unless you've managed to conjure up an additional caravanserai, I don't know how we're going to accommodate a thousand unexpected arrivals."

"I just met with the steward in charge of the palace grounds," Muntadhir replied. "I think we should set up a travelers' camp in the front gardens. The Daevas will be horrified, of course, and it would take some time to restore the grounds afterward, but it could be done beautifully: conjured silk tents between the palms, a water garden and courtyard where we could have merchants selling traditional crafts and maybe a storyteller and some musicians performing the old epics." He smiled hesitantly. "I thought it might be a nice homage to our roots—and the sheikhs could hardly claim offense if we put them next to our own palace."

A wistful expression had drifted across his father's face. "That is an excellent suggestion. Very good, Muntadhir. I'm impressed. You've been doing fine work with the Navasatem preparations."

Muntadhir smiled fully, perhaps the most genuine smile Ali had seen cross his face in months, as though a load had been lifted from his shoulders. "Thank you, Abba," he said sincerely. "I hope only to make you proud and honor our name."

"I am certain you do." Ghassan tented his hands. "However, *after* the holiday, Muntadhir, I expect you to turn your attention and charm back to your wife."

The brief pleasure that had bloomed in his brother's face vanished. "My wife and I are fine."

Ghassan eyed him. "This is my palace, Emir. I know everything that goes on within its walls, which means I'm aware you and Nahri haven't visited each other's beds in over four months.

I married the two of you to *unify* our tribes, understand? It's been nearly five years. I had two children by Hatset in less time."

Ali cleared his throat. "Can I . . . leave?"

Neither man looked at him. Muntadhir was staring at their father's desk, a muscle working in his jaw. "These matters take time, Abba," he said finally.

"They're *taking time* because you spend your nights with everyone who isn't your wife, something I've warned you about more than once. Should another person—another Daeva—be distracting you from your duties . . . well, that person can easily be removed."

Muntadhir's head jerked up, and Ali started at the barely checked fury in his brother's face. "There's no one distracting me," Muntadhir snapped. He was gripping Ghassan's desk so hard his knuckles had turned white. "And I am well aware of my duties; you've been beating their importance into me since I was a child."

Ghassan's eyes blazed. "Should you find your position burdensome, Emir," he started coldly, "I have another who can replace you, one I suspect would happily take over your marital duties and whose company your wife already prefers."

Ali's ears burned at the insinuation. "That's not what—"

Disdain twisted Muntadhir's face. "My wife prefers Queen Hatset's endless purse and a fool she can manipulate into building her hospital." He turned to look at Ali. "And after it's completed, she'll have no use for either."

The cruel words landed, piercing something insecure and vulnerable deep in Ali's heart. "She is worth ten of you," he responded, hurt surging forward and crashing past his self control. "What she's doing is brilliant and brave, and you couldn't even pull yourself from your courtesans long enough to visit—"

The office door burst inward, slamming hard against the wall. Ali spun, unsheathing his zulfiqar as he moved between his family and the doorway. But it was only Wajed who appeared, looking stressed and alarmed.

"Abu Muntadhir," he greeted Ghassan in Geziriyya. Somewhere behind him, Ali could hear a woman wailing, her cries echoing through the corridor. "Forgive me, there's been a terrible crime."

"My lady, please!" Ali stiffened at the sound of Kaveh's voice. "You cannot go before the king like this!"

"Yes, I can!" a woman shouted. "It is my right as a citizen!" A string of Divasti followed, broken by sobbing.

Ghassan stood up as a Daeva woman in a blood-soaked chador came stumbling into sight. Kaveh was at her side, pale and tense, as were a handful of other Daevas and two members of the Royal Guard.

"What's going on?" Ghassan demanded, switching to Djinnistani.

Kaveh stepped forward as the woman sank to her knees in front of them, crying into her hands. "Forgive my tribeswoman, my king," he pleaded. "She lost her wits begging to come before you."

"She is welcome to come before me," Ghassan replied. Ali could hear true concern in his voice. "My dear woman, whatever has happened? Are you hurt? I can have the Banu Nahida summoned . . ."

The woman began to cry harder. "It is too late for that. My husband is already dead. They took him, they cut his throat."

Wajed looked grim. "A few of my men found them. Her husband . . ." He shook his head. "It was bad."

"Did you catch them?" Ali asked quickly.

Wajed paused. "No. It . . . we found them near the Geziri Quarter. They'd gone to shop for pearls and . . ."

"This didn't happen in the Geziri Quarter," Kaveh snapped. "I know where you found them, Qaid."

Ghassan's voice was intent. "Who attacked you, my lady?"

"*Shafit*," she spat. "We wanted to see the Nahid hospital, but we didn't get halfway through their workcamp before these filthy men were pulling at our clothes and dragging us into a back alley. They threatened . . . they threatened to dishonor me. Parvez begged them, told them he would give them everything we had . . ." She shook her head as if to dispel the image, and her veil briefly fell from her face.

Shocked recognition stole through Ali, and his gaze darted to the grand wazir. No. It wasn't possible.

Muntadhir had crossed the office to pour a glass of water from the pitcher on the windowsill. He returned and pressed it into the woman's hands with a few soft words of Divasti. She took a shaky breath, wiped her eyes, and then drank.

And with that second glimpse of her face, Ali was certain. He'd seen this woman twice before. Both had been rather memorable occasions. The first time had been at the Daeva tavern he'd visited with Anas, where she'd been laughing and gambling with a group of courtesans. The second time had been at his apartment; she'd been waiting in his bed after his first morning in court, sent to "welcome" him to the palace.

A "welcome" arranged by Kaveh e-Pramukh.

It was Kaveh who spoke next. "I tried to warn the Banu Nahida about that camp," he said, his voice rising as he wrung his hands. "The dirt-bloods are dangerous. It is unnatural to work with them, and now they have killed a Daeva man in broad daylight. The whole place should be torn down."

Ali cleared his throat, fighting for calm. "Were there any witnesses?"

Kaveh eyed him incredulously. "Is her word not enough?"

Not when you're involved. But Ali didn't say that; instead touching his heart and speaking truly, "I meant no offense toward your employee, Grand Wazir. But it could help us catch—"

"I am not his *employee*," the woman declared. "What is that supposed to mean? I am a woman of noble blood! I belonged to none but my Parvez!"

Ali opened his mouth, but Ghassan held up a hand. "*Were there witnesses?* I do not doubt your account, my lady. But it would help us find the perpetrators."

Wajed shook his head. "No witnesses, my king. None who would speak to us anyway, though it was fairly chaotic when we arrived." He hesitated and then added, "A rather *large* number of Daevas were gathering to demand whoever did this be found and held accountable."

Alarm sparked in Ali. "The shafit in that camp are under our protection. There are hundreds of women and children there."

"They have no business being there," Kaveh retorted. "This is your fault. You whispered your poisonous opinions into my Banu Nahida's ear, and now a Daeva man is dead."

Suspicion gripped Ali. Kaveh had made his opposition to Nahri working with the shafit clear at the Grand Temple. But surely he couldn't be so hateful as to plot something like this. . . .

Aware of how tenuous the situation was, Ali switched to Geziriyya so that the Daevas couldn't understand him. "Abba, I know that woman," he said softly. "*Kaveh* knows that woman. He arranged for her to come visit my bedroom when I first moved back into the palace." Ghassan's eyes flickered to his, his face not betraying a hint of emotion, and Ali pressed on. "Muntadhir, surely you recognize her. You were there too. If she were to remove her veil, I know you would remember her."

Muntadhir stared at him, seeming to contemplate the situation.

And then a ruthless calm swept his face. "I have made very clear how I feel about your judgment regarding the shafit." He abruptly squared his shoulders, calculated outrage twisting his face. "And I am *not* going to ask this poor woman to disrobe because you think she's a prostitute!"

His final words—uttered in Djinnistani rather than Geziriyya—cracked across the room. Kaveh gasped, and the woman let out a shrill cry.

Ali whirled around, seeing horror in the faces of the growing number of people who'd been drawn by the woman's wails. "I-I didn't say that," he stammered, stunned by Muntadhir's betrayal. "I only meant—"

"How dare you?" Kaveh accused. "Have you no shame, Prince Alizayd? Do you hate the Daevas so much that you'd dishonor a weeping woman while her husband's blood still stains her hands?"

"That's not what I meant!"

Muntadhir deftly brushed past him to kneel at the woman's side. "We will find and punish whoever did this," he promised, sincerity in every line of his handsome face. He glanced back at Ghassan. "Kaveh is right, Abba. I have tried to warn you and Nahri both. The shafit are dangerous, and something like this was bound to happen. Ali is delusional. His fanaticism has been infecting everyone around him."

Ali gaped at him. "*Dhiru . . .*"

"Alizayd, leave us," Ghassan said curtly. "You and your companions are confined to the palace until I say otherwise." His eyes flashed. "*Understand?* Directly to your apartment; I will not have you further enflame this situation."

Before Ali could protest, his brother grabbed him, dragging him toward the doors. "Abba, don't!" he cried. "You heard Wajed, there's a mob growing. Those people are innocent!"

Ghassan didn't even look at him. "It will be handled."

Muntadhir shoved him out, pushing Ali hard enough to knock him off balance. "Is there any situation you can't make worse?" he snapped in Geziriyya.

"You lied," Ali accused, shaking with emotion. "I know you—"

"You know *nothing* about me." Muntadhir's voice was low and venomous. "You have no idea what this position has cost me. And I'll be damned if I'm going to lose it to some shafit-obsessed zealot who can't hold his tongue."

He slammed the door in Ali's face.

Ali staggered back, fury in his heart. He wanted to rip open the door and drag his brother through it. He had never before felt such a physical need to hit someone.

The delicate water table—a new, rather lovely addition to the corridor, a beautifully conjured construct featuring painted crystal birds that appeared to flit as they bathed in the still waters of a mosaic pool—promptly exploded, the water sizzling into mist.

Ali barely noticed. *It will be handled,* his father had said. What did that mean? Ali thought of his workers and their families facing a Daeva mob, of Subha and her little daughter. He wasn't supposed to be reckless, not anymore. But how could he let violence befall the people he'd sworn to protect? He knew his father's politics; Ghassan wasn't going to risk the fallout of letting the Royal Guard loose on mourning Daevas just to protect the shafit.

But there was someone else those Daevas might listen to. Nerves fluttered in Ali's chest. Muntadhir would kill him, if Ghassan didn't first.

It doesn't matter. Not now. Ali jumped to his feet and ran for the infirmary.

23

NAHRI

Daeva or not, Nahri was fairly certain she was never going to like horses.

As if hearing her thoughts, their mount put on a burst of speed, dashing around the next corner at a breakneck pace. Squeezing her eyes shut, Nahri tightened her grip around Ali's waist.

He let out a choked sound of protest. "I don't understand why you couldn't take your own horse," he said for what seemed like the tenth time. "It would have been more appropriate."

"This is faster," she said defensively, not wanting to admit her shortcomings as a rider. It was a skill other Daevas prided themselves on. "Muntadhir's always going on about how much he loves this horse. He says it's the fastest in Daevabad."

Ali groaned. "You might have told me it was his favorite *before* we stole it."

Her temper flared. "Maybe you should have worried about that before bursting into my infirmary ranting about conspiracies."

"But you believe me?" Ali asked, hoping rising in his voice.

I believe Kaveh is up to no good. The grand wazir had made his hostility to the shafit clear, though Nahri wasn't sure she believed he could have plotted such a vile act. There had always been something she hadn't quite trusted about him, but he didn't seem to be a cruel man.

She settled for a different answer. "It's such a monumentally absurd story—even for you—to concoct that I'm assuming there's a chance it's the truth."

"How gracious of you," Ali muttered.

They ducked to avoid a low-hanging line of laundry. They were taking a back passage through the Geziri Quarter that Ali believed was faster, and the windowless expanses of the broad stone mansions loomed up around them, the faint scent of refuse clinging to the air. The horse jumped a wide drainage canal, and Nahri swore, hugging Ali tighter to hook her fingers around his weapons belt. That was an item she knew he'd keep secure.

She heard him murmur a prayer under his breath. "Do you have to do that?" she hissed into his ear, fighting embarrassment. Nahri was not going to pretend the prince was the most . . . objectionable person to hold tight. She was a grown woman; she could quietly note the positive effects daily sparring might have on a man without getting worked up about it. *Ali* was the one making this unnecessarily awkward. "You know, for someone with such a clear recollection of one of Kaveh's courtesans, you're acting pretty prim."

Ali sputtered. "I didn't do anything with his courtesans!" he said, defending himself. "I would never. Forgive me for remembering a face!"

She felt mildly insulted at the heat in his voice. "Do you have something against Daeva women?"

"I . . . no, of course not," he stammered back. Ali shifted as if to put space between their bodies, but another lunge of the horse sent them hard against each other. "Can we . . . can we not talk about this right now?"

Nahri rolled her eyes but let it go. Fighting with Ali wasn't going to help her face down a Daeva mob.

Nerves fluttered in her stomach. Nahri knew the Daevas listened to her—and she had a fair amount of confidence in her ability to persuade—but the prospect of confronting an angry crowd scared even her.

It won't be like that, she tried to assure herself. *You'll swear on your family's name to see justice done and then order them to go home.* The most important thing was to prevent this from spiraling out of control.

It wasn't long before the alley began to widen. They turned another corner, and Ali slowed the horse. Just past an open archway, Nahri caught a glimpse of the street. The horse's clattering hooves softened.

The sound was immediately replaced by wailing. Nahri inhaled sharply, smelling blood and smoke on the warm air. Ali spurred the horse out of the alley, a choked cry of denial on his lips . . .

They were too late.

THERE WAS NO DAEVA MOB. NO CORDON OF ROYAL Guard trying to establish order. Instead what had been a happy, lively neighborhood of workshops and new homes this morning had been reduced to smoldering husks. The air was choked with smoke, a gray haze obscuring much of the camp.

"No," Ali begged softly as he slid from the horse. "God, no . . ."

Nahri jumped off after him. She could hear a baby crying, and sick with fear for Subha's family, she lunged forward.

Ali caught her wrist. "Nahri . . ." His voice was heavy with emotion. "We're alone. If people blame you, if they want revenge . . ."

"Then they want revenge." Nahri glared at him. "Let me go—and don't ever try to stop me again."

He dropped her wrist as if it had burned him. "I'm sorry."

"Good. Come on."

They entered the camp silently.

Smoking workshops and tents loomed around them; one of the pumps Ali had installed had been smashed and was going wild, spraying water in a wide arc. The muddy road had been churned up by hooves and it sucked at her slippers as she passed smashed furniture and broken pots. And yet, it looked like most of the damage was confined to the main thoroughfare, a small mercy; perhaps the Daevas who attacked had been too frightened to get off their horses or venture into the narrow side lanes. Shafit, shocked and covered in dust and blood, were salvaging what they could from their ruined homes, while others simply sat in stunned disbelief.

A hush descended as more and more people recognized them. Ahead she saw a small group of shafit gathered around a prone form on the ground. A body.

Nahri stumbled. Burned beyond recognition, it looked like it might have been a young man, his gaping mouth trapped in a permanent scream.

"They burned him alive."

Nahri whirled around to see Subha. The shafit physician was filthy, her clothes and skin coated in ash, a bloody apron tied around her waist. "A boy younger than you," she spat at Ali. "A boy who could barely string two words together. I would know. I delivered him myself and unwrapped the cord that was around his neck . . ." She trailed off, looking anguished as she tore her gaze from the murdered youth. "Of course, that was after they set fire to our homes and smashed through our workshops. When they rode down those who would not answer their questions and beat those who didn't speak quickly enough. And when that boy couldn't answer, they decided he was their culprit. He did *nothing*." Her voice broke as she raised an accusing finger at both of them. "We came here to help you. To build *your* hospital under *your* protection."

"And we failed you." There were tears in Ali's eyes, though his voice didn't shake. "I'm so sorry, Subha, from the depths of my soul."

The doctor shook her head. "Your words won't bring him back, Alizayd al Qahtani."

Nahri couldn't look away from the murdered boy. "Where are your injured?" she asked softly.

Subha jerked her head toward the remains of a makeshift tent, a tattered tarp all that protected the two dozen or so bloodied people lying in its shade. "Over there. Parimal is bringing more supplies."

"I don't need supplies." Nahri approached the group. A boy lay alone on a dirty blanket closest to her. He seemed to be in shock; his lip was split and his jaw bloodied and bruised. He clutched a second, blood-soaked blanket to his abdomen.

Nahri knelt and pulled it away. He'd been stabbed, very nearly disemboweled. It was a miracle he wasn't already dead. Purple swelling ballooned the skin, and she could smell torn intestine. Subha couldn't help him, even with supplies.

But Nahri could. She took a deep breath, aware of the step she was about to take and what it would mean.

And then she laid her hands upon his body.

Heal. The skin immediately twisted beneath her fingertips, the swelling vanishing, the torn muscles and flesh rushing back together. The young man let out a strangled gasp, and she felt his racing heartbeat even out. Nahri opened her eyes, meeting Subha's stunned expression.

She cleared her throat. "Who's next?"

BY THE TIME THE CALL TO MAGHRIB PRAYER ECHOED across Daevabad, Nahri had lost track of how many shafit she had healed. The injuries were brutal: broken bones, crushed limbs, and gruesome burns. From what Nahri could gather, the rampage had been short but savagely effective: a mob of riders racing through and throwing conjured balls of fire before seizing and murdering the young man they declared guilty.

Twenty-three were dead, a number that likely would have been twice as high without her intervention, and the fact that a third of the camp had fled into the hospital, taking refuge behind the doors that the Daeva raiders hadn't dared pass. "Why didn't everyone do so?" Nahri had asked.

"The men said they rode in the name of the Nahids," had been Subha's blunt answer. "We weren't sure a Nahid hospital was safe."

Nahri hadn't inquired further. And by the time she was done—her last patient a six-year-old with a skull fracture who'd been found in the arms of her dead father—Nahri was drained in every manner a person could be.

She sat back from the girl and took several deep breaths, trying to steady herself. But the acrid smell of smoke and blood turned her stomach. Her vision blurred, and she squinted, trying to see past a wave of dizziness.

Subha put a hand on her shoulder. "Easy," she said as Nahri swayed. "You look ready to faint." She pressed a waterskin into her hands. "Drink."

Nahri took it gladly and drank, pouring some into her hands to splash onto her face. "We will catch and punish the men who did this," she promised. "I swear."

The other doctor didn't even bother to feign a nod. "Maybe in another world."

Too late, Nahri registered the sound of hoofbeats. There were a few alarmed cries, and Nahri dropped the waterskin as she whirled around, half fearing the mob had returned.

It was almost worse. It was Ghassan.

The king wasn't alone, of course. The Qaid and a contingent of the Royal Guard, all very well armed, were behind him, as were Muntadhir and Kaveh. Her blood raged at the sight of the grand wazir. If Kaveh had a hand in the attack that had led to this awful reprisal, he would pay. Nahri would make damn sure of it. But she'd also be careful—she wasn't going to shout accusations she couldn't prove like Ali had and then have them used against her.

She straightened up. "Subha, your family is in the hospital?"

The other doctor nodded. "They're with Razu."

"Good." Nahri wiped her hands on her smock. "Would you join them? I think it best you not draw the king's attention right now."

Subha hesitated. "And you?"

"I need to put some men in their place."

But Ghassan didn't even glance her way as Nahri ducked out of the tent and approached. He was off his horse and striding across the bloody cobblestones straight for his son, as if there was no one else in the street.

Ali seemed to notice a half-moment too late. Covered in blood and dust, he had not stopped moving since they arrived, doing whatever the shafit asked of him: cleaning debris, repairing tents, distributing blankets.

He raised his hands. "Abba—"

Ghassan struck him across the face with the metal hilt of his khanjar.

The crack echoed across the street, the camp going silent at the sound. Nahri heard Ali gasp, and then his father hit him again and he staggered back, blood streaming down his face.

"On your knees," Ghassan snapped, pushing Ali to the ground when he didn't move fast enough. He unsheathed his zulfiqar.

Horrified, Nahri ran toward them, but Muntadhir was faster, jumping from his horse and striding forward. "Abba, wait—"

"*Do it.*" Ali's voice, wracked with anguish, cut his brother off. He spat blood and then glared at his father, his eyes blazing. "End this *facade*," he choked, his voice breaking on the word. "Just do it!"

Ghassan's hand stayed on the zulfiqar. "You disobeyed me," he accused. "I told you I would handle things. How dare you come here? How dare you risk your brother's wife?"

"Because your way of handling things is to let people die! To let everyone who is not us spend so much time fighting each other that they can't oppose you!"

The charge hung in the air like a lit match. People were staring in visible shock at the Qahtani men.

It looked as if it took Ghassan every bit of self-control he had to lower his zulfiqar. He spun around, turning his back on his son and motioning to the Royal Guard. "Take Prince Alizayd to the dungeon. Perhaps a few months sleeping with the corpses of those who've defied me will teach him to hold his tongue. And then tear the rest of this place down."

Nahri stepped directly in his path. "Absolutely not."

Ghassan gave her an annoyed look. "Stand down, Banu Nahri," he said condescendingly. "I do not have the patience for one of your self-important speeches right now. Let your husband punish you as he sees fit."

It was exactly the wrong thing to say.

The ground below her feet gave a single, angry jolt. There were a few cries of surprise as some of the horses were startled and reared. Filthy and fed up, Nahri barely noticed. Energy was crackling down her limbs, the city pulsing angrily in her blood. She had not come to this place—to the hospital they'd rebuilt on the bones of their slaughtered ancestors—to be brushed aside. She had not publicly broken her people's most deeply held taboo to be told to "stand down."

"No," she said flatly. "You won't be tearing this place down.

No one's touching my hospital and no one's dragging my partner off to rot in the dungeon."

Ghassan looked incredulous—and then his face hardened in a way that had once turned her blood to ice. "I beg your pardon?"

A whisper rustled through the group behind them, and then Kaveh came forward, looking aghast.

"Tell me it's not true," he implored. "They are saying you healed a shafit here with your own hands. Tell me they're lying."

"I healed about fifty," she corrected coldly. Before he could respond, Nahri raised her scalpel and cut a deep gash into her palm. Barely three drops had fallen to the dust before the wound closed. "And yet seemingly the Creator has not seen fit to take my abilities."

Kaveh looked horrified. "But at the Temple, you promised—"

"A promise like that means nothing when people are dying. My tribe committed a heinous crime—one whose source you and I will *definitely* be discussing. For now, I did what I could to rectify it." She shook her head in disgust. "Do you understand? What happened was a tragedy that *you* let spin out of control. A few criminals attack an innocent couple and that justifies a war in the streets? Is that who we are?" She gave Ghassan a defiant look but chose her next words carefully. "What happened to the king who was ready to move us past all this?"

It was both a challenge and an opportunity, and Nahri prayed they'd seize on the latter. She couldn't read Kaveh's expression; she suddenly wondered if she'd ever read anything about him correctly.

But Ghassan . . . his expression was one of open appraisal. As though he was seeing her for the first time.

Nahri met his stare. "I have dealt with you fairly at every turn, King Ghassan," she said, lowering her voice. "I renounced my Afshin. I married your son. I *bow my head* while you sit on a shedu throne. But if you try to take this from me, I will rip this city and your family apart."

Ghassan narrowed his eyes and drew nearer; it took every ounce of courage Nahri had not to step back.

"You cannot be so foolish as to threaten me," he said, softly enough that only she could hear. "I could reveal you as shafit right here."

Nahri didn't drop her gaze. And then in a single, petrifying moment, she decided to call his bluff. Nahri could read a mark, djinn king or not, and she was still willing to bet Ghassan al Qahtani would rather be known as the king who united their tribes than the one who destroyed the last Nahid.

"Then do it," she challenged, keeping her voice equally low. "Let us see who the Daevas believe now. Who your children believe. I've kept my word. Do this and it will be *you* acting in bad faith, not I."

Perhaps moved to interfere by the deadly expression brewing on his father's face, Muntadhir approached. He looked sick, his horrified eyes tracing the blood-spattered street and smoldering buildings. "Abba, it's been a long day. Let me take her back to the palace."

"That sounds like an excellent suggestion." Ghassan didn't take his eyes off her. "You're correct, Banu Nahida," he continued, his voice diplomatic. "You *have* acted in good faith, and I'm certain your actions here were only intended to save lives." He shrugged. "Perhaps one day the Daevas will even forget you completely disobeyed Suleiman's code to do so."

Nahri refused to flinch. "My hospital?"

"You may keep your little project, but you won't be returning to it until it's completed." Ghassan shot a glance at Ali, still kneeling on the ground. "Nor will you be *leaving* it unless it is at my command. A contingent of the Guard—and not ones your mother has managed to pay off—will arrest you if you try." He looked between Ali and Nahri. "I think it's best we put some distance into this . . . partnership. Should you need to discuss the work, you may communicate through a messenger . . . one I assure you will be very much in my service."

Muntadhir grabbed her hand, pulling her away. "Understood," he said quickly, perhaps seeing the defiance still bright in her eyes. "Nahri, let's—"

"I'm not done," Ghassan cut in, his voice freezing her blood. But his attention was back on Ali. "The Banu Nahida may have acted in good faith, but you did not. You disobeyed me, Alizayd, and I am not unaware as to who's been whispering in your ear and putting gold in your hands. That ends today."

Ali shot to his feet, his eyes burning. "Excuse me?"

Ghassan stared back at his son. "You've made clear your life means nothing to you, but you can't act so heedlessly and not expect to hurt others." His expression sharpened. "So you can be the one to tell your sister she'll never see her mother again." He turned on his heel, striding back to his horse. "Kaveh, arrange a ship. Queen Hatset will be leaving for Ta Ntry tomorrow."

24

DARA

The lake Dara had ravaged six months ago was already recovering. The gash he'd torn into its bed was barely visible, hidden beneath a sinuous net of sea-green waterweeds that reached out and twisted across opposite ends to knit together like lace. The surrounding trees were blackened, skeletal things, and the beach itself was dusted with ash and littered with the tiny bones of various aquatic creatures. But the water was returning, cool, blue, and smooth as glass, even if it only came to his knees.

"Did you think it would not heal?"

Dara shuddered at the sound of the marid's raspy voice. Though they'd been told to return here, he hadn't been certain what they'd find.

"I thought it might take more time," Dara confessed, clasping his hands behind his back as he gazed at the horizon.

"Water is unstoppable. Eternal. It always returns. *We* return." The marid fixed its dead eyes on him. It was still in the form of its murdered human acolyte, the body now reduced to salt-bleached bones and rotting gristle in the places where it wasn't armored with shell and scales. "Water brings down mountains and nurtures new life. Fire burns out."

Dara returned his gaze, unimpressed. "You know, I grew up on stories where the marid appeared as fetching mermaids or terrifying sea dragons. This decaying corpse is quite the disappointment."

"You could offer yourself to me," the marid replied smoothly, its coat of shells clacking together in the biting wind. "Give me your name, daeva, and I'll show you anything you wish. Your lost world and slain family. Your Nahid girl."

A finger of ice brushed his spine. "What do you know of any Nahid girl?"

"She was in the mind and memories of the daeva we took."

"The daeva you took . . ." Dara's eyes narrowed. "You mean the boy you used to murder me?" His mouth twisted. "Alizayd al Qahtani is no daeva."

The marid seemed to still, even the shells and bones falling silent. "Why would you say such a thing?"

"He is a djinn. At least, that is what his fool tribe call themselves."

"I see," the marid said, after another moment of considered silence. "No matter. Djinn, daeva . . . you are all the same, shortsighted and as destructive as the element that smolders in your hearts." It ran its bony hands through the water, making tiny ripples dance. "You will leave my home soon, yes?"

"That is the plan. But if you try to deceive me, I assume you understand what I'll do." Dara pinned the marid with his gaze.

"You've made your intent clear." A pair of tiny silver fish darted between its hands. "We will return you to your city, Darayavahoush e-Afshin. I pray you content yourself with spilling blood there and never return to our waters."

Dara refused to let the words land. "And the lake? You will be able to re-create the enchantment I asked about?"

The marid cocked its head. "We will bring down your stone tower. And then understand we are done. We will bear no more responsibility for what your people do."

Dara nodded. "Good." He turned away, the wet sand sucking at his boots as he headed back to the camp they'd pitched on a grassy bluff set back from the water. At Dara's suggestion, they had packed up and left their mountain encampment less than a week after Mardoniye's death. Though the mist of copper vapor had been fading by then, its very existence had provoked questions among his men that he couldn't answer. So they'd moved, biding the final weeks before Navasatem here.

And now the generation celebrations began in three days. In three days, they would enter this water and be transported back to Daevabad. In three days, he would be home. In three days, he would see Nahri.

In three days, you will once again have the blood of thousands on your hands.

He closed his eyes, trying to shut away the thought. Dara had never pictured feeling such despair on the eve of a conquest he'd desired for centuries. Certainly not back when he was the Scourge of Qui-zi, the cunning Afshin who'd bedeviled Zaydi al Qahtani for years. That man had been a dashing rebel, a passionate leader who'd picked up the shattered pieces of his tribe and knit his people back together with promises of a better future. Of a day when they would sweep into Daevabad as victors and seat a Nahid on the shedu throne. Back then, he'd had quieter dreams for himself as well. Fleeting fantasies of re-claiming his family's house, taking a wife and raising children of his own.

None of those dreams would ever be now, and for what Dara had done—for what he was about to do—he had no right to them. But Nahri and Jamshid would have such dreams. His soldiers would. Their children would be the first Daevas in centuries to grow up without a foreigner's foot pressed down on their necks.

He had to believe it.

The sun blinked crimson behind the mountains, and a deep, rhythmic drumming came from the firelit camp, a welcome distraction from his grim thoughts. Their group was gathering while Manizheh prepared for sunset ceremonies at a makeshift fire altar. It was little more than a brass bowl set atop a circle of rocks, and Dara could not help but think wistfully of the magnificent gleaming altar back in Daevabad's Grand Temple.

He joined the line of weary soldiers, plunging his hands into the fiery ash in the brazier and sweeping it over his arms. There was a subdued air to the gathering, but that didn't surprise him. Mardoniye's death had been the first time most of his warriors had witnessed what a zulfiqar could truly do. Add the whispers he was trying to quash surrounding the vapor that had killed the Geziri scouts, and it made for a tense, grim atmosphere within the camp.

Manizheh caught his eye, beckoning him closer. "Did you find the marid?" she asked.

He wrinkled his nose. "Decomposing on the rocks on the opposite shore and no less self-righteous. But they are ready to assist us. I made clear the consequences should they betray us."

"Yes, I have no doubt you made yourself quite clear." Manizheh's black eyes twinkled. She had returned to treating Dara with her typical warm affection the very morning after they fought. And why not? She had won, after all, putting him firmly back in his place with a few swift words. "And are you ready?"

His response was automatic. "I am always ready to serve the Daevas."

Manizheh touched his hand. Dara caught his breath at the burst of magic, a sweep of calm similar to a drunken ease surging through him. "Your loyalty will be rewarded, my friend," she replied softly. "I know we've had our disagreements, and I see you standing on the edge of bleakness. But our people will know what you've done for them. *All* of them." Her voice was intent. "We are indebted to you, and for that I promise you, Dara . . . I will see you find some happiness."

Dara blinked, the feelings he'd tried to suppress on his walk back rising and churning within him. "I do not deserve happiness," he whispered.

"That's not true." She touched his cheek. "Have *faith*, Darayavahoush e-Afshin. You are a blessing, our people's salvation."

Emotions warred in his heart. By the Creator, did he want to seize her words. To throw himself back into that belief wholeheartedly, the faith that had once come so easily and now seemed impossible to grasp.

Then force yourself to. Dara stared at Manizheh. Her worn chador and the battered brass bowl before her might have been a far cry from the splendid ceremonial garb and dazzling silver altar found in the Grand Temple, but she was still the Banu Nahida—Suleiman's chosen, the Creator's chosen.

He managed some conviction. "I shall try," he promised. "Actually . . . I would like to do something for you all after the ceremony. A gift, to brighten your spirits."

"That sounds delightful." She nodded to the rest of their group, seated on the grass. "Join your fellows. I would speak to you all."

Dara took a seat next to Irtemiz. Manizheh raised a hand in blessing, and he bowed his head in unison with the rest, bringing together his hands. The emerald on his ring caught the dying light, gleaming past the soot coating his fingers. He watched as Manizheh went through the sacred motions, pouring fresh oil in the glass lamps bobbing along the simmering water and lighting them with a stick of burning cedar. She pressed it to her brow, marking her forehead with its sacred ash. She closed her eyes, her lips moving in silent prayer.

And then she stepped forward.

"You all look terrible," she said flatly. The shoulders of a few of the surrounding Daevas slumped at her words. But then her mouth quirked in a rare true smile. "That's all right," she added gently. "You're entitled to feel terrible. You've followed me on what must seem a fool's dream and you've done so with an obedience that will earn you admittance into the Creator's eternal gardens. You've held your tongues when you must have so many questions." She gazed at them, letting her eyes fall on each man and woman in turn. "And for that you have my promise, my children . . . whether in this world or the next, you and yours will be provided for. Our people will speak of your names in stories and light tribute to your icons in the Grand Temple.

"But not yet." She moved past the altar. "I suspect some of you worry we are rushing this. That we are resorting to dark and cruel methods. That to attack when people are celebrating a cherished holiday is wrong.

"My answer is: we are out of time. With each passing day, Ghassan's persecution of our people worsens. His soldiers have taken to rampaging through our lands and looting our homes. To speak against him is to invite death. And were that not enough, Kaveh tells me that his half-tribe son, the radical who dares call himself 'Afshin-slayer,' has returned to Daevabad to further rile up his dirt-blooded supporters."

Dara tensed. That was *not* what Kaveh had said, and though Dara was not blind to what she was trying to do, the ease with which she spun the lie reminded him far too much of the current occupant of Daevabad's throne.

Manizheh continued. "Another time, this news might please me. Indeed, little would delight me more than to see the Qahtanis ripped apart by their own bloody fanaticism. But that is not how sand flies operate. They mob and they swarm and they devour. Their violence will spread. It *has* spread. It will envelop our city in chaos." Her voice was low and intense. "And the Daevas will pay the price. *We always do.* The icons of too many martyrs already line the Grand Temple, and those of you in the Daeva Brigade witnessed firsthand the savagery of the shafit when you were thrown out of the Citadel."

Manizheh gestured to the last rays of the vanished sun and then knelt, gathering a handful of sand. "This is *our* land. From the Sea of Pearls to the dust of the plains and the mountains of Daevabad, Suleiman granted it to our tribe, to those who served him most faithfully. Our ancestors spun a city out of magic—pure *Daeva* magic—to create a wonder unlike the world had ever seen. We pulled an island out of the depths of a marid-haunted lake and filled it with libraries and pleasure gardens. Winged lions flew over its skies and in its streets, our women and children walked in absolute safety.

"You've heard the Afshin's stories. The *glory* Daevabad once was. The marvel. We invited the other tribes to partake, we tried to teach them, to guide them, and yet they turned on us." Her eyes flashed, and she released the dust. "They betrayed us in the worst of ways: they *stole* our city. And then, not content with breaking Suleiman's law in their land, they let their shafit spawn defile ours. To this day, they keep these pitiful creatures around to wait on them hand and foot. Or worse! They pass them off as djinn children, irrevocably polluting their bloodlines and risking us all."

She shook her head, sadness sweeping her face. "And yet for so long, I saw no way out. The city would call to me, call to my brother, Rustam, with a strength that made our hearts ache. But it seemed dangerous to even dream of a better future. For the safety of us all, I bowed my head as Ghassan al Qahtani lounged on the throne of my ancestors. And then . . ." She paused. "Then the Creator granted me a sign impossible to ignore."

Manizheh beckoned for Dara to rise. He did so, coming to her side.

She laid a hand on his shoulder. "Darayavahoush e-Afshin. Our greatest warrior, the man who made Zaydi al Qahtani himself tremble. Returned to us, freed of Suleiman's curse, as mighty as our legendary forbearers. My people, if you are looking for proof of the Creator's favor, it is here in Dara. We have difficult days ahead. We may be forced to acts in ways that seem brutal. But I assure you . . . it is all necessary."

Manizheh fell momentarily silent, perhaps gauging the impact of her words. Dara saw some of the faces before him shining with wonder, but not all. Many looked uncertain, anxious.

He could help her with that.

He took a deep breath. The pragmatic thing would have been to leave his favored form, but the thought of doing so before their entire camp shamed him, and so instead he raised his hands, letting the heat dance from them in smoky golden waves.

They touched the fire altar first and the jumbled rocks melted together into a shining marble base, the battered bowl shifting into a proper silver vessel, glimmering as it formed from the dying sunlight. The smoke swirled around Manizheh, turning her plain garments into the delicate blue-and-white silks of ceremonial dress before cresting over the rest of their followers.

Dara closed his eyes. In the blackness of his mind, he dreamed of his lost city. Sharing meals and laughter with his Afshin cousins between training sessions. Holidays spent with his sister, sneaking tastes of their favorite dishes while his mother and aunts cooked. Racing his horse across the plains outside the Gozan River with his closest companions, the wind whistling past them. Not a single person in those memories had survived the sack of Daevabad. He gave magic to the yearning in his heart, to the ache he expected would always be there.

There were gasps. Dara opened his eyes, fighting a swoon as the magic drained him.

The Daevas were now seated upon the finest of carpets, spun from green wool the color of spring grass, tiny living flowers woven into the shimmering threads. The men wore matching uniforms, the patterned gray-and-black coats and striped leggings the same ones his Afshin cousins had donned. A feast was spread on white linen behind them, and Dara could tell from a single sniff of the air that the dishes were his family's recipes. The plain felt tents had been replaced by a ring of silk structures that billowed in the air like smoke, and in a marble-screened corral, dozens of ebony horses with flashing golden eyes pranced and snorted.

No, not just pranced. Dara's gaze locked on the horses. They had *wings*—four undulating wings each, darker than night and moving like shadows. The Afshin in him saw the immediate benefit in the marvelous creatures: they would speed his soldiers more swiftly to the palace. But in his heart, oh, the traitorous part of his heart . . . how he suddenly wished to steal one and flee this madness.

Manizheh gripped his shoulder, seizing upon her followers' visible awe. "*Look*," she urged, her voice carrying on the still air. "Look at this wonder, this sign of the Creator's blessing! We are going to Daevabad. *We are taking it back*." Her voice rang out, echoing against the growing dark. "We will rip the Citadel from its moorings and the Qahtanis from their beds. I will not rest until those who have hurt us, those who threaten our women and children in the city that is *ours*—by the Creator's decree!—have been thrown in the lake, their bodies swallowed by its waters." Smoke was curling from her collar. "We will greet the next generation as leaders of all djinn, as Suleiman intended!"

A youth near the front stepped forward, throwing himself into prostration before Manizheh.

"For the Nahids!" he cried. "For the Lady!"

Those nearest followed suit, falling in a wave before Manizheh. Dara tried to picture Nahri and Jamshid at her side, the young Nahids not only safe but wrapped in the glorious heritage they'd been too long denied.

But the sick burning was already sweeping through him. He choked it down as Manizheh's gaze lit on him, expectation—and a slight challenge—in her eyes.

He fell to his knees in obedience. "For the Nahids," he murmured.

Satisfied triumph filled her voice. "Come, my people. We will take our blessings and then enjoy the feast our Afshin has conjured. Be merry! Celebrate what we are about to do!"

Dara stepped back, fighting to keep from stumbling and struggling for a lie that would allow him to escape before his weakness was noticed. "The horses . . . ," he blurted out, aware that it was a thin excuse. "If you don't mind . . ."

He staggered away. Fortunately, the rest of the Daevas were busy swarming Manizheh and Dara spotted enough jugs of wine as he passed the feast that he suspected no one would miss him for some time. He slipped between the tents, letting the encroaching dusk swallow him. But he barely made it four more steps before he fell to his hands and knees, retching.

His vision blurred. He closed his eyes, the drums beating painfully in his head as he clutched at the dirt.

Transform, you fool. Dara could not recover from the magic he'd just done in his mortal form. He tried to shift, desperate to pull the fire that pulsed in his heart over his shivering limbs.

Nothing happened. Stars were blossoming before his eyes, a metallic ringing in his ears. Panicking, he tried again.

The heat came . . . but it wasn't fire that wrapped his limbs. It was an airy whisper of nothingness.

And then Dara was gone. Weightless. Formless, and yet more alive than he'd ever been. He could taste the buzz of an approaching storm on the air and savor the comforting heat from the campfires. The murmur of creatures unseen seemed to call to him, the world glimmering and moving with shadows and shapes and an utter wild freedom that urged him to fly . . .

He slammed back into his body, flames flickering over his skin. He lay there, his hands over his face.

"Suleiman's eye," he whispered, stunned. "What was that?" Dara knew he should have been terrified, but the brief sensation had been *intoxicating*.

His people's legends flooded his mind. Stories of shapeshifting, of traveling across the desert as nothing more than a hot wind. Is that what he had just done? Had just been?

He sat up. Dara wasn't exhausted or sick now; he felt almost giddy. Raw, as though he'd touched a spark of energy, and it was still coursing through him. He wanted to try it again, to see what it might feel like to fly along the cold wind and race over the snow-dusted peaks.

Laughter and music from the feast caught his ear, a reminder of his people, as insistent as a leash.

But for perhaps the first time in his life, Dara didn't think about his responsibilities to his people. Bewitched and seduced, he grabbed for the magic again.

He was gone even faster this time, the weight of his body vanishing. He spun, laughing to himself as soil and leaves swirled and danced around him. He felt vast and yet remarkably light, the breeze carrying him away the moment he allowed it. In seconds, the lake was nothing but a gleaming mirror of moonlight far below.

And by the Creator . . . the glory spread before him. The forbidding mountains now looked inviting, their sharp peaks and ominous shadows a maze to dash through, to explore. He could sense the very heat seeping through the ground's thick crust, the sea of molten rock flowing beneath the earth, sizzling where it met water and wind. It all pulsed with activity, with life, with an untamed energy and freedom that he suddenly desired more than anything else.

He wasn't alone. There were other beings like him, in this state of formlessness. Dara could sense them, could hear whispered invitations and teasing laughter. It would be nothing to take the ghost of a hand, to race off and travel realms he hadn't known existed.

Dara hesitated, longing tearing through him. But what if he couldn't return? What if he couldn't find his way back when his people needed him most?

Manizheh's resolve—her threat—closed around him. He could see her unleashing the poison and failing to take the city. He could see an enraged Ghassan ripping away his copper relic before it killed him and then seizing Nahri by her hair. Dragging her before her mother and plunging a zulfiqar through her heart.

Fear, thick and choking, snared him, and with it, a panicked wish to return. This Dara did with far less grace, shifting back into his mortal form while still airborne. He slammed into the ground so hard it knocked the air from his lungs.

Gasping and wracked with pain, Dara wasn't sure how long he lay there, blinking at the thick cluster of stars above, before a chuckle drew his attention.

"Well . . . ," a familiar voice drawled. "I suppose it took you long enough to learn that." Vizaresh stepped forward, peering over his body. "Need some help?" he offered lightly, extending a clawed hand. "I suggest next time you land before shifting."

Dara was so stunned he actually let the ifrit help him into a seated position, leaning heavily against the trunk of a dead tree. "What was that?" he whispered.

"What we once were." Yearning filled Vizaresh's voice. "What we were once capable of."

"But . . ." Dara fought for words. No speech seemed worthy of the magic he'd just experienced. "But it was so . . . peaceful. So beautiful."

The ifrit narrowed his yellow eyes. "Why should that surprise you?"

"Because that's not what our stories say," Dara replied. "The original daevas were troublemakers. Tricksters who deceived and hunted humans for their own—"

"Oh, forget the damn humans for once." Exasperation creased Vizaresh's fiery visage. "Your people are obsessed. For all your laws about staying clear of humanity, your kind are just like them now, with your petty politics and constant wars. This—" He gripped Dara's hand, and with a surge of magic, it turned to flame. "*This* is how you were made. You were created to burn, to exist between worlds—not to form yourself into armies and pledge your lives to leaders who would toss them away."

The words struck too close to the misgivings Dara tried to keep buried. "Banu Manizheh is not tossing our lives away," he defended her sharply. "We have a duty to save our people."

Vizaresh chuckled. "Ah, Darayavahoush, there are always people to save. And always cunning men and women around who find a way to take advantage of that duty and harness it into power. If you were wise—if you were a true daeva—you would have laughed in the face of your Manizheh the moment she brought you back and vanished on the next wind. You would be *enjoying* this, enjoying the possibility of all the lovely new things you could learn."

Dara caught his breath against the sharp tug of longing in his chest. "A purposeless, lonely existence," he said, forcing disdain he did not entirely feel into his voice.

"A life of wandering, of wonderment," Vizaresh corrected, hunger in his eyes. "Do you think I don't know what you just experienced? There are worlds you can't see as a mortal, beings and realms and kingdoms beyond your comprehension. We took mates when we desired companionship, parted amicably when it was time to travel the winds again. There were entire centuries my feet didn't touch the ground." His voice grew nostalgic, a smile curving his lips. "Though admittedly when they did, it *was* typically because of the lure of human entertainment."

"Such entertainment brought the wrath of one of the Creator's prophets upon you," Dara pointed out. "It cost you this existence you paint so lovingly."

Vizaresh shook his head. "Dallying with the occasional human was not why Suleiman punished us. Not the entire reason anyway."

"Then what was the reason?"

The ifrit gave him a wicked smile. "Are you asking questions now? I thought all you did was obey."

Dara checked his temper. He might despise the ifrit, but in a small way, he was beginning to understand them—or at least, to understand how it felt to be the last of your kind.

And he was truly curious as to what Vizaresh had to say. "And I thought *you* wanted me to learn new things," he said archly. "Unless this is all bluster and you know nothing."

Vizaresh's eyes danced. "What will you give me for telling you?"

Dara grinned. "I won't smash you against a mountain."

"Always so violent, Darayavahoush." Vizaresh regarded him, pulling and twisting at a length of flame between his hands as if it were a toy. Abruptly, he dropped to sit across from Dara. "Fine, I will tell you why Suleiman cursed us. It was not for playing with humans—it was because we warred with the marid *over* those humans."

Dara frowned. This was not a story he'd ever heard before. "We went to war with the marid over *humans*?"

"We did," Vizaresh replied. "Think, Darayavahoush. How did Aeshma summon the marid of this lake?"

"He had me kill one of its acolytes," Dara said slowly. "A human acolyte. He said the marid would be obliged to respond."

"Precisely."

"Precisely what?"

Vizaresh leaned in close, as though confiding a secret. "Bargains, Darayavahoush. Debts. A human summons me to poison a rival and later I take their corpse as a ghoul. A village with dying crops offers the blood of one of its screaming members to the river, and the marid promptly flood it, filling their fields with rich silt."

Dara drew back. "You speak of evil things."

"I'd not thought you so sensitive, Scourge." When Dara glared, he shrugged. "Believe it or not, I once agreed with you. I was content with my own innate magic, but not all daevas felt similarly. They enjoyed the thrall of human devotion and encouraged it where they could. And the marid did *not* like that."

"Why not?"

Vizaresh toyed with the battered bronze chain he wore around his neck. "The marid are ancient creatures, older even than daevas. The human practices that fed them were established before humans even began raising cities. And when some of those humans began to prefer *us*?" He clucked his tongue. "The marid have an appetite for vengeance that rivals that of your Nahids and Qahtanis. If a human turned from them to beg intercession from a daeva, they'd drown its entire village. In retaliation, our people started doing the same." He let out an exaggerated sigh. "Flood and burn down a few too many cities and suddenly you're getting dragged before some ranting human prophet in possession of a magic ring."

Dara tried to take that all in. "If that's true, it sounds like the punishment was rather deserved. But I do not understand . . . if the marid were also responsible, why were they not disciplined?"

Vizaresh flashed him a mocking grin, his lips pulling back over his curved fangs. "Who says they weren't?" He seemed delighted at Dara's confusion. "You would make for a better companion if you were clever. I would laugh to see the chaos a true daeva would wreak in your position."

I would cause no chaos. I would leave. Dara shoved the thought away as soon as it came. "I'm not like you." His gaze caught on the chain Vizaresh was still fingering, and his irritation sparked. "And were *you* clever, you would not wear that in my presence."

"This?" The ifrit pulled the chain free from his bronze chest plate. Three iron rings hung from its length, crowned with emeralds that winked with unnatural malice. "Trust me, Darayava-housh, I am not fool enough to touch one of your followers even if they should beg it of me." He caressed the rings. "These are empty now, but they have saved me during bleaker centuries."

"Enslaving the souls of fellow daeva *saved* you?"

True anger flashed in the ifrit's eyes for the first time. "They were not my fellows," he snapped. "They were weak, mewling things who threw their allegiance to the family of so-called healers, the Nahid blood poisoners who hunted my *true* fellows." He sniffed. "They should have been glad for the power I gave them; it was a taste of what we once were."

Dara's skin crawled at Vizaresh's words, but he was thankful for it. What was he doing letting Vizaresh fill his mind with dreams and likely lies that would pull him away from Manizheh? Was Dara so foolish as to forget how deceptive the ifrit could be?

He rose to his feet. "I may not remember much of my time in slavery, but I assure you I was not *glad* to be forced to wield magic—no matter how powerful—in the service of violent human whims. It was despicable."

He walked away, not waiting for Vizaresh's response. Ahead, Dara could hear laughter and music from the feast beyond the tents. Night had fallen, a thin sliver of moon and thick cluster of stars making the pale tents and bone-white beach glow with reflected celestial light. The scent of spiced rice with sour cherries and sweet pistachio porridge—his family's recipes—sent a newly sharp ache into his heart. Suleiman's eye, how was it possible to still miss them so much?

A closer—rather drunken—giggle caught his ear.

"—what will you do for it?" It was Irtemiz, teasingly holding a bottle of wine behind her back. Bahram's arms were around her waist as they staggered into view, but the young man went pale when he noticed Dara.

"Afshin!" He stepped away from Irtemiz so fast he half stumbled. "I, er, we didn't mean to intrude upon you. Your brooding." His eyes went bright with embarrassment. "Not brooding! That's not what I meant. Not that there's anything wrong with—"

Dara waved him off, admittedly a little chastened. "It is fine." He eyed them, noting that Irtemiz's coat was already open and Bahram's belt missing. "Are the two of you not enjoying the feast?"

Irtemiz offered a weak smile, color rising in her cheeks. "Just taking a walk?" she offered. "You know, to better . . . er, prepare ourselves for such heavy food."

Dara snorted. Another time, he might have tried to put an end to such trysts—he didn't need lovers' spats among his soldiers. But considering the deadly mission that loomed in just a few days, he decided there was no harm in it. "Choose another direction to walk. Vizaresh is lurking back that way." Though he was slightly disgruntled, he could not help but add, "There is a lovely cove if you follow the eastern beach."

Bahram looked mortified, but Irtemiz grinned, her dark eyes sparkling with mirth. She grabbed the young man's hand. "You heard our Afshin." Laughing, she dragged Bahram off.

Dara watched them go. A quiet sadness stole into his soul as he stood alone. His fellows suddenly seemed so young, so different.

This is not my world. It was clearer to him than it ever had been before. He cared for these people, loved them, but the world he was from had vanished. And it wasn't coming back. He would always be slightly apart.

Like the ifrit. Dara hated the comparison but knew it was an apt one. The ifrit were monsters, no doubt, but it could not have been easy to watch their world destroyed and remade, to spend millennia trying to recapture it while steadily, one by one, they perished.

Dara was not ready to perish. He closed his eyes, remembering the giddy sensation of being weightless and the way the dark mountains seemed to beckon. This time he couldn't tamp down the longing in his heart, so he let it remain, laced under a new veneer of determination. Forget the games of the ifrit and the marid's long-lost secrets—they belonged to a past he wouldn't let claim him again.

Dara would end this war for his people and see them safe.

Then perhaps, it would be time to discover what else the world offered.

25

ALI

Ali gazed upon the room that was to be Nahri's office with quiet approval. The completed window seat had been placed in the cozy alcove overlooking the street this morning, and he sank down upon the cushioned bench, pleased at how comfortable it was. Shelves within easy reach lined the alcove—this place would be perfect for reading.

I hope she likes it. Ali gazed beyond the room, past the balcony that overlooked the hospital's inner courtyard. The sounds of construction—the final stages—came to his ears. *I hope this hospital is worth the price we paid for it.*

He sighed, turning to peer through the wooden screen that looked out at the street below. It was as close as Ali could get to the slowly recovering shafit workcamp—his father had made clear he would personally double the death toll from the attack if Ali so much as opened his mouth about it.

There was a knock and then Lubayd called out from beyond the archway. "Can I come in? Or do you need a minute?"

Ali rolled his eyes. "Come in." He turned away from the window. "Aye, not with your *pipe*," he scolded. He chased the other man back through the archway, waving the offensive fumes away. "You'll stink the place up!"

Lubayd's eyes twinkled with amusement. "Well, aren't you protective of your little Nahid's sanctuary?"

"I'm protective over everything here," Ali shot back, unable to check the defensive heat in his voice. Knowing Lubayd to be merciless in his teasing when he spotted weakness, Ali quickly changed the subject. "You shouldn't be smoking in the hospital anyway. Doctor Sen said she'd toss you out the next time she caught you."

Lubayd inhaled. "What is life without risk?" He tilted his head toward the stairs. "Come. Aqisa is back from the palace and waiting for you."

Ali followed him out, returning the various salaams and nods of workers as they passed through the hospital complex. His home and prison for the past two months, the hospital was now all but complete. Attendants were preparing for tomorrow's opening ceremony, rolling out embroidered silk carpets and conjuring delicate floating lanterns. A few musicians had arrived to practice, and the steady beat of a goblet drum echoed through the courtyard.

He caught sight of Razu and Elashia sitting in a swing deep in the shade of a lime tree. Ali touched his brow in greeting as he passed, but neither woman appeared to notice him. Razu was tucking one of the tree's silky white flowers behind Elashia's ear, the ever-silent Sahrayn woman giving her a small smile.

It must be nice to have such a close friendship, he thought reflectively. Ali had Lubayd and Aqisa, of course, and they were truer and more loyal friends than he deserved. But even they had to be kept at an arm's length; his many secrets were too dangerous to reveal entirely.

Aqisa was waiting in the shadow of the large foyer, dressed in plain robes, her braids tied up and bundled under a turban. "You look dreadful," she greeted him bluntly.

"It's the eyes," Lubayd agreed. "And the shambling walk. Were he a bit bonier, he'd make a convincing ghoul."

Ali glowered at them. Between his nightmares and the race to finish the hospital, he was barely sleeping, and he was not unaware his appearance reflected such a thing. "It's good to see you too, Aqisa. How are things at the palace?"

"Fine." Aqisa crossed her arms, leaning against the wall. "Your sister sends her greetings."

His heart twisted. The last time Ali had seen Zaynab was when he'd been forced to break the news of their mother's imminent banishment. Though Hatset had remained grimly calm, telling them both to be strong—and that she'd be back, no matter Ghassan's orders—Zaynab had broken down in front of him for the first time in his life. "Why couldn't you have just listened to him?" she'd wept as Ali was forcibly escorted back out. "Why couldn't you have held your tongue for once?"

Ali swallowed the lump in his throat. "Is she okay?"

"No," Aqisa said flatly. "But she's surviving and is stronger than you give her credit for."

He winced at the rebuke, hoping she was right. "And you've had no issues getting in and out of the harem? I worry you're risking yourself."

Aqisa actually laughed. "Not in the slightest. You may forget it at times, but I *am* a woman. The harem exists to keep out strange, dangerous men; the guards barely pay me any mind." She caressed the hilt of her khanjar. "If I do not point it out often enough, your gender can be remarkably stupid." The humor left her face. "No luck with the infirmary, however."

"Still guarded?" Ali asked.

"Day and night, by two dozen of your father's most loyal men."

Two dozen men? A wave of sick fear—his constant companion since the attack—rolled through him. He was even more worried for Nahri than he was for himself; despite their strained relationship, Ali suspected his father was still unwilling to directly execute his own son. But Nahri wasn't his blood, and Ali had never seen *anyone* publicly challenge Ghassan the way she had in the ruins of the shafit camp. He could still remember her—small in comparison to his father, exhausted and covered in ash, but thoroughly defiant, heat rippling through the air when she spoke, the stone street shivering with magic.

It was one of the bravest acts he'd ever witnessed. And it petrified him, for Ali knew all too well how his father handled threats.

Ali turned on his heel, pacing. It was driving him mad to be locked up here, trapped on the other side of the city from his sister and Nahri. A sheen of dampness erupted down his back, and he shivered. Between the day's rain and his roiling emotions, Ali was struggling to check his water abilities.

Automatically, his gaze went to the corridor that led to Issa's room. At Hatset's request, the Ayaanle scholar had stayed behind to continue looking into Ali's "problem." But Ali wasn't optimistic. He didn't have his mother's touch with the erratic old man, and the last time he'd tried to check on Issa's progress, he'd found the scholar surrounded by a massive circle of parchment forming a family tree of what must have been every person even tangentially related to Ali. He'd rather impatiently asked what in God's name his ancestry had to do with getting the marid out of his head, and Issa had in turn hurled a globe *at* his head, rudely suggesting that as an alternative.

A shadow fell across them, the shape of a large man stepping into the shaft of sunlight coming from the garden. "Prince

Alizayd," a deep voice rumbled. "I believe your father made his orders clear."

Ali scowled, turning to glare at Abu Nuwas, the senior Geziri officer sent to "watch over" him. "I'm not trying to escape," he said acidly. "Surely, standing near the entrance is permitted?"

Abu Nuwas gave him a surly look. "A woman is looking for you in the eastern wing."

"Did she give you a name? This place is crawling with people."

"I am not your secretary." Abu Nuwas sniffed. "Some grandmotherly-looking shafit." He turned away without another word.

"Oh, don't be rude," Lubayd said when Ali rolled his eyes. "He's only following your father's orders." He blew out a ring of smoke. "And I rather like that one. We got drunk together a few weeks ago. He's an excellent poet."

Ali gaped. "Abu Nuwas is a *poet*?"

"Oh, yes. Wonderfully scandalous stuff. You'd hate it."

Aqisa shook her head. "Is there anyone in this city you haven't befriended? Last time we were at the Citadel, there were grown warriors fighting to take you out for lunch."

"The emir's fancy crowd won't have me," Lubayd replied. "They think I'm a barbarian. But regular Geziri folk, soldiers . . ." He grinned. "Everyone likes a storyteller."

Ali rubbed his temples. Most of Lubayd's "stories" were tales meant to bolster Ali's reputation. He hated it, but his friend only doubled his efforts when Ali asked him to stop. "Let me go see about this woman."

The eastern wing was fairly quiet when Ali arrived, with only a pair of tile workers finishing a last stretch of wall and a small, older woman in a faded floral headscarf standing near the railing overlooking the garden, leaning heavily on a cane. Assuming she was the woman Abu Nuwas had meant, Ali crossed to her. Maybe she *was* someone's grandmother; it would not be the first time an older relative had come here searching for work for a ne'er-do-well youth.

"Peace be upon you," Ali called out as he approached. "How may I—"

She turned to face him, and Ali abruptly stopped talking.

"Brother Alizayd . . ." Sister Fatumai, once the proud leader of the Tanzeem, stared back at him, her familiar brown eyes sharp as knives and simmering with anger. "It's been a long time."

"I'M SORRY TO HEAR YOU'RE HAVING TROUBLE WITH supplies," Ali said loudly as he led Sister Fatumai away from the curious workers, ushering her toward a room packed with fresh linens. He was almost impressed he could lie considering how rattled he was, but knowing the spies his father had filled the hospital with, he had little choice. "Let's see what we can spare . . ."

He ushered the Tanzeem leader into the room, and after quickly checking to make sure they were alone, shoved the door closed and whispered a locking enchantment under his breath. A half-filled oil lamp had been left on one of the shelves, and Ali quickly lit it. The conjured flame danced down the wick, throwing weak light across the small chamber.

He turned to face her, breathing hard. "S-sister Fatumai," Ali stammered. "I . . . I'm so sorry. When I heard what happened to Rashid . . . and saw Sheikh Anas's masjid . . . I assumed—"

"That I was dead?" Fatumai offered. "A fair assumption; your father certainly tried his best. And honestly, I thought the same of you when you left for Am Gezira. I figured it was a story told to hide the truth of your execution."

"You're not far from the truth." He swallowed. "The orphanage?"

"It's gone," Fatumai replied. "We tried to evacuate when Rashid was arrested, but the Royal Guard caught up with the last group. They sold the youngest as servants and executed the rest."

Her gaze grew cold. "My niece was one of the ones they murdered. You might remember her," she added, accusation lacing into her voice. "She made you tea when you visited."

Ali braced himself on the wall, finding it hard to breathe. "My God . . . I'm so sorry, sister."

"As am I," she said softly. "She was a good woman. Engaged to marry Rashid," she added, leaning against the wall as well. "Perhaps a small consolation that they entered Paradise as martyrs together."

Ali stared at the ground, ashamed.

She must have noticed. "Does such speech bother you now? You were once one of Sheikh Anas's most devout students, but I know faith is a garment worn carelessly by those who live in the palace."

"I never lost my faith." Ali said the words quietly, but there was a challenge in them. He'd only met Sister Fatumai after Rashid, another member of the Tanzeem, had tricked him into visiting their safe house, an orphanage in the Tukharistani Quarter. It was a visit designed to guilt the wealthy prince into funding them, a tour to show him sick and hungry orphans . . . but conveniently *not* the weapons he'd learned they were also purchasing with his money. Ali had never gone back; the Tanzeem's use of violence—possibly against innocent Daevabadis—was not a line he would cross.

He changed the subject. "Would you like to sit? Can I get you something to drink?"

"I did not come here to enjoy Geziri hospitality, Prince Alizayd." She shifted on her feet. Beneath the tired exterior and silver hair, there was steel in Fatumai, and it chastened him as much as it concerned him. There had been heart in the Tanzeem. They'd saved and sheltered shafit children, put books in hands and bread in mouths. Ali didn't doubt for a second that they were believers, as God-fearing as he was.

He also didn't doubt that quite a few of them had blood on their hands. "Are the rest of the children safe?"

She laughed, a hard sound. "You really don't know your father, do you?"

Ali almost couldn't bring himself to ask the question. "What do you mean?"

"Do you think it mattered to Ghassan that some were children?" She clucked her tongue. "Oh no, Brother Alizayd. We were a *danger*. A threat to be tracked down and exterminated. We came into his home and stole the heart of his youngest, so he sent his soldiers tearing through the shafit district in pursuit of us. Of anyone related to us. Family, neighbors, friends—he killed scores. We were so desperate to escape we tried to flee Daevabad itself."

"Flee Daevabad? You were able to hire a smuggler?"

"'Hire' is not the word I'd use," she said, a deadly finality in her voice. "Not that it mattered. I volunteered to stay behind with those who were too young for such travel and the ones who had too much magical blood to be able to pass in the human world." Her voice quivered. "The rest . . . I kissed their brows and wiped their tears . . . and watched as your father's firebirds burned the boat."

Ali reeled. *"What?"*

"I'd rather not repeat it if you don't mind," she said flatly. "Hearing their screams as the lake tore them apart was bad enough. I suppose your father thought it was worth it to take out the handful of Tanzeem fighters who were with them."

Ali abruptly sat down. He couldn't help it. He knew his father had done some awful things, but sinking a ship full of fleeing child refugees was pure evil. It didn't matter who Ghassan had been hunting.

He should not be king. The blunt, treasonous thought burst into Ali's head in a moment of terrible clarity. It suddenly seemed simple, the loyalty and complicated love for his father that Ali had long struggled with snipped away as someone might cut a strained rope.

Fatumai paced farther into the chamber, oblivious to his pain or perhaps rightfully uncaring about the prince having a breakdown on the floor. She ran her hands along the stacked supplies. "A lively, organized place this seems," she commented. "You have done extraordinary work, work that has truly changed the lives of innumerable shafit. Ironic, in a way, that it happened here."

That immediately pulled him from his thoughts. "Meaning?"

She glanced back. "Oh, come, brother, let us not pretend. I am certain you know what once happened to the shafit in this so-called hospital. Your namesake certainly did, though it is absent from the songs spun about his mighty deeds." She shrugged. "I suppose there's little glory in tales of plague and vengeance."

Her words were far too precise to be a mistake. "Who told you?" he asked haltingly.

"Anas, of course. Do you think you're the only one with a skill for combing through old texts?" She leveled her gaze on Ali. "He thought it was a story that should be spread far more widely."

Ali closed his eyes, his hands clenching into fists. "It belongs to the past, sister."

"It belongs to the present," Fatumai returned sharply. "It is a warning of what the Daevas are capable of. What your *Nahid* is capable of."

His eyes shot open. "What we are *all* rather capable of. It was not Daevas who murdered your children on the lake. Nor was it Daevas who burned this place to the ground and slaughtered everyone inside fourteen centuries ago."

She stared at him. "And why, brother? Tell me why the Geziris and shafit torched this place with such fury."

Ali couldn't look away and yet he couldn't not answer. "Because the Nahid Council experimented on shafit here," he confessed softly.

"Not just experimented," Fatumai corrected. "They created a poison here. A pox that could be mixed with paint. Paint that could be applied to what, exactly, my warrior friend?"

"Scabbards," he answered softly, sickness rising in his chest. "Their soldiers' scabbards."

"Their *Geziri* soldiers," she clarified. "Let's get our facts straight. For that's all the Nahid Council said your tribe was good for. Fighting and, well . . . we'll not say the impolite term, but *making* more soldiers to fill the ranks." She met Ali's stony gaze. "But the pox wasn't designed to kill the purebloods who wore those scabbards, was it?"

Water was pooling in his hands again. "No," he whispered. "It wasn't."

"That's right, it didn't do a damn thing to those soldiers," Sister Fatumai replied, a savage edge rising in her voice. "They happily headed home to Am Gezira, that insolent, restless little province. One filled with too many shafit, and too many djinn relatives who would spirit them away into the desert when Daeva officials came to drag them to Daevabad." She tilted her head. "Zaydi al Qahtani had a shafit family, didn't he? His first family?"

Ali's voice was thick. "He did."

"And what happened when *he* returned home on leave? When he let his children play with his sword? When he removed his scabbard and touched the beloved wife he hadn't seen in months?"

"He woke beside their bodies the next morning." Ali's gaze flickered unwillingly to the hilt of his own sword. Ali had read of their fate in a misplaced biography when he was a child, and it had given him nightmares for weeks. To see the people you loved most dead at the hands of a contagion you'd unknowingly given to them . . . it was something that would drive a man mad. Would drive a man to return to his garrison and put his khanjar through the throat of his Daeva commander. To lead a revolt that would reshape their world and ally them with the marid against his fire-blooded fellows.

To perhaps, in the dark quiet of his soul, purposely allow the slaughter of a hospital.

Fatumai was studying him. "You've told no one of this, have you? Afraid your shafit friends would rightfully run your Banu Nahida out?"

Her words struck—but that hadn't been the reason. The excitement in Nahri's voice, the cautious interest he'd seen from Subha when they first visited . . . Ali hadn't had the heart to destroy those things. And for what? To point out for the hundredth time the ghastly acts their people had committed so long ago?

"No, I wasn't afraid. I was *tired*." Ali's voice broke on the word. "I'm tired of everyone in this city feeding on vengeance. I'm tired of teaching our children to hate and fear other children because their parents are our enemies. And I'm sick and tired of acting like the only way to save our people is to cut down all who might oppose us, as if our enemies won't return the favor the instant power shifts."

She drew up. "Bold words for the son of a tyrant."

Ali shook his head. "What do you want from me?" he asked wearily.

She gave him a sad smile. "Nothing, Prince Alizayd. Respectfully, all that would make me trust you again would be seeing your father dead by your hand. I am finished with the politics of this city. I have ten remaining children who depend on me. I will not risk them."

"Then why are you here?"

Fatumai touched a tray of tools. "I came to pass on a warning."

Ali tensed. "What warning?"

"Your little speech about vengeance, Alizayd. There are shafit who don't long to work at your hospital, ones who would make the

Tanzeem look like Daeva sympathizers. People whose anger could bring this city to its knees and who would never forgive a Nahid for the past, no matter how many shafit she heals. I've lost some of my older children to them. They watched their friends die on the lake, their neighbors sold on that auction block, and they want nothing more than to see you so-called purebloods suffer. And your Nahid should fear them."

Ali was on his feet the next moment, but Fatumai held up a hand. "There are whispers that an attack will happen during Navasatem," she explained. "I will not reveal who I learned it from, so do not ask."

"What kind of attack?" Ali asked in horror.

"I don't know. It is a rumor and a thin one. I only pass it on because the thought of what the Daevas and the Royal Guard would do to us in retribution terrifies me." She turned to go, her cane tapping the stone floor.

"Sister, wait. Please!"

Fatumai was already pulling open the door. "That is all I know, Alizayd al Qahtani. Do with it what you will."

Ali paused, a thousand responses hovering on his lips.

The one that made it through was a surprise to him. "The little girl we saved. The girl from Turan's tavern. Is she all right?"

The cold grief in Fatumai's eyes told him the truth before she uttered the words.

"She was on the boat your father burned."

NIGHT HAD FALLEN, THE SKY IN THE WINDOW BEHIND Ghassan the silver-purple color of twilight and heavy with fog from the day's warm rain. Ali had all but paced holes in the hospital's courtyard before realizing that, however little he wished to see his father, security for Navasatem rested here.

Ghassan looked unconvinced. "An attack during Navasatem? Who told you this?"

"A friend," Ali said flatly. "One I will not be able to track down again. And she knew nothing more anyway."

Ghassan sighed. "I'll pass your concerns to Wajed."

Ali stared at him. "That's it?"

His father threw up his hands. "What else would you have me do? Do you know how many vague threats we get about the Daevas? About Nahri? Especially after the attack in your workcamp?"

"So increase her security. Cancel the procession. Cancel anything during which she'll be exposed!"

Ghassan shook his head. "I will not be canceling any Daeva celebrations on your word. I care not to hear Kaveh screeching about it." A vaguely hostile expression flitted across his face. "Besides . . . Nahri seems to think rather highly of herself lately. Why should I protect someone who so openly challenges me?"

"Because it's your duty!" Ali said, aghast. "You are her king. Her *father-in-law*."

Ghassan scoffed. "Considering the state of their marriage, I am hardly that."

Ali couldn't believe what he was hearing. "She's a woman under our roof. Her protection is part of our highest code, our most sacred—"

"And I will *speak to Wajed*," Ghassan interjected, in a tone that indicated the conversation was over. He rose to his feet, making his way to the windowsill. "But on another matter, your timing is good. The hospital is ready for tomorrow's opening ceremony?"

"Yes," Ali said, not bothering to conceal the bitterness in his voice. "I can report to the dungeon after it's over if you like."

Ghassan picked up a black velvet case that had been resting near the window. "That's not where I'm sending you, Alizayd."

There was a grim decisiveness to his voice that put Ali on edge instantly. "Where are you sending me?"

Ghassan opened the case, staring at whatever lay inside. "I had this made for you," he said softly. "When you first returned to Daevabad. I had hoped, I had even prayed, that we might find a way past all this as a family." He pulled free a magnificent length of dyed silk, patterned blue, purple, and gold twisting together over its shimmering surface.

A turban. A royal turban like the one Muntadhir wore. Ali's breath caught.

Ghassan ran his fingers over the silk. "I wanted to see you wear this during Navasatem. I wanted . . . so much to have you at my side once again."

At my side. Ali fought to keep his face blank. Because for the first time in his life, those simple words—that reminder of his duty as a Geziri son, the offer of one of the most privileged and safe positions in their world . . .

It filled him with absolute revulsion.

There was a tremor in his voice when he finally spoke. "What do you plan to do with me, Abba?"

Ghassan met his gaze, a storm of emotion in his gray eyes. "I do not know, Alizayd. I am near equally torn between declaring you my emir and having you executed." When Ali's eyes widened, he pressed on. "Yes. You are beyond capable for the position. It's true you lack in diplomacy, but you have a keener command of military matters and the city's economy than your brother ever will." He dropped the turban cloth. "You are also the most reckless and morally inflexible person I have ever come across, perhaps the greatest danger to Daevabad's stability since a lost Nahid strolled in with an Afshin at her side."

His father came around the desk, and Ali found himself stepping back, the air sharp and dangerous between them. And, God forgive him—as Ghassan moved, Ali's gaze fell on the dagger at his father's waist.

Zaydi al Qahtani's rebellion had started with a dagger through a throat. It would be so simple. So quick. Ali would be executed, he'd probably go to hell for killing his own father, but Daevabad's tyrant would be gone.

And then Muntadhir would take the throne. He could see his brother doing so, panicked, grieving, and paranoid. He'd almost certainly lash out, arresting and executing anyone associated with Ali.

Ali forced himself to look into his father's eyes. "I've only ever tried to act in Daevabad's interest." He wasn't sure whether he was speaking to his father or the dark urge in his mind.

"And now I'm going to invite you to act in your own," Ghassan said, seemingly unaware of the deadly thoughts swirling within his son. "I'm sending you back to Am Gezira after Navasatem."

Whatever Ali had expected . . . it was not that. "What?" he repeated faintly.

"I'm sending you back. You will formally renounce your titles and find a way to thoroughly sabotage your relationship with the Ayaanle, but you will otherwise return with my blessing. You may marry a local woman and tend to your crops and your canals with whatever children God grants you."

"Is this a trick?" Ali was too stunned to even be diplomatic.

"No," Ghassan said bluntly. "It is the last resort of a man who does not wish to execute his son." He looked almost imploringly at Ali. "I know not how to get you to bend, Alizayd. I have threatened you, I have killed your shafit allies, banished your mother, sent you to be hunted by assassins . . . and still you defy me. I am hoping your heart proves weaker than your sense of righteousness . . . or perhaps wiser."

Before Ali could stop himself, he saw Bir Nabat in his mind. His students and his fields, himself laughing over coffee with Lubayd and Aqisa.

A wife. A family. A *life*—one away from Daevabad's blood-soaked history and marid-haunted lake.

Ali felt like he'd been punched in the stomach. "And if I refuse?"

Ghassan looked exasperated. "It is not an offer, Alizayd. You are going. For God's sake . . ." A desperate note entered his voice. "Will you let me give at least one of my children some happiness? You wanted to go back, didn't you?"

He had. Desperately. Part of Ali still did. But he'd be leaving his home to a king he no longer believed deserved to rule it.

"Do not offer me this," he begged. "Please."

Ali's warring desires must have been plain on his face, because a quiet remorse swept his father's. "I suppose I've forgotten there are situations for which kindness is the most powerful weapon."

Ali was shaking. "Abba . . ."

But his father was already leading him out. "My men will take you back to the hospital. Your conditions remain."

"Wait, please—"

This time, the door closed softly in his face.

26

NAHRI

Nahri crossed her arms, staring skeptically at the saddle that had been placed on the stack of cushions piled before her. "Absolutely not."

"But it's safe!" Jamshid persisted. Clutching the handholds set in the saddle's frame, he hauled himself into the seat. "Look." He gestured to the raised back. "It's designed to compensate for the weakness in my lower body. I can bind my legs and use a crop to ride."

She shook her head. "You'll fall and break your neck. And a *crop*? You can't control a horse with some stick alone."

Jamshid eyed her. "My dear Banu Nahida . . . I say this with the utmost respect, but you are perhaps the last person in Daevabad I would take riding advice from." Nahri scowled, and he laughed. "Come now . . . I thought you'd be pleased. I got the design from that shafit doctor of yours. We're exchanging skills!" he teased. "Isn't that what you wanted?"

"No! I thought we might try some of her therapies so that in a few years you would be back on a horse *without* the need for a stick."

"I'm pretty sure the Navasatem procession will be over by then." Jamshid shifted in the saddle, looking pleased with himself. "This shall do nicely. Oh, what?" he asked when she glared at him. "You're not my mother. I don't need your permission." He brought his hands together as if holding imaginary reins. "I'm your elder anyway."

"I'm your Banu Nahida!" she argued back. "I could . . . I could . . ." She trailed off, thinking fast.

Jamshid—the former priest in training—turned to face her. "You could do what?" he asked politely, his eyes dancing. "I mean, what precisely could you do, according to the protocols of our faith?"

"Let him be." Nisreen's soft voice interrupted them, and Nahri glanced back to see her mentor standing at the curtain. Her eyes were locked on Jamshid, her face shining with warmth. "You should ride in the Navasatem procession if that's what you desire. It does my heart good to see you like this—even if your current stallion leaves much to be desired," she added, nodding to the stack of cushions.

Nahri sighed, but before she could respond, the sound of retching came from across the infirmary.

Jamshid glanced over. "It looks like Seyyida Mhaqal is sick again."

"Then you better get over there," Nahri replied. "If you have time to construct horses out of cushions, my brilliant apprentice, you have time to deal with fireworms."

He made a face but slipped from the saddle, heading for the sick patient. He didn't take his cane, and Nahri could not help but feel a quiet sense of triumph as he made his way steadily across the room. It might not be happening as quickly as Jamshid liked, but he *was* getting better.

She glanced at Nisreen, wanting to share her happiness. But Nisreen quickly dropped her gaze, collecting the glasswork Nahri had been using to prepare potions earlier.

Nahri moved to stop her. "I can do that. You shouldn't have to clean up after me."

"I don't mind."

But Nahri did. She pulled the pair of beakers from Nisreen's hands and set them down, taking the other woman's arm. "Come."

Nisreen made a startled sound. "But—"

"No *but*. You and I need to talk." She snatched up one of the bottles of soma that Razu had gifted her; it was proving a rather effective pain management technique. "Jamshid," she called. "You're in charge of the infirmary."

His eyes went wide over the bucket he was trying to maneuver beneath Seyyida Mhaqal. Curly gold fireworms clung to his wrists. "I'm what?"

"We'll be right outside." She escorted Nisreen to the balcony, pulling her to a bench, and pressing the bottle of soma into her hands. "Drink."

Nisreen looked indignant. "I beg your pardon?"

"*Drink*," Nahri repeated. "You and I clearly have some things to say to each other, and this will make it easier."

Nisreen took a delicate sip, making a face. "You have been spending too much time with djinn, to be acting thus."

"See? Aren't you happy you got that off your chest?" Nahri asked. "Tell me I've ruined my reputation. That the priests are saying I've strayed and Kaveh is calling me a traitor." Her voice grew slightly desperate. "None of you can meet my eyes nor want to talk to me, so surely that's what's being said."

"Banu Nahri . . ." Nisreen sighed—and then took another swig of the soma. "I don't know what you want me to say. You laid hands on dozens of shafit in broad daylight. You broke Suleiman's code."

"*To save lives,*" Nahri said, defending herself fiercely. "The lives of innocent people attacked by members of our tribe."

Nisreen shook her head. "It is not always as simple as that."

"Then you think I'm wrong?" Nahri asked, trying to keep the tremble from her voice. "Is that why you've barely been speaking to me?"

"No, child, I don't think you're wrong." Nisreen touched Nahri's hand. "I think you're brilliant and courageous and your heart is in the right place. If I hold my tongue, it's because you share your mother's stubborn streak and I would rather serve quietly at your side than lose you altogether."

"You make me sound like Ghassan," Nahri replied, stung.

Nisreen passed over the bottle. "You did ask."

Nahri took a long drink of the soma, wincing as it burned down her throat. "I think I went too far with him," she confessed; Ghassan's cold eyes as he gazed at her in the ravaged workcamp were a thing not easily forgotten. "The king, I mean. I challenged him. I had to do it, but . . ." She paused, remembering his threat to reveal her as a shafit. "I don't think he's going to let it pass unpunished."

Nisreen's expression darkened. "Did he threaten you?"

"He doesn't need to. Not directly. Though I suspect he sent Hatset away in warning to me, as well as to Ali. A reminder of the place of queens and princesses in his court, no matter how powerful their family." Nahri's lips thinned in distaste. "Right now, he and I hold each other in check, but should things shift . . ." She took another swig of the soma, her head beginning to swim. "I'm so tired of this, Nisreen. All this plotting and scheming just to keep breathing. It feels like I'm treading water . . . and, God, do I want to rest."

That lay between them for a few long moments. Nahri stared at the garden, the setting sun throwing it in shadow. The air smelled rich, the soil wet from the day's unexpected rain. The soma in her veins tingled pleasantly.

A tickle at her wrist drew her attention, and Nahri glanced down to see a morning glory's tender vine nudging her arm. She opened her palm, one of the bright pink flowers blooming in her hand.

"The palace magic has been responding to you more often," Nisreen said softly. "Since that day."

"It probably likes me picking fights with the Qahtanis."

"I would not be surprised." Nisreen sighed. "But on that . . . things will get better here. I promise. Your hospital is nearly complete. And though I don't agree with your involving the shafit, you've brought back something vital, something incredibly important to our people." She lowered her voice. "And for what you've done for Jamshid, you should be blessed. It was the right thing to take him under your wing."

Nahri let go of the flower, still glum. "I hope so."

Nisreen touched her cheek. "It was." Her eyes turned intent. "I'm proud of you, Nahri. Perhaps in all our disagreements, that's not a thing I've made clear, but I am. You're a good Banu Nahida. A good . . . what is your human word? Doctor?" She smiled. "I think your ancestors would be proud too. A little horrified . . . but proud."

Nahri blinked, her eyes suddenly damp. "I think that's the nicest thing you've ever said to me."

"Happy Navasatem," the other woman offered dryly.

"Happy Navasatem," Nahri repeated, raising the bottle. "To the start of a new generation," she added, trying to stifle the slight slur in her voice.

Nisreen pulled the bottle from her hands. "I think that's enough."

Nahri let her take it, working up the courage to ask her next question. "You said I was stubborn . . . do you—do you think I'm being too proud?"

"I don't understand."

Nahri stared at her hands, feeling self-conscious. "If I had any sense, I'd be patching things up with Muntadhir. I'd be *returning* to Muntadhir. I'd find a way to give Ghassan the grandchild he wants."

Nisreen hesitated. "That strikes me as a terrible reason to bring a child into this world."

"It's the pragmatic one. And that's what I'm supposed to be," Nahri pointed out, bitterness stealing into her voice. "Pragmatic. Heartless. That's how you survive in this place. It's how I've survived everything."

Nisreen's voice was soft. "But what do *you* want, Nahri? What does your heart want?"

Nahri laughed, the sound slightly hysterical. "I don't know." She looked at Nisreen. "When I try to imagine my future here, Nisreen, I see nothing. I feel like the very act of envisioning the things that make me happy will destroy them."

Nisreen was looking at her with open sympathy. "Oh, Banu Nahida, don't think like that. Listen, Navasatem begins tomorrow. Enjoy it. Enjoy your hospital and the parade. Ghassan will be too busy overseeing everything to scheme." She paused. "Try not to fret over your future with the Qahtanis. Let's get through the next few days, and we can sit and discuss all this after." Her voice caught. "I promise you . . . things are going to be different very soon."

Nahri managed a nod, Nisreen's calm words dissipating some of the fear that gripped her heart. They always did; Nisreen had been a steadying presence at Nahri's side since her first day in Daevabad. She'd saved her from the various plots of the harem and guided Nahri's trembling hands through countless procedures. She'd rinsed Dara's ashes from Nahri's tear-streaked face and quietly told her what to expect on her wedding night.

And yet it suddenly struck Nahri that for all the times she'd unburdened herself to Nisreen, there was still so little she knew about her mentor. "Nisreen, can I ask you something?"

"Of course."

"Are *you* happy here?"

Nisreen looked surprised by the question. "What do you mean?"

"I mean . . ." Nahri wrung her hands. "Do you ever regret staying in Daevabad after my mother healed you?" Her voice gentled. "I know you lost your parents in the attack on your village. But you could have returned home and had your own family instead of serving mine."

Nisreen grew very still, her gaze contemplative. "I would be lying if I said there weren't times I feared I'd taken the wrong path. That I never dreamed of something else, never mourned the other lives I might have lived. I don't think that's an uncertainty anyone loses." She took a sip of the soma. "But I've led an astonishing life here. I've worked alongside Nahid healers, witnessing the most miraculous, incredible things magic is capable of. I've saved lives and consoled the dying." She smiled again, taking Nahri's hand. "I've taught the next generation." Her eyes grew wondrous, seeming to gaze into a distance Nahri couldn't see. "And there are even greater things to come."

"Does that mean you plan to stay?" Nahri asked, a mix of jest and hope in her voice. "Because I could really use another Daeva at my side."

Nisreen squeezed Nahri's hand. "I will always be at your side."

SITTING STIFFLY WITH MUNTADHIR IN THE MASSIVE throne room, Nahri watched the oil in the tall glass cylinder burn low.

A hush had descended upon the crowd below, an expectant and excited buzz. Though court had been held as usual, the day's business was done with a wink, the petitions getting silly as was apparently the custom on the last day of a generation. The throne room was packed, eager crowds spilling out into the entrance gardens.

Nahri was struggling to share their excitement. For one, she'd drunk a little too much soma last night and her head was still swimming. But worse was being in the throne room itself. It was here she'd been forced to denounce Dara, and the more she learned about her people, the more obvious the room's Daeva design became. The open pavilion and manicured gardens so similar to those of the Grand Temple; the elegant columns carved with Nahids riding shedu, archers sporting ash marks, and dancers pouring wine. The green marble floor cut through with canals of rushing ice water brought to mind the green plains and cold mountains of Daevastana, not Am Gezira's golden sands. And then there was the throne itself, the magnificent, bejeweled seat carved to imitate the mighty shedu her ancestors had once tamed.

To be a Nahid in the throne room was to have her family's stolen heritage thrust in her face while she was forced to bow down before the thieves. And it was a humiliation she hated.

She could feel Ghassan's gaze on her now, and she tried to bring a happier expression to her face. It was tiring to play the part of the joyful royal wife when she hadn't spoken to her husband in weeks and she was fairly certain her father-in-law was contemplating assassinating her.

Standing at Ghassan's side was Kaveh. Ever diplomatic, the grand wazir had greeted her warmly when she arrived. Nahri had smiled back, even as she considered trying to brew up one of her ancestors' truth serums to slip into his wine. Nahri wasn't certain if Ali's accusations about Kaveh's complicity in the workcamp attack were true, but her instincts told her there was more ruthless cunning behind Kaveh's politely loyal mask than she had previously suspected. Not that she knew what to do about it. Nahri meant what she'd said to Subha: she was determined to find some justice for the camp's victims. But under virtual imprisonment in the palace infirmary—Ghassan would not even let her go to the Temple to speak to her people—she wasn't sure how to accomplish that.

She looked around the chamber once more. Ali was missing, an absence that concerned her. Per Ghassan's orders, they hadn't seen each other since that day, though they'd been exchanging letters through the king's messenger fairly often. In a petty move, they'd resorted to writing out their words in Egyptian Arabic, but Ali's messages were all business: hospital updates and construction news. As far as anyone could tell, he'd been brought into line, chastened by his mother's banishment and his own confinement in the hospital.

Nahri didn't believe that for a minute.

There was a flicker of light, and then a cheer broke out across the room, drawing her attention back to the now extinguished cylinder.

Ghassan rose to his feet. "I call to a close the twenty-ninth generation of Suleiman's Blessing!"

A roar of approval greeted his words, cheers and ululations ringing across the chamber. Sparks flew as people clapped—an already drunk few cackling as they sent up glittering conjured fireworks.

Ghassan lifted his hand. "Go home, my people. Sleep at least one night before we all lose ourselves in merriment." He smiled—for once it looked a little forced—and turned away.

Nahri stood—or tried to. Her aching head protested and she winced, her hand going to her temple.

Muntadhir caught her shoulder. "Are you all right?" he asked, sounding at least half concerned.

"Fine," she muttered, though she let him help her.

He hesitated. "Preparations for the parade tomorrow are going well?"

Nahri blinked. "They are . . ."

"Good." He bit his lip. "Nahri . . . I expect the next few days will be a whirlwind for us both, but if possible, I would like to take you up on your offer to visit the Grand Temple."

She crossed her arms. "So you can stand me up again?"

"I won't, I promise. I shouldn't have before." She raised a skeptical brow at the half apology and he made an annoyed sound in his throat. "All right, Jamshid has been harassing me to make peace with you, and this seems like a good first step."

Nahri considered that, her conversation with Nisreen running through her mind. She wasn't sure how she wanted to proceed with Muntadhir, but visiting the Temple with her husband didn't mean she had to jump back into bed with him. "All right."

A whisper of magic fluttered through the throne room, setting the hairs on the back of her neck on end. The air suddenly warmed, movement near the floor drawing her gaze.

Her eyes went wide. The water in the nearest fountain, a pretty stone octagon covered in starlike mirrored tiles, was boiling.

There was a startled cry behind her. She whirled around to see djinn hastily backing away from the trench fountains lining the perimeter walls. Water was boiling in those fountains as well, the enchanted ice floating in their depths steaming away so quickly that a white haze rose from the floor.

It lasted only seconds. There was a whistling, cracking sound as the scorching water let out enormous clouds of steam and then abruptly drained away, vanishing into jagged gashes at the bottom of the fountains.

Muntadhir had drawn closer. "Please tell me that was you," he whispered.

"No," she replied, her voice shaking. In fact, the familiar warmth of the palace magic seemed briefly gone. "But the palace does that sometimes, doesn't it?"

Muntadhir looked uneasy. "Of course." He cleared his throat. "Magic is unpredictable, after all."

Nervous laughter was breaking out across the throne room, the odd moment already dismissed by the majority of the festive crowd. Ghassan was gone, but Nahri spotted Kaveh standing beside the throne. He was staring at the smoking fountain closest to him.

And he was smiling.

It was grim and it was brief, but there was no denying his expression and the cold pleasure in it sent ice snaking around her heart.

Truth serum, she decided. As soon as the holiday was over. She touched Muntadhir's hand. "I'll see you at the hospital party tonight?"

"I wouldn't miss it for the world."

27

ALI

Ali's head was pounding as he stumbled into his small room at the hospital. The late afternoon light burned his eyes through the window, so he yanked the curtains shut, exhausted from supervising preparations for tonight's opening.

A mountain of paperwork greeted him on the desk. He picked up the first piece of parchment. It was an invitation from one of the Sahrayn trade ministers, a suggestion they meet after Navasatem to discuss some thoughts Ali had on restoring the city's port.

Bitterness swept through him, hard and fast. There would be no "after Navasatem" for Ali.

The words swam before him. Ali was exhausted. He'd pushed himself to the breaking point trying to fix things in Daevabad and now none of it mattered. He was being tossed out either way.

He dropped the letter and then collapsed onto his bed cushion. *It does matter,* he tried to tell himself. The hospital was complete, wasn't it? Ali could at least give Nahri and Subha that.

He closed his eyes, stretching out his limbs. It felt heavenly to lie flat and still for a moment, the allure of sleep tempting. Irresistible.

Just let yourself rest. That's what everyone had been telling him to do anyway. He took a deep breath, settling deeper into the cushion as sleep stole over him, wrapping him in a peace as cool and still as water . . .

The lake is quiet when he arrives, emerging from the silty current that brought him here. The chill of it is a shock, a sharp departure from the warmer waters he prefers. Though this lake is sacred to his people, the Great Tiamat's dazzling cloak of shed scales lining the bottom, it is not his home. Home is the vast twining river that cuts through desert and jungle alike, with waterfalls that crash into hidden pools and a spread of delta that blossoms to greet the sea.

He moves with the current, cutting through a school of rainbow-hued fish. Where are the rest of his people? The lake should be thick with marid, scaled hands and tentacled limbs grasping him in welcome, sharing new memories in quiet communion.

He breaks the water's surface. The air is still, laden with the fog that drifts over the lake like an ever-present storm cloud. Rain-soaked emerald mountains loom in the distance, melting into a pebbly beach.

A crowded beach. His kin have swarmed it, hissing and snapping teeth and beaks and claws. On the shore itself is a sight he has never seen in this holy place: a group of humans, protected by a thick band of fire.

Disbelief washes through him. No humans should be able to cross into this realm. None should be able to, save the marid. He swims closer. The dryness encroaching upon his skin hurts. The fire before him is already changing the atmosphere, sapping the air of its life-giving moisture.

A ripple dances over the lake's surface when the other marid spot him, and he is pulled forward on a current. As he is embraced, he opens his mind to his people, offering them memories of the rich flood he gifted his humans last season in ex-change for the boats and fishermen he devoured.

The visions they offer in return are not as pleasant. Through the eyes of his kin, he sees the mysterious invaders arriving on the beach, crossing over the threshold as though it were nothing. He sees one of them accidentally venture past the fire's safety and then tastes its flesh when it is dragged into the water, seized by tendrils of seaweed and drowned, its memories consumed for information. What those memories reveal is shocking.

The invaders are not humans. They are daevas.

Such a thing should be impossible. The daevas are supposed to be gone, van-quished by the human prophet-king Suleiman a century earlier. He studies them again from the waterline. Suleiman has changed them, has taken the fire from their skin and left them shadows of the fiends they once were.

One moves. Anger swirls inside him as he recognizes her from the dead daeva's memories. It is Anahita the thief; a so-called healer who'd spent centuries luring away the marid's human worshippers. She's been reduced to a slip of a thing, a ragged young woman with unruly black curls barely checked by the faded shawl draped over her head. As he watches, she lights a stick of cedar from a brass bowl of flames and presses it to the brow of her dead fellow, her lips moving as if in prayer.

Then she stands, her attention turning to the lake. She steps over the protective ring of fire.

Water snakes, his elders and mates, instantly rush at her. They hiss at her bare, mud-splattered feet, twining around her ankles.

Anahita hisses back, "Be still."

He freezes, along with the rest of his kin. For her words come out in the marid's tongue, a language no daeva should be able to speak.

Anahita continues. "You know now what we are . . . trust that I know you as well." Her eyes burn. "I know the scaled wraiths who caught the feet of wading chil-dren in the Euphrates, the ones who swallowed merchant ships as a passing curiosity. I know you . . . and Suleiman knew you too. Knew what you did." She raises her small chin. A dark mark stands out on her cheek, a stylized star with eight points. "And he tasked me with bringing you to heel."

Her arrogance is too much. His kin swarm the shore, churning the lake into waves that flash pointed teeth and sharp silver spines. Creatures from times forgotten, from when the world was simply fire and water. Plated fish and massive snout-nosed crocodiles.

"Fool," another marid whispers. "We will drag you into our depths and extinguish everything that you are."

Anahita smiles. "No," she replies. "You won't." The star symbol on her cheek flashes.

The world breaks.

The sky shatters into smoking pieces that dissipate like dust in water as the veil comes falling down, revealing a painfully azure sky from the realm beyond. The mountains groan as dunes of golden sand rush to swallow them, their life snuffed out.

The lake is next, evaporating from around them in a hot mist. He screams as pain wracks his body, and the holiest of their waters vanishes in the blink of an eye. The creatures of their domain—their fish and their snakes and their eels—shriek and die twitching. Sprawled on the cracked mud, he watches Anahita stride towards the lake's center.

"Here," Anahita declares as the earth buckles before her, rocks and debris racing to pile upon one another. She climbs them, a path smoothing before her feet. She glances back and the mark on her face abruptly stops glowing. "This is where we will build our city."

The lake dashes back. The sky and the mountains reassemble. He slips gratefully into the water, longing to fully immerse himself in its depths, to soothe his wounds by burrowing into the cold mud at the bottom. But there is something new, something dead and oppressive, in the heart of their sacred lake.

An island, growing to dwarf the woman who stands on a rocky precipice. Anahita closes her eyes, her fingers spinning a hot wind into a smoky boat that she blows back to her followers. She makes her way down to the new shore and then sits, lifting her face to the sun—now bright as it has never been before. She trails one hand through the water. A shining black-and-gold pearl winks from a brass ring upon her finger, and a searing pain tears through him when it dips beneath the lake's surface.

Anahita must see their helpless rage, for she speaks again. "You are being called to account as my people were by Suleiman. You will aid in the construction of my city, let my people sail unimpeded, and in return we shall have peace."

The lake sparks with heat, a crackle of lightning splitting the blue sky. It strikes the beach, consuming the daeva they killed in a blast of sacred fire.

"But know this." The flames reflect in Anahita's black eyes. "If you take another daeva life, I will destroy you."

Dead fish dot the lake. Horror is rising through his people. He senses lesser marid hurrying to the bottom, spring sprites and pond guardians desperate to escape into the streams that run far below the earth, below mountains and plains, and deserts and seas.

Streams that are steadily closing up, trapping them here with this daeva demon.

But he is no spring sprite. His is the river of salt and gold and he will not see his people subjugated. He calls to the lake, urging it to fight, to swallow these invaders whole.

Scaled hands grab him, tentacles wrapping his limbs. NO. It is a command, the voices of the lake's elders weaving together into a collective. GO. BEFORE SHE SEES YOU.

He tries to wrestle free, but it is useless. They are dragging him down, using the dying shreds of their magic to wrench open one last portal. He is shoved through.

FIND A WAY TO SAVE US. He gets a final glimpse of the dark lake, the pleading eyes of his people. THEY ARE COMING BACK.

"Ali, wake up. Wake up!"

Ali howled in rage, lashing out at the creatures holding him. "Get off me!" he hissed, his voice coming out in a breathless, slippery tongue. *"GET OFF ME."*

"Lubayd, *shut him up.*" It was Aqisa, barring the door, her dagger drawn.

"Prince Alizayd!" There was knocking on the door. "Is everything all right?"

Aqisa swore out loud and then yanked her turban away, her black braids spilling to her shoulders. Concealing the dagger behind her back, she pulled open the door just enough to reveal her face. "We do not wish to be interrupted," she said brusquely and then slammed it shut.

Ali writhed against the hand Lubayd had clamped over his mouth. Water was pouring from his skin, tears streaming down his face.

"Ali, brother." Lubayd was trembling as he held Ali down. A gash marred his cheek, four straight lines as though claws had swept across his face. "*Stop.*"

Still shaking, Ali managed a nod and Lubayd dropped his hand. "They were burning the lake," Ali wept, the marid's raw grief still roiling within him.

Lubayd looked bewildered and afraid. "What?"

"The lake. The marid. They were in my head and—"

Lubayd's hand instantly went back to Ali's mouth. "I didn't hear that."

Ali pulled free. "You don't understand . . ."

"No, *you* don't understand." Lubayd jerked his head toward the rest of the room.

His small bedroom was in chaos. It looked like a tropical storm had blown through, leaving the curtains in wet tatters and a pool of glimmering water on the floor. Most of his belongings were soaked, and a foggy mist clung to the bed.

Ali's hand went to his mouth in shock and then he recoiled, smelling blood on his fingertips.

Horrified, Ali looked again at Lubayd's face. "Did I . . ."

Lubayd nodded. "You . . . you were screaming in your sleep. Shouting in some language I've never—"

"No, he wasn't." Aqisa's voice was sharp. Intent. "You had a nightmare, understand?" She headed for the windows, tugging down the ruined curtains and letting them drop to the floor. "Lubayd, help me clean this up."

Nausea rose swift and punishing in Ali's stomach. The air smelled of salt, and a cold sweat broke out across his brow. The nightmare was growing murkier by the minute, but he could still feel the marid's despair, its ache to get back to its people.

They are coming back. Those were the only words he remembered and the warning echoed in his head, dread he didn't understand wrapping tight around his heart. "Something's wrong," he whispered. "Something is going to happen."

"Yes, you're going to get thrown in the lake if you don't shut your mouth." Aqisa shoved aside the wet curtain she was using to mop the floor and then tossed her turban cloth to Lubayd. "Wipe that blood off your face." She looked between the men. "No one can see this, understand? *Nothing happened.* We're not in Bir Nabat and this isn't some new spring we can all pretend you were lucky enough to discover."

The words pierced Ali's daze, upending the delicate dance he and his friends usually did around this subject. "What?" he whispered.

Lubayd was stuffing ruined papers into a dripping cloth sack. "Ali, brother, come on. There was a damn oasis bubbling beneath your body when we found you in the desert. There are times you don't emerge from the water in the cistern back home for hours."

"I—I didn't think you noticed," Ali stammered as fear sent his heart racing. "Neither of you ever spoke—"

"Because these are not things to be discussed," Aqisa said bluntly. "Those . . . creatures. You cannot speak of them, Ali. You certainly can't run around shouting that they're *in your head.*"

Lubayd spoke up again, looking almost apologetic. "Ali, I don't spin my wild stories just to annoy you. I do it so people don't spread *other* stories about you, understand? Tales that might not have a happy ending."

Ali stared at them. He didn't know what to say. Explanations, apologies, they ran through his mind, leaving him at a loss.

The adhan came then, calling the faithful to maghrib prayer. Across the city, Ali knew court would be ending, his father announcing the official beginning to Navasatem as the sun dipped below the horizon.

Aqisa straightened up, coming around the bed cushion with a garment bag. "These are the clothes your sister sent you for tonight's ceremony." She dropped it in his lap. "Get dressed. Forget what we discussed here. You're about to have your family and every gossiping, back-stabbing noble in this city crawling through these corridors. You can't be trembling like a leaf and rambling about the marid." She eyed him. "It was a nightmare, brother. Say it."

"It was a nightmare," he repeated, his voice hollow. He'd been having them for months, hadn't he? He was overworked, he was exhausted. Was it any surprise that a dream might have been more visceral today? More gut-wrenching? That his water abilities might have reacted accordingly?

It was a nightmare. Only a nightmare. It had to be.

28

NAHRI

The festivities were in full swing by the time Nahri arrived at the hospital, the complex vibrant with the magical frenzy the djinn excelled at. Bewitched glass dragonflies with wings of colorful conjured fire flitted through the air, and the fountains flowed with date wine. A trio of musicians played instruments that looked as if they'd been fished from an aquatic kingdom: the drums were made from the bellies of impossibly large shells, the sitar carved from pale driftwood and strung with sea silk. A life-size brass automaton in the shape of a sly-eyed dancer crushed sugarcane into juice, the liquid pouring from one glittering, outstretched hand. A banquet had been set up in one of the chambers, the aroma of spices carrying on the warm air.

The crowd of merrymakers was no less impressive. Nobles from the city's oldest families and merchants from the richest mingled and argued with political elites in the garden courtyard, while Daevabad's most popular poets and artists gossiped and challenged each other to impromptu competitions from satin cushions. Everyone was dressed in their enchanted finest: fragrant capes of living flowers, sparkling scarves of harnessed lightning, and glittering robes of mirrored beads.

Muntadhir and Nahri were immediately swept into the packed courtyard. Her husband, of course, was in his element, surrounded by obsequious nobles and loyal friends. At the fringe of the circle, Nahri stood up on her toes in a vain effort to see the completed hospital over the heads of laughing partygoers and dashing servants. She thought she might have caught a glimpse of Razu dealing twinkling playing cards before a group of enthralled onlookers, but deciding to respect whatever scheme the other woman had devised, Nahri stayed put.

That was not the case, however, when Nahri finally saw Subha, scowling at the crowd from beneath a shadowed archway.

"Emir, if you'll excuse me a moment . . ." Distracted by an Agnivanshi minister's exaggerated tale of simurgh hunting, Muntadhir offered what might have been a nod, and Nahri slipped away, winding through the mob until she reached Subha's side.

"Doctor Sen!" she greeted her affectionately. "You look as happy as I expected."

Subha shook her head. "I cannot believe we rushed to complete this place for a party." She glared at a pair of giggling Geziri noblewomen. "If they break anything . . ."

"Ali wrote to assure me all the equipment would be safely packed away." Nahri grinned. "The two of you must like working together. Neither of you have any sense of fun." She laughed when the other healer threw her a dirty look. "Though you do look lovely." Nahri gestured to Subha's clothes, a deep purple sari patterned in maroon and gold diamonds. "This is very pretty."

"Do you know that when you speak, you sound like a fruit peddler trying to sell me overripe produce?"

"One person's overripe is another person's sweet," Nahri said dryly.

Subha shook her head, but her grumpiness took on a slightly warmer edge. "You're quite a sight yourself," she said, nodding at Nahri's attire. "Are the Daevas making gowns of gold now?"

Nahri brushed her thumb over the thickly embroidered sleeve. "Seems like it—and it's as heavy as you might imagine. I'll be eager to trade it for a medical smock as soon as we can start seeing patients here."

Subha's expression softened. "I never imagined working in a place like this. Parimal and I have taken to touring the apothecary and supply closets just to admire how well stocked everything is . . ." Her tone grew a little sad. "I wish my father could have been here."

"We'll do his legacy proud," Nahri said sincerely. "I'm hoping you can share some of his wisdom when it comes to training apprentices. And on that note . . . Jamshid!" she called out, seeing him approaching. "Come! Join us."

Jamshid smiled, offering a bow as he brought his hands together in blessing. "May the fires burn brightly for you both."

Nahri glanced at Subha. "I heard I have you to thank for that dangerous saddle he's insisting on using."

"You did wish us to exchange skills."

Nahri shook her head, managing not to roll her eyes. "Where's the final member of our team?"

Subha's face fell. "I don't know. I haven't seen the prince since this afternoon. I wouldn't be surprised if he finally fell asleep somewhere. He seems determined to work himself to death."

"And what a shame that would be," Jamshid murmured.

Subha suddenly smiled, her gaze fixing on her husband as he emerged from a door on the other side of the courtyard carrying their daughter. The baby's dark eyes went wide and mesmerized at the sight of the magical feast.

Nahri nudged her shoulder. "Go say hi. We'll catch up later." As Subha moved away, Nahri turned to Jamshid. "You really don't like Ali, do you?" This was not the first time she'd seen him react negatively to mentions of the prince.

Jamshid hesitated. "No," he said. "I do not. I didn't mind him when he was younger—he was always intense, but he was Muntadhir's little brother, and Muntadhir adored him. But that night you saved him . . ." His voice lowered. "Nahri, he made me throw a man into the lake. A man I'm not certain was even dead."

"A man who tried to assassinate him," Nahri pointed out. "A shafit. Do you have any idea what Ghassan would have done if he found out a shafit nearly killed his son?"

Jamshid looked unconvinced. "I still don't like him being in Daevabad. I don't like the effect he's had on Muntadhir, and I worry . . ." He pressed his lips into a thin line. "He's a very ambitious man."

Nahri could not deny that Ali's return had sent her husband into a spiral, but she wasn't sure it was a justified one. "Muntadhir is going to be king, Jamshid. And he is a better politician than you give him credit for. Though if you're so concerned about his well-being . . ." Her voice turned crafty. "Perhaps you might go distract him a bit."

Jamshid eyed her knowingly. "You're trying to get away."

"I'm the Banu Nahida. I have a Creator-given right to explore my own hospital."

He exhaled, but it was a feigned grouchiness. "Go on then," he said, inclining his head toward the opposite corridor. "Now, when no one's looking."

Nahri brought her hands up in blessing. "May the fires burn *very* brightly for you."

The corridor he suggested was empty. Nahri quickly slipped off her sandals so her footsteps wouldn't be heard and had no sooner pressed a bare sole to the cool marble floor than the pale walls lit up, glowing softly in the dark as if to lead the way.

She grinned. Wouldn't that be convenient when she had a patient emergency in the middle of the night? She traced her hands along the wall, the rosy hue brightening where her fingers made contact. Her hospital—her ancestors' hospital—was restored. A dream she'd been almost too nervous to voice six months ago had been realized and now stood gleaming in the moonlight, Daevabad's most powerful citizens laughing within its rooms. It all seemed so outrageous, so audaciously hopeful, that it scared her.

Stop. Nisreen's calm words came back to her. Nahri could enjoy a night of happiness. Her many problems would still be there in the morning, whether or not she took a few hours to savor this rare success.

She wandered on, following a twisting staircase she was fairly certain led to the hospital's library. The sounds of celebration faded behind her; she was obviously the only fool creeping through empty hallways instead of enjoying the party.

She emerged in the library, a wide, airy room with lecture space for dozens of students. A wall of shelves had been built into the opposite side, and Nahri went to them, curious to see what volumes had been collected.

Then she stopped. Across the library was a small archway, tiled in a black-and-white pattern reminiscent of Cairo's buildings. Odd. She didn't remember seeing this room on any of the plans. Intrigued, she crossed to investigate.

Her breath caught the moment she stepped over the threshold. It wasn't just the archway that was reminiscent of Egypt.

It was *everything*.

A mashrabiya that might have been plucked from Cairo's heart overlooked the street, the cozy window seat covered in red and gold cushions, its intricate wooden screens hiding a private nook. Brightly embroidered tapestries—identical to the ones she'd seen in the markets back home—adorned the walls, and a stunning teak desk inlaid with glinting vines of mother-of-pearl anchored the room. Miniature reeds and bright purple-blue Nile lotus blooms grew lush within a raised marble fountain that lined the wall, the clear water inside passing over warm brown stones.

A glimmer of silver moved in the shadows of the mashrabiya. "Nahri?" a sleepy voice asked.

She jumped in surprise. "*Ali?*" She shivered. Restored or not, the dark, empty hospital was still an eerie place to stumble upon someone unexpectedly.

She opened her palm, conjuring a handful of flames. Small wonder she hadn't seen Ali: he was seated deep in the window box, pressed against the wooden screen as though he'd been gazing out at the street. Nahri frowned. Though he was dressed in a formal dishdasha, his head was uncovered and he looked . . . well, terrible. His face was gray, his eyes almost feverish.

She stepped closer. "Are you all right?"

Ali sat up. His movements were slow, bone-weary exhaustion written into every line of his body. "I'm fine," he murmured. He scrubbed his hands over his face. "Sorry, I wasn't expecting anyone to come up here."

"Well, you picked a poor time for a nap," she said lightly. "You might remember there's a party going on downstairs."

He blinked, still looking dazed. "Of course. The opening celebration."

Nahri studied him again. "Are you *sure* you're all right?"

"I'm sure," he replied quickly. "I just haven't been sleeping well. Nightmares." He rose to his feet, stepping into the light. "But I'm glad you found me. I was actually hoping to . . ." His gray eyes went wide, tracing over her. "Oh," he whispered. "You . . . you look—" He abruptly shut his mouth, averting his gaze. "Sorry . . . so, ah, how do you like your office?"

She stared at him in confusion. "My *office*?"

He inclined his head. "Your office. I thought you might like somewhere private to steal away between patients. Like the orange grove you have at the palace infirmary. The one I, er, intruded upon," he added, embarrassment in his voice.

Nahri's mouth fell open. "You built this place? For *me*?"

"I'd say the entire hospital is for you, but yes." Ali drifted closer, running his hands through the water in the fountain. "I came across a few shafit artisans from Egypt and told them to let their imaginations run wild." He glanced back with a small smile. "You always did seem so fond of your old land."

My old land. Nahri gazed at the mashrabiya again; in that moment, if she squinted just the right way, she could almost imagine being home. Could imagine hearing men joking in Cairo's distinctive cadence and smelling the spices and herbs of Yaqub's apothecary.

Homesickness rose inside her, sharp and fast. "I miss it so much," she confessed. "I keep thinking I'll stop, that I feel more settled here . . ." She leaned against the desk. "But there are days I'd do almost anything to go home. Even if it was just for an afternoon. A few hours of joking with people in my language and sitting next to the Nile. Of being anonymous in the streets and bartering for oranges. We had the best fruit, you know," she added, her throat catching. "Nothing in Daevabad tastes as sweet."

Ali was looking at her with open sympathy. "I'm sorry."

She shook her head, embarrassed to find herself fighting tears. "Forget it," she said, roughly wiping her eyes. "By God, you must think I'm mad, pining for human citrus when I'm surrounded by every luxury the magical world contains."

"I don't think you're mad." Ali assured her, crossing to join her at the desk. "They're your roots. They're what make you who you are. That isn't something you should have to cut away."

Nahri tipped the flames in her hand into a lamp on the desk. How much easier things would be if that were true here. Struggling to tamp down her emotions, she glanced around her office again. It really was lovely, the tapestries glowing in the light of the flickering lamp. A fresco had been painted on the opposite wall, a replica of a scene she might have seen in one of Egypt's ancient temples.

It touched her more than she thought possible. "Thank you," she finally said. "This . . . this was incredibly kind of of you."

Ali shrugged. "I was happy to do it." He smiled again, the shadows in his tired face lessening slightly. "As you are fond of pointing out—I *do* owe you."

"You'll always owe me," she said, pushing up to sit on the desk. "I have a talent for extending the debts of powerful people indefinitely."

His grin widened. "That I believe." But then his smile faded. "I'm happy to finally see you again. I've been worried about you."

"I'm fine," Nahri said, forcing indifference into her voice. She'd already been emotional enough in discussing her nostalgia for Egypt. "Besides, I'm not the one falling asleep in empty offices. How have *you* been? Your mother . . ."

Pain flashed in his eyes. "We're both still alive," he replied. "Which is more than I can say for a lot of people here."

If that wasn't the bitter truth. Nahri sighed. "For what it's worth, I think we were right to intervene. A lot more people would have died if you hadn't brought me to the camp when you did."

"I know. I just hate that choosing to do the right thing in Daevabad always seems to come with a steep price." His face fell. "Zaynab . . . she decided not to come tonight. I don't think she'll forgive me for our mother's banishment."

Genuine sympathy swept through her. "Oh, Ali, I'm sure that's not true." Nahri reached out to touch the sleeve of his dishdasha; it was an elegant pale silver, chased through with midnight-colored stripes and belted with a teal sash. "After all, she was clearly the one who picked this out."

Ali groaned. "Is it that obvious?"

"Yes. The only time you're not wearing something stark and streaked with dirt, it's because someone else has dressed you." Embarrassment colored his face again, and she laughed. "It's a compliment, Ali. You look nice."

"You look incredible." The words seemed to slip unthinkingly from his mouth, and when she met his gaze, a little startled by the emotion in his voice, he looked away. "Your garments, I mean," he explained quickly. "The headdress. It's very . . . intricate."

"It's very heavy," Nahri complained, reaching up to touch the gold diadem holding her shimmering black chador in place. The smoky fabric was enchanted to appear as though it were smoldering, the ruby and diamond ornaments glittering like fire. She lifted the diadem free, placing it beside her on the desk, and then slid her fingers under the chador to rub the aching spot where the metal had pressed. Catching sight of Ali watching her, she scolded him. "Oh, don't you judge. Your turbans are probably light as a feather in comparison to this thing."

"I . . . I'm not judging." He stepped back from the desk, clearing his throat. "Though while you're here, do you mind telling me what's being done to protect you given that threat?"

It took Nahri a moment to process his words, taken aback by the abrupt change in subject. "Threat? What threat?"

"The one from my shafit acquaintance." When she squinted in confusion, alarm flashed in Ali's face. "The one I passed on to my father. Surely he told you."

"This is the first I've heard."

"The first you've *heard*?" Anger crossed his face. "Is the king here? Did you see him below?"

"Not yet, but—wait!" She grabbed Ali's wrist when he turned

for the door. "Will you stop trying to get tossed in the dungeons?" She pulled him back. "Tell me about this threat."

"A woman I know said she heard some shafit were planning to attack you during Navasatem."

She waited for him to elaborate, but he stayed silent. "And that's it?" she asked. "Nothing more?"

"Isn't that enough?" Ali sounded incredulous.

Nahri looked him in the eye. "No. Ali, I get threats every day. My entire tribe does. But Kaveh, Muntadhir, and Wajed have been harping about security for an entire year, and they've told me their plans. Kaveh panics over everything, and Muntadhir is my husband. I trust them, on this issue at least."

Ali looked unconvinced. "It only takes a few angry people. And after what happened in the workcamp, Nahri, there are a *lot* of angry people."

"I'll be well guarded," she assured him. "I promise."

He sighed. "Would you at least consider having Aqisa join you tomorrow for the procession? I'd offer to come myself, but I don't think your people would like it."

Nahri pondered that, trying to imagine the reaction Ali's fierce friend from rural Am Gezira would have on the crowd of mostly city-raised Daevas. Not to mention what it might suggest to Muntadhir. "Ali . . ."

"Please."

She let go of his wrist, raising her hands in defeat. "Fine. As long as she keeps her dagger on her person unless I give the order." She frowned again. With the moonlight falling on his face, she could see that Ali was trembling. "Ali, what's really going on? You're acting even stranger than usual."

He actually laughed, the sound hollow, and then ran his hands over his face. "It's been a rough few days."

Nahri hesitated. They weren't supposed to be friends, not

anymore. But the despair radiating from the prince tugged at her heart. Despite the circle of companions and family that surrounded him, it was obvious Ali had secrets. And Nahri knew all too well secrets were a burden lonely to bear.

And he *had* built her this lovely office. "Do you want to talk about it?" she asked.

His gaze darted to her, the desperation in his eyes unmissable. "Yes," he said hoarsely. "No. I don't know. I wouldn't even know where to start."

She pulled him toward the cushioned seat next to the screened window. "How about by sitting?" She sat across from him, pulling up her knees. "Is this about your father?"

Ali let out a deep sigh. "Part of it is. He's sending me back to Am Gezira."

"You're going back to Am Gezira?" she repeated in surprise. Ali certainly hadn't been acting like a man going anywhere; he seemed to have a thousand plans for the future of Daevabad. "For how long?"

"Forever?" His voice broke, as if he'd tried to make a joke out of it and failed. "My father doesn't want me stirring up any more trouble. I'm to give up my titles and go back to the village I was living in after Navasatem." Ali's shoulders slumped. "He told me to marry and have a family. To have a peaceful life that doesn't include fomenting dissent in Daevabad."

Both his words and the unexpected jolt of emotion in her chest at the thought of his leaving threw her wildly off balance. She struggled to find the right response. "The village . . . Bir Nabat?"

He looked surprised. "I didn't think you'd remember the name."

Nahri rolled her eyes. "There's not a soul working at the hospital who hasn't heard you wax poetic about the ruins and canals of Bir Nabat." She shook her head. "But I don't understand why you wouldn't want to go back. You clearly love it there. Your letters were always—"

Ali started. "You read my letters?"

Nahri knew she couldn't hide her slip. She let out a huff of frustration at both herself and him. "I . . . All right, I read them. They were interesting," she said, defending herself. "You put in information about local healing plants and stories about the humans to lure me in."

A sad half-smile twisted his mouth. "I wish I was even half as subversive as you think I am. I'd do a lot better in Daevabad."

"But you have a chance to *leave* Daevabad." She nudged his shoulder when he scowled. "So why do you look so upset? You get to have a *life*. A peaceful one, in a place you love."

Ali was silent for several heartbeats, his gaze fixed on the floor. "Because this is my home, Nahri, and I . . ." He squeezed his eyes shut, like whatever he was about to say caused him pain. "I don't think I can leave it while my father still rules."

Nahri would swear the temperature in the room plummeted. She jerked back, instinctively glancing around, but they were alone. She was already shaking her head, the fear Ghassan had carved into her an instinctual response.

"Ali, you can't talk like that," she whispered. "Not here. Not ever."

Ali looked back at her, beseeching. "Nahri, you know it's true. He's done terrible things. He's going to keep doing terrible things. That's the only way he knows—"

Nahri actually clapped her hand over his mouth. "Stop," she hissed, her eyes darting around the room. They might be alone, but God only knew the form Ghassan's spies took. "We're already in his sights. *I'm* already in his sights. Was what he did at the shafit camp not enough to convince you to back down?"

He pushed her hand away. "No," he said fervently. "It did the opposite. A good king wouldn't have allowed that bloodshed.

A good king would ensure justice for both the Daevas and the shafit, so that people didn't resort to taking vengeance into their own hands."

"Do you know how naive you sound?" Nahri said desperately. "People aren't that virtuous. And you can't fight him. He is capable of things you can't imagine. He'll destroy you."

Ali's eyes blazed. "Aren't there some things worth that risk?"

All of Muntadhir's warnings about his younger brother came flooding back to her. "No," she said, her voice so cutting she barely recognized it. "Because a hundred others will pay the price for your risk."

Bitterness creased his face. "Then how do we fight, Nahri? Because I know you want better for Daevabad. I heard you in the Temple, I watched *you* confront my father." He gestured to the rest of the room. "Was not the whole point of building the hospital to move forward?"

"The hospital was meant to be a *step*," she countered. "It was meant to provide a foundation to build some peace and security between the Daevas and shafit for the day your father *doesn't* have his boot on our neck. We're not there, Ali. Not yet."

"And how many more people will die while we wait for that day?"

Their gazes locked. There was nothing but conviction in the warm gray of his eyes. No cunning, no deception.

It terrified her. Because whatever history was between them, Nahri did not think she had it in her to watch the kind man who'd built her this office, this quiet homage to the home she still loved—the man who'd taught her to read and helped her summon flames for the first time—be executed in the arena.

Nahri sat back down. "Ali, you say you owe me your life," she started, fighting a tremble in her voice. "I'm going to collect on that debt. Go back to Am Gezira."

He let out an exasperated sigh, turning away. "Nahri . . ."

She reached out, taking his chin in one hand and forcing him to look back at her. He visibly jumped at her touch, his eyes going wide.

"Take your father's offer," she said firmly. "You can help people in Am Gezira without getting killed. Marry some woman who will love to hear you ramble about canals, and have a whole band of children you'll undoubtedly be too strict with." She cupped his cheek, her thumb brushing his beard. She didn't miss the sudden racing of his heart.

Nor the sadness rising in her own.

Ali seemed speechless, his eyes flickering nervously across her face. It would have to do. She stood up, dropping her hand as she stepped away, the sudden sting of tears in her eyes. "Go steal some happiness for yourself, my friend," she said softly. "Trust me when I say the chance doesn't always come back."

29

ALI

"So you still haven't told me where you were last night," Lubayd said as they made their way to the arena. "Aqisa and I were looking for you at the celebration."

"I didn't go," Ali replied. "I didn't feel up to it."

Lubayd halted in his tracks. "Another nightmare?"

"No," Ali said quickly, hating the fear in his friend's expression. "No nightmares. But I was exhausted and didn't trust myself not to say something inflammatory to my father. Or my brother." He made a sour face as they kept walking. "To anyone really."

"Well, then I'm glad you slept in and avoided getting arrested. Though you did miss quite the party." He stretched, cracking his neck. "Is Aqisa meeting us at the arena?"

"Later. I asked her to guard the Banu Nahida during the parade this morning."

"That's the one meant to reenact Anahid's arrival in Daeva-bad, right?" Lubayd snorted. "In that case, will you and your little healer be fighting to the death at some point to represent the latter half of our history?"

Ali flinched at the joke. *Go back to Am Gezira, Ali. Steal some happiness for yourself.* Ali had been replaying those words and the memory of Nahri's hand cradling his jaw in his mind since last night. Which—he had to give credit to her—had rather effectively interrupted his brewing thoughts of rebellion.

He closed his eyes. God forgive him, she had looked so beautiful last night. After not seeing her for weeks, Ali had been struck speechless at the sight of her standing in the darkness of that quiet room, dressed in the finery of her ancestors. She'd looked like a legend brought to life, and for the first time, he'd been nervous—truly nervous—in her presence, struggling not to stare as she smiled her sharp smile and slid her fingers under her chador. And when she'd touched his face . . .

Muntadhir's wife. She's Muntadhir's wife.

As if his thoughts had the power to conjure, a familiar laugh sounded ahead, one whose lightheartedness cut through Ali like a knife.

"—I'm not mocking you," Muntadhir teased. "I think the 'Suleiman just threw me across the world look' has its appeal. Your rags even smell!" Muntadhir laughed again. "It's all very authentic."

"Oh, be quiet," he heard Jamshid return. "There's more where these rags came from and your steward owes me a favor. I'll have them used to line your fancy turban."

Ali peered around the corner. Muntadhir and Jamshid were across the corridor, framed together in a sunlit arch. He frowned, shading his eyes against the sudden brightness. For half a second, he'd swear he saw his brother's hands on Jamshid's collar, his face inclined toward his neck as though jokingly smelling him, but then Ali blinked, sunspots blossoming across his vision, and the two men were apart, neither looking very pleased to see him.

"Alizayd." His brother's disdainful gaze flickered up and down Ali's rumpled dishdasha. "Late night?"

Muntadhir always seemed to know a new way to make him feel small. His brother was immaculately turned out as usual in his ebony robes and brilliant royal turban. He'd looked even more stylish last night, dressed in an ikat-patterned waistcloth and brilliant sapphire tunic. Ali had seen him at the party, had watched from an upper balcony after Nahri left as his brother laughed and caroused like he'd built the hospital himself.

"As always," Ali replied acidly.

Jamshid's eyes flashed at his tone. The Daeva man was indeed dressed in rags, his black tunic torn and smeared with ash and his pants with unfired brick dust—a nod to the human temple that Suleiman had ordered their ancestors to build.

Muntadhir cleared his throat. "Jamshid, why don't you head to the procession? We'll meet later." He squeezed the other man's shoulder. "I still want to see that saddle."

Jamshid nodded. "Until then, Emir-joon."

He left, and Muntadhir ignored Ali, sweeping through the entrance that led to the arena's royal viewing platform.

Lubayd snickered. "I suppose emirs don't like to be interrupted, same as everyone else."

Ali was baffled by the amusement in his friend's voice. "What do you mean?"

"Well, you know . . ." Lubayd stopped and studied Ali. "Oh . . . you don't know." Spots of color rose in his cheeks. "Forget it," he said, turning to follow Muntadhir.

"What don't I know?" Ali asked, but Lubayd ignored him, suddenly very interested in the spectacle below. To be fair, it was a sight: a half-dozen Daeva archers were competing, putting on a show to amuse the packed crowd while they waited for the procession to arrive.

Lubayd whistled. "Wow," he said, watching as a mounted Daeva archer on a silver stallion raced across the sand, aiming a flaming arrow at a hollow gourd mounted on a high pole. The gourd was stuffed with kindling and painted with pitch; it burst into flames, and the crowd cheered. "They really are demons with those bows."

Ali glowered. "I'm well aware."

"Alizayd." Ghassan's voice rang across the pavilion just as Ali was about to take a seat with a few of the officers from the Royal Guard. His father was at the front, of course, leaning against a silk-covered bolster, a jade cup of ruby-colored wine at hand. "Come here."

Lubayd grabbed his wrist before he could move. "Careful," he warned. "You seem a little surlier than usual this morning."

Ali didn't respond. It was true he didn't trust himself to say anything to his father, but he had no choice other than to make his way to the front. Muntadhir was already seated, flashing his charming grin at a pretty servant as she passed. She stopped with a blush and smile to pour him a cup of wine.

He makes that look so easy. Not that Ali wanted to go around enticing attractive women into pouring him wine—every part of that was forbidden. But he knew Muntadhir wouldn't have been reduced to a stammering wreck in front of Nahri last night. And as he watched his brother, Ali was unable to deny the jealousy clawing in his chest. Muntadhir had leaned over to whisper in the cupbearer's ear, and she giggled, playfully bumping him with her shoulder.

You have a wife. A beautiful, brilliant wife. Though Ali supposed when everything else was offered to you on a silver platter, beautiful, brilliant wives weren't blessings to be cherished.

"Everything going well with the procession?" Ghassan asked Muntadhir, paying no attention to Ali as he sat down stiffly on a plain prayer mat, forgoing the soft cushions closer to the pair.

Muntadhir nodded, taking a sip of his wine as the cupbearer

moved away. "The priests and Nahri led dawn ceremonies at the lake. Kaveh was to make sure they all boarded their chariots, and Jamshid just left to escort them here with another group of archers." A small smile broke his face. "He's riding today."

"And security for the procession?" Ghassan pressed. "Did you speak with Wajed?"

"I did. He assured me he has soldiers lining the parade route and that no shafit would be permitted to join."

Ali struggled not to roll his eyes. Of course, banning the shafit from the festivities would be the type of "security" the palace enacted. Though Ali supposed he should be happy his brother and not his father was overseeing Navasatem. Ghassan probably would have chosen to execute on sight any shafit who strayed within five blocks of the procession route.

All too aware he was in the exact mood that Lubayd had warned him to guard against, Ali tried to direct his attention to the arena. The Daeva archers were dressed in the age-old style of their ancestors, dashing about as if they were part horse themselves in wildly striped felt leggings, dazzling saffron coats, and horned silver helms. They rose to stand in painted saddles as they galloped in sweeping arcs and intricate formations, ornaments flashing in their horses' manes as they drew back stylized silver bows.

Unease pooled in Ali's stomach. Though not Afshins themselves—Darayavahoush's family had been wiped out in the war—the men below were the clearest inheritors of his legacy. One of the men let a scythe-ended arrow fly at a target, and Ali could not help but cringe. He didn't know which kind of arrows Darayavahoush had shot through his throat, but he'd bet one of them was down below.

"Not to your taste, Zaydi?" Muntadhir was watching him.

The sarcasm with which his brother spoke his nickname cut

deep, and then the punch of another arrow tearing through a target made his stomach clench. "Not quite," he said through his teeth.

"And yet to hear it, you're the finest warrior in Daevabad." Muntadhir's tone was light, but malice lurked underneath it. "The great Afshin-slayer."

"I never trained much with the bow. You know that." Ali had learned to use one, of course, but he was meant to be Qaid, and archery took time, time Wajed had preferred Ali spend on the zulfiqar and strategy. The Daeva men before him had likely been in saddles since they were five, given toy bows at the same age.

A servant came by with coffee, and Ali gratefully took a cup.

"You look as though you need that," Ghassan commented. "I was surprised not to see you at the hospital's opening last night."

Ali cleared his throat. "I wasn't feeling well."

"Unfortunate," Ghassan said. "I have to say I was pleased; it's an impressive complex. Regardless of your recent behavior, you and Banu Nahri have done fine work."

Ali checked the resentment growing inside him, knowing he'd be smarter to take advantage of his father's seemingly amicable mood. "I am glad to hear that." He took another sip of his coffee, savoring the bitter, cardamom-scented tang. "On a related note, I was wondering if you'd seen my proposal."

"You'll have to be more specific," Ghassan replied. "I think I have fifty proposals from you on my desk at the moment."

"The one giving official recognition to the shafit guilds in the workcamp. I'd like them to be able to compete for government contract—"

"My God, do you *ever* stop?" Muntadhir cut in rudely. "Can we not have a day's break from your yammering about the economy and the shafit?"

Ghassan raised a hand before Ali could speak. "Let him be.

As it is, he's not wrong to be thinking about the economy." He cleared his throat, his gaze going a little distant. "I've received an offer for Zaynab's hand."

Ali instantly tensed; there was nothing he liked in the careful way his father had delivered that news. "From who?" he demanded, not caring that he sounded curt.

"Nasir Ishak."

Ali blinked. "*Who?*"

"Nasir Ishak." Muntadhir had gone pale as he repeated the name. "He's a spice merchant from Malacca."

"He's more than a spice merchant," Ghassan corrected. "He's king of the djinn in those islands in all but name. Daevabad's control has always been tenuous there."

Malacca. Ali looked between his father and brother. They couldn't be serious. "Daevabad's control is tenuous there because it's *across the ocean*. Zaynab will be lucky to visit here once a century!"

Neither man answered him. Muntadhir looked like he was fighting to keep his composure. "You told me you had decided against his offer, Abba," he said.

"That was before . . . recent events." Ghassan's mouth thinned in displeasure. "We need to start looking beyond Ta Ntry for allies and resources. Nasir is an opportunity we can ill afford to turn away."

"Does Zaynab get a say in this?" Ali could hear the edge in his voice, but this was too much. Was this another reason his mother had been banished? So that she wouldn't be able to protest her daughter being shipped across the sea to fill the Treasury's coffers?

"I've spoken with Zaynab about this possibility," Ghassan replied tersely. "I would never force her. I would never have to. She takes her loyalty and duty to our family far more seriously than you, Alizayd. And quite frankly, your stunt in the shaft camp and your mother taking half the Ayaanle delegation back to Ta Ntry has forced my hand." He turned back to Muntadhir. "Nasir is arriving next week for the holiday. I'd like you to spend time with him and get to know what kind of man he is before I decide anything."

His brother stared at his hands, emotions warring on his face. Ali watched him, silently begging: *Say something. Anything. Give some sign that you can stand up to him, that you won't become him.*

Muntadhir cleared his throat. "I'll talk to him."

"Coward." The moment the word slipped from his lips, Ali knew it wasn't fair. But he didn't care.

Muntadhir stared at him in shock. "What did you just say to me?"

"I said you're a—" From below, another arrow struck the target, making a solid thunk as it tore through the flesh of the gourd. Ali instinctively flinched, the moment stealing his words.

Ghassan had drawn up, glaring at Ali with open contempt. "Have you lost all sense of honor?" he hissed under his breath. "I should have you lashed for speaking with such disrespect."

"No," Muntadhir said sharply. "I can handle this, Abba. I should have already."

Without another word, his brother rose to his feet and turned to face the packed pavilion. He aimed a dazzling smile at the crowd, the change in his expression so sudden it was as though someone had snuffed out a candle.

"Friends!" he called out. The Qahtani men had been speaking quietly in Geziriyya, but Muntadhir raised his voice, switching to Djinnistani. "The great Afshin-slayer is anxious to show his skills, and I do believe you deserve a spectacle."

An expectant hush fell across the crowd, and Ali suddenly realized just how many people were watching them: nobles always eager to witness some drama from Daevabad's royals.

And Muntadhir knew how to draw their attention. "So I'd

like to issue my little brother a challenge . . ." He gestured to the archers below. "Beat me."

Ali stared at him in incomprehension. "You want to compete with *me*? In the arena?"

"I do." Muntadhir put his wine cup down with a flourish, his eyes dancing as if this were all a joke. "Come on, Afshin-slayer," he goaded when Ali didn't move. "Surely you're not afraid?" Without waiting for a response, Muntadhir laughed and headed for the steps.

The eyes of the rest of pavilion were on Ali, expectant. Muntadhir might have done it in jest, but he'd issued a challenge, and Ali would lose face if he didn't address it—especially one so seemingly innocent.

Ali rose to his feet slowly.

Ghassan gave him a warning look, but Ali knew he wouldn't interfere; Geziri men didn't back down from such a public contest, and princes in the line of succession certainly did not. "Remember yourself," he said simply.

Remember what? That I was always meant to be beneath him? Or that I was meant to be his weapon—one who could defeat any man?

Lubayd was at his elbow in a second. "Why do you look like you just swallowed a locust?" he whispered. "You can shoot an arrow better than that gold-draped fool, can't you?"

Ali swallowed, not wanting to confirm his weakness. "I-I was shot, Lubayd. By the Afshin," he stammered, the memories coming to him in a swift punch. "It was bad. I haven't touched a bow since."

Lubayd blanched, but there was no time for him to respond. Muntadhir was already joining the Daeva riders. They grinned as he greeted them in the Divasti that Ali couldn't speak, gesturing back toward Ali with laughter. God only knew what Muntadhir was saying to them. They were probably his friends, the wealthy nobles with whom he liked to wine and dine in the salons of courtesans and poets. A world that didn't look kindly upon men like Ali.

And though he knew he'd provoked his brother, a hurt Ali rarely acknowledged made itself known, the knot of resentment and jealousy he tried so hard to disavow threatening to come undone. The times he'd forced himself to smile when Muntadhir's companions teased him growing up, asking how many men he'd killed at the Citadel and if it was really true he'd never touched a woman. The countless family celebrations that ended with Muntadhir sleeping in a silken bed at the palace and Ali on the floor of his barracks.

Stop. Because of those barracks, the arena right here is your home. Muntadhir and his friends couldn't take that from him. Archery might not be Ali's specialty, but surely he could beat his spoiled, soft brother.

One of the riders slipped from his saddle, and without missing a beat, Muntadhir swung into his place. His brother was the better horseman, that Ali knew. Ali could ride well enough but had never shared Muntadhir's love for the sport. His brother kept his own stable and had probably spent countless hours racing outside the city walls, laughing and trying stunts with Jamshid—who was an even more talented rider—while Ali labored at the Citadel.

Muntadhir's horse cantered up. "Why so glum, Zaydi?" His brother laughed, spreading his arms. "This is your thing, isn't it? You used to talk when you were a kid about these martial competitions. How you would sweep them and earn your place as my Qaid. I'd think the greatest warrior in Daevabad would be smiling right now." Muntadhir drew nearer, his grin fading. "Or maybe you've been intruding upon *my* world for so long—insinuating yourself with my wife, embarrassing me before Abba—that you've forgotten your place." He said the final words in Geziriyya, his voice low. "Maybe you need a reminder."

It was the wrong thing to say. Ali glared back even as the other

Daeva men rode up, joking in Divasti as their horses circled him, kicking sand. "I spent my childhood training to serve you," he shot back. "I'd say I know my place quite well; I was never permitted to have another. Something I suspect Zaynab is about to learn as well."

He'd swear uncertainty flickered in his brother's eyes, but then Muntadhir shrugged, looking nonchalant. "So let's begin." He wheeled his horse around and raised his voice so the crowd could hear him. "I was just telling my companions here that I think it is time a few sand flies tried their hand at this." His brother winked, flashing a mesmerizing smile at the thousands of djinn arrayed in the arena seats. He was the dashing emir again, and Ali heard more than a few women sigh. "Try to contain your laughter, my people, I beg you."

Another Daeva came riding out, carrying a long, wrapped parcel. "Here you are, Emir."

"Excellent," Muntadhir replied. He addressed the crowd again. "I heard the Daevas have a weapon that I thought my brother might like to see. Our dear Zaydi does love his history." He took the parcel, pulling free the cloth and then holding it out to Ali.

Ali felt a catch in his throat. It was the bow from the Afshin's shrine. The exact replica of the weapon with which Darayavahoush had shot him.

"Do you like it, akhi?" Muntadhir asked, a soft edge of cruelty in his voice. "Takes a little getting used to but . . ." He abruptly raised it, drawing the string back in Ali's direction.

Ali jerked, the motion throwing him back into that night. The silver bow glittering in the light of the burning ship, Darayavahoush's cold green eyes locked on him. The searing pain, the blood in his mouth choking his scream as he tried to grab Muntadhir's hand.

He stared at Muntadhir now, seeing a stranger instead of his brother. "May I borrow a horse?" he asked coldly.

The Daevas brought him one at once, and Ali pulled himself into the saddle. The animal danced nervously beneath him, and he tightened his legs as it reared. They'd probably given him the worst-tempered one they had.

"I think maybe he does not like crocodiles," one of the Daevas mocked.

Another time Muntadhir would have harshly rebuked the man for such words, Ali knew. Now his brother just chuckled along.

"Ah, let us give Zaydi a minute to get used to riding a horse again. A bit different from the oryxes in his village." Muntadhir pulled free an arrow. "I should like to try this bow out."

His brother was off like a shot, the sand churning in his wake. As he neared the target, he raised the bow, leaning slightly sideways to aim an arrow upward.

It hit the exact center of the target, the enchanted pitch bursting into a sparkle of blue flames.

Ali's mouth fell open. That had been no lucky shot. The audience's applause was thunderous, their surprised delight clear. Where in God's name had Muntadhir learned to do that?

The answer came to him just as quickly. *Jamshid.* Ali swore under his breath. Of course Muntadhir knew how to shoot; his best friend had been one of the best archers in Daevabad—he'd trained with the Afshin himself.

Muntadhir must have seen the shock in Ali's face, for triumph blossomed in his own. "I suppose you don't know everything, after all." He tossed Ali the bow. "Your turn, little brother."

Ali caught the bow, his sandals slipping in the stirrups. But as the horse stepped nervously, Ali realized it wasn't just his sandals slipping, it was the entire saddle. It hadn't been tightened enough.

He bit his lip. If he dismounted to check it, he was going to look either paranoid or as if he didn't trust the Daevas who'd saddled the horse in the first place.

Just get this over with. Ali pressed his heels to the horse ever so slightly. It seemed to work for a moment, the horse moving at a slow canter. But then it picked up speed, galloping madly toward the target.

You can do this, he told himself desperately. He could ride and fight with a sword; a bow was only a bit more complicated.

He tightened his legs again. Ali's hands were steady as he nocked an arrow and raised the bow. But he'd never been taught how to adjust for the movement of the horse, and the arrow went embarrassingly off target.

Ali's cheeks burned as the Daeva men laughed. The mood was openly hostile now; they were clearly enjoying the spectacle of the sand fly who'd murdered their beloved Afshin being humiliated by his own kin with a weapon they cherished.

Muntadhir took the bow from him. "It was a good attempt, Zaydi," he offered with mocking sincerity. His eyes glittered. "Shall we try it backward?"

"Whatever you wish, Emir," Ali hissed.

Muntadhir rode off yet again. Even Ali had to admit his brother cut a striking figure, his black robe billowing behind him like smoky wings, the brilliant colors of the royal turban glimmering in the sunlight. He executed the move with the same ease, rising in his saddle as if he were the damned Afshin himself, turning backward and again striking the target. The arena burst into more applause, a few ululations coming from a knot of Geziris close to the ground. Ali recognized Muntadhir's cousin, Tariq, among them.

Ali glanced at the screened balcony above the royal platform. Was Zaynab there? His heart twisted. He could only imagine how his sister felt watching this after trying so hard to make peace between her brothers.

Muntadhir tossed the bow at him with more force than necessary. "Good luck."

"Fuck you." The crude words slipped from Ali's mouth in a flash of anger, and he saw Muntadhir startle.

And then smile yet again, a glimmer of spite in his brother's eyes. "Oh, do you not enjoy being embarrassed, Zaydi? That's odd, as you don't seem to mind doing it to me."

Ali didn't take the bait, riding off without another word. He couldn't ride as well as Muntadhir, he knew that. But he could turn around and aim a damn arrow. Drawing back on the bow, he whirled to face the target.

He did so too fast . . . and his saddle slid free.

Ali fell with it, dropping the bow and pulling his feet from the stirrups. The spookish horse reacted the exact way he imagined the Daevas had hoped for, putting on a burst of speed as the saddle slipped further. He saw a blur of hooves, the ground too close to his face. Several people screamed.

And then it was over. Ali landed hard on his back, rolling to narrowly avoid being trampled as the horse bolted away. He gasped, the air knocked clear from his lungs.

Muntadhir leaped lightly from his horse to retrieve the bow from where Ali had dropped it. "Are you all right?" he drawled.

Ali climbed to his feet, biting back a hiss of pain. He could taste blood in his mouth from where he'd bitten his tongue.

He spat it at the ground. "I'm fine." He wrenched the bow from his brother's hands, picking up the arrow from where it had fallen in the dust. He marched toward the target.

Muntadhir followed, staying at his shoulders. "I am surprised you haven't trained more on the bow. You know how your Banu Nahida loves her archers."

The pointed words struck much deeper than they should have. "That has nothing to do with me," he said heatedly.

"No?" Muntadhir retorted softly in Geziriyya. "Because I can give you some pointers. Brother to brother."

"I don't need your advice on how to shoot an arrow."

"Who says I was talking about archery?" Muntadhir continued as Ali drew back the bowstring. His voice was deadly quiet, his words again for Ali alone. "I was talking about Nahri."

Ali sent the arrow hurtling into the wall. A wave of laughter greeted his blunder, but Ali barely noticed. His face burning at the insinuation, he whirled on his brother. But Muntadhir was already there, taking the bow back.

He hit the target dead center, barely taking his gaze from Ali's. "I do believe I win." He shrugged. "I suppose it's fortuitous you're not going to be my Qaid after all."

Ali had no words. He was more hurt than he thought he could ever be, feeling younger and more naive than he had in years.

Muntadhir was already turning away, as if to return to the platform.

Ali stalked after him, keeping his gaze down and defeated though rage burned in his heart. Muntadhir wanted to see the Citadel-trained part of him?

Very well.

The two of them were only out of eyesight for a second, in the shadow of the stairwell, but it was enough. Ali lunged at his brother, shoving a hand against his mouth before he could scream and kicking open the door to a weapons' closet he knew was located under the stairs. He pushed Muntadhir inside, pulling the door closed behind them.

Muntadhir stumbled back, glaring. "Oh, have you something to say to me, hypocrite? Going to give me a lecture on righteousness while you—"

Ali punched him in the face.

His heart wasn't entirely in it, but the blow was enough to make Muntadhir reel. His brother swore, reaching for his khanjar.

Ali knocked it out of his hands but made no move to take it. Instead, he shoved Muntadhir hard into the opposite wall. "What, isn't this what I'm supposed to be?" he hissed. "Your weapon?"

But he'd underestimated his brother's own anger. Muntadhir wrenched free and threw himself on Ali.

They fell to the dirt, and Ali's fighter instincts swept over him; he'd spent too many years battling for his life in Am Gezira to not immediately react. He rolled, snatching up the khanjar and pinning Muntadhir to the ground.

He had the blade at his brother's throat before he realized what he was doing.

Muntadhir seized his wrist when Ali moved to jerk back. His gray eyes were wild. "Go on," he goaded, bringing the blade closer to his neck. "Do it. Abba will be so proud." His voice broke. "He'll make you emir, he'll give you Nahri. All the things you pretend you don't want."

Shaking, Ali fought for a response. "I . . . I don't—"

The door burst open, Lubayd and Zaynab framed in the dusty light. Ali immediately dropped the khanjar, but it was too late. His sister took one look at them sprawled on the floor, and her eyes flashed in a mix of fury and disappointment that would have made their mother proud. "Thank you for helping me find my brothers," she said flatly to Lubayd. "If you wouldn't mind permitting us a moment . . ."

Lubayd was already backing through the door. "Happily!" He pulled it closed behind him.

Zaynab took a deep breath. "*Get off of each other this instant.*" When both princes promptly separated, she continued, her voice seething, "Now would one of you *please* explain what in God's name just happened in the arena?"

Muntadhir glared at him. "Zaydi found out about Nasir and lost his mind."

"Someone had to," Ali snapped back. "And don't you act all innocent! Do you think I don't know my saddle was loosened? You could have killed me!"

"I didn't touch your damned saddle!" Muntadhir shot back,

climbing to his feet. "Don't make an enemy of half the city and then be surprised when people try to sabotage you." Fresh outrage crossed his face. "And you have some nerve accusing me of anything. I've tried to tell you a dozen times to back off and then you go and call me a coward to Abba's face when all I'm doing is trying to clean up your mess!"

"I was trying to stand up for Zaynab, and for that, you embarrassed me in front of the entire arena!" Hurt rose in Ali's voice. "You insulted Nahri, you let your friends call me a *crocodile* . . ." Even saying it stung. "My God, is this what Abba has turned you into? Have you been imitating him so long that cruelty is now your first instinct?"

"Alizayd, enough," Zaynab said when Muntadhir jerked back as though Ali had slapped him. "Can *Zaynab* get a word in edgewise, since apparently *my* future is the one that sparked this latest fight?"

"Sorry," Ali muttered, falling silent.

"Many thanks," she said acidly. She sighed, peeling back the veil she'd worn in front of Lubayd. Guilt rose in Ali's chest. His sister looked exhausted, more than he'd ever seen before. "I know about Nasir, Ali. I don't like it, but I don't need you running your mouth about it before even speaking with me." She glanced at Muntadhir. "What did Abba say?"

"That he's arriving this week," Muntadhir replied glumly. "He told me to spend time with him and find out what sort of man he is."

A muscle worked in Zaynab's cheek. "Maybe you can let me know as well."

"And that's *it*?" Ali asked. "That's all either of you are prepared to do?"

Muntadhir glared at him. "You'll forgive me for not taking political advice from someone who's been living in a village for five years and whose foot is all but attached to his mouth." His expression twisted. "Do you think I *want* to become like him, Zaydi? Do you have any idea of what *I've* had to give up?" He laced his hands behind his head, pacing. "Daevabad is a tinderbox, and the only way Abba keeps it from exploding is by holding it tight. By making sure everyone knows that if they risk its safety, they risk the lives of everyone they love."

"But that's not who you are, Dhiru," Ali protested. "And that's not the only way to rule."

"No? Maybe we should try it your way, then?" Muntadhir turned back, his gaze cutting through Ali. "Because I think *you're* more like Abba than you want to admit. But where Abba wants stability, you want justice. *Your* version of justice—even if you have to drag us there kicking and screaming. And let me tell you, little brother . . . I'm getting pretty damn clear eyed where you're concerned. You're enjoying the favor of a lot of angry people with weapons and grievances in this city . . . and how convenient, then, that you have the Ayaanle ready and willing to financially support you."

"The *Ayaanle*," Zaynab said, her voice biting, "are a great deal more nuanced than you give us credit for, and this one in particular has been scrambling to make peace between you two idiots for months." She closed her eyes, rubbing her temples. "But things were getting worse in Daevabad before Ali came back, Dhiru. I know you don't want to see it, but they were."

Muntadhir threw up his hands. "And what would you have me do? Ruin a financial alliance we need because my sister will be lonely? Make Alizayd my Qaid again and rightfully lose all my supporters for handing my army to a fanatic?" His words rang with true desperation. "Tell me how to fix this between us because I don't see a way."

Ali cleared the lump growing in his throat. "We're not the problem." He hesitated, his mind racing. The cold realization he'd had with Fatumai after learning what his father had done to the Tanzeem children. His conversation with Nahri last night. All the charges Muntadhir had neatly laid out. There was really only one thing it led to, a conclusion clear as glass.

He met his brother's and sister's expectant eyes. "Abba needs to be replaced."

There was a moment of silent shock and then Zaynab let out a choked, aghast sound he'd never before heard from his ever-refined sister.

Muntadhir stared at him before dropping his head into his hands. "I can't believe it. I can't believe you actually found a way to make this conversation worse." His voice was muffled through his fingers.

"Just listen to me," Ali rushed on. "He's been going astray for years. I understand his concerns about Daevabad's stability, but there is only so long this tactic of trampling anything that opposes him can work. You can't build anything on a cracked foundation."

"And now you're talking like a poet," Muntadhir moaned. "You really have lost your mind."

"I'm tired of watching innocent people die," Ali said bluntly. "I'm tired of being complicit in such suffering. The Daevas, the shafit . . . do you know he had a boat full of refugee children burned merely to execute a few Tanzeem fighters? That he ignored a threat I passed on regarding Nahri's safety because he said she was growing arrogant?" He glanced at Zaynab, knowing his sister shared at least a few of his views. "He's crossed too many lines. He shouldn't be king."

Zaynab's face was conflicted, but she took a deep breath. "Ali's not entirely wrong, Dhiru."

Muntadhir groaned. "Oh, Zaynab, not you too." He crossed the floor to start rifling through one of the supply chests, pulling free a small silver bottle and ripping open the top. "Is this liquor? Because I want to be completely intoxicated when Abba gets wind that his children are plotting a coup in a fucking closet."

"That's weapons polish," Ali said quickly.

Zaynab crossed to Muntadhir's side, knocking the bottle out of his hands when he seemed to still be evaluating it. "Stop. Just listen for a moment," she insisted. "Between the three of us, we might have the support. If we presented a united front, Abba would be hard-pressed to oppose us. We'd need to get the majority of the nobles and the bulk of the Citadel on our side, but I suspect those whose hearts aren't amenable might find their purses are."

"Do you think we could do that?" Ali asked. "We've already spent a fair bit on the hospital."

"Little brother, you'd be surprised how far the illusion of wealth will take you even if the deliverance of such promise takes longer," Zaynab said archly.

"Ayaanle gold," Muntadhir cut in sarcastically. "Well, I suppose I know which way the throne will be swinging."

"It won't." Ideas were coming together in Ali's head as he spoke. "I don't know who should rule or how, but there have to be voices besides ours shaping Daevabad's future. Maybe more than one voice." He paused, thinking fast. "The Nahids . . . they had a council. Perhaps we could try something like that."

Zaynab's response was sharp. "There are a lot of voices in Daevabad who don't think very fondly of us, Ali. You start giving power away and we could end up getting chased back to Am Gezira."

"*Enough.*" Muntadhir shushed them, darting a glance around. "*Stop scheming.* You're going to get yourselves killed, and for nothing. There's no overthrowing Abba unless you can take Suleiman's seal ring from him. Do you have any idea how to do that?"

"No?" Ali confessed. He hadn't thought of the seal ring. "I

mean, he doesn't wear it on his hand. I figured he kept it in a vault or . . ."

"It's in his heart," Muntadhir said bluntly.

Ali's mouth fell open. That was not a possibility that had occurred to him.

Zaynab recovered first. "His *heart*? The seal is *in* his heart?"

"Yes." Muntadhir looked between them, his expression grave. "Do you understand? There's no taking Suleiman's seal unless you're willing to kill our father for it. Is that a price you'd pay?"

Ali struggled to push that shocking information aside. "Suleiman's seal shouldn't matter. Not for this. Stripping your citizens of their magic isn't a power a political leader should have. The seal was meant to help the Nahids heal their people and fight the ifrit. And when it comes time for it to be passed again . . . the person that ring belongs to isn't in this room, and you both know it."

It was Zaynab's turn to groan. She pinched the bridge of her nose, looking exasperated. "Ali . . ."

Muntadhir gestured rudely between them. "Now do you believe me?" he asked Zaynab. "I told you he was smitten with her."

"I'm not smitten with her!"

There was a pounding on the door and then it abruptly opened, revealing Lubayd again.

"Ali, Emir Muntadhir!" he gasped, leaning on his knees and fighting for breath. "You need to come quickly."

Ali shot to his feet. "What's wrong?"

"There's been an attack on the Daeva procession."

30

NAHRI

Nahri wouldn't have admitted it to him, but *maybe* Kartir had a point about the Navasatem procession being fun.

"Anahid!" came another cry from below her. "Anahid the Blessed!"

Nahri smiled bashfully from underneath her chador, making a blessing over the crowd. "May the fires burn brightly for you!" she shouted back.

It was an almost unbelievably lovely morning, with not a cloud in the bright blue sky. Nisreen and a coterie of laughing Daeva women had awoken her hours before dawn with milk-sweets and pepper-scented tea, pulling her from bed despite Nahri's weary protests and dressing her in a soft, simple gown of undyed linen. Before the sun had risen, they'd joined an excited and growing throng of Daevas at the city's docks in order to wait for the sunrise. As the first pale rays crossed the sky, they'd lit colorful boat-shaped oil lamps of translucent waxed paper, setting them adrift

on the lake—glowing a pale pink in the dawn sun—and trans-
forming the water into an enormous, dazzling altar.

The joy of the crowd had been infectious. Children chased
each other, gleefully smearing wet handfuls of the muddy mortar
that signified the temple their ancestors had built for Suleiman
across arms and faces, while boisterous vendors hawked the sugared barley cakes and rich plum beer traditionally consumed for
the holiday.

Chanting and singing, they'd made their way to the chariots
that would carry the procession to the palace. They'd been constructed in secret; it was Daeva tradition that the chariots were
designed and built by older Daevas and ridden by youth: a literal
celebration of the next generation. There were thirty in total, one
to signify each century of freedom, and they were utterly spec-
tacular. Because her tribe was not one for half measures, the ve-
hicles were also enormous, resembling moving towers more than
anything else, with room for dozens of riders, and wheels twice
the height of a man. Each was dedicated to an aspect of Daeva life:
one boasted a grove of jeweled cherry trees, golden trunks peeking out from beneath a canopy of carved jade leaves and gleaming
ruby fruit, while the one behind hers spun with cavorting brass
horses. Their quicksilver eyes flashed, white jasmine blossoms
heavy in the rich black tassels of their manes.

Nahri's chariot was the largest, and embarrassingly so, crafted
to look like the boat Anahid might have once sailed across the
lake. A blue-and-white silk flag billowed above Nahri's head, and
standing proud at the stern was a magnificent carved wooden
shedu. She was currently sitting on it, cajoled and harassed into
doing so by the ring of thrilled little girls at her feet. Traditionally one of them would have stood in for Anahid, but Nahri's attempts to convince them to do the same this time had been met
only with disappointed pouts.

But her people's delight was infectious, so embarrassment

aside, Nahri was having a good time, a thing her warm cheeks and silly grin betrayed. She waved to the crowds on the street, bringing her hands together in blessing as she passed by groups of cheering Daevas.

"This is not what I was told to expect," Aqisa groused from Nahri's side, picking at one of the many garlands of flowers the little girls had—at first timidly and then with great exuberance when the warrior woman didn't stop them—draped around her neck.

Nahri bit back a laugh at the sight of the pink blossoms tangled across Ali's terrifying friend. "Don't they celebrate Navasatem in Am Gezira?"

The other woman cast a dismayed look at a pair of drunk young men on the float behind them. They were giggling madly, spinning around the brass horses, each with a bottle of plum beer in hand. "We do not celebrate anything in such a manner."

"Ah," Nahri said softly. "Small wonder Ali likes it there."

"You are enjoying yourself?" she heard Nisreen call from below. Nisreen was riding alongside the chariots with the rest of the Daeva elders, their horses draped in shimmering cloth the color of the rising sun.

Nahri leaned over to shout down to her. "You might have mentioned I'd be seated on a shedu," she complained. "Ghassan is going to burn something when he sees this."

Nisreen shook her head. "It's all in good fun. The first night of the new moon is always the wildest." She nodded at the drunken youths. "By this evening, more Daevas than not will look like them. It doesn't leave us much of a threat to the king."

Nahri sighed. "I look forward to spending all night tending to their injuries." She'd already found herself contemplating how quickly she would be able to get to the young men behind her when one of them inevitably fell and cracked his skull open.

"I'd say that's a fair possibility. But we have Jamshid in the

infirmary with us tonight, and we'll make sure none of us leave."
Nisreen paused. "Maybe you could ask that shafit healer you're
collaborating with to join us. She could bring her family."

Nahri glanced down in surprise. "You want me to ask Subha
and her family to spend the night in the infirmary?" It seemed a
bizarre request, especially considering the source.

"I think it's a smart idea. We could use the extra hands, and
you've mentioned her child is still nursing."

Nahri considered that. It would be good to have Subha's help,
and she'd been wanting to show the doctor the infirmary anyway.
"I'll send her a message when we get back to the palace."

She straightened back up, peering at the street ahead and trying to get her bearings. It looked like they were almost at the
midan.

Nearly out of the shafit district. Nahri flushed, hating how quickly
the thought—and the relief—had come. Ali's worry had seemed
sincere, but it was difficult to parse out his warning from the *rest*
of their conversation, and that was a subject she refused to think
about today.

Even so, she glanced around at the crowd. It was mostly
Daeva, though there were plenty of purebloods from the djinn
tribes pressed against the barricades, spinning starry sparklers
and sharing cakes and beer. A line of soldiers separated them
from the shafit onlookers, many of whom were also cheering but
were held far back.

Guilt stabbed at her. That wasn't right, regardless of the
threat. Nahri would have to see if there wasn't some sort of bonus
celebration she could put together for the shafit to make up for it.

She shifted on the wooden shedu, pulling her chador past
her rounded ears. It was unusually and mercifully light—no
heavy gold ornaments draped over her head today. Stitched together from layers of silk so delicate they were nearly transparent

and dyed in a beautiful array of colors, the chador was meant to give the appearance of shedu wings. Nahri lifted her face to the sun, listening to the delighted chatter of the Daeva children around her.

I wish Dara could have seen this. The thought rose in her head unbidden and unexpected, and yet oddly enough did not fill her with the tumultuous mix of emotions that memories of Dara usually did. She and Dara might have been of very different minds about the future, but she could not help but hope the Afshin would have been proud to see her sitting upon a wooden shedu today.

Movement caught her eyes ahead; a line of Daeva riders was approaching to join the procession. Nahri grinned as she recognized Jamshid among them. She waved, catching his eye, and he lifted his cap in acknowledgment, gesturing with a wide, giddy smile at the horse beneath him.

A loud bang sounded, an explosive rumble both strange and distantly familiar. God only knew what it was. Some Daeva had probably conjured a set of flying drums.

The noise came again, and this time there was a shout—and then a scream, accompanied by a burst of white smoke from the balcony directly across the street.

A dark projectile smashed into the carved balustrade above her head.

Nahri shouted in surprise, shielding her head from a rain of wooden shards. There was movement on the balcony, a glint of metal and then another explosion of white smoke.

Aqisa yanked her off the shedu. "Get down!" she cried, throwing herself over Nahri.

In the next moment, the shedu shattered, another projectile hitting the head with enough force to cleave it off. Stunned and with Aqisa pinning her hard against the wooden deck, Nahri lay still. She heard more screaming and then another cracking sound.

Gunfire, she finally recognized, her memories of Cairo catching up to her. The hulking Turkish cannons, the deadly French muskets . . . not things an Egyptian girl like her, living on the streets and already evading the authorities, would have ever touched, but weapons she'd seen and heard many times. The type of weapons barely known to djinn, she recalled, remembering Ali's fear when she'd handled the pistol at the Sens.

There was another shot, this one hitting the base of the juggernaut.

They're targeting me, Nahri realized. She tried to push Aqisa off, to no avail. "They're after me!" she shouted. "You need to get the children away!"

An object crashed to the wooden deck an arm's length from her face. Some sort of cracked ceramic jug, with a fiery rag stuffed in one end. Nahri caught the eye-watering smell of pine and tar as a dark sludge seeped out. It touched the flames.

The fireball that exploded was enough to sear her face. Instinctively, Nahri rolled, dragging a shocked Aqisa to her feet. The pieces came together horribly in her head, the pitch-filled pots and wild flames immediately familiar from her people's worst stories about the shafit.

"Rumi fire!" she screamed, trying to grab the little girls. Another jar struck the street, fire engulfing a pair of riders so quickly they didn't even have time to scream. "Run!"

And then it was chaos. The surrounding crowds broke, people pushing and shoving to get away from the spreading flames. Nahri heard the Royal Guard shouting, trying to impose order as their zulfiqars flashed in the light.

Nahri choked down her panic. They had to save the children. She and Aqisa swiftly led them to the other side of the chariot. Daevas on horseback had already thrown up ropes, men climbing to help them down.

Aqisa grabbed her collar. "Water!" she said urgently. "Where is the nearest pump?"

Nahri shook her head, coughing as she tried to think. "Water doesn't work on Rumi fire."

"Then what *does* work?"

"Sand," she whispered, gazing in rising horror at the damp stone streets and wooden buildings surrounding her. Sand was the only thing misty Daevabad didn't have in abundance.

Aqisa abruptly yanked her back again as a metal ball slammed into the wood where Nahri's head had just been. "They're up there," she warned, jerking her head toward a balcony. "Three of them."

Nahri dared a quick peek. A trio of men were hunched inside the screened structure, two of them armed with what looked like muskets.

Rage burned through her. From the corner of her eye, she spotted an Agnivanshi soldier with a bow quickly climbing the jeweled trees of the chariot next to hers. He pulled himself onto one of the branches, nocking an arrow in the same movement.

There was a shout, and then one of the attackers fell from the balcony, an arrow buried in his back. The archer turned for the other men.

A blast of a musket brought him down. As Nahri cried out, the soldier fell dead to the ground, the bow tumbling from his hands.

"Get down, Nahri!" Nisreen yelled, drawing her attention back as another shot splintered off the deck and the last of the children were spirited away.

Nahri jumped, Aqisa urging her into a sprint as the chariot cracked in half from the heat of the spreading flames.

A knot of Daevas pulled her into their midst. Nisreen was there, ripping Nahri's distinctive chador off. "Get the Banu Nahida away," she ordered.

"No, wait—" Nahri tried to protest as hands pushed her onto a horse. Through a break in the crowd, she spotted Jamshid. He was riding hard—dangerously hard—one hand clutching his saddle while he dipped to reach for the bow on the ground . . .

A clay jar of Rumi fire struck him directly in the back.

"*Jamshid!*" Nahri lunged forward as he toppled from the horse. His coat was on fire, flames dancing over his back. "No!"

Everything seemed to slow. A riderless horse galloped past, and the smell of smoke and blood thickened on the air. Nahri caught herself from swooning, the sudden presence of torn bodies, broken bones, and slowing hearts threatening to overwhelm her Nahid senses. The streets her ancestors had carefully laid down were burning, engulfing fleeing parade-goers. Ahead, Jamshid was rolling in a vain attempt to put out the fire spreading across his coat.

Fury and desperation rose inside her. Nahri shoved free of the Daevas trying to wrestle her away.

"Jamshid!" Sheer determination brought her to his side as he writhed on the ground. Not caring if she risked herself, Nahri grabbed the unburnt edge of his collar and wrenched the burning jacket off him.

He screamed, the smoldering fabric taking a good part of the skin on his upper back with it, leaving his flesh bloody and exposed. But it was better than being consumed by Rumi fire—not that it mattered; the two of them were surrounded now, the flames hungrily licking up the surrounding buildings.

A heavy object crashed to the ground before her: the remains of the burning shedu she'd ridden to emulate her ancestors. But as Nahri watched the chaos around her, helplessness threatened to suffocate her. Nahri was no Anahid. She had no Afshin.

She had no idea how to save her people.

Afshin . . . like a burst of light, one of her last memories of Cairo came to her: the warrior with striking green eyes, whose name she had not yet known, standing amid the tombs of her human home, raising his arms to conjure a storm.

A *sand*storm. Nahri caught her breath. *Creator, please*, she prayed. *Help me save my city.*

She inhaled, bowing her head. Acting on instinct, she tried to see the city as she might have seen a patient, tried to visualize the dirt between its cobblestones and the dust gathering in every corner.

She *pulled*. The wind immediately picked up, lashing her braids against her face, but she could still sense resistance, her hold on the magic just a touch too weak. She cried out in frustration.

"Nahri," Jamshid breathed, his voice hoarse as he clutched her hand. "Nahri, I don't feel right . . ." He choked, his fingers tightening on her own.

A raw punch of magic hit her so hard she nearly fell back. She gasped, reeling as she tried to maintain her control. It was both familiar and not, a jolt as if she'd plunged her hands into a vat of ice. It raced through her veins with a wild madness, like a creature too long caged.

And it was the exact push that she needed. Nahri didn't hesitate, her eyes locking on the burning streets. *Heal*, she commanded, pulling hard.

Every speck of sand in her family's city rushed to her.

It whirled into a racing funnel of smothering dust. She exhaled and it collapsed, raining down to cover the street and the ruined chariots, blowing into dunes against the buildings and coating the bodies of fleeing and burning djinn and Daevas alike. Extinguishing the fire as thoroughly as if she'd dunked a candle into a pool of water.

It did the same to Nahri. Her hold on the magic collapsed, and she reeled, exhaustion sweeping her as black spots burst across her vision.

"Banu Nahida!"

Nahri blinked, catching sight of Nisreen racing toward her, still holding her bright chador. At her side, Jamshid struggled to sit up, his shirt hanging in scorched tatters across his chest.

And across his perfectly healed back.

Nahri was gaping at his unmarred skin when there was another crack of the musket. Jamshid shoved her down.

But the shot hadn't been aimed at them.

The time between seeing Nisreen racing toward them and seeing her mentor fall seemed to take hours, as if to effectively sear itself on her mind's eye. Nahri tore away from Jamshid, lunging to Nisreen's side without recalling moving.

"Nisreen!" Black blood was already soaking through her tunic. Nahri ripped it open.

She went completely still at the sight of the stomach wound. It was ghastly, the human weapon damaging the other woman's flesh in a way Nahri hadn't thought possible in the magical world.

Oh God . . . Not wasting a moment, Nahri laid her hand against the blood—and then immediately jerked it back as a searing pain slashed across her palm. The smell, the burn . . .

The attackers had used iron bullets.

There was a cry and then the remaining men on the balcony fell to the ground, their bodies riddled with arrows. Nahri barely noticed. Her heart in her throat, she ignored the pain to lay hands on her mentor again. *Heal*, she begged. *Heal!*

A bloody scrape on Nisreen's cheek instantly did, but from the bullet wound, nothing. The bullet itself stood out like an angry scar against the rest of Nisreen's body, a cold, alien intrusion.

Jamshid sank down next to her, dropping the bow. "What can I do?" he cried.

I don't know. Terrified, Nahri searched Nisreen's face; she needed Nisreen to guide her through this. She needed Nisreen, period. Tears filled her eyes as she took in the blood at the corner of her teacher's mouth, the black eyes that were filled with nearly as much shock as pain.

The answer came to her in an instant. "I need pliers!" she screamed to the crowd. "A spike, a blade, something!"

"Nahri . . ." Nisreen's voice came in a heartbreaking whisper. She coughed, more blood dripping from her mouth. "Nahri . . . listen . . ."

Blood was soaking through Nahri's clothes. Someone, Nahri didn't even care who, thrust the handle of a knife into her hand. "I'm sorry, Nisreen," she whispered. "This is probably going to hurt."

Jamshid had taken Nisreen's head in his lap. With quiet horror, Nahri realized he was praying softly, giving her last rites.

Nahri refused to accept that. She banished her emotions. She ignored the tears running down her cheeks and the steady, horrible slowing of Nisreen's heart.

"Nahri," Nisreen whispered. "Nahri . . . your—"

Nahri inserted the knife, her hands mercifully steady. "I have it!" With a rush of blood, she pulled free the bullet. But the movement cost her. Nisreen shuddered, her eyes brightening in pain.

And then, even as Nahri spread her fingers across the wound, Nisreen's heart stopped. Roaring in anger, Nahri let loose the magic she had left, commanding it to restart, for the torn vessels and frayed flesh to connect.

Nothing.

Jamshid burst in tears. "Her heart," he sobbed.

No. Nahri stared at her mentor in dull disbelief. Nisreen couldn't be dead. The woman who had taught her how to heal could not be the one person she couldn't help. The woman who, for all their many, *many* fights, had been the closest thing to a mother Nahri had ever had.

"Nisreen," she whispered. *"Please."* She tried again, magic rushing from her hands, but it did nothing. Nisreen's heart was still, blood and muscles slowing as the bright pulses in her head steadily blinked out—Nahri's abilities telling her clearly what her heart wanted to deny.

Nisreen was gone.

31

ALI

Ali ripped the hospital door open, grabbing the first person he saw. "The Banu Nahida! Where is she?"

A bloodied Parimal started, nearly dropping a tray of supplies. Ali quickly let him go.

Parimal's expression was grave. "In the main chamber. She's unharmed, but it's bad, Prince. Many are dead."

That Ali knew. He and Muntadhir had rushed to the procession but the streets had been in turmoil, and they'd finally arrived to learn Nahri was already back at the hospital treating victims.

Muntadhir had stayed behind to assist Jamshid in restoring some order while Ali continued to the hospital, passing the ruins of the celebration turned to carnage with growing despair. The dead lay where they'd fallen, their bodies still being shrouded. Ali had counted at least fifty.

One of the dead, Jamshid grimly told them, had already been

quietly taken to the Grand Temple, her still form covered in the Banu Nahida's own chador. Nisreen's name landed hard in Ali's heart, the scope of the violence done today unimaginable.

"May I ask . . ." Parimal was staring at him, looking sick and hesitant. "The attackers . . . were they identified?"

Ali met his gaze, all too aware of what Parimal was really asking. It had been the same awful prayer in the darkest part of Ali's heart.

"They were shafit," he said softly. "All of them."

Parimal's shoulders dropped, his expression crumpling. "Oh no," he whispered. "It's terrible, but I'd hoped . . ."

"I know," Ali cleared his throat. "Where is she?"

Parimal nodded to his left. "The main examination room."

Ali hurried off, through the halls whose construction he'd personally overseen. He'd looked forward to seeing the hospital operational, but God . . . not like this.

The chamber was packed, the hundred pallets full and more patients lying on woolen blankets on the floor. The vast majority were Daeva. He caught sight of Nahri bent over a crying young boy being held by his mother. She had a pair of forceps in her hands and seemed to be removing bits of wooden shrapnel from his skin. He watched her set aside the forceps and touch the little boy's face before pushing slowly to her feet, exhaustion in every line of her body. She turned around.

Her eyes had no sooner met his than Nahri's face crumpled in grief. Heartsick, Ali rushed to her side. She trembled, shaking her head and looking like it was taking every bit of strength she had not to cry.

"I can't," she choked out. "Not here."

Wordlessly, Ali took her hand. She didn't resist, letting him lead her out of the room and into the garden. They had barely closed the door when she broke down sobbing.

"They killed Nisreen," she wept. "They shot her and I couldn't do anything. I couldn't . . ."

Ali pulled her into his arms. She started to cry harder and they sank slowly to the floor.

"She taught me everything," Nahri gasped through her sobs. "*Everything*. And I couldn't do a damned thing to save her." She shook violently against him. "She was scared, Ali. I could see it in her eyes."

"I'm so sorry, Nahri," he whispered, at a loss for anything else to say. "I'm so, so sorry." Not knowing what else to do, he simply held her as she cried, her tears soaking through his dishdasha. He ached to do something, *anything*, that would make this better.

He wasn't sure how long they'd been sitting there when the call to asr prayer came. Ali closed his wet eyes, letting the muezzins' call wash over him. It put a little steadiness back into his spirit. Today's attack was awful, but the adhan was still being sung. Time wasn't stopping in Daevabad, and it would be up to them to make sure this tragedy didn't shatter the city.

The adhan seemed to bring Nahri back to herself as well. She took a shaky breath, pulling away to wipe her eyes.

She stared at her hands, looking utterly lost. "I don't know what to say to them," she murmured, seemingly as much to herself as to Ali. "I told my people we could trust the shafit. But we were just attacked with human weapons, with Rumi fire, when we were celebrating *our* holiday in *our* city." Her voice was hollow. "How can I call myself a Banu Nahida if I can't protect my own people?"

Ali reached out, taking her chin in his hands. "Nahri, you're not responsible for this. Not in any way. A few twisted souls exploited a security weakness that, to be honest, we should have prepared for the first time those damnable weapons showed up in this city. It has no bearing on your outreach to the shafit, no bearing on your position as Banu Nahida. You saved lives," he assured her. "I heard what you did to put out the fire. You think anyone but a Banu Nahida could have done that?"

Nahri didn't appear to hear him, lost in whatever darkness clouded her mind. "This can't happen again," she muttered. "Never again." Her expression abruptly sharpened, her eyes fixing on his. "The woman who warned you . . . where is she? I want to talk to her."

Ali shook his head. "She knew nothing more."

"She clearly knew enough!" She jerked free of his hands. "Maybe you couldn't get any more information from her, but I bet I can."

The vengeance in her voice unsettled him. "She wasn't behind this, Nahri. And I couldn't find her if I tried."

"Then what's her name? I'll have my people search for her if you won't."

Ice crept over Ali's skin. Right now, he would have done almost anything to help Nahri . . . but he couldn't give her that. He bit his lip, fighting for words. "Nahri, I know you're grieving—"

"You know?" She shoved away from him. "What do you know about grief?" Her wet eyes flashed. "Who have you lost, Ali? Who's died in your arms? Who have you begged to come back, to look at you one last time?" She staggered to her feet. "The Daevas bleed, the shafit bleed, and there the Geziris stand. Safe in their deserts back home, secure in the palace here."

Ali opened and closed his mouth, but that was not a charge he could dispute. "Nahri, please," he begged. "We . . . we'll fix this."

"And what if we can't?" Her voice cracked in exhaustion. "What if Daevabad is just broken in a way that can't be repaired?"

He shook his head. "I refuse to believe that."

Nahri just stared at him. The anger was gone, replaced by a pity that made him feel even worse. "You should leave, Alizayd.

Escape this awful place while you still can." Bitterness creased her features. "I know I would." She turned for the door. "I need to get back to my patients."

"Nahri, wait!" Ali shot to his feet, desperate. "*Please.* I'll make this right. I swear to God."

She pushed past him. "You can't make this right." She wrenched open the door. "Go back to Am Gezira."

LUBAYD AND AQISA WERE WAITING FOR HIM WHEN ALI left the hospital.

Lubayd took one look at him and then grabbed Ali's arm. "Is she okay?"

Ali's mouth was dry. "She's alive."

Go back to Am Gezira. Suddenly, in a moment of weakness, Ali wanted nothing other than that. It would be easy. The city was in chaos; the three of them could slip out in an instant. His father wouldn't blame him—he had told Ali to leave and would probably be quietly relieved he didn't have to force his son to obey his wishes. Ali could be back in Bir Nabat in weeks, away from Daevabad and its constant bloody heartache.

He rubbed his eyes. Ahead, the sight of the shafit camp caught his eye. It had been rebuilt—expanded—after the attack and was bustling now with tense workers streaming into and out of the hospital.

Sick fear crept into his heart. The Daevas had attacked this place before, killing a score for the death of a single man.

What would they do to the shafit for the destruction wrought today?

They could go to war. It was his father's constant concern, Ali knew. The Daevas and the shafit made up the majority of Daevabad, thoroughly outnumbering the rest of the djinn, and the Royal Guard might not be able to stop them. Ghassan might not even be inclined to let them *try* and stop them. Ali knew their world's cold calculus; the Guard would be sent to watch over the other quarters, to keep the purebloods of the djinn tribes safe while the "fire worshippers" and the "dirt-bloods" had their final fight.

But his first instinct will be to stop this. To brutally stamp out anything that might escalate.

The door opened again, Subha stepping out to join them.

The doctor took a deep breath. "I didn't think I'd ever see worse than the attack on the camp," she confessed by way of greeting. "I can't imagine the demons who planned such a thing. To attack a parade full of children . . ."

They were children themselves only a few years ago. Ali knew in his heart this traced back to the Tanzeem. The few twisted souls who'd watched their sheikh murdered, their orphanage burned, and then their adopted brothers and sisters die on Daevabad's lake, just as Sister Fatumai had said.

"I think we've got the survivors out of danger for now," Subha continued, her expression heavy. "I wish I'd been there," she said softly. "Lady Nisreen . . . I probably could have gotten the bullet out."

"Please don't tell Nahri that," Ali said quickly.

Subha shook her head. "I can tell you it's already on her mind. When you lose a patient like that, you never stop wondering what you could have done differently. And if it's someone you love . . ."

Ali flinched. "Will you stay with her?" he asked. "With Nahri?"

"Where are you headed?"

He hesitated, trying to think. "The Citadel," he finally decided. He wasn't welcome at the hospital and didn't trust his father not to lock him up if he returned to the palace. "I want to see what we can do to keep people from each other's throats while we figure out who's responsible for this."

Aqisa narrowed her eyes. "Are you allowed at the Citadel?"

Ali took a deep breath. "I think we're about to learn exactly how popular I am with the Royal Guard."

THE SOLDIERS AT THE GATE CERTAINLY DIDN'T STOP him from entering; indeed, there was open relief on the faces of a few.

"Prince Alizayd," the first man greeted him. "Peace be upon you."

"And upon you peace," Ali replied. "Is the Qaid here?"

The man shook his head. "You just missed him heading back to the palace." He paused. "He seemed upset. He went tearing out of here with a few of his most senior officers."

Ali's stomach dropped, uncertain what to think about that. He nodded and then continued on, striding into the heart of the Citadel, the place that in many ways had been a truer home to him than the palace. Its tower stood proud, stark against the setting sun.

A knot of Geziri officers were just inside, arguing loudly over a scroll. Ali recognized all of them, particularly Daoud, the officer who'd made a point of thanking him for his effort with his village's well when he first arrived in Daevabad.

"Prince Alizayd, thank God," the man said when he caught sight of Ali.

Ali made his way over cautiously, raising a hand to stop Lubayd and Aqisa from following him. He was here as a soldier now, not as a civilian from outer Am Gezira. "The Qaid has gone to the palace?"

Daoud nodded. "We received orders from the king that troubled him."

"What orders?" Ali asked, instantly concerned.

Barghash, one of the louder, brasher captains spoke up. "He wants us to raze the neighborhood in which the attack took place. It is unnecessary. We found the shafit who lived in the apartments with their throats cut. The attackers must have killed them. And the attackers themselves are dead! We've been asked to slaughter scores of shafit for no reason other than—"

"That's enough," Abu Nuwas interrupted. "You took an oath when you joined the Guard to obey the king."

"That's not quite the oath he took," Ali corrected. "He pledged to serve God and the security of his people. And the shafit are also our people."

Abu Nuwas gave him an annoyed look. "Respectfully, Prince Alizayd, you hold no rank here. You are not even supposed to *be* here. I can have you escorted to the palace if you like."

The threat was clear, and Ali saw more than a few men bristle . . . though their barbed glances were not for him.

Ali paused, seeing Muntadhir and Zaynab in his mind. Their father.

Bir Nabat and the life he might have lived.

God forgive me. God guide me. "I'm very sorry, Abu Nuwas," he said quietly. Ali's hand dropped to his khanjar. "But I'm not going back to the palace."

He cracked the other man across the skull with the hilt of the blade.

Abu Nuwas fell unconscious to the dust. Two of the officers immediately went for their zulfiqars, but they were outnumbered, the remaining officers and several infantrymen lunging forward and restraining them.

"Please make sure he's all right," Ali continued, keeping his voice calm. He picked up the scroll from the ground, his eyes scanning the repulsive order, his father's signature clear on the bottom.

It burst into flames in his hand, and Ali dropped it to the ground.

He gazed at the shocked soldiers around him. "I didn't join the Royal Guard to murder innocents," he said flatly. "And our ancestors certainly didn't come to Daevabad to raze shafit homes while their children sleep inside." He raised his voice. "We *keep the peace*, understand? That's all that's happening right now."

There was a moment of hesitation among the men. Ali's heart raced. Aqisa reached for her blade . . .

And then Daoud nodded, swiftly making the Geziri salute. "Your prince has issued a command," he declared. "Draw up!"

The soldiers in the courtyard, slowly at first and then moving at the speed with which they would have obeyed Wajed, took their places.

Daoud bowed. "What would you have us do?"

"We need to secure the shafit district. I won't have anyone seeking vengeance tonight. The gates to the midan will need to be closed and fortified—fast. I'll need to send a message to the king." *And to my siblings*, he added silently, praying he'd made more headway than he thought while arguing with them in the closet.

"What about the Geziri Quarter?" Daoud asked. "There are no gates separating us from the shafit."

"I know." Ali took a deep breath, considering his options and suddenly wishing he'd done a bit more scheming with Zaynab. He fidgeted with the prayer beads around his wrist. Whose support *could* he count on?

His fingers stilled on the beads. "I need you to get me every Geziri muezzin you can find."

32

NAHRI

You're a good Banu Nahida.

Nisreen's words from the other night rang in Nahri's mind as she stared at the sink. *A good Banu Nahida.* The shock in her mentor's face, the way the spark—the jesting and the weary patience, everything that made her Nisreen—had vanished from her dark eyes, the hands that had guided Nahri's now growing cold in the quiet of the Grand Temple.

"You need a break." Subha's voice yanked her from her thoughts. She threw a towel at Nahri. "You could have washed your hands a hundred times for how long you've been standing here staring at the water."

Nahri shook her head, drying her hands and retying her apron. "I'm fine."

"I'm not asking." Nahri glanced at the other doctor, startled, and saw only determination in her eyes. "You wished to work with another healer? Fine, then I'm acting on behalf of our patients. You are not fit to treat anyone right now."

Before Nahri could protest, the doctor took her by the arm, all but depositing her in a low couch. A cup of tea and platter of food waited on a nearby table.

Subha nodded to it. "The camp workers have been bringing food and clothing by. They thought your people could use it."

The gesture moved her. "That was kind," she said softly. She picked up the tea, too weary to resist, and took a sip.

Subha sat beside her. She sighed, wiping a line of ash from her sweat-streaked brow. "If I've not said it yet, I'm terribly sorry." She shook her head. "I spoke a bit with Lady Nisreen last night." A small smile played on her lips. "It was only slightly confrontational; in all, she seemed very capable and quite kind."

Nahri stared at her tea. "She taught me everything I know about the Nahid sciences." Emotion rose in her voice. "She was the closest thing to family I had in Daevabad, and I couldn't save her."

Subha touched her hand. "Don't lose yourself in what you might have done for a patient, especially not one you loved." She cleared her throat. "Trust that I speak from experience. After my father . . . I felt useless. I wasted weeks on self-pity and grief. You don't have weeks. Your people need you now."

Nahri nodded, finding relief in the direct words. They were certainly more useful than weeping on Ali's shoulder in the garden.

A weakness. That's what Nisreen had called Ali, and clearly she'd been right. Had Nahri been the Banu Nahida her people needed, she would have forced the name of that informant from Ali's lips.

"Banu Nahida?" A familiar voice called from the knot of people bustling about the entrance to the exam chamber.

Jamshid. Someone must have given him a shirt, but it was covered in blood and ash, and he looked as exhausted as Nahri felt. His gaze fell on hers, and then he was across the room in seconds, with such swift agility that Nahri nearly dropped her teacup. Forget the burns, Jamshid wasn't even *limping*.

"*Jamshid?*" She gaped, looking him up and down. Closer now, she could see he was trembling, his eyes bright with barely checked panic.

Subha frowned. "Nahri said you were struck with Rumi fire and badly burned." She rose to her feet, reaching for him. "Would you like us to—"

He jerked back. "I'm fine," he said hoarsely. "Quite, quite fine," he added, sounding slightly hysterical. "How are you?"

Nahri stared at him. He certainly didn't *sound* fine. "We're doing what we can," she replied. "Are they finished at the procession site?"

Jamshid nodded. "The final count is eighty-six dead," he said softly. "Muntadhir and the king were leaving when I did. They only found the three attackers."

"Nearly a hundred people dead at the hands of *three*?" Nahri put down her tea, her hands shaking. "I don't understand how this could happen."

"It never has before," Jamshid said, his voice sorrowful. "I don't think anyone expected anything like this."

Nahri shook her head. "I'm glad to have been present when Daevabad's people discovered a new low in slaughtering one another."

Jamshid stepped closer, laying a hand on her shoulder. "I'm so sorry about Nisreen, Nahri." He blinked back tears. "I can't even really believe it. It's difficult to imagine returning to the infirmary and not seeing her there."

Nahri struggled to keep her voice from thickening. "We'll have to manage. Our people need us."

He flushed. "You're right, of course. But Nahri . . . if things are under control here, do you have a minute to talk? Alone?" he clarified, nodding to the corridor.

"Of course." Nahri stood. "If you'll excuse me, Doctor Sen."

The moment they were outside, Jamshid whirled on her. "Nahri, are you sure it was Rumi fire in those containers?"

Nahri was as taken aback by the question as she was by the fear in his eyes. "Yes? I mean, what else could have burned like that?"

He was wringing his hands. "Do you think there could have been anything else in it? Some sort of . . . I don't know . . . healing serum?"

She blinked. "Because of your back?" In the chaos of the attack and Nisreen's death, Nahri had hardly given thought to how swiftly Jamshid's burns had vanished.

He'd gone pale. "No, not just because of my back . . ." His mouth opened and closed as if he was struggling for words. "Nahri, you're going to think I'm mad, but—"

"Banu Nahida!" It was Razu this time. "You need to come quickly," she said, switching to Tukharistani. "This one's father is throwing a fit outside."

Jamshid spun on Razu. "Then tell him to wait!"

The words had no sooner left Jamshid's lips than he gasped, clapping a hand over his mouth. Nahri's eyes went wide. He'd just spoken in a perfect imitation of Razu's ancient dialect of Tukharistani—a language she'd heard not a soul save Razu and herself speak.

"Jamshid, how did you—"

"Jamshid!" Kaveh came racing into the corridor. "Banu Nahida! Come, there's no time to waste!"

Jamshid still looked too astonished to speak, so Nahri did. "What's going on?"

Kaveh was pale. "It's the emir."

JAMSHID WAS IN FULL PANIC AS THEY GALLOPED TO-
ward the midan, whatever he'd been trying to tell her clearly gone

from his mind. "What do you mean, he collapsed?" he demanded of Kaveh again, shouting over the clatter of hooves.

"I am telling you all that I know," Kaveh replied. "He wanted to stop and visit with survivors outside the Grand Temple, and then he passed out. We brought him inside, and I came for you as soon as I could."

Nahri tightened her legs around her horse, clutching the reins as the Geziri Quarter passed by in a blur. "Why would you not bring him to the infirmary or the hospital?"

"I'm sorry, we weren't thinking."

They passed through the Geziri Gate. The midan was eerie in its emptiness, like many of the streets had been, glowing faintly in the deepening night. It should have been filled with celebrations, with Daevas who'd had a bit too much plum beer dancing on the fountains and children conjuring fireworks.

Instead it was entirely still, the smell of burned flesh and smoke hanging on the dusty air. A handcart selling delicate garlands of blown-glass flowers lay abandoned on its side. Nahri feared there was a good chance its owner lay under one of the eighty-six blood-soaked shrouds outside the Temple.

The sound of chanting suddenly drew her ear. Nahri raised a hand, slowing her horse. It was the singsong intonation of the call to prayer . . . except isha prayer had already been called. It wasn't in Arabic either, she realized.

"Is that Geziriyya?" Jamshid whispered. "Why would the muezzins be calling in Geziriyya? And why now?"

Kaveh had grown paler. "I think we should get to the Temple." He spurred his horse toward the Daeva Gate, the two shedu statues throwing bizarre shadows against the midan's copper walls.

They hadn't gotten halfway across when a line of horsemen moved to intercept them. "Grand Wazir!" a man called. "Stop."

The Qaid, Nahri realized, recognizing him. Six members of the Royal Guard stood with him, armed with scythes and zulfiqars, and as Nahri watched, another four archers stepped out from the other gates. Their bows were not yet drawn, but a whisper of fear went through her anyway.

"What is the meaning of this?" she demanded. "Let us pass. I need to get to the Grand Temple and make sure my husband is still breathing!"

Wajed frowned. "Your husband is nowhere near the Grand Temple. Emir Muntadhir is at the palace. I saw him just before we left."

Jamshid pushed forward on his horse, seemingly heedless of the way the soldiers instantly moved their hands to their blades. "Is he all right? My father said he had taken ill at the Grand Temple."

Baffled confusion on Wajed's face, and a flush of guilt on Kaveh's, were all Nahri needed. "Did you lie to us?" she demanded, whirling on the grand wazir. "Why in God's name would you do such a thing?"

Kaveh shrank back, looking ashamed. "I'm sorry," he said hurriedly. "I needed to get you to safety, and Muntadhir was the only way I could think of to get you both to leave the hospital."

Jamshid drew up, looking shocked and wounded. "How could you let me think he was hurt?"

"I'm sorry, my son. I had no—"

Wajed interrupted. "It doesn't matter. None of you will be going to the Grand Temple. I have orders to have the two of you escorted to the palace," he said with a nod to Kaveh and Nahri. He hesitated, looking weary and worn down for a minute, before he continued. "Jamshid, you're to come with me."

Kaveh instantly edged in front of his son and Nahri. "I beg your pardon?"

The call came again, haunting waves of Geziriyya breaking the tense silence. Wajed stiffened, a muscle working in his face, as if whatever was being said caused him pain. He wasn't the only one. Half the men were Geziri, and they too looked visibly un-settled.

One went further, the sole Geziri archer standing in the frame of the neighboring Tukharistani Gate. He shouted some-thing in their language. Wajed returned a terse response.

The archer clearly wasn't mollified. He argued back, gestur-ing at them and then at the gate that led back to the shafit neigh-borhoods. Nahri had no clue as to what he was saying, but it was seeming to resonate. The other Geziris shifted uncomfortably, a couple darting uncertain glances at each other.

Abruptly, the archer threw down his bow. He turned on his heel, but he didn't get far because with a single curt word from Wajed, another soldier shot him dead.

Nahri gasped, and Jamshid drew his sword, instantly moving closer to her.

But the Qaid wasn't looking at them, he was glaring at his men. "That is the penalty for treason, understand? There will be no ar-rests and no forgiveness. I do not care what you hear." He eyed the soldiers. "We take commands from only one man in Daevabad."

"What in the Creator's name is going on, Wajed?" Nahri de-manded again. She, Kaveh, and Jamshid had drawn as close as they could on horseback.

"You can direct your questions to the king when you see him." Wajed hesitated. "Forgive me, Banu Nahida, but I have my orders."

He raised a hand, and the rest of the archers drew their bows, their arrows targeted on the Daevas.

"Wait!" Nahri cried. "What are you doing?"

Wajed drew a pair of iron-laced binds from his belt. "As I said, the king has requested that you and Kaveh be taken to him. Jamshid is to come with me."

"*No.*" Kaveh sounded desperate. "Ghassan isn't taking my son. Not again."

"Then I have instructions to shoot the three of you dead," Wajed said quietly. "Starting with the Banu Nahida."

Jamshid slid from his saddle. "Take me," he said immediately, dropping his sword to the ground. "Don't hurt them."

"No! Wajed, *please*, I beg you," Kaveh beseeched. "Just let him stay with me. We're no threat to you. Surely whatever Ghassan has to say to me and Nahri . . ."

"I have my orders, Kaveh," Wajed cut in, not ungently. "Take him," he said to his men and then glanced at her. "And I'd suggest you keep any possible sandstorms to yourself. We're all rather quick with our weapons." He tossed the iron cuffs to her. "You'll be putting those on if you care about their lives."

Kaveh lunged for his son. "Jamshid!"

A soldier hit him hard across the back of his skull with the flat of his blade, and Kaveh crumpled to the ground.

"Baba!" Jamshid sprang for his father but hadn't taken two steps before a pair of men grabbed him, pressing a knife to his throat.

"Your choice, Banu Nahida," Wajed said.

Jamshid's worried gaze darted between his father's slumped form and Nahri. "Let them take me, Nahri. Please. I can take care of myself."

No. Thinking quickly, she spun back on Wajed. "I want to speak to my husband," she insisted. "The emir would never permit this!"

"The emir does not command me," Wajed replied. "The cuffs. *Now,*" he clarified as the knife pressed harder into Jamshid's throat.

Nahri cursed under her breath but slipped them on. The iron burned against her skin, her magic not gone, but deadened. A pair of soldiers instantly descended upon her, binding her wrists tightly so that she couldn't take the cuffs off.

Nahri glared at Wajed. "I will kill your king if you hurt him. I swear it to you, Qaid, on my ancestors' ashes. I will kill your king and then I will kill you."

Wajed merely inclined his head. Another pair of soldiers was binding Jamshid's hands.

"I'm going to get you out," she declared. "I promise. I'll get word to Muntadhir."

Jamshid swallowed. "Take care of yourself first. Please, Banu Nahida!" he shouted as they pulled him away. "We need you alive."

33

ALI

From a window at the top of the Citadel's stone tower, Ali sur-
veyed the lake below. On this moonless night, it was darker than
usual, a perfectly still pane of black reflecting the sky. In the
distance, a narrow band of golden beach was all that separated
it from the equally dark mountains.

He inhaled, the crisp air bracing. "The gates are closed?"

"Yes, my prince," Daoud replied. "The shafit district is as
secure as possible. The gate in the Grand Bazaar has been sealed
with magic and fortified with iron bars. Our people did the
same." He cleared his throat. "The recitation of your speech by
the muezzins had quite an effect."

The recitation of my speech will be the first charge they read at my trial. Ali
had ordered his father's cruel plans revealed to the entire Geziri
Quarter: sung by its muezzins and cried out by every imam and
sheikh who knew him—respected clerics whose word would be
trusted. The plans were followed by a far simpler call:

Ghassan al Qahtani asks that you abide the slaughter of our shafit kin.

Zaydi al Qahtani asks you to stop it.

His plan very much had the desired effect . . . more than even Ali had anticipated. Whether his people were feeling nostalgic for the proud cause that had brought them to Daevabad, fed up with corruption, or simply believed the Afshin-slayer who'd wandered their land digging wells and breaking bread with their relatives was the right man to follow, Ali couldn't say. But they had revolted, Geziri men and women spilling into the streets and seizing any soldiers who tried to stop them from going to the shafit district. Both neighborhoods were now under his control, a mix of soldiers loyal to Ali and well-armed civilians taking up positions throughout.

"The hospital?" he asked, disquiet rising in his heart. "Was the Banu Nahida . . ."

"She had just left," Daoud replied. "With the grand wazir and his son. They apparently went rushing out in some haste. We have soldiers positioned outside the hospital, but per your orders, none will go inside. The freed slave Razu is guarding the entrance and threatening to turn anyone who crosses her into a spider." The man said these words with a nervous glance, as if expecting Razu to pop out and transform him into an insect right then and there.

"Good. Make it known that if a single Daeva is harmed tonight by one of our men, I'll execute the perpetrator myself." The thought of the wounded Daevas still inside the hospital made Ali sick. He couldn't imagine how terrified they must have been to learn they were trapped in the building while the surrounding neighborhoods rebelled under the leadership of the "Afshin-slayer."

Ali's gaze fell on Wajed's desk. Needing access to its wealth of city maps, Ali had taken over the Qaid's office, but doing so felt like carving out a piece of his heart. He could not stand in this room without recalling the hours he'd spent staging battles with rocks and sticks as a young child while the Qaid worked above him. He'd read every book in here and examined every battle diagram, Wajed quizzing him with a far gentler affection than his own father ever had.

He will never forgive me for this, Ali knew. Wajed was loyal to the end, his father's closest companion since their shared childhood.

He turned to Lubayd. "Do you really think Aqisa can sneak into the harem?"

"I think Aqisa can do pretty much anything she sets her mind to," Lubayd replied. "Probably better than you or I."

Good. Ali needed Aqisa to get his letter to Zaynab; his sister would at least try to help him, this he knew. "God willing, my sister can convince Muntadhir to support us."

"And then?" Lubayd crossed his arms. "*You've* taken the Citadel. Why are you going to hand it back to anyone, let alone the brother you've been fighting with for months?" His gaze grew pointed. "People aren't taking to the street to make Muntadhir king, Ali."

"And I'm not doing this to be king. I want my brother and sister on my side. I *need* them on my side." For Ali was fairly certain his father had a plan in place on the chance Ali rebelled and took the Citadel. He'd made his opposition to the king quite clear and it was no secret he was well liked by the soldiers with whom he'd grown up. He knew his father; there was no way Ghassan hadn't come up with a strategy to defuse him.

But for Muntadhir, his devoutly loyal emir? For the Princess Zaynab, the proclaimed light of his eyes? Ali suspected his father's reaction would be murkier, slower, and emotional. Ali might have taken the Citadel, but success lay with his siblings. His *life* lay with his siblings. He'd offered terms to his father—a letter outlining the steps he wanted to take to ensure security while they investigated the attack—but Ali knew the moment he ordered the muezzins to reveal Ghassan's plans for the shafit that there was no going back. His father would not forgive such a breach in loyalty.

"I pray your brother has better sense than you." It was Abu Nuwas, bound on the floor and very angry. Ali had brought him up in what he suspected would be a futile effort to learn what his father might do next. "You brash fool. You should have gone to your father yourself rather than having those charges read aloud. That is not our people's way."

"I'd say a fair number of Geziris disagree with you," Ali argued. "As well as the majority of the Guard."

Abu Nuwas snorted. "You offered to double their salaries. I'd avoid the moral high ground if I were you, Prince Alizayd."

"My father erred when he chose to let his army go hungry rather than force the rich to pay their share." Ali drummed his fingers on the desk, restless. There was not much to do besides wait for a response from the palace, and yet every minute dragged like an hour.

You should enjoy them, he thought darkly. *There is a strong possibility they will be your last.* He paced before the wide window, contemplating his options. It had to be near midnight.

A pair of flies flew lazily past his face. Ali batted them away, but movement caught his eye outside the window, along with a growing buzz. He stepped over to the sill.

Lubayd joined him. "What is *that*?"

Ali didn't respond. He was just as astonished as his friend. What appeared to be hundreds, perhaps even thousands, of flies were swarming above the lake, buzzing and zipping as they rose steadily higher in the air, moving in skittering bursts toward the city.

A few more flew through the window. Lubayd caught one in his hands and then shook it hard to stun it. It fell to the stone sill.

"It looks like a sand fly, like one of the ones from back home." Lubayd poked it and the fly crumbled into ash. "A *conjured* sand fly?"

Ali frowned, running a finger over the remains. "Who would bother conjuring up an enormous swarm of sand flies?" Was this some sort of bizarre Navasatem tradition he wasn't aware of? He leaned out the window to watch as the last of the flies made their way past the lake and into the city itself.

Then he froze. Hidden by the twitching mass of flies overhead, something *else* had begun to move that had no business doing so. Ali opened his mouth to call out.

A presence thundered to life in his head.

He dropped to his knees with a gasp, the world going gray. He clutched his skull, crying out in pain as sweat erupted across his body. A scream that was not a scream, an urgent warning in a language without words, hissed in his mind, urging him to run, to swim, to flee.

It was gone nearly as quickly as it came. Lubayd was holding him, calling his name as he braced himself on the windowsill.

"What happened?" he demanded, shaking Ali's shoulder. "Brother, talk to me!"

Abruptly, all the flies in the room fell dead, a rain of ash tumbling around them. Ali barely noticed, his gaze locked on the window.

The lake was moving.

The dead water shivered, shaking off its stillness as the lake danced, small swells and currents playing on its surface. Ali blinked, convinced his eyes were playing tricks on him.

"Ali, say something!"

"The lake," he whispered. "They're back."

"Who's back? What are you . . ." Lubayd trailed off. "What in God's name is *that*?" he cried.

The water was rising.

It lifted from the earth in an undulating mass, a body of rushing black liquid that pulled from the shore, leaving behind a muddy bed of jagged crevasses and the bones of ancient shipwrecks. It rose higher and higher, blocking the stars and mountains to tower over the city.

The rough outline of a reptilian head formed, its mouth opening to reveal glistening fangs. The bellowing roar that followed shook Ali to his bones, drowning out the alarmed cries from the sentries below.

He was too shocked to do anything other than stare in disbelief at the utter impossibility before him.

They turned the Gozan River into a beast, a serpent the size of a mountain that rose to howl at the moon. The seemingly ridiculous story of a now-dead Afshin and the girl who declared herself Manizheh's daughter ran through Ali's head as the lake-beast howled at the sky.

And then it abruptly turned, its terrifying visage aimed directly at the Citadel.

"Run!" Lubayd shouted, dragging him to his feet. "Get out!"

There was a violent tearing, and then the floor buckled beneath him. The room spun and Ali tumbled through the air.

He slammed hard against the opposite wall, the wind knocked from his lungs. He caught a glimmer through the window, the black water rushing up . . .

And then Ali crashed into darkness.

34

NAHRI

Nahri glared at the guards. "I'm excellent with faces," she warned. "Be assured I won't forget yours."

One of the men snickered. "Good luck getting out of those binds."

Fuming, Nahri returned to pacing the low stone parapet. She and a still unconscious Kaveh e-Pramukh had been dragged back to the palace and deposited at a pavilion high upon the walls overlooking the lake to await the king. It was the same place she had once stargazed with Ali, though there was no hint of the fine furnishings and sumptuous feast she remembered. Instead they were alone with four Geziri warriors bristling with weapons, warriors whose eyes had yet to leave her.

She stopped at the edge, staring over the distant, deadly water as she tried to shift the iron cuffs lower, wincing at the burn. But far worse than the pain was her feeling of helplessness. She and Kaveh had been here for what felt like hours, Nahri watching the sky grow an inky black while Jamshid was taken God only knew where.

The still lake caught her eye. Had it not been cursed, she might have been tempted to jump for her freedom. It was a long fall that would likely break a bone or two, but she was a Nahid. She could always heal.

Except that it is cursed and will tear you into a thousand pieces. Frustrated, Nahri turned back, fighting the urge to burn something.

The look on her face must have been obvious. "Watch yourself, fire worshipper," one of the guards warned. "Believe me when I say none of us have patience for the Scourge's whore."

Nahri straightened up like a shot. "Call me that again and I'll see you dead before dawn."

He instantly moved forward, his hand dropping to the hilt of his zulfiqar before one of his fellows hissed a warning in Geziriyya, pulling him back.

"Banu Nahida?" Kaveh's voice was weak from where he lay slumped against the wall.

Forgetting the Geziri guard, Nahri hurried to the grand wazir's side. His eyes had blinked open, and he looked dazed. Unable to heal him, Nahri had settled for ripping a strip of cloth from his shirt and binding it around his head. Blood had soaked through the cloth in black splotches.

"Are you okay?" she asked urgently.

He touched his head and winced. "I . . . I think so." He sat up slowly. "What . . . where is Jamshid?"

"I don't know," Nahri confessed. "Wajed took him from the midan, and we've been up here since then."

Kaveh drew up, alarm flashing across his face. "What time is it?"

"Midnight, perhaps? Why?" she asked when alarm flashed across his eyes.

"Midnight?" he whispered. "Creator, no. I have to find him."

He grabbed her shoulder with his bound hands, and Nahri jumped at the breach in etiquette. "I need you to think, Nahri. Did they say anything about where they might be taking Jamshid? Anything at all?" His face looked gaunt in the dim light. "It wasn't the Citadel, was it?"

She jerked free. "I don't know. And you're not the only one with questions. Why did you lie about Muntadhir being hurt?"

Kaveh looked only slightly remorseful. "Because I needed you and Jamshid somewhere safe tonight. Lady Nisreen . . . she was supposed to stay with the two of you in the infirmary, but . . ." Sorrow creased his features. "The Grand Temple seemed the next safest option."

"Are you worried the shafit are planning another attack?"

Kaveh shook his head. He was toying with a ring on his hand, a gold band crowned with what appeared to be a copper-striped agate. "No, Banu Nahri. Not the shafit."

The door opened just then, the guards bowing their heads as Ghassan entered the pavilion. Nahri drew back, dread coursing through her. There was open rage in his eyes—an expression that contrasted sharply with the weary slump of his shoulders, and one that sent a shiver down her spine. Ghassan al Qahtani was not a man who easily betrayed his emotions.

He drew to a stop, looking coldly down at the Daevas on the ground. "Leave us," he snapped to the guards.

The soldiers were gone the next moment, closing the door behind them.

Nahri struggled to her feet. "What do you want?" she demanded. "How dare you drag us here when our people are wounded and grieving because of a lapse in *your* security?"

Ghassan tossed a scroll at her feet. "Are you responsible for this?" he asked.

Nahri picked it up. She recognized Ali's handwriting immediately. She read it . . . and then she read it again, convinced she'd misunderstood. The well-thought-out plans to spearhead an investigation into today's attacks and ensure security for the city until passions had died down.

The calm assurances that he would return his father's army when he was convinced there would be no retribution against the shafit.

Nahri stared at the words, willing them to rearrange. *You fool. You could have gone to Am Gezira. You could have found some doting wife and lived a peaceful life.*

"What?" Kaveh prompted, sounding worried. "What is it?"

Nahri dropped the scroll. "Ali took the Citadel."

Kaveh gasped. "He did *what*?"

Ghassan cut in. "The question remains, Banu Nahida. Are you and my son working together?"

"No," she said acidly. "Believe it or not, I did not have much time today between shrouding the dead and treating burned children to participate in a coup."

"Is that why you dragged us here?" Kaveh demanded, glaring at the king. "You've lost control of your fanatical son—a danger you should have dealt with years ago—and you're trying to pin the blame on us?"

Ghassan's eyes lit with challenge. "Oh, has my simpering grand wazir finally grown a spine? A rather rich accusation, Kaveh, considering the part you played in inflaming people's passions." His face grew stormy. "Did you think I wouldn't follow up on Ali's suspicions about the attack on the shafit camp? Did you think you could light a spark like that in this city—*my* city—and not have it explode in your face?"

Nahri's stomach dropped. It was one thing to hear the accusation from Ali—he could be a little overwrought—but the certainty in Ghassan's voice and the flush in Kaveh's cheeks confirmed what her heart had wanted to deny. She might not have trusted the grand wazir, but he was a fellow Daeva, a friend of Nisreen's, and Jamshid's father.

"You faked the attack on the Daeva couple," she whispered. "Didn't you?"

Kaveh's face was bright red. "You and Jamshid needed to see the truth about the shafit, and it would have happened sooner or later on its own—it has today! How can you possibly defend the dirt-bloods after what they did to the procession? They have no business being anywhere near your ancestors' hospital; they have no place in our world at all!"

Nahri jerked back like she'd been slapped.

But Kaveh wasn't done. He glared at Ghassan. "Nor do you. Daevabad has not seen a day of peace since Zaydi al Qahtani bathed it in Daeva blood, and you are as treacherous as your barbarian forefather." Emotion ripped through his voice. "I almost believed it, you know. Your act. The king who wished to unite our tribes." Nahri watched as angry tears filled his eyes. "It was a lie. Twenty years I served you; my son took half a dozen arrows to save yours, and you *used his life* to threaten me." He spat at Ghassan's feet. "Do not pretend you care for *anyone* but your own, you filthy sand fly."

Nahri instinctively took a step back. No one spoke to Ghassan like that. He did not brook the slightest dissent, let alone open insults from an upstart Daeva wazir.

That Ghassan smiled instead of opening Kaveh's throat was petrifying.

"You've wanted to say that for a long time, haven't you?" the king drawled. "Look at you, all full of spite and indignation . . . as if I have not accommodated your tribe's frivolous grievances again and again. As if *I* wasn't the one to lift you and your son out of your sad lives as petty provincial nobles." He crossed his arms. "Let me return the favor, Kaveh, for there is something I have also *long* wanted to tell you."

"Enough of this," Nahri interrupted. Jamshid was missing and Ali was in open revolt; she wasn't wasting time over whatever history Ghassan and Kaveh shared. "What do you want, Ghassan? And where is Jamshid?"

"Jamshid . . ." Ghassan's eyes glittered. "Now, oddly enough, there is a Daeva I like. Certainly more loyal than either of you, though I can't imagine from whom he inherited such wisdom. It clearly doesn't run in his family."

At her side, Kaveh tensed and Nahri frowned. "What's that supposed to mean?"

Ghassan paced closer, reminding her uncomfortably of a hawk stalking something small and fragile. "Did it never strike you as strange how confident I was of your identity, Banu Nahri? So *immediately* confident?"

"You told me I resemble Manizheh," Nahri said slowly.

The king clucked his tongue. "But enough that I'd make a scene in court having only spotted you from a distance?" He glanced at Kaveh. "What do you think, Grand Wazir? It seems you knew Manizheh *very well*. Does our Nahri resemble her strongly?"

Kaveh looked like he was having a hard time breathing, let alone answering. His hands were clenched into tight fists, his knuckles pale and bloodless. "Yes," he whispered.

Ghassan's eyes flashed in triumph. "Oh, come now, you can lie better than that. Not that it matters. She has something else. Something her mother had, something her uncle had. Not that either of them was aware of it. Bit embarrassing actually." He tapped the black mark on his temple, Suleiman's eight-pointed star. "You think you own a thing, and well . . ."

A frisson of danger tingled across her skin. Hating that she was playing into his game but seeing no way out, she pressed. "Why don't you try speaking straight for once?"

"Suleiman's seal, child. You bear a shadow of his mark . . . right here." Ghassan reached out to touch the side of her face, and

Nahri jerked away. "To me, it is clear as day." The king turned back to Kaveh, his gray eyes simmering with triumph and something else, something vicious and vindictive. "They all bear it, Grand Wazir. Every single person with Nahid blood. Manizheh. Rustam. Nahri." He paused, seeming to savor the moment. "Your Jamshid."

Kaveh shot to his feet.

"Sit back down," Ghassan snapped. The cruel humor was gone from his voice in an instant, the merciless cold of a despot replacing it. "Or the only place Jamshid—your Baga Nahid—will end up is in a shroud."

Nahri reeled, her hand going to her mouth. "Jamshid is a *Nahid*?" Bewildered and shocked, she struggled for words. "But he has no . . ."

Abilities. The word died on her tongue. Jamshid's desperate questions about the Rumi fire that had burned him and his abruptly healed wounds. The ancient Tukharistani he'd spoken to Razu . . . and the raw burst of power Nahri had felt when he clutched her hand and she summoned a sandstorm.

Jamshid was a Nahid. Nahri's eyes were suddenly wet. Jamshid was *family*.

And there was no way he knew it; he wasn't that good of a liar. She whirled on Kaveh. He'd dropped back to the ground at Ghassan's command but looked no less fierce. "You hid it from him," she accused. "How could you?"

Kaveh was shaking now, rocking back and forth. "I had to protect him from Ghassan. It was the only way."

The king scoffed. "Fine job you did of that; I knew that boy was a Nahid the moment you brought him to my court. The rest was rather easy to figure out." Hostility leached into his voice. "The summer of his birth was when Saffiyeh died. The summer Manizheh ignored my pleas to return to Daevabad early to save her queen."

"Saffiyeh was never her queen," Kaveh shot back. "And Manizheh got barely a week with her own child before she was forced to return to you once again."

"It was clearly enough time for her to do something to conceal Jamshid's abilities, wasn't it?" Malice twisted Ghassan's face. "She always considered herself so clever . . . and yet her son might have used those abilities when Darayavahoush turned on him. An irony in that: the last Baga Nahid nearly killed by his Afshin, all while trying to save a Qahtani."

Nahri looked away, heartsick. Dara probably would have thrown himself on his own sword if he'd known that truth. She leaned against the parapet, her legs suddenly weak. Ghassan and Kaveh were still arguing, and Nahri knew she should be paying attention, but suddenly all she wanted to do was escape this awful palace and find her brother.

"You should be grateful," Ghassan was saying. "I gave the two of you a life here. Wealthy, respected, powerful . . ."

"As long as we danced to your tune," Kaveh snapped. "Forget *our* desires, *our* ambitions; everything is in thrall to Ghassan al Qahtani's grand plans." His voice was cruel. "And you wonder why Manizheh refused you."

"I suspect the reason she refused me—however disappointing—sits in front of me now." Ghassan was eying Kaveh dismissively, but there was a resentment in his gray gaze that he couldn't entirely mask. "Manizheh clearly had a peculiar . . . taste."

Nahri's patience abruptly vanished. "Oh, get over yourselves," she hissed. "I'm not standing here listening to some old men bicker about a long-lost love. *Where is my brother?*"

Ghassan's expression darkened, but he answered. "Somewhere secure. Where he'll be staying, with people I trust, until the city is calm again."

"Until you beat us back into obedience, you mean," Nahri

said bitterly. "I've been down this path with you before. Why don't you just tell us what you want?"

Ghassan shook his head. "Direct as always, Banu Nahri . . . But I know your people. Right now, I imagine a good number of Daevas are hungry for shafit blood, and it's clear the shafit feel similarly. So let us settle things down." He turned to Kaveh. "You'll be taking the blame. You will confess to faking the camp assault and arming the shafit who attacked your procession."

"I had *nothing* to do with what happened to the procession," Kaveh said heatedly. "I would never!"

"I don't care," Ghassan said flatly. "You will take responsibility. The ruined grand wazir, driven to destruction by his own twisted fanaticism. You will confess to plotting against your Banu Nahida, and after unburdening yourself so, Kaveh . . . ." He nodded coolly toward the wall. "You will take your own life."

Kaveh's eyes went wide, and Nahri swiftly stepped forward. "I'm not going to let you—"

"I am not done." Something different, more complicated to read, flickered across Ghassan's face. "For your part, Banu Nahida, I am going to need you to send a letter to my youngest and inform him that you have been arrested and charged with being his co-conspirator in an attempted coup. And that you will be executed tomorrow at dawn should he not surrender."

Nahri felt the blood drain from her face. "*What?*"

Ghassan waved her off. "Believe it or not, I would rather not involve you, but I know my son. Ali might be happy to martyr himself, but I have no doubt he will no sooner see that letter in your handwriting than throw himself at my feet."

"And then?" she pressed. "What do you intend to do with him?"

The cold humor vanished from Ghassan's face. "He will be the one executed for treason."

No. Nahri exhaled, pressing her hands into fists. "I'm not going to help you trap him," she replied. "I'm glad he's taken the Citadel. I hope he takes the palace next!"

"He's not going to be able to take it by dawn," Ghassan said evenly. "And you'll not only write that letter, I'll have you dragged to the midan so you can weep for him to save you if necessary. Or I'll kill your brother."

Nahri recoiled. "You wouldn't." Her voice was shaking. "You wouldn't do that to Muntadhir."

Ghassan's brows lifted in faint surprise. "Not one to miss much, are you? Though, yes, Banu Nahida, I would. Indeed, Muntadhir would be wise to learn to keep his heart closer. He risks himself with such affections in this world."

"What would you even know about affection?" Kaveh cut in, his eyes wild. "You're a monster. You and your father used Manizheh's love for her brother to control her and now you plan to do the same to her daughter?" Kaveh glared at Ghassan. "How could you ever claim to care for her?"

Ghassan rolled his eyes. "Save me the false pieties, Kaveh. You've too much blood on your hands."

But Kaveh's words were the reminder that Nahri needed.

She closed her eyes. She'd tried so hard to wall herself off from the king, to mask her vulnerabilities and make sure there was no chink in the armor she drew around herself. He already had the fate of her tribe in one fist, had used the threat of violence against them to force her into obedience more than once for years.

But her efforts hadn't mattered. Because he had always had something so much closer. Precious. He'd built a chink into her armor from the start, and Nahri had never even known it was there.

She tried to think. If Ali had taken the Citadel, this was no mere palace revolt; the bulk of the Royal Guard was now out of

Ghassan's hands. She remembered the haunting waves of Gezi-riyya drifting over the air, recalling what she knew of Daevabad's neighborhoods. Ali could already be in control of the Geziri Quarter. The shafit district.

She opened her eyes. "You think he can do it, don't you?" she asked Ghassan. "You think Ali can beat you."

The king's eyes narrowed. "You're very out of your depth, Banu Nahida."

Nahri smiled; she felt sick. "I'm not. I used to be very good at this, you know. Reading a mark, spotting weaknesses. You and I actually have that in common." Her throat hitched. "And Jam-shid . . . I bet you savored that secret." She inclined her head toward Kaveh. "I bet you delighted in it every time you saw him, contemplating the ways you could revenge yourself on the man who had the love of the woman you wanted. You wouldn't give that up easily."

Ghassan drew up. The king's face was calm, but Nahri didn't miss the heat in his voice. "None of this posturing will get your brother back any sooner."

I'm sorry, Jamshid. I'm so sorry. Nahri exhaled, fighting the deep, awful sadness wrapping her heart. "I won't help you."

Ghassan's eyes flashed. "I beg your pardon?"

"I won't help you," she repeated, hating herself. "I won't let you use my brother against me. Not for any reason."

Ghassan abruptly stepped closer. "If you don't do this, Banu Nahida, I'm going to kill him. I'm going to do it slowly and I will make you watch. So you may as well do us all the favor of simply obeying now."

Kaveh scrambled up, alarm twisting his expression. "Banu Nahri—"

Ghassan backhanded him across the face. The king was obvi-ously stronger than he looked; the blow sent Kaveh sprawling to the floor, a burst of blood on his mouth.

Nahri gasped. But the casual, brutal violence only made her more determined. Ghassan was a monster. But he was a desperate one, and Nahri trembled to think what he would do to Daevabad in the wake of a failed coup.

Which meant she'd have to do all she could to make sure it didn't fail. "You're wasting your time, Ghassan. I'm not going to break. This city beats in my family's blood. In my blood." Her voice shook slightly. "In my brother's blood. And if the last Nahids need to die to save it . . ." She stilled her trembling, lifting her chin in defiance. "Then we'll have served our people well."

Ghassan stared at her for a very long moment. His expression wasn't inscrutable now, and he didn't bother arguing with her. Nahri had read her mark.

And she knew he was about to destroy her for it.

He stepped back. "I'm going to tell Jamshid who he really is," he said. "Then I'm going to tell him how his sister, having grown tired of sleeping with the man he loves, betrayed them both to save a man he hates." The words were crude—the last attempt of an angry old man who'd traded decency for a throne that was about to be wrenched away by his own blood. "Then I will finish the job your Afshin started and have your brother scourged to death."

"No, Ghassan, wait!" Kaveh threw himself before the king. "She didn't mean it. She'll write the letter—ah!" He cried out as Ghassan kicked him in the face, stepping around his body and reaching for the door.

With a wail, Kaveh smashed his hand against the stone. Nahri heard a sharp crack, his ring shattering.

A strange coppery haze burst from the broken gem.

In the time it took Nahri to draw a quick breath, the vapor had bloomed to engulf the grand wazir.

"Kaveh, what is that?" she asked sharply as copper tendrils darted out like a dancer's hand, reaching, searching. There was something familiar about the movement, about the metallic shimmer.

The king briefly glanced back, looking more annoyed than anything.

The vapor rushed at the copper relic bolted through his ear.

It instantly melted, and Ghassan cried out, clasping his head as the liquid metal surged into his ear. Suleiman's seal flashed on his cheek, and Nahri swooned, her magic gone.

But it didn't last. The king's eyes went wide and still as a haze of copper veiled their gray depths.

Then Ghassan al Qahtani fell dead at her feet.

Her abilities slammed back into her. Nahri covered her mouth with a startled cry, staring in shock as copper-flecked black blood poured from the king's ears, mouth, and nose.

"By the Most High, Kaveh," she whispered. "What have you done?"

"What had to be done." Kaveh was already crossing to Ghassan's body, stepping into the pool of spreading blood without hesitation. He retrieved the king's khanjar, quickly using it to slice through the binds on his wrists. "We don't have much time," he warned. "We need to find Jamshid and secure Muntadhir."

Nahri stared at him. Had he lost his mind? Ghassan's guards were just outside the door. They weren't getting away, let alone finding Jamshid and "securing" Muntadhir, whatever that meant. "Kaveh, I think—"

"I do not care what you think." The barely checked hostility in his voice shocked her. "Respectfully . . ." It sounded like he was struggling not to shout. "You're not the one making decisions tonight. A thing that is clearly for the best." He glanced at her, his eyes simmering with anger. "You will answer for the choice you just made. Not tonight. Not to me . . . but you will answer."

A fly buzzed past her ear. Nahri barely noticed; she was speechless. Then another swept past her face, brushing her cheek.

Kaveh turned to look at the sky. More flies were coming, a swarm from the direction of the lake.

Grim determination swept his features. "It is time."

There was an angry shout from beyond the closed door.

Nahri instantly recognized the voice. "Muntadhir!" She lunged for the door. His father might be lying in a pool of blood on the ground, but right now Nahri trusted her estranged husband far more than the mad wazir who'd orchestrated a riot and assassinated a king.

"Nahri?" Muntadhir's voice was muffled through the door, but from his tone, he was clearly arguing with the guards on the other side.

Kaveh shoved himself between Nahri and the door. "Muntadhir cannot come in, Banu Nahri. He cannot be exposed to this."

"Exposed to *what*?" she cried. "The fact that you just murdered his father?"

But as she tried to wrestle past him, she suddenly spotted what Kaveh meant.

A coppery haze was reforming above the dead king. Glittering particles, like minuscule metal stars, swirled up from Ghassan's pooling blood, forming a cloud twice the size of the one that had escaped Kaveh's shattered ring.

Nahri instantly backed away, but the vapor flowed harmlessly past her and Kaveh, separating and undulating around her waist like a wave. The flies zipped over them all, dozens now.

Muntadhir broke down the door.

"I don't care what he said!" he shouted, trying to shove past a pair of guards. "She's my damned wife and . . ." Muntadhir recoiled, his eyes locking on his father's bloody body. "*Abba?*"

The guards reacted more swiftly. "My king!" Two flew to Ghassan, the other two going for Nahri and Kaveh. Muntadhir didn't move from the door frame, falling heavily against it as if it was all that was keeping him on his feet.

The flies suddenly flickered into flashes of fire, dissolving into a rain of ash.

"Muntadhir, I didn't do it!" Nahri cried as one of the guards grabbed her. "I swear! I had nothing to do with this!"

A roar broke the air, a scream like the crash of ocean waves and the bellow of a crocodile. It sounded dully distant, but it set every hair on her body on end.

Nahri had heard that roar before.

The vapor struck again.

The guards who'd gone to Ghassan screamed, clutching their heads. The soldier who'd seized her dropped her arm and backed away with a cry, but he wasn't fast enough. His relic dashed into his ear with vindictive speed. He shrieked in pain, clawing at his face.

"No." Kaveh's horrified whisper cut through the wails. His gaze locked on Muntadhir, still framed against the door. "This wasn't how it was supposed to happen!"

Muntadhir's eyes went bright with fear.

Nahri didn't hesitate. She shot to her feet, running across the pavilion as the coppery cloud, now tripled in size, flew at her husband.

"Banu Nahida, wait!" Kaveh cried. "You don't—"

She didn't hear what else he had to say. The vapor just behind her, Nahri threw herself at Muntadhir.

35

NAHRI

Too late, Nahri remembered that the door opened on to a staircase.

Muntadhir grunted as she hit him hard in the stomach and then he cried out as he lost his balance. They tumbled down the stairs, various limbs bashing against the dusty stone before they landed in a heap at the bottom.

Pinned beneath her, Muntadhir swore. Nahri gasped, the wind knocked from her lungs. Her abilities were still dulled from the iron cuffs, and she was bruised and battered, a searing pain running down her left wrist.

Muntadhir blinked and then his eyes went wide, locking on something past her shoulder. "Run!" he cried, scrambling to his feet and yanking her up.

They fled. "Your relic!" Nahri wheezed. In the opposite corridor from the one they'd taken, someone cried out in Geziriyya.

Then, chillingly, the wail abruptly cut out into silence. "Take out your relic!"

He reached for it as they ran, his fingers fumbling.

Nahri glanced over her shoulder, horrified to see the coppery haze lapping toward them like a hungry, malevolent wave. "Muntadhir!"

He yanked it out, hurling the copper bolt away just as the vapor engulfed them. Nahri held her breath, terrified. And then it passed, rushing down the corridor.

Muntadhir fell to his knees, shaking so hard Nahri could hear his teeth rattling. "What the hell was that?" he gasped.

Her heart was pounding, the echo throbbing in her head. "I have no idea."

Tears were running down his face. "My father . . . *Kaveh*. I'll kill him." He staggered to his feet and turned back toward the way they had come, one hand braced on the wall.

Nahri moved to block him. "That's not what's important right now."

He glared at her, suspicion crossing his face. "Did you—"

"No!" she snapped. "Really, Muntadhir? I just threw myself down a stairwell to save you."

He flushed. "I'm sorry. I just . . . he . . ." His voice cracked, and he wiped his eyes roughly.

The grief laced in his words dulled her temper. "I know." She cleared her throat, holding her bound wrists out. "Would you get this off me?"

He pulled free his khanjar, quickly slicing through the cloth binds and helping her out of the iron cuffs. She inhaled, relieved as her powers burned through her veins, her blistered skin and dark bruises instantly healing.

Muntadhir had opened his mouth to speak again when a voice echoed down the hall. "Banu Nahida!"

It was Kaveh.

Nahri clapped a hand over her husband's lips, dragging him into the shadows. "Let's not find out if he has any other tricks up his sleeve," she whispered. "We need to warn the rest of the Geziris in the palace."

Even in the shadows, she could see his face pale. "You think it will spread that far?"

"Did it look like it was stopping?"

"Fuck." It seemed an appropriate answer. "My God, Nahri . . . do you know how many Geziris are in the palace?"

She nodded grimly.

There was a sudden rumble, the floor shuddering beneath their feet. It lasted only a second, and then was gone.

Nahri braced herself. "What was *that*?"

Muntadhir shuddered. "I don't know. It feels like the entire island just shook." He ran a hand nervously over his beard. "That vapor . . . do you have any idea what it might be?"

Nahri shook her head. "No. It looked somewhat similar to the poison used on your brother, though, didn't it?"

"My brother." Her husband's expression darkened and then panic swept his face. "*My sister.*"

"Muntadhir, wait!" Nahri cried.

But he was already running.

ZAYNAB'S APARTMENTS WEREN'T CLOSE, AND BY THE time they made it to the harem garden, Muntadhir and Nahri were both thoroughly out of breath. The scarf she'd tied around her head in the hospital was long gone, her curls plastered to her damp skin.

"Jamshid was always telling me I should exercise more," Muntadhir panted. "I should have listened."

Jamshid. His name was like a knife to her heart.

She darted a look at Muntadhir. Well, there was one situation that had just grown more complicated. "Your father had him arrested," she said.

"I know," Muntadhir replied. "Why do you think I was banging down the door? I heard Wajed took him out of the city. Did my father tell Kaveh where?"

"Out of the *city*? No, your father said nothing about that."

Muntadhir groaned in frustration. "I should have stopped all this sooner. When I heard he had you as well . . ." He trailed off, sounding angry with himself. "Did he at least tell you what he wanted with Jamshid?"

Nahri hesitated. Ghassan might have been a monster, but he was still Muntadhir's father, and Nahri didn't need to add to her husband's grief right now. "Ask me later."

"If we're alive later," Muntadhir muttered. "Ali finally lost his mind, by the way. He seized the Citadel."

"It would seem an excellent night to be in the Citadel instead of the palace."

"Fair point." They crossed under the delicate archway leading to the pavilion that fronted Zaynab's apartment. A rich teak platform floated over the canal, framed by the wispy fronds of slender palm trees.

Zaynab was there, perched on a striped linen couch and examining a scroll. Relief coursed through Nahri, followed swiftly by confusion when she saw who was seated with the princess.

"*Aqisa?*"

Muntadhir marched across the platform. "Of course you're here. Doing my brother's dirty work, I assume?"

Aqisa leaned back, a move that revealed the sword and the khanjar belted at her waist. Looking unbothered, she took a leisurely sip of coffee from the paper-thin porcelain cup in her hand before responding. "He asked me to convey a message."

Zaynab deftly rolled the scroll back up, looking uncharacteristically nervous. "It seems Ali was quite inspired by our last conversation," she said, tripping over the last words. "He wants us to remove Abba."

Muntadhir's face crumpled. "We're beyond that, Zaynab." He sank into the couch beside his sister, gently taking her hand. "Abba is dead."

Zaynab jerked back. "What?" When he didn't say anything further, her hand flew to her mouth. "Oh God . . . please don't tell me Ali—"

"Kaveh." Muntadhir reached for his sister's relic, carefully removing it from her ear. "He unleashed some sort of magical vapor that targets these." He held up the relic before hurling it away into the depths of the garden. "It's bad, Zaynab. I watched it kill four guards in a matter of seconds."

At that, Aqisa ripped out her own relic, sending it flying into the night.

Zaynab had started to cry. "Are you sure? Are you sure he's really dead?"

Muntadhir hugged her tightly. "I'm sorry, ukhti."

Not wanting to intrude on the grieving siblings, Nahri edged closer to Aqisa. "You came from the Citadel? Is Ali all right?"

"He has an army and isn't trapped in a palace with some murderous mist," Aqisa replied. "I'd say he's doing better than we are."

Nahri looked out at the dark garden, her thoughts roiling. The king was dead, the grand wazir was a traitor, the Qaid was gone, and Ali—the only one of them with military experience— was involved in a mutiny across the city.

She took a deep breath. "I . . . I think that leaves us in charge."

The night sky abruptly darkened further—which Nahri thought a rather apt response. But when she glanced up, her mouth went dry. A half-dozen smoky, equine shapes with wings of flashing fire were racing toward the palace.

Aqisa followed her gaze and then grabbed her, pulling her swiftly inside the apartment. Zaynab and Muntadhir were right behind them. As they bolted the door, they heard several thudding crashes and the distant echo of screams.

"I don't think Kaveh is working alone," Muntadhir whispered, his face ashen.

Three pairs of gray-toned eyes settled on her. "I have nothing to do with this," Nahri protested. "My God, do you really think I'd be in your company if I did? Surely you both know me better than that."

"I believe that," Zaynab muttered.

Muntadhir sank to the floor. "Then who *could* he be working with? I've never seen magic like this."

"I don't think that's what's most important right now," Zaynab said softly. There were more shouts from somewhere deep in the palace, and they all went quiet for a moment listening before Zaynab continued. "Nahri . . . could the poison spread to the rest of the city?"

Nahri recalled the wild energy of the vapor that had chased them and nodded slowly. "The Geziri Quarter," she whispered, voicing the fear she could see in Zaynab's eyes. "My God, if it reaches there . . ."

"They need to be warned at once," Aqisa said. "I will go."

"As will I," Zaynab declared.

"Oh no, you won't," Muntadhir replied. "If you think I'm about to let my little sister go dashing off while the city is under attack—"

"Your *little sister* isn't asking permission, and there are people who will believe my word more readily than Aqisa's. And you're needed here. Both of you," Zaynab added, nodding at Nahri. "Dhiru, if Abba is dead, you need to retrieve the seal. Before Kaveh or whoever he's working with figures out how to do so."

"Suleiman's seal?" Nahri repeated. She hadn't even given a thought to that—the king's succession seemed a world away. "Is it with your father?"

Muntadhir looked like he was about to be sick. "Something like that. We'd need to get back to him. To his body."

Aqisa locked eyes with Zaynab. "The chest," she said simply.

Zaynab nodded and beckoned them farther into her apartment. It was as rich and finely appointed as Muntadhir's, though not as cluttered with artwork. Or wine cups.

The princess knelt beside a large, elaborate wooden chest and whispered an unlocking charm over it. As the lid sprang open Nahri peered inside.

It was entirely filled with weapons. Sheathed daggers and scimitars wrapped in silk rested beside an oddly lovely mace, a crossbow, and some sort of barbed, jeweled chain.

Nahri didn't know whose expression was more shocked, hers or Muntadhir's. "My God," she said. "You really are Ali's sister."

"What . . . where did you . . . ," Muntadhir began weakly.

Zaynab looked slightly flustered. "She's been teaching me," she explained, nodding to Aqisa.

The warrior woman was already selecting blades, looking unbothered by Nahri and Muntadhir's reactions. "A Geziri woman her age should have mastered at least three weapons. I have been making up for an abominable lapse in her education." She pressed a sword and the crossbow into Zaynab's hands and then clucked her tongue. "Stop trembling, sister. You'll do fine."

Nahri shook her head, and then considered the chest, knowing well her limitations. Quickly, she pulled out a pair of small daggers, the heft reminding her of something she might have used to cut purses back in Cairo. For a moment, she thought longingly of Dara's blade back in her room.

I wish I'd had a few more knife-throwing lessons with him, she thought. Not to mention that the legendary Afshin would have probably made for a better partner in a palace under siege than her visibly skittish husband.

She took a deep breath. "Anything else?"

Zaynab shook her head. "We'll sound the alarm in the Geziri Quarter and then head to the Citadel to alert Ali. He can lead the Royal Guard back. Warn every Geziri you see in the palace, and tell them to do the same."

Nahri swallowed. It could be hours before Ali returned with the Guard. She and Muntadhir would be on their own—facing God only knew what—until then.

"You can do this," Zaynab said. "You have to." She hugged her brother. "Fight, Dhiru. There will be time for grief, but right now, you're our king, and Daevabad comes first." Her voice grew fierce. "I'll be back with your Qaid."

Muntadhir gave a jerky nod. "God be with you." He glanced at Aqisa. "Please keep my sister safe." He nodded toward the pavilion. "Take the stairs we came from. There's a passage close by that leads to the stables."

Zaynab and Aqisa left swiftly. "Are you ready?" Nahri asked when she and Muntadhir were alone.

He laughed as he strapped a wicked-looking sword to his waist. "Not in the slightest. You?"

"God, no." Nahri grabbed another needle-sharp dagger and flipped it into her sleeve. "Let's go die."

36

ALI

Ali floated peacefully in warm darkness, wrapped tight in the embrace of the water. It smelled of salt and mud, of life, gently teasing and tugging at his clothes. A pebbly soft tendril stroked his cheek while another twined around his ankle.

A throbbing at the back of his head slowly brought him to the present. Dazed, Ali opened his eyes. Darkness surrounded him. He was submerged in water so deep and so clouded by muddy silt that he could barely see. Memories came to him in pieces. The watery beast. The Citadel's tower tumbling through the air . . .

The lake. He was in Daevabad's lake.

Sheer panic tore through him. He thrashed, trying desperately to free himself from whatever held him. His robe, he realized, blindly fumbling. The crumbled remains of some sort of brick wall had pinned it to the lake bed. Ali wrenched it off, kicking madly for the surface. The smell of ash and blood grew thicker on the water, but he ignored it, fighting past floating debris.

He finally broke through. He gasped for breath, pain surging through him.

The lake was in chaos.

Ali might as well have emerged onto a scene from the darkest circle of hell. Screams filled the air, cries for help, for mercy, in all the djinn languages he knew. Layered over them were moans, feral, hungry sounds that Ali couldn't place.

Oh, God . . . and the water. It wasn't just debris that surrounded him, it was bodies. Hundreds of djinn soldiers, floating dead in their uniforms. And when Ali saw the reason, he cried out, tears springing to his eyes.

Daevabad's Citadel—the proud symbol of Zaydi al Qahtani's rebellion, of the Geziri tribe, Ali's home for nearly two decades— had been destroyed.

Its once mighty tower had been ripped from its moorings and dragged into the lake, only a crumbled hump remaining above the water. Jagged gashes, as if from the claws of some massive creature, had raked through the remaining buildings, through the soldiers' barracks and across the training yards, making furrows so deep that the lake had filled them. The rest of the complex was on fire. Ali could see skeletal figures moving against the smoke.

Tears ran silently down his cheeks. "No," he whispered. This was a nightmare, another awful vision from the marid. "Stop this!"

Nothing happened. Ali took in the sight of the bodies again. Djinn murdered by the marid's curse did not remain floating upon the water; they were torn apart and swallowed by its depths, never to be seen again.

The curse on the lake was gone.

"I see someone!"

Ali turned toward the voice to spot a makeshift boat, one of the carved wooden doors of the tower, making its way toward him, crewed by a pair of Ayaanle soldiers wielding broken beams as oars.

"We've got you, brother," one of the soldiers said, hauling him aboard. His golden eyes went wide when he glanced at Ali. "Aye, praise God . . . it's the prince!"

"Bring him over!" Ali heard another man cry from some distance away.

They paddled awkwardly through the water. Ali had to turn away from the sight of the door pushing through the thick clutter of bodies, his fellows in uniform, too many of their faces familiar.

This isn't real. It can't be real. But it didn't feel like one of his visions. There was no alien presence whispering in Ali's head. There was just bewilderment, grief, and carnage.

As they neared the ruins of the Citadel, the remains of the toppled tower grew larger, rising from the lake like a lost island. A shattered section of its exterior shielded the few dozen warriors who'd gathered there. Some were curled around themselves, weeping. But Ali's gaze immediately flew to the ones who were fighting, several soldiers fending off a pair of thin, wraith-like creatures whose tattered shrouds clung wetly to their wasted bodies.

One was Lubayd, swinging his sword wildly. With a disgusted cry, he decapitated one of the leering creatures and kicked the body back into the lake.

Ali could have wept with relief. His best friend, at least, had survived the Citadel's destruction.

"We found the prince!" the Ayaanle soldier at his side cried. "He's alive!"

Lubayd whirled around. He was there by the time they arrived, yanking Ali to his feet and throwing his arms around him in a tight hug.

"Ali, brother, thank God . . . ," he choked out. "I'm sorry . . . the water came so fast, and when I couldn't find you in the room—"

Ali could barely manage a response. "I'm all right," he croaked.

A scream cut the air, a plea in Geziriyya. "No, don't! God, please!"

Ali lurched to the edge of the ruined tower, catching sight of the man who'd cried out: a Geziri soldier who'd managed to make it back to the beach only to be mobbed by the skeletal beings. They surrounded him, dragging him to the sand. Ali saw teeth and nails and mouths bearing down . . .

And then he couldn't watch, his stomach rising. He spun back around as the djinn's guttural cry was cut short.

"They . . . are they—" He couldn't even say the word.

Lubayd nodded. He looked shattered. "They're ghouls. It's what they do."

Ali shook his head in denial. "They can't be ghouls. There are no ifrit in Daevabad to summon ghouls—and certainly no dead humans!"

"Those are ghouls," Lubayd said firmly. "My father and I came upon a pair devouring a human hunter once." He flinched. "It's not a sight one forgets."

Ali felt faint. He took a deep breath; he couldn't fall apart. Not now. "Did anyone see what attacked the Citadel in the first place?"

Lubayd nodded, pointing to a thin Sahrayn man rocking back and forth, his arms wrapped tightly around his knees. "He was the first one out, and the things he's saying . . ." He trailed off, looking nauseated. "You should talk to him."

His heart in his throat, Ali approached the Sahrayn man. He knelt at his side, laying a hand on his shivering arm. "Brother," he started softly. "Can you tell me what you saw?"

The man kept rocking, his eyes bright with terror. "I was keeping watch on my ship," he whispered. "We were moored over there." He pointed to the ruined pier where a broken Sahrayn sandship had been driven up onto the shattered docks. "The lake . . . the water . . . it spun itself into a monster. It attacked the Citadel. Ravaged it, pulling what it could back into its depths." He swallowed, shaking harder. "The force of it threw me in the lake. I thought the curse would kill me . . . When it didn't, I started swimming . . . and then I saw them."

"Saw what?" Ali pressed.

"Warriors," the man whispered. "They came racing out of the lake on the backs of smoky horses with their bows drawn. They started shooting the survivors and then . . . and then . . ." Tears were rolling down his cheeks. "The dead came from the water. They swarmed my boat as I watched." His shoulders shook. "My captain . . ." He started to weep harder. "They tore out his throat with their teeth."

Ali's stomach plummeted, but he forced himself to peer through the darkness at the beach. Yes, he could see an archer now: a racing horse, the glimmer of a silver bow. An arrow went flying . . .

Another scream, and then silence. Fury surged through Ali, burning away his fear and panic. Those were his people out there.

He turned to study the ruined Citadel. And then his heart stopped. A ragged hole had been punched into the wall facing the street.

Ali grabbed the Sahrayn man's arm again. "Did you see any-thing go through there?" he demanded. *"Are those things in our city?"*

The sailor shook his head. "The ghouls, no . . . but the riders . . ." He nodded. "At least half of them. Once they were past the city walls . . ." His voice turned incredulous. "Prince Alizayd, their horses—they *flew* . . ."

"Where?" Ali demanded. "Where did you see them fly?"

The pity in the man's eyes filled Ali with awful, knowing dread. "The palace, my prince."

Ali shot to his feet. This was no random attack. He couldn't imagine who—or what—was capable of something like this, but he recognized a strategy when he saw one. They'd come for the Guard first, annihilating the djinn army before it could muster to protect the next target: the palace.

My family. "We need to get to the beach," he declared.

The Sahrayn man looked at him as though he'd gone insane. "You won't be able to get to the beach. Those archers are shooting everything that moves, and the few djinn who make it out are being eaten alive by ghouls the moment they step out of the water!"

Ali shook his head. "We cannot let those things into our city." He watched as a soldier dispatched another pair of ghouls when they attempted to climb upon the ruined tower, their gaping mouths full of rotted teeth. The man did so fairly easily, a single sweep of his blazing zulfiqar severing both in two.

They are not invincible, Ali noted. *Not at all.* It was their numbers that gave them an advantage; a single, terrified djinn, exhausted from navigating a gauntlet of arrows, stood no chance against dozens of hungry ghouls.

Across the water, another djinn was attempting to climb onto a floating bit of wreckage. Ali watched helplessly as a torrent of arrows cut him down. A small band of the mysterious archers had set themselves up on a section of broken wall that ran between the water and the ruined Citadel complex. Right now, Ali and his fellow survivors were safe, a shell of the tower curving up to protect them from the archers' view. But he didn't imagine their reprieve would last for long.

He examined the stretch of water separating their small sanctuary from Daevabad's shore. It was a manageable swim if not for the fact that anyone who tried would be visible to the archers the entire time.

A decision settled upon him. "Come here," he said, raising his voice. "All of you."

Ali waited for them to do so, taking advantage of the moment to study the survivors. A mix from all five of the djinn tribes, mostly men. He knew nearly all by face, if not by name—they were all Royal Guard except the Sahrayn sailor. A few cadets, a handful of officers, and the rest infantry. They looked terrified and bewildered and Ali couldn't blame them. They'd trained all their lives as warriors, but their people hadn't seen true war in centuries. Daevabad was supposed to be a refuge from the rest of the magical world: from ghouls and ifrit, from water-beasts capable of dragging down a tower that had stood for centuries.

He took a deep breath, well aware of the near suicidal nature of the counterattack he was about to propose. "I don't know what's happening," he started. "I don't think any of us do. But we're not safe here." He gestured to the mountains, looming far from the distant shore. "The curse might be gone from the lake, but I don't think many of us could make that swim. The mountains are too far away. The city, however, is not."

The Sahrayn sailor shuddered again. "Everyone who's made it to that beach has been slaughtered." His voice rose. "We should just take blades to each other's throats—it's a better fate than being eaten alive."

"They're picking us off," Ali argued. "We stand a better chance if we fight together . . ." He eyed the men around him "Would you stay here only to be killed later? Look at what they did to the Citadel. Do you think that wasn't deliberate? They came after the Royal Guard first, and if you think whatever is attacking us is going to have mercy on a band of stranded survivors, you're a fool."

A Geziri captain with a nasty gash across his face spoke up. "We'd be in view of those archers. They'll see us swimming and have us riddled with arrows before we even get close to the shore."

"Ah, but they won't see me coming." Ali kicked off his sandals. It would be easier to swim without them. "I'll stay under the water until I get to the wall."

The captain stared at him. "Prince Alizayd . . . your courage is admirable, but you can't swim that length underwater. And even if you could, you're just one man. I counted at least a dozen of those warriors and probably a hundred ghouls. It's suicide."

"He can do it." It was Lubayd, his voice intense. He met Ali's gaze, and from the mix of grief and admiration in his friend's eyes, Ali could tell Lubayd knew what he was preparing to do. "He doesn't fight like the rest of us."

Still seeing uncertainty on too many faces, Ali raised his voice. "Daevabad is our home! You all took oaths to defend it, to defend the innocents within who are about to be butchered by the same monsters who just killed so many of our brothers and sisters. You *will* get back to that beach. Gather all the weapons you can. Help each other swim. Paddle on pieces of wood. I don't care how you do it, but get across. *Fight.* Stop those things before they get into the city."

By his last words, a good number of the men were rising to their feet, grim but determined, but not all.

"We'll die," the Sahrayn sailor said hoarsely.

"Then you will die a martyr." Ali glared at those still sitting. "Stand up!" he roared. "Your fellows lie dead, your women and children are defenseless, and you're sitting here weeping for yourselves? Have you no shame?" He paused, meeting each of their gazes in turn. "You all have a choice. You can end this night a hero, with your families safe, or you end it with them in Paradise, their entrance bought with your blood." He drew his zulfiqar, fire blazing down its length. *"STAND UP!"*

Lubayd raised his sword with a wild—and slightly frightened—cry. "Come, you puffed-up city-born brats!" he goaded. "What happened to all the crowing I've been hearing about your bravery? Don't you want to be sung about in the stories they'll tell of this night? Let's go!"

That brought the rest of them to their feet. "Prepare yourselves," Ali ordered. "Be ready to go as soon as they're distracted."

His heart racing, he shoved his zulfiqar back into its sheath, ripping a length from his ruined dishdasha to secure his blades.

Lubayd grabbed his wrist, pulling him close. "Don't you fucking die, Alizayd al Qahtani," he said, pressing his brow to Ali's. "I did not drag your starving ass from a crevasse to see you eaten by ghouls."

Ali fought the tears pricking his eyes; they both knew there was little chance he was making it off the beach alive. "God be with you, my friend."

He turned away. Before he could show the fear coursing through his blood, before the others could see even a second of hesitation, Ali dove into the lake.

He swam deep, the motion throwing him back into his memory of the marid nightmare. Though the water was dark with silt, he caught sight of the lake bed below. It was muddy and gray, a pale imitation from the lush marine plain of his dream.

Could the marid be behind all this? Ali wondered, remembering their rage. Had they returned to take back their home?

He kept swimming. Ali was fast and it wasn't long before he caught sight of the wall he was looking for. He took care to press himself close against it as he silently broke the water's surface.

Voices. Ali listened closer. He wasn't sure what he expected— the gibberish of some unknown demons, the slithering tongue of the marid—but what he heard froze his blood.

It was Divasti.

They were being attacked by *Daevas*? Ali glanced up, past a narrow lip of overhanging rock, and caught a glimpse of a young man. He looked as though he could be a Daeva, dressed in a charcoal-colored coat and black leggings, the dark colors blending perfectly with the shadows.

How in God's name did a band of Daevas come through the lake armed with ghouls and flying horses?

The Daeva man suddenly drew up, his attention narrowing on the lake. He reached for his bow . . .

Ali was out of the water in the next breath. He pulled himself onto the wall before the shocked eyes of the man, drew his zulfiqar, and plunged the fiery blade into the archer's chest.

The man didn't have a chance to scream. Ali shoved him off the end of his zulfiqar and knocked him into the water. He'd turned to face the others before a splash even sounded.

Daevas, three of them. Another archer—a woman with a long black braid—and two men armed with a broadsword and a mace. They looked taken aback by his arrival, aghast at their comrade's death. But not afraid.

And they reacted a *lot* faster than he would have imagined.

The first drew his broadsword, the acrid smell warning Ali of iron before it sparked hard against his zulfiqar. The man danced back, careful to avoid the poisoned flame. It was a move Ali associated with other Geziris, with warriors who'd trained against zulfiqars.

Where had a Daeva man learned *that*?

Ali ducked, narrowly avoiding the studded mace that swung past his face. The Daevas neatly fanned out to surround him, moving in perfect unison without saying a word.

Then the remaining archer hissed in Djinnistani. "It's the Afshin-slayer." She let out a mocking laugh. "Bit of a disingenuous title, sand fly."

The swordsman lunged forward, forcing Ali to block him, and again the mace-bearer used the distraction to attack. This time the mace clipped Ali's shoulder, the studs tearing out a patch of flesh.

Ali gasped at the burn, and one of the Daeva men leered at him. "They'll eat you alive, you know," he said, gesturing to the ghouls below. "Not us, of course. Orders and all. But I bet they smell *your* blood on the air right now. I bet it's making them ravenous."

The three warriors stepped closer, forcing Ali to the edge of the wall. He didn't know who had trained the Daevas, but they'd done a damn good job, the soldiers moving as if they were of one mind.

But then the swordsman pressed too close. Ali dropped, seeing his opening and lunging at the man holding the mace. He caught him clean across one thigh, the poisoned flames leaving a line of swiftly blackening flesh in their wake.

"Bahram!" the archer cried in horror. The man looked shocked, his hand going to the fatal wound. Then he glanced at Ali, his eyes wild.

"For the Banu Nahida," he whispered and rushed forward.

Caught *completely* off guard by the man's declaration, Ali was ill-prepared for his desperate charge. He raised his zulfiqar in defense, but it didn't matter. The man took the strike through the stomach, throwing himself on Ali and sending them both tumbling over the wall.

Ali landed with a bone-jarring impact on the wet sand. A wave passed over his face, and he choked on the water, his shoulder throbbing. His zulfiqar was gone, stuck in the body of the Daeva man he'd killed, now lying deeper in the shallows.

A high-pitched moan had him struggling to his knees, the hungry whines and tongueless shrieks of the undead ghouls growing louder. Ali turned his head.

His eyes went wide. There were scores of ghouls running for him—some bloated corpses of putrefied flesh and bloody teeth, others reduced to skeletons, their clawed hands sharp as knives. And they were only seconds away from closing in. They'd eat him alive, rip him apart, and be waiting for his friends—the few who survived the archer he saw even now nocking an arrow.

No. This couldn't be their fate. His family, his city. Ali thrust his hands into the wet sand, the water surging through his fingers.

"Help me!" he begged, crying out to the marid. The ancient monsters had already used him; he knew their assistance would come with a terrible price, but right now Ali didn't care. "Please!"

Nothing. The water stayed silent and lifeless. The marid were gone.

But in a small corner of his mind, something stirred. Not the alien presence he expected, but one that was familiar and comforting. The part of Ali that delighted in wading through the flooded fields of Bir Nabat and watching the way the water made life bloom. The memory of the little boy whose mother had carefully taught him to swim. The protective instinct that had saved him from countless assassins.

A part of him that he denied, a power that frightened him. For the first time since falling in the lake that awful night . . . Ali embraced it.

When the next wave broke, the world was quiet. Soft and slow and gray. Suddenly, it didn't matter if he didn't have his zulfiqar at hand. If he was outnumbered.

Because Ali had *everything* else. The water at his feet that was like a deadly, angry animal pacing its cage. The moisture in the air that was thick and heady, coating every surface. The veins of underwater streams that were spikes of power and pulsing life and the springs in the rocky cliffs eager to burst their stony prison.

His fingers curved around the hilt of his khanjar. The ghouls surrounding him suddenly seemed insubstantial smoky nothings, the Daevas not much more. They were fire-blooded, true, burning bright.

But fire could be extinguished.

Ali screamed into the night, and the moisture in the air burst around him, pouring down as rain that licked his wounds, soothing and healing his battered body. With a snap of his fingers, he raised a fog to shroud the beach. He heard the archer cry out, surprised by her sudden blindness.

But Ali wasn't blind. He lunged for his zulfiqar, yanking it from the dead man's body just as the ghouls attacked.

With the zulfiqar in one hand and the khanjar in the other, droplets of water spinning off their wet blades, he cut through the crowd of undead. They kept coming, relentless, two new ghouls pushing through for every one he decapitated. A furious flurry of snapping teeth and bony hands, seaweed wrapping their decayed limbs.

The Daevas on the wall above him ran, the heat from their fire-blooded bodies vanishing. There were others; Ali could sense another trio rushing to join them and five already in the remains of the Citadel. Ten in total, that he knew.

Ali could kill ten men. He cut off the head of the ghoul blocking his path, kicked another in the chest, and then raced after the Daevas.

He stopped to fling his khanjar at the closest, catching the man in the back. Ali plunged it deeper when he caught up, twisting the dagger until the man stopped screaming before yanking it free.

Pounding caught his attention. He glanced back through the gloom he'd conjured to see two archers on smoky horseback racing along the water's edge. One drew back his bowstring.

Ali hissed, calling to the lake. Watery fingers snaked around the horses' legs, dragging the archers into the depths as their enchanted mounts disappeared in a spray of mist. He kept running. Two of the fleeing Daevas stopped, perhaps inspired by a burst of courage to stand their ground and defend their fellows.

Ali put his zulfiqar through the heart of the first, his dagger opening the throat of the second.

Seven men left.

But the ghouls caught up with him as he lunged for the wrecked outer wall of the Citadel, snatching him back as he attempted to climb it. There was a blur of bone, the scent of rot and blood overwhelming as they tore into him. Ali screamed as one bit deeply into his already wounded shoulder. They were everywhere, and his hold on the powerful water magic dipped as panic seized him.

Daevabad, Alizayd, his father's voice whispered. *Daevabad comes first.* Bleeding badly, Ali gave more of himself up, embracing the raw magic coursing so wildly within him that it felt like his body would burst.

He was given a gift in return. The sudden awareness of a rich vein of water beneath him, a hidden stream snaking deep, deep under the sand. Ali called to it, yanking it up like a whip.

Stone and sand and water went flying. Ali lashed it at the ghouls, taking out enough to escape the horde. He scrambled over the ruined Citadel wall.

Another pair of Daevas had been left to deal with him, their bravery rewarded with two swift strikes of his zulfiqar that took their heads. Blood was running down his face, torn patches of flesh burning under his tattered dishdasha.

It didn't matter. Ali dashed toward the breach, arrows raining down on him as he navigated the broken courtyard where he'd first learned to fight. The bodies of his fellow djinn were everywhere, some pierced with arrows, some torn apart by ghouls, others simply crushed in the violent mayhem the lake-beast had unleashed upon the complex. Grief and rage flooded his veins, pushing him on. And though the archers might have been able to see in the summoned fog, one nearly struck true, an arrow tearing past his thigh. Ali gasped.

But he didn't stop.

He vaulted over a ruined pile of sandstone, what he dimly recognized as the sunny diwan in which he'd attempted to teach economics to a bored group of cadets. The swordsman who'd mocked him stood there now, shaking as he raised his blade.

"Demon!" the Daeva screamed. "What the hell are y—"

Ali silenced him with his khanjar.

Four left. He inhaled, taking a moment to survey his surroundings. A glance revealed two archers still standing on the Citadel wall, a position from which they'd be able to easily target the soldiers landing on the beach. The remaining two Daevas had swords in their hands. They were steps from the breach in the Citadel wall that led into the city, a mob of ghouls on their heels.

Ali closed his eyes, dropping his blades, sinking to the ground and plunging his hands into one of the pools of water left by the lake's attack. He could feel his fellows in the distance, the last survivors of the Royal Guard staggering out of the water. But none were close to the Citadel. Not yet.

Good. He called to the lake again, feeling it pace in his mind. It was angry. It wanted vengeance on the stone island marring its heart.

Ali was about to let it take a small piece. He beckoned to the waves lashing the wall. *Come.*

They answered.

The water roared as it crashed over the Citadel, dashing the archers against the stone courtyard. It parted as it neared him, rushing past to grab the ghouls and smash them to bits. A single scream rent the air as it swallowed the last Daevas and raced to the breach, eager to devour the rest of the city.

It took everything Ali had to rein it in. There was a howl in his head, and then he was the one screaming, clawing at the ground as he wrenched the lake back the way it had come. The water fell at his feet, surging into the sand and swirling into ruined, rocky crevices.

His hold on the magic disintegrated and Ali collapsed. Blood and sweat poured from him in equal parts as he sprawled on the ground. His ears were ringing, the scars the marid had carved in his body throbbing. His vision briefly blurred as his muscles seized.

And then he was lying still upon the cold, wet ground. The sky was a rich black, the spread of stars beautiful and inviting.

"Alizayd!"

Though Ali heard Lubayd shout his name, his friend seemed a world away. Everything did, save the beckoning stars and the warm blood spreading beneath him.

There was a crack of thunder. Odd, he dimly noticed, as the night sky was cloudless.

"Ali!" Lubayd's face swam into view above his. "Oh, brother, no . . ." He glanced back. "We need help!"

But the ground was already turning cold again, water seeping up through the sand to embrace him. Ali blinked, his mind a degree clearer. The spots dancing before his eyes faded as well—just in time for Ali to notice an oily black smoke rising behind Lubayd. The tendrils danced, twisting together.

Ali tried to croak out his friend's name. "Lu-Lubay—"

Lubayd hushed him. "It's okay, just hold on. We're going to get you to that Nahid of yours, and you'll be fine." He tucked Ali's zulfiqar back in his belt, and a smile cracked across his face, doing little to erase the worry in his eyes. "Don't you be letting this—"

A jarring, crunching sound stole Lubayd's words. His friend's expression froze and then his body jerked slightly as the crunch came again, a terrible sucking noise. Lubayd opened his mouth as if to speak.

Black blood spilled from his lips. A fiery hand shoved him out of the way, and his friend crumpled.

"By the Creator . . . ," a smoky voice drawled. "What are *you*— you lovely, destructive bit of chaos?"

Ali gaped at the creature looming over him, its clawed hand

clutching a bloody war ax. It was a skinny wraith of a thing, with limbs that looked like pressed light and golden eyes that flared and flashed. And there was only one creature in their world that looked like that.

An ifrit. An ifrit had crossed the veil into Daevabad.

The ifrit seized him by the throat, and Ali gasped as he was lifted into the air. It pulled him close, its glittering eyes inches from Ali's face. The smell of blood and ash washed over Ali as the ifrit ran a tongue over its sharp teeth, unmistakable hunger and curiosity in its feral expression.

It inhaled. "Salt," it whispered. "You're the one the marid took, aren't you?" One of its razor-sharp claws pressed hard against his throat, and Ali got the impression it would be nothing for the demon to rip it open. "But this . . ." He gestured to the ruined courtyard and drowned Daevas. "I've never seen *anything* like this." Its other hand ran down Ali's arm, a quick examination. "Nor anything like the magic simmering off you." The fiery eyes gleamed. "I'd love to take you apart, little one. See how that works, layer by layer . . ."

Ali tried to wrench himself free and caught sight of Lubayd's body, his glassy, unseeing eyes fixed on the sky above. With a choked cry of denial, Ali reached for his zulfiqar.

The ifrit's fingers abruptly tightened on his throat. It clucked its tongue disapprovingly. "None of that now."

"Prince Alizayd!"

As Ali grappled with the iron grip the demon had on his throat, he glimpsed a band of men running in the distance: the rest of the survivors from the Royal Guard.

"*Prince?*" the ifrit repeated. He shook his head, disappointed. "A shame. There's another after you, and he's got a temper even *I* won't cross." He sighed. "Hold on. This is most *certainly* going to hurt."

There was no time to react. A searing bolt of heat raced over

Ali, consuming them both in a swirl of fire and sickly green clouds. Thunder crashed in his ear, shaking his very bones. The beach vanished and the cries of his men fell away, replaced by the blur of rooftops and the roar of the wind.

And then it was gone. They crashed, and the ifrit released him. Ali landed hard, sprawled on a stone floor. Disoriented, he tried to stand, but nausea rose, swift and fierce inside his roiling stomach, and it was everything Ali could do not to vomit. Instead, he squeezed his eyes shut, trying to catch his breath.

When he opened them again, the first thing he saw was the familiar doors of his father's office. They'd been torn off their hinges, the room ransacked and set ablaze.

Ali was too late.

The ifrit who'd murdered Lubayd was striding away. Still dizzy, Ali tried to track his movement, the scene coming to him in pieces. A knot of young warriors dressed in the same mottled black uniforms of the Daevas on the beach surrounded another man, their commander perhaps. He stood with his back to Ali, barking out what sounded like orders in Divasti.

An enormous silver bow, horribly familiar, was strung across his broad shoulders.

Ali jerked his head in denial, sure he was dreaming.

"Have I got a prize for *you*," the ifrit crowed to the Daeva commander, jerking a thumb back at Ali. "This is the prince your Banu Nahida is after, yes? The one we're supposed to lock away?"

The Daeva commander whirled around, and Ali's heart stopped. The cold green eyes from his nightmares, the black tattoo that declared his position to the world . . .

"It is not," Darayavahoush e-Afshin said in a low, lethal voice. His eyes blazed, a flicker of fire-yellow beneath the green. "But he will do just fine."

37

DARA

Dara had taken two steps toward Alizayd before he stopped himself, hardly believing the blood-covered Ayaanle man before him could be the self-righteous royal brat he'd sparred with in Daevabad years ago. He'd grown up, losing the childish hint to his features that had stayed Dara's hand from ending that match in a more lethal manner. He also looked terrible, like something Vizaresh might have fished from the lake, half dead. His dishdasha hung in soaked rags, his limbs covered in bleeding gashes and bite marks.

His eyes, though—they were the Geziri gray Dara remembered. His father's eyes, Zaydi al Qahtani's eyes, and if Dara doubted it, the zulfiqar hanging at Alizayd's waist was confirmation enough.

The prince had pushed himself to a sitting position. He seemed thoroughly disoriented, his dazed eyes sweeping over Dara in shock.

"But you're dead," he whispered, sounding stunned. "I killed you."

Anger surged into Dara's blood, and he clenched his hands into smoldering fists. "Remember that, do you?" He was struggling to hold on to his mortal form, aching to submit to the flames that wanted to consume him.

Nahri's hands on his face. *We'll leave. We'll travel the world.* Dara had been close, so close to escaping all this.

And then Alizayd al Qahtani gave himself to the marid.

"Afshin?" the tentative voice of Laleh, his youngest recruit, broke through his haze. "Did you want me to lead my group to the harem?"

Dara exhaled. His soldiers. His duty. "Hold him," he said flatly to Vizaresh. He would deal with Alizayd al Qahtani himself, but only after giving his warriors their orders. "And take that damned zulfiqar off him immediately."

He turned around, briefly squeezing his eyes shut. Instead of the blackness of his closed lids, Dara saw through five sets of eyes, those of the smoky beasts he'd conjured from his blood and let loose with each group of warriors. He caught a reassuring glimpse of Manizheh—who'd insisted on separating from them immediately to head for the infirmary—riding atop the galloping karkadann he'd shaped for her.

The creatures pulled hard on his consciousness, the magic wearing on him. He would need to give up his mortal form soon, even if it was only to recover.

"Break apart," he said in Divasti. "You heard the Banu Nahida. Our first priority is finding the grand wazir and Ghassan's body. Laleh, your group will search the harem. Gushtap, take yours to the pavilion on the roof that Kaveh mentioned." He eyed them. "I expect you to remember yourselves. Do what's necessary to secure the palace and keep our people safe, but no more." He paused. "Such mercy does not extend to any survivors you spot from the Royal Guard. Kill them at once. Do not give them a chance to draw their blades. Do not give *any* man a chance to draw a blade."

Gushtap opened his mouth, saying, "But most men wear weapons."

Dara stared at him. "My order remains."

The other warrior bowed his head. Dara waited until his soldiers had vanished before turning back around.

Vizaresh had taken Alizayd's zulfiqar and was holding it near the prince's throat, though the bleeding djinn didn't look capable of putting up much of a fight; he didn't even look like he could stand. The realization made Dara pause. It was one thing to cut down a hated enemy in combat; executing a wounded young man who could barely keep his eyes open was another matter.

He is dangerous. Rid yourself of him. Dara freed the short sword at his side. And then he abruptly stopped, taking in the sight of the soaked prince more carefully.

Bite marks. He whirled on Vizaresh. "You were supposed to be with my soldiers and your ghouls at the beach. Have they secured what remains of the Citadel?"

Vizaresh shook his head. "Your soldiers are dead," he said bluntly. "And my ghouls are gone. There was no point in staying. The djinn were already retaking the beach."

Dara stared at him in disbelief. He'd looked upon the ruins of the Citadel himself and sent his warriors in with a hundred ghouls. They should have been more than a match for whatever survivors remained. "That cannot be." He narrowed his eyes and then lunged at Vizaresh. "Did *you* abandon them?" he snarled.

The ifrit raised his hands in mock surrender. "No, fool. You've *this* one to blame for killing your warriors," he said, jerking his head in Alizayd's direction. "He had command of the lake as if he were marid himself. I'd never seen anything like it."

Dara reeled. He'd sent a dozen of his best to the beach. He'd sent *Irtemiz* to that beach.

And Alizayd al Qahtani had killed them all with marid magic. He shoved Vizaresh aside.

Alizayd finally staggered up, lurching toward the ifrit as if to grab his zulfiqar.

He didn't make it. Dara struck him across the face, hard enough that he heard bones crack. Alizayd fell sprawling to the floor, blood pouring from his shattered nose.

Too angry to hold his form, Dara let his magic loose. Fire swept down his limbs, claws and fangs bursting from his skin. He barely noticed.

Alizayd certainly did. He cried out in shock, crawling backward as Dara approached again. Good. Let Zaydi's spawn die in terror. But it wouldn't be with magic. No, Dara was going to put metal through this man's throat and watch him bleed. He grabbed Alizayd by his torn collar, raising his blade.

"*Wait.*" Vizaresh's voice was so softly urgent that it cut through the haze of Dara's rage.

Dara stopped. "*What?*" he spat, turning to look over his shoulder.

"Would you really kill the man who cut you down before your Nahri and slaughtered your young soldiers?" Vizaresh drawled.

"Yes!" Dara snapped. "That's *exactly* what I'm going to do."

Vizaresh stepped closer. "You'd give your enemy the very peace you've been denied?"

Smoke curled past Dara's hands, heat rising in his face. "Are you looking to join him? I do not have patience for your damned riddles right now, Vizaresh!"

"No riddles, Darayavahoush." Vizaresh pulled the metal chain out from under his bronze chest plate. "Merely another option."

Dara's eyes locked on the emerald rings that hung from the chain. He caught his breath.

"Give him to me," Vizaresh whispered in Divasti. "You know his name, do you not? You can take the killing blow yourself and obey Manizheh, but let me take his soul first." He drew nearer, his voice a low purr. "Take the vengeance you deserve. You've been denied the peace of death. Why should your enemy be granted it at your hands?"

Dara's fingers shook on the knife, his breath coming fast. Manizheh was getting her revenge on Ghassan; why shouldn't Dara have his? Was it any worse than what they were already doing? What he had already done?

Alizayd must have realized something was wrong. His gaze darted between Dara and the ifrit, finally dropping to the chain of slave rings.

His eyes went wide. *Wild*, sheer terror coursing through them. He jerked back with a gasp, trying to tear himself from Dara's grip, but Dara easily held on, pinning him hard to the ground and pressing the blade to his throat.

Alizayd shouted, writhing against them. "Get off me!" he screamed, seemingly heedless of the knife against his neck. "Get off me, you—"

With a single brutal motion, Vizaresh grabbed the prince's head and slammed his skull into the ground. Alizayd instantly fell silent, his dazed eyes rolling back.

Vizaresh let out an annoyed sigh. "I swear, these djinn make even more noise than humans, though I suppose that's what happens when you live too close to those earth-blooded insects." He reached for Alizayd's hand, slipping the ring over his thumb.

"Stop," Dara whispered.

The ifrit glared at him, his fingers still closed around the ring. "You said he wasn't the prince you were after. I have not touched any of your people. You can give me this one."

But if the cold way Vizaresh had smashed the young prince's head into the floor—indeed, as one might swat a fly—had already pulled Dara back to himself, the angry possessiveness in the ifrit's voice made him recoil. Was that how Qandisha had thought of him? A possession, a toy to enjoy, to toss to humans as a plaything, only to delight in the chaos it would cause?

Yes. We are the ancestors of the people who betrayed them. The daevas who chose to humble themselves before Suleiman, to let a human forever transform them. To the ifrit, his people—djinn and Daeva alike—were an anathema. An abomination.

And Dara had been a fool to ever forget that. However he'd been brought back to life, he was no ifrit. He would not allow them to enslave another djinn's soul.

"No," Dara said again, revulsion coursing through him. "Get that disgusting thing off him. *Now*," he demanded when Vizaresh didn't move. Instead of obeying, the ifrit jerked up, his attention caught by something behind them. Dara followed his gaze.

His heart stopped.

38

NAHRI

"Are you sure this leads back to the outer wall?" Nahri whispered as she and Muntadhir crept through the twisting servants' passage. Save for a bit of fire she'd conjured, it was entirely dark.

"I've told you twice," Muntadhir replied snippily. "Which of us spent our entire life here again?"

"Which of us used this to sneak into random bedrooms?" Nahri muttered back, ignoring the annoyed look he threw her. "What, am I wrong?"

He rolled his eyes. "This passage ends soon, but we can take the next corridor all the way to the east end and access the outer steps there."

Nahri nodded. "So, Suleiman's seal . . . ," she started, trying for a light tone. "How do we retrieve it? Do we have to carve it from your father's face or—"

Muntadhir made a choking sound. "My God, Nahri, really?"

"You were the one who got all queasy when you first brought it up!"

He shook his head. "Are you going to stick a dagger in my back and run off the moment I tell you?"

"If you keep saying things like that, very possibly." Nahri sighed. "Can we try being on the same side for *one* night?"

"Fine," Muntadhir grumbled. "I suppose someone else *should* know, all things considered." He took a deep breath. "It has nothing to do with his cheek; the mark shows up there once the ring is taken."

"The ring? Suleiman's seal is on a ring?" Nahri thought back to the jewels she'd seen adorning Ghassan over the past five years. Quietly assessing the valuables another person was wearing was a bit of her specialty. "Is it the ruby he wears on his thumb?" she guessed.

Muntadhir's expression was grim. "It's not on his hand," he replied. "It's in his heart. We have to cut it out and burn it. The ring re-forms from the ash."

Nahri stopped dead in her tracks. "We have to do *what*?"

"Please don't make me repeat it." Muntadhir looked ill. "The ring re-forms, you put it on your hand, and that's that. My father said it can take a few days to recover from the magic. And then you're trapped in Daevabad forever," he added darkly. "Now do you see why I was in no hurry to be king?"

"What do you mean, you're *trapped in Daevabad*?" Nahri asked, her mind racing.

"I didn't ask." When she stared at him in disbelief, he threw up his hands. "Nahri, I don't think I was older than eight when he told me all of this. I was more preoccupied with trying not to be sick in terror than with interrogating him about the exact strings attached to wearing a ring I was supposed to pull from his bloody corpse. What he told me was that the ring can't leave

the city. So unless someone is willing to leave their heart behind . . .”

"How poetic," she muttered as they continued moving down
the dim passageway.

He stopped outside the grimy, barely visible contours of a
door. "We're here."

Nahri hovered at his shoulder as he gently eased it open. They
stepped into the darkness.

Her face fell. A Geziri woman in a steward's robe lay dead on
the stone floor, blood running from her ears.

"The poison has been through here," she said softly. This
wasn't the first body they'd found. Though they'd been able to
warn a handful of Geziri nobles, they were finding far more dead
than alive: soldiers with their zulfiqars still sheathed, a scholar
with scrolls scattered around her, and—most heartbreaking—a
pair of young boys in feast clothing, clutching unlit sparklers in
their hands, tendrils of the hazy copper vapor still clinging to
their small feet.

Muntadhir closed the woman's eyes. "I'm going to give Kaveh
to the karkadann," he whispered savagely. "I swear on my father's
name."

Nahri shivered; she couldn't argue with that. "Let's keep
going."

They'd no sooner stood up than Nahri heard footsteps. At
least three people were approaching from around the bend. With
no time to duck back inside the passage, they swiftly pressed
into a darkened niche in the wall. Shadows rushed over them, a
protective response from the palace, just as several figures came
around the bend.

Her heart dropped. Daevas, all of them. Young and unfamiliar, they were clad in uniforms of mottled gray and black. They
were also quite well-armed, looking more than capable of taking
on the emir and his wife. It was a conclusion Muntadhir must

have come to as well, for he made no move to confront them and stayed quiet until they had vanished.

Finally, he cleared his throat. "I think your tribe is conducting a coup."

Nahri swallowed. "It does seem that way," she said shakily.

Muntadhir looked down at her. "Still on my side?"

Her gaze fell on the murdered woman. "I'm on the side that doesn't unleash things like that."

They kept walking, following the deserted corridor. Nahri's heart was racing, and she didn't dare speak, especially since it was now clear there were enemies creeping through the palace. An occasional scream or abruptly cut-off warning broke the air, carried through the echoing halls of the labyrinthine royal complex.

A strange buzz swept her skin, and Nahri shivered. It was an oddly familiar feeling, but she couldn't place it. She moved her hand to one of her daggers as they continued. She could hear the beat of her heart in her head, a steady pounding. Like the tap-tap-tap of a warning.

Muntadhir threw out his arm. There was a muffled cry in the distance.

"Get off me!"

He gasped. "Nahri, that sounds like—"

But she was already running. There was the sound of arguing, another voice, but she barely heard it. She threw up her arm as they rounded the corner; the sudden light was blinding after so much time stealing through the dark.

But the light wasn't coming from torches or conjured flames. It was coming from two ifrit who had Ali pinned to the ground.

Nahri jerked to a halt, stifling a scream. Ali was a bloody wreck, lying too still beneath a large ifrit inexplicably dressed in the same uniform as the Daeva soldiers and holding a knife to the prince's throat. A skinnier ifrit in a bronze chest plate was clutching Ali's hand, holding the prince's wrist at what must have been a painful angle.

Both ifrit turned to stare at the royal couple. Nahri gasped when she spotted the green gem gleaming on one of Ali's fingers.

A ring. An emerald slave ring.

The ifrit dressed in Daeva clothing opened his mouth, his eyes flashing brighter. "Nah—"

She didn't let him finish. Fury flooding through her, she dragged her dagger hard across her palm, breaking the skin. Then she charged forward, throwing herself on him without hesitation.

She and the ifrit tumbled backward together, Nahri landing on his chest. She raised the bloody dagger, trying to plunge it into his throat, but he easily knocked it out of her hand, his own knife still in one of his.

She scrambled for it, but he was stronger. He let the knife go and it clattered to the floor as he grabbed her wrists and then rolled her over, pinning her beneath him.

Nahri screamed. The ifrit's fiery eyes met hers, and she caught her breath, startled by what looked like grief swirling in the depths of their alien color.

And then the scorching yellow vanished, his eyes turning the shade of green that haunted her dreams. Black curls sprouted from his smoky scalp, and the fiery light was snuffed from his face, leaving his skin a luminescent light brown. An ebony tattoo marked his temple: an arrow crossed with the wing of a shedu.

Dara stared back at her, his face inches from hers. The scent of cedar and burnt citrus tickled her nose, and then he spoke one word, one word that left his lips like a prayer.

"*Nahri.*"

NAHRI HOWLED, SOMETHING RAW AND SAVAGE RIPPING through her. "Stop!" she screamed, writhing underneath him. "Get rid of that face or I'll kill you!"

He held her hands tight as she attempted to claw at his throat. "Nahri, stop!" the ifrit cried. "It's me, I swear!"

His voice shattered her. God, it even sounded like him. But that was impossible. *Impossible.* Nahri had watched Dara die. She'd raked her hands through his ashes.

This was a trick. An ifrit trick. Her skin crawling at his touch, Nahri tried to twist free again, spotting her bloody dagger near her feet.

"Zaydi!" Muntadhir flew to his brother's side only to be promptly thrown across the corridor by the second ifrit. He smashed hard into one of the delicate fountains, water and glass bursting around him.

Thinking fast and desperate to get the ifrit off her, Nahri brought her knee up hard where his legs met his body.

He gasped, his still-green eyes lighting with pain and surprise, and jerked back enough for her to scramble free. A glance revealed Muntadhir back on his feet, running for Ali as the younger prince slowly rolled over, blood streaming down his face. The second ifrit reached for the war ax hanging across his back . . .

"*STOP!*" The corridor trembled, echoing with the first ifrit's command. "Vizaresh, stand down," he snapped as he climbed to his feet. The second ifrit instantly did so, stepping back from the Qahtani brothers with a splash, the water from the broken fountain puddling at his feet.

The ifrit wearing Dara's guise turned back to Nahri, his gaze imploring. "Nahri," he choked out, her name leaving his mouth like it caused him pain. He took a step toward her, reaching out like he wanted to take her hand.

"Don't touch me!" The sound of his voice was physically painful; it was everything she could do not to cover her ears. "I don't know who you are, but I'll blood-poison you if you don't change your appearance."

The ifrit fell to his knees before her, bringing his hands up in the Daeva blessing. "Nahri, it's me. I swear on my parents' ashes. I found you in a Cairo cemetery. I told you my name in the ruins of Hierapolis." The same hollow grief swirled into his eyes. "You kissed me in the caves above the Gozan." His voice broke. "Twice."

Her heart twisted, fierce denial running through her. "It's not." A sob tore from her chest. "You're dead. *You're dead.* I watched it happen!"

He swallowed, sadness rippling across his face as his haunted eyes drank her in. "I was. But no one seems content to leave me in that state."

Nahri swayed on her feet, jerking back when he moved to help her. Too many pieces were coming together in her head. Kaveh's careful treachery. The well-armed Daeva soldiers.

Dara. The dashing warrior who'd taken her hand in Cairo and spirited her away to a land of legend. Her broken Afshin, driven to destruction by the crushing politics of the city he couldn't save.

He spoke again. "I'm sorry, Nahri." That he seemingly registered whatever little change was in her expression—for Nahri didn't easily give up her mask—was its own proof.

"What *are* you?" she whispered, unable to conceal the horror in her voice. "Are you . . . are you one of *them* now?" She jerked her head toward the ifrit, almost afraid to hear the answer.

"No!" Dara closed the distance between them and took her hands, his fingers hot against hers. Nahri did not have it in her to pull away; it looked like it was costing Dara everything not to grab her and *run* away. "Creator, no! I . . . I am a daeva," he said faintly, as though the words made him ill. "But as our people once were. I am free of Suleiman's curse."

The answer made no sense. *None* of this made any sense. Nahri felt as though she'd stumbled upon a mirage, a mad hallucination.

Dara drew her closer, reaching for her cheek. "I am sorry. I wanted to tell you, to come straight away—" His voice turned desperate. "I could not cross the threshold. I could not come back for you." He rushed on, his words growing more incomprehensible. "But it is going to be okay, I promise you. She is going to set it all right. Our people will be free and—"

"Fuck," Muntadhir swore. "It is you. Only you would come back from the dead a second time and immediately start another damn war."

Dara's eyes flashed, and ice stole into Nahri's heart. "You're working with Kaveh," she whispered. "Does that mean . . ." Her stomach twisted. "The poison killing the Geziris . . ." *No, please no.* "Did you know?"

He dropped his gaze, looking sick with regret. "You were not supposed to see it. You were supposed to be with Nisreen. Safe. Protected." He said the words frantically, as though trying to convince himself as much as her.

Nahri jerked free of his grip. "Nisreen is *dead.*" She stared at Dara, aching to see a glimmer of the laughing warrior who'd teased her on a flying carpet and sighed as she kissed him in the quiet dark of a secluded cave. "The things they say about you are true, aren't they?" she asked, her voice thick with rising dread. "About Qui-zi? About the war?"

She wasn't sure what she expected: denial, shame, perhaps overly righteous anger. But the flicker of resentment that flared in his eyes—that took her by surprise.

"Of course they are true," he said tonelessly. He touched the mark on his brow, a grim salute. "I am the weapon the Nahids made me. Nothing more, nothing less, and apparently for all of eternity."

With his usual poor timing, Ali chose that moment to speak. "Oh, yes," he croaked from where he sat on the floor, leaning heavily against his brother. His gray eyes were wild with grief, standing out starkly against his blood-covered face. "You poor, pitiful murdering—"

Muntadhir clapped a hand over Ali's mouth, but it was too late.

Dara whirled on the Qahtani princes. "What did you say to me, you filthy little hypocrite?"

"Nothing," Muntadhir said quickly, clearly struggling to keep his brother's mouth shut.

But Ali had drawn their attention . . . though it wasn't his words that held it.

The water from the broken fountains was *rushing* for him. It streamed across the floor, surging into his bloody clothes, tiny rivulets dancing over his hands. Ali seemed to suck for breath, dipping his head as the air abruptly cooled.

Then he jerked his head back up, the movement unnaturally sharp. An oily black mingled with the gray in his eyes.

There was a moment of shocked silence. "I did try to tell you," the ifrit spoke up, "that there was something a little different about him."

Dara was staring at Ali with naked hate. "It is nothing I cannot handle." He stepped away from Nahri. "Vizaresh, take the emir and the Banu Nahida away. I will join you in a moment." His voice softened. "They do not need to see this."

Nahri sprang up to stop him. "No!"

She didn't even get close. Dara snapped his fingers, and a burst of smoke wrapped her body, tight as rope.

"Dara!" Nahri tripped, falling hard to her knees, stunned that he'd used magic against her. "Dara, stop, I beg you! I *order* you!" she tried, pulling desperately for her own power. There was a rumble from the ancient bricks. "*Afshin!*"

Fire licked down Dara's arms. "I am truly sorry, Nahri," Dara said, and she could hear it, the heartbreak in his voice. "But yours are not the orders I follow anymore." He started after Ali.

Ali staggered to his feet, shoving Muntadhir behind him.

The oily color flashed across his eyes again, and then his zulfiqar flew to his hand, a burst of water behind it like he'd cut through a wave. Flames licked down the copper blade.

Vizaresh hadn't moved to follow Dara's command. He looked between them now, his wary yellow eyes taking in the two warriors.

Then he shook his head. "No, Darayavahoush. You fight this one on your own. I will not quarrel with one the marid have chosen to bless so." Without another word, he vanished in a crack of thunder.

Ali rushed forward. As Nahri cried out, he raised his zulfiqar . . .

And then he fell back, as though he'd smashed into an invisible barrier. He stumbled, looking stunned, but without hesitation, gathered himself and sprang forward again.

This time, the barrier knocked him back completely.

Dara hissed. "Yes, your marid masters couldn't do that either." He lunged at the prince, ripping the zulfiqar from Ali's hands. The flames soaring as if he were a Geziri man himself, Dara swung it up. Nahri screamed again, writhing against the smoky binds as the magic of the palace built in her blood.

Muntadhir hurled himself between Ali and the zulfiqar.

There was the smell of blood and burning flesh. A flash of pain in her husband's eyes and then a wail from Ali, a sound so raw it didn't seem real.

Rage ripped through her. And just like that, her magic was there. The smoky binds that had dared to confine her—her, in her own damned palace—abruptly burst apart, and Nahri inhaled, suddenly aware of every brick and stone and mote of dust in the building around her. The walls erected by her ancestors, the floors that had run black with their blood.

The corridor shook, hard enough to send the plaster crumbling from the ceiling. Flames twisted around her fingers, smoke curling past *her* collar. Her clothes flapping madly in the hot breeze spinning out from her body, she raised her hands.

Dara turned to her. She could both see him and *sense* him, standing bright and furious on the edge of her magic.

Nahri threw him across the corridor.

He hit the wall hard enough to leave a dent in the stone and crumpled to the floor. A piece of her heart broke at the sight, still traitorously linked to the man who kept finding new ways to shatter it.

And then Dara got back up.

Their gazes met. Dara looked stunned. Betrayed. And yet, still grimly determined, a warrior committed. He touched the golden blood dripping down his face and then threw his hand out, a wave of black smoke wrapping his body. There was a glimmer of scales and flash of teeth as it doubled in size.

In an explosion of plaster and stone, Nahri brought the ceiling down on him.

She collapsed as the dust rose around her, the magic draining.

Ali's screams brought her back. Pushing aside the grief threatening to tear her open, Nahri staggered to her feet. Muntadhir had fallen to his knees, leaning against his brother. Blood was spreading across his dishdasha.

Nahri ran to him, ripping open the cloth. Tears sprang to her eyes. Had he been attacked with anything but a zulfiqar, Nahri would have breathed a sigh of relief; it was a clean gash stretching across his stomach, and though it was bloody, it wasn't deep.

But none of that mattered. Because the skin around the wound was already a sick blackish green, the color of some awful storm. And it was spreading, delicate tendrils tracing the lines of veins and nerves.

Muntadhir let out a dismayed sound. "Oh," he whispered, his hands shaking as he touched the wound. "Suppose that's ironic."

"No. No, no, no," Ali stammered the word as if the whispered denial would undo the awful scene before them. "Why did you do that? Dhiru, *why did you do that?*"

Muntadhir reached out to touch his brother's face, the blood from his hands staining Ali's skin. "I'm sorry, akhi," he replied weakly. "I couldn't watch him kill you. Not again."

Tears ran down Ali's face. "It's going to be okay," he stammered. "N-Nahri will heal you."

Muntadhir shook his head. "Don't," he said, clenching his jaw as she reached for him. "We all know you'll be wasting time."

"Would you let me at least *try*?" she begged, her voice breaking on the word.

Muntadhir bit his lip, looking like he was struggling to hide his own fear. He nodded, a small motion.

Nahri instantly spread her hands, concentrating on the pulse and heat of her husband's body, and yet she'd no sooner done so than she realized the futility of it. She couldn't heal his torn flesh and poisoned blood, because she couldn't sense the wound. His body seemed to end where the darkening flesh began, its edges pushing back at her consciousness as it advanced. It was worse than her struggles with Jamshid, worse even than her desperate fight to save Nisreen. Nahri—who'd just thrown a man across the room and conjured a sandstorm—could do nothing to fight the zulfiqar's poison.

Muntadhir gently pushed her hands away. "Nahri, stop. You don't have time for this."

"We have time," Ali cut in. "Just try again. Try harder!"

"*You don't have time.*" Muntadhir's voice was firm. "Zaydi, look at me. I need you to listen and not react. Abba is dead. You need to go with Nahri and retrieve Suleiman's seal. She knows how."

Ali's mouth fell open, but before he could speak, there was a rumble from the pile of debris.

Muntadhir paled. "Impossible. You dropped a damned ceiling on him."

Another rumble seemed to answer, dust and plaster shivering.

Ali reached for his brother. "We need to get you out of here."

"That's not happening." Muntadhir took a steadying breath and then pushed himself into a seated position. He glanced around, his gaze settling on an object glimmering in the dust.

A silver bow.

A hint of vindictiveness flitted across his face. "Nahri, would you hand me that bow and see if you can't find the quiver?"

Feeling sick, she nonetheless complied. She knew in her heart whose bow this was. "What are you doing?" she asked as he staggered to his feet holding the bow, determination and pain etched across his features.

Muntadhir swayed, pulling free his khanjar. He beckoned Ali closer and then shoved it in his brother's belt. "Buying you time." He coughed, then nodded at the khanjar. "Take that and your zulfiqar, akhi. Fight well."

Ali didn't move. He suddenly looked very young. "Dhiru, I . . . I can't leave you," he said, his voice trembling, as if this was something he could argue away. "I'm supposed to protect you," he whispered. "I'm supposed to be your Qaid."

Muntadhir gave him a sad smile. "I'm pretty sure that means you have to do as I say." His expression softened. "It's okay, Zaydi. We're okay." He nocked an arrow, something broken in his face even as he winked. "Hell, I think this means I might even make it to your Paradise."

Tears were running unchecked down Ali's cheeks. Nahri quietly picked up his zulfiqar and then stepped forward, taking his hand. She met Muntadhir's eyes, a look of understanding passing between them. "We'll get Suleiman's seal," she promised. "And I'll find Jamshid. You have my word."

At that, Muntadhir's eyes finally grew damp. "Thank you," he said quietly. "Please tell him . . . " He took a deep breath, rocking back slightly, obviously struggling to gather himself. When his gaze met hers again, there was a mix of regret and apology there. "Please tell him I loved him. Tell him I'm sorry I didn't stand up for him sooner." He wiped his eyes with his sleeve and then drew up, looking away. "Now go. I can count my short reign a success if I manage to convince the two most stubborn people in Daevabad to do something they don't want to do."

Nahri nodded, her own vision clouding as she dragged Ali away.

"Dhiru," he choked out again. "Akhi, please . . ."

The rubble gave a giant shake and then a horrible, heart-wrenchingly familiar—and very angry—roar.

"*Go!*" Muntadhir shouted.

They ran.

39

DARA

Agony, the kind of pain Dara hadn't felt since being dragged back to life, was the first thing he was aware of. Crushed limbs and broken teeth, torn flesh and a throbbing in his head so strong he nearly wanted to succumb back to the blackness.

He twitched his fingers, feeling the rough stone and splintered wood beneath them. His eyes blearily winked open, but Dara saw nothing but darkness. He grunted, trying to free the arm twisted painfully underneath him.

He couldn't move. He was pressed in, crushed from all sides.

Nahri. *She brought the ceiling down on me. She actually brought the* ceiling *down on me.* He'd been shocked by the sight of her looking like some sort of wrathful goddess, smoke twisting around her hands, her black curls blowing wildly in the scorching wind she'd summoned. She'd looked like a Nahid icon he might have bowed to in the Temple.

But the hurt in her eyes, the betrayal . . . that was the woman from Cairo.

You are going to be risking the woman you actually serve if you do not get out of here. The thought of Manizheh and his mission was enough to get Dara moving again, pain be damned. The fate of Daevabad hung in the balance. He inhaled, catching the smoky scent of blood as he struggled to free himself.

His blood. *Creator, no.* Dara closed his eyes, reaching out, but there was nothing.

He'd lost his hold on the conjured blood beasts. Suleiman's eye, there'd been half a dozen. Karkadann and zahhak and rukh. They were mindless, destructive things when they escaped his control, a lesson he'd learned early in his training with the ifrit. And now they were wild at the side of his warriors and Manizheh.

Swearing under his breath, Dara tried to wrench free but only succeeded in shaking the debris nearest him and making his body ache worse.

Embrace what you are, you fool. The brief moments he'd spent in his other form had been an instant balm. Dara needed that power.

The fire sparked in his blood, flushing through his skin. His senses sharpened, claws and fangs sprouting. He touched the crumbling bricks above his head, and they exploded into dust.

He climbed out far more slowly than he liked, his body stiff and the pain still present. It was a frightening reminder: Dara was strong but not invincible. He finally hauled himself out of the ruin, coughing on dust and trying to catch his breath.

An arrow tore through his arm. Dara yelped in surprise, hissing as his hand flew to the wound.

The arrow jutting out of it was one of his own.

A second one flitted past his face, and Dara jerked back just before it went through his eye. He flung himself behind a ruined piece of masonry, peering through the rubble.

Muntadhir al Qahtani was shooting at him with his own bow. Dara spat in outrage. *How dare that lecherous, dishonorable wretch—* An arrow flew at his hiding spot.

Dara ducked, cursing out loud. Had he not struck Muntadhir with the zulfiqar? And since when did some sand fly know how to handle a Daeva bow that way?

Gritting his teeth, Dara broke the fletch off the arrow in his arm and then yanked it out, biting back a grunt of pain. His fiery skin closed over the wound, leaving a black scar like a line of charcoal. That it healed was a small relief, but Dara tipped his arrows in iron, and he'd just had a very necessary reminder of the limits of his body. He didn't want to learn what would happen if Muntadhir managed to catch him somewhere more vulnerable than his arm.

Why don't you try shooting in the dark, djinn? Dara pressed his hands to the pile of debris, urging the wood to burst into flame. It burned dark, the oily paints and ancient masonry sending up a choking wall of thick, black smoke that Dara directed toward the emir.

He waited until he heard coughing and then shot to his feet, staying low as he charged. Muntadhir sent another arrow spinning in his direction, but Dara ducked and was wrenching the bow from the other man's hands before he could shoot a second. He used it to backhand the emir across the face, sending him to the floor.

Dara was on him the next second. He banished the smoke. The front of Muntadhir's dishdasha was ripped open and his stomach bloodied, the dark green lines and cracking ash around the wound grisly confirmation that Dara had indeed struck him with the zulfiqar.

Nahri and Alizayd were nowhere to be seen. "Where are they?" Dara demanded. "Your brother and the Banu Nahida?"

Muntadhir spat in his face. "Fuck you, Scourge."

Dara put a knee against Muntadhir's wound, and the emir gasped. *"WHERE ARE THEY?"*

Tears were rolling down the other man's face, but Dara had to give him his due—he held his tongue even as his eyes blazed in pain.

Dara thought fast. Nahri and Alizayd were clever. Where would they go?

"Suleiman's seal," he whispered. Dara immediately drew away his knee, remembering his mission. "Is that where they went? Where is it?"

"In hell," Muntadhir choked out. "Why don't you go look for it? You must be a frequent visitor."

It took all of Dara's self-control not to throttle the other man. He needed Muntadhir's help. And Qahtani or not, Muntadhir had stayed behind with a painful, fatal wound so his little brother and wife could escape.

He leaned closer to Muntadhir. "Your people have lost; I will be catching up with your brother either way. Tell me how to retrieve Suleiman's seal and Alizayd dies quickly. Painlessly. On my honor."

Muntadhir laughed. "You have no honor. You brought an *ifrit* into our city. There are Geziri children who should be lighting fireworks now lying dead in the palace because of you."

Dara recoiled, trying to reach for the justifications Manizheh had offered. "And how many Daeva children died when your people invaded? Far more than the Geziri children who will be lost tonight."

Muntadhir stared at him in shock. "Do you *hear* yourself? What sort of man plots that calculus?" Hate filled his gray eyes. "God, I hope it's her in the end. I hope Nahri puts a goddamned knife through whatever passes for your heart."

Dara looked away. Nahri had certainly seemed capable of

that, glaring at him from across the corridor with flames whipping around her hands as if he were a monster.

She was wrong. She doesn't understand. This mission *had* to be right, it had to succeed. Everything Dara had done for his people, from Qui-zi through tonight's attack, could not be for nothing.

He refocused on Muntadhir. "I know you know what happened to my little sister when Daevabad fell. You took pains to remind me when last we met. Give *your* little brother an easier death."

"I don't believe you," Muntadhir whispered, but Dara's words seemed to have an effect, worry creasing the emir's face. "You hate him. You'll hurt him."

"I'll swear on Nahri's life," Dara replied swiftly. "Tell me how to retrieve Suleiman's seal, and I'll grant Alizayd mercy."

Muntadhir didn't speak, his eyes searching Dara's face. "All right," he finally said. "You'll have to get the ring first." His breathing was becoming more ragged. "The palace library. Go to the catacombs beneath. There's a—" He gave a shuddering cough. "A staircase you'll need to take."

"And then?"

"Follow it. It's quite deep; it will go for a long time. You should feel it getting warmer." Muntadhir grimaced, curling in slightly on his stomach.

"And after?" Dara prompted, growing impatient and a little panicked. He wasn't going to lose time going after Nahri and Alizayd only to have Muntadhir die before giving him an answer.

Muntadhir frowned, looking slightly confused. "Is that not the way back to hell? I assumed you wanted to go home."

Dara's hands were at Muntadhir's throat the next moment. The emir's eyes shone feverishly, locking on Dara's in a last moment of defiance.

Of triumph.

Dara instantly let go. "You . . . you are trying to trick me into killing you."

Muntadhir coughed again, blood flecking his lips. "Astonishing. You must have been quite the brilliant tactician in your—ah!" he screamed as Dara kneed his wound again.

But Dara's heart was racing, his emotions a mess. He didn't have time to waste torturing a dying man for information he was loath to give up.

He drew back his knee, looking again at the smoking green-black edges of Muntadhir's wound. This was not the fatal strike that had felled Mardoniye so quickly. It was the zulfiqar's poison that would take the emir, not the cut itself.

How fortunate then, that Muntadhir had been delivered to a man who knew intimately how long such a death could take. Dara had nursed more friends than he cared to recall through their last moments, easing their seizing limbs and listening to their suffering last gasps as the poison slowly consumed them.

He reached out and snatched Muntadhir's turban, shaking the cloth loose.

"What the hell are you doing?" Muntadhir panted as Dara began binding the wound. "God, can you not even let me die in peace?"

"You're not dying yet." Dara hauled the emir to his feet, ignoring how he shook with pain. "You might not tell *me* how to retrieve Suleiman's seal. But there is another, I suspect, who can make you tell her anything."

40

NAHRI

They ran, Nahri dragging Ali through the dark palace, her only thought to put as much distance as possible between the two of them and whatever it was that Dara had become. Her ancestors' magic pulsed through her blood, offering ready assistance in their flight: stairs rising with their strides and narrow passageways bricking up behind them, removing their trail. Another time, Nahri might have marveled at such things.

But Nahri wasn't certain she'd ever marvel at anything in Daevabad again.

At her side, Ali stumbled. "I need to stop," he gasped, leaning heavily against her. Blood was dripping from his broken nose. "There." He pointed down the corridor toward an unassuming wooden door.

Her dagger at the ready, Nahri shoved the door open, and they tumbled into a small sunken courtyard of mirrored fountains and jewel-bright lemon trees. She slammed the door behind them and sank down to catch her breath.

And then it all caught up with her. Nahri squeezed her eyes shut, but she could still see him. His haunted green eyes above her, the swirl of smoky magic and the defiant set of his features right before she brought the ceiling down on him.

Dara.

No, not Dara. Nahri could not think of the Afshin she'd known and the fiery-visaged monster who'd struck down Muntadhir and arrived in Daevabad on a wave of death as the same man.

And Muntadhir . . . Nahri pressed a fist to her mouth, choking back a sob.

You can't do this right now. Her husband had put himself before the deadly Afshin to buy his wife and brother time. Nahri would honor that sacrifice. She had to.

At her side, Ali had fallen to his knees. A glimmer of copper caught her eye.

"Oh my God, Ali, *give me that.*" Nahri lunged for the relic in his ear, pulling it out and flinging it at the trees. She shuddered, horrified to realize he'd had it in the entire time they were running. Had they come upon the vapor . . .

Pull yourself together. Neither she nor Ali could afford another mistake.

She laid her hands lightly on his brow and left shoulder. "I'm going to heal you."

Ali didn't respond. He wasn't even looking at her. His expression was dazed and vacant, his entire body shivering.

Nahri shut her eyes. Her magic felt closer than usual, and the veil between them, the odd cloak of salty darkness that the marid possession had drawn over him, immediately dropped. Underneath, he was a mess: his nose shattered, a shoulder sprained and badly punctured, and two ribs broken between the innumerable gashes and bites. Nahri commanded them to heal, and Ali caught his breath, grunting as his nose cracked into place. Her power, the healing ability that had denied her twice today, swept out bright and alive.

She let go of him, fighting a wave of exhaustion. "Nice to know I can still do that."

Ali finally stirred. "Thank you," he whispered. He turned to her, tears glistening in his lashes. "My brother . . ."

Nahri violently shook her head. "No. Ali, we don't have time for this . . . *we don't have time for this*," she repeated when he turned away to bury his face in his hands. "Daevabad is under attack. *Your people* are under attack. You need to pull yourself together and fight." She touched his cheek, turning him back to face her. "Please," she begged. "I can't do this alone."

He took one shuddering breath, and then another, briefly squeezing his eyes shut. When he opened them again, there was a touch more resolve in their depths. "Tell me what you know."

"Kaveh unleashed some sort of poisonous vapor similar to what nearly killed you at the feast. It's spreading fast and targets Geziri relics." She lowered her voice. "It's what killed your father."

Ali flinched. "And it's spreading?"

"Fast. We came upon at least three dozen dead so far."

At that, Ali jerked upright. "Zaynab—"

"She's fine," Nahri assured him. "She and Aqisa both. They left to warn the Geziri Quarter and alert the Citadel."

"The Citadel . . ." Ali leaned against the wall. "Nahri, the Citadel is gone."

"What do you mean, it's *gone*?"

"We were attacked first. The lake . . . it rose up like some sort of beast—like what you said happened to you at the Gozan when you first came to Daevabad. It pulled down the Citadel's tower and ripped through the complex. The majority of the Guard is dead." He shivered, silvery drops of liquid beading on his brow. "I woke up in the lake."

"The lake?" Nahri repeated. "Do you think the marid are involved?"

"I think the marid are gone. Their . . . presence . . . feels absent," he clarified, tapping his head. "And the lake's curse was broken. Not that it mattered. The few of us who didn't drown were set upon by ghouls and archers. We were taking the beach when that ifrit grabbed me, but there were fewer than two dozen of us left." Grief swept his face, tears again brimming in his eyes. "The ifrit killed Lubayd."

Nahri swayed. Two dozen survivors. There had to have been hundreds—*thousands* of soldiers in the Citadel. Scores of Geziris in the palace. All dead in a matter of moments.

It's true what they say about you, isn't it? About Qui-zi? About the war? Nahri closed her eyes.

But it wasn't heartbreak coursing through her right now. It was determination. Clearly, the man Nahri knew as Dara was gone—if he'd ever truly existed in the first place. This Dara was the Afshin first, the Scourge. He'd brought a war to Daevabad's doorstep and declared himself a weapon of the Nahids.

But he had no idea what kind of Nahid he'd just set himself against.

Nahri rose to her feet. "We need to retrieve Suleiman's seal," she declared. "It's our only hope of defeating them." She glanced down at Ali, reaching out her hand. "Are you with me?"

Ali took a deep breath but then clasped her hand and climbed to his feet. "Until the end."

"Good. We'll need to find your father's body first," she said, trying not to think about what they'd need to do after that. "Last I saw him, we were on the platform where you took me stargazing."

"We're not far, then. We can take a shortcut through the library." He ran a hand anxiously over his beard and then recoiled, dropping his hand to pull the emerald ring off his thumb.

"Ali, wait!" But Ali had yanked it off and tossed it away before Nahri could finish her protest. She braced herself as it clattered on the tiled floor, half expecting Ali to turn to ash. But he stayed solid, staring at her in surprise.

"What?" he asked.

"*What?*" She threw up her hands and then crossed to retrieve the ring. "What if part of the slave curse is still lingering between you and this, you idiot?"

"It's not," Ali insisted. "They'd barely gotten it on my thumb when you arrived. I think they were arguing about it."

Arguing about it? God, she almost hoped so. She never could have imagined Dara giving another djinn to the ifrit that way. Not even his worst enemy.

"I'd still like to keep it close," she said, slipping the ring into her pocket. She pulled free the zulfiqar she'd awkwardly laced into her belt. "You should probably take this."

Ali looked ill at the sight of the zulfiqar that had struck down his brother. "I'll fight with another weapon."

She leaned forward and pressed it into his hands. "You'll fight with this. It's what you're best at." She met his eyes. "Don't let Muntadhir's death be for nothing, Ali."

Ali's hand closed over the hilt, and then they were moving, him leading her through a door that opened into a long, narrow passageway. It sloped downward, the air growing colder as they descended. Floating balls of conjured fire hissed overhead, setting Nahri's nerves on edge.

Neither of them spoke, but they hadn't been walking long when a boom sounded and the ground shook slightly.

Ali held out a hand to stop her, putting a finger to his lips. There was the unmistakable noise of a heavy object dragging along the dusty stone somewhere behind them.

Nahri tensed. That wasn't all she heard: from beyond the library's silver door at the end of the passageway, a shriek sounded.

"Maybe we should find another way," she whispered, her mouth dry as dust.

The door burst open.

"Zahhak!" A Sahrayn scholar ran at them, his eyes wild, his robes flaming. "*Zahhak!*"

Nahri broke apart from Ali, each of them flattening against the wall as the scholar raced by. The heat from his burning robes seared her face. Nahri turned back, opening her mouth to shout for him to stop . . .

Just in time to see a smoky snake, its body nearly as wide as the corridor, come around the bend. The scholar didn't even have a chance to scream. The snake swallowed him whole, revealing glittering obsidian fangs longer than Nahri's arm.

"Run!" she shrieked, pushing Ali toward the library.

They ran full bore, diving through the door. Ali slammed it shut behind them, shoving himself against the metal as the massive snake crashed against it, rattling the frame.

"Tell your palace to do something about this!" he shouted.

Nahri quickly pressed her hands against the door's decorative metal studs, hard enough to break her skin. She had yet to succeed in completely mastering the palace's magic; it seemed to have its own mind, responding to her emotions with its own distinctive quirk.

"Protect me," she pleaded in Divasti.

Nothing happened.

"Nahri!" Ali cried, his feet slipping as the snake rammed the door again.

"PROTECT ME!" she shouted in Arabic, adding a few choice curses that Yaqub would have lectured her for using. "I command you, damn it!"

Her hands began smoking, and then the silver melted, spooling out to meld the door into the wall. She turned and fell back against the frame, breathing hard.

Her eyes shot open. A creature the size of the Sphinx was careening through the air toward them.

This had to be a nightmare. Not even in enchanted Daevabad did smoky beasts capable of devouring a village fly free. The creature soared on four billowing wings, crimson fire flashing beneath glimmering scales. It had a fanged mouth large enough to swallow a horse and six limbs ending in sharp claws. As Nahri watched, it shrieked, sounding lost as it dived for a fleeing scholar. It caught him in its claws and then flung him hard into the opposite wall as a surge of flames burst from its mouth.

Nahri felt the blood drain from her face. "Is that a dragon?"

At her side, Ali gulped. "It . . . it looks like a zahhak actually." His panicked eyes met hers. "They are not usually that big."

"Oh," Nahri choked out. The zahhak shrieked again and set the lecture alcove next to them ablaze, and they both jumped.

Ali raised a shaking finger at a row of doors on the other side of the massive library. "There's a book lift just beyond there. It goes to the pavilion we want."

Nahri eyed the distance. They were several stories up and the floor of the library was in complete chaos, a maze of broken, burning furniture and fleeing djinn, the zahhak diving at everything that moved.

"That thing will kill us—no," she said, seizing Ali's wrist when he went to lunge in the direction of a young scribe the zahhak had just snatched up. "You run out there now and you're no good to anyone."

A crack drew her attention. The serpent was still bashing the barricaded door and the metal was starting to strain.

"Did anything in your Citadel training prepare you for fighting giant monsters of smoke and flame?"

Ali was staring intently at the eastern wall. "Not at the Cita-del . . ." He looked pensive. "What you did to the ceiling back there . . . do you think you can do it to that wall?"

"You want me to bring down the library wall?" Nahri repeated.

"The canal runs behind it. I'm hoping I can use the water to extinguish that thing," he explained as the zahhak veered a little too close.

"*Water?* How do you expect to control . . ." She trailed off, remembering the way he'd summoned his zulfiqar while fighting Dara and registering the guilt in his expression now. "The marid did nothing to you, right? Isn't that what you told me?"

He groaned. "Can we fight about this later?"

Nahri gave the shelves on the eastern wall a forlorn last look. "If we live, you're taking the blame for destroying all those books." She took a deep breath, trying to focus and pull upon the palace's magic like she had in the corridor. It had been a surge of rage and grief over Muntadhir that had finally pushed her abilities.

Across the room, a knot of scholars hiding behind an over-turned table on the second floor caught her eye. Entirely in-nocent men and women, many of whom had fetched her books and patiently instructed her in Daevabad's history. This was her home—this palace now filled with the dead she hadn't been able to protect—and she'd be damned if she was going to let that zahhak take another life under her roof.

Her skin prickled, magic simmering through her blood, tick-ling at her mind. She inhaled sharply, almost tasting the old stone. She could feel the canal, the cold water pressing hard against the thick wall.

Ali shivered as though she'd touched him. "Is that you?" A glance revealed his eyes had once again been swept by the oily dark film.

She nodded, examining the wall in her mind. The process felt suddenly familiar, much like the way she'd examine an arthritic spine for weak spots, and there were plenty here; the library had been built over two millennia ago. Roots snaked through crumbling bits of brick, rivulets of canal water stretching like grasping tentacles.

She *pulled*, encouraging the weak spots to crumble. She felt the wall shiver, the water churning on the other side. "Help me," she demanded, grabbing Ali's hand. The touch of his skin, cold and unusually clammy, sent an icy jolt down her spine that made the entire wall shake. She could see the water fighting its way in and worked to loosen the stone further.

A small leak sprang first. And then, in the time it took for her heart to skip, an entire section of the wall came down in a burst of broken bricks and surging water.

Nahri's eyes shot open. Had she not been concerned for both her life and the priceless manuscripts being swiftly destroyed, the sudden appearance of a stories-high waterfall in the middle of the library would have been an extraordinary sight. It crashed to the floor, rushing in a turbulent whirlpool of broken furniture and cresting whitecaps.

The spray caught the zahhak as it flew too close. It screeched, aiming a torrent of flames at the thundering water. Ali gasped, lurching back as if the fire caused him physical pain.

His movement attracted the zahhak's attention. The creature abruptly spun in the air and flew straight for them.

"Move!" Nahri grabbed Ali, pulling him out of the way just as the zahhak vaporized the shelves they'd taken shelter behind. "Jump!"

They jumped. The water was cold and swiftly rising, and Nahri was still struggling to her feet, hampered by her wet gown, when Ali shoved her head back under the water just as another fiery plume shot at them.

She emerged, gasping for breath and ducking a broken

wooden beam that rushed by. "Damn it, Ali, you made me break my library. Do something!"

He rose to face the zahhak, moving with a deadly grace, drops of water clinging to his skin like honey. He raised his hands, fixing his gaze on the zahhak as it came flying back at them. With a thunderous crack, the waterfall spun out like a whip across the air and cut the zahhak in two.

Their relief was short-lived. Ali swayed, sagging against her. "The door," he managed as she sent another burst of her own healing magic through him. "The door!"

They hurried on, wading as fast as they could through the makeshift river. Nahri lunged for the handle as the door came into reach.

A spray of arrows thudded into it, narrowly missing her hand.

"Suleiman's eye!" She whirled around. A half-dozen riders on smoky steeds were coming through the library's main entrance, silver bows drawn and ready in their hands.

"Just go!" Ali wrenched open the door and shoved her through. He slammed it shut behind them, piling various pieces of furniture to block it as Nahri caught her breath.

They'd entered a small, perfectly circular chamber. It resembled a well, the ceiling disappearing into the distant gloom. A rickety metal staircase climbed in a spiral around two softly glowing columns of amber light. Baskets overflowing with books and scrolls drifted in their midst, one column taking the baskets up while the other brought them down.

Ali nodded to the steps. "That goes straight to the pavilion." He unsheathed his zulfiqar. "Ready?"

Nahri took a deep breath, and they started climbing. Her heart raced with every shuddering groan of the staircase.

After what seemed like hours but was surely only minutes, they drew to a stop in front of a small wooden portal. "I hear voices," she whispered. "It sounds like Divasti."

He pressed an ear to the door. "At least three men," he agreed softly. "And trust me when I say the Afshin trained his soldiers well."

Nahri quickly considered their options. "Take me captive."

Ali looked at her as though she'd gone mad. "Excuse me?"

She shoved herself into his arms, bringing his khanjar to her throat. "Just play along," she hissed. "Give them a rant about fire worshippers and sin. Your reputation precedes you with my people." She kicked open the door before he could protest, dragging him with her. "Help me!" she cried pitifully in Divasti.

The Daeva warriors whirled around to stare at them. There were three, dressed in the same dark uniforms and armed to the teeth. They certainly looked like men Dara might have trained; one had an arrow aimed at them in a second flat.

Thankfully, Kaveh was nowhere to be seen. "Drop your weapons!" she begged, writhing against Ali's arm. "He'll kill me!"

Ali reacted a bit more smoothly than Nahri found comfortable, pressing the blade closer to her throat with a snarl. "Do it, fire worshippers!" he commanded. "Now! Or I'll gut your precious Banu Nahida!"

The closest Daeva gasped. "Banu Nahri?" he asked, his black eyes going wide. "Is that really you?"

"Yes!" she cried. "Now put down your weapons!"

They glanced at each other uncertainly until the archer swiftly lowered his bow. "Do it," he ordered. "That's Banu Manizheh's daughter."

The other two instantly complied.

"Where is my father?" Ali demanded. "What have you done with him?"

"Nothing, sand fly," one of the Daevas spat. "Why don't you let go of the girl and face us like a man? We threw the bodies of your father's men in the lake, but you still have time to join your Abba."

He stepped aside to reveal the dead king, and Nahri recoiled in horror. Ghassan's body had been abused, bloody boot marks staining his clothes, his jewelry and royal turban stripped away. His glassy, copper-hued gray eyes stared vacantly at the night sky, his face coated in blood.

Ali abruptly released her, and a look of rage unlike any she'd seen from him before, twisted his face.

He'd thrown himself at the Daeva soldiers before she could think to react, his zulfiqar bursting into flames. They moved fast, but they could not quite match the speed of the grief-stricken prince. With a cry he cut through the man who had spoken, yanking the blade free and swinging back to behead the archer who had recognized her.

And with that, Nahri was catapulted back into the night of the boat. The night she'd seen firsthand what Dara was truly capable of, the way he'd torn through the men surrounding him like some instrument of death, impervious to the blood and screams and brutal violence that surrounded him.

She stared at Ali in horror. She couldn't see anything of the bookish prince, the man who was still sometimes too shy to meet her eyes, in the raging warrior before her.

Is this how it starts? Was this how Dara had been undone, his soul stripped away as he watched the slaughter of his family and his tribe, his mind and body forged into a weapon by fury and despair? Is this how he'd been made into a monster who would visit that same violence on a new generation?

And yet Nahri still found herself lunging forward when the last Daeva raised his sword, preparing to strike. Nahri grabbed the man's arm, throwing him off balance as he spun to look at her, his expression one of utter betrayal.

Ali plunged the zulfiqar into his back.

Nahri stepped away, her hand going to her mouth. Her ears were ringing, bile choking her.

"Nahri!" Ali took her face in his hands, his own now wet with the blood of her tribesmen. "Nahri, look at me! Are you hurt?"

It seemed a ludicrous question. Nahri was beyond hurt. Her city was collapsing and the people dearest to her were dying or turning into creatures she couldn't recognize. And suddenly she wanted more than anything to flee. To race down the steps and out of the palace. To get on a boat, a horse, any damn thing that would take her back to the moment in her life before she decided to sing a zar song in Divasti.

The seal. Retrieve the seal and then you can sort all this out. She jerked back from his hands, pulling free one of her daggers as she moved automatically toward Ghassan's body.

Ali followed her, kneeling at his father's side. "I should have been here," he whispered. Tears came to his eyes, and something of the friend she knew returned to his face. "This is all my fault. He was too busy trying to deal with my rebellion to anticipate any of this."

Nahri said nothing. She had no assurances to offer right now. Instead, she cut a slit in Ghassan's bloody dishdasha, straight across the chest.

Ali moved to stop her. "What are you doing?"

"We have to burn his heart," she said, her voice unsteady. "The ring re-forms from the ash."

Ali dropped his hand as if he'd been burned. "What?"

She was able to summon up enough pity to soften her voice. "I'll do it. Between the two of us, I've a bit more experience carving into people's bodies."

He looked sick but didn't argue. "Thank you." He shifted away, taking his father's head in his lap, closing his eyes as he began to softly pray.

Nahri let the quiet Arabic words wash over her—reminding her of Cairo, as always. She worked quickly, cutting through the flesh and muscle of Ghassan's chest. There wasn't as much blood as she would have expected—perhaps since he'd already lost so much.

Not that it mattered. Nahri had been bathed in blood today. She expected its stain would never completely fade.

Even so, it was grim work, and Ali looked ready to pass out by the time she finally plunged her hand into Ghassan's chest. Her fingers closed around his still heart, and Nahri would be lying if she said she didn't feel a small twinge of dark pleasure. The tyrant who had toyed with lives as though they were pawns on a game board. The one who had forced her to marry his son because her own mother had denied him. The one who had threatened her brother's life—more than once.

Unbidden, a burst of heat bloomed in her palm, the dance of a conjured flame. Nahri quickly pulled her hand free, but his heart was already ash.

And clenched in her hand was something hard and hot. Nahri uncurled her fingers, her own heart racing.

The seal ring of the Prophet Suleiman—the ring whose power had reshaped their world and set their people at war—glistened in her bloody palm.

Ali gasped. "My God. Is that really it?"

Nahri let out a shaky breath. "Considering the circumstances . . ." She stared at the ring. As far as jewels went, Nahri wouldn't have necessarily been impressed by this one. There were no fancy gems or worked gold; instead a single battered black pearl crowned a thick dull gold band. The pearl had been carefully carved, something she didn't think possible, the eight-pointed star of Suleiman's seal gleaming from its surface. Etched around it were minuscule characters she couldn't read.

She trembled and she'd swear the ring vibrated in return, pulsing in time with her heart.

She wanted nothing to do with it. She shoved it at Ali. "Take it."

He leapt back. "Absolutely not. That belongs to you."

"But you . . . you're next in line for the throne!"

"And you're Anahid's descendant!" Ali pushed her fingers back over it, though she saw the flash of longing and regret in his eyes. "Suleiman gave it to your family, not mine."

A denial so strong it neared revulsion ran through her. "I can't," she whispered. "I'm not Anahid, Ali, I'm a con artist from Cairo!" And *Cairo* . . . Muntadhir's warning flashed through her mind. He said the ring couldn't leave Daevabad. "I have no business touching something that belonged to a prophet."

"Yes, you do." His expression turned fervent. "I believe in you."

"Have you met *you*?" she burst out. "Your belief is not a mark in my favor! I don't want this," she rushed on, and suddenly it was damnably clear. "If I take that ring, I'll be trapped here. I'll never see my home again!"

Ali looked incredulous. "This *is* your home!"

The door crashed open. Nahri had been so focused on her warring heart that she hadn't heard anyone approaching. Ali yanked his father's robe over the ghastly hole in his chest, and Nahri stumbled back, slipping Suleiman's ring into her pocket just before a group of Daeva warriors burst in.

They abruptly stopped, one holding up a fist as he took in the sight before him: the dead king and the very bloody young people at his feet. "He's up here!" he shouted in Divasti, directing his words to the staircase. "Along with a couple of djinn!"

A couple of djinn . . . no, Nahri supposed right now there was little to mark her out. She rose to her feet, her legs wobbly beneath her. "I am no djinn," she declared as another pair of warriors emerged. "I'm Banu Nahri e-Nahid, and you'll put your weapons down right now."

The man didn't get to respond. Her name was no sooner uttered than a slight figure pushed through the door. It was a Daeva woman, her eyes locked on Nahri. Dressed in a dark uniform, she made for an arresting sight, a silky black chador wrapping her head underneath a silver helmet. A steel sword, its edge bloodied, was tucked into her wide black belt.

She pulled the cloth away from her face, and Nahri nearly crumpled to the ground. It was a face that could be her own in another few decades.

"Nahri . . . ," the woman whispered, black eyes seeming to drink her in. She brought her fingers together. "Oh, child, it has been too long since I've looked upon your face."

THE DAEVA WOMAN CAME CLOSER, HER GAZE NOT leaving Nahri's. Nahri's heart was racing, her head spinning. . . .

The smell of burning papyrus and cries in Arabic. Soft arms pulling her into a tight embrace and water closing over her face. Memories that didn't make sense. Nahri found herself fighting for air, tears that she didn't understand brimming in her eyes.

She raised her dagger. "Don't come any closer!"

She immediately had four bows trained on her. She stepped back, stumbling against the stone parapet, and Ali grabbed her wrist before she lost her balance. The parapet was low here, the knee-high stone wall all that kept her from plunging into the lake.

"Stop!" The woman's curt command snapped like a whip, belying the softness in her voice when she'd spoken to Nahri. "Stand down. You're frightening her." She glared at the warriors and then jerked her head toward the door. "Leave us."

"But, my lady, the Afshin won't be happy to learn—"

"It is *I* you take orders from, not Darayavahoush."

Nahri did not know men could move so fast. They were gone in an instant, clattering down the steps.

Ali pressed closer. "Nahri, who is that?" he whispered.

"I . . . I don't know," she managed. She also didn't know why every Cairo-honed instinct in her was screaming at her to get away.

The woman watched the warriors leave with the sharpness of a general. She shut the door behind them and then pricked her finger on the sharp metal screen.

It surged together, instantly locking.

Nahri gasped. "You're a Nahid."

"I am," the woman replied. A soft, sad smile came to her lips. "You're beautiful," she added, seeming to take Nahri in again. "Marid curse be damned—you still have his eyes. I wondered if you would." Grief filled her face. "Do you . . . do you remember me?"

Nahri wasn't sure *what* she remembered. "I don't think so. I don't know." She knew she shouldn't be confessing anything to the woman who claimed to be in command of the forces attacking the palace, but the fact that she claimed to be a Nahid wasn't doing much for Nahri's wits. "Who are you?"

The same broken smile, the look of someone who'd been through far too much. "My name is Manizheh."

The name, both unbelievable and obvious, punched through her. *Manizheh.*

Ali gasped. "Manizheh?" he repeated. "Your *mother*?"

"Yes," Manizheh said in Djinnistani. She only now seemed to realize Ali was there, her gaze leaving Nahri's for the first time. Her dark eyes scanned him, lingering on his zulfiqar. She blinked, looking taken aback. "Is this Hatset's son?" she asked Nahri, returning to Divasti. "The prince they call Alizayd?" She frowned. "You were to be in the infirmary with Nisreen. What are you doing with him?"

Nahri opened her mouth, still reeling. *Manizheh. My mother.* It seemed even more impossible than Dara rising from the dead.

She fought for words. "He . . . he's my friend." It was a ridiculous answer and yet it was the first that came to her. It also seemed wiser than admitting they were here stealing Suleiman's seal. "What are *you* doing here?" she demanded, feeling a little of her sharpness return. "I was told you were dead. Kaveh told me he found your murdered body decades ago!"

Manizheh's expression turned solemn. "A necessary deception and one I pray you can eventually forgive. You were taken from me as a child by the marid, and I feared I'd lost you forever. When I learned you'd fallen into Ghassan's hands . . . the things I'm sure he has subjected you to . . . I am so sorry, Nahri." She stepped forward as if she wanted to take Nahri's hand and then stopped as Nahri cringed. "But I promise you—you're safe now."

Safe. The word echoed inside her head. *My mother. My brother. Dara.* In the space of a few hours, Nahri had gone from being the only living Nahid to having a whole family of relatives to form a council again, with a damned Afshin to boot.

Her eyes were wet, the constant loneliness she carried in her chest expanding to the point where it was difficult to breathe. This couldn't be possible.

But the brutal evidence was before her. Who else but a Nahid would be capable of creating the poison dealing death to the Geziri tribe? Who else but the Banu Nahida rumored to be the most powerful in centuries would be able to bring Dara back from the dead, to make him obey completely?

Suleiman's seal ring burned in her pocket. It was the only ace Nahri had. Because no matter what this woman said, Nahri did not feel like they were on the same side. She had meant what she said to Muntadhir: she wasn't on the side of anyone who'd arranged for the deaths of so many innocents.

Manizheh raised her hands. "I mean you no harm," she said carefully. She switched to Djinnistani, her voice cooling as she addressed Ali. "Put down your weapons. Surrender yourself to my men, and you won't be hurt."

That had the predicted response, Ali's eyes flashing as he raised his zulfiqar. "I won't surrender to the person who orchestrated the slaughter of my people."

"Then you will die," Manizheh said simply. "You have lost, al Qahtani. Do what you can to save those Geziris left." Her voice turned persuasive. "You have a sister in the palace, and a mother I once knew in Ta Ntry, do you not? Believe me when I say I would rather not inform another woman of her children's deaths."

Ali scoffed. "You mean to make us into pawns." He raised his chin defiantly. "I would rather die."

Nahri had absolutely no doubt that was true; she also had no doubt most of the surviving Geziris would feel similarly. Which meant they needed to get off this damned wall and away from Manizheh.

Take the ring, you fool. She could thrust her hand into her pocket and claim Suleiman's seal for herself in the same time it would take Manizheh to lunge for it.

And then? What if she couldn't call upon it correctly? Nahri was guessing the prophetically granted abilities of a magical ring likely had a learning curve. She and Ali would still be stuck on this pavilion with a vengeful Banu Nahida and a swarm of warriors below.

She stepped between Ali and Manizheh. "And that's what you're after?" she demanded. "If we surrendered . . . could you contain the poison?"

Manizheh spread her hands, stepping closer. "But of course." Her gaze returned to Nahri. "But I'm not after *your* surrender, daughter. Why would I be?" She took another step toward them, but stilled as she spotted Ghassan's body.

Her entire expression changed as her eyes swept his face. "Suleiman's mark is gone from his brow."

Nahri glanced down. Manizheh spoke the truth; the black tattoo that had once marked Ghassan's face had vanished.

"Did you take the seal?" Manizheh demanded. Her voice had shifted, barely concealed desire evident beneath her words. "Where is it?" When neither one of them responded, she pursed her mouth in a thin line, looking like she was growing exasperated with their defiance. The expression was almost maternal. "Please do not make me ask again."

"You're not getting it," Ali burst out. "I don't care who you claim to be. You're a monster. You brought ghouls and ifrit into our city; you have the blood of thousands on your—"

Manizheh snapped her fingers.

There was an audible pop, and then Ali cried out, collapsing as he clutched his left knee.

"Ali!" Nahri spun, reaching for him.

"If you try to heal him, I'll break his neck next." The cold threat sliced the air, and Nahri instantly dropped her hand, startled. "Forgive me," Manizheh said, seeming sincere. "This is not at all how I wanted our first meeting to go, but I will not have you interfere. I have planned too many decades for this." She glanced again at Ali. "Do not make me torture you before her eyes. The ring. Now."

"He doesn't have it!" Nahri shoved her hand in her pocket, her fingers running over the two rings there before plucking one out. She thrust her fist over the parapet, letting the ring dangle precariously from her finger. "And unless you're willing to spend the next century searching the lake for this, I'd leave him alone."

Manizheh drew back, studying Nahri. "You won't do it."

Nahri raised a brow. "You don't know me."

"But I do." Manizheh's tone was imploring. "Nahri, you're my daughter . . . do you imagine I've not sought stories of you from every Daevabadi I've met? Dara himself can hardly stop speaking of you. Your bravery, your cleverness . . . In truth a more devoted man I've rarely met. A dangerous thing in our world," she added delicately. "To make plain your affections. A truth Ghassan was always too willing to make cruelly clear to me."

Nahri didn't know what to say. Manizheh's words about Dara felt like salt on a wound, and she could feel the other woman reading her, evaluating her every flinch. Ali was still clutching his knee, breathing heavily against the pain.

Her mother came nearer. "Ghassan's done that to you as well, hasn't he? It's the only way he had to control women like us. I *know* you, Nahri. I know what it's like to have ambitions, to be the cleverest in the room—and have those ambitions crushed. To have men who are less than you bully and threaten you into a place you know you don't belong. I've heard of the extraordinary strides you've made in just a few years. The things I could teach you; you'd be a goddess. You'd never have to lower your head again."

Their gazes met, and Nahri could not deny the surge of longing in her heart. She thought of the countless times she'd bowed to Ghassan while he sat on her ancestors' throne. The way Muntadhir had dismissed her dreams for the hospital and Kaveh had condescended to her in the Temple.

The smoky binds Dara had dared conjure to hold her. The magic that had raged through her blood in response.

Nahri took a deep breath. *This is my home.*

"Why don't we compromise?" she suggested. "You want the Nahids in charge again? Fine. I'm a Nahid. *I'll* take Suleiman's seal. Surely, I can negotiate a peace more effectively than a woman who abandoned her tribe and returned only to plot the slaughter of another."

Manizheh stiffened. "No," she said. "You can't."

"Why not?" Nahri asked archly. "This is about what's best for the Daevas, isn't it?"

"You misunderstand me, daughter," Manizheh replied, and Nahri inwardly swore because try as she could to read it, there was nothing in this woman's face that gave her thoughts away.

"You cannot take the seal yourself because you are not—entirely—daeva. You're shafit, Nahri. You have human blood."

Nahri stared at her in silence. Because with those words—those utterly confident words—Nahri knew the woman before her was not lying about being her mother. It was a secret only Ghassan had known, the truth he said Suleiman's seal made clear.

"What do you mean, she's *shafit*?" Ali gasped from the ground.

Nahri didn't respond; she didn't know what to say.

"It's all right," Manizheh assured her gently as she approached them. "It's not a thing anyone else need ever know. But you cannot take that seal. Possessing it will kill you. You simply aren't strong enough."

Nahri jerked back. "I'm strong enough to use Nahid magic."

"But enough to wield Suleiman's seal?" Manizheh pressed. "To be the bearer of the object that reshaped our world?" She shook her head. "It will tear you apart, my daughter."

Nahri fell silent. *She's lying. She has to be.* But by the Most High, if Manizheh hadn't struck doubt into her soul.

"Nahri." It was Ali. "Nahri, look at me." She did, feeling dazed. This was all too much. "She's lying. Suleiman himself had human blood."

"Suleiman was a prophet," Manizheh cut in, echoing with brutal effectiveness the insecurity that Nahri herself had expressed. "And no one asked you to involve yourself in a Nahid matter, djinn. I have spent longer than you've been alive reading every text that ever mentioned that seal ring. And all of them are clear on this point."

"And that's rather convenient, I'd say," he shot back. He stared up at Nahri, beseeching. "Don't listen to her. Take the—ah!" He yelped in pain, his hands wrenching from his shattered knee.

Manizheh snapped her fingers again, and Ali's hands jerked to the khanjar at his waist.

"What-what are you doing to me?" he cried as his fingers

cracked around the dagger's hilt. Beneath his tattered sleeves, the muscles in his wrists were seizing, the khanjar coming free in shuddering, spasming movements.

My God . . . *Manizheh* was doing that? Without even touching him? Instinctively Nahri sought to pull on the magic of the palace.

She didn't so much as make a stone shiver before her connection was abruptly severed. The loss was like a blow, a coldness seeping over her.

"Don't, child," Manizheh warned. "I have far more experience than you." She brought her hands together. "I do not wish this. But if you don't hand the ring over right now, I will kill him."

The khanjar was nearing Ali's throat. He wriggled against it, a line of blood appearing below his jaw. His eyes were bright with pain, sweat running down his face.

Nahri was frozen in horror. She could feel Manizheh's magic wrapping around her, teasing at the muscles in her own hand. Nahri was not capable of *anything* like that—she didn't know how to *fight* someone capable of anything like that.

But she knew damned well she couldn't give her Suleiman's seal.

Manizheh spoke again. "They have already lost. We have won—*you* have won. Nahri, hand over the ring. No one else will ever learn you're shafit. Take your place as my daughter, with your brother at your side. Greet the new generation as one of the rightful rulers of this city. With a man who loves you."

Nahri wracked her mind. She didn't know who to believe. But if Manizheh was right, if Nahri took the seal and it killed her, Ali would swiftly follow. And then there'd be no one to stop the woman who'd just slaughtered thousands from gaining control of the most powerful object in their world.

Nahri couldn't risk that. She also knew that, shafit or not, she had her own skills when it came to dealing with people. In going after Nahri the way she had, Manizheh had made clear what she believed her daughter's weaknesses to be.

Nahri could work with that. She took a shaky breath. "You promise you'll let the prince live?" she whispered, her fingers trembling on the ring. "And that no one will ever know I'm a shafit?"

"On our family's honor. I swear."

Nahri bit her lip. "Not even Dara?"

Manizheh's face softened slightly, with both sadness and a little relief. "I'll do my best, child. I have no desire to cause you further pain. Either of you," she added, looking as genuinely moved as Nahri had yet seen her. "Indeed, nothing would please me more than to see you find some happiness together."

Nahri let the words slide past her. That would never happen. "Then take it," she said, tossing the ring at her mother's feet.

Manizheh was as good as her word. The ring had no sooner left Nahri's hand than the khanjar dropped from Ali's throat. Nahri fell to his side as he gasped for breath.

"Why did you do that?" he wheezed.

"Because she was going to kill you." As Manizheh bent to retrieve the ring, Nahri swiftly moved as though to embrace him, taking the opportunity to shove his weapons back in his belt. "Are you sure the curse is off the lake?" she whispered in his ear.

Ali stiffened in her arms. "I . . . yes?"

She pulled him to his feet, keeping her hand on his arm. "Then forgive me, my friend."

Manizheh was straightening up with the ring in her hand. She frowned, studying the emerald. "This is the seal ring?"

"Of course it is," Nahri said airily, pulling the second ring— Suleiman's ring—from her pocket. "Who would lie to their mother?" She shoved the ring onto one of Ali's fingers.

Ali tried to jerk free, but Nahri was fast. Her heart gave a single lurch of regret, and then—just as Manizheh glanced up—she felt the ancient band vanish beneath her fingers.

Shocked betrayal blossomed in her mother's eyes—ah, so Manizheh had emotions after all. But Nahri was not waiting for a response. She grabbed Ali's hand and jumped off the wall.

She heard Manizheh cry her name, but it was too late. The cold night air lashed at her face as they fell, the dark water looking a *lot* farther away than she remembered. She tried to steel herself, all too aware that she was in for a great deal of pain and some temporarily broken bones.

Indeed, she hit hard, the crash of the water against her body a cold, painful thrust like a thousand sharp knives. Her arms flew out, tangling in Ali's as she submerged.

She shuddered with pain, with shock, as the memory Manizheh had triggered came briefly again. The smell of burning papyrus, the screams of a young girl.

The sight of a pair of warm brown eyes just before muddy water closed over her head.

Nahri never broke the surface. Darkness whirled around her, the smell of silt and the sensation of being seized.

There was a single whisper of magic and then everything went black.

41

DARA

Dara was not going to last another minute with Muntadhir al Qahtani.

For an actively dying man, the emir was running his mouth at remarkable speed, gasping out an unending stream of barbs obviously calculated to goad Dara into killing him.

"And our *wedding night*," Muntadhir continued. "Well . . . nights. I mean, they all started to blend together after—"

Dara abruptly pressed his knife to the other man's throat. It was the tenth time he'd done so. "If you do not stop talking," he hissed. "I'm going to start cutting pieces off of you."

Muntadhir blinked, his eyes a dark shadow against his wan face. He'd paled to the color of parchment, ash crumbling on his skin, and the green-black lines of the zulfiqar poisoning—creeping, curling marks—had spread to his throat. He opened his mouth and then winced, falling back against the carpet Dara had enchanted to speed them to Manizheh, a flash of pain in his eyes perhaps stealing whatever obnoxious response he had planned.

No matter—Dara's attention had been captured by a far stranger sight: water was gushing through the corridor they flew down, the unnatural stream growing deeper and wilder the closer they came to the library. He'd raced to the infirmary only to be told that a panicked, rambling Kaveh e-Pramukh had intercepted Manizheh and sent her here.

They soared through the doors, and Dara blinked in alarm. Water was pouring through a jagged hole near the ceiling, crashing against the now flooded library floor. Broken furniture and smoldering books—not to mention the bodies of at least a dozen djinn—lay scattered. Manizheh was nowhere to be seen, but he spotted across the room a knot of the warriors who'd been accompanying her.

Dara was there in seconds, landing the rug as gently as possible on an island of debris and splashing into the water. "Where is the Banu—"

He didn't get to finish the question.

A tremor tore through the palace, the ground beneath him shaking so violently he stumbled. The entire library shuddered, piles of debris collapsing and several of the massive shelves breaking free of the walls.

"Watch out!" Dara cried as a cascade of books and scrolls rained down upon them. Another tremor followed, and a crack ripped across the opposite wall with such force that the floor split.

The quake was over in seconds, an eerie hush hanging over them. The water drained away, surging toward the rent in the floor like an animal fleeing. And then . . . as though someone had blown out a lamp he couldn't see, Dara felt a shift in the air.

With a bone-jarring popping sound, the globes of conjured fire that floated near the ceiling abruptly went out, crashing to the ground. The fluttering black al Qahtani banners grew still, and the door ahead of him flew open. All the doors did, whatever locking enchantments had been set seemingly broken.

A chill went down his spine at the silence, at the odd, empty coldness that had stolen through the room. Dara conjured a handful of flames, the firelight dancing along the scorched and water-stained walls. Ahead, his men appeared to be struggling to do the same, gesturing wildly at the dark.

"Can you conjure flames?" he heard one ask.

"I can't conjure anything!"

A far more shocked cry caught his ear. Dara whirled around. Muntadhir had staggered to his feet, swaying as he held out his arms to gape at his body.

In the dim light of the ruined library, the deadly dark lines of the magical poison that marked the emir's skin were retreating.

Dara's mouth fell open as he watched the utterly impossible sight before him. Like a spider curling in on itself, the poison was leaching away, creeping back from Muntadhir's shoulders and down past his chest. Muntadhir ripped away the cloth binding his stomach just in time to reveal the dark green hue lifting from the wound altogether. And then—with the barest hint of smoke—it vanished entirely.

The emir dropped to his knees with a choked sob. He touched his bloody stomach, weeping with relief.

Dread rose in Dara's heart. Something had just gone *very* wrong. "Bind that man!" he managed to snap at his soldiers. Dara didn't need any more surprises when it came to Muntadhir and weapons. "*Now*. And where is the Banu Nahida?"

One of his men raised a finger toward a darkened set of stairs. "I'm sorry, Afshin," he said, his arm trembling wildly. "She ordered us away when we found Banu Nahri."

Nahri. Muntadhir instantly forgotten, Dara raced through the door and then ducked as the remains of an enchanted pulley system came crashing down around him. Heedless of the destruction, he took the steps two at a time, arriving at another door.

"Banu Nahida!" he called loudly. When there was no response, he kicked the door in.

Manizheh stood alone and very still, her back to him, among a tangle of bodies. Fear clawed up in his throat as Dara forced himself to examine their faces. *No, Creator, no. I beg you.*

But Nahri wasn't among the dead. Instead, they were his own men. They'd been slaughtered, still-smoldering slashes rending their bodies.

A zulfiqar. *Alizayd.* Dara knew it in his bones. And it was entirely his fault. He should have killed the prince the second he had him, instead of letting Vizaresh delay him with fantasies of vengeance.

Mardoniye. His warriors on the beach. Now these three. Dara clenched his fists, fighting the heat aching to burst free. This had all gone so wrong—and not just because of the ifrit.

It had gone wrong because in his heart, Dara had known this invasion was a mistake. It was too rushed and too brutal. They'd allied with creatures he didn't trust and used magic he didn't understand. And he had gone along, had bowed his head in submission to a Nahid again and dismissed the disquiet in his soul. Now it had blown up in his face.

It wasn't even the first time. His own history had taught him nothing.

Manizheh had yet to move. She just stood there, staring at the dark lake. "Banu Manizheh?" he spoke again.

"It's gone." Her voice was an uncharacteristic whisper. "*They're* gone. She gave the seal to that sand fly."

Dara staggered back. "*What?* You can't mean . . ."

"I mean exactly as I say." There was an edge in Manizheh's voice. "I should have known better," she murmured. "I should have known not to trust her. She deceived me, *mocked* me, and then gave Suleiman's seal—our ancestors' seal—back to the people who stole it."

Dara's gaze fell again on the murdered men and for the first time, he felt a sting of true betrayal. How could Nahri have given something so powerful, so precious, to a man she'd watched slaughter her own people?

He swallowed, pushing his roiling emotions down. "Where are they?" he asked, trying to check the tremor in his voice. "Banu Nahida, *where are they?*" he pressed when she didn't answer.

She raised a trembling hand, gesturing to the dark water. "They jumped."

"They did *what?*" Dara was at the parapet in seconds. He saw nothing but the black water below.

"They jumped." Manizheh's voice was bitter. "I tried to reason with her, but that djinn had his claws in her mind."

Dara fell to his knees. He clutched the stone, and a stir of movement caught his eye, small swells and eddies glimmering on the dark lake.

He let out his breath. "The water is moving," he whispered. Dara leaned out farther, examining the distance. Surely, a Nahid healer could survive that fall. If she'd jumped clear of the rocks, if she landed the right way . . .

Hope and grief warred in his chest. *Creator, please . . . let her be alive.* Dara didn't care if she greeted him with a dagger to his heart; after tonight, part of him would welcome it. But this couldn't be how Nahri's story ended.

He rose unsteadily to his feet. "I am going to find her."

Manizheh grabbed his wrist. "Stop."

The flat word, uttered as one might issue a command to some sort of animal, broke the fragile grip he had on his emotions.

"I have done everything you asked!" he choked out, wrenching free of her grip. "I have been your Afshin. I have killed your enemies and bloodied our home. You can grant me a few moments to find out whether she still lives."

Manizheh's eyes lit in outrage, but her voice remained cool. "Nahri isn't what's important right now, Darayavahoush." She abruptly pointed up. "That is."

Dara glanced up.

The sky above the palace was shattering.

It looked like a smoky glass dome cracking, the inky midnight peeling away to reveal the warmer hues of dawn, the glow of a desert sky instead of the murky fog that lurked, ever present, above Daevabad. It was spreading, rippling out across the horizon. And as his gaze followed the falling sky, he noticed rooftop fires were winking out across the city. A camp of travelers' tents, magical creations of silk and smoke, collapsed, as did two conjured marble towers.

Dara was utterly bewildered. "What is going on?" He glanced at Manizheh, but she wasn't looking at him. As Dara watched, she drew her sword, pricking her thumb on the blade. A well of black blood blossomed. And then another.

The color left her face. "My magic . . . it's gone."

Coldness swept him as he watched more fires blink out. The stillness that had fallen over the library, the poison that had drained from the emir . . .

"I do not think it is your magic alone," he whispered. "I think it is all of Daevabad's."

EPILOGUE

Consciousness tickled at Nahri, the rich smell of mud and sweet birdsong pulling her from darkness.

The pain came next, her back and shoulders aching. Her head. Her arms. Everything, really.

And that damned sun. Too bright. Brighter than any sun in Daevabad had any right being. Nahri shaded her eyes with one hand, blinking as she tried to sit up.

Her other hand sank into mud. What in God's name . . . Nahri looked around as sunspots cleared from her eyes. She was sitting in some sort of flooded marsh, waist deep in cloudy water. Just behind her was a grove of tall, bristling palm trees, scrubby greenery growing unchecked over a crumbling mud-brick wall.

Ahead was a wide river, its current languid as it stretched to flow across its floodplains. A narrow emerald band of greenery bordered the opposite bank, beyond which was desert, gleaming golden in the bright sun.

Nahri stared at the river in utter incomprehension. She must have taken a blow to the head. Because she would *swear* that it looked like . . .

"No!" A familiar voice broke the still air, ending in a wail. "*No!*"

Ali. Nahri scrambled to her feet, aching all over. What was wrong with her healing abilities? The mud sucked at her legs, and she clambered past the marsh to firmer land. She caught sight of more ruined structures between the trees: a cracked pigeon coop and the bare brick outlines of what might have once been small homes.

She pushed through a cluster of palm fronds. Just ahead was what looked like a village mosque—one long abandoned. Its minaret was broken, its dome cracked open to the sky.

Relief coursed through her—Ali was inside, his back to her as he peered past the top of the minaret. She staggered forward, her limbs protesting every jolt and her skin crawling. Nahri didn't know where they were—it certainly didn't look like Daevabad—but she felt as though she'd been here before.

She climbed up the ruined minaret's stone steps. Thoroughly out of breath by the time she reached the top, Nahri stumbled forward, reaching for his shoulder as she wheezed out his name. "Ali."

He was sobbing when he spun on her.

Suleiman's seal burned bright on his temple.

The events of the night before came together too fast, too horrible, and then Ali was lunging at her, putting his hands on her shoulders like he never had before.

"You have to take us back!" he begged. Closer now, Nahri could see that his face was feverish, his entire body twitching. "Nahri, please! They have my sister! They have every—*ah*," His voice broke as he clutched at his heart, gasping for air.

"Ali!"

He shoved himself away from her. "I can't control this." The smoky mark of the seal shimmered on his skin. "You should never have given me that ring! You should never have taken us away!"

"I haven't taken us anywhere!"

Ali raised a shaking hand. "Then why are we *here*?"

Nahri glanced where he was pointing. She stood.

The sight before her on the not-so-distant horizon was immediately familiar. The ancient stone mosques and towering minarets. The forts and palaces of long-dead sultans and generals, dynasties lost to time. The countless blocks of multistoried buildings, all an earthy warm brown, a *human* warm brown, that Nahri knew rose over twisting, busy streets of jostling shopkeepers, gossiping coffee drinkers, and racing children. Over apothecaries.

Tears sprang to her eyes. *It's not possible.* Her gaze immediately darted from the city she'd have known anywhere to the swollen river at its banks. The river for which she'd been jokingly named by fishermen who'd plucked her out of it as a child.

On the opposite shore, standing unmoving and eternal against the dawn sky, were the three Pyramids of Giza.

The words came to her in Arabic first, of course. "Ya masr," she whispered softly as the Egyptian sun warmed her cheeks, the scent of the Nile's silt on her skin. "I'm home."

GLOSSARY

Beings of Fire

DAEVA: The ancient term for all fire elementals before the djinn rebellion, as well as the name of the tribe residing in Daevastana, of which Dara and Nahri are both part. Once shapeshifters who lived for millennia, the daevas had their magical abilities sharply curbed by the Prophet Suleiman as a punishment for harming humanity.

DJINN: A human word for "daeva." After Zaydi al Qahtani's rebellion, all his followers, and eventually all daevas, began using this term for their race.

IFRIT: The original daevas who defied Suleiman and were stripped of their abilities. Sworn enemies of the Nahid family, the ifrit revenge themselves by enslaving other djinn to cause chaos among humanity.

SIMURGH: Scaled firebirds that the djinn are fond of racing.

ZAHHAK: A large, flying, fire-breathing lizard-like beast.

Beings of Water

MARID: Extremely powerful water elementals. Near mythical to the djinn, the marid haven't been seen in centuries, though it's rumored the lake surrounding Daevabad was once theirs.

Beings of Air

PERI: Air elementals. More powerful than the djinn—and far more secretive—the peri keep resolutely to themselves.

RUKH: Enormous predatory firebirds that the peri can use for hunting.

SHEDU: Mythical winged lions, an emblem of the Nahid family.

Beings of Earth

GHOULS: The reanimated, cannibalistic corpses of humans who have made deals with the ifrit.

ISHTAS: A small, scaled creature obsessed with organization and footwear.

KARKADANN: A magical beast similar to an enormous rhinoceros with a horn as long as a man.

NASNAS: A venomous creature resembling a bisected human that prowls the deserts of Am Gezira and whose bite causes flesh to wither away.

Languages

DIVASTI: The language of the Daeva tribe.

DJINNISTANI: Daevabad's common tongue, a merchant creole the djinn and shafit use to speak to those outside their tribe.

GEZIRIYYA: The language of the Geziri tribe, which only members of their tribe can speak and understand.

General Terminology

ABAYA: A loose, floor-length, full-sleeved dress worn by women.

ADHAN: The Islamic call to prayer.

AFSHIN: The name of the Daeva warrior family who once served the Nahid Council. Also used as a title.

AKHI: "My brother."

BAGA NAHID: The proper title for male healers of the Nahid family.

BANU NAHIDA: The proper title for female healers of the Nahid family.

CHADOR: An open cloak made from a semicircular cut of fabric, draped over the head and worn by Daeva women.

DIRHAM/DINAR: A type of currency used in Egypt.

DISHDASHA: A floor-length man's tunic, popular among the Geziri.

EMIR: The crown prince and designated heir to the Qahtani throne.

FAJR: The dawn hour/dawn prayer.

GALABIYYA: A traditional Egyptian garment, essentially a floor-length tunic.

GHUTRA: A male headdress.

HAMMAM: A bathhouse.

ISHA: The late evening hour/evening prayer.

MAGHRIB: The sunset hour/sunset prayer.

MIDAN: A plaza/city square.

MIHRAB: A wall niche indicating the direction of prayer.

MUHTASIB: A market inspector.

NAVASATEM: A holiday held once a century to celebrate another generation of freedom from Suleiman's servitude. Originally a Daeva festival, Navasatem is a beloved tradition in Daevabad, attracting djinn from all over the world to take part in weeks of festivals, parades, and competitions.

QAID: The head of the Royal Guard, essentially the top military official in the djinn army.

RAKAT: A unit of prayer.

SHAFIT: People with mixed djinn and human blood.

SHAYLA: A type of women's headscarf.

SHEIKH: A religious educator/leader.

SULEIMAN'S SEAL: The seal ring Suleiman once used to control the djinn, given to the Nahids and later stolen by the Qahtanis. The bearer of Suleiman's ring can nullify any magic.

TALWAR: An Agnivanshi sword.

TANZEEM: A grassroots fundamentalist group in Daevabad dedicated to fighting for shafit rights and religious reform.

UKHTI: "My sister."

ULEMA: A legal body of religious scholars.

WAZIR: A government minister.

ZAR: A traditional ceremony meant to deal with djinn possession.

ZUHR: The noon hour/noon prayer.

ZULFIQAR: The forked copper blades of the Geziri tribe; when inflamed, their poisonous edges destroy even Nahid flesh, making them among the deadliest weapons in this world.

THE SIX TRIBES
OF THE DJINN

THE GEZIRI

Surrounded by water and caught behind the thick band of humanity in the Fertile Crescent, the djinn of Am Gezira awoke from Suleiman's curse to a far different world than their fire-blooded cousins. Retreating to the depths of the Empty Quarter, to the dying cities of the Nabateans and to the forbidding mountains of southern Arabia, the Geziri eventually learned to share the hardships of the land with their human neighbors, becoming fierce protectors of the shafit in the process. From this country of wandering poets and zulfiqar-wielding warriors came Zaydi al Qahtani, the rebel-turned-king who would seize Daevabad and Suleiman's seal from the Nahid family in a war that remade the magical world.

THE AYAANLE

Nestled between the rushing headwaters of the Nile River and the salty coast of Bet il Tiamat lies Ta Ntry, the fabled homeland of the mighty Ayaanle tribe. Rich in gold and salt—and far enough from Daevabad that its deadly politics are more game than risk, the Ayaanle are a people to envy. But behind their gleaming coral mansions and sophisticated salons lurks a history they've begun to forget . . . one that binds them in blood to their Geziri neighbors.

THE DAEVAS

Stretching from the Sea of Pearls across the plains of Persia and the mountains of gold-rich Bactria is mighty Daevastana—and just past its Gozan River lies Daevabad, the hidden city of brass. The ancient seat of the Nahid Council—the famed family of healers who once ruled the magical world—Daevastana is a coveted land, its civilization drawn from the ancient cities of Ur and Susa and the nomadic horsemen of the Saka. A proud people, the Daevas claimed the original name of the djinn race as their own . . . a slight that the other tribes never forget.

THE SAHRAYN

Sprawling from the shores of the Maghreb across the vast depths of the Sahara Desert is Qart Sahar—a land of fables and adventure even to the djinn. An enterprising people not particularly enamored of being ruled by foreigners, the Sahrayn know the mysteries of their country better than any—the still lush rivers that flow in caves deep below the sand dunes and the ancient citadels of human civilizations lost to time and touched by forgotten magic. Skilled sailors, the Sahrayn travel upon ships of conjured smoke and sewn cord over sand and sea alike.

THE AGNIVANSHI

Stretching from the brick bones of old Harappa through the rich plains of the Deccan and misty marshes of the Sundarbans lies Agnivansha. Blessedly lush in every resource that could be dreamed—and separated from their far more volatile neighbors by wide rivers and soaring mountains—Agnivansha is a peaceful land famed for its artisans and jewels . . . and its savvy in staying out of Daevabad's tumultuous politics.

THE TUKHARISTANIS

East of Daevabad, twisting through the peaks of Karakorum Mountains and the vast sands of the Gobi is Tukharistan. Trade is its lifeblood, and in the ruins of forgotten Silk Road kingdoms, the Tukharistanis make their homes. They travel unseen in caravans of smoke and silk along corridors marked by humans millennia ago, carrying with them things of myth: golden apples that cure any disease, jade keys that open worlds unseen, and perfumes that smell of paradise.

ACKNOWLEDGMENTS

Two years ago, I tentatively sent the first book in what would become the Daevabad Trilogy off for submission. Never in my wildest dreams did I imagine my five-hundred-plus-page homage to the medieval Islamic world would gain the extraordinary reception it has, and as I put the finishing touches on its sequel, I am humbled and grateful for the opportunity I've been given to share the story and characters who've lived in my head with the rest of the world. It has been a journey and one that would have never been possible without an amazing group of readers, fantastic fellow writers, a crack publishing team, an extremely understanding family, and quite frankly, the grace of God.

First, to all the readers, reviewers, bloggers, fan artists, and booksellers who loved and spread the word about my book, thank you. You're what makes this all worth it.

A huge thanks as well to all the amazing scholars and "Twitterstorians" who helped me hone this book, whether by helping me track down incredibly specific views of the Cairo waterfront in the nineteenth century or crafting jokes in Akkadian. Your love of history and willingness to share knowledge with the public sphere is exactly what we need nowadays.

To the amazing Brooklyn Speculative Fiction Writers, particularly Rob Cameron, Jonathan Hernandez, and Cynthia Lovett, who came to my aid when I was in the thick of Book 2 despair . . . you're the absolute best and I look forward to your own books flying off shelves one day.

I've been blessed to make the acquaintance of a truly wonderful number of fellow authors in the past few years whose blurbs, words of advice, or simply sympathetic ears made a world of difference to this fretting rookie. S. K. Ali, Roshani Chokshi, Nicky Drayden, Sarah Beth Durst, Kate Elliot, Kevin Hearne, Robin Hobb, Ausma Zehanat Khan, Khaalidah Muhammad-Ali, Karuna Riazi, Michael J. Sullivan, Shveta Thakrar, Sabaa Tahir, Laini Taylor, Kiersten White . . . I am so, so grateful. Fran Wilde, you are an actual treasure and your mantra has gotten me through so many rough patches.

Jen Azantian, my incredible agent and friend, I owe you more than I can ever say for seeing me through the past two years—and too, Ben, for helping us both out! To my editor, Priyanka Krishnan, I have been honored to work with you, know you, and watch my characters and world come to life under your careful hand. To everyone at Harper Voyager on both sides of the Atlantic, particularly David Pomerico, Pam Jaffee, Caro Perny, Kayleigh Webb, Angela Craft, Natasha Bardon, Jack Renninson, Mumtaz Mustafa, Shawn Nicholls, Mary Ann Petyak, Liate Stehlik, Paula Szafranski, Andrew DiCecco, Shelby Peak, Joe Scalora, and Ronnie Kutys, thank you for taking a chance on me and for all your hard work. To Will Staehle, thank you for knocking it out of the park with another gorgeous cover.

To my wonderful and very forgiving family, who has been

spectacularly supportive as I've grown more absentminded and stressed, thank you so, so much. Mom and Dad, I would never have been able to do this without you. Much gratitude as well to my grandmother and mother-in-law, who helped take care of me while I was injured and trying to finish this book.

To my husband, Shamik, my best friend and first reader, thank you for keeping my feet on the ground and for pushing me when I needed it. I love getting to dream and plot in this weird fictional world you've helped me create. For Alia, my little Nahri-in-training, you are the light in my life, my love, and your stories are even grander than my own.

Finally, to my fellow Muslim fantasy nerds: I wrote this story for you, for us, and I have been incredibly humbled and honored by your response. I thank you, from the bottom of my awkward convert's heart. May we all have the grandest of adventures!

About the author

About the book

Insights,
Interviews
& More . . .

Read on

Meet S. A. Chakraborty

Melissa C. Beckman

S. A. CHAKRABORTY is a speculative fiction writer from New York City. Her debut, *The City of Brass*, is the first book in the critically acclaimed, bestselling Daevabad trilogy, and has been nominated for the Locus, World Fantasy, Crawford, and Campbell awards. When not buried in books about Mughal miniatures and Abbasid political intrigue, she enjoys hiking, knitting, and re-creating unnecessarily complicated, medieval meals for her family. You can find her online at www.sachakraborty.com or on Twitter @SAChakrabooks where she likes to ramble about history, politics, and Islamic art. ∾

The Kingdom of Copper: Recipes

If the feast scene has you hungry, have no fear! Here are three recipes inspired by medieval cuisine from the Middle East that will have you eating like a Daevabadi royal—Nahid poison *definitely* not included!

Judhaba
(roast chicken with a savory bread pudding)

You're going to end up roasting your chicken over the filling, and unless you have a medieval kitchen, this might take a little creativity. I prepare the bread pudding in a large, shallow Dutch oven and then suspend the chicken on an oven grate over it, but you could also use a roasting pan or simply lay the chicken on top of everything.

4 cups chopped pitted dates and dried apricots

1 to 2 tablespoons pomegranate molasses

¼ cup plus 2 teaspoons sugar

4 to 5 pound whole chicken, innards removed, rinsed and thoroughly dried

2 tablespoons plus ¾ cup rose water

Olive oil

1 tablespoon ghee or butter

1 teaspoon salt

2 good size pinches of saffron, divided

½ cup chicken broth

1 tablespoon sumac

Dash of honey

Enough pita bread to cover your roasting pan twice, torn into 1-inch pieces (Use semolina bread if you can and nothing too thick or chewy.)

Chopped mint and toasted, slivered almonds for garnish

1. Prepare the fruit filling. Put the dates, apricots, and pomegranate molasses in a medium saucepan. Fill with enough water to cover and simmer for 20 to 30 minutes. Lightly mash with ¼ cup sugar. Remove from heat.▶

The Kingdom of Copper: Recipes *(continued)*

2. Rinse and thoroughly dry your chicken. In a small bowl, mix 2 tablespoons rose water, 1 tablespoon olive oil, 1 tablespoon ghee, 1 teaspoon salt, a pinch of crumbled saffron, 1 tablespoon sumac, and a dash of honey and then use it to baste your chicken inside and out.

3. Preheat oven to 425°F. This is when I usually lightly toast half the bread pieces, by spreading them out on a sheet pan for 5 to 8 minutes. Don't toast the other half!

4. Roast the chicken on a separate pan, uncovered, for 30 minutes.

5. While the chicken is roasting, prepare the bread pudding. Lightly oil your roasting pan or Dutch oven and then put down a layer of the toasted bread pieces. Pour over the chicken broth.

6. Layer in the date-apricot mixture over the bread and then pour over the remaining ¾ cup rose water (with another pinch of saffron dissolved in it). Sprinkle the remaining sugar over it. Cover with a layer of untoasted bread pieces.

7. After about 30 minutes, the chicken juices should be starting to run. Remove the chicken (very carefully, it will be hot!) and tip the accumulated juices from the pan and bird over the bread and fruit mixture. Place the chicken on top to continue roasting.

8. Reduce the temperature to 325°F and tent chicken with foil if it's browning too quickly. Cook 30 minutes, then turn chicken over to cook breast side down, again letting juices drip over bread. Cook another 20 to 30 minutes, or until fully cooked. (Your meat thermometer should read 165°F.)

9. Remove from oven and let the whole thing rest 10 minutes. Then carve chicken and serve atop the bread pudding, garnished with mint and toasted slivered almonds.

Pistachio-Stuffed Date Fritters

2 cups blanched, peeled pistachios

½ cup regular sugar (or to taste)

Rose water

1 pound dates (about 24, pits removed
*   (Medjool or another bigger, sweeter type is best)*

2 cups flour

2 teaspoons baking powder

1 tablespoon corn starch

1 cup milk

Sugar syrup (2 parts sugar to 1 part water, or add less water to make it thicker, if desired; you can also add lemon juice or rose water)

Powdered sugar, optional

Unrefined sesame oil, for frying

1. Make the filling: Grind the pistachios (make sure they're dry!) with ½ cup sugar and 1 to 2 tablespoons rose water in a food processor for 5-10 minutes, or until paste-like.

2. Stuff the pitted dates with the pistachio mixture. Do not overstuff! Press the dates closed and then chill for an hour or so in the refrigerator uncovered on a plate.

3. Make the crepe batter. In a medium bowl, mix flour, baking powder, and corn starch together. Whisk in milk until batter is thin enough to cling to the dates without being too watery.

4. Prepare your oil for frying and line a plate with paper towels. You'll be dipping things back and forth and letting them rest, so make some room.

5. Dip the stuffed dates in crepe batter, then fry them until nicely browned. Let them drain on paper towel–lined plate for a few minutes, then dip them in sugar syrup. Let cool on wax paper.

6. Repeat step 5 to rebatter the dates and then fry and dip in syrup again.

7. Let cool and then serve with sprinkled powdered sugar. Delicious warm or cold the next day!

Tamarind Juice

Particularly popular during Ramadan, people make this a number of different ways. You can make it as thick or thin as you like and vary the sweetness to your taste.

16 ounces (1 pound) tamarind pulp; this typically comes in a block with seeds and is different than tamarind paste

Sugar, or another sweetener

Lemon juice and/or rose water, optional

1. Break up the tamarind pulp with your hands into small pieces. Soak in 4 cups water for 8 hours or up to overnight. Stir and mash apart occasionally to separate out seeds and pieces.▶

The Kingdom of Copper: **Recipes**(*continued*)

2. Strain out the seeds and pulp using a fine mesh strainer or cheesecloth, keeping the liquid. You might have to stir and scrape through the mixture a bit in order to get all the juice.

3. Over low heat, mix the tamarind liquid, 2 to 4 additional cups of water, and then sweeten to taste (I use ¾ cup sugar). You can add some fresh lemon juice and/or rose water to taste.

4. Chill and serve over ice. ᘉ

Reading Group Discussion Questions

1. *The City of Brass* ends in climactic fashion: Dara is seemingly killed, Nahri is left under Ghassan's cruel thumb, and Ali is changed by the marid and then cast out to be assassinated. With *The Kingdom of Copper*, what did you make of the beginning and how it dealt with building off those plotlines? What sort of emotions did you feel entering this world again?

2. In *The City of Brass*, we got only Ali's and Nahri's perspectives. However, in *The Kingdom of Copper*, S. A. Chakraborty included Dara's perspective as well. What more do you learn about this complex, multifaceted character through these chapters? Does your judgement of him change throughout the story?

3. What is your takeaway from Nahri's marriage to Muntadhir? Do you think marrying him was the correct choice for Nahri? Would you have done it, if you were in her position?

4. In the beginning, Manziheh and Dara have a conversation that leads her to ask if he would die for Nahri and then to warn him of the risks of personal attachment. What do you make of this conversation and their relationship throughout the novel? Do you think these characters act the way they do to protect those they love, or is it to further their own ambitions?

5. After traveling with Lubayd and Aqisa, Ali returns to Daevabad. How did you react to his homecoming? Was it what you expected it would be?

6. As Nahri and Ali's relationship strengthens further in *The Kingdom of Copper*, what commonalties do they share, if any?

7. Nahri and Dara don't interact for most of the book, so how does that strengthen or weaken their relationship? What do you think their future looks like together? ▶

Reading Group Discussion Questions *(continued)*

8. There are many moral gray areas in the book—often, Ali, Dara, Nahri, and other characters are stuck in situations where the line between right and wrong is blurred. How does this common dilemma help with their personal growth? Were there times when you felt unsure about what you would do? Were there times you would have made different choices than the characters?

9. Who do you think has grown the most since *The City of Brass*? Is there a particular character that stands out in *The Kingdom of Copper*?

10. Toward the end, Nisreen dies during an attack. What was your reaction to this scene? How do you think her death will impact Nahri in the future?

11. How did the ending of *The Kingdom of Copper* make you feel? Was it the ending you expected from the beginning?

12. After reading *The City of Brass* and *The Kingdom of Copper*, how do you think the Daevabad trilogy will end? ❧

An Excerpt from
The Empire of Gold

PROLOGUE

Manizheh

Upon the palace that had always been hers, Banu
Manizheh e-Nahid gazed at her family's city.

Bathed in starlight, Daevabad was beautiful, the
spread of the dazzling cityscape—the jagged lines
of towers and minarets, domes and pyramids—
astonishing from this height, like a jumble of
jeweled toys. Beyond the sliver of white beach, the
dappled lake shimmered with movement against
the black embrace of mountains.

She spread her hands on the stone parapet. This
was not a view Manizheh had been permitted while
a prisoner of the Qahtanis. Even as a child, her
defiance had made them uneasy; the palace magic's
open embrace of the young Nahid prodigy and
her obvious talent curbing her life before she was
old enough to realize the guards that surrounded
her day and night weren't for her protection. The
only other time she'd been up here had been as
Ghassan's guest—a trip he'd arranged shortly after
he became king. Manizheh could still remember
how he'd taken her hand as they gazed at the city
their families had killed each other for, speaking
dreamy words about uniting their peoples and
putting the past behind them. About how he'd
loved her since they were children, and about how
sad and helpless *he'd* felt all those times his father
had beaten and terrorized her and her brother.
Surely, she must have understood that Ghassan had
no choice but to stay silent.

In her mind's eye, Manizheh could still see his
face that night. They'd been younger; he'd been
handsome. Charming. *What a match*, people would
have said. Who wouldn't want to be the beloved
queen of a powerful djinn king? And indeed, she'd
laced her fingers between his and smiled—for she
still wore such an expression in those days, her eyes
locked on the mark of Suleiman's seal, new upon his
face.▶

And then she'd closed his throat.

It hadn't lasted. Ghassan had been quicker with the seal than she'd anticipated, and as her powers fell away, so did the pressure on his throat. He'd been enraged, his face red with betrayal and Manizheh remembered thinking that he would hit her. Fearing he'd do worse, simply taking what he wanted from her there on the roof, and that it wouldn't have mattered if she screamed—he was king now and no one would cross him.

But Ghassan hadn't done that. He hadn't needed to. Manizheh had gone for his heart and so Ghassan did the same with ruthless effectiveness: having Rustam beaten within a hair of his life as she was forced to watch, breaking her brother's bones, letting them heal and then doing it again, torturing him until Rustam was a howling mess and Manizheh had fallen to her knees, begging Ghassan for mercy.

When he finally granted it, he'd been even angrier at her tears than her initial refusal. I wanted things to be different between us, he'd accused. You shouldn't have humiliated me.

She took a sharp breath at the memory. He's dead, she reminded herself. Manizheh had stared at Ghassan's bloody corpse, committing the sight to memory, trying to assure herself that her tormentor was truly gone. But she wouldn't have him burned, not yet. She intended to examine his body further, hoping for clues to how he'd possessed Suleiman's seal. Manizheh hadn't missed that his heart had been removed—carved from his chest with surgical precision, making fairly clear who'd done the removing. Part of her was grateful. Despite what she'd told Nahri, Manizheh knew almost nothing about how the seal ring was passed to another.

And now because of Nahri, Manizheh knew the first step—after finding her anyway—would be to cut out the heart of her djinn prince.

She returned her gaze to the city. It was startlingly quiet, adding an eerie façade to the entire experience. Daevabad might have been a city at peace in the dead quiet of night, safe and still under the helm of its rightful guardians.

A lie the occasional wail betrayed.

A distant scream came again. The cries had otherwise finally started to fade, the violence of the night likely giving away to sheer shock and terror. Frightened people—hunted people—didn't scream. They hid, hunkering down with their loved ones in whatever shelter they could find, praying the darkness might pass them. Everyone in Daevabad knew what happened when cities fell. They were raised on stories of vengeance and their enemy's rapacity; depending on their roots, they were told hair-raising tales of Zaydi al

Qahtani's violent conquest of Daevabad, Darayavahoush e-Afshin's scourging of Qui-zi, or the innumerable sacks of human cities. No, there wouldn't be screaming. Daevabad's people would be hiding, weeping silently as they clutched their children close, the sudden loss of their magic only one more bewilderment.

They are going to think another Suleiman has come. It was the conclusion any sensible person would arrive at. Had Suleiman's great judgement not started with the stripping of their ancestors' magic? They probably expected to see their lives shattered, their families torn apart as they were forced to toil for another human master.

Manizheh pressed her palms harder against the cold stone, aching to feel the palace's familiar magic. To conjure dancing flames or the shimmer of smoke. It still seemed impossible that her abilities were gone. Manizheh could only imagine the injuries piling up in the infirmary; injuries she now couldn't heal. For a woman who'd endured the ripping away of everything she loved—the shy country noble she might have married, the dark-eyed infant whose weight in her arms she'd ached to feel again, the brother she'd betrayed, her very dignity as she bowed before the Qahtanis year after year—the loss of her abilities was the worst. Her magic was her life, her soul—the power beneath the strength that had enabled her to survive everything else.

Perhaps an apt price to pay for using healing magic to kill, a voice whispered in her head. Manizheh pushed it away. Such doubt wouldn't help her or her people right now. Instead she'd lean on anger, the fury that coursed in her when she watched years of planning upended by a quick-fingered shafit girl.

Nahri. The defiance in her dark eyes. The slight, almost rueful shrug as she shoved their family's most cherished treasure onto the finger of an unworthy sand-fly.

I would have given you everything. Everything you could have possibly wanted. Everything I never had.

"Enjoying your victory?"

Aeshma's mocking voice set her teeth on edge, but Manizheh didn't so much as twitch. She'd been dealing with the ifrit long enough to learn how to handle him—how to handle everyone, really. You simply offered nothing—no weaknesses, no doubt. No allies or loved ones. She kept her gaze forward as he joined her at the wall.

He exhaled. "A long time I've waited to look upon Anahid's city." There was cruel triumph in his voice. "But it's not quite the paradise of the songs. Where are the shedu rumored to patrol the skies and the gardens of jeweled trees and rivers of wine? The fawning marid servants conjuring rainbows of waterfalls and a library teeming with the secrets of creation?"

Manizheh's stomach twisted. Gone, for centuries now. She'd immersed herself in the great stories of her ancestors and they▶

painted an utterly unfamiliar Daevabad to what she saw now. "We will bring them back."

A quick glance revealed cold pleasure rippling across his fiery visage. "She loved this place," he continued. "A sanctuary for the people she dragged back together, her carefully tended paradise that allowed no sinners."

"You sound jealous."

Aeshma's eyes flashed, fixing on hers. "Three thousand years I dwelled in the land of the two rivers with Anahid, watching the floods recede and the humans rise. We warred with the marid and traveled the desert winds together. And it was all forgotten in the face of Suleiman's command."

"You chose different paths."

"She betrayed her people, her closest friends."

She saved her people. And I intend to do the same. "Here I thought we were finally setting that aside and making peace."

Aeshma scoffed. "And how do you propose to do that, Banu Nahida?" He turned to face her. "Do you think I don't know what's happened? You cannot summon as much as a flame, let alone hope to fulfill your bargain with me." He raised a palm, a tendril of fire swirling between his fingers. "A shame your people haven't had three millennia to learn other ways of magic."

It took everything Manizheh had not to stare at the flame, hunger eating through her soul. "Then how fortunate I have you to teach me."

He laughed. "Why should I? I have been helping you for years now and I've yet to gain a thing."

"You've gained a glimpse of Anahid's city."

Aeshma grinned. "There is that, I suppose." His smile widened, his sharp teeth gleaming. "I could gain even more right now. I could throw you from this wall and kill her most promising descendant."

Manizheh didn't flinch; she was too accustomed to men trying to threaten her. "You would never escape Darayavahoush's wrath. He would track down every ifrit left, torture and slaughter them before your eyes, and then spend a century killing you in the most painful way he could imagine." She said the words plainly, for it was the truth and they both knew it. "You would die at the hands of the magic you desire most."

That seemed to land, a scowl replacing his mocking grin. It always did; Manizheh knew Aeshma's weaknesses as well as he knew her secrets.

"Your Afshin does not deserve such abilities," he snapped. "The first daeva freed from Suleiman's curse in three thousand years and he's an ill-tempered, overly armed fool. You might as well have given such abilities to a rabid dog."

Manizheh pressed her mouth into a thin line. She didn't like the analogy—and she definitely didn't like the defiance newly simmering below Dara's usual absolute loyalty. But the Afshin was a man who wore his desires and fears plainly, and Manizheh did not doubt she could handle him.

Aeshma was another matter. "If you desire Dara's abilities, you should stop issuing worthless threats and help me get Suleiman's seal back. I cannot free you from the curse without it."

He dropped his gaze to stare at her. "Perhaps you cannot free me from it at all."

She kept her face carefully blank. "You were the one who came to me," she reminded him. "And you've seen what I'm capable of."

He snorted. "Indeed, I have. Enough that I'm not particularly eager to see you master my kind of magic, as well. Especially not for the mere promise you'll do your best to free me and my people from our curse. If you want me to teach you blood magic, I'm going to need something far more tangible in return."

More tangible. For the first time in a very long time, Manizheh's stomach knotted. She had already lost so much. What she had left—who she had left—was precious. "What do you want?"

The ifrit's cold smile curled again as his gaze drifted over Daevabad, the eagerness in it sending a hundred warnings through her mind. "I think of that morning every day, you know," he said softly. "That raw power scorching the air, screaming in my mind. I hadn't felt something like that since Anahid pulled this island from the lake with her own hands." He ran his fingers along the parapet in a caress. "There's nothing quite like Nahid magic, is there? A drop of Nahid blood poisons me. Nahid hands raised this city, brought untold masses back from the brink of death. A Nahid life . . . imagine all the things that could do." He paused to twist the knife deeper. "The things it already has done."

Manizheh went cold, and now she did flinch. How quickly it all came back. The smell of burned flesh and sticky blood coating her skin. The twinkling city seemed to disappear, replaced by a scorched plain and smoky sky—the dull color reflected in her brother's vacant, unseeing eyes. Rustam had died with an expression of faint shock on his face and seeing it had broken what was left of Manizheh's heart, reminding her of the little boy he'd once been. The Nahid siblings who'd lost their innocence too soon, who'd stuck together through everything only to be ripped apart at the end.

She cleared her throat. "Speak plainly."

"I want your daughter." He was brusque now, any coyness gone. "And now that she's proven herself a traitor, you need her gone. Your Scourge is obsessed. If she was clever enough to deceive you, how do you imagine that lovesick fool will fare should she make a play for his loyalties?"▶

Poorly. But Aeshma's words played through her mind. A traitor. How simple it was for the ifrit to declare such a thing. He hadn't seen a trembling young woman in a torn, bloodied dress. He hadn't stared into frightened, achingly familiar eyes.

She betrayed you. Indeed, Nahri had done worse, tricking her with a sleight of hand more appropriate for a low-born shafit thief than a Nahid healer. But Manizheh could have forgiven that, would have forgiven that had Nahri taken the ring for herself. Creator knew she could not judge another woman's ambitions.

But Nahri hadn't taken Suleiman's seal for herself. No, she'd given it to a Qahtani. To the son of the king who'd tormented her, who'd stolen any chance Manizheh had at a happy life and driven the final wedge between her and her brother. Manizheh couldn't forgive that. In time, perhaps she could move on.

But Daevabad didn't have time.

A glimmer caught her eye—a fiery shard of sun emerging from behind the eastern mountains. She was taken aback. Sunrise was not typically so bright in Daevabad, the shimmer of its protective magic veiling it off from the rest of the world. But it wasn't just the brightness—something else felt wrong.

Silence. Manizheh waited a few heartbeats, but it didn't abate. Neither the Grand Temple's drumming nor the djinn adhan had welcomed the sun's arrival, and the quiet sent more dread into her heart than all the blood that had dripped from her unhealed finger. Nothing stopped the drums and the call to prayer; they were part of the very fabric of time in Daevabad.

Until Manizheh's conquest ripped that fabric to shreds. Daevabad was her home, her duty, and she'd broken part of its heart. It was her responsibility to fix it.

No matter the cost.

She closed her eyes. Manizheh had not prayed since she'd watched two djinn scouts bleed out in the icy mud of northern Daevastana, dead at the hands of the poison she'd designed. She'd defended her plan to Darayavahoush, she'd gone forward with bringing an even worse wave of death to Daevabad. But she had not prayed through any of that. It felt like a link she had broken.

And she knew the Creator would not help her now. She saw no alternative, only the path she'd forged and had to keep walking.

She took a deep breath. Forgive me, Rustam. I tried, I really did.

"I can offer you her name." Manizheh's voice was steady; she would not show the ifrit the wound he'd struck. "Her true one. The name her father gave her." ∽